CAN I KEEP YOU?

THE STALKER'S PLAYLIST

D. C. POWERS

CONTENT NOTE

Some content within this novel may be disturbing or triggering for readers. Reader discretion is advised.

This book should not be used as a reference guide for anything. Recommended reading age: 18 years and older

Trigger warnings: graphic violence, explicit language, homicide, topic of suicide, depression, homophobia, abuse, abandonment, prior discussions of rape, consensual sex, bondage/ropes, masturbation, oral, sex toys, stalking, gang activity, hit and run, kidnapping, squirting, revenge, forced proximity, flashback of miscarriage, mind games, making light of diabetes, torture, bodily fluids, death, sex with inanimate objects, bullying, family drama, lies, PTSD, bigotry, cheating, disabled FMC, disabled MMC, alcohol & tobacco use, overdosing, genital piercings, misuse of military gear, male on male relations, female on female relations, bribery, & copious amounts of candy consumption.

This book may cause hunger. Proceed with snacks.

D.C. Powers

THE PLAYLIST

This book was written with music as its heart. When you encounter words **bolded** within the text, give that song a listen. You may find some songs have underlying meanings, aiding the plot. The playlist is in sequential order with the story.

https://www.tunemymusic.com/share/JHZLL7nDCQ

The Stalker's Playlist

Pixies - *Where is my mind?*
Semisonic - *Closing time*
Stone Temple Pilots - *Vasoline*
Beck - *Loser*
Sam the Sham & the Pharaohs - *Lil' red riding hood*
Marcy Playground - *Sex & candy*
The Human League - *Don't you want me*
The Flys - *Got you*
OMC - *How Bizarre*
Radiohead - *Creep*
Edwyn Collins - *A girl like you*
Radiohead - *Karma police*
Kinks - *All day and all of the night*
Spin Doctors - *Two princes*
Elastica - *Connection*
Toadies - *Possum Kingdom*
Highly Suspect - *My name is Human*
NIN - *Terrible Lie*
311 - *Don't Stay Home*
Deftones - *Change*
Silverchair - *Tomorrow*
Ozzy Osbourne - *No More Tears*
Depeche Mode - *Policy of Truth*
Incubus - *Pardon Me*
The Verve - *Bitter Sweet Symphony*
Chevelle - *The Red*
Blink 182 - *Dammit*
White Town - *Your Woman*
Primitive Radio Gods - *Standing Outside a Broken Phone Booth with Money in my Hand*
Our Lady Peace- *Superman's Dead*
No Doubt - *Don't Speak*
Red Hot Chili Peppers - *Otherside*
Yeah Yeah Yeahs - *Maps*

GLOSSARY:

Masshole- A contemptible or obnoxious person from Massachusetts.

Póg- In the Irish language means "kiss."

Pockabook- A purse or handbag.

De facto- Describes a powerful figure, rule, or situation that exists and holds authority in practice.

Dia is Muire Duit- A traditional Irish response to a greeting, meaning "God and Mary be with you."

Ar dheis Dé go raibh a hanam- A traditional Irish phrase meaning, "may she rest in peace."

Sláinte- Gaelic used as a toast, similar to "cheers."

Suppah- A late evening meal, such as dinner.

Bastardo- An Italian or Spanish word meaning "bastard."

Fica- Italian slang for "pussy."

Puttana- A vulgar Italian word that translates to "whore."

Omerta- Practiced by the Mafia; a code of silence about criminal activity and the refusal to give evidence to authorities.

Bogtrotters- A disparaging and offensive term for a person of Irish birth or ancestry.

Capo- In the Mafia, a capo is a high-ranking leader who manages a crew.

Guappo- An Italian word for "thug" or "bully."

Mo Shearc- An Irish term of endearment that translates to "my love."

Mick- An ethnic slur for Irish people.

Leanbh- an Irish word that means "child."

Figlio di puttana- Translated from Italian, "son of a bitch/whore."

Stronzo- A colorful Italian word which can mean anything from, "asshole, shit, prick, fucker, etc…"

Cosa Nostra- Also known as the "Mob" or the "Mafia," evolved from the Sicilian Mafia.

BRODI

One year ago...

"Kelly lands his first shot right out of the gate!" The crowd roars and screams. "Cook may be the heavy weight in the ring tonight, but Kelly is quick on his feet."

"Bullshit," I mutter to myself, watching this unjust fight unfold.

"Looks like Cook is blocking every body-shot Kelly is throwing. If he keeps up at this rate, he's going to tire before the next round," the ring announcer speculates. Kelly's erratic, pushing Cook back to gain center ring. "Cook's calm and controlled movements make for a good defense against Kelly's combination work."

The bell marks the end of the first round, sending the boxers to their corners for a minute to hydrate and hear from their trainers.

I don't know why I bothered watching the fight; I already knew who was going to win. In one ear I had, T.O.P.- DOOM DADA, blasting as to keep me from being bored to tears.

Spectators move around trying to get a better viewing angle, before the second round begins. One pair of eyes scanning the crowd locks onto mine, then moves quickly to my position in the back of the room.

"I would never have thought a beast like Cook would have to work so hard to come out on top," Alex says.

I cross my arms, not meaning for the chuckle to escape.

"No... Really? They're fixing it for Kelly?"

I look down at nothing in particular and shrug, already annoyed by this man's inability to notice anything of significance, like me trying to be left the fuck alone. I clear my throat, remove the transceiver, and put it in my pocket.

"It's not my fault you put your money on a name who wasn't already tied to the Murrays."

Alex is the kind of guy everyone knows, but no one can really rely on. Mostly *because he has no allegiance to anyone. He's a drifter. Knowing a little bit about a lot of things and using that as his calling card on the streets. No gang will have him, but it's no mystery he wants to be in whatever group that'll have him. I'm confident he would turn on his own grandmother if it meant a payday.*

"Well, fuck me sideways..."

I grimace.

"What can I do to have you move my bet to Kelly?" His wide pleading eyes make the dark circles below them look even darker on his thin aging skin. Fool.

"No way. I'm not ending up like the last bookie."

The second round begins, and the horde of people screams Cook's name. His sharp movements open up an opportunity for him to deliver an uppercut to Kelly's jaw, causing blood to drip from the victor's nose. He better reel himself in real quick or this is going to be his last time ever fighting. "Good shot from Cook! Kelly is going to have to claw back into this and do some damage."

I look over at Alex, who watches the fighters with hope in his eyes, as they dance around the ring. Like a switch is flipped, they go from toe-to-toe to unnaturally primed. Cook all but pulls his hits, as Kelly begins landing blow after blow.

Alex looks back to me. "I put everything I had into this match! Switch my wager to Kelly and... I'll give you something significant."

My eyebrow raises accompanied by a reluctant smile, because nothing this guy says is valuable. "Tell me now and I'll consider it."

Alex combs his thinning hair back with his fingers, all the while looking around for something, or someone who may make him not want to divulge this secret.

"Things are not looking good for Cook, folks!" The announcer bellows.

"I know you're skimming the top of the bets..."

I see red. This slimy motherfucker is going to blackmail me! Instantly my arms unfold, I crack my knuckles within each palm, while deciding where I'm going to dump this asshole's body.

"Woah! Keep your assless chaps on, biker boy. My lips are sealed if you can do this for me. Plus, I have some historic news about that banging brunette you're seeing."

How the fuck does he know about Cindel? Is he watching me when I'm not at the Bay Boxing Club? I've only ever brought around girls for hire, never wanting any of this to get entangled with my personal life.

"Ooooo. That overhand left from Kelly has clipped Cook, leaving him looking a bit buzzed," the announcer proclaims, right before the bell signals the end of the second round.

I watch Cook return to his corner, looking like a lame dog that's being taken out to pasture. I hate when they force the obviously better opponent to lose. It makes me wonder what Cook did to deserve this, or maybe in this industry it all just comes down to who you know.

Alex leans closer. I wish I was smoking, just so I could blow the smoke in his face, but I am out at the moment.

"What do you know about the Lombardis?"

I sneer before regaining a foot of space between him and I. "I know enough about the stories, but they're ghosts now. What do they have to do with any of this?" I snap.

His smile turns feline as he beckons me closer to whisper into my ear. I hear the third round commence, just as he ardently reveals everything my girl has to do with the Murrays, and the Lombardis. He also proudly discloses how he found out from his cousin Craig, who just so happened to have gone to high school with her mother, Terri. Craig, apparently rejected by Terri, was bitter. Knew she chose Charles over him. When Cindel applied to work at the store Craig managed, he was able to make the connections. The roar of the crowd becomes distant; the ring announcer sounds as if he's underwater. How can this possibly be true?

Kelly lands the final hit that knocks out the boxer who should be the title-holder. I guess that's how life goes. No matter how big and bad you may think you are, there will always be someone who has your balls within their grasp. Alex, for being as blind as he seemed, figured out my game without even trying. Perhaps I misjudged what he's capable of. If he's right, I have valuable intel which could prove to be useful, if I find myself facing down the barrel of a gun.

"Consider this an early Christmas gift," he teases, just as two of Murray's notorious thugs walk by. Each guy has more height and muscle than him and I put together. Alex stands ramrod straight, looking out toward the concluded fight with a smug grin. "Be sure to handle that bet for me. Oh—do say hi to Cindel as well."

Fuck... I need to look into this shit myself to validate his claim.

After the warehouse is void of drunken fans and irate gamblers, who lost a small fortune, one of the Murray's lackeys strides up to me. This guy was a little more doughy than the other, but I liked him better. He was kinda fun to play cards with and had jokes for days. Though, I'm not a dumb fuck, I would never want to be caught in a ring with him. I've seen him train and worse; I've seen what he's capable of when someone did the Murrays dirty.

"Brodi!" He bellows, lopping the toothpick in his mouth from one corner to the other.

I rise from my seat at a small table, having just finished counting out the night's winnings, before stuffing the bills into a green zippered pouch. "Gar-

ron." I hold out the money for him to take, just like he's collected so many times before. "Ten thousand tonight," I declare.

"For this big of a fight?! Damn. Boss isn't going to be too happy."

I shove my hands deep into my front pockets, feeling the small roll of bills I've taken for myself. "Word on the street is the fight was rigged."

He opens up the pouch while chewing on the wooden stick. "Word on the street, huh?" He raises an eyebrow at me after flipping through the money. I nod, so fucking thankful I'm dealing with him as opposed to his less friendly accomplice. He shrugs, taking my word for it. Then turns toward the hallways where the safe resides. I've never seen it, nor would I dare enter that damn room. That's Eamon's office.

My phone buzzes and I look down to find a message from my girl.

> Cindel: Hey, I know you're at work, but could you maybe come over and watch a movie with me?

I let out a lengthy sigh and set down the phone to rub my fingers into my eyes. I know why she wants me to come over. She's sad. It's close to the anniversary of her brother's death. I'm fucking terrible at this shit. It wasn't so bad at first, mostly because we spent a lot of our time fucking, but as time went on and the fire didn't burn quite as hot, she wanted to talk more. Started sharing her desire to build a future on trust or some shit. She was actually a little freakier than I thought, even got jewelry for her snatch. We experimented a bit, but I couldn't really get on the same page as her. I'm a simple kind of guy and I know what I like. This past Thanksgiving, she invited me to the Catskills to meet her parents. Rather than suck it up and go, like any good boyfriend would, I made up an excuse. "Sorry, babe. They have me stuck at work that whole holiday weekend." In actuality, I was at work, just buried deep inside a bombshell blond, with double D's. I never claimed to be a good man, but I seemed to make her happy. Now that I know how special she is, I have no intention of giving her up.

I look up to the opened ceiling. Squiggles of light float around the exposed ductwork, from rubbing my sockets too hard. Phone in hand, I write out a response for my needy girlfriend.

> Brodi: Hey sunshine! I'm feeling kind of lousy all of a sudden. Think I may be coming down with something. When I'm better, I promise to go with you to feed the ducks.

Not waiting for a response, I shove the phone into the inner liner of my jacket, and leave. Between the fight, Alex's news, and the misappropriation of the house's winnings, I'm too wired to sleep. After watching someone get unjustly fucked into fifty shades of black and blue, I was heading to Cha-Cha's where I planned to cum down Destiny's throat.

ONE

CINDEL

I don't want to be here. Not today. It's been exactly six months since Brodi disappeared. I'd rather be back in my apartment, buried in blankets with a bag of candy corn, nibbling away, one color at a time.

The bar is warmer than the outside autumn air, allowing me to part with my frayed sweater. Underneath I wear a form fitting top with a plunging neckline, and lace that covers me just enough. I upcycle a lot of my clothes and this one always brings in good tips. It's early enough in the evening that older couples, as well as after-work gatherings, were just finishing up. This meant the younger, rowdy crowd would be filling up the space in no time. They were the ones that generously tipped.

Tonight, I am stationed behind the counter. Patrons line the bar trying desperately to get my attention. Naturally, the more eager you appear, the longer I make you wait. Women also took priority in my book. They never called me "baby" or insisted I smile when I'm just trying to do my damn job. A tablet sat on the bar for customers to place their drink orders. Although, I wished the ones that were too impatient to communicate with me used it.

I've been here half a year, so The Black Sheep's regulars know me. I like when they make sure, I can see their faces. It's even better when customers position themselves to the right of the bar, which has better lighting.

From what I understand, March is the busiest time here. People flock to Southie's prevalent Irish area, visiting local pubs and bars to celebrate. I've seen the lines for myself, snaking past the deli shop around the corner. That week my usual tips doubled. On St. Patrick's Day, I hit an all-time record: most money earned in one day. Didn't even have to snap a single picture of my feet! Now we're back to business as usual. Fall is here, the weather is brisker by the day, and the tavern is filled with familiar faces. Occasionally, we'll have a Salem enthusiast passing through, but I've learned not to expect any fat tips from tourists.

I move with ease mixing cocktails, tilting bottles at just the right angle to add flare, all while serving with a smile. This isn't my first time in the food service industry. In fact, it's probably my eighth or ninth, with a few odd jobs mixed in. I had a brief position at a pet store when I was fresh out of college. I've also worked at a drugstore and as a waitress where I acquired my bartending license, before they closed from increasing rent prices.

The worst job was when I accepted a position as a receptionist at a hotel. I pretty much answered phones the whole time. After making countless booking errors, the last straw was when I reserved a room for an important client under the name '*I buff.*' Well… I was let go, to put it lightly. Shia LaBeouf showed up for his suite, only to be informed, he had no such reservation. Can I just say, he's not quite as likeable without Bumblebee by his side.

Dribbles of alcohol sit at the bottom of the glasses decorating the bar. For every drink I serve, three freshly drained ones appeared. I happened upon this bartending gig, shortly after Brodi went missing. It was a good thing too, because I had just been let go from the resort and Star Mart wasn't paying me enough. I also was looking to fill my schedule to the brim.

It didn't help, though. I still think about him almost every day. The police weren't interested in helping a distressed girlfriend with a missing person's case. "Did you consider that maybe he just took off?" They would ask me. No…! Maybe? Would he?

Graduated nearly two years ago, I never thought I'd still be here… pouring drinks instead of completing my passion projects, which mostly remained unfinished in the deepest parts of my bedroom closet.

Music reverberates through the bar; I know it's unnecessarily loud because my rib cage rattles with the bass. I love music. It somehow manages to extinguish any concerns or present frustrations. Listening to music nonstop has catalogued songs within an unintentional memory folder. Without much effort, I can sing along with almost any song. Besides country music, because I was never able to get into a song about a pickup truck, or an ex running off with their dog. The heavy rhythm doesn't allow any room for feelings, let alone thinking. And, if I'm lucky, I may get a short reprieve from my tinnitus.

Tinnitus is when people experience perpetual buzzing or ringing in their ears. Some people may even get a static sound. Mine is a high-pitched bell, which ironically likes to get louder during stressful or quiet times. Like when I'm trying to sleep. Sometimes, the ear-splitting sound goes silent. It doesn't last very long, but it's a sort of heaven on earth feeling when it happens. During those few moments of bliss, I hold my breath, wishing the silence would stay. Doctors think the cause is due to a temporary muscle spasm in the ear. The only thing that seems to last in my life is hearing impairment. Oh… and anxiety with a side of depression. That is, according to the countless therapists I've seen over the years. Really… it would be so nice for something useful to come into my life and stick around. Something that's good for me.

Hands on the bar top, I can feel a tremor moving through the counter. I look up to find a customer, slamming his hands on the surface to grab my attention. His features are intense and paired with an edgy buzzed in slit within one eyebrow and a too tight purple V-necked shirt. He looks like a Jersey boy who got separated from his bros on the way to the shore. I watch as his mouth moves, transfixed on how his thin lips are able to maneuver despite his taut, Botox filled face.

"Hey! Bangs!" he repeats.

The tortuous roaring of bells plays even louder. Why can't people just use the tablet to order?! Standing before the impatient man, I ask what I can get started for him. "Hey, what can I—"

He slams his hands down on the bar top again. "Lemme... An ol fash—" he slurs, barely understandable.

Reaching deep to retrieve my *best customer service skills*, I say, "I'm sorry... Could you repeat your drink, please?"

His wayward mouth made it impossible to read his lips. "Ol'-d! F-asshh-oo-n-d!" He enunciates, like I'm nothing more than a piece of machinery that has teased the ends of his patience.

Arming my lungs with air, hoping to limit how hot I feel my face becoming, I make my way to a clean stack of glasses. First, I overfill the cup with ice, add too many bitters, too little liquor, and not a grain of sugar, then sparsely garnish the drink before handing it to the insufferable patron. "That'll be nineteen. Would you like to open a tab?"

The inebriated man slams a crumbed twenty on the counter. "Keep the change. Dumb—"

He spins around only to be met by a thick arm jutting out from the crowd. It appears as if a mystery man has *old-fashioned* by the jaw, causing his words to cease and his body to be fixed in place. The enigma of a man, dips his two large fingers into the glass, retrieving the miniscule cherry, then slowly opens his perfect pouty lips to pop the sugared trimming into his mouth. The bigger man's smile turns feline as he hums.

"I think you owe her an apology." His voice is deep, resonating, and somehow sexy.

The stunned, inebriated man now has a vein bulging from his temple. Either from embarrassment or anger, I'm not sure which. He attempts to move his jaw to form words around the grip of the other man. "I... I didn't think... I did anythin "

My eyes bounce between each person, unsure if I needed to grab help, or maybe my manager to intervene. *Old-fashioned* is lifted a little higher off the ground.

"Try again," the mystery man all but growls.

"I sor—ma'. I'm sorr—I'm sorry, ma'am!" the boorish man finally manages to get out.

The vigilante releases the stuttering man, nearly tossing him to his buddies located nearby. As if they knew what to do, they escorted the crude customer out of view, most likely into the street. Good.

The very good looking, cherry thief makes his way toward me. "Here." He places a crisp fifty-dollar bill on the bar before giving me a seductive grin from his perfectly chiseled face. He has the kind of looks that should only belong to those marbled statues in museums. The custom designer suit tells me he comes from money. No one should look like that.

"Thanks, but I don't need someone to swoop in and rescue me. I also don't need your charity." I think I decided at that moment that a pretty face usually comes with a catch. Crossing my arms over my chest, I find that I'm finally able to do something with my body, other than gawk at this man's gall.

He runs a palm down each side of his head, as if to fix the already perfectly groomed buzzed sides and short sandy comb back. Leaning onto the counter between us, his eyes skate over every inch of my body, making me feel exposed. Seen. "A Scotch, please… Neat." His emerald eyes make me feel like I've finally reached the city to meet the wizard. The one who can help me get home. I'm mesmerized by the way his cheekbones perfectly accentuate his stupidly beautiful face.

I reach for the scotch; our eyes still locked, as if I've entered some sort of unofficial staring contest. Placing the drink between us temporarily ceases whatever moment we just had. He watches me as he places the glass on his full lips. He sips the golden liquid, tightening muscles creating dimples on his cheeks, before it finally works its way down his throat. I'm enamored by his Adam's apple as it bobs on a swallow. God… Oh shit, am I drooling?

"It's cute," he states, shaking me from my trance, then pushing the fifty closer to me.

"The drink?" I inquired, confused how a beverage could be cute.

"The bangs," he states plainly.

Heat washes over me, starting at my neck and working downward toward my core. Am I having trouble accepting a compliment or is it because a breath-taking stranger is giving it?

He drains the rest of the amber colored liquid. Stands and turns to leave, without so much as a goodbye. He's gone just as quickly as he came. Joined by the two guys from earlier, who most likely threw the impossible patron out of the bar. One of the men who flanked his side seemed content to be there. Chewing on a toothpick, as his gaze seems to catch on any pretty face that happens by. While the other guy looks disinterested. He was bigger in size than his accomplice, and I swear, I catch his steely eyes lingering on me right before they leave.

The sea of people seems to part as the three dapper men make their way out of my line of sight. It's been a while since someone of the opposite sex complimented me. I find myself biting the inside of my mouth, just to fight back a ridiculous girlish smile.

After multiple months at The Black Sheep, I've learned to rotate regularly to keep the bar tops free of too many unaccompanied drinks. I collect and stack glasses high in my arms to carry to the back for washing, when I notice something small and white behind the tower of cups. I set down my fragile collection, only to find an abandoned earbud on the bar top. I swear, I have the same kind, but I know mine are safe at home on their charger. At the bar, I exclusively wore my hearing aids; they're lighter and do a better job at filtering out background noise. Now, if I wanted to listen to music, I could use my hearing aids, but my earbuds had a better range. Plus, they do an overall better job of deterring unwelcome conversations from strangers.

I place the item just under the counter, where misplaced wallets and keys get stored. The rest of the night is pretty uneventful, aside from a pack of inebriated women with matching shirts reading: *bachelorette party crew.* They are retracing their steps, going from bar to bar, trying to find the maid of honor's cell phone. When I return it, they are so grateful, they gift me a pair of beaded, penis necklaces.

It still didn't top my interaction with Mr. Neat. After closing, I count out my tips before reporting to my manager Cassie. Tipping out allows staff like Connor, our barback, to be included. Since he helps ensure the staff on the floor have clean glasses, no spills, and are well stocked all night. I inquire with everyone working, if anyone is missing an earbud.

"Nope," Brittany said.

"I don't bring music to work," Jada retorts.

Well… If it didn't belong to any of my coworkers and no one came back to collect it, I'll just take it home. I figure it could come in use if I ever lose one of mine. They appear to be the same generation that I just received from my parents last year. Charge it, pair it, done. Easy. Dropping the lonely earpiece into my bag, I pull on my sweater, before saluting my coworkers, and make my way out onto the vacant streets, in the early morning hours.

My apartment is dark. I instinctively drop my bag on the narrow entryway table, pull off my boots, and remove my hearing aids. They fit well enough but wearing them for too long is always uncomfortable. I have a charging station near the front door as well as in my bedroom. I nestle the aids within the one near the door, feeling instant relief with them off.

A red glow illuminates the room just enough for easy navigation farther into the living space. Gently, I tap my fingernail against the glass of a tank to say hello to Thelma. Two furry legs stretch out from her hide, while her stabby, bug munchers move up and down in a form of greeting.

My eyelids feel heavier within my home, knowing my bed is within reach. I force my sleep deprived body toward the bathroom, where I halfheartedly brush my teeth before bed. The house is still, as I reemerge to retrieve my phone from my bag off the modest console. I'm so tired.

As I pull the phone out, the solo earbud rolls onto the entryway rug. I bend down to pick up the white device, inspect it, then wipe it off on my shirt. It looks brand new. Like it's never been used prior. The long antenna part has a tiny "R" on its side. I inserted the white bud into my right ear. Nothing. I don't know what I expect to hear. Would anything be able to play on it? I wouldn't know until I paired it with my phone. It's probably dead, too.

I shuffle my way into my bedroom, enjoying the motionless city outside during sleepy hours. I pull closed the window covering and drop to my bed. Not having the energy to undress, I lie there for a moment, staring at the ceiling. My blinks become longer as I recall the shade of green of Mr. Neat's eyes. Somewhere between visions of his dimpled smile and my dark purple walled room, I drift to sleep.

I startle awake, feeling as if I forgot something. The ever-present, earsplitting ring welcomes me to the waking world as I sit up, still in yesterday's clothes. I find my phone somewhere on the bed and open the calendar to see what is on today's agenda.

I always have some kind of job, or an errand to attend to. Keep busy. You won't have time to think of much else. Fortunately, I woke up with enough time to bathe and feed myself before my other job. Light pours through the cracks of the curtains. I must have passed out last night. It's not the first time I've forgotten to set my alarm. One time, I slept four hours into my morning shift at Bravo Pharmacy. When I finally arrived, they canned me on the spot.

My hands run up and over my face, where I find the earbud still securely in place from last night. Pulling out my nightstand drawer, I feel around until I find the charger case for my earbuds. Removing my own set, I rummage through the drawer again to find a marker. Mystery tech in hand, I use my teeth to uncap a purple Sharpie and draw a small star on the *foreign* earbud. Now, I can tell the difference between mine and this one. Dropping the bud in my charger, I feel sudden vibrations within the apartment. Like someone is running.

I quickly take off, out of my room, and into the main living area of the apartment. There, I find a silver haired young woman, in nothing more than an oversized Metallica shirt. She waves a tea towel close to an opened window, silently mouthing "sorry," while attempting to waft smoke from the kitchen to outside. The source appears to be an undeserving, frozen waffle in the toaster. Why am I not surprised…

While the smoke drifts out the window, I try to help by unplugging the appliance and shaking its contents into the sink. Running water over the circular briquette, I ensure it's no longer a fire hazard. Once the cooking chaos subsides, I fetch my fully charged hearing aids from their charger. I hear my roommate shut the window. We convene in the kitchen, where we both stare at the soggy, charred toaster pastry.

Andrea is shorter than me, but still, she attempts to throw a toned arm over my shoulder before speaking. "Benny's? My treat."

I look down at her perfect skin. A cute bob frames her face. "Sure…"

Her nose wrinkles. "You smell like a bar."

I take the opportunity to wrap myself around her.

"Ewww!" She effortlessly pushes me off.

"Payback for making our home smell like your gym bag was lit on fire."

She scoffs, grabs a spray from under the kitchen counter, and proceeds to spray the air in front of us.

"Great, now it smells like smoky lemons in a gym bag," I retort.

She grabs one of my arms and lifts it just high enough to spray the deodorizer under my armpit. "There! Now we can go have breakfast at Benny's."

TWO

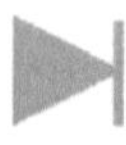

ANDREA

I sat across from my roommate and closest friend in a diner about two blocks from our apartment.

Cindel wasn't too keen to start the day smelling like a combination of Febreze and smoke, so I waited in my room for her to shower and get ready for breakfast. A call came through right as I was in the middle of reading an article about my favorite movie star. Apparently, there is speculation about her partnering back up with Mr. Reeves to make a Speed 3!

"Hello, sir… No, I'm alone," I say, pulling on a pair of dark leggings as I listen. "Yes, sir."

I hold the phone to my head and tuck the tail of my shirt in, then search for a pair of clean socks.

"Correct… I plan to head over there today."

I reluctantly smell a rolled-up pair of white socks I find beneath the bed. Clean enough.

"I'll keep you informed."

The phone call ends as I hear Cindel's bedroom door close from the other side of the apartment.

"Ready!" she hollers.

Between my cooking skills and our wacky work hours, we find ourselves at Benny's at least three times a week.

Since I can't bear to look at another waffle and it's so close to noon, I decide on the lunch menu.

Cindel orders her usual stacked pancakes with maple syrup. My friend is blessed with the ability to eat loads of empty calories, without so much as an added inch to her waist. With how much she's been through, I think she deserves to eat as much sugar as a child would on their birthday.

After we order, I watch her across the table, I can't help but notice how quiet and withdrawn she's being today. I reach across the laminate surface and take her hand in mine.

"How are you?" I ask, searching her face for an indication of how she may be doing.

Her soft smile pulls on my heart's strings. I know yesterday was hard for her. It's been about six months since Cindel's boyfriend, Brodi, up and disappeared. She's still holding onto hope, convinced that one day, he'll just show up with some kind of whirlwind story explaining why he's been missing. Call me a pessimist, but I'm confident the little weasel is dead.

I rub my thumb over the top of her hand in reassuring circles as I continue to wait patiently for her to share. I know Cindel well, probably better than she knows herself. I can practically see the wheels turning in her overactive brain, as she imagines all the outcomes of the conversation before she attempts to speak. She always does this… overthinks everything.

This isn't the first time we have spoken about this. We've had countless conversations about Brodi, however, the more I share my opinion on the matter, the more she pulls away. Lately, I'm trying to listen more than I'm trying to make her change her mind.

"I'm just…" she finally starts. "I'm just so tired." Her eyes float up toward the grid patterned ceiling. She blinks a few times before attempting to look back at my face. "I know he's gone. Probably ran off with… someone else."

Damn. Why did I have to put that idea in her head? She wouldn't come out of her room for a week when I stupidly suggested that.

"I just feel weird. Like something's different?"

I have to wonder what could have possibly changed at her jobs, or with me, to make her feel this way.

She gingerly pulls her hand from mine, indicating she's not in the mood for being *touchy feely*. Instead, her hands fall below the chrome edged table. I can only hope she's not mutilating her cuticles again.

This year has affected her worse than the one before. The circles under her eyes don't seem to ever reduce no matter how much sleep she gets, while her clothes continue looking baggier and baggier. She's hurting and honestly, I don't know how to help her emotionally. I'm able to protect her, but this? This is foreign territory for me.

I remember when we first met, she had the ability to light up any room she entered. Her professors used her work as examples, while her classmates fought for the chance to partner with her. She had this way about her that just made you feel good, simply by being in her presence. Everyone wanted to know the girl with a bubbly personality and ambitious goals. Cindel and I became real close, real quick. People thought we were a *thing* in college, because we were always together. *That* was never going to happen with her, that's not why I'm here.

We moved into our current apartment about five years ago and have been together ever since. It's been about three years since her brother died; no one saw it coming. Mental illness is real, but I never saw the signs with him.

My mom was unwell, never really met my dad, but mom tried to do right by me. She left this world when I was too young to understand. That's why I value Cindel so much. She's like the sister I never had and her folks, the family I so desperately needed.

Things were different after Theo was gone. Cindel was lost. She met Brodi shortly after her he died. I think she was still going through a crisis. Looking for something exciting. Something dangerous. Brodi was the quintessential bad boy covered in tattoos, rode a Harley, and had a habit of getting into trouble. She fell hard and fast for him. I strongly advised against the pairing, but she wouldn't hear it. Whatever the reasoning, she clung to Brodi like a lifeline. I couldn't fathom taking anything from her that brought her happiness, so I let it go.

Cindel attempted to keep her relationship with said miscreant, from her parents. The very ideal was comical! Nothing gets past them. At first, Cindel tried ignoring their phone calls when Brodi was around. She even went so far as to feign an illness to get out of a visit from her mom. The ruse didn't last long though; Mama Terri showed up within the week to chew her daughter out. I *may* have been the one to inform them about her biker boy.

But despite the intervention, Cindel kept seeing him. Just because he made her happy, didn't mean he was good for her. He had these grandiose ideas. Constantly telling her, when he gets enough money saved, they'll move to Montana, live off the land on the side of some mountain. He said it so often; she actually started to believe him.

During their relationship, her personal goals went out the window, replaced with pipe dreams from a man with Peter Pan syndrome. She started replacing her wants with his needs. I even had a short stint of learning to pickle foods in our apartment. Unfortunately, during one of her homesteading extravaganzas, she knocked over a huge jar of pickled eggs, causing the apartment to reek of vinegar and garlic for weeks.

But she was on cloud nine with that piece of trash. Hell, I'm surprised she didn't brand her skin with a traditional Japanese dragon to match his. At least as far as I know, she hadn't done anything that permanent.

After graduation, I was able to fall into freelancing positions. Companies in the city always seemed to need a graphic designer, in one form or another. Cindel, however, struggled to find her footing in the fashion world. She took on any and every job, just to scrape by. Sadly, it seemed as though each job she accepted took her father away from her dream career.

Her parents took a huge step back from her life. They didn't have to explain themselves to me; I knew why. Cindel didn't. But I was here for the long haul, no intention of leaving Cindel to face this city alone. She is the one who insisted on staying here in Boston, after her parents left. I may not agree with her uninformed choices, but I'm here for her.

When Brodi disappeared, a part of my best friend went with him. Now, it feels like I have to reach deep inside just to get any idea of what's going on with her. I desperately want to uncover the Cindel I once knew in there. I swear that fucker Brodi better be dead, because if I find him alive, I'll kill him myself.

Cindel and I barely speak until our meals arrive, both of us are lost in our thoughts.

I dig into my veggie hummus wrap while she douses her meal in sticky amber colored goo. Girl is gonna have diabetes before forty at the rate she consumes sugar.

We eat, I pay, and we find ourselves once again at a loss for words, just outside the diner. I look up at my best friend, who is even taller than me with her beloved Doc Martens on.

"Is there anything I can do to help?"

She chews on her bottom lip while she thinks about my question. She looks so... broken. Long minutes pass before she finally makes eye contact with me. Her tired eyes wrinkle at the corners while her mouth strains into a smile.

"No... thank you. For always being there for me." She throws her arms around me in a tight embrace, before she leaves, heading to her other shit job.

The giant calendar on the fridge in our apartment displays her work schedule for the month. Today, she's at Star Mart. A supermarket chain with multiple locations. She started working at the one off Washington Street about a year or so ago.

I make sure I always know where she is, but she can't say the same for me. Cindel rarely knows my whereabouts. In fact, I have an important errand to run today that she, thankfully, has no idea about.

THREE

Six months ago...

It's just after midnight, and I'm still at the shop. I've been a mechanic at Rick's Rides for damn near four years, but it didn't pay worth shit. Not like being a bookie for the Murray's. Sure, they were a bunch of seedy assholes, but I knew an opportunity when I saw one. As long as they stayed in the dark about what I was doing, things were going swell. I've been busting my ass for too long and I deserve to eat better than a steady diet of microwaved noodles with saltines. Plus, I like boxing in my free time, keeps my mind sharp. Especially when I become so bored of the same remedial tasks.

Bike comes in; replace the filter, empty the old engine oil, refresh fluids, and inspect the rear drive belts. Same shit day in and day out. Don't get me wrong, I'm good at what I do, but I know I'm destined for better things. Rick was a good guy and that's why I stayed loyal to him for so many years.

Rick tossed me the keys an hour ago, after he threw an arm around his old lady and headed home. I sit behind my boss's wooden desk, lounging in a worn, ripped leather seat. Between my legs bobs a raven-haired vixen that smells of cheap perfume and cloves. She has wicked curves in all the right places and an even more wicked mouth. My phone buzzes with a text; Doe-eyes looks up at me.

"Everything okay?" she coos.

I suck in a short breath through my teeth from the sudden loss of her warm mouth around my dick. "Everything's fine. Fuck, don't stop."

I collect her hair in my hand and force her back down, encouraging her to work me faster this time. Her cheeks hollow out, allowing my cock to slip deeper into her throat and she attempts to swallow, tugging on the head of my dick, while her hand fondles my balls. I firmly press the back of her head down, as she starts making a gurgling sound. Knowing this bitch is choking on *my cock causes a tingling sensation to start at the base of my spine. She hums, knowing exactly how I need it, vibrating the sensitive tip.*

"Fuck. Right there."

I can feel my balls draw up and I close my eyes, lost in the feeling. With a final wet gag from her, I unload down the bitch's gullet. I hold her head in place as the once forceful jabs become slow, shallow pumps until she's consumed every drop of me. She pops off and leans back onto her bargain heels.

"Damn, woman... do you always have to tag my dick with your hooker paint?"

She giggles in response before she retrieves a tissue from her purse, and hands it to me.

Like this could possibly help.

I fervently rubbed the traces of her lipstick off my cock, as I watched the little minx reapply her crimson stain.

This one came with me to one of the fights this past week but bailed early. I told her she owed me a blowjob for it, so she showed up at Rick's to deliver. If I couldn't get my dick wet in an alley behind The Bay Boxing Club, I had to wait until my boss had me close the shop.

Cindel was in my bed currently, so going back to my place was out of the question.

I tuck myself back into my pants before I fasten them and lean back in the chair, propping my boots up onto Rick's desk. It's such a relic; he won't even notice any wear to its surface.

"Don't wait too long to call me this time, sugar."

I don't bother to respond. Destiny has never held power over me.

Lacing my fingers behind my head, I enjoy the view of her skin-tight, cheetah print ass, as it bounces toward the exit.

She turns and blows a kiss before disappearing through a side door, into the night.

My eyelids lower once again, relishing in the fact I get to go home and sink into another warm hole.

I hear the heavy door swing open, then slam shut abruptly. I opened one eye.

"You forget something?"

I sit up, surprised, to find a broad-shouldered man in a form-fitted suit. I knew I should have locked that damned door. Lucky for me, I recognized the brooding guy from the club.

"Daxton! This fuckin' guy! How the hell are ya?!"

I spring from my seat, round the desk, and smack him on the back. Like a wall of muscle, he hardly flinches.

"You've been... busy this evening," he states dryly, smoothing the front of his jacket.

"You know how it is! Women can't keep their hands off me. Hard to choose just one, right? Come, sit."

My unannounced guest ignores my invitation to sit in one of the smaller wooden chairs, instead taking a seat at the end of the desk, where I resided moments ago.

"Soooooo, how's business? I understand one of the bars is doing well now."

His expression remains unreadable, but I did catch a tick along his jawline. Shit. Not one for small talk, I see. I rub the back of my neck, feeling the room becoming increasingly hot. Did they know?

"Cut the crap, Brodi. You know why I had to come all the way out here. Where's the rest of the money?"

Fuck. I look at the hardened man, trying to gauge if this is a warning visit or something else entirely. Is he here alone?

I lean forward, placing an elbow on each knee, fisting my hands together, all while mirroring his steely glare. If I lie, I know I won't be walking out of here. I need to be smart. Use what I know and get the hell out of here.

"Look man, I've come across some information... something that will make the Murrays very happy." I say sitting back, casually throwing an arm over the neighboring chair and resting one foot on the opposite knee. "Let's just say, this information has been under wraps for a loooong time."

He crosses his arms over his muscular chest and lifts an eyebrow.

He's biting, so I continue, "It's the kind of intel that could make everyone forget about any misplaced funds."

His jaw moves side to side, as if his teeth are grinding.

I pushed on. "The Lombardis were more involved than the Murrays suspected," I state firmly.

"How so?" His mouth barely moves as he asks, speaking through gritted teeth.

"My source..." I almost say the poor sap's name before catching myself. "Someone has told me that a Lombardi is responsible for Mary Murray's death."

His face is unreadable; he looks past me.

I turn slightly to find nothing in particular before I turn back to his unsettling stare.

"The rat responsible for that, has already been dealt with." He looks bored, like this information wasn't as important as I initially thought. "Who's your informant?" He asks pointedly, leaning back in the worn chair causing it to emit a high-pitched screech.

Shit. Maybe they already know. I need something more substantial if I don't want to wind up in an underwater grave. That's what I heard about these goons. You do them wrong, and they'll fillet you before sinking you to the bottom of the bay, like the rest of the idiots dumb enough to.

"I'm an asset, you know! How about this?! You tell your boss to wipe my slate clean, and I'll tell you where to find a Lombardi. There's one still here in the city, right under your noses."

The man's once indecipherable features become calculated. His eyes narrow to slits, pinning me in place. "Which one?" He all but growls.

I didn't plan on ever using this knowledge, but desperate times call for desperate measures. I'm out of options to save my own ass.

"The young, pretty kind," I divulge, feeling a small pang of regret that I've just royally fucked up her life, all because I can't handle my own shit.

His eyes automatically darken. I can no longer tell if I'm digging myself an escape route, or my own grave.

I should pack a bag and leave tonight. Tell Cindel to go back to her parents in New York. My legs begin to bounce, so I decide to stand instead. I roll my shoulders, as if it might make me appear bigger against this manslayer.

"Wow! Would you look at the time! I need to close up the shop. So... if you don't mind? Ya know... Fucking off?" I train my eyes to remain on the pin-up girl in the center of the clock, but I can still feel his eyes watching me. His stare boring into the side of my head.

The chair groans when he stands.

Can I grab my knife in time?

He slowly rounds the desk, and I listen to his footsteps as he makes his way past me. I dare not look away from the clock as I watch the seconds lazily go by. Only once I hear the scrape of metal against metal, followed by a thundering slam does time return to normal. I blink. The hand is once again, moving at a normal pace around the face of the clock. Voices outside carry past the thin bay doors. Perhaps he wasn't alone, the idea of taking on more than one of him unsettles me.

Tires crunch over gravel, just as I crack the door and see a dark colored Audi pulling onto the roadway. I stand there watching as the taillights disappear down the darkened road.

Fuck me; I thought for sure I was a dead man when he brought up the money. I know an opportunity when I see one, and right now I see the moment to leave.

I knew my fate was sealed when I started skimming from the bets placed at the club. Eamon asked me to be the new bookie a few months back, I never intended to do it this long, but when I saw my stash growing, I naturally became greedy. I had shit parents and couldn't depend on anyone but myself.

The way the Murrays throw money around is fucked up. I deserve more than the table scraps they throw me.

My plan had always been to save enough to leave; build a cabin in the mountains, maybe even bring my girl. Live an honest life.

I guess I shouldn't be too surprised the money started burning a hole in my pocket, and I found myself at Cha-Cha's three times a week with enough coke up my nose to put down an elephant. I'm cut from the same cloth as my folks, I suppose. Shit human beings through and through. What I squirreled away would have to suffice. I wasn't about to stick around and see what the Murrays had in store for me once they learned my hand was in their cookie jar.

Grabbing my keys and phone off the desk, I throw on my leather jacket, lock the door, and make my way to the Harley out-front. I straddle the bike, briefly checking my phone notification from earlier, when I was preoccupied.

Cindel: I saw another Harley today! I think it was a "Fat Bob." I could actually hear it coming! I'm at your place. Waiting in bed for you.

Chewing on the inside of my cheek, I steel my spine and text back.

Brodi: Hey, sunshine. I figure you'd be sleeping by now. I'm going to be later than usual. You should go home.

She sends back a sad face emoji.

Brodi: I'll meet you at Benny's tomorrow.

I add, knowing by then I'll be halfway to Ohio.

I tuck the phone inside the inner pocket of my jacket, pull my helmet on, and secure the strap beneath my chin.

Sticking the key into the ignition, I check for neutral before I turn the fuel tap on. Engaging the choke, I use my right foot to kickstart the bike. It roars to life, instantly shaking away my swirling thoughts.

I love this bike, even though the solo headlamp has become foggy as of late. It's overdue for a cleaning, it's barely bright enough to light my way on these winding roads. Though I know each turn like the back of my hand, you still have to be cautious for the occasional opossum hanging out in the middle of the road. Those little fuckers could definitely throw you from your ride.

My feet rest on the pegs, as I add just enough throttle to bring me through the first of many turns. My cares fall away as I ride past darkened warehouses and empty side streets. It's late. Businesses are closed and most people are asleep at this hour; it's just me and the open road.

Just as I emerge from a banked corner, a blinding set of lights comes on from down one of the side streets. The unforeseen vehicle peels out from its current position and comes straight for me!

I straighten my front, while attempting to add enough throttle to get out of the way but not lose traction. The mystery vehicle barrels toward me, and I know I can't get out of the way. The car hits me from the back; my bike ejects me onto the hood of their ride. They slam on the brakes, and I slide from the vehicle's dented hood, and onto the road in front of it.

My body screams at me from every joint, and I can't feel my left arm. A succession of car doors slam, while orbs of light dance across my vision. Where's my bike? Is it salvageable? Who the fuck hit me?

Fuck my arm! It's definitely dislocated.

Footsteps approach, scraping along the grooved road edges, where I apparently lie. The assholes stop on either side of me, as I attempt to blink away the starry light show. I heard a shutter sound, as if a phone was taking a picture.

Two silhouettes stand over me, outlined by the car's headlights. One figure walks away, with a phone held to their ear. I can barely make out a masculine voice say, "we have it handled."

"Hey!" I try to yell, only to be met with debilitating pain. Feels like I cracked at least one rib. "What the fuck, man?!"

The shadowed kneels, over my broken body, but I can't make out a face. Using my good arm, I discreetly reach for the switchblade that I always have strapped to my ankle. I get the feeling they are not going to be calling an ambulance for me.

A deep, menacing voice comes from above me. "You're not an asset, Brodi, you're a liability."

Fuck. They are going to kill me!

I lie perfectly still, letting them think they rendered me immobile. With all the strength I can muster, I grit my teeth and push up slightly. I whip my working arm across the man's form, making contact with his neck. My blade opens his throat, and a crimson waterfall begins flowing onto me and the street.

The man finally comes into focus, and I watch him desperately grasp at the hanging flesh, trying to put himself back together.

I pull back again, ready to stab him in his fucking eye, when I hear a metallic scrape. I look up, just in time to see the other guy swinging a bat, straight for my head.

CINDEL

A short walk from the diner and I'm at my neighborhood Star Mart. This supermarket chain can be found throughout Boston and New England. Working here, it's easy to pick up extra hours, but you're just a number, so if you don't show up for a shift, you're blacklisted. Meaning, they won't schedule you again because you fucked up.

I prefer stocking the shelves over working the checkout lanes, less human interaction results in less drama all around, and my coworkers are nice enough. I've worked here longer than I have worked at The Black Sheep, but I've yet to forge any lasting friendships. Management is tolerable at best, as long as I don't have to deal with Craig. The Star Crew calls him *Creepy Craig* behind his back, because he's just downright weird. I mean, who the fuck brings a can of tuna to work each shift, then proceeds to coat their crackers without any mayo or seasoning? Psychopaths, that's who! I mean, at least change it up a little… a turkey sandwich is a safe bet… or really anything that doesn't make the whole backroom smell like cheap fish.

The nickname stuck for me, right around my ninety-day review. Craig sat in a folding chair, right beside me, the entire shift. He said it was to "grade" my work ethic. From stocking, to bagging, and even mopping, *Creepy Craig* was right there beside me. He insisted it was company policy but, from what I heard, no one else had to face such scrutiny. No one wants to be watched that closely; it's uncomfortable. Lucky for me, Craig hasn't shared too many of the same shifts as me after that. So, I keep showing up at work.

Today's schedule is posted in the backroom; I'm on register three. Grabbing one of the required green aprons from the hook on the wall, I push my head through the top and leave the laces to hang at my sides. Next, I shove my purse into a drawer at the bottom of the filing cabinet and make my way to the front.

The words '*Star Crew*' lie across my chest in big white block letters. I was embarrassed to wear it at first, but when I saw everyone else had to endure the same sin against fashion, I grew used to the idea.

Joining the floor, I saw Mairead. She's one of the newer girls who started this month. Her name is pronounced like "parade" but with an "m" instead of a "p" and she is sweet as can be. Red curly hair and a genuine laugh that warms my very soul. Mairead is just easy to like. Seeing her on the register beside me gives me hope that perhaps my shift will go by quicker than usual.

"Hey Cindel." She gives a small wave as I approach.

"Hey Mairead. It's nice they put us together for once." I tie my apron into a bow behind my back.

"I know, right?!" She agrees, opening a compact to check her face, while slightly crouching behind the register. "Hey… I never had a chance to get your number. I barely saw you last time we worked together." She pulls a phone from the front pocket of her apron and reaches across my lane to hand it to me. "Here."

I enter my contact info and hand it back, with an exaggerated bend over the conveyor belt. She looks down at the new contact; her smile doesn't quite reach her eyes. Then she tucks it back into her apron, just as a customer with an overflowing carriage pulls into her lane.

I log into my register with my employee number, but before I can turn on the numbered light, I notice something. A small box with a piece of paper attached sits just below the cash drawer. Sometimes my coworkers will store a can of pop there, but that's about it.

I pick up the small black box, and see my name is on the tag. Clippings of mismatched letters are arranged on the manila paper. I look around to see if anyone is watching me. Mairead, still busy with her customer's large transaction but, no one else in sight. Slowly, I lift the top of the box off to find purple, sparkly tissue paper within.

Unwrapping its contents, I finally set eyes on the item within. What the—

"Are you open?"

My eyes jump up at the voice that caught me off guard. Tired, deep-set eyes stare back at me. An older gentleman in suspenders, juggling a carton of eggs and two bunches of bananas, waits patiently for me to respond. I nod, since apparently, I am unable to form words. I ball up the note with the mismatched letters forming my name and toss it into the pail. Then I pushed the lid onto the small box and tucked it back where I found it.

I'm on autopilot, unable to think. I scan the customer's items without even uttering "hello". I find myself unable to function.

The man lifts an eyebrow in question, and I realize he's waiting for the total.

"Oh. Sorry. That will be… four dollars and sixty-two cents, please."

He digs into his pocket, pulling out a leather coin pouch.

"Turn on your light!"

I spin around to find Craig hovering, mere inches behind me. "Light," he repeats.

I nod, still not firing on all cylinders, reach forward and flip the switch for my lane light on. The customer begins counting his change on the conveyor belt with pennies, nickels, and a few quarters.

"Smile. We want our guests to feel welcome here at Star Mart," Craig says through a phony customer service smile. He's never pleasant unless someone who doesn't work here is watching. His face is too close to mine. How does his breath already reek of tuna? My afternoon shift has just started!

Eventually, Craig shuffles off to creep someone else out, and I'm able to return to my job. Sorting the money into the register, I place the man's items into a paper bag, then flip my light off, again.

"I need to go to the bathroom," I whisper to Mairead, who is now thumbing through one of the magazines from the rack in her lane.

"Got it," she replies with a thumbs up.

I sweep the confounded box with purple insides into my front apron and quickly make my way to the facilities.

Once I'm inside the women's bathroom, I check underneath each stall, making sure I'm alone. Turning the lock, I rest my back against the closed door. My breaths are shaky and I'm questioning what I'm doing here in the first place. I attempt to slow my breathing, in through my nose till my lungs ache from the sheer amount of oxygen in them, before blowing out a smooth, unrushed stream. I repeat this process three times, despite the unpleasant scent of bleach.

The lighting in here has never been kind, but I look more like one of those female leads in a slasher movie who barely escaped alive. Really, Cindel? Get a hold of yourself. I splash some cool water onto my hot, flushed skin. Then pull out a few paper towels from the dispenser to dab the drips from my reddened face. It's probably just a coincidence, I tell myself.

Reaching into the pocket of my apron, I retrieve the black box. Holding it in my hand, I slowly remove the lid, as if something is going to jump out at me. I set the lid on the edge of the sink and allow a finger to slide in past the tissue paper, until I can feel what's inside I close my eyes and pull out the small device. I count down, "3...2...1..." before I force open my eyes.

An earbud sits in my hand, and there, on the stem is the same purple star I drew just this morning. How?! This can't be the same one. It's in my bedroom... on the charger.

Is this a joke? Oh my god! Did someone break into our apartment? My mind races through possible scenarios and explanations on how this thing has sprouted legs. Is someone watching me? Following me?

I feel... unwell. I push into one of the stalls, under the impression that I'm about to lose my sticky flapjacks when I hear something. It could be distant, or perhaps close, but very soft. Do my aids need to be recalibrated?

I stare at the impossible item in my hand, suddenly realizing that the source of sound is its tiny speaker. I hold it closer to my ear.

"Stop!" the tiny device commands. The once ill feeling turns into dread. Should I drop this damned thing into the toilet and flush it? It definitely can't find its way back to me then. But this doesn't explain how it showed up at my job, instead of staying put where I left it. This whole situation is nuts.

The earbud is still making noise. Despite myself, I remove the dome from my ear, letting the receiver wire dangle while I slip the curious tech into my ear. Maybe I've finally cracked?

I hold my breath, both nervous about what I may hear and tired of the unpleasant bathroom smell. I… I can hear it. I can hear it? The only way that could happen is if the device was calibrated for my ears, meaning someone would have to manually input an audiogram result, based on me. And yet, I can hear the music loud and clear.

Without meaning to, I take a deep breath in, feeling like I might once again lose my stomach contents because I can taste Lysol in my mouth.

Pixies - "Where is my Mind?" Plays through the disturbing device. What am I doing?! Take it out of your ear and drop it!

I used to like this song, but I have a feeling I won't want to hear it again after today. Flush it down the toilet. Flush it! My inner voice of reasoning repeats.

The song continues playing as I internally battle between rational thought and my uncanny ability to be recklessly curious. What good has being inquisitive ever done for me? Where is your mind, Cindel?!

The eerily disoriented ooooo's in the song make me feel as if I'm floating above my body. Watching this situation unfold without the ability to choose. Goosebumps break out along my arms. Just as the song fades, I feel myself slipping back into control. I yank the earbud from my ear, like it has the ability to poison me if it stays a second longer; it falls into the toilet. The water ripples as it sinks to the bottom and I don't hesitate; I flush the fucking thing. I pick up the wrappings from the floor and sink area before tossing them in the trash can.

After washing my hands, I attempt to smooth down my hair before making my way back onto the floor. I'd like to think this will be the end of it, but from my past experiences, nothing is ever that easy.

Mairead appears worried when I return. How long was I even gone? "Craig came looking for you. I told him your pussy was bleeding."

I slap my hand over my mouth before a wild sound comes out. "You did not!" I jeered.

She shrugs and goes back to flipping through a different tabloid, as I return to my lane. I didn't tell her why I was in the ladies' room so long, the very idea sounds insane, even to me. She could apparently tell that something is off and suggested I go home, but I need the money. Plus, being here vs. my apartment wouldn't make much of a difference. I had a feeling that whatever just happened would follow me.

The rest of the day goes by painfully slow. Mairead talks a lot, mostly about shopping, her favorite restaurants, and about some places she's traveled to in the past. I haven't so much as ventured off the east coast, only going as far as Florida once to visit a beach. She's been to other continents. Maybe her family is loaded?

I try to focus on present tasks, pushing thoughts about invasions of privacy and robbery from my mind. I half pay attention to my pleasant colleague between bouts of customers. Giving her responses like, "Oh, I didn't know that" or "That sounds wonderful."

I am being a shitty person, that's the only way to put it, but my mind is running rampant trying to make sense of why the earbud is appearing in places it shouldn't be.

Mairead changes into an adorable sundress after we clock out together. Then we make our way out into the chilly evening.

"You look great!" I secretly wonder if she is cold, but she is an adult and can dress herself without my advice. "Do you have a date or something?" I inquire, pulling my bag onto my shoulder.

"Nope, just like to look my best. Never know who you'll bump into." She gives a spin, causing her dress to lift and fan out from the action.

I envy that carefree feeling, wishing I too could twirl around in my favorite flowy skirt without a care in the world. How could someone with such an infectious personality want to work at a B Grade grocery store, like Star Mart? Clearly, she's from money, but why here? She belongs selling vacations or designer handbags that are worth triple my monthly rent.

"Let's grab lunch one day soon," she suddenly suggests, pulling me from my super judgy thoughts.

Don't be a bitch. I tell myself. You don't know her. "I'd like that," I say as we walk side by side, down the sidewalk.

"I'll text you!" She sings songs.

Right, she has my number now. I nod and smile, before she says, "Byeeee." Seeming to dance away down a side street, while I continue walking the path toward my apartment building.

I don't need a key to get into my building. It's nice, especially in the colder months when you just want to get inside and warm up. Someone always has the lobby door propped open with a brick or something they've found lying around in the street. More often than not, someone was accidentally locking themselves out or forgetting their key, so the tenants informally agreed the easiest solution was to leave the door ajar. Sure, it's not exactly safe, but most of the neighbors know one another, and we don't exactly get a lot of visitors to our building. If someone they don't know comes around, people have no trouble asking what their business is here.

I slip past the entry, replacing the tire iron in the door, before stopping by the collection of metal mailboxes. Most are stuffed to the brim with letters, while boxes line the edges of the lobby floor. Since packages don't fit in the building's meager, slotted compartments, they go on the floor. It was all based on the honor policy. We always get our mail, so the system works.

A small sticky note was inside our mailbox, indicating one of those staged packages was for us. I reached down, picking up and turning over each cardboard box, until I found a shoebox sized one, with my name and address. Placing the rest of the mail under my arm, I make my way up the stairs to our third-floor apartment. Inside, I retrieve a pair of scissors from the kitchen, to open the mystery shipment. No return address. I didn't think you could mail anything without a return address. It has my information on it, but I don't recall ordering anything. When my parents send me something, my mom calls twice a day to make sure it arrives on time. So, I can count them out as senders. It was very light, considering the size of the package. Running the scissor along the taped seam. I opened the box. Inside, sat another box. This one was white and looked brand new, like it was just purchased from a postage store. Slicing the tape along its edges, I pull out yet another box, slightly smaller than the last. This box, however, was black. No tape, just held together with a purple ribbon. I pull at the bow and lift the lid of the box, finding it filled with purple, sparkly tissue paper. My heart stills and I drop the package to the floor. Stepping back, I all but grasped the scissors in my fist, whirling around expecting to defend myself. From what or who, I'm not sure. I'm met with a still, quiet apartment, just how it was when I arrived.

Wow, I am paranoid! I put down the impromptu weapon and went to Andrea's door. Knocking softly, I wait. No answer. I'm home alone. Why is she never here when I need her? Picking up the fallen box, I pull back the tissue paper to reveal a neatly folded note. Tiny cut-out letters were arranged to form words. *Try not to lose this one,* it reads.

"No," I whisper.

I pull out the tissue slowly, until I find what I suspected would be inside. Was this some kind of fucked up game? I stand frozen in utter disbelief, as the purple star mocks me from the stem of the earbud sitting just inside the box.

I feel sick and confused. This joke isn't funny. I haven't felt this vulnerable since I was little. When my life changed. Is someone trying to trick me?

I recheck the locks on the front door, I need to know that no one can get to me. I reread the note, trying to discern who would do something like this. Andrea would never play such a cruel joke on me. She's always inquiring about who I'm with or where I'm going. It's like having an extra mom away from mom. Whoever is doing this must have known I got rid of it. Don't those things have trackers? If I keep it, will they leave me alone?

I pace the length of the small apartment kitchen while I think. After some time, I decide to keep the infernal thing, but I refuse to use it again. What other choice do I have? I put the white bud back in its smallest box, open my bedroom door and chuck it onto my bed before slamming the door shut.

My ears were sore, and I felt a headache coming on. I remove my hearing aids, place them in the charger by the door, and attempt to busy myself. My brain is short-circuiting, and I need to do anything other than spiral into insanity. I'll occupy myself the best way I know how. Cleaning.

Starting off easy, I begin breaking down the mind fuckery number of boxes and set them by the door for recycling. Then I move onto wiping down the kitchen counters and replacing the garbage bag beneath the sink. Once I finish in the kitchen, I march over to the small storage closet beside the bathroom and pull out the cordless vacuum.

On this episode of Cindel teetering on madness, join us as we watch her rage clean the whole damn apartment, so she doesn't have to face her current circumstances. I'm sweating. I focus on sucking up every single dust bunny as I extend the nozzle beneath Andrea's bed. She has lots of junk under here. I can't hear the whirring of the vacuum, but the tones of bells are forever present.

A tap on my shoulder causes me to jump back and a scream rips from my throat. I turn to find my perturbed roommate.

Turning off the vacuum, I give her the "one minute" finger, scurrying through our home, appliance in hand, to retrieve my hearing aids. Aids in place, I gingerly slide the rocker switch as I find Andrea before me in the living room.

Her eyes bounce around the room, admiring the results of my cleaning bender. "Wow!" I can now hear her say. "That bad of a day?"

Our apartment is never this tidy.

"Something like that."

I tuck the vacuum back into the closet and come to sit next to her on the couch.

"Was it Creepy Craig?" she inquires.

"Tuna breath was tame today."

She skates her knuckle back and forth over her lips.

"Was someone mean to you? Do I need to hurt them?!"

I laugh at the suggestion. She was the kind of friend who couldn't hide what she was thinking from her face. Her features were intense, as she probably debated accompanying me to work next time. Andrea has never had a problem speaking her mind.

"Easy, tiger. No one was mean." I take a deep breath, deciding what to tell her. "It was an uneventful workday," I lie. I can't right now. My legs are sore, and I just sweat my butt off, so I wouldn't have to think about this, I'm not about to bring it back up.

"I think I'm…" I pause, suddenly feeling guilty. My best friend just wants to know I'm okay. Do I share my hypothesis with her?

I imagine how I would sound. *Help, I think I have a stalker! They've sent me a menacing earbud twice!* Really, Cindel, listen to yourself.

"When's the last time you saw your therapist?" I can practically hear my mother ask me. I'm troubled enough without bringing my best friend into whatever this is.

"I'm tired," I finally say. "I think I need a break."

She looks thoughtfully at me, almost a little sad that she can't fix what's going on. "Look, I have tomorrow off. I'll stay in, rest, and get some crafting done."

She crosses her arms against her chest. "You work too hard," she chides.

This I know to be true, but If I don't work both these jobs, we won't make rent. We would have to start skipping at least one meal each day.

"I know, but so do you… you're never here. Always off, saving the world with your graphic designs!"

Andrea pulls me into a tight hug. Her embrace is progressively becoming tighter.

"Thank you for always being there for me. You're my best friend."

She holds me tighter still.

"I don't know what I did to deserve you, but… I do deserve air. Air! Need air!" I squeal.

She laughs, releasing me from her loving crush of death. She holds my shoulders as I intake big gulps of precious oxygen.

"Cindel, you are my whole world. It's me who doesn't deserve your friendship."

Maybe I'm just tired or reading too much into things, but she looks sad for a brief moment. Like some kind of over-caffeinated bunny, Andrea hops up from her place beside me.

"I'm going to start heating up the leftover Chinese. You pick a movie. Make sure it's something with lots of action, but ends happily," she instructs.

"Yes, ma'am!"

I searched through our collection of DVDs before deciding on a classic from 1994. A dashing Keanu Reeves navigates a dangerous situation on a bus full of people with such ease; it makes my current dilemma seem miniscule.

The smell of artery clogging takeout fills our living space, as she carries over the containers of lo mein, spring rolls, and the last bit of wonton soup.

"Oooo, good choice! I just read that there's talk of a Speed 3 coming out!" She informs me before plopping down on the couch.

Andrea falls asleep about an hour into the movie. She was either tired, or her body went into some kind of food coma due to the rarity of having fast food.

I mute the sound, letting the closed captions continue. I don't want to wake her. I prefer reading the words on the screen anyway, as opposed to struggling to hear the soft voices, in contrast to the booming sound effects.

The ending is, of course, joyful. Although, I have to wonder if all their perilous situations helped thrust the two lead characters together or was there also an underlying chemistry? Regardless, it was a wild ride that ended well for everyone, except the bad guys. Too bad, Mr. Reeves can't show up and help me with my shitty situation.

I hadn't been in my bedroom since I threw the black box onto my bed. Entering the room, I immediately grab the disturbing gift and bury it in my closet. It now sits behind three shoe boxes, a collection of unfinished crafts, and a heavy pile of thrifted clothes I have yet to upcycle. There. Out of sight, out of mind!

I draw my curtains and double check the locks on the windows, and the front door before crawling into bed.

Andrea was out for the night, and her soft snores were the last thing I heard before disconnecting.

My body felt heavier than my mind, struggling to sync with the hum buzzing in my head. I imagine myself, a beautiful young Sandra Bullock just opening my eyes after a catastrophic explosion. In this scenario, no one is screaming or crying. Everyone is elated they made it out alive. The danger is gone, and everyone can continue living their perfectly normal lives. Sickly inaccurate, depiction. My story isn't so pretty.

FIVE

CINDEL

My phone vibrates on my end table, way too early in the morning. The words *"Take a Deep Breath,"* fill my screen and I do just that, as I hit the speaker button.

"Yes?" I mumble, not even bothering to move my mouth away from my pillow.

"Is that any way to answer a call? Honestly, Cindel." The words scroll across the screen, so I don't miss any piercing words from my mother.

I pop in one of my paired earbuds because, apparently, I'm a glutton for punishment. "Hello, Mother." I sing songs. My body protests as I try to sit up, reminding me how few hours of sleep I managed.

"Your father is here too. Say hi, Charles."

"Good morning, Cinnabun!" I hear him holler in the background.

Cinnamon bun is my nickname. From as far back as I could remember, weekend mornings were for my dad and I. Rising before the rest of the family, my dad would turn on Boston 25 News, while we made massive cinnamon buns, drenched in cream cheese frosting. The aroma would fill the house, beckoning my mom and brother from their beds. We'd enjoy the sweet, swirled pastry on the porch together, listening to the birds talk with one another.

"Sweetie, we need you to come watch Kingston this weekend. Your father and I are going to Martha's Vineyard to celebrate our very overdue anniversary."

I was taken aback by the implication that I can just up and leave with such short notice. Kingston is the black Russian Terrier that my dad insisted on adopting after one of their client's dogs had a litter. Kingston and my dad do everything together. Morning walks, trips to the local hardware store, but my mother draws the line when it comes to bedtime. He sleeps on his own plush cushion, on my dad's side of the bed. She'd probably like the fur ball a little more if he didn't develop a habit of sampling my mom's expensive shoe collection. That week my dad slept on the couch, with his delighted shoe connoisseur alongside him.

"Can't you drop Kingston off to me on your way there?" I suggest.

"No, no, no... you know Kingston needs lots of room to stretch his legs. That tiny apartment you have won't be adequate. Plus, it gives you a chance to get out of the city and breathe that fresh mountain air. It will do you a world of good."

After my brother's death, I think my parents couldn't bear to be in Boston anymore. They sold one of my favorite houses we ever lived in and have been 'changing it up' ever since. Now, they're home sitters in the Catskills. The places they take care of are usually people's second, if not third homes. Clients with too much money, who need to hire strangers to come live in and care for their possessions while they are away on some lavish vacation.

I couldn't imagine leaving Southie. Hell, I haven't left the state in years. The one time I could have gone on a thrilling adventure was in college. The school offered educational trips for students to explore fashion on a global level, beginning in Paris. I was so excited to go, but then things changed. The idea of leaving was unfathomable.

Boston is where I grew up, even just passing by the local cinema reminds me of my brother and I sneaking into rated R movies before we were old enough or stopping by Mike's Bakery every Friday morning for a fresh cannoli.

The memories were painful at first, but now I relish them. To feel like he's still here. I don't want to forget these kinds of things, but apparently my parents are fine leaving those reminders behind. The only remaining family I have in town is my uncle. We try to catch up once a month over breakfast. He actually doesn't mind how much I talk about Theo. The thought that I haven't been to visit his grave in a while sends a swell of consuming guilt through me.

"Darling! Are you there?"

It's too early for all this. "Yes... I've been kind of busy lately. Picking up extra shifts at Star Mart, and I'm also preparing for the upcoming Grand Bazaar. I really should be a vendor more often. The event is in—"

"You know, your father and I haven't taken a proper vacation for years..." she cuts in.

Oh, here we go.

"We've made countless sacrifices. You have no idea what we've been through. We also sent you to the college of your choosing, then... then, your brother..."

I can hear her sniffling on the other side of the line. I've been down this road and it's not pretty. I take a deep breath as I do many times on these calls, hence the contact's name. I haven't asked for any time off either of my jobs. I'm sure they can find coverage and free up my weekend.

"Fine. Okay. Text me the time you need me and the address. I'll come watch Kingston."

As quickly as turning off a faucet, she collects herself and responds. "Wonderful! We'll see you soon then. Oh, do tell Andrea we said, hello."

I don't know why I bother; they sometimes talk to her more than me.

"Love you, Cinna!" I hear my dad say farther away than before.

"Love you, too," I reply. Great, a multi-day trip to the middle of nowhere is exactly what I need right now.

With the drapes drawn, I can't tell how late I have slept. I'm actually surprised when I glance at the time and see it's just after ten in the morning. I rarely sleep this late. Pushing my feet within the plush, purple slippers beside my bed, I make my way out into the kitchen.

No sign of Andrea, which wasn't a shocker. Unlike me, the schedule on the refrigerator says she works today. It's interesting that she claims I'm *over-worked*, when I swear, her erratic working hours have me wondering if she's part robot.

I find a pot of stale coffee on the burner. After sweetening the bean water to my liking, I check on Miss Thelma. She's a Chilean rose-hair tarantula, who was originally my brother's pet before he died. Andrea's not a fan of things with more than four legs and can easily hide inside a shoe, so I do all the feedings and cleaning for Miss Thelma. To my surprise, she is out and sitting atop the faux, skull hide, indicating she is hungry. It's good to always have something squiggly on hand to nourish her. This week's menu offers a choice between mealworms and crickets. She's really no trouble to care for. Mostly active at night, thus it was strange for her to be up at this time of day. Over the years, I've learned what she prefers, but Thelma was still *Theo's* pet. She'll let me hold her temporarily but won't hang out with me like she would him. My parents wouldn't take her when my brother passed. In fact, it was such a hard no, that my mom wouldn't even sit near the enclosure when she came to visit me. Fortunately, that was a rare occurrence.

After feeding the fuzzy little insomniac, I fill my tummy with raisin bran and start the task I have put off too long. Starting in my closet, I sort my inventory for the upcoming bazaar. I plan to make silk woven earrings, bracelets, as well as a shit ton of embroidery hoops. Some customers like to display my art more than they like wearing it. So far, I have a few solid pieces that I have upcycled from my years of thrifting.

I lay out five vintage band shirts, cropped and trimmed with lace. Three necktie skirts, adorned with metal studded waistlines and four bedazzled jackets.

Of course, I held onto my stud setter from childhood. Ordinary pieces can easily be jazzed up with a row of rhinestones. My favorite piece to date is the one that brings all the warm and fuzzies back for me. The notorious world of

Lisa Frank had my mom pulling out her hair over the number of stickers I littered my bedroom furniture with. How could she be mad when she played a part in creating this monster? I was given all the trapper keepers, folders, and pencils available on the market. My childhood was colorful, and I was clearly spoiled, but it brought me joy.

Now I chase that high, making wearable art in an attempt to return to a simpler time. Dolphins leap from the water in the shape of a heart, on the back of a consigned jean jacket. It took nearly an entire day to paint the back, plus some bedazzling to tie it all together. I planned to display this magnificent piece in my booth at the event. After sorting and pricing the items that are ready to go, I lay out the unfinished projects on my bed.

Definitely a lot more work than I remember. Andrea is handling the new banner for my booth, designing and printing it at one of the companies she freelances with. She drew the logo herself, insisted it's a gift and my money is no good to her.

I push the majority of the projects aside; I'm in the mood to embroider today. Customers seem to like those catchy phrases to hang up in their houses. Sayings such as; *Shoes Off Bitches* or *Come Back With a Warrant.* They're easy enough to make, and even grandmas find the idea absolutely hilarious.

I begin setting out different colored threads, various needle types, wooden hoops, and yards of fabric onto the coffee table in the living room. Thelma nestles back inside her little skull cave, only leaving her little legs poking out. I sail through chain stitches, which I normally struggle with, and finish by adding French knots around the word *BITCHES* for emphasis. The satin stitch takes the longest, but it looks so clean and vibrant when you add bold faced words in your embroidery. Eight hoops with hilarious catchphrases take me all the way to nightfall.

My body feels stiff from remaining in the same spot most of the day. Andrea sometimes makes it home for dinner, so I decide to be a good house-wife and make food. Leaving the projects right where they lie, I scrounge the kitchen for ingredients. Once I find what I need, I set to work on broccoli and cheese soup. My brother taught me how to make it when we were young. With him being five years older, our parents put him in charge when they were working or traveling.

My parents worked in real estate and dabbled in investments. Their long list of clients meant late nights at the office and little time for family bonding. As we grew older, they were gone even more, only retiring shortly after Theo died. Now, with no ties to Boston or any responsibilities, they get to enjoy the finer things life has to offer. How nice for them.

I grab milk, butter, cheese, carrots, and broccoli from the fridge. As well as an onion and garlic bulb from the macrame basket, hanging beside the kitchen sink. The remaining ingredients sit atop a slightly unlevel shelf we have yet to get around to fixing, even though we've lived here for a number of years. I set to work, chopping veggies, grating cheese, and melting butter on the stove.

"Pleeeaaase... I promise I'll be careful!" I begged my brother to let me chop the veggies, while he worked the stove. "I'm the Susan chef and you're the head cook!" I instructed my big brother. Placing a chef's hat on the counter for him to wear.

I loved making things. Whether it was out of paper or food, I desired to create something new. He looks back at me, and I see the corner of his lip pull up into a small smile.

"I think you mean sous-chef." My brother signs, 'second chef' before beckoning me over to the cutting board beside him.

I place my paper hat upon my head, causing my bangs to push down slightly into my vision. At least I could still see well enough if I tilted my chin slightly toward my chest. Standing on a stool, my brother hovered over me, holding my hand on the knife, while the other was positioned atop a carrot, curling my fingertips inward so they were out of harm's way. He guided me through three cuts before letting go, allowing me to experience the force behind the slice. I had to lean all my weight forward to make it through the root.

"Good. Keep going. Careful not to cut yourself." He instructs, while he seared the meat and transferred the drippings to a Dutch oven, I wanted to make something special too.

I used the tip of the sharp knife to make the carrot slices into star shapes, by carving out little triangles around the edge. I had six stars finished before I glanced up to tell him about it. Not looking at my next cut, the circular veggie got away from me and my finger wasn't clear of the knife. Blood welled from the edge of my ring finger. Ahead of my cry, Theo was by my side, kitchen towel in hand.

"Shhhh." He cradled my hand, examining the finger to make sure it's not too bad. "Look, it's still there. Just a small cut."

I was more upset with myself for making a mistake than I was about the pain. I used my free hand to pull the paper chef hat off my head, causing it to tumble to the floor.

Theo looked at me, not tenderly but with something different in his eyes. "Do you see this?"

My blurry vision attempted to focus on the orange shape in his hand.

"This couldn't have happened without this." He held up my sheltered hand, next to the carrot. The red complimented the orange, tragic, yet somehow beautiful. "You can't grow without some pain, Cindel." He looked mad, but I knew he wasn't. "Don't stop pursuing what you love because you're scared of getting hurt. Use it as a lesson and keep going."

I know now the look he gave me was one of determination. Someone who knew life could be ugly and cause discomfort but also knew not to take it for granted. He always understood life was precious.

The pad of my thumb rubs idly over the tiny, raised scar on my ring finger. I couldn't discern if it was the onions in the pan or the recollection of my brother behind my fresh wave of tears. Regardless, I continue through the cooking steps, occasionally patting the corner of my eyes with my sleeve. Before long, I had a pot full of cheesy goodness. Turning the dial to low, I decide to hop in the shower since Andrea still isn't home. My stomach growls in protest, after I emerge dressed. Still no, Andrea. I shouldn't be surprised; she told me she had some big projects coming up. I pulled out my phone to text my missing roommate.

> Cindel: Hey, I made your fav! Broccoli and Cheese Soup. Are you on your way home?

I watch little dots appear. Disappear. Appear. Then a text comes through.

> Andrea: Hey, sorry! I'm going to be a little longer. Go ahead and dig in. I'll have a bowl when I get home. Thanks!

I text back a thumbs up emoji, before dishing myself a heaping serving, and cuddling up on the couch to enjoy my favorite show, *The Sopranos*. Andrea doesn't understand my appeal to the show; she says it's unrealistic. As if her preferred happy-ending genres are any better. My eyes race along the words on the screen, absorbing every dramatic gangster scenario Tony finds himself in. Somehow, I find the show cathartic, even though logically, I know it's morally wrong. I'm not about to become some sort of criminal. The family stuck to a code which made it predictable when someone went astray.

I finish my bowl of soup and set it down beside my collection of stitched hoops. Just as the next episode begins, I feel my eyes growing heavy. I tell myself if I just rest my eyes, I can make it through one more episode. I can't fight it... losing track of time between scenes of 'not being able to refuse a request on his daughter's wedding day' and Johnny being dragged out of the wedding reception.

I startle when I feel someone touching me. Opening my eyes, I find Andrea sitting just in front of me, rubbing my upper arm gently.

"Hey." She smiles down at me.

"Hey," I reply sleepily.

The sun is up, despite feeling as though no time had passed. I must have fallen asleep on the couch.

"Were you knitting all day and night?" She gestures toward the table that looks like a craft store threw up. Everything was as I left it last night. Even the pot of soup remained abandoned since I passed out mid episode.

Without being asked, she stands to tidy up. "Did you turn off the TV when you got in last night?" I ask as I rub the sleep from my eyes, stretching toward the ceiling.

In the kitchen sink, my roommate fills my bowl to soak. Likely containing cemented cheese from last night's dinner.

"I… actually, I just got in."

Just got in? Shouldn't the DVD be stuck on the main menu? I was only on season six; it should still be playing. Shouldn't it?

I make my way to the kitchen and put my hand over the top of the pot to find it still warm. "At least the soup is still edible." I give a weak smile. "So, you were at work all night?" I lean against the fridge watching her serve herself a ladle full.

"Ahuh." She nods, as she blows and samples from her spoon. "Okay… do you work nights now too?"

She shrugs, while cautiously slurping at the thick stew. It's not like her to be so vague.

"Are you not telling me something?"

She stops eating all together, places her bowl down and walks over to me, taking my hands in hers. "Cindel, I was just working. I promise." She squeezes my hand slightly. "If I get laid… you'd probably catch me in the act," she teases, then becomes serious, leveling me with a look. "I'm not doing drugs, and I promise you don't need to worry about my safety." She can read me like a book.

I bite my bottom lip, causing a twinge of pain, as I fight off any sign of hurt that may be collecting along the corner of my eyes. "I know. I just. I worry." I rub the tip of my tongue along the swollen part of my lip I just created. Andrea looks at me with sympathetic eyes.

"I'm right here. You won't lose me." She pulls me into a hug, and I feel the dam I've been holding back release.

She doesn't say another word but starts to sway like a mother rocking an infant. I didn't want to cry again. I thought I was past this. Moments become minutes as I regain my composure and slow my breathing. My sleeves still prove to be an adequate tissue. I'll need to wash this now.

"It's not knitting," I finally say once I manage to collect myself.

She pushes back from me with a puzzled look. "What?"

"You called it knitting, I wasn't knitting all night, it's called embroidery. It's different."

She releases me, picking up her bowl of broccoli and cheese soup before striding off to her room.

"Whatever you say, dork." She slams the door.

"I heard that!"

I swear, we fight like siblings more than my brother and I ever did.

The door opens a crack, and she puts her hand out with her pinky extended, middle and ring finger down, and her thumb and pointer out. Sign language letters: *I, L, & Y*. Together it's, *I love you*, in sign language.

I yell through the door that separates us, "Love you too, wifey!"

SIX

CINDEL

I was in a surprisingly cheerful mood today. Could be because I had a day to recharge my batteries, or maybe it's from the two sprinkle donuts I put down with a regular on my way to The Black Sheep.

Unlike Star Mart, The Black Sheep has no compulsory uniform, so I am free to have fun with my outfits. Today, I chose to wear one of my upcycled pieces. At first, I had debated whether or not to sell the Ozzy shirt from 92', but instead I adorned the sleeves and bottom edging with lace trim. Then sort of forgot about it until I sorted through my closet on my day off. I paired the oversized top with cobalt tights and my standard, black combat boots, I knew as soon as I saw my reflection that Mr. Osbourne was a keeper. It screamed, casual rocker with a hint of city chic. A small braid snaked down the right side of my head, making me feel like a badass Viking lady. Usually, I opt to wear my hair down. It was easier, safer, and allowed me to blend in. Right now, I feel confident, and I could care less what anyone thinks about me, or my hearing aids. I like how I look, and I'll dress however I damn well please.

I pull open the red wooden door, to find Jada drying glasses behind the bar and Brittany removing stools from the tops of tables. A woman in her late forties is behind the cash register, making sure the drawer is in order and we have enough change for tonight's crowd.

Cassie runs a tight ship. When she is on the floor, everyone does their best. She doesn't take any b.s. from the crew. No excuses. No slacking. If she caught you chewing gum on the clock, you would be in charge of scrubbing graffiti off the bathroom stalls that very night. A little unreasonable of a punishment if you ask me, but I respected her, nonetheless. Even the customers are wary of her. If someone got fresh with her or anyone under her watch, she had no problem throwing them out on their ass. She is a fire-cracker. Not quite as spirited with her outfit choices, I noticed she stuck to skinny jeans and a company shirt, embroidered with a tiny black sheep.

I quickly make my way to the back, tossing my coat and bag in the back-room with the rest of the girls' belongings, before jumping in to help with opening tasks. I'm not late by any means, but I'm not super early like everyone else seems to be. Cassie walks over to where I've started refilling the ice bin and places something down. I look at her, then down at a black box, then back up. She watches with a raised eyebrow. My gaze jumps back to the dark package. The box has a purple ribbon tied around its sides, with a neat bow atop. I'm at a loss for words. The gesture reminds me of a beloved pet presenting their owner with a grotesque gift, like a dead bird or half chewed up squirrel. How could you deny their present when they're just trying to please you? My mouth opens and closes without a single utterance.

"This was left for you," she informs me, pushing it closer with a red painted finger.

Words finally tumble from me. "Di-Did you happen to see who left it?" I stare at her mouth, unable to blink, ensuring I don't miss a single syllable.

"No, sorry. It just had a wrinkled note with the letters of your name. Wanted to get it to you before one of the delivery guys made off with it." My teeth rake over my top lip as Cassie tilts her head to the side. "You're not sure who it's from? Probably just some fella that fancies ya. I used to get plenty of gifts in my younger days. Enjoy the attention, dear." She pats my hand that rests beside the uncanny black box, before striding off to check on the rest of the staff's progress. Right. Enjoy being stalked. Sure.

Pulling at the purple velvet ribbon, I opened the box to see the same creamy, folder paper as before. I open the note slowly. My hand trembles. Finding various fonts extracted from magazines, just like last time. *You left this behind.* Beneath the note, I find exactly what I suspected. From the moment Cassie put down that black box, I knew what was inside. The ever-looming white earbud nestled within purple tissue paper.

I close my eyes, taking slow even breaths before opening it again. I should put the lid on the box. Tuck it away and go on with my work tasks, but I don't. Instead, I reach into the box, lift the tech by the long part, then rotate the item within my fingertips. The star. How? I threw the note away... even buried the box in my closet! Is this some kind of twisted game? Is a creepy suited puppet going to roll out from a dark corner on a tricycle and ask me to play? My hand continues to shake as I rotate the damned thing, trying to rationalize that maybe it's not the same one. Maybe someone has lots of right earbuds and they simply keep sending me a new one. That still doesn't explain the star. I drew that in my room. In my bed! Is some perv watching me? I feel light-headed, realizing I stopped breathing somewhere between examining my purple Sharpie work and having a full-blown panic attack.

I set the device back in the box and scurry to the backroom to have a moment to think. I chance taking a seat in Cassie's chair within the cramped storage room. Beyond the icemaker, there's barely enough space back here for a desk, filing cabinet, commercial dishwasher, and mop bucket. Sitting in the tweed chair, the box before me, I recall my breathing exercises from therapy. Count back from ten, focusing on your breath, while using your sense of touch to ground you. Ten... nine... eight... What if he watches the whole apartment? Shit... seven... is Andrea in danger? Six...there's no getting rid of this. I've tried that already. Fuck counting. This isn't helping.

What if... what if I played along? Would they leave me alone if I comply? Could doing this keep my roommate safe? Will we be okay?

Completely abandoning all calming techniques, I decided, then and there to just play the stupid game. I just wasn't too sure I wanted to win the stupid prize that came along with it.

"Fine! Message received," I whisper-shout at the inanimate object. I flip the rocker switch on my exposed ear, remove the receiver, and place my hearing aid within the little black box. Whether I truly want to or not, I consciously make the choice to replace my medical device, with a potential gateway to a stalker. With my hearing aid now in the box, I place it with the rest of my belongings ahead of going back out to the floor.

There's still much to do before The Black Sheep welcomes patrons, so I need to move quickly to finish any remaining tasks. I carry a bucket of ice with me, hoping that no one noticed I was gone in the back for a little longer than necessary. Only being here, a little under six months, I wanted my coworkers to like me.

"Cindel!" Cassie hollers to me, just as I finish filling the underbar ice bin. "You're on the floor tonight."

I nod with a curt smile. If I had a choice in the matter, I prefer to be behind the bar. My back toward shelving and storage, I only had one direction to interface with customers. Although I do make better tips when I'm moving around serving tables, it can also be extremely overwhelming. So many moving bodies and sounds that I don't even realize when a party may be trying to get my attention. So, I rotate. Regularly. My attentiveness was usually rewarded with a fat tip.

By nine o'clock, the bar is packed. I find myself scarcely able to weave through the crowd with a tray full of drinks. The horde is becoming rowdier by the minute and making it that much more difficult to decipher each customer's drink order. Balancing a multitude of drinks, each a different size and color, I warily navigate my way back to table six.

Without warning, I start to feel my foot slip on something wet beneath my shoe. In slow motion, the tray I'm holding begins to tilt, while my body ambles forward. I try to regain my footing, scared I am going to lose all the drinks, when a hand shoots out and steadies my tray. Spring colored, clover eyes look back at me, as I clumsily right myself with the extra support. His perfectly chiseled face appears regal, and his intense stare bores into me.

Rising to his full height, he rolls his shoulders, while effortlessly saving the whole table's order. No drinks tipped, but some liquid now dances around the ring of the tray. I look from his face to my hand resting upon his, like some kind of debutante at their first ball. Neither of us speak.

Move your hand, Cindel, I scream internally. I do just that, clearing my throat, I stammer, "Mr. Neat."

He bows his head, as if pleased I remember our previous interaction. Taking the tray from him before Cassie noticed, I was not about to scrub toilets for allowing a customer to hold my tray of drinks.

Casually, he settles his hands into the front pockets of his jacket. As if he didn't just save me from an embarrassing situation.

"Thank you for the hand," I offer.

When I turn back toward the direction of the table, I feel a large hand curl around my free wrist. I freeze on the spot and turn to look at him. The extremely handsome customer points to my ear.

"Do you like music?" he asks the words slowly, as if he already knew it's hard to hear in here and wants to make sure I can read his lips.

Suddenly remembering I have the troublesome device in my ear, I respond, "Yes."

He nods as if to himself, unsure what direction to take next with this inter-action. It's odd how this man has sought me out twice now, without bringing his '*A*' game. Considering how brutally sexy this man is, shouldn't he have his choice of anyone? Why single out the server girl?

"I'd like to see you again," he admits, catching me off guard. I did not expect this, but before I could respond, he continued. "Not here, though. Like out… maybe a meal?"

I look around, unsure if anyone is watching, especially my boss. I find Jada watching me from the bar. Is she… leering? As if she knew what was happening here?

"Umm." A body slides between my coworker and I, allowing me to focus back on the point of contact along with the question. "I think I'd like that."

His smile is devious, almost as if he already knew I'd say yes.

I go to turn when I remember something concrete on my schedule coming up.

"Not Thursday," I blurt. "Once a month, I meet with my uncle at Benny's for a stack of pancakes."

Well, I get the pancakes; he gets eggs. Sometimes a bowl of yogurt or avocado toast. He has to watch his sugar intake. He's my only family here, after everyone else left, in some sort of capacity. I haven't missed a single month since Theo died.

His eyebrow lifts as he studies me, like he's not used to anyone giving him parameters. His verdant eyes trail over me. Damn, this tray is growing fucking heavier by the second. A smile blooms upon his perfect face, and he gives a single nod. "I'll see you at the end of your shift."

Turning toward a very impatient table six, who had to sit by and watch the awkwardly flirtatious exchange, I place down each drink. My shoulder is instantly relieved. I give an apologetic smile and make my way back to the bar. Brittany has apparently joined in watching me, leaning with her back against the counter while hugging an empty tray to her chest.

"Ooooo, what's going on there, Miss Mari?"

I blow air through my lips, making a trilling sound. "Last time a guy gave me his number, you called him and pretended to be me!"

Jada's upturned smile and crossed arms tell me she's in a bad mood. Regardless, they're both constantly on me about putting myself out there, and I wasn't about to give them anything that could initiate an onslaught of questions.

"That was one time!" Brittany retorts, throwing out a defensive arm.

I know they mean well, but at the rate they eat up men, I wasn't ready to join their casual cannibal club. I haven't been ready to entertain the idea of dating again. Am I ready?

I didn't see Mr. Neat the rest of the night, but I did serve his buddies that took up space at the end of the bar. A collection of glasses gathered around the friends after a lengthy time just sitting. The chatty one chewed on a toothpick, shamelessly hitting on anything that walked by with tits. His companion, however, was as unreadable as he was the previous time I laid eyes on him. It looked as if the conversationalist ordered for both of them, having no issues with filling the air space. Occasionally, the chatterbox would elbow the reserved man, lifting his eyebrows suggestively when a miniskirt hovered too close to the duo. I watched as the quiet ones piercing gray eyes never actually looked at any of the women in question but instead scanned the room with feigned interest. A few times, I swear his gaze landed on me. An hour 'til closing, most of the customers have finished their last drink and left, including Mr. Neat's comrades at the bar.

My ear ached from the foreign earbud, I wish I had taken it off earlier and switched back to my hearing aid. It was too busy this evening and I honestly didn't have a moment to do so.

I didn't expect to see him again, until he emerged from the bathroom hallway, walking straight up to me with all the confidence of a man who knows what he wants. I stand fixed in place, watching him as he reaches into his front pocket and withdraws his cell phone. He unlocks it and hands it to me. He was serious...

I haven't been on a date with another man in forever. Not since Brodi. Even then, he never really took me anywhere. He did at first, but things started changing over time. I look down at the phone. An emotional slurry mixing around inside. I haven't felt wanted in an awfully long time. Before I talk myself out of it, I enter my number and hand it back to the smooth operator.

"Cindel. Do I have it right?" he asks.

I can't help but tilt my head, slightly confused. "Yeah. I'm surprised you pronounced it right. Most people say *Citadel* or *Kindle*."

He slips the phone back into his pocket. "What can I say? I know more than anyone should. Guess I'm not just a pretty face after all."

Oh, this guy is going to be trouble. He winks at me before striding toward the front door of the bar. When the door swings open, I'm able to see the two other men just outside, apparently waiting for their friend. No one should be that cocky or good looking.

"Shit," I mutter. He knows my name, but I didn't get his.

Wait, I didn't type my name. Did I? Maybe he asked about me. Perhaps one of my coworkers told him my name? That would explain how he got the pronunciation right. Great conversation skills, Cindel! You couldn't even ask his name?

I continue wiping down sticky tables and collecting empty glasses, when I'm taken aback by the sound of a piano. It isn't coming through the bar's sound system. Cassie already ensured it was off when we came to the last call of the night. She claims it encourages people to leave faster. Take away the ambience and the clientele goes with it.

Music was playing through me. Personalized just for my ears. The notorious 90's single from the American rock band **Semisonic** plays **"Closing Time."** The song is unsettling. Suggesting, I was taking someone home tonight. Was the person who gave me this here? Am I being watched right now?

I now know better than to try to get rid of the musical device, like I did before. Instead, I attempt to finish cleaning my section in spite of the pounding of my heart. The last few customers gather themselves before stumbling out into the chilly, darkened streets.

When the song ends, I bolt into the backroom to grab my bag. Jada and Brittany are already gone, so I ask Cassie if she needs any more help before I leave.

"No thanks, dear. Enjoy your night."

With my pepper spray clutched in my fist, I walk home on edge. It was the only song I heard, not being able to keep that thing in my ear another moment. I tossed it into my purse and replaced it with my hearing aid.

A young couple approaching on the sidewalk, causes me to cross over to the other side of the street. I don't want anyone near me. Especially if it was someone I don't know. I walk so fast, I don't see anyone else as I approach my building.

Even though the streets are quiet, it doesn't help this sinking feeling that I am being watched. Followed.

I'm panting by the time I enter the apartment. Fortunately, I am alone, so as not to cause my roommate to notice my distressed state. Sometimes I wish she was here, though. That I could tell her what was happening right now, but with our schedules never aligning, we barely cross paths lately. Conversations with her are becoming sparse and I can feel us becoming distant.

I check the locks before making my way to the window that looks down to the street. Barely finding anyone on the walk home, I didn't expect to see a form standing beside a tree on the opposite side of the building. The person was just standing there. No dog. Not smoking. Were they… looking up at me?

I gasp, closing the curtain in response. I rub my eyes, trying to make sense of what I just saw. Okay, this is how the girl dies in these kinds of movies. Should I take a look to see if the shadowy figure is still there? Nope. Not going to help this plot move forward. I argue with myself that I have an over-active imagination and need to eat something, because my brain is obviously starved of logic. I force myself to walk away from the drawn shade. Pull off my boots and tights, ahead of reheating the broccoli and cheese soup in the microwave. While the hum of the microwave promises me nourishment, I queue up *The Sopranos* DVD to distract myself from the present. I select the episode that I last watched but fell asleep to, then tuck my phone beside me just in case Andrea needs to get ahold of me.

Pressing play, the episode begins, and I dig into my hot meal. A delighted Johnny Sack has been given permission to temporarily leave prison to attend his daughter Allegra's wedding. Two distinct families are merging, promising drama filled moments to occupy my tireless mind. The phone vibrates against my leg, as I attempt to put a much too hot spoonful of cheese into my mouth. Carefully, I place down the bowl expecting to see a message from Andrea, but to my surprise, it's not her. It's a message from an 'unknown' number. Could this be the guy from the bar? I open the message.

> Unknown: As much as I like The Sopranos, we've seen this episode before.

Instantly, I stand and the phone slips from my hand before knocking the spoon out of the bowl in front of me. It flips hot cheesy lava onto my bare skin.

"Owww, shit fuck!" I hobble to the kitchen, submerge a hand towel beneath cold tap water, and press the cooling cloth to my skin. After a few blissful moments of relief, I check to see that my thigh is super red but not terribly burnt.

Before I even consider cleaning up flecks of food from the living room, I march over to the window. I yanked back the curtains to peer back down in the spot I last saw someone, but there was no one. The sidewalk is void of bodies, nothing out of the ordinary to see. No menacing characters, just garbage cans on the street. In that moment, an older man dottles by with a leash in hand. An elated golden retriever trots in front of him, probably pleased as punch to get his master out of bed at such an hour. I step back, pulling the curtains closed and bend down to pick up my phone, feeling like I'm the butt of someone else's joke. I feverishly write a response to the "unknown" number.

> Cindel: Who is this? Are you the creepy stalker who gave me the earbud?

I hold my breath, awaiting a reply. The phone shakes slightly in my hand when dots appear and dance on the screen. It vibrates within my grasp, just as the next message pops up.

> Unknown: Did you know that the band playing on the stage during the episode "Mr. & Mrs. John Sacrimoni Request," is a real-life band? They go by the name 'Double Down.' The band has a classic Frank Sinatra style, while adding a fun twist to modern songs. It's truly a beautiful fusion of jump-swinging numbers and talented tributes. I know you like music.

What. The. Actual. Fuck?! I type back my response without much forethought.

> Cindel: Look, psycho, I don't need Soprano fun facts. Tell me who the fuck this is, or my cop friend is going to trace this number!

My heart is hammering so hard, I can feel it in my stomach. More dots tease at the bottom of the screen. Then, they go away. More dots pop up. I can't help but begin to pace. Waiting for a reply, I find myself once again looking out the window.

> Unknown: You hate cops. Let's not start this relationship on lies. Finish your soup and go to bed, Cindel.

I can feel the blood drain from my face, just as an impending boiling sensation begins working its way up from my belly.

Instantly, I sprint to the bathroom, making it just in time to regurgitate any food I had consumed up until that point. The burning, churning sensation dissolves, but it doesn't help this consuming awareness of being toyed with. Staggering back into the kitchen, I begin opening cabinet after cabinet, until I set eyes on what I am looking for. Pulling the heavy, stone-made item from its place on the shelf, I set it on the counter, before retrieving the last thing I need from my purse. Got it!

I drop the white earbud with its meaningless star into the hollow bowl. Standing up onto the balls of my feet, I bear my weight down on the mortar and pestle, as I begin to grind the earbud into dust. It takes much more effort than I hoped for, but completely worth it to watch the scraps of technology go down the drain, along with my vomit. If there's a tracker, maybe the weirdo will follow it into Southie's sewer system, where they'll live out the rest of their days. Tomorrow, I had every intention of going to my phone provider's store and changing my number. In the meantime, I'll shut off my phone.

After I clean up and finally make it back into my room, I can't settle. Instead, I rearrange my furniture, so I have my bed in front of the bedroom door and a large chest of drawers in front of the window. I don't own a gun or anything, but I do have my pepper spray from my purse. I also may have brought a large kitchen knife to bed with me. Just in case.

As I lay in bed, my eyes are unwilling to close, I feel overwhelmingly lonely. Andrea's never around, and Brodi... Brodi was no prince charming. In fact, the way we met was unexpected, but I never felt unsafe with him. When we started dating, we went out often. Whenever someone was too close at a club or trying to hit on me, Brodi instantly stepped in.

He was protective, strong, and often a little too hot-headed for his own good. Sometimes he would visit me during my lunch break at the hotel. It was really sweet how he'd bring a sandwich and share it with me, until he wasn't able to come around anymore. He got banned after punching a guest in the face when he came to visit me. An older gentleman asked if I conduct the bed turndown service myself. Brodi overheard and connected his first with the man's nose. I was lucky I didn't get fired, but we lost a client and Brodi couldn't come back. The perv had it coming! Maybe I should have quit and left with Brodi then and there. I still got let go a few weeks later. Things could have been different if I had just given the hotel the 'middle finger' and walked out?

Brodi and I were drawn to each other physically. Whether it was something I should have done on my part or an external factor. Seeing him less hurts. A few months before he disappeared, I actually thought I was ready to leave Boston. Make a new life with him. Then, it was like his polarity switched; he started pulling away. Half the time he seemed to have dumb excuses as to why he couldn't see me, but when we were together, it was good. Not magical, but better than a lot of relationships.

I'd like nothing more right now than to be in the crook of his thick, motor oil smelling, tattooed arms. My eyes burn and my pillow is wet. I'm tired. Once the sun's morning rays relentlessly pierce through the edges of my blinds, I feel a little safer knowing it's daylight, but I can't fight the exhaustion any longer. The sandman creeps in, and I soon find myself slipping within my recurring nightmare.

Spring was here. The scent of blooming cherry blossoms lingered just outside our playroom window. I was spread out onto the floor with crayons and drawing paper, as I created various designs of gowns and dresses. I liked to create outfits that princesses would wear, just like in the movies. Sunlight spilled across the wooden floor, warming the slats beneath me. I felt like the heroine of a fairy tale, bathed in my own magical glow.

My brother commonly played games on the small TV in front of the couch. Connected only by a wire, he could lead four green turtles through the city streets, battling ninjas, and devouring pizza along the way. We could be in that room for hours, me on the floor creating and him pleasantly engulfed in his game. It was wordless companionship, but I knew we still enjoyed having each other there.

Today, however, I designed whimsical attire alone. Theo wasn't allowed to play his usual console games in the rec room since he got into a fight at school. Donovan Polinsky was picking on a girl in their class, all because she wore pigtails. During lunch, Donovan wouldn't stop pulling the girl's hair. That is, until Theo stepped in. Theo, like a knight in shining armor, went straight up to Donovan and poured a carton of milk down the back of his shirt. Donovan swung at my brother. Playing all those video games must have made Theo quick, because he dodged the hit, causing Donovan to stumble forward, catching his chin on the lunch table. Donovan chipped a tooth, and Theo was briefly suspended. Mom and Dad were upset he got in trouble, but I heard Dad also saying he was proud of him for doing the right thing. Theo had a lot of chores that week, including polishing the fancy silverware, dusting the bookshelves, and scrubbing the baseboards on both floors of the house.

Outside, tiny chirps indicated baby birds were hungry from the trees below. I, too, was hungry for lunch, but I needed to decide which shade of blue would best suit the massive tulle gown.

Little specks of dust stole my attention, as they danced between the opened window and my drawing, creating an unexpected performance. I blew little puffs of air, watching the once graceful spots, spin and twirl with velocity. The star of the show, a large fleck of gray rocking from side to side, just outside my little rectangle of sunshine. Pushing my art to the side, I watch in amazement as the dust piece slowly made its way toward the window, before being caught by a breeze and rushing outside.

It was suddenly so bright. I felt as if all the air was sucked from my lungs, like that one time I fell backward off a swing. My throat felt dry, unable to form words while I remained still, my body unable to move. The worst part was the sound. It was both the loudest and the quietest thing I had ever heard, all at once. The ringing was unbearable, no matter how much I tried to cover my wet ears, the sound wouldn't relent. Smoke filled my vision. As it cleared near the floor, pairs of feet came rushing toward me. I lay there watching the situation unfold, my parents' mouths moved, but I was unable to hear anything but ear-splitting bells. A slew of dust flecks filled the room now, but none of them danced. Not quite like they did before.

CINDEL

I wake, covered in sweat, legs bound, with something awkward and hard poking me in my chest, I glance around the room finding that everything has been rearranged. As I attempt to kick off the cocoon of blankets, I find the cause of my discomfort is the travel-sized pepper spray I previously clung to.

Pulling at my clothes, I groan, hating the feeling of how the fabric sticks to my clammy skin. Everything appears the same as I left it last night.

Somehow, I managed to fall asleep, but I didn't feel rested. I've been reliving the same day, in my dreams, for damn near eighteen years. It's the only dream I can seem to remember after waking. Sometimes the nightmare can alter, but the ending is never happy.

Locating a loose hair tie in my bed, I pull up my hair before finding my phone. It's off.

Oh right… I remember now, a psychopath was texting me. Hence, the redecorated bedroom.

I peeked under my bed to find the kitchen knife I stashed, in case anyone was stupid enough to break in. It was a good thing I stored the weapon there instead of keeping it with me.

I sleep like I'm *wrestling a bear*. Andrea's description of how I sleep, not mine.

My phone comes to life after pressing the power button, and I hold my breath, hoping there are no new messages. Relief washes over me when I don't see anything but a calendar reminder. I worked at the market and the bar today. Shit. It's going to be a brutal day.

Pushing my bed back from the door, I emerge to find our living quarters quiet and still. Secretly, I hoped to find Andrea panicking in the kitchen. Responsible for some form of transgression, against an unsuspecting breakfast staple.

I pad my way across the room, then gently tap my knuckles on her door, listening for any indication of life.

No answer.

Slowly turning the knob, I poke my head through to find black painted toes poking out from beneath a disheveled comforter; she's asleep. Carefully turning the knob, I ease the door closed and breathe a sigh of relief that she is home. Safe.

It's not just my safety I need to be concerned about this weirdo leaving me presents and sending unnerving messages. If I knew she was home... I should have stayed up. This isn't just about me anymore.

This person knows where I live. I need to tell her. She's my best friend.

I get a whiff of myself as I cross the open space, on the way back to my room. Phew! If a crazed lunatic did come into my room last night, they would have instantly abandoned ship.

In the shower, I try to visualize what information I 'do' have. Like laying cards out on a table, I sort them based on what I've seen, heard, and know to be true. Nothing connects. None of it makes sense, and the more I think about it, without concrete evidence, I sound rather insane.

I debate on how I should tell Andrea... or when for that matter. Seeing her lately has been more erratic than using the Orange Line. Unreliable. From track problems to weather delays, you'd be better off taking a shuttle bus to your destination.

The longer I let this go, the messier it will become.

I could handle it if she's pissed, but what if she sees me in a negative light?

Stepping out of the shower, I towel off and head to my room. I don't think I should say anything... at least not yet. Andrea is very protective. If I'm going to bring her into this, I need more information. I won't derail our friendship on a hunch.

I have a stop to make before heading into work.

For now, I'll stick to the allegorical bus. Predictably reliable, although don't put anything on the floor... who knows what that mystery substance is. It's better to keep all your belongings on your lap.

Leaving early for Star Mart, I have enough time to swing by the cell store when it opens and change my phone number.

Approximately fifteen minutes after entering the bright yellow store, I was walking out with a new number and a little less anxiety about being messaged by a 'potential' stalker.

The sidewalks are covered with brightly colored leaves, still dewy as I walk to work. I love this time of year. Parents hold their little ones' hands as they walk through the park. Others walk their dog or jog for sport. Although we're all on the same path, each person obviously leads a very different life. I watch each of them. Wondering if the young man jogging has early onset heart disease and was actively trying to change a possibly bleak future. Then my gaze catches on an older woman pushing a stroller.

Suspecting that she, like many women, has faced hurdles, prior to becoming a mother.

Some people climb mountains, while most are simply trying to avoid potholes on the road of life. I understand this makes us who we are, but I can't help wondering if my destination would be different if my path wasn't filled with bear traps and snake pits. Could I be the one pushing a stroller or was I meant to be more health-conscious, exercising daily in the park?

Maybe someone who didn't constantly question why I'm still here.?

I stopped briefly at a bench to enjoy my last few moments outside.

I pull out my phone and shoot off a quick text to my parents, Andrea, and even my uncle, letting them know my new phone number. Andrea instantly replies.

Andrea: How do I really know it's you?

Cindel: You slept with our Art History professor during our first semester.

Andrea: No one should look that good in loafers.

Making my way to the backroom, I place my belongings in the metal filing cabinet's bottom bin.

Next, I throw on the atrocious apron and make my way out to the lane that coincidentally is furthest from Mairead.

I swear… as soon as a manager learns you get along with someone, they either put you on completely different shifts or place you as far from that person as humanly possible.

It's surprisingly busy for a weekday. If I didn't already know Mairead was assigned to the first lane, I wouldn't be able to see her over the troves of early risers, carrying baskets and pushing carriages full of items.

The morning goes by rather quickly. It's a sea of unfamiliar faces, until…

"Hello, Cindel."

I look up to find a sharply dressed man with sandy-blond hair. He looked just as handsome as he did when I saw him at the bar.

"Hello…" I still don't know what to call him, so I settle on, "Mr. Neat."

His grin looks even more radiant in the brighter setting of the store.

"It's Eamon actually," he says as he begins unloading the items from his basket onto the conveyor belt.

"Well, 'Eamon actually…' it's nice to finally put a name to your face."

I scan three jars of cherries, a container of coarse salt, four jars of olives, and weigh ten lemons.

His smell of leather finds me, even on the other side of the counter.

"So, you're having people over?" What an obvious question. Nice job making small talk, Cindel.

His head cocks slightly. "You could say that." He pulls his wallet out and chuckles to himself.

I chew the inside of my cheek at a loss of words. How is it that I have worked in the service industry for my entire adult life, but I still have the uncanny ability to be this socially awkward?

"Did you get my text?"

I look down at my phone seeing no new messages. Is he the one who sent that message from the unknown number? Suddenly, I realize… shit.

"I changed my number."

His once exultant appearance slips, as he gathers his bags.

"I can take a hint." His mouth gathers on one side of his face. "It's okay if you don't want to—"

Omg! He thinks I'm brushing him off.

"Wait! It's not that. I changed my number this morning."

My inner cheek finds its way back between my molars. I'm really going to create a canker sore, if I don't reel in these harmful habits.

"It's just that…" I start.

He all but leans over the conveyor belt, the only thing separating us. Eamon is watching me, and I can't help but stumble over my words as I watch his lips part.

Is it hot in here, because he's not even touching me and I'm misfiring already?!

He must read that I'm having trouble constructing a sentence because he all but purrs the next phrase.

"Are you avoiding someone, Cindel?"

Oh, sweet baby Jesus, what was I was trying to say? Am I drooling?

"I… let me…"

Reaching into the front pocket of my apron, I pull out my phone and unlock it. "Here."

He reluctantly takes my phone from my hand, lifting an eyebrow as if he's able to see straight into my wheelhouse, struggling to work through hostile conditions.

"Is there something else going on, Cindel?"

How is it my name has never sounded quite as sensual as it does coming from this man's mouth?

"Well… It's kind of hard to explain."

His thumb rubs across his lower jaw, ending on his dimpled chin.

I wonder what his fine layer of stubble would feel like against my skin.

Someone joins the line behind him, causing us to pull away from one another.

He quickly types his number into my phone before handing it back to me.

I look down to find he's created and sent a new message. Texting the word *'Marco'* to himself so he has my new number as well.

He gathers his two bags, coming around the lane to stand just before me. Even on the rubber slip mat, he's so fucking tall!

Reaching out, his hand comes up to meet my cheek, his fingers skate down my face, lifting my chin gently to look up at him.

"Let me know if someone else is bothering you, Cindel. I should be the only one doing that."

He steps back and all the warmth, along with the leathery scent, goes with him.

The customer clears her throat, and I spin around to see a vast collection of dish soaps, air fresheners, and toilet paper rolls. Ugh, One of those! The couponing biddies were older ladies who came in regularly with multiple clippings from that week's paper. They also insisted on paying with pre-rolled coins and crumpled singles. I didn't mind that they wanted to save money, just that I had to validate their change. This usually causes an unnecessarily long line to form behind them.

As if on cue, she places her hanging glasses onto her nose, opens up her foldable wallet, and begins shuffling for said vouchers.

I begin scanning, unable to help watching the former, more handsome customer heading toward the sliding glass doors. I pull out my phone, open up the newest message and type, *'Polo.'* I hold it just below the register, because I wasn't exactly wanting to advertise that I was using my phone on the floor.

His body stops on a dime as he reaches for his phone, upon me sending the message. A smile blooms across his chiseled face, as his thumbs race across the phone.

My phone vibrates in my hand. He instantly wrote back.

> Unknown: If you ever feel like a fish out of water…
> please tell me.

Tell him? I haven't even told my best friend… would I really discuss anything like this with Eamon?

It was so crowded in Star Mart. Everyone likes to stop at this one as opposed to the other one off of Huntington Ave. It was hard to see, but I could have sworn I saw Mairead on the other side of the store, sticking her tongue out at Eamon from her lane.

Was he shaking his head? Exiting through the sliding doors, he disappears down the street.

See? This is what a shitty night of sleep does to you.

Your imagination is getting away again.

Once the coupon queen finishes paying in quarters and questionably weathered singles, I check my phone again.

> Andrea: Any hot customers wearing loafers?

I bite back a grin, quickly messaging her back.

> Cindel: None yet. Have you tried the Financial District?

Dots appear before a message pops up.

> Andrea: NO WAY! They walk like they have a stick up their ass. Plus, they're not even into strap-ons.

A laugh bursts out of me, just as Craig happens by.

I try to discreetly slip my phone back into my front apron pocket but based on how quickly he's waddling toward my lane, I know I've been caught.

"Miss Mari, was that a personal phone I just saw on the floor? Per company policy, all employees are to leave their electronic devices within their designated cubbies in the backroom."

No one used those things. Half the time our stuff turns up missing. That's why most of the girls shove their purses in the bottom of a filing cabinet.

His voice is ridiculously loud, causing customers to look in our direction. I hate when there's unnecessary attention on me.

Craig just stands there with his hands on his hips. It feels more like a disappointed coach, who was waiting for an excuse as to why their star athlete went against the play he just carefully laid out.

Don't chew on yourself, Cindel. Speak!

"I was sending a message to my uncle! He's sick..." I fib.

"Do you commonly laugh when your family gets sick?" His too shiny face glistens beneath the store's fluorescent lighting, as he continues his reign of middle management terror. "Hm?"

This guy really takes his job too seriously.

"It was kind of an inside joke. Sorry. I'll put it away now."

He licks his top set of teeth then gives his pants a small lift around the belt.

"I'm glad you're choosing compliance. Flip off the switch for your lane light and follow me."

I let out a small sigh. Reluctantly doing as I'm told. The guests clear just enough for me to see Mairead's look of confusion from across the store. As if to say, "Where the fuck are you going?"

I follow the real life Humpty Dumpty, with a stache, to the far back corner of the store, where we find another Star Crew member busily cutting open boxes. The pimple-faced teen is working around glops of fallen contents and broken containers, in an attempt to shelve more products in the baby section.

"Christopher needs his fifteen," he tells me, once again adjusting even higher on his waist. "I'd like you to clean up this mess while he's gone."

The pubescent boy mirrors my astonished look. Like, really…? She's cleaning it up, not me? I attempt to replace the look of shock from my face. I won't give Craig the satisfaction of thinking he's winning with this form of punishment.

"It's Vaseline! How am I supposed to clean this?"

He walks away. Temporarily disappearing, then reappearing with a yellow bucket on wheels and mop.

"That should do the trick." He thrusts the wooden handle into my hand. "Come on, Christopher. I don't need the state slapping my hands, every time a minor doesn't get their little breaks."

They both head toward the backroom, on the other side of the store. Leaving me with an impossible mess and the most useless cleaning tool ever. This is so unfair. There's petroleum jelly everywhere! The floor, the shelves… just as I'm taking in the extent of this god-awful mess, I notice something on the shelf. Something that doesn't belong. Past a row of diapers, just above a huge glob of oily goo, I see purple. Shifting the shelved items to the side, I find a small, black box with a violet ribbon.

No! It can't be.

Instinctively, I look down the aisle both ways, seeing no one in sight. I crushed and flushed the last one.

"Argh!"

Of course, another would show up. I pull at the loose bow end, flip off the top, and see it. The earbud. The insulting device with the purple mark, that might as well be a boomerang. No matter how hard I try to get rid of the thing, it just keeps coming back.

Craig is looming and I don't want to be caught doing something else unregulated. The last thing I need is to be fired.

Tucking my hair behind my ear, I carefully remove my hearing aid and drop it into the front pocket of my apron. Despite my better judgment, I nestle the cursed earbud into my vacant ear, then push the box back, behind a line of disposable diapers.

Not wanting to give him a chance to *write me up*, I set to work mopping the floor. Instantly, the water has a sheen to it, regardless of how many times I ring out the mop. All I'm doing is smearing the gloopy contents in circles. I can feel myself becoming stinky and hot with this impossible task.

Looking for relief, I hastily pulled my hair back into a ponytail, prior to ringing out the mop again. I startle when I hear the sound of drums, paired with a familiar guitar riff. Of course, this 'plague of a device' is playing music again! I know this song.

Thanks to sharing a wall with my brother, I had the pleasure of listening to this song a great deal of times, when he was in high school. He would commonly become obsessed with songs to the point that he would play them over and over. Once everyone became utterly sick of hearing it, he moved onto his next hyper fixation.

"Really?!" I all but whisper yell to no one in particular. "**Vasoline**?!" I object. "I don't think **Stone Temple Pilots** meant it like this?"

I was quite literally squabbling with an empty aisle. As the song plays, I grow more irritated by the second. I drop the handle of the mop, just before peeking down each aisle for anyone who may be watching me. Obviously, my stalker thinks they're funny. Whoever it is has to be close by!

Turning the corner, I peered around a tower of boxed stuffing. Beyond a customer, Craig catches sight of me.

"Shit. Shit. Shit."

I scurry back to the mess on aisle nine, hoping he didn't realize it was me. Unfortunately, as soon as I reach down and pick up the wooden handle, there he is. Red faced and slightly panting. Did he run?

"Are we finished already?" he says between short breaths.

Yes, he definitely ran… or rolled. How is he so quick?

He crosses his arms and pins me with a look.

"That was awfully fast. I thought it would have taken you at least—" He stops mid-sentence, staring at the side of my face like a bug was on it. "Are you listening to music, Miss Mari?"

Oh crap. I was so focused on the mess, then the song played… I didn't think about covering the earbud with my hair. Before I could even respond, he looks past me, where small puddles of water and shining swirls of Vaseline has only grown in size.

Just like before he shuffles off momentarily, only to return with a yellow caution sign.

"Please follow me to my office."

Craig pivots and starts toward the backroom.

He didn't have an office. He was a supervisor at a shitty grocery store! Damnit, I'm going to lose another job. I cross my arms over the top of my apron, hiding the words, *Star Crew*. I wasn't in the mood to direct any naive customers to the bread aisle when I was on my way to getting fired.

My balding manager was more round than tall with a superiority complex that caused subordinates to hate him while corporate adored the man. Christopher, not quite done with his break, was evicted from the room mid granola bar and ordered to promptly clean up the impossible mess.

"Have a seat, Miss Mari."

I put myself into the slightly rusted metal chair, just in front of the breakroom's lunch table, with him on the other side. The plastic table was riddled in mysterious smears of food, while Craig snagged the only semi-comfortable chair in the whole space.

He scoots forward, leaning his upper body onto the table, with thick, meaty forearms. Being this close to him was so much worse than him sitting and grading me on my performance. At least then I had distance.

"How long have you been with us, Miss Mari?" he asks, with all the confidence of a man who already knew the answer. Seeing as he's the one controlling the questioning, I sense a power trip coming.

"Just Cindel, please." I find myself unable to look away from his yellow, crooked smile. "I'm not sure. A little under a year?" I force myself to look away, desperate to find anything else in the room to keep my attention. My focus settles on a dollop of dried ketchup, on the edge of the heavily used table.

"Nine months and twenty-one days to be exact." He rebuts, with his grotesque grin still on display.

Why would he know the exact timeframe down to the day? Did he plan on firing me and look up my hire date?

"Have you read the handbook? The one you signed when you were hired at this establishment?" His fingers barely laced together as he sets them in front of himself. He reminds me of a fat house cat that likes to play with its food but too spent to actually give chase.

"Yeah, I kind of remember signing—"

He leans forward instantly interjecting, "Section eight, third paragraph. Employees will adhere to rules and regulations put in place by Star Mart, including but not limited to any personal use of electronic devices during working hours."

What? Who would memorize that? Apparently, this guy. I bet he lives in his mom's basement. I was very much over this one-sided conversation.

"If you're going to fire me, just do it."

He puts his hands in a defensive motion. "Woah… Hold on right there, little miss. I feel like there's been a misunderstanding here. You've become an essential Star Crew member here at Star Mart. Also, I feel like we've become close as of late. Let's not be so quick to throw all that away."

Close? He can't be serious! "Excuse me?" I lean back, feeling the room becoming uncomfortably smaller than before. As if he could read my thoughts from my physical response, he reacts.

His arm shoots across the table, like a frog's tongue snatching a bug. He has me by the wrist, securing me to the table.

"Let. Me. Go."

I try to yank my arm back, using my other hand to try and pry him off me, only to have that arm also pinned down by his slimy grasp. With both hands holding me firmly on the surface, he leans over the table. I want to leave, but I can't break from his hold. He takes his bottom teeth and rakes them over the ends of his gross mustache, combing it in a downward motion.

I look over my shoulder to find I'm completely alone. My throat burns as acid begins to climb its way up. How did I not notice the door to the back-room was closed?

Nice job following Creepy Craig to a secluded location, Cindel. Why don't you just make an extra key to your apartment for your stalker while you're at it?!

His breathing has become heavy, but he remains unnervingly calm. Such a contrast to my panicking struggle to break free.

"I'll scream!" I warn him.

"That wouldn't do either of us any good. I plan to inform corporate of your delinquency."

Delinquency? What delinquency?

He didn't need me to defend myself, because he could read it from my expression.

"Won't they be surprised when they learn you've been skimming your drawer for months." His feline smile displays each one of his yellowed teeth, and I want nothing more than to knock them out with my boot.

"That's not true and you know it!" I growl.

He tightens his grip on my wrists before standing. Then without warning, he moves to the door faster than a man of his size should. Now he stands between me and any chance of leaving this room.

I back up. Trying to put as much distance between me and this disgusting liar of a man. He could ruin my life. Any chance of getting a job in this city if he reports this. I'll be labeled as a criminal. A thief. Could I do jail time?

I take inventory of what's around me and how I can get out. I'll worry about the slander later.

He's watching me. His chest shakes slightly, and an unsettling chuckle tumbles from him.

"Maybe I shouldn't have told Alex about you. Others may want you for themselves." His lips purse, soon morphing into a sickening grin across his pockmarked face.

"I'll tell you what?... No one needs to ever know about the little 'money issue,' if you do something for me."

What could I possibly do for him? Also… who would want me and who the fuck is Alex?

My breath comes out in short huffs. That's when I noticed… it.

His tan trousers are tented. He's fucking aroused?! Fuck! I may actually vomit. I felt hot and cold all at once.

"Just like her… pretty with a little bit of fight in ya! I like that," he admits.

My ears are ringing much too loud for me to think straight.

His vile mouth continues moving, but I've tuned it out.

Move, Cindel! Grabbing the first thing within reach, I remove the red canister from the wall.

He's starting to stroke himself, ahead of undoing his belt. I don't want to see what happens next.

Pulling the clip, I start unloading the backroom's fire extinguisher onto him.

"Ah, what the fuck?!!!" He tumbles forward, as if the door is pushed from the other side. My revolting manager hits the floor, face first with a cry. "You bitch!"

Unknowingly, a head of bouncing red curls pops through the ajar door. "What's going on in here?!" She marvels at the scene before her.

The metal canister drops to the ground with a thud as I rush toward my savior. I leap over the blubbering oaf, who's complaining about his nose or whatever. As I step past the threshold I declare, "I quit, asshole!"

Mairead squats next to him, whispering something to his foam-covered form. I couldn't hear what was said, but as if she knows the drill, she grabs our belongings and we get the hell out of that fucking place.

We stand before the store for what feels like longer than necessary. With adrenaline still coursing through my body, I am sure if I am waiting for the police to show up or if I might act on my impulsive urge to light the whole damn building on fire. I know neither would be good.

I turn to Mairead who seems pleased as punch to be out in the sun.

"What'd you say to him?" I finally asked.

She proceeds to remove her apron and drops it to the ground. Without a word, she rummages through her bag for various items. Types on her phone in front of taking a rip from a vape stick. I didn't even know she smoked. It smells like watermelon. As calmly as someone could be who just quit their job on a whim, she replies, "I told him to enjoy his last fucking can of tuna while he still can."

I can't help but laugh. It was funny. A little creepy, but I needed the distraction.

Mairead threw her head back and laughed wildly. Both of us must have looked high or like we just committed a crime. I liked her from the start, but now she has my admiration. She was exactly the kind of friend I needed right now. Friendly, sweet, but capable of kicking ass and taking names. All of this is wrapped within a seemingly innocent package. There's more to this girl than I initially thought.

EIGHT

CINDEL

Today has been… interesting to say the least. After escaping from the nauseatingly uncomfortable interaction with my now ex-manager, Mairead and I used our newfound freedom to hit the town. We didn't hit the clubs, nor did we attempt to find our truths at the bottom of the glass at the neighboring bar. I was surprised she didn't want to do any of that, when most girls her age are just breaking in their fake IDs.

I'm only a couple years older, and I know *age is just a number*, but I feel a lot older than I actually am. Hell, I all but took a personal oath after my brother died, to never drink or do drugs again, at the ripe age of twenty.

Authorities said it was a drug-overdose. The evidence was all there, they said, but I just can't fathom my brother doing such a thing. Sure, I objected. Insisting they look into it further, but when my parents decided to move shortly after his death, it was hopeless. No one listened to a desperate, young girl. I felt abandoned in my pursuit of knowledge.

Once my mind stops reeling, I remove the earbud from my ear and drop it into my bag. With my hearing aid removed from my apron and back on my right ear, I pushed the horrendous uniform into a nearby trash can on the street.

"Fuck you, Star Crew!" I hold out both middle fingers for the inanimate object. I'm sure I looked nuts, but it made me feel a little better.

Trust was a funny thing. The people you were expected to trust; law enforcement, authority figures, managers… were, more often than not, the ones who spit in your face when you're vulnerable. Whereas acquaintances and even complete strangers have shown me more patience and kindness than I've experienced in a long while.

As I follow this free-spirited girl through the streets of Southie, I suddenly realize that I put my faith into her. I didn't mean to… it just sort of felt right.

Mairead spares no expense during our Boston bender. We seem to stop at every establishment along the way. I try to pay my share when we get a coffee or when there is an entry fee, but she straight up refuses.

As I first suspected, her family has a shit ton of money. She only took this most recent job to *fuck with their heads*. I wish my parents were wealthy.

The first stop is the Boston Tea Party Museum. Apparently, it's a must-see. Tourists have the opportunity to throw fake crates of tea off the side of a ship. I've lived here my whole life and have never been. Well, when Mairead learned this, she wouldn't take *no* for an answer. She is having so much fun, she's throwing other things into the water, too. Of course, the actors aren't too keen on having to fish extra things out of the channel, in turn yelling at Mairead.

Let's just say I won't be coming back anytime soon, due to the fact that she cut the ropes that secured the ship's tarp, temporarily trapping staff and unsuspecting visitors. Not to mention, she also manages to make off with one of the actor's hats as we both fled the scene. Over the past thirty minutes, she's been popping out of corners, surprising random city goers with an *Argh!* Pretty sure that's not what the colonists said while objecting to British taxation and policies.

Next up, I follow Mairead as we explore the Freedom Trail. I feel like I am on a field trip through the city. Exploring the historical neighborhoods and sites, along red-bricked paths, that I never had the time to appreciate before. It is actually really nice. We stop along the way to check out a bookstore, with a lovely section of used books nestled between two brick buildings. Almost instantly, I have three in my hand. Then I remember I am now 'down a job' and in turn reshelve them. Mairead stubbornly grabs the books back off the shelf and pays with a fifty. She doesn't even wait for the change, just pulls me to the next thing that catches her eye.

We stand beneath massive concrete pillars for the entrance to the Granary Burying Ground, when suddenly Mairead takes off. After all the walking we have done thus far, I don't understand how her legs and feet aren't sore. I'm starting to regret spending so many hours on my feet, prior to bartending tonight.

My energized friend continues at a brisk pace, almost as if looking for something. Passing each marker, she pauses momentarily beside a headstone, before moving onto the next. Finally, she stops, allowing me precious moments to catch up to her. She pulls out a small pad of paper from her bag and draws a line. Like a wind-up toy, Mairead's off again! Continuing on to the next row of markers, stopping briefly, drawing a line, and so on. The only similarity I can find between the two graves she hesitated at was the name '*Mary.*' She repeats this process for what feels like forever!

There must be over two thousand markers here. We learned about this historical burial ground when I was in school. Mostly Revolutionary War-era patriots are laid to rest here; however, there are thousands more buried in unmarked graves. I couldn't imagine not knowing where my loved one ended up.

It looks like I was going to be here for a while, so I make myself comfortable on a stone bench and pull out one of the newly purchased books, while Mairead finishes with whatever she is doing.

This one is a classic from Agatha Christie. It's about a young woman who survives, despite facing multiple close calls from someone trying to murder her. An unsuspecting man gets pulled into the mix, helping her untangle the mess and solve the mystery.

I love reading and was thrilled to finally have a few moments to get back into the habit. I guess I'll have more time to read now that I work less. Shit. Will I be able to make my half of the rent this month? Just as I hit Chapter 7; *Tragedy*. Black, Mary Jane shoes appeared in front of me.

"One hundred and three," she proclaims.

Her cheeks are pink from the cold, while her once tight curls appear frizzier at the ends. Yet despite her sad state, the ridiculous hat still remains atop her head. Her coat lies next to me, along with her bag. It would have served her better on her body. I tuck my book away and drape the coat over her shoulders.

"Come on then. Let's get you warmed up." I guide her toward a glowing coffee shop, just a block over, hoping to warm her from the inside out.

The sun disappears below the horizon, as I order two regulars. Sitting us at a high top, we watch as the street progressively becomes illuminated by orangey globes. Reds from the setting sun melt into deeper blues as night takes over.

An advantageous ending to a calamitous day.

At this point, she doesn't argue about me paying. She is still for once. Calm. We sit quietly, enjoying each other's company as the steam rises over our drinks. Mairead's color returns to her face about halfway through her cup before she starts speaking.

"My mom's name was Mary; she died a while back." She shrugs off the jacket from her shoulders, letting it fall to the chair beneath.

"I'm very sorry," I say, but it doesn't come out quite as sincere as it should. "Losing someone is life altering."

Her lashes are wet, but I witness no tears actively falling. All the while she looks upon the dark streets. Headlights are the only light I find in her eyes.

"Were you close?" I press, hoping maybe she can learn to trust me too.

She nods her head, chewing on her bottom lip. "She understood me. Trusted me to do the right thing. She believed I was perfect... just the way I am."

I study her soft features. Button nose, light dusting of freckles, and long lashes. The kind of beauty that could never be bought. I'm at a loss for words.

"I just wish everyone else knew me the way she did," she admits.

My heart rips at its seams. That I got. I rest my hand on hers.

"You're not what I expected, Cindel." I turned my head slightly, unsure if she meant it to come off as it did.

"Thank you?"

She throws her head back with a startling, infectious laugh. The hat tumbles behind her, as if she wasn't just discussing her deceased mother a moment ago.

I force a smile. I was getting ready to tell her about Theo, to share how I knew exactly what loss felt like, but she was past it. Much like the setting sun, the powerful moment had dissipated, and she was onto the next 'exciting' thing.

Leaping up from her seat, she retrieves her stolen accessory off the floor. Placing the eccentric hat on my head, she proceeds to stand like a flamingo before speaking.

"The night is young! Where to now?!" Her mood is as erratic as the wind is from the sea.

"Mairead… I've had a lot of fun. Thank you for the interesting afternoon, but I need to get to work."

Her posture slouches slightly, becoming that of a child who needs to come inside and do their chores instead of playing.

"I have bills to pay. Not all of us have a rich family to help us out," I tease, paired with a playful shove of her balancing leg. This was very much a move my brother would have done to me.

"Ugh. The Black Sheep blows! Come get a new job somewhere else with me!"

Though that did sound kind of nice, there's something about the bar. When did I tell her about the bar? I must be forgetting things, I really need to get a good night's sleep. Maybe it's just me being sentimental, but I feel like I've landed right where I belong.

"Ooooo! How about the arcade we passed today? Wouldn't that be fun?!" She exclaims.

"No, thank you. Too many extra noises and the blinking lights would give me a migraine." I pause. "Maybe this is a sign? A push for me to pursue my real passion."

Mairead appears to be having trouble holding still. Back to her exuberant self, she rolls up on the balls of her feet before rocking back to the heel of her buckled shoe. Maybe caffeinating her was a bad idea.

We gather our items and head out, saying our goodbyes outside the coffee shop.

"There has to be at least one company looking for an entry level seamstress," I accidentally wonder out loud.

She suddenly squeals and begins hopping from foot to foot. "I looooove clothes! I didn't know you sew!"

Confirmed. Just like from the movie Gremlins, I will not be hydrating Mairead after dark again. Especially not with coffee.

"Yeah… I actually went to school for fashion." I check the time, realizing I have a mere twenty minutes to get across town to The Black Sheep.

"Here!" She places the colonial hat on my head she five-fingered, just hours prior. "It's going to be a trend; I can feel it…" she promises.

I give her a tight smile in return.

"Let's get together later this week. We can do each other's makeup ooooor go to Copley Place to shop! I'll text you now that I have your new number. We're going to have so much fun together! Just you wait and see." She pulls me into a tight hug before skipping off down the street.

Jesus, I was ready to sleep for an entire week after the day we just had and it still wasn't over. My body is exhausted… Mairead's idea of fun was inconceivable.

"Nice hat!" Jada calls out upon me entering the bar.

Schooling my features, I bring a slightly opened hand to my face, before closing fingers together beside my mouth, signing *shut up*.

When I started here, my coworkers were eager to learn some basic sign language. It made it easier to communicate on busy nights from across a room. Of course, they were more interested in learning curse words like *bitch* and *pussy*. Purely so they could talk shit about problem customers, without them being ever the wiser.

Jada blows me a kiss in response.

Brittany has warmed up to me over the past few months, but Jada can be downright unpleasant at times. I hope she's more bark than bite and with time, she'll learn to like me too.

I head straight to the ladies' room to get changed. I'm glad I brought an extra outfit with me in my bag today. Between rage quitting and sightseeing as a local, there was absolutely no time to run home before my second shift. I set my bag on the edge of the sink, pulling books and clothes out one by one, just as something topples to the floor. I crouched down to pick up the lost item. Turning the earbud in my fingers, I can't help but consider a different course. No matter what I do… this little piece of plastic will not stay away. I'm accustomed to accepting horrible things at this point. From losing my ability to hear without assistance, to losing my brother, then Brodi, just up and vanishing. Why should this be any different?

"Why do you get to call the shots?" I say to the petite microphones.

Maybe Mairead rubbed off on me a bit today or possibly poor judgment from lack of sleep, but I was done. Is this me dancing in the rain?

"Give me your worst," I proclaim, as I switch out my hearing aid for the small earbud.

After I change into green, crushed velvet pants, and my weathered *Nine Inch Nails* shirt, I tug on my trusty combat boots. I just manage to fit everything back into my bag, including the ridiculous hat. Eat your heart out, Mary Poppins. I toss my bag in the backroom before joining my coworkers on the floor.

Unlike Star Mart, I'm allowed to have my phone on me, while on the clock. If you're playing on your phone, you're not making good tips, so there's no use in making a rule about it when money talks. We're not open yet, so I audited my phone for any messages. One message from the contact: *It's Eamon actually*. I saved his information earlier, when I was waiting for Mairead to finish tallying headstones. It seemed like the most appropriate contact, plus it made me smile.

> It's Eamon actually: I'm glad I had a chance to see you today. I guess I'll be visiting Star Mart a lot more for groceries.

My smile from his text quickly turns into a frown.

> Cindel: Feel free to shop, but I won't be there.

A question mark comes through.

> Cindel: I quit today. My manager was an asshole.

I was being vague. I didn't feel like expanding upon the whole, 'blackmail' and 'boner' part.

> It's Eamon actually: I'm sorry, Cindel. Can I help?

My smile returns.

> Cindel: No. It's okay. I'm at the bar tonight. Maybe swing by and say hi?

Dots appear, dancing across the bottom of the screen for long moments before a message pops up.

It's Eamon actually: Sorry. I have a big event tonight at my club. I wish I could come and watch you work.

I wondered which club he meant, so I asked. His expensive suits and confidence screamed businessman.

It's Eamon actually: It's a boxing club. I own a few different businesses around the city.

Cindel: Any I would know?

It's Eamon actually: I guarantee it.

A winky emoji was added.

"Cindel!"

My name rings out more clearly on my left side.

"Can you help by chopping the limes? I need to go grab a lager to stock the mini fridge before we open." Brittany is a hard worker and is kind of amazing at delegating tasks.

Slipping the phone into my back pocket, I head to the small chopping board to take over garnish duty.

Jada was by the front, spraying and wiping away last week's drink specials on the A-Frame sign.

I scanned the room, anticipating Cassie taking inventory with a clipboard or high up on a ladder changing a lightbulb, but instead she was sitting. I've been here almost six months and not once have I seen that woman sit. Even on her smoke breaks, she stands in the back alley. Literally, her motto is: "If there's time to lean. There's time to clean."

I walk over as she starts to cough uncontrollably. She curls into herself, attempting to cover her cough. It looks like she's truly unwell.

"Cassie… can I get you anything? Water perhaps?"

Unable to speak between fits of coughs, she just manages to shake her head *no*.

"Would you like to go outside and get some air?"

She shakes her head vigorously again, unwilling to accept any help I offer. My manager is a chain-smoker, but I've never witnessed her struggle like this.

Connor, the barback, appears at our side a moment later. He snakes an arm around her back, helping her to stand.

"I'm going to drive her to her house. She needs a breathing treatment," he states, as if it's no big deal.

Cassie continues coughing, appearing even more pale than before.

"Can I do anything to help?"

He shakes his closely shaven head. "Naw… I should be back in about an hour or so. I called in help with coverage tonight."

Looking between Jada and Brittany, we all look slightly stunned. We open in minutes with just the three of us.

After they leave, we pick up the bar menus from the tables. We collectively agree that we weren't going to serve tables tonight. If they want to order, they will need to come to one of us at the bar. Luckily, it is the middle of the week. That fact alone could make this undermanned shift doable.

The hour goes by and still no Connor. Jada and I stay behind the bar while Brittany runs the room, cleaning up discarded drinks and spills.

By ten o'clock we accept that it is just us for the rest of the shift. The reasonable flow of weeknight customers becomes increasingly busier by the hour.

Did a bus let off a bunch of people in front of The Black Sheep? What is going on?

We are having trouble keeping up with collecting and sanitizing the glasses before a new drink gets ordered.

Brittany, being the superstar she is, runs the dishwasher in the back.

Jada and I improvise, using martini glasses to serve drinks that have no business in that glassware. It is so busy, I'm amazed when I notice two familiar faces at the end of the bar. One chews the usual toothpick, while the other just looks offended to be here.

"What can I get you?"

Adjusting the toothpick to the corner of his mouth, the chatty brute answers, "Two Guinness, doll."

"Is it okay if it's in a copper mug? We're a little short on glasses." I ran another customer's card while taking the duo's order.

"Like a mule? You can't serve me Guinness in that! What about them, over there?!" He points to a stack of dirty glasses off to the side.

"Sorry, those are unwashed. We're a little short on help today."

His friend remains quiet, typing away on his phone as if he could care less if he even had a drink at all.

"Then pop-off and wash 'em, doll. I'll wait." He leans back on his stool, chewing on the tiny sliver of wood.

"Look! You can either have your beer in a shiny mug, or you can get it somewhere else," I say through gritted teeth.

"I'm here, aren't I? I'm not going anywhere!" The wisecracker leans forward onto the bar, attempting to grab a bottle of whatever is within reach.

His companion who once couldn't be bothered to look up, abruptly slams down his hand onto the top of the bar. The slapping sound makes me jump, finding his smokey gaze fixed on me. Without a word, he stands from his chair and proceeds to walk down the length of the bar, only to come around to the employee's side.

"Hey! You can't be back here!" I shout, stomping over to the audacious man before the bar sinks.

Standing beside him, I didn't feel quite as brave. He's big. Intense... with broad shoulders, he's a wall of muscle. My eyes naturally travel over his body. What do I do? Push him to the other side of the counter?

"Please, leave!"

He ignores my rants and pleas, only to begin filling one of the sink vats with hot water.

Am I invisible or is there just a small sign on my forehead reading, *DOORMAT*?!

Jada and Brittany both lift an eyebrow, still they carry on serving drinks and taking orders.

This has in fact been the longest day ever and it's not even midnight. I'm not paid enough for this shit.

The introverted dishwasher stands there until we have nearly every available glass cleaned and stacked on the rubber mat, atop the counter. We are finally able to serve the right drink in its appropriate glass, but I also felt helpless within this man's presence, as desperate as we were or not. Honestly, this random guy probably secured all of us getting home before 3 a.m. With a bar towel draped over his shoulder, he helps himself to a tap, two clean glasses in tow.

As he comes close, my eyes track down to his neck. Something is there; barely visible in the dim light. A jagged pink scar spans the front of his throat. I coughed, in a feeble attempt to cover the fact that I forgot how to breathe. What is wrong with me?

He proceeds to pour two perfect Guinness for himself and his unhelpful friend, who now has a bleach blond with huge knockers sitting on his lap.

Clearly, he has moved on from the glass debacle, paying no mind to his friend who just did manual labor for his dark, malt beverage.

The reserved man, passes by me again, returning to his stool, sits beside his friend; like nothing transpired.

Connor shows up shortly before closing, explaining how he needed to take Cassie to the ER because her at-home treatment wasn't working.

As relieved as we are to have him back, we are all worried about Cassie's health.

Most of the customers funneled out long before closing time, including the brutes who occupied the space at the end of the bar.

We have most of the final tasks underway, as I hear the jingle of the door's bell.

I look up to find the same devilishly handsome man, It's Eamon actually, stride into The Black Sheep.

"Hey." He stops at the bar and takes a seat on the stool in front of me.

"Hey back." I continue cleaning the nozzles as he watches me carefully.

"Last call was five minutes ago, I hope you didn't want a drink."

He smiles. "It's okay. I wasn't in the mood for a drink. Sorry I wasn't here sooner."

I shake my head. "It's okay, you already said you had an event at your club tonight." I start covering the containers of the lemons, cherries, and olives with plastic wrap.

"I understand you were short staffed tonight."

It's hard not to get lost in his mesmerizing eyes.

"Wow, word gets out fast." Were customers complaining about their service tonight?

"Connor reached out."

What? Now I am lost. How does he know Connor? "Do you know Connor?"

He laughs to himself, poking his tongue into the side of his cheek before answering. "Cindel… do you know who owns The Black Sheep?"

I was a little taken back by his question, but I answer regardless. "Cassie?"

Jada struts by, tracing a finger along the shoulders of the good-looking man in front of me.

"Hey, Eamon." She coos in her flirty voice I've heard her use multiple times before, trying to bait a guy into buying her a shot, too.

My eyes bounce from Jada to Eamon, unsure if this is some kind of joke.

His jaw ticks as he takes a seat at the bar. Green eyes travel up to meet mine. With a perfectly fitted suit in a royal blue, he looks regal. Outlandishly confident.

"No, little one. Cassie does not own this bar… I do."

He moves toward the register.

As if that was the closing line to a movie, my right ear hums to life.

A melody I've heard during my high school years at Boston Charter, **Beck – "Loser"**, plays only for me to hear. With its catchy rhythm, combined with verbal diarrhea that made about as much sense as what this insanely attractive man just told me. I couldn't discern if I was short circuiting, because I was stuck cleaning the same area on the tabletop.

I've been wearing this earbud all night and now the musical stalker plays this?! There's no message! It's just layer upon layer of nonsensical madness. Like cake tiers filled with inedible ingredients of nails and glass. I know I told myself I was accepting this… running headfirst toward the danger, but already I've hit a wall. I'm beyond frustrated.

The song ends and I can't hold in the words that tumble out of me.

"Yes, you are a loser," I grumble, just as Eamon appears before me. Oh shit.

NINE

EAMON

Slowly, she's beginning to realize that she's a fish out of water. The starry-eyed girl looks more surprised than anything. Almost muttering to herself.

The staff carries on with their nightly tasks. The girls restock the liquor shelves, Connor empties the ice bins, and Cindel struggles to get through the most mundane of tasks. It looks as if she's been wiping down the same table for the past five minutes.

Since Cassie's gone, I tally the cash drawer. I've depended on her to manage things in my absence. I've never been too fond of The Black Sheep, however Cindel working here has encouraged me to come around more.

She stumbles slightly as her shoe catches a stool. I fight the urge to smirk. She's too busy watching me out of her peripheral, as opposed to watching where she's going.

She's a sweet kid. I know I shouldn't be here. Making myself known to her. Doing any of this, but I feel responsible. Like her well-being was handed over to me long ago. Once her boyfriend was out of the picture, I arranged for her to take this job. It's actually thanks to him that I found her at all. Life sure has a sick sense of humor. Exchanging wants for needs. Loss paired with ill-begotten gains.

I have bled, poured my everything into this life, only to watch the foundation slowly begin to crumble. I'll be damned if I let anything else I care about be eradicated. Just between the Bay Boxing Club and The Black Sheep, I have kept myself busy over the past couple years. When my dad went back to Ireland to bury my mother, I was left to clean up in his wake. Handle everything alone…

My sister isn't very reliable when it comes to business. Instead, I have a few entrusted men to help. Kilkenny Castle wasn't built overnight, but over generations. Ultimately, it's my turn to make things better. It's no easy task, but I push myself each day to learn more, be more.

I do it because I can't accept the past. We have all been deceived. This way of life has rules. A code to follow. It was broken. When I finally unravel this web of lies, someone is going to join the rest of the massholes buried beside the interstate.

As despicable as some people may appear, I don't believe everyone is guilty. Cindel was closer to a delicate piece of china vs. the city's Teflon skin. I know she's faced unspeakable things. Still suffering from the loss of her brother, even years later. I understand better than most, but if she doesn't play along, this game, this life… will consume her. I hope she can make it out of this unscathed. Then, I might be able to get some fucking sleep at night.

Getting close to her is the first phase. Learn everything she knows. It feels so wrong, but I've been chasing ghosts for way too long. If the rest of my family had their say, they would have already burnt this city to the ground, but I owe it to someone important… to take a different road. If you told me just a few years ago that I would be here today with this empty, cavernous feeling inside… I would have laughed in your face! Probably bash your teeth in too for saying something so impudent. But now…? Right now, I would trade my very soul, just to be at peace.

How could anyone anticipate their future? Especially when you couldn't ever fathom yourself there in the first place. When you have everything in life handed to you on a silver platter, you feel invincible. I was a damn fool. No one is immortal. I can't get back what's gone, but I refuse to allow anything to happen to the nescient. Acceptance doesn't create empires, but integrity helps pave the way.

My phone vibrates and I see a new message.

Connor: Cassie has passed, sir.

God damnit. I don't have time to manage my own shit, let alone handle the affairs of this bar. Cassie was a good one, never asked too many questions, and did a damn good job of keeping this place in tip top shape. She was on borrowed time. Lung cancer. That woman was a force. When she found out, she insisted that I keep it to myself. Like a Viking earning their way into Valhalla on the battlefield. She didn't want to lay down and accept her fate, but stand tall, work, and live her life as normal as possible. I'm sure it didn't help that she was constantly having to bail her adult son out of trouble. Hopefully the loss can rattle his cage just enough to set him on the straight and narrow. Not that I have ever had the freedom to choose, but I knew all too well how the deceased can call from their grave for you to do better.

I slide the device back into the inner pocket of my jacket. A decision will need to be made soon. Cindel has moved onto wiping down another table. With her back to me, I decide at that moment to walk over to her. She appears startled when I reach her and I could have sworn she muttered, "Yes, you are a loser." I ignore it.

"Can we talk? I ask and I can't help but notice how her body is more rigid as I stand closer to her. She's still cleaning the same spot as we speak.

"Oh… Sure!" She adjusts her chestnut hair to cover the earbud. "What's up?" Her smile is sweet but forced.

"You did great tonight." I already made up my mind; I just have to inform her. "I'd like to make you a manager."

Suddenly, she stops buffing the countertop. "Excuse me?"

I sit on the bar stool, so I'm eye level with her. The color of her eyes is a flawless match.

"I can't be a manager. Is Cassie going to be out for a while? Plus… Jada and Brittany have both worked here longer than me."

I hold up my hand before she can continue. "You are capable. I wouldn't have chosen you, otherwise."

She searches my face, probably thinking this is some kind of trick. I'm drowning in those hauntingly familiar oceans. I revert my gaze, unable to tolerate the blue pools any longer and check my phone. Shit, I need to get back.

"Do you accept?"

Cindel's mouth opens and closes a few times, validating the nickname I've given her. So fucking adorable. My heart splinters.

She surveys the room, then comes back to me. "I guess…as long as Cassie comes back soon."

I place my hand on hers and squeeze gently. Poor thing looks like a deer in its last moments before the headlights reached them.

"I'll let the rest of the staff know. You'll be acting as manager beginning the next shift. Sorry, but I have to run. I have a gathering to attend." I turn on my heel, leaving Cindel to recover from the shell shock. I should have stayed and talked with her, but I have my crew waiting for me.

I salute Connor as I stride toward the red, wooden door.

Dax leans against the brick wall, waiting for me. Garron is already back at the boxing club, readying for our arrival.

Garron has been an essential part of the family since we were boys. His dad worked for my parents, and so it's expected that the next generation would roll right into the position effortlessly.

Dax, on the other hand, was somewhat newer to the crew. The last guy, Finnegan, had an unfortunate accident. He may have taken a midnight dance with a train after he had the bollox to póg my little sister. Another reason why I didn't want her around any of this. I like Dax better, anyhow. Sometimes reserved, he still has my trust. He earned that shit.

Dax gets into the passenger seat while I start the car. I preferred the blue version of the Audi R8, but the white one went just as fast. Maybe after a few more big events, the house will have enough to buy another blue one. My previous R8 had an unfortunate accident when the front end was smashed last Spring. Maybe after a few more big events, the house will have enough to buy another one in my preferred color.

We take off in the direction of Kilby Street, toward the Bay Boxing Club. I requested the crew stick around for a little after party, once the event was through. I just hope they didn't have too much fun while I was away handling the matter at the bar.

I pull up shortly after one in the morning. Although the place is dark from the outside, I know my men were bustling within the steel walls. Dax at my side, we make our way to the side alley door. It swings open without even having to announce our presence. There's a camera on every corner of this building. They already knew I was here.

The familiar sound of a grown man begging fills the space as I pass hung bags and matted walls. Then we weave through nearly a hundred arena chairs. My crew vacated the ring once I entered the building, now, the only thing at its center is a restrained, middle-aged man. The spotlight accentuates his greasy thin hair, while the dark spots on his skin tell me he's spent a great deal of time on the streets. His lip is split. One eye purple with the onset of swelling causing the lid to shut, in addition, three of his fingers face an unnatural direction.

Garron and the boys roughed him up just enough to loosen his tongue, but they saved the grand finale for me.

"Alex! Sorry for my tardiness. I see my boys got you the best seat in the house while you waited."

The weak man starts cursing despite his current predicament. Once the sharp words leave his mouth, he apologizes a moment later, as if realizing it will only make things worse. He follows up with a plea. How very predictable. I tsk.

"I need you to take a deep breath, Alex, because I'm going to ask you something and if you lie to me, I'm going to remove an ear."

The disgraceful man begins blubbering and I haven't even touched him yet. I like this part… taking my time, I circle the chair, only stopping once the giant man-child manages to collect himself. That tiny sliver of hope they hold onto is fascinating. Why can't they just accept it?

Poised behind the chair, I grasp one of the only working fingers he has left, snapping it with little effort. He wails and then proceeds to piss himself. Lowlifes disgust me. I step back and speak slowly so the incompetent man follows.

"Not only have you been changing your bets, effectively stealing from my house for months, but now I learn you're some kind of wannabe gangster! The

Mafia?! Really, Alex…?! You're an empty suit. No one wants someone who never shuts their mouth! You've always been a piece of shit." I stare into his desperate tired eyes, witnessing the faith he once held onto slowly slip away.

The fucking Mafia. The only name that held actual power went into hiding damn near eighteen years ago. Maybe it's just another gang, simply trying to find their footing in this city? It can't be them. I've done my fair share of 'taking out' any form of competition that has come our way over the years. I have no plans to go into business with another family again.

We weren't always like this; unwilling to play nicely with anyone. In fact, there was a time when the Murrays worked closely with another.

When I was very young, I would sometimes sneak out of bed and listen among the staircase railing, while our families would talk business. The Lombardis and the Murrays each had their own territory within South Boston. Our family's main store front was the boxing club. If someone wanted to gamble with their hard-earned money, we had the means. The club hosted events bringing in big names, along with high bidders, at least once a week. Most of the patrons left happy, and we were raking in the cash. My father told me, "It's important to diversify." Have your money working in different corners of the market, so that's where more bars came in.

At one point, the Murray family had eight places cleaning their money. The Lombardis were known for their stronghold on anything having to do with land and construction. Also, drugs. From what I understood, the family sourced out those dealings since they had a family to care for. I'm not sure who the kingpin was then nor do I know now, but one thing is for certain... The drugs never stopped flowing through this city.

It's de facto… if anyone steps in your yard, fucking around in your business, they're gonna be tucked in nice and tight. Taking a permanent sleep within a new row of townhouses' concrete foundation. That was the Lombardis M.O. Real estate. Every building sale in Southie or investment into land, the money always passed through the Lombardis hands. Hell, if it weren't for them, my grandparents wouldn't even have had the properties that they did.

Both crime families needed one another. When I was ten, it all changed. The Lombardi family had some kind of hit put on them, causing them to effectively disappear. Power shifted, making business messier for us. It seemed as if someone new was capitalizing on their family being gone. Whoever it was had no honor, because our fronts started facing monthly raids from the cops over suspicion of drugs, of all the fucking things to charge us with. Our soldiers either turned up in the slammer or went missing. I'd like to say that our men are fiercely loyal, but one rat can bring down the whole house.

When my father left for Ireland and I took over., I salvaged what we had and attempted to make a few of the businesses better, while most closed. The Bay Boxing Club is my baby. It was no easy feat, but I managed to make it my own. Murray's even got a facelift. Changing the bar name to The Black Sheep. It was a fitting name as I planned to create change. Figure out who broke the code and destroyed my family. I've never had a desire to fit in, and if I have to, I will shift the tides, alone. In this life, you only have two choices. You're a rat, much like Alex before me, or you can end up in the slammer. Either way, you're going to wind up dead. That's the only way out of all of this. In a body bag.

In the meantime, while I await the day it's my turn to leave this shit-stained planet, I'll search for answers. Bloodying my hands daily is just a bonus. I've changed. Long gone is the kid who valued friendship or any semblance of love. Now, I'm consumed by suspicion, filled with malice, and left with poor quality sleep.

The cobalt, Armani suit jacket lay neatly on a chair just outside of the perimeter. Rolling up the sleeves of my shirt, I'm reminded of the obligation to my family, as a skull with two tiny shamrock shaped eyes stares back at me. On my eighteenth birthday, my dad had one of his buddies come over and decorate my skin to match the one on my old man's bicep. "It's a family tradition," he told me. His father had done the same to him, so naturally shit runs downhill and going against traditions is an insult.

Sleeves pushed up past my elbows, I stand in front of the pathetic man while his head hangs low. Grasping a handful of his finely matted hair, I cock his head back to look within his reddened eyes. "Think before you answer, because you only have two ears."

His busted bottom lip quakes, causing spit to gather around the corners of his mouth, like the foam between cresting waves.

I delivered my first question with a soothing tone. "Are you Brodi's *informant?*"

He attempts to shake his head up and down very slowly, while I still have a fist full of hair. Progress.

I continue, "How did you stumble upon such a secret?"

He wets his lips before saying, "Lombardi. The Lombardi family. It... it was them all along."

Not possible! The Lombardis were effectively retired. I yank at his scalp, sending the chair flipping over with him still clinging on. I'm left holding a tangled, disgusting clump of brown hair.

Garron approaches, offering me my favorite tool. Shaking the hair to the floor, I press my dress shoe to the side of his face, before taking the double-edged blade from my accomplice.

Alex struggles to wiggle away. He's probably running on pure adrenaline. I'm confident his hands and fingers are now shattered beneath the weight of his body and the chair. The ring smells of body odor and piss, while my patience is at breaking point.

I squat down with my sole still pressed against the side of his jaw. I hover my prized blade above his ear. "I need a name." Each word pushes through my clenched teeth.

"I don't know, man! Oh god, please! I don't fucking know his name!"

I pinch the tip of his ear and lift, as if he's a disobedient child. With little effort, I drag the knife through the underside of his ear, from sideburn to jawbone. The shrieking causes a migraine to set in. Screams and mumbled curses fill the room, as the sobbing man shakes involuntarily. I'm delighted he's still conscious. Most likely now in shock, he wasn't going to last much longer. I was done with this anyway. I flip his head to the other side and reposition my shoe against his other cheek.

"W-Wait! Wait! I know what he looks like! I can help. Please…!"

My sleeves and chest have splatters of crimson despite my best efforts to keep clean. I step back, wondering how this nark can possibly help me find someone's face out of thirty-three thousand Southies.

All at once, the repugnant man vomits, coating the side of my fucking Prada shoes! Dax jumps into the ring, delivering a punishing swing from his steel-toed boot. A muffled scream bubbles from the restrained form. The heap ceases movement after a few seconds, while the pool of blood grows wider. I step back, because I can wash out vomit a lot easier than blood.

A cavernous hole is all that remains where the man's face used to be. "You caved his goddamned face in, man." I grumble at an unfazed Dax.

He grabs a corner rag from the side and proceeds to wipe off his shoe. Garron giggles like a hyena as he regards us just off to the side. Normally, he is the one to jump in, hot headed and without forethought. I drop the blade to the floor, leaving the mess behind.

"Clean this up!" I spit, stepping off the raised platform and making my way to the back office for a clean shirt.

After removing my soiled shirt and adding it to the pail to be burned later, I sit at the desk with my phone. I need to know more, and I only have one way of doing that. My thumbs hover over the text thread with Cindel. I haven't even bothered to clean the drying blood from my hands.

> Eamon: Hey, little fish, sorry I had to leave so abruptly.

> Cindel: It's okay.

> Eamon: Would you like to have dinner with me?

It takes a few moments until another message comes through.

> Cindel: Now? It's almost 2 a.m.! Plus, I thought you had a meeting?

I'm sure she's curious what kind of encounter happens at this hour, but she doesn't ask. I snicker to myself as I type back.

> Eamon: Got off on the wrong foot with a new client. The meeting ended earlier than expected.

Dots dance along the bottom of the screen as she appears to be typing, erasing, and retyping her response.

> Cindel: Today has been the longest day in history for me. I need to get some sleep.

I agree. It has been a taxing day. She doesn't deserve this. My search for answers will have to hold off until another day.

> Cindel: I also have this breakfast thing in the morning.

Right... the Thursday thing with her uncle. I wonder what other family she has that I didn't know about. It may be wise to spend time with her in a new setting, outside of work. We have a lot of regulars, and you can never be too careful. You never know who may be watching.

> Eamon: How about dinner this weekend?

She doesn't wait to respond. Dots dance ahead of a lengthy response.

> Cindel: Shit. Sorry... I'm sure you didn't know. I told Cassie earlier this week that I needed the weekend off. I'm going to the Catskills. My parents need me to dog sit.

Is that where they ran off to all those years ago? I debate telling Cindel that Cassie is gone, but I think better of it. She's had a rough day already. Damn, now I need to hire more help.

Finally, I responded.

> Eamon: Next week, then. Goodnight, beautiful.

I felt foul outside as well as within. I rest my head against the walnut desk, trying to quiet the swarm of bees taking up residence in my brain, when the damn phone begins to buzz violently.

"What?" I answered. Rubbing at my temples; soon realizing my hands are still splattered with blood and now it's surely on my face now.

"Sup, loser?!" a high-pitch voice replies.

"Make it quick, I'm a little busy." Pressing the phone to my ear before migrating to the office bathroom. Retrieve a towel, I begin to wipe at the evidence off me, trying to do right by my family.' Fuck. Going to have to burn this brand-new hand towel now.

"Yeah. Yeah. Important gang shit to do. Blah. Blah." The teasing voice plays through the speaker. I throw the towel down into the sink.

"What the fuck do you want?!" I turned back just in time to see Garron and Dax have entered the room, both taking seats in front of my desk.

"Okay, geeze! I thought you should know that Dad's coming. He said something about you being out of your wheelhouse. Says he needs to come and sort this shit, himself."

I march over to Garron, pushing his feet off the edge of my desk. "Yeah... how about, no! You tell him—" I begin, only to be cut off by a shrill voice on the other line.

"I'm not your fucking pigeon, Eamon! Tell him yourself when he's standing in front of you within the next couple hours!"

I sighed heavily. There was a time when we weren't at each other's throats. I bet Mom is turning in her grave with how we are to each other now. "Sorry. It's just... I got a lot of moving pieces right now and I'm trying to get more intel."

The line is quiet for a moment. I can hear her quick, angry breaths through the phone. "Whatever, fuck face."

I try to say thanks for the heads up, but she already ended the call.

"Go!" I demand through gritted teeth.

Although these are the only two people who seem to risk being this close to me these days, I didn't want them here. "Go get ready... my father will be here soon."

Alone again, I find myself back in the bathroom. Taking in my reflection within the modest mirror. Each year I look more like my father. The lines on my forehead are deeply creased despite my face being at rest. Dark circles mark each eye that I never had before. I thought it was just the way my father's face looked, but now I understand why he always appeared so haggard, edged with weariness. It must come from a lifetime of making hard decisions or neglecting things that so desperately needed your attention.

My father took everything for granted... but so have I. There's no redo button. No winding back the clock. I've grown more resentful over the past couple years, and I'm not sure there's a way of coming back. I scowl at the man in the reflection, draw back my fist and attempt to shatter the person I've become.

TEN

CINDEL

I'm cross-legged on the couch, fixing the hem of a flared pair of jeans as I consider my interaction with Eamon at the bar last night. The way his eyebrows drew together. How his mouth popped open and closed when he stood before me. Did he hear me? Does he actually think I called him a loser? It was the song, dammit! I'd probably still be mortified over that part if it wasn't for the fact that I was offered a position as manager. Manager! He complimented me. Said I did a good job. Was this a permanent thing? How long until Cassie came back? Why me?! He could have just as well offered it to Brittany or Jada. I haven't even been there for a year and he chose me?! So much unexpected shit keeps piling up this week.

Ten tiny, black toes appear in my peripheral, forcing me from my thoughts. Andrea is wrapped in a dark satin robe with wiggling toes. I wonder if it's in response to the stagnantly cold floors in our apartment or if she's uncomfortable interacting with me. Both seem feasible. Folding over the hem onto the self-sticking tape, I finally looked up. Arms crossed, her mouth moving without a sound.

Shit. I flip the rockers on my hearing aids to hopefully catch up on what I missed.

"—distant." She chews on her lip, clearly waiting for me to respond.

"Sorry, can you repeat that?"

Understanding as always, she repeats herself. She starts over, "I didn't mean to... I'm sorry that I've been so distant." She lowers herself onto the coffee table just in front, now at eye level with me.

"I know you've been busy at work. It's okay—" She holds up her hand to stop me.

"No. It's not okay. Yes, I have more on my plate lately, along with urgent deadlines but still..." She looks down at her nails, pushing a cuticle back that looked fine to begin with. "It's not an excuse to be a bad friend," she confesses.

I push forward, throwing my arms around her silk covered form. "You've never been a bad friend," I contest. "I think part of this tension between us has been my own paranoia too. Worried that If I don't know what's going on... I might lose you too."

She pulls back, placing each of her hands on my shoulders. "I would fight my way back from hell to be by your side, Cindel. You don't need to worry about me. I'm here for the long haul."

I glance at the clock on the stove. "Can we talk tonight... maybe pig out on junk food while some ridiculous, romantic comedy plays in the background?"

A tight smile forms on her face. "Sure. I'll see you tonight." Her words are soft and unsure.

Andrea has always been good at sniffing out lies. Does she know I'm keeping something from her? Was the offer of watching her favorite genre too much? Even though I'd love to mend fences with my long-time best friend, I have a feeling candy, and a movie isn't going to cut it. Something about the past few interactions with her has left me apprehensive. I can't shake this feeling that she's keeping something from me too. It makes me resistant to confiding in her. To tell her about the earbud, the texts, the songs, and the whole potential stalker thing. Hypocritical of me? Absolutely. Although, I barely trust myself to make the right decision. My fail safe is to remain closed off. It's one of the reasons my therapist recommended journaling, so I could at least learn to trust myself. Pouring all of me onto pages that wouldn't judge me or let me down. Maybe this is my way of holding onto her. Too afraid that if I tell her..., show her, she won't like what she sees. In the meantime, I'll keep pretending like everything is okay.

Raising off the couch, I visit my room to change into the tailored jeans and grab my belongings before leaving for breakfast with my uncle. We swapped awkward grins with one another before I slipped out the door.

Out of breath, I enter Benny's just a few minutes after nine. My uncle is already seated in our usual corner booth, in the back of the diner. He gives me a small welcoming wave, as I navigate to the table. Standing to greet me with a tight squeeze, we sat down together, and he handed me a menu. There were already two steaming cups of coffee at the table and a glass of orange juice.

"I hope you don't mind... I already put in our orders. I have an important meeting this morning."

Unlike my dad, my uncle isn't retired. Which is surprising considering he's quite a bit older. He works in investing. Like at one of those big banks. He tried explaining what he did to me once, but I became lost when he started using words like subsidiaries and prospectus. That's what I like about my uncle; he's never dumbed things down for me or been vague about life in general. He actually listens when I speak. Even if it's the same discussion, time and time again. My uncle doesn't steer away topics, no matter how happy or sad they may be. As opposed to my parents, who like to move past uncomfortable conversations. They've never been the type to *work through feelings* or dwell on unsavory events. They are either really good at compartmentalizing, or they really just don't give a shit about anything significant to me.

"No, I don't mind," I insist. "Sorry I was late."

He passes his hand in front of himself. "Don't you fret, kid. Tell me what's new with you?"

I start emptying packets of sugar and all the tiny creams from the little bowl on the table, into the bitter drink. He never uses them. "I quit one of my jobs or got fired, depending on how you look at it. The manager was a real piece of work. I hated working there." He nods, listening just as patiently as always. "Funnily enough... I got a promotion at The Black Sheep."

A smile blooms across his aging face. Over the years, his forehead has expanded while his hairline has decreased, but he's still somehow magnetic.

He sits up in his seat. "You're kidding, that's great! Look at how everything works out, isn't that what I'm always telling ya?!"

I nodded while recalling past times he told me that very thing. "You worry too much about things you have no power over, Cindel. Just let it be. Everything happens for a reason," he would say.

Our food arrives just as I'm telling my uncle about Eamon. He leans over to sniff my warm, syrup-drenched pancakes before returning to his less exciting over-easy egg on avocado toast.

"Would you like a bite?" I held out my fork offering a stack of triangles.

"No, thanks, kid. Don't want to spike my blood sugar first thing in the morning." He sips from his black coffee and scans the room, for what I'm not sure. Maybe it's just a protective thing? Knowing your exits; monitoring movement in a room.

By the time our plates are clear and the check arrives, I feel stuffed. I reach into my bag to cover my half of the bill, only to have my uncle wag his finger. He always covers breakfast, but it doesn't stop me from offering. After laying down two crisp twenties, he studies me for a moment.

"Something wrong, kiddo?"

Am I really that easy to read? I play with the strap on my purse, deciding what to say without sounding like I belonged under a twenty-four-hour psychiatric hold.

"I... would it?" I chew the inside of my cheek.

The dark circles under my uncle's eyes seem darker. I wonder if he's tired. Working a full-time job at his age, probably isn't easy. He leans back, placing his arms on either side of the sparkly, plastic bench. Even his mannerisms are different from his brother's. Confident, powerful, and sure of himself.

My father was adopted by my grandparents when he was a baby. It's ironic how, over the past couple years, I've grown to know the man in front of me better than my own parents. Perhaps because of our proximity to one another? Him being the only remaining family I had left in the city. Regardless, I see him more than I ever did as a kid, and he never pushed me away.

I take a deep breath in and breathe out slowly, just like I was instructed to do over multiple years of therapy. Don't close him off too, Cindel. Say it!

"I feel like I'm being followed."

He raises a bushy eyebrow, just like anyone would do after making such a claim.

"I know it sounds crazy, but there was this earbud and then songs started playing."

He rubs his freshly shaven face. Even though it appears smooth, you can still make out pores of black along his neck and jaw. "Songs?"

I nod. "Yes, songs." I respond. "Every time I try to get rid of it, the thing just keeps coming back. So, I figured what the hell, I'll just listen and…" I pause, stifle through my bag and locate the item in question. "Here."

I place the earbud in the middle of the table between us; he picks it up and begins turning it over, examining it. His other thick eyebrow raises to match the first. "Have you called the police?" He leans forward, handing the quaint, polar device back to me.

"You know how helpful they are." I stopped trusting law enforcement to uphold the law long ago. "They didn't even look into my brother's death!" I seethe.

"Shhhh…" He inclines forward earnestly, reaching for my hands like a man desperate to cling to something real. His silvery eyes search mine. "Cindel, Cindel, Cindel… You know he took his own life. You've seen the report. He overdosed. When's the last time you saw your therapist, kiddo?" He gives my hands a gentle squeeze, his eyes taking on a soft, pitting look. "I hate to see you letting your imagination get in the way of your successes. Focus on that promotion you just got. Maybe that stalker fellow is just some admirer? Don't overthink it. This isn't one of your TV shows. No one's watching you." He lets go of my hands suddenly and taps his chin with a crooked finger. "Ya know what? I bet it's that boy you told me about. Your boss?"

He can't be serious. Eamon? No. He doesn't have time for that. He's running his businesses. Plus, looking as he does, I'm sure he has tons of girls throwing themselves at him. He wouldn't waste his time stalking me. Would he?

Looking down at his Rolex, he pats his mouth with a napkin, then extracts himself from the booth, and pulls on his overcoat. I follow, pulling my bag onto my shoulder and standing along with him. He closes the gap, takes a gentle hold of my face, and kisses each temple before looking down into my eyes. "I like when you share with me, kid. Same time next month?"

I nod and force a smile. For the first time, I didn't feel better after one of our breakfast dates. Pushing up a pair of aviators, he strides toward the door and down the street. Maybe things will be different in a month. Till then, I'll try to follow his advice. Don't let my imagination get carried away and focus on the opportunity in front of me.

I voluntarily go to The Black Sheep before my scheduled shift. With Eamon offering me the position as manager, I had a lot to learn before my first day in the new role. Walking in, I find Eamon standing just behind the bar with Connor.

"You two look sweaty, were you moving kegs?" They both answer with a "yeah" in unison, as Connor disappears behind the swinging door.

"You're early!" Eamon exclaims.

"Good morning to you too…" I tease.

From the first time I saw Eamon, he has always been dressed to the nines. Tailored suit, expensive designer shoes… however, today he is dressed down. He's wearing a cotton tank-top which reveals toned arms and a bar towel is thrown over his shoulder. Corded muscle runs the length of each forearm. Is that a tattoo? As I approach, the lower half of his body reveals itself as, gray sweatpants. My belly somersaults as I try desperately not to home in on his crotch area. He crosses his arms and leans back resting the sole of his shoe against a storage cabinet behind him. It's giving 'I'm sexy even in casual attire' vibes.

"Since I was promoted to a manager position just last night, I figured I would come in early! Try to get a jump on things, like understanding my new responsibilities." I take a seat on a bar stool, then proceed to pull out a small spiral notebook and pen.

A smile plays at the corner of his mouth. "Okay…" he starts. "Are you familiar with balancing the drawer?"

I nod. "I've watched Cassie do it a multitude of times. One night, I had to tally up the drawer myself. Cassie had to run out for only a couple hours. Her son wound up in jail, again."

He breaks his hold, bringing up a hand to rub his jaw. His face is unshaved; he looks, troubled or maybe just tired.

Moving with the grace of a predator, he rests his hands on either side of my spot at the bar. Leaning forward, he's mere inches from me. I can't help but notice one of his knuckles looks bruised, with new small cuts and scrapes around the knuckles. Should I ask? That's really not my business. His gaze on me feels heated, but what he says next doesn't match how he looks at me.

"There's not much left besides making the schedule and delegating. If you see someone not pulling their weight in one area, rotate them. They won't always like it, but I've got a business to run, not friendships to keep." I jot down a couple of notes as he talks. "Don't sweat it! You're going to do great tonight!"

Why does everyone keep telling me to relax in different ways? Do I really seem to be wound that tightly? "Wait... you're not going to be here?"

He looks down at me, and I feel my face warming under his intense stare. God, he's handsome. "No, little fish. I won't. My father just flew in, and we have some catching up to do. Connor will be here all night, though."

I shake my pen between my fingers while I think. "What about those two guys you're always with?"

His eyebrow lifts in response. "Who? Garron and Dax? No, they'll be with me. It's a slow night; you shouldn't run into any trouble. If you do, find Connor. He's a tough cookie."

I nod. Understanding that 'I'm covered but also feeling a little nervous about being in charge. I'm not as tough as Cassie, nor am I as knowledgeable about what it takes to run a place like this.

He takes my hand, causing the pen to tumble to the bar top and gently rests a warm kiss upon my knuckles. I'm ensnared by this man's proximity. His eyes are such a lovely green. "When you get back from the Catskills, I have our first date all planned." Although the bar separates us, it feels extremely intimate. I'm sure my face is already bright red.

"I look forward to it." I just manage to sputter as Connor clears his throat, emerging from the back swinging door.

"Can I take her for a bit? I wanted to go over the scheduling software with her on the computer?"

Eamon releases my hand just before folding his arms again. His eyes fixated on me as I gather my things and follow Connor to the back. I may need to climb inside of the ice machine, just to extinguish the burn from that man's energy.

Connor is a wealth of information; I feel bad for pinning him as *only a barback* over the time I've worked here. He not only knows what needs to be ordered each month, but he even knows the banking info and safe combination. After he walks me through the scheduling software, he places a set of keys with a clover keychain attached in front of me.

"Any questions?"

I'm sure I had at least twenty, but he covered everything. I also didn't want to be a bother when he had already taken time away from his tasks to help me.

"Great! Jada and Brittany are in tonight. Oh, yeah... we also hired two new girls to help out when you're gone. They'll continue through the holiday season too."

Jesus! It hasn't even been twelve hours?! I guess when you run a popular watering hole like The Black Sheep, you have back up. Maybe the bar isn't so different from the grocery market. There's always someone to take your place when you don't show up. Would they replace me if I didn't do a good enough job at managing things while Cassie is away? I wasn't sure which was worse, working my first shift as acting manager with my once equals or supervising two new hires? I don't want to fuck this up and have everyone hating me by the end of the night.

"Go get some lunch, then get back here so we can go over bar licensing."

Eamon is already gone by the time I emerge from the backroom.

Two blocks over, I find a short line at a deli counter that has one of the best pastrami on rye sandwiches this side of Boston. I need brain fuel before I continue with my *learning to manage a bar in less than twenty-four hours* crash course.

The line moves fairly quickly, a man in a hoodie in front of me and two ladies arguing about wearing white after Labor Day just behind. Sandwich in hand, I shuffle over to the counter to pay. I grab a black and white cookie beside the register before fishing my wallet out.

"All taken care of," the man in the stained apron informs me. Then proceeds to motion for the chatty women to come forward.

"Wait. I'm sorry… you said it's taken care of? Like someone paid for my food? Who?" I step aside, making room for the ladies to move up, as the man smashes keys on the register.

"One of those pay-it-forward folks. He was just in front of you."

I grab the paper bag holding my lunch order and rush out to the busy street. Looking each way, I see no sign of the hooded figure. I had no one to thank at that moment, but I had a feeling I knew who the stranger was.

Just outside The Black Sheep, I devour my sandwich. I decide to save the chocolate side of the dinner-plate sided cookie for, after Connor was through info dumping about things I never intended to learn. I will need the sugary pick-me-up!

My notebook sits on my lap as I flip through pages of chicken scratch and bolded reminders about this new position. Connor is a great teacher, and he knows a lot about The Black Sheep. I am curious as to how he is such a wealth of knowledge for being a barback. Maybe all the employees who have tenure learn these things.

I was prepared but not PREPARED. To be honest, I was a mess internally. Questioning whether or not Eamon has made a mistake, asking me to step in as manager, and also when will Cassie be back? With a nearly full notepad, learning too much about negotiating supplier contracts, and proper safety regulations, my brain was fried! I treat myself to the dark side of the cookie, while Connor is in the alley, pressure cleaning the floor mats before opening.

I am just finishing my treat before Jada and Brittany enter together. I wave while attempting to choke down the last bite; however, they don't wave back.

Instead, I am met with a tight-lipped smile from Brittany, and Jada didn't even bother to look my way. They make their way to the backroom, carrying on as if I am not even in the room. I pocket my notepad and join my coworkers in the backroom, secretly hoping this wasn't the beginning of an ugly working environment.

"Hey," I say upon entering. "I wanted to ask you both where you would like to be stationed tonight? I know the schedule usually determines where everyone is, but today I wanted to—" I trail off.

Brittany appears deeply pained, rubbing her upper arm with a downcast gaze, while Jada's narrowed eyes lock onto mine. Her lips narrow at the corners before words form like darts being thrown at its target.

"What makes you so special?!" Jada all but spits. Her arms cross over her chest as she steps forward.

"I'm… What?" I expected tension, but she already has her claws out, and we aren't even open yet!

She continues, "You haven't been here as long as I have been! Even as long as Brittany. What makes you so qualified?!" Any semblance of a friendly working relationship has all but turned sour overnight. Brittany seemed to shrink back slightly.

"I didn't ask for this!" I protest.

"Sure, you didn't… but I'm positive that sleeping with the boss helped."

Is that what they think?! My hands shoot out from my sides. "I'm not sleeping with Eamon!" This time, both girls share a look.

"Right… just couldn't even wait until Cassie's funeral to steal her job!"

My next words get stuck in my throat. All the comebacks I had cued up vanished. I hold myself steady, clutching at my upper arms.

"Wait… what?" I look between Brittany and Jada, but neither regards my shock.

"Oh…" Jada's downturned mouth instantly flips to that of the Cheshire Cat. "Your Eamon didn't tell you?"

Tell me what? I couldn't voice.

"Cassie is dead!"

The room seems to sway. Like ripples that follow along the top of the water when you drop a heavy rock into a lake. I lean against the ice machine for stability. The two simply stroll past me and push the swinging door outward.

I remain in the backroom while I collect my thoughts.

Dead? How?! She was fine! Has been fine. Now she's gone! I could feel myself growing more upset by the minute. I was, of course, sad. Sad for her son. Upset how I'll never see her again, yet I'll have to be reminded of her endlessly each time I work at The Black Sheep. Then my mind diverts… instantly going to Theo… Brodi. The pain of another loss begins to fester in my stomach, and I don't want to go there. Not now… Not today! Why? Determined, I swap out my anguish for anger. Why? He must have known! He could have just told me?!! Eamon lied to me!

The monotonous ringing in my head seems to be getting louder by the second. Not giving myself a second to think better of it, I pull out my phone and send a strongly worded message to Eamon. Then slip it back into my back pocket. I don't want to see the response. Too filled with everything right now, I am confident I would say something that could get me fired.

I go to my bag, apparently disconnected completely at this point from my prefrontal cortex. Switching out my right hearing aid, for the piece of tech that bears the purple star. There was no plan, no analysis of what putting this earbud back on meant, just doing. Acting. Perhaps I was searching for something, but as soon as the plastic antenna hung from my ear, I felt soothed. Will I hear something? Only time will tell, but as of late this thing… whatever is happening… has been the only situation I can count on.

I peek through the port window of the backroom door, finding both Jada and Brittany beginning the opening tasks for the evening. Spying made me feel like I was back in grade school. Not wanting to leave the bathroom because I knew all the kids were talking about me. They thought I wouldn't notice. The way they would turn just enough, so their backs were to me or using only a whisper voice; believing that I couldn't hear the mean things they said about me. I'm deaf, not dumb! Plus, I learned how to read lips pretty quickly. I knew what they said about me. The names. The jokes. The isolation. As I got older, I tried to steel myself, ignoring the banter. If I didn't give them a reaction, they would eventually stop. When my brother found out, he wanted to get back at them. I never figured out how he learned about the teasing, but the main one's responsible wound up with gum in their hair or their clothes being riddled with itching powder.

I don't care for this empty feeling and right now, I would prefer just about anything to take up this space.

Tonight is a brutally slow night. I don't even have to bother Connor with any silly questions the entire shift. Both Jada and Brittany insist on being on the floor, in turn making me behind the bar alone. I know they want to be as far away from me as possible. They barely even speak to me the whole night, besides the reluctant drink request that they can't fill themselves.

Even my musical stalker was radio silent! For once, I wanted to interact beyond, "What can I get you?" But tonight had to be quiet.

I counted the drawer twice at closing and still I couldn't get it to balance. Admitting defeat, Connor came to my rescue and recounted. That's all I need right now… a short drawer on my first shift as the "acting" manager.

I check my phone. Disappointed that not even Eamon has attempted to communicate. Rereading my text, I doubt if I should have even sent it, until I tell myself that he is the one that withheld information. I shouldn't feel bad, but I kind of do.

Connor totaled the drawer with the initial count I made, finding two sticky twenties that most likely caused the discrepancy. I'm both thankful and embarrassed.

Jada flips each chair onto the small tables with a spin, causing the stool to make an unnecessary tottering sound. Connor notices me wince. He snaps his fingers loudly across the bar at Jada, telling her to drop the attitude. She does.

Brittany gives me a small wave before walking out the door with Jada, who doesn't spare a single glance in my direction. I couldn't have picked a more perfect time to take time off.

Connor sticks around a little later than usual, even watching me lock up. He's a pretty nice guy and I'm thankful for his help today. We go our separate ways, him slipping down a side street while I continue along my usual path to my apartment building.

Alone again, I walked quickly. Hoping to find Andrea already home, snuggled up with her fuzzy bat blanket waiting for me on the couch. We're overdue to catch up. I don't care if we talked or watched a movie. I'm desperate for any positive interaction. A movie would be perfect. What's the name of the one where two unlikely partners suck at communicating, get caught up in embarrassing situations, and eventually the two wind up perfectly matched right before the ending? Miss Congruent? No. Miss Congenerous? Whatever its name is, I really don't see her appeal to these types of movies, but I was willing to sit through the film just to spend time with her.

Pushing my key within the lock, I realize I am holding my breath. Whether it's because I am anxious about her not being there or actually being present was debatable. I let the air out slowly as I push the door open to our apartment. Both will be difficult... and there she is! Like the sighting of a silvery-haired nymph in their natural habitat, but instead of a magical aura, she was cast in the glow of the television. The small adjacent table was covered with a candy-filled charcuterie board, complete with plastic skeleton.

"No way!" I skip to the table, half haphazardly removing my shoes and dropping my bag to the floor. "Are those gummy worms crawling out of its mouth?"

She nods her head.

"With Twizzler pull n' peel for intestines?!" I marveled.

Her cheeks raise, causing her eyes to nearly disappear. Her smile disintegrates any current worries. "Couldn't think of a more delicious organ," she admits.

I let myself fall on top of her and proceed to plant a big kiss on her forehead. "You're a genius!" I tell her.

Without delay, I unwrap a Rolo and pop it into my mouth. I love the way the chocolate oozes out caramel, when I crush it within the inside of my cheek.

Andrea doesn't have much of a sweet tooth. She'll cheat occasionally by adding extra chocolate chips to one of her protein shakes, but she's all about gain and rarely misses her gym days.

This entire spread is all for me. So sweet of her! Figuratively and literally. I move onto the mountain of candy corn, surrounding the skeleton's plastic skull, as Andrea cues up a movie. The words "Miss Congeniality" fill the screen.

"That's it!" I shout at no one in particular. "Congeniality!"

She shakes her head, clearly not understanding that I finally have clarity, after struggling to remember the name of this freakin' movie on my walk home. My generous roommate drapes a blanket over both of us, in preparation for Gracie to transition from a demoted FBI agent to beauty queen in one short montage. Unexpectedly, the hole I once felt earlier this evening feels a little less profound, as we watch a pageant contestant befriend the abrasive, very unladylike Gracie. In the long run, the undercover agent foils the copycat terrorist's plan and even bags the cute guy; all in four-inch heels. How is it that Andrea has managed to dupe me into watching not one, but two Sandra Bullock movies in the past week? Just as Gracie's superior was about to pull the plug on the whole mission, I knew what I had to do. Andrea extended an olive branch, so I needed to give her the same courtesy.

I all but blurt out… "I'm involved with someone."

Robotically, she reaches forward, grabs the remote, and clicks off the movie. Not paused, just off. Her head swivels toward me; she pushes a few silver strands behind her ear and simply glares at me. "Pardon me, I think my best friend just dropped news so big, my brain malfunctioned."

A nervous laugh bubbles out of me. I push my back against the side armrest of the couch, facing her fully.

"I'm pretty sure I would know if you were dating someone. You know how nosy I can be," she admits while also giving me a light shove on the shoulder.

"I didn't say dating. I said *involved*."

"Isn't that the same thing?" Her head turns at an angle that reminds me of a dog trying to figure out why you're not also offering them food as you eat.

"No. It's way different!" I pull my legs into a crossed position. "It's kind of complicated. He's kind of my boss. Well, he *is* my boss, but it might not necessarily—"

Her head turns in the other direction, still just as befuddled. "Connor? I thought he was gay."

What? "No. Connor? I actually don't know his sexual orientation. Plus, Connor's not my boss."

She holds her palm out, encouraging me to continue.

"Eamon. I actually didn't even know he owned the bar up until recently. He's interesting. Devilishly handsome and also funny at times. He calls me little fish and…"

Andrea looks sick. Her eyes look toward me, but it feels more like she's looking through me.

"Hey. Are you okay? You look like you're not feeling too well."

She stands suddenly and starts to pace the small area in front of Thelma's tank. Is she pissed?

I try to turn back the clock. "I know I should have mentioned something sooner, but it's new and we really haven't even officially been on a date yet. I think it's an awkward stage." Mostly because I'm not sure if I can trust him. Is it possible that Eamon is the one who left the earbud, like my uncle suggested? Is he capable of playing multiple roles? Maybe I should have kept my mouth shut or told her something less impactful like, I had a delicious pastrami on rye today! If it's not some banal thing, it is monumental. At least as of late. Everything from my ex-manager expecting some kind of sexual favor in the backroom of Star Mart, to the returning earbud that transmits cryptic music, and even learning my new managerial position is more permanent than I initially thought, because Cassie actually died!

My roommate finally halts her parading, after practically burning a hole in one of the Persian rugs we got last summer. "What about Brodi?!"

Wow. That's the last thing I expected her to come back with. She never cared for him. As she continues, her voice becomes progressively louder. "What if he turns up? Aren't you crazy about him still?!"

I am aghast… Andrea?! Making a case for Brodi? This week has been outlandish!

"Are you sure you're ready to be with someone again so soon?" Her voice turns softer while her words fall flat.

Things were strained between Brodi, and I before he disappeared. I was the one forcing the square peg in the round hole. Yes, I miss him, but I think I'm realizing I missed the *old* him. If he showed up today, I would still be begging for his attention, even though he was the one that up and left. This behavior was very unlike Andrea. Not aligned with the *live for today* mantra, she has attempted to instill in me over the past few months.

"You're the one reminding me it's been half a year. I never thought you'd be the one telling me to keep up hope. You thought he was a sleaze bag anyways." I fired back.

She folds her arms, and I can't help but notice the way her fist clenches. Like when she's ready to go, *let it all out*, on the punching bag in her room. Her response isn't sharp like mine. "Just… try to remember how you felt when he first disappeared. I think seeing someone so soon after him is a poor choice."

I see red. I find myself standing the next second, my body language mirroring hers. "Says the girl who told me all about how she slept with her last three clients at work!" If she was able, I'm sure that piercing glare could shoot lasers through me. Shit.

Before I can even get out another word, she spins on her heel and slams the door to her bedroom. Like any rationally unsettled person, I begin stress cleaning! I fold blankets, fluff pillows, and even store the remaining candy within multiple Ziplock bags. When I'm done, I say goodnight to Thelma before dropping in two small grasshoppers.

Andrea's room has faint snapping sounds coming from the other side. I can't help but rest my ear against the door. The sound grows into louder pops and cracks. She is definitely getting good use out of that punching bag. I back away, returning to my side of the apartment and close myself in my room.

I feel like a cruel friend. Not only am I not being forthcoming about what is actually going on with me, but now I need to apologize on top of it! It's not my business who she sleeps with, but she can't judge me for trying to move on. I need to sleep. Tomorrow requires me to operate heavy machinery.

I am not looking forward to the long drive to the Catskills, to watch my parents' dog Kingston. I'm drowning in thoughts as I lie in bed. Playing with feasible outcomes and scenarios based on choices I simply didn't make. The limitless possibilities fill me up until I sink to the bottom. I can't swim. It's too much and none of it makes any sense. My hearing aids are on the charger, but it's never silent. The resonating sound in my head matches the waves of light, momentarily painting my ceiling in amber tones, as cars pass by on the streets below. Why? I wonder. Why wasn't it me? My brother was incredible. Never doubted himself. He would have used these past few years to make a difference. He was stronger. Smarter. Just... better. It should have been me.

Sleep eventually finds me, but I wish I would never wake up.

ELEVEN

EAMON

I leave the Black Sheep with enough time to grab a shower and some lunch before meeting up with Garron and Dax at the Bay Boxing Club. My father should be arriving shortly based on the live flight tracker.

Cindel caught me off guard today, showing up early like that. Each time she turns up, those easy eyes of hers make my job that much harder. It would be simpler if she wasn't around to see the destruction I leave in my wake.

Steam fills the shower as I stand beneath the stream, watching the droplets roll off me and onto the tile floor. I need to clear my mind. My hand finds my dick, recalling memories from earlier this morning. Squeezing gently, I glide over the head back and forth until I find my release.

Time is a fucked-up construct. It was only a couple years ago I was present in my life and shockingly happy. I had a purpose and felt like I was grounded.

Now, I would freely lob off my own hand to go back during a time that stood still. Keeping business and pleasure separate, my apartment was on the other side of town off Liberty Drive. Unless I intended for that person to suck my dick, no one came here but me.

I dress in a black button-up and tan slacks, forgoing the formal business jacket for my father's arrival. I like to give him the middle finger in any subtle way possible. I close the clasp on the band of my Rolex and make my way to the main room. Thanks to the designer, my kitchen has top of the line appliances, microwave drawer, and my favorite: a countertop ice ball maker for my whiskey. Hell, even the fridge has a television in it. I open the stainless-steel doors to find a couple bottles of water, a withered apple, and expired leftovers. I don't like cooking or being in the kitchen; it was never a part of my repertoire. I do know that everything works mainly, because my last partner was an excellent cook. During that season of my life, I barely wore pants. I was either fucking or too well fed, to bother with slacks and a belt.

I pull out my phone to place an order from one of my regular takeout spots. Maybe I should send for someone to at least stock my fridge. I shake away the idea, with the realization that this kitchen will never see activity like it had before. Grabbing my keys, I look back at the large empty sink in the island which at one time would have been filled faucet high with dishes. It was once used, cluttered, and chaotic, but full of laughter too. Now, it's devoid of everything. Lifeless, clean, and quiet. I hate this place

Parking just outside the steel building, I quickly make my way inside. One of the larger grunt workers who goes by *The Barber,* holds the side door open for me upon approach. He earned his name by having at least two straight razors on him at any given time. Last time I saw him in action, he managed to peel back a man's scalp from his hairline to the nape of his neck, before his victim finally expired. We always get the information we need thanks to The Barber's fine craftsmanship. Glad to have him, because I'd never want to be on the receiving end.

Inside, five men are poised around a small table engaged in a game of Gin Rummy. Smoke bellows up from another area in the back, as a few of my crew members dismantle and clean their pieces. Garron is shirtless and laying into one of the hanging bags just off the side of the ring. Walking up to the side of him, I grab a towel off a chair and throw it into his face. "Clean yourself up. Patrick should be here any minute."

He starts wiping away the sweat from his brow then, patting his armpits. He nods in understanding.

"Where's Dax?" I scan the room to see if maybe I missed him, in this club full of bodies. I requested they all be present for today.

"Not here, sir. I can text him."

I put up my hand, refusing his help. Garron takes that as his cue to go freshen himself for my father's arrival. Frustrated, I retrieve my phone and shoot off a text to the tardy man in question.

Moments later, the large doorman opens the ingress to welcome my father. Patrick Murray is flanked by six men on each side, most as big if not bigger than *The Barber*. My father oozes money, never sparing a cent when it comes to displaying power or wealth. I'm sure there's at least two Range Rover limousines parked outside as we speak.

He stands in front of me with his smug face, tailored ivory Giorgenti suit, and handmade green, leather shoes. It's funny to think that not too long ago he would use a shoe like that to whoop me, now he looks weak from this side of the room. His thinning skin is speckled with dark patches, while the scar along his temple, from a deal gone wrong, is still pink and defined through his fine hair. I don't care for the way his men study me, seeming to size me up. This is my turf, he thrust this onto me when he left; he doesn't get to show up and reign the same as he once did.

The once playful roar of voices settles down as father and son, position themselves before one another like some form of standoff. A thick eyebrow lifts on his face as he takes in my outfit. Clearly not pleased I forgone the jacket. I fight back a grin.

"Dia is Muire Duit!" My father exclaims as he reaches for me, grabbing each side of my head and giving me a little shake.

"Da..." I force myself to nod respectfully.

Garron does a slow jog toward the group, looking much more put together than before.

Smiling and throwing his head back, my father embraces Garron with a big hug and a pat on the back. "My boy! You look well, lad." He holds his shoulders while looking him over. "How's your mother?" he asks softly.

Garron bobs his head. "Not too bad. She's living comfortably with the time she has left, thanks to you."

Patrick swipes his hand in front of his face. "Ah, It's nothing. You're family!"

Garron goes down the line of my father's crew, giving each man a fist bump while dad looks around.

"Where's that kid, Dax?" As if he were summoned, he pops in through a side door. "Daxton! My boy. Come, let's have a look at ya!" He motions for the straggler to come over to the group.

Dax walks over, locking eyes with me; he knows I'm not too keen on tardiness. He stands before my father, significantly taller than him, but Patrick has more mass around the middle.

"I like that you're still standing, even after what happened."

Dax tilts his head forward.

"Tell me, did the party responsible get what they deserved?"

Dax puffs out his chest slightly.

In response, Patrick slaps him on the back. "Wonderful! Man of few words... I like this guy. Bet he keeps all the best secrets."

He motions for his men to take up residency on the chairs in the lounging area. My men immediately stand, clearing the table of cards, and rush out of the way. Smart move.

Garron walks up with a small wooden box, offering his *father-figure* a cigar, then proceeds to light a match.

My phone vibrates in my front pocket. I discreetly check to see what it is. It's a message from her.

> Cindel: Cassie is dead?! Why didn't you tell me?! Am I now the permanent manager?

I shoved the phone back into my jacket pocket, not wanting to handle two nuclear fallouts at once. Later, I tell myself.

My father removes his suit jacket and tumbles back onto a too low chair.

Clumsily, he attempts to cross his opposite ankle over his knee before finally relaxing against the eggplant-colored seat. The woodsy aroma wafts around us as he experiments with the smoke, to create unsuccessful ringlets.

"A little birdie told me you found a hidden Lombardi. What have you learned so far?" My father takes a methodical toke of his thick cigar.

"Yes... I did find a Lombardi, however, I haven't learned much. I'm working on that." I feel like I'm ten again, standing in the kitchen as my father chastises me for yanking the head off of one of my sibling's dolls.

"Your sister thinks you're fucking this up," he proclaims, holding the smoking stick between his yellowed teeth.

Of course she would say that to him. Ever since mom died, she's been just as unhinged as he is. If anything, she's worse! My sister doesn't care about the business side of things. I bet she would be just fine with watching it all become ash. I may be the big brother, but when she makes up her mind about something, she can be scary as fuck if you get in her way.

"She doesn't need to be involved in this," I say, through gritted teeth.

"Oh, but she does and she is."

I hear whispers around me from my crew. He hasn't even been here for five minutes and already he's trying to make me seem incompetent.

"I just need a bit more time."

He places his suspended jade shoe, back down to the floor. Then, placing both hands on his opened thighs with the stogie between the fingers of one hand, he leans in. He speaks softly at first, but gradually his voice rises to an untethered shout. "How about this... I'll keep your sister on a leash, for now... but I will be staying here until I have FUCKING VENGEANCE!" Spit flies from the mouth of his beet red face.

I breathe in through my nose and out through my mouth, ever so slowly. "Yes sir." I look down at the floor, instinctively.

Like a switch has been flipped, he goes back to lounging and puffing on his smoke. "Ah! Please tell your sister we'll be having dinner tonight at seven sharp, and for your sanity and mine put a fucking tail on that Lombardi cunt!"

After being chummy with my crew, drinking my whiskey, and smoking my Cubans, the brute of a man finally makes his way up to the loft suite, positioned on the second floor of the boxing club. Once out of ear shot, I swung at the first bag within reach, giving a jab, cross, hook! Anger bubbles deep within me, I've lost my touch, and I let him get to me too easily.

My father's men took off to enjoy all that Boston has to offer, while I go back to business as usual.

Once we open the doors, paying members trickle in over the next hour to work on their techniques through practicing drills. I have some fish to fry, so I am out of there before Patrick wakes from his nap.

I push open the door, walking promptly to my car.

"Need us, boss?!" Garron jogs toward me, through the parking lot with Dax a few steps behind.

"No, I've got this on my own. You two… do whatever the fuck you both do when I'm not around."

Garron salutes me as I slide into my white Audi.

As I'm driving, a text comes through.

> Sis: Nice job making Daddy mad. Will you be joining us for dinner tonight?

At the traffic light, I write back.

> Eamon: No. Stop putting your nose where it doesn't belong!

Immediately, a message comes through.

> Sis: Whatever do you mean?

Followed by a smiley with a halo emoji.

I lobbed the cell phone down to the passenger seat's footwell. Fuck.

I didn't really know where I was heading, but I knew it wasn't The Black Sheep. I didn't want her to see me, not when I was wound so tightly. She wouldn't be safe.

I find myself back in my living room overlooking the harbor. Yachts and fishing charters bob in the reflective water just outside my executive suite. The panoramic ocean and city views just weren't as breathtaking anymore. I pull the floor to ceiling curtains closed, encasing myself in darkness before making my way to my room. This bedroom is my favorite; it's the only room I told the designer she couldn't lay a fucking finger on. Unlike the rest of the apartment, it has gray wainscot walls, dim lighting, and a low-profile bed. I kept it simple, no wall art; allowing the dark moody vibe to take center stage. Small wooden dressers adorn each side of the tufted, upholstered headboard. The ceiling reflects the earthy tones covering the bed. That mirror sure did make for some fun times.

Without much thought, I find myself throwing open drawers and stuffing clothes into a duffle bag from my closet. Between family shit, business, and my quest for answers; I couldn't stand to be here a minute longer. All those memories came rushing back like a wave and I'm tired of choking on the salted water. I'm going on a little trip and will only return once I have clarity.

103

TWELVE

CINDEL

Three hours and sixteen minutes in a rental that smells like sourdough and menthols. I opt to drive with my hair up and the windows down. Thank my lucky stars this shit box has Bluetooth capabilities, allowing my temporary torture chamber to at least have quality tunes.

Living in the city, I've never had the need to own a car, but my parents were sure to teach my brother and I how to drive. Theo, of course, excelled at the task. He even had a short stint being a valet driver until he got fired for backing a Porsche into a light pole. I enjoy driving but know my skills haven't flourished past automatic, base-model cars.

I wear my crimson, striped sweater, a pair of thick tights, and a pleated skirt. I really need to get to the laundromat because most of my clothes were beginning to reek like The Black Sheep. Hopefully, my parents don't cringe at the odor of cloves and stale beer clinging to the fabric. They know I've had a lot of jobs since college and after a while, they kind of stopped keeping track. I'm sure my mom would have *choice words*, if she actually knew the kind of place I worked at.

As I drive, my thumbs make themselves at home, forging a new hole right through each sleeve. My knuckles are covered, as I battle to stay warm against the chill that whips through the car. I refuse to close the windows and be imprisoned with this stench. My weekend bag sits on the passenger seat, over-flowing with clothes, a charger, two books, and the materials I require to finish up a project for the Craft Bazaar, coming up next week.

Three hours and sixteen minutes morph into four hours and some change, when an overturned maple syrup truck blocks both lanes. Traffic piles up, and we are sitting ducks until a tow truck arrives, and the state's road crew are able to scrape the road for one lane to pass. When I tell my mom, she becomes anxious to leave, since they would have to take a slightly different route. They want to arrive at Martha's Vineyard before dark.

So, with a quick, *sorry we can't stay any longer*! Followed by a, *love you*, exchanged via text, they head out.

My karaoke skills are becoming fine-tuned over the long drive, as I sing along with Gwen Stephani and Shirley Manson. As I continue into the more mountainous terrain, a song comes on, I don't recall adding to my curated playlist. It starts with a howl, then a tambourine joins in. Slow, eerie lyrics about a little girl in red being in the woods, all alone. The words scroll by the screen with the song name: **"Lil' red riding hood."** Not bothering to change it, I focus on making the right turns, according to the GPS, so I don't wind up in the wrong place. I did however plan to remove the ever so creepy song from my playlist, so I wouldn't have to listen to it again.

The red marker off the side of the main road indicates I have arrived at my destination. I pause momentarily, since no one is behind me. Taking in the long winding driveway, lined with oak trees. Cautiously I follow the path up the side of the mountain, to a gravel parking area. A short stone wall separates me from a magical, single-story home. Ivy cascades down every surface of the structure; lattice windows hold wavy glass, while wooden arched doors made the charming home present as, cozy and inviting. My parents told me a little about the historical home. Originally built in the 1920s, it was the kind of place out of a storybook with a blissfully ignorant princess and a fleet of tiny grumpy men, obsessed with treasure.

After I park, I grab my bag and start down the lush path toward my new residence for the next few days. Trees shade the home from every angle. With moss-lining the cobbled path, it seems that even sunny days aren't enough to warm the grounds.

My dad did a wonderful job maintaining the gardens. Even though the cooler temperatures slowed down a majority of growth, the foliage is still breathtaking. Purple ghost shaped flowers line the walkway in front, while a small garden along the side of the house, overflows with rainbow Swiss chard. It looks like nature's candy, although I don't recall ever eating it. Surrounding the property and well into the valley below, is a canvas of fall colors. Shades of yellow, crimson, and pumpkin-orange cover the expansive mountain views.

I show myself in, using a key underneath the small pelican statue, to the left of the front door. Just where my parents said it would be. Little specks of dust try to dance across the soft lit room as I step into the classical dwelling. It appears as if the flecks of lint are attempting to spin and swirl, much like the memory I commonly revisit at night.

I hear something… snapping me from my thoughts, Kingston urgently trots up with happy tail wags. I oblige by collapsing to the floor and burying my face in his Frito scented fur. I love his delicious *bagged chip* smell. After a substantial number of good boys and belly rubs, I find my way to the kitchen, where I set my stuff down. I also sent a quick text to my parents and Andrea.

Arrived Alive!

I happily wander around the massive house to get a lay of the land, Kingston right beside me. The largest bedroom is right off the kitchen and appears to be the most lived-in. It must be where my parents reside while watching this home. Attached to the sleeping area is a lovely sunroom with an antique, wooden table and matching chair. I could see myself sitting out here, finishing up projects for the Craft Bazaar. Kingston follows every step of the way, being the best tour guide. Just past the kitchen is the living room, complete with reading nook and a grand, navy-blue fireplace. This house has to be worth over a million bucks! An extra bedroom just off the sitting area is set up as a study, but my mom mentioned a guest suite outback was made up for my stay.

Hot on my heels, Kingston and I race from the back door to the guest house, about a hundred feet away from the main structure. He wins.

The door opens right into the sleeping area, resembling a miniature version of the house I just toured. The room is large enough to be comfortable for a short stay, but you have to go from one dwelling to another if you want to access food. My favorite part is the romantic, clawfoot tub in the corner of the bathroom. I look forward to washing the stench of the 'rental car' off me, in that incredible bath. After unpacking a few of my things and participating in a spirited round of fetch in the yard with Kingston, I plan to use the rest of the daylight hours to craft, out on the deck.

My parents were right; it is very peaceful here. It was an ideal time to "get away." Andrea and I didn't part on good terms. I regret not trying to see her before I left this morning. I replay our conversation, trying to analyze if it's something I said or was she blowing this whole, *new guy thing* out of proportion. Should I have led with the earbud and stalker bit? Of course not, because that sounds like a situation that would incite a whole lot more concern than some innocent flirting with your boss.

Okay. Let's play devil's advocate. If it's not Eamon… then. Who else could it be? A regular customer at the bar? Someone from Star Mart? No one comes to mind, but it only takes one misinterpreted smile to make some weirdo become obsessed with someone who is just trying to do their job.

Really… is it only one-sided? I was stupid enough to take the lonely device home. If I just left it there… I wouldn't be having this perpetual feeling of being followed or watched wherever I go. I played a part in this. Be that as it may, trying to get rid of it has backfired each time.

Technology was much simpler when I was younger, although it was extremely cumbersome. Back then, headphones had to rest over my hearing aids. Now, everything is so advanced I can use my hearing aids to listen to music or earbuds as hearing aids. They have the capability of doing both. Although, my earbuds have a better sound quality and farther range. It's also nice to wear them and appear as if I'm occupied. I find people don't bother interacting with me, if they see the little antenna hanging from my ear. After a while, they do become uncomfortable. My hearing aids are made for my ears, so I can tolerate them for a much longer period. Technology may have come far… but it also has the capability of being truly terrifying.

Placing my sparkly Caboodle onto the corner of the wooden desk, I run my hands along the surface appreciating the grooves and notches that the natural wood birthed. Whether it is the view of the mountains, the cold-crisp air, or the pleasant home; I am keen to create art. Especially atop something so instinctively beautiful.

I line up rows of rainbows, silk threads on the desk, then carefully arrange earring hoops and metal teardrops in a small dish next to me. Most of my larger handmade items were back at the apartment, but I want to add accessories, so my booth's table wasn't bare at next week's event. After some trial and error, I taught myself how to make silk thread and tassel earrings. Items like these not only draw people into your tent but increase the quantity of items sold per customer.

The bottom tray in my glimmering box has a sea of beads to rummage through. I am searching for pearl-colored accents on the first piece. My fingertips glide over the filled container, pushing around colored plastic, when I feel something that doesn't belong. My hand stills above the uniquely shaped item. No… there's no way! I left it at home! This weekend was meant for me to get away… away from everything.

I close my eyes, willing myself to slow my breathing, my heart picking up pace. Opening my eyes as I let out the air evenly, pulling the item from its obscure location.

The white tech sits in the palm of my hand, with exactly as I feared would be on it. A crude purple star on the long side.

Before I can think better of it, I quickly stand from the desk, startling poor Kingston in the process. He tilts his head, probably wondering why such a peaceful moment warrants such urgency.

I open the outer door to the windowed room and throw the stowaway headphone into the yard.

There! Instant regret racks through me. Wait… was this just a means to an end? I already realized those things have trackers in them. Oh fuck! I scurry outside and begin searching frantically for the stupid earbud.

"Where is it?! Where is it?!" I mutter, as I crawl around on hands and knees, pushing past fallen leaves, parting dormant blades of grass. It might as well be a needle in a haystack! I wasn't sure if I was shaking from anger at myself or fear; that someone could know precisely where I was because of that blasted device. I need to find it! Consequences be damned, I have to destroy it!

My mind keeps circling back to the unknown. Did they already know where I was? Out here in the middle of nowhere, alone.

The trees dance slowly to a song I can't hear. When the sun begins to set, I make my way back inside. Shit. Shit. Shit. I couldn't find it. The shadows soon disappear along with the last trace of light. Perhaps if I busy myself with making earrings again, I won't think about it… but I am thinking about it.

I find myself paying more attention to the tree line than embellishing earrings with beads. I feel uneasy. Watched.

Kingston whines to be let out and fed. I take the opportunity to rummage around in the kitchen for something to eat. Canned soup seems to be the only thing my parents have.

I sit in the bay window enjoying the microwave bowl of soup, while Kingston's shadow sporadically moves about the grounds. He's likely sniffing out a mole or locked onto the scent of something that has passed through. Golden lights automatically come on, illuminating a narrow perimeter around the house, but not much of the expansive mountainside yard.

I polish off the contents of roasted lentils, place my phone in the waistband of my skirt and call for Kingston to come in. Hanging half out of the back door, that's when I notice something glowing on the ground. Kingston runs past me into the house for his own meal; however, my feet are moving in the opposite direction. Toward the source of the white light. It beckons me out to the edge of the yard, where I reach down to the illuminated object. Is it really…?

I pick it up, turning it over in my hand, and I find the purple taunting star. It lights up?! Someone is toying with me. Now that I've found it, I must get rid of the thing. I wasn't going to play this game any longer. I march over to the end of the property that overlooks the tree capped valley. Making sure to keep back far enough from the edge. It was dark and I wasn't about to fall off the side of a mountain. Just as I wind my arm back to throw the earbud into the abyss, my phone vibrates against my hip.

I freeze, unsure what to do next. I palm the illuminated tech and withdraw my phone. *Take a deep breath*, fills my screen. I hit accept.

"Hi, Mom." I scan the area while walking quickly back toward the house with my cell phone to my ear.

"Hi, sweetie! We arrived a little while ago. Sorry, we didn't call right away; we ran into some old friends from Boston. Do you remember the Colbys? Such a nice family. They have a son around your age."

I have no idea who she's talking about, but that doesn't stop her from rambling on. Standing with my back against the door, inside the locked house, I stare at the haunting earbud in the palm of my hand. I am barely listening to the person on the other line at this point. What am I going to do with this damned thing?!

"So, he's being a good boy?"

Her question pulls me away from my racing thoughts. "What?" I ask.

"Kingston!" She repeats. "Is he being a good boy for you?"

I look toward the black shaggy dog, who now squiggles along the carpet, in a sort of interpretive dance, joyful over a full belly. "Yeah! He's a great dog."

A deeper voice now asks, "What do you think of the view?" My dad is on the phone now.

I rechecked the lock on the door. "It's umm…" I walk over to a kitchen drawer and toss the confounded thing in before slamming it shut with my hip. Finally, my brain can think clearly. "We definitely don't have views like this back in Southie," I say. Sounding more deranged than carefree.

"Well… enjoy it and thanks for making the trip. Love you, Cinnabun."

"Love you too, Dad. Enjoy your trip. Talk to you later."

After checking every lock in the house, twice, I commence closing each and every curtain. If there was no drape, I block the window with throw pillows, so there was no possible way to see into the house. As I covered the last window, I swear I see something moving. Maybe I'm tired…

It was most likely just a deer or maybe a black bear? My dad said they are prevalent in these areas. If I'm being honest, it looked like it was on two legs. Like a person. I peek around the pillow one more time, and I swear I see the silhouette of a large figure, standing right where I previously found the earbud.

My breath feels like it's caught in my throat. As I've practiced so many times before, I close my eyes and count to ten. When I open them and scan the tree line again, the shadowy figure is gone.

I feel trapped. Caged in this house. Is my mind playing tricks on me or am I being stalked for real?!

Kingston is ready to turn in, curling up in his plush, flannel dog bed by the fireplace. The kitchen drawer is outlined in light from where I shoved the earbud. I could just leave it in there for the rest of my stay, or I could destroy it. Do old 1920's remodeled homes have garbage disposals? Would pulverizing this one break the link between me and my deranged stalker? I grab a wooden spoon out of the utensil container on the counter. Open the drawer, ready to shred this thing into a thousand pieces, when my phone vibrates again. I grab it off the table, expecting my parents to have forgotten to tell me something, but instead, it's a text from an unknown number.

> Unknown: Be a good girl and put the earbud in.

I slammed the drawer shut, as if a snake was within it. I make my way to a window; moving the curtain to the side, I scan the dark yard for any signs of movement. I do this from each window but find nothing.

The tired dog whines. Poor Kingston probably thinks we were waiting for someone to arrive.

Soon, I find myself yawning uncontrollably. Just as before, I powered down my phone. I already changed my number, and I did not want to receive any more messages. Once I was confident no one was outside, I too curled up in the living room to fall asleep. There was no way I was walking outside, in the dark, to get to the guest suite.

What if someone breaks in? The best thing I had was a set of wrought iron and fireplace tools.

I pull the stand over to the couch before wrapping myself in a throw blanket and using the underside of a scratchy embroidered pillow of a mallard, for my head. My eyes feel so heavy that regardless of my fears, I stand no chance of remaining awake. At least Kingston is here. Surely, he would wake me. With that slight piece of mind, I soon drift off.

THIRTEEN

FROM THE SHADOWS

I already knew she was coming out here, and I was fortunate to have enough time to myself to follow her. It's not often I'm on my own. I rented a small cabin as close as possible, having to pay triple the usual cost when I learned it was already rented for the weekend. Money talks, so naturally it was mine in the end.

Cindel sets herself up in the sunroom, allowing me a chance to watch her from afar. She plays with the ends of her hair, running the strands through her fingers, like an endless loop. I've seen her do this before. She does this whenever she's thinking, or sometimes nervous. I'm captivated by everything she does… everything she is.

I smile from the shadows as she throws my gift into the yard, mere feet from my hiding spot. Tortured as I watch her bent over form, crawl around the lawn, trying to find it again. Sometimes she doesn't make sense, but that's what I love so much about her. Unable to predict what she's going to do next, and that fascinates me. I am mildly concerned my dick might fall off with how hard it's been over the course of the last hour. Fuuuuck. Her body is all I can see when I close my eyes and now, she's freely giving me more material. On her hands and knees. I was ready to take it out right here, but I know if I move too much with the sun still above the horizon, there is a chance she could see me.

Cindel is vigilant. Scanning the property, trying to find me, but I'm nothing if not disciplined. With the earbud connected to my phone, I open up the app and select the 'light up' function. I want her to find it. She needs to know I'm here. Watching. She may be freaked out by my tactics, but it's necessary. I just wish she would do as she's told and keep the damn earbud with her. It's quite taxing to get a new pair each time, calibrate it just for her, and deliver it discreetly. Hacking into her hearing aids felt too personal, so I settled on the earbud idea. It allows the illusion of free will, but she's a curious girl, and I knew she would take it home the night she found it. I picked the right ear because I'm rather fond of the little freckle she has on the right side of her neck. She only puts her hair behind her ears when she has an earbud in. Otherwise, her hair is down, covering her usual hearing aids.

I can't for the life of me figure out why she'd hide any part of herself. She's fucking perfect just the way she is.

I'm not particularly good with words… but I like music. As if creating a mosaic, each song I select is the perfect piece…. bringing her closer to seeing the big picture.

If she destroys another earbud, it's a setback. Time is running out so to speak. I fold, take out my phone and tell her to be a good girl, and put the little device in.

It's kind of adorable… her little temper tantrums. The way she stomps around after an interaction with me or how she attempts to keep me out by rearranging her room. Now, she's using pillows to keep me out. I'm curious if she will stop pushing me away once I finally introduce myself.

No. Fucking stupid idea. I need to stay hidden, at least my identity, for as long as possible. Only one person knows how I actually fit into this equation, and they have no idea what I've been up to. Yes, I was tasked with watching her, but my intentions are quite different than the one who gives the orders.

I was raised to be a tool. A pawn in a game I never agreed to play, but what young child has a say in how they are brought up. I went along with it for a while, too. Never complained a single fucking time, either.

Three years ago, everything changed. When Cindel was thrust into this, I threw the damn rule book out the window. She was never supposed to be brought into this.

I'm drawn to her. From the first time I saw her, I felt the pull.

Right now, it isn't any different. Once I am confident, she is asleep, I stalk toward the darkened house. A copy of the key in hand. I actually have a set of keys to multiple houses in the vicinity.

"I want access to these homes, just in case," he told me.

It was my first assignment, after I was well enough to be out and about.

Turning the key in the lock, I enter the cottage quietly and slip off my boots by the door. Not wanting to chance leaving my car nearby, I hiked up here and my shoes are filthy.

Cindel's soft nasally breathing remains steady as I inch closer.

Kingston, as if on cue, lifts his head and begins to show teeth. I came prepared. Placing a beefy marrow bone in front of him, his attention is quickly diverted to the offered morsel. Good boy. I pat the top of his head.

Her body is strewn across the emerald, green couch. If she opens her eyes right now, she will see my face. I only have a black hoodie on. Next time, I plan to be a little more creative. Only a blanket covers the top half of her body; tights and schoolgirl skirt are still on from earlier. I grin to myself, knowing she must be out if she was too tired to bother undressing. Just as well, I would have little restraint if Cindel was lying here in nothing but her undergarments.

Next, I notice the tools for the fireplace are pulled close to her. Cute. It's hard to ward off intruders when you pass out, and your pooch is food motivated.

I'm impressed more than anything. The way she thinks ahead. Always on guard. For someone who's faced so much… she survived. She's fragile… but fragile like a bomb.

My fingers twitch and I reach for her. With the back of my knuckles, I touch her. Starting at the petite bone of her ankle. My hand glides up her calf slowly. I want to feel her skin. The separation between us is both torture and a blessing.

My stomach does that dipping thing. Like when you're driving and you go down a hill, only for the road to rise again instantly.

The back of my hand continues to explore past her knee. Her body moves slightly and I freeze. She groans but doesn't wake. Gently I progress up to her thigh, wishing desperately to delve beneath that tempting skirt, where I truly ache to be. My cock is rock hard now, without even touching her flesh. The curve of her hip is the widest part of her small frame. Cinched waist and small chest. I want nothing more than to sink my teeth into her.

I have a feeling that she has dark desires. Like I'm the only one who can satiate them. They're there; she just needs a bit of an awakening. I've witnessed the last guy she was with. A minute man who fucked his way through Cha-Cha's in the back alley of clubs. Pathetic. When she's mine, she will never have to beg for my affection. Her needs come first.

Cindel is stunning… lips slightly parted as she sleeps. I should leave. If she wakes up and finds me, everything will be ruined. Despite my better judgment, I brush my thumb along her bottom lip, making it bounce. Her tongue juts out to lick her lips, and I can't help but mirror the action. Fuck! That mouth. I wonder how it would look around my dick. A sleep filled groan escapes her as she tries to power through my toying.

Okay… I've had my fun for the night. I adjust my cock before going over to the kitchen drawer to retrieve the piece of tech she's just going to have to learn to accept. I carefully remove and place her hearing aid on the table beside us, then nestle the little bud into her right ear. I admire her freckle.

Her eyes flutter, from my touch, but she doesn't wake. My insides burn for this woman.

Gently, I place my lips against her forehead. As if saying the words against her will make them more powerful. My mouth moves lightly on her skin as I soundlessly deliver my message. Listen better, Princess.

Just as stealthily as before, I pull my boots back on and exit the house.

After locking up, I head over to the guest suite. There are a few surprises I have in store for her.

FOURTEEN

CINDEL

Whoever this home designer was, definitely didn't have people sleeping in the living room in mind. How am I supposed to sleep past seven in the morning, when a gigantic skylight engulfs the room in a cheerful morning glow?

I pull my sore body off the stiff couch and shuffle to the kitchen to find some kind of jet fuel, seeing as the sun has tortured me awake. Sifting through the cabinets, I manage to find some expired instant coffee. I put a teapot on the burner and began to pull up my hair, as I search for sweetener. Just as I guide the strands into a high pony, my fingers brush against my ear. Wait. I try to recall last night. Didn't I? I yank open the kitchen drawer where I last left it.

"No, no, no…" It's not there! My shaky fingers dance over my right ear, removing the item. I hold the haunting piece of plastic out in front of me; the periwinkle doodle mocks me. How? Did I—I glanced back to the emerald, green couch I spent last night on, eyes catching on the hearing aid upon a side table. I can't breathe.

Kingston trots up to me, tail wagging, probably oblivious to my impending heart attack. He just wants to be let out. Taking a staggered breath before attempting to move my feet, Kingston nearly drops something big on my foot.

"Ah! Careful, boy. What's this?" I picked up the slimy, smelly item. "Where'd you get this?" It's a pre-chewed marrow bone and Kingston is just delighted to show me. He begins scratching the door. "Okay. Okay." I let the dog outside, put the mystery bone back down on the ground, and washed my hands.

I all but throw the earbud onto the large dining table. Fetching my hearing aid, I sit in the too bright room as my brain struggles to keep up. I didn't put it on last night. It was supposed to be in the drawer!

"Someone was here," I speak into the empty room. I distinctly remember leaving my hearing aids on before bed, so I was able to hear anything out of the ordinary. My eyes bounce around the room, landing on the massive bone in the kitchen. I never saw that yesterday. I toured the house. Kingston didn't have a bone. Where could he have found this? Nothing made sense. When I finally stand, I grab a wrought-iron poker stick before surveying the house. What if someone is still here?

Cautiously, I peek around each corner, making sure I don't see anything before progressing. The main bedroom and bathroom… clear. The kitchen and living room… clear. The last room is the study. The door is closed. Okay. If someone is in there… swing!

I throw the door open with a shove and hold out the metal stick in a defensive move. I tried fencing once in high school, but this is much heavier. Stillness. Entering slowly, I scan each corner of the room. I glimpse under the large desk then make my way to the closet. Someone had to have been here, but would they be stupid enough to stick around? I place my hand on the knob of the wooden accordion closet. Ready to pull back and protect myself at the same time… without warning, a high-pitched whistling makes me jump!

Instinctively, I drop the wrought iron tool, and it tumbles to the floor, landing roughly on my foot. "Ahhhh, Fuck!" I'm so on edge; the damn tea kettle gives me a jump scare. My foot instantly pulses with pain and already I can see the top part, beginning to swell.

I hobble to the kitchen and throw open the freezer door. Grabbing a bag of frozen peas, I drop it onto the top of my foot. Then proceed to drag myself to the screeching pot and remove it from the stove. A compilation of scratching sounds at the door causes me to gasp. It's just Kingston. He's pawing at the door, indicating he was done with his business and ready to come inside. Jesus.

I pivot and hop on one foot to let him in. This time, I choose to stay on the floor. A happy pooch with his bone and a skittish girl with her bag of frozen veg.

A few hours of elevating my foot and rotations between frozen peas, corn, and butternut squash; the swelling has gone down, but I'm left with a giant bruise and a limp. I don't know if I'm madder at myself or the situation at hand, but I know I can't leave. Any sane person may try to call the police, but my past experiences with law enforcement were less than ideal. Basically, they're fucking useless.

They barely investigated my brother's death. Simply closing the case as a classic overdose. I later found out the coroner's report read: *Suicide*. I didn't want to believe it. Even after three years, I still have my doubts, but I learned one thing… unless concrete evidence was served up on a silver platter, the police don't care. I can see it now… officer, I feel like I'm being watched, and I keep losing track of my earbud. Yeah, I sound absolutely bananas.

I thrust myself into my work instead. Finishing up a substantial collection of earrings, a little after lunch. I am pleased with how they turned out for my first go. They're going to make a nice addition at the craft fair. After I have another can of soup, with some saltines I found in the cupboard, I go out to the garden. I spend a long while just sitting on a stone bench, staring at the guest house. Trying to convince myself to take a shower.

All my stuff is in there and I haven't been back since I locked myself up in the main house last night. With a push and a groan, I hobble to the door of the guest house. To my surprise, it was unlocked. I must have forgotten to lock it. Entering the small suite, I am taken aback. Every kind of sour candy and chocolate mini bar I could think of, decorated the bed. I feel lightheaded. I'm not going crazy. It wasn't like this before!

Scanning the yard between me and the main house, I see no signs of movement aside from birds landing in their feeder. Promptly, I close myself in the suite and lock the door behind me. As quickly as I can muster, I limp around the room closing the curtains. I check under the bed and confirm, I'm alone.

My foot screams at me to get off my feet. I am tired and in pain. This whole situation is ludicrous, to be quite frank. Fuck it. I draw a bath, while I wait for the water to fill the claw footed tub I attempt to slow my mind.

See if I can make sense of anything from last night. This person… this stalker knows an uncomfortable amount of information. No one has paid this close attention to me for a long time. Whatever their intentions, they don't seem to want to hurt me. I mean, I was sleeping and they didn't do anything but put the earbud in my ear. They even locked the house door. All I know is they aren't here now. So, I undress. Removing everything, including my hearing aids. Carefully, I slid my aching form into the warm water.

The tub back at the apartment isn't quite as large. I can completely submerge my whole body into this one. Filling my lungs, I descend into the water, head and all… hoping for clarity. Weightless. Only the endless roaring to keep me company. Plunged into abandonment, I'm still overwhelmed. My mouth opens, releasing a forced, hollow scream. It's silent. Meant for no one. I can only feel it tear through me. I wished to be more comfortable with myself. It's always been Theo and me. Then Andrea and me, and now it's just… now it's just me.

I've never desired attention, but there is something about having at least one person who gets you. Someone who recognizes what makes your soul sing, grasps your sense of humor, and is okay to sit idly by your side, when and if you need it. I feel like I've lost that, the older I become. Could I learn to be content on my own? Why did the idea of a stranger desiring me make me feel something? Confused, curious, and yearning? Breaking the surface, I come back to reality.

Instantly, I'm hit by a wave of overpowering emotions. The loss of my brother, my parents leaving Boston, countless dead-end jobs, Brodi disappearing on me, nearly being assaulted by my manager, Cassie dying, Andrea and I not being as close, and now... whatever the hell is going on here. I can't handle any more; I need to escape these intrusive thoughts. My psyche is spiraling down the drain and my god damned foot hurts. I just want to stop thinking... feel better.

My hand begins to travel down my curves to the space between my legs. Desperate for a distraction. I need to be released from this mindset. My slender fingers dip inside, curling at just the right angle. My body is begging to move toward the good instead of the bad. Gradually, I switch between moving my fingers in and out, to making small circles on my clit. I totter my piercing back and forth, concentrating on pushing myself to the edge. My phone was still in the house, so I have to use my imagination instead of porn to get me there. I lack control over where my mind goes when I'm feeling troubled. I want desire, I need passion. Someone who only has eyes for me.

My brain creates a movie. I picture Eamon pinning me against the wall. His eyes crazed as he took what he wanted from me. My fingers move in faster circles, causing my hips to rise. Guiding myself toward a release. Using my other hand, I press my palm right above my pubic bone, feeling that delicious pressure. The tension drives me further toward the edge. My imagination morphs my pursuer, as he paws at my tits while lifting me to position himself at just the right angle. I picture a tall, shadowed figure, pulling my panties to the side and sliding himself in with nothing but a fist full of spit. His sinful groan resonates through me, conquering any sound of ringing in my mind. I unravel. Falling headfirst into pleasure. A muted scream tears through me, and I can sense the stress leaving my body. Straight away I'm relaxed. I don't think I've done that in months.

IN THE SHADOWS

I scared her to the point that she injured herself. Although not directly my fault, I still plan to bring her something later tonight, to aid her.

I watch from the edge of the tree lined property as she shuffles to the guest house to find my sweet treats. I also left behind two hidden cameras as a present to myself. If I can't touch her more, I can at least watch. The cameras are as small as a fingernail. She won't find them. Even with the curtains closed, I can still see what she is up to on my phone, in real time.

And wouldn't luck just have it, my girl wants a bath soon after my discreet installation. I opt to hit 'record' when I see her start to undress. I might want to rewatch it in the future.

I throw the curly haired dog one more bone, before coming to stand just on the other side of the wall. Fuck, she's a vision, I watch her climb in then proceed to submerge herself completely underwater. She is under the water for a concerning amount of time. It takes everything in me not to bust down the door, when she lets out a muffled scream from beneath the water. She's a rollercoaster of emotions and I'm willingly along for the ride. Finally, she withdraws, taking in a big gulp of air before lounging within the vat of water.

I lean against the side of the guest house, holding my portal to her, while enjoying the show unfolding before my eyes. Cindel begins touching herself. And my dick revolts against the restricted environment it is in. Screw it. I oblige, releasing my stiff member before spitting in my hand to play along with this siren's song. I start off slow as I witness her dip her fingers into herself before moving to her bundle of nerves. My fist pumps faster, all the while her legs begin to twitch as she chases her release. Her hips lift and legs open slightly as she raises herself above the surface of the water. Holy shit. Her pussy on full display, fingers moving against something unexpected, back and forth. She's pierced! That was *very* unexpected.

A million ideas flash across my mind. What I could do with that shiny treat. I can't hold out any longer. Her free hand presses on her lower belly and she cracks. I tumble right behind her, letting out a painful, soundless groan.

Ribbons of my seed shoot onto a Dogwood sapling before me. Fuck. I'm no arborist, but I hope my *reject spunk* doesn't kill the young tree.

I tuck myself away as I watch her chest slow on my feed to a normal rhythm. No one else will have her again but me. Cindel doesn't know it yet… but she's mine. Before making the trek back to my cabin, I slip into the modest building. I place the earbud in the middle of the candy-covered bed, along with a walking stick just outside the guest suite's door.

By the time I reach my cabin, she is toweled and, in the bedroom, staring down the elephant in the room. Be a good girl. Put it on. As if I willed her with my mind, she puts the earbud in her right ear, and I can't help but smile. I open up the app and play the most appropriate song for this scenario; **Marcy Playground – "Sex & candy."**

These plans I'm making… this game I'm playing, is nothing compared to the lengths I would go to for her. I do hope she likes her big gift. Perhaps, she'll have less to concern herself with when she learns what I've done for her.

CINDEL

My last full day in this place is filled with cable TV reruns and binging on possibly compromised candy. I'm sorry, but after eating canned soup for two days, I wasn't about to pass up on the offering.

Kingston was also living the *high life*. Spoiled with yet another tasty marrow bone. He carries them wherever he goes, likely concerned they'll disappear just as quickly as they appeared. We share a look. Something between guilt or perhaps gluttony.

I texted Andrea once or twice during my stay, but she wasn't very chatty, which I expected. My foot no longer has a heartbeat, which makes me feel way better about driving home tomorrow. Creepy stalker even gifted me a carved walking stick. It was resting against the stoop of the guest suite. With a crick in my neck from spending the night on a stiff sofa and there being little success in keeping anyone out, I decided to sleep in the guesthouse. Of course, I let Kingston join me. He was elated that I let him up in bed with me, although he's not much of a guard dog. His love has easily been bought with food, twice now.

Wait… If I'm eating the candy, does that mean I'm no better than a food-motivated pet?

My parents will be here in the morning to relieve me from dog duty, so tonight I packed and returned everything to the way I found it. I also sent Eamon a message.

> Cindel: Hey… I'd like to talk when I get back in town tomorrow. Are you at work?

No response all day. He hasn't even texted back about Cassie. Against my better judgment, I have kept the earbud. Ever since it appeared on the bed after my bath, I've been wondering how to handle it. I was vulnerable but whoever placed it there still left me alone. No different than a grandma who insists on serving you another slice of pie once you're full. If you try to say no, she's just going to insist you're too skinny. So, you might as well admit defeat, shut up, and eat the pie. When I comply, whomever it is, seems to stay away. Aside from the occasional song, that seems to poke fun at whatever situation I find myself in. Like, literally being caught in 'Vaseline' or 'Closing Time' during the end of my shift at the bar. Clearly, he thinks he's funny. Could it be a he? Would it make a difference if it isn't?

Regardless, I am ready to go home! Through being alone in the mountainous woods, eating soup, and accepting candy from strangers. Just after sunset, I sleepily make my way to the guest house with Kingston at my heels and lock us in for the night. I strip down to a T-shirt and began brushing my teeth, when the earbud comes to life.

The Human League – "Don't you want me" begins playing and the words paralyze me. The lyrics, *Don't you want me baby*, repeat over and over in a song talking about a girl who works at a bar, and her refusal of said relationship. This creep doesn't just want to play games from a distance; it feels like they really want to pursue me.

"No!!! No, I don't want you!" Toothpaste splatters across the mirror as I shout at no one but my own reflection. As the song plays through, I abandon brushing and go to my bag... collect the remainder of the candy from the song stalker and throw it into the trash can. I won't be conditioned into obedience.

I finish brushing, wash my face, recheck the lock, and climb into the bed. Kingston curls up at my feet with his bones.

"Traitor," I proclaim. This stalker knows me. Could it be someone close to me? Would Eamon be capable of all of this? I work tomorrow night. If he's there... he has some explaining to do.

SEVENTEEN

CINDEL

My parents come back bearing gifts. They picked out a basket chock full of locally made soaps, Martha's Vineyard signature salad dressing, and chocolates from the island's premier chocolatier. I know my dad was the one who picked the sweets, because it was something I actually liked. Andrea might actually enjoy the rest; maybe it can be a sort of olive branch in lieu of our last interaction.

Kingston performs zoomies all over the house when they first arrive. Mom is anxious the couch will be ripped from the dog's repetitive jumping. Dad actually interacted with me.

"Don't be a stranger," he says.

While Mom insists, I look for jobs in the area. "Not only will you be closer, but you could meet a nice boy and settle down."

Gee, Mom, why don't you just offer me up to someone's rich son in the area, so I don't wind up as a spinster?

"Are you still working at the market, Cinnabun?" My dad stands with me just outside the house, after helping me carry my belongings to the rental car.

"I'm just at the bar now, actually."

He nods understandingly. "You're too good for those places, kiddo."

Sometimes I wish they were just proud of me for where I am… not where I 'could' be. "I got a promotion."

My dad lights up. "Wow, that's awesome! Does it make you happy?"

I think for a moment. There's something about the bar that I do love. I nod earnestly. "Yes. Yes, I do think it makes me happy. It's just a bit of an adjustment period. Some of my coworkers are a little salty toward me right now."

My dad widens his stance and pretends to shoot guns, using finger hands. "Do I need to have someone taken care of? Pew Pew!"

I laugh. "You're such a dork. I love you, Dad."

I fall into his outstretched arms feeling safe and whole. A twinge of guilt settles in, knowing that before this weekend, I didn't even want to come here, let alone wake up. As sad as I may feel at times, I couldn't imagine leaving my parents with the pain of losing both their children. Especially my dad, who has done nothing but shower me with encouragement and love. As distant as they are, they're still my parents and I know they've always tried to do right by me and my brother. One last hug before the road and I am on my way.

Sometimes I make happy little mistakes, like leaving the windows cracked during my stay. It actually made the scent in the car a lot more tolerable, but I'm counting my lucky stars it didn't rain. I would not be able to swing damage charges on top of the rental cost. Before I left, dad tried to sneak me some cash. I absolutely refused the offer, knowing they themselves make peanuts as house sitters for the rich and wasteful.

The drive is much easier on the way home, I think I was ready to get back to the city and away from that haunted house of surprises. For once, I am not in the mood to listen to music. Instead, I reflect. Alone with my thoughts for hours. Approaching Boston, I feel like I have clarity. I think I worked out what to say to Andrea and I also decide to keep my dinner plans with Eamon. This stalker business could go one of two ways. One, I figure out it's Eamon and confront him about his ridiculous games or two, it's not, and I learn I am in fact in danger of being lowered down into a hole and offered lotion or the hose. There is a small possibility the stalker sees Eamon around me, causing them to lose interest. It's not exactly a solid strategy, but it might work. The earbud sits at the bottom of my purse, in the passenger seat, where it's been since it played the last disturbing song.

By the time I drop off the rental and make my way back to the apartment, I am ready for a nap. Poor quality sleep, a foot injury, and fucked up mind games were not on my bingo card for a weekend off from work.

I trudge up the three flights of stairs, which is fortunately easier with the walking stick in hand. I appreciate the intricate whittled designs on the top. That's why I brought it back to Southie with me. Not because it was forced upon me by a pushy stalker, but I understand the time and commitment that goes into making something this special.

Reaching my floor, I pause temporarily to shuffle through my bag for keys. When I look up, I find someone sitting against the adjacent wall, from my apartment door. I stride closer to the mop of red hair.

"Mairead?"

The sprightly girl pops up, brushing her bouncy curls back from her face. "Cindel, hiiiiii!" She wraps her arms around me tightly, paying no mind to my hands being full.

"What are you doing here?" I attempt to shift my weight onto the walking stick, unsure if this was a quick chat or if I was inviting her in. Was I up for a visit? No. It's been a long day already. I was hoping to relax and put my foot up.

She wears a yellow A-line dress, thigh-high with pink polka dots. It fits her frame well, with lovely, puffed sleeves. A little too summery for a chilly fall day, but she rocks it, nonetheless.

She fiddles with her hands behind her back, as she gently twirls the dress while speaking. "Well. I was in the area, and I got this great idea! We could take the train to Salem! I've always wanted to go. I read that they have reenactments of the Salem Witch Trials! I'm confident they would have burned me at the stake, if I lived during that time. Oooo, let's wear costumes. Can we check your closet?" She steps forward, touching the walking stick with her fingers. "Cool staff! You should bring that with us."

My foot is starting to ache at this point. "I kind of just got home. I was away watching my parents' dog and—"

She suddenly notices me juggling an overnight bag and then some. "Oh. Let me help you!" She starts taking things from me, freeing up my hands to unlock the apartment door.

She invites herself in. I lean the wooden walking stick in the corner behind the door and set everything else onto the entryway table.

Andrea is in the kitchen, sitting cross-legged on the counter, actively shoveling a hardboiled egg into her mouth. Did Mairead try to knock, or did my roommate have no idea someone was just looming outside our apartment's door? She looks bothered that someone new is standing in our kitchen. Okay. Based on her expression, I don't think Andrea knew anyone was out there. Mairead gives an exaggerated wave, and Andrea lifts an eyebrow while attempting a "hello," with a mouth full of dry egg.

"I like your place!" She kicks off her ballet flats and starts meandering around the apartment like it's a department store. She reads the spine of a few books on the bookshelf, opens a drawer or two, and gives a gentle tap on Thelma's enclosure.

Andrea mouths to me, "Do you know her?"

I respond with a nod and an unsure smile.

She plops down on the couch and hugs a throw pillow to her chest. "So how long until you're ready to go? If we're quick, we can make it to Salem before it gets dark."

"Salem?!" Andrea blurts around another bite of egg.

"Actually… Mairead, your trip idea sounds nice, but I'm really tired after a day of traveling, and I have work tonight. Can I take a raincheck?"

Mairead makes a humph sound, followed by throwing her head back and staring up to the ceiling at nothing in particular.

Andrea gives me another 'what the fuck' look and I shrug.

As if she is zapped with electricity, Mairead springs from the sofa and asks to use the bathroom.

"Sure… First door on the right," I Instruct.

Andrea immediately starts signing to me. Asking things like, "Who the fuck is this?" and "Why are you going on a trip with someone I've never met?"

I quickly reassure her that she's a co-worker from my last job and I didn't plan to travel with anyone. At least not today.

"Oh my god!" Mairead hollers from the other room.

Andrea and I quickly move toward the call to see what the unexpected house guest is yelling about.

We find her in my room of all places, with her bottom in the air, pulling bins out from under my bed. "These are so funny!" She holds up different sized embroidery hoops, which I have been working on for the Craft Bazaar. "Welcome to the Shit Show! I Cross Stitch so I don't Kill People! O-M-G, Can I have this one?!"

Andrea and I share a look as I reply, "Umm yeah. Sure."

She gives a high-pitched squeal before standing to prance in place.

Andrea actually fights back a laugh, most likely at my expense.

"Mairead, I'd really like to settle in, since I just got back. Do you mind… if we hang out another day?"

I am too exhausted to question why the energetic girl is in my room, let alone being confrontational, it was just not in my wheelhouse.

"Okie dokie," she replies, clutching her embroidered art and happily making her way toward the front door.

Andrea follows behind, quietly taking in everything as it unfolds.

As I go to close the door, wishing Mairead a final farewell, she pops her head back through. "Oh shit. I forgot to tell you. Remember Craig?"

Well, yeah how could I forget the awful manager that tried to manipulate and assault me, before I quit. "Yeah. What about him?" Now, I need a nap.

"He's dead."

Okay, now I am awake.

"I heard he died during a closing shift. One of the cashiers found him in the morning all blue and unresponsive. The cops thought he choked while eating, but the coroner found something that points to a homicide!"

Craig was an absolutely repulsive human, but I don't think he deserved to be murdered. Well… maybe. No. God, my moral compass is fucked up. "Did they figure out who did it?"

She examines her perfectly pink, manicured nails like this kind of discussion bores her, instead of being the heinous topic it is. "Not sure… BUUUT, do you want to hear what they found in his throat?!"

I'll bet my collection of embroidery hoops, it was tuna.

The words tumble from her, like she just can't hold onto it any longer. "An earbud! Isn't that wild?!"

My head begins to tingle. It feels cold, as if all the blood rushed from my face.

"K, bye!" Mairead turns and frolics down the hall, and her red waves bounce out of sight.

"Your friend is… weird," Andrea says, as I close our apartment door.

I don't feel much like going to work this evening. I try to relax, but instead I just feel ill. I've felt this way sense Mairead's visit. Not sure if it was the diet of soup and candy over the weekend, or the news she casually dropped on her way out, but there is no point in trying to nap. Painkillers didn't even help diminishing this splitting headache and I rarely take anything, even ibuprofen.

I replay Mairead's visit, trying to sort out if I too, was in immediate danger. It was obviously my music stalker who murdered Creepy Craig. Oh crap, what if I had the matching earbud in my possession? Was I considered an accessory to murder? Could I be charged or even arrested!? I wasn't even in town! I was hours away in the Catskills. He must have killed my ex-manager then came out to the woods to mess with me. Is that why Eamon wouldn't respond to me? Could he be behind all of this? Is my boss a murderer?

Geeze, this sounded closer to the premise of a B-grade slasher movie that would play at the discount theatre. Focus! I tell myself.

Ugh. I am so drained. The last thing I need is for Jada or Brittany to be just as spicy as they were the last time I worked. How am I going to get through this shift? Oh right… I'm a manager. My mind jumps to Cassie. The sassy, yet wise woman, who was wonderfully predictable to work beside. I never had a proper moment to grieve the fact that I will never hear her clipped, sarcastic voice again. Why do my managers keep dying?

I reapply my under-eye coverage twice, because my dark, puffy eyes keep exposing how truly exhausted I am. Andrea left at some point when I was in the bathroom, so I guess I'll have to wait to give her the soap and dressing from my parents.

While walking to The Black Sheep, I go over the questions I would like Eamon to answer when I see him next. I also opt for leaving the earbud at the bottom of my purse, instead of actually putting it in my ear. It's been a whole day since I last heard from my stalker or should I say Eamon. Speak of the devil!

I enter the bar to find Eamon comfortably nestled at a back table with the same two men that always seem to be by his side. Garron and Dax, I believe? They're always around. Were they like bodyguards or something? Why would the owner of a bar and club need protection?

Before I can talk myself out of it, I march right up to the group of men and address Eamon. "Can I talk to you… alone?!"

The men both look to Eamon. The one with the toothpick smirks like he's delighted to see his buddy in trouble, while the quiet one just scowl, as per usual. Eamon lifts his hand to indicate for the other men to leave the table.

My first question rolls off my tongue, even before we're out of earshot. "Why didn't you answer my texts?!"

He reaches forward and crushes the cigarette he was currently smoking, into the ashtray in the middle of the table. Blowing out slowly, his eyes skate over my face. "I didn't want to upset you."

I cross my arms over my chest and shift my weight to one side. "That's not a good enough answer. Do you want me to go to dinner with you or not?" Holy smokes, I can't believe I said that out loud. To my boss no less. Overwhelmed and slightly grumpy Cindel, clearly isn't sticking to what she planned to say during the multi hour drive back to Boston.

The corner of his mouth curves up slightly. Is he... pleased with me? "Yes." His voice is gravelly and deep. "I do want to take you to dinner." He begins collecting the cards on the table that appear to have been dealt for a game that I interrupted. "You're right. It's not good enough. I was worried you wouldn't take the job if you knew."

I unfold my arms and step closer to the table. "Know what?" I urge.

"That Cassie was sick. She had cancer. It was her wish to keep it secret. She wanted to save face with the people around her. Didn't want their pity, she said."

Oh god! She was sick! I had no idea. "It still doesn't explain why you kept her passing from me," I declare.

His jaw ticks and he nods. "You're right. I'm sorry. I should have been up front."

"I'm not fragile, you know! I've faced enough loss in this life. I have a right to know."

He looks down to the table speaking so softly, "I know, kid."

Without warning, a crashing noise comes from the backroom. Followed by a scream. Eamon jumps from his seat, and we both sprint to the back. The first thing we see is Jada. She's on the floor by the ice machine, whaling and holding her ankle. "Ahhhh! Fuuuuck...!" Tears stream down her face as she grits her teeth. Everyone gathers in the backroom, standing around an injured Jada.

"What happened?" Eamon barks. Connor answers while drying his hands on a towel, "Ice machine appears to be leaking. She came to the back to grab more glasses but probably didn't see the puddle. She slipped. I'll get this mopped up and fixed right away."

Eamon nods before kneeling to scoop Jada in his arms. He proceeds to carry her out to the bar. She looks like she is in a lot of pain, but also has this smug look about her, while being carried by our extremely handsome boss.

Jada is taken to the nearby walk-in clinic by Eamon and seen immediately. She apparently has a small ankle fracture. They said she'll need at least six weeks to heal. That's not good. The new hires weren't experienced enough for busy nights, and I was a little concerned about being down a seasoned staff member. I could manage on weekdays, but weekends were a whole different story.

Garron and Dax take up residence at their usual spot along the bar top, while Brittany does the job of two people on the floor. She doesn't seem to be salty at all this evening and I'm thinking that's thanks to Jada being gone. A couple hours later, Eamon returns from dropping Jada off at her house. She has two roommates to help her get around over the next couple of weeks. Eamon joins his friends at the bar and motions for me to come over to him.

"What will it be, sir?" I ask with a touch of playful sarcasm.

A smile plays on his lips, while his buddies watch our interaction from behind their drinks. "I'd like your favorite drink," he proclaims.

"I don't have a favorite," I state dryly.

"When you're not on the clock, then. What would you make yourself?" He presses.

"Soda or water usually. I don't drink."

Garron all but shoots beer through his nose. The other men pull back slightly. Garron grabs a fist full of bar napkins in an attempt to pat his face dry.

"You don't drink?" Eamon inquires.

Dax raises an eyebrow, curiously but still seems unfazed by this revelation.

"I... I lost my brother some years back to an overdose. I haven't touched alcohol since. Drugs either."

Garron's the first to pipe up, "Well, you didn't die! So, I don't see the point in—" Garron is cut off as his face thrusts forward slightly from Eamon, giving him a good whack to the back of his head. In an authoritative tone I haven't heard before, Eamon commands Garron to go for a long walk. Garron stands with his damp shirt and walks out the door without question.

Eamon reaches out, resting his hand on the bar top, silently inviting me to place mine in his. I do, and he lifts it to his lips, pressing a gentle kiss to my knuckles. "I apologize for my ox-headed friend. Losing someone you love can be a lifelong battle." He continues holding my hand lightly, rubbing a thumb over my knuckles. "Now, about that dinner."

I get lost in his jaded eyes and sharp, masculine features.

"I already got a table at the Oceanfront Steakhouse, this Wednesday for dinner. Does that work for you?"

Very presumptuous of him to make a reservation before we get through this whole, *keeping things from me*, issue. Although, it would be ideal to spend time with him somewhere other than the bar. For the first time in a while I have butterflies fluttering in my stomach. I nodded, probably smiling too wide. I have more to ask him. Eamon looks pleased.

Dax sets down the glass he was sipping from, hard. I thought for sure it was going to shatter. He pushes back from the bar and walks out the big red door, following the same path Garron went.

"What's up with your friend?" I inquire.

"He can come off as difficult at times. He doesn't speak. There was an incident a while back, his vocal cords were damaged."

I think back to the first couple times we've interacted. I guess… yeah, I've never heard him utter a word.

Eamon continues, "He's a furiously loyal friend."

I chew on my bottom lip. "Does he know sign language? I had a tutor who practiced with me when I was younger. I became fluent. Even though hearing aids allow me to hear, I still wanted to have another way of communicating."

He takes out his phone, bringing the productive conversation to a halt. I miss the warmth of his touch, instantly.

"Not sure actually…" he finally replies. "Sorry, little fish, I have something urgent to attend to on the other side of town." He stands from his seat. "I'll pick you up at your place. Eight o'clock."

I smile again.

"Great. It's a date." He turns to stride away, then stops suddenly, returning back like he forgot something. He puts out his hand for me to place mine in his again, kissing each knuckle individually, as he watches my reaction. "See you soon, beautiful."

My cheeks heat and I can't help but admire the way those slacks hug his delicious ass as he walks out of the bar.

EIGHTEEN

EAMON

My father has my men eating from the palm of his hand by the time I arrive back in town.

I had to get away long enough that I could figure out what I was doing next, without my father breathing down my neck. I'd say my time was rather productive; I have a direction now.

Patrick told stories about his heyday as *Paddy Muscles* and how any man that dared square off with him, never saw another sunrise. His face beams as he reveals how the harbor's fishermen love our families' secret recipe. The chumbuckets we provide lead to bigger fish being caught.

He kept the story about the Murrays and Lombardis until I came back. I guess he thinks I need a refresher, as if I had forgotten; I haven't. I know how the families used to get along. Even work together. Hell, I'm pretty sure our mothers had already planned marriages to one another's children. Now, Patrick spits on their family name with distaste, saying they never deserved to be in this city in the first place. I hate hearing their names thrown around so carelessly, especially from his mouth.

When he isn't reminiscing about his iron fist reputation, he is emptying bottles of my top shelf whiskey. He's only been here five days and he's already cleaning me out. I'll have to ask Connor to drop off another case before the end of the day.

It's a quiet Wednesday, at the Bay Boxing Club, so Patrick Murray called for a sit down. He wants to discuss what he's been up to over the past few years in Ireland.

My father sits at the head of the custom marble conference table, leading the meeting about how he's revolutionizing the gambling business. His head is so far up his own ass, he doesn't realize it's all been done before. He's established a niche with speakeasies, making gambling easier for the international market. Money taken in is ushered to an offshore bank account, through webserves located in Costa Rica where betting is legal. I tried not to yawn too wide during his speech.

"I would like to see all operations go virtual. It makes it much more complicated for law enforcement to track."

Men gathered around the table turn to one another, either nodding their heads or muttering in agreement. Everyone is simply trying to pacify the technology challenged man.

"As eager as I am to implement this method here, that's not why I've made this trip…" His once relaxed position becomes more rigid, as he leans forward in his chair, forcing his thick fingers to fold together on top of the long table. He wets his lips before speaking, "Son, your mother, Ar dheis Dé go raibh a hanam…"

Everyone at the table briefly closes their eyes and respectfully gives a moment of silence in lieu of my father's words.

"She supported this plan wholeheartedly."

I shake my head and calling his bullshit. "No, she supported *you*, not what you're trying to do."

He wasn't used to being talked back to. His face turns shades of purple even while he tries to school his features. The boorish man speaks concisely, breathing heavily in between each word. "We evaded the Maxi Trial so we can continue with dignity."

I've heard enough. I stand from my chair; my men mirror the action.

In turn, my father's men bounce from their seats.

"SIT DOWN!" Patrick bellows. His voice booms through the small meeting room. Everyone looks at one another with suspicion. Slowly, bodies begin to lower into their chairs along the long table. "This will be happening!" He informs the room, but it's primarily directed at me. "I've already put things in motion. Honor is putting family first!"

My blood boils within my veins.

With a wave of his hand, he releases everyone to their prior obligations.

I remain in my seat staring at this stranger of a man.

He removes a handkerchief from his pants pocket and pats at his forehead. What makes him think he can just walk back into our lives after being gone for years and take control back? Even has the balls to throw around the word *honor*. When I came of age, he was nothing but a shit father. I felt as if the heat within me was ready to explode. Fuck this!

"When your mother was alive, she told me about you and that Lombardi boy. Tell me, do you think your actions may be why we're all here today?"

My heart is hammering in my chest so hard; I think it might puncture a rib. I only see red. Slamming my hands on the table, I stare into the hollow eyes of the man who I vowed to never become. Not thinking, I just react. Lunging toward my father, I instantly realize I am a damned fool.

A revolver appears on the table between us.

My fiery insides solidify, holding me in place. Would he? He's become a different person since his wife left this Earth. I wouldn't put it past him to take me out.

"How about you take that pent up anger and put it where it belongs, boy." With one hand resting on the gun, he leans back casually. Patrick is ruthless, desperate, and in turn has become careless.

I don't bother wasting my breath. Teeth clenched so tightly, I'm sure I could crack a molar.

He continues, "You have one month until I release the red wolf. Do you understand?"

My vision blurs and my jaw aches, but I nod despite my urge to fight this. I won't let him fuck up everything. I've worked too hard over the past three years to let any innocents get caught up in this. My hands are dirty enough, thanks to him. I spit on the ground beside his seat at the table, then leave the room without sparing my obstinate father a second glance.

A black Tom Ford suit was one of my sharpest pieces. I pair the wool-silk twill with a black shirt, and emerald cufflinks. The combination of pieces commands the attention of everyone in the room. My hair was trimmed and styled, along with a clean shave from a modest barber shop, on the way home.

About twenty 'til I left to meet Cindel outside her apartment. Everything was already arranged, along with the reservation at the Oceanfront Steakhouse on the North end of the city. Two dozen, long stem roses sit in the passenger seat as I pulled up right at eight p.m., to find a small framed, radiant girl standing outside her building. I couldn't discern if I was a danger to her or is she was a danger to me. She texted me in advance to ask what color I was wearing, so she could plan accordingly. I guess it's a thing couples do.

Her sheer long sleeved dress shimmered from passing headlights. With only a tank top and mini skirt layered underneath, I felt uneasy. Too much of her was on display. Should I suggest she looks cold? Throw my jacket over her body? In her hand, she held a deep-green bag along with her signature, scuffed up combat boots. I don't think I've ever seen her without them. Cindel's evening attire complimented mine. It's possible that she may get more looks than me tonight.

I've learned she has an affinity for clothes. For only shopping at thrift stores, she sure does a damn good job of slapping together a showstopper.

Putting the car in park, I round the Audi to open the passenger door for her. "You look lovely tonight, Cindel." Her cheeks turn a subtle shade of pink, as she scoots the roses to the side and climbs in.

As soon as I'm back in the driver's seat, she speaks quickly, "Thank you. For picking me up and for the roses. It's sweet of you."

I chuckle to myself over how seamlessly honest this girl is.

"The night's just getting started," I quip.

After having the car valeted, I pull the innocent girl to my side and guide her into the posh establishment. The hostess recognizes me upon entry, ushering us to my usual table near the back with the best views of the bay. It's quieter, there are fewer prying eyes, and it is close to an exit if the situation ever arose.

Cindel looks a little uneasy. She shifts the conversation to work, talking about how much she has learned the past few days. Was she nervous about the upscale dining or being around me? I wasn't sure. She goes on to tell me how she's already found a way to save around two hundred dollars a month by ordering from a different distributor for The Black Sheep's beer and liquor. This girl is talented and wicked smart. Any guy would be lucky to have her as their date, but there's no one else. Just me. I'm the one across from her at the table. I know she has things she'd like to ask me, because I have the same line of questioning ready.

Taking her hand in mine, I lean forward, gazing into those comforting eyes. "Let's not talk about business tonight. How about you tell me about your family… I'd love to know more about you."

She taps her chin. "Have you ever heard of Mari Real Estate? Well, that was my parents'. My dad worked in investing a little too, but they mostly did the real estate stuff. Not so long ago, they were an unstoppable duo. They had a hand in most of the sales throughout South Boston. They were very popular."

I nod. Having heard it all before, I still try to be polite and engage. "No kidding?" The shortened name was a nice touch.

"Well… my parents retired three years ago. Right after my brother passed."

I unbutton the top button of my collared shirt, feeling suddenly too warm. I take a large swig from my wine glass and clear my throat.

"The reason you don't drink or smoke?"

She nods tentatively. "Right." Cindel shifts in her seat, pushing her hair behind her ears, and sips from her iced water. Long moments pass before she continues. "He… he overdosed." She combs her hair behind her ears again, even though not a single strand has slipped free. "Sorry. This isn't exactly a first date topic. We can talk about—"

I stupidly blurt out. "Do you believe it?"

She cocks her head while furrowing her eyebrows. "Believe what? That he's dead? I mean, I was present at the funeral. So, yeah, I believe it."

My foot starts bouncing under the white linen tablecloth. "No. Do you believe it was a drug overdose?"

She studies me for a moment, opening her mouth before closing it again. She attempts to manipulate her hair behind her ears ahead of speaking. "That's an oddly specific question. If I'm being completely honest, no. The coroner's report was vague, and authorities refused to look into any other possibilities. They wrote it off as an unfortunate accident."

I finish off the glass of wine, raising my glass for the waitress to top me off. It's hard to swallow, but I ask anyway. "You think there was foul play?" My breath stills… awaiting a response.

She nods just as the waitress tops off my glass and asks Cindel if she would like a refill. I wait until they leave us alone.

Finally allowing myself air, I whisper the next part, "Do you miss him?"

She looks up to the high ceiling, before bringing her now glossy eyes back to mine.

"Every day."

I understood wholeheartedly how she felt. Our food arrives shortly after that, putting a temporary hold on any questions she may have for me. I have Wagyu beef with seared veggies and petite potatoes, while Cindel opted for honey glazed salmon, sweet potato risotto, and carrots. We kept the rest of the conversation lighter. Chatting about clothing, what's in style, and her side hustles in the world of passion projects. She even invited me to some little craft event coming up. I shared what it's like running the Bay Boxing Club. Leaving out any incriminating details about the true nature of the businesses. The best lies are woven from truths after all. She has a good sense of humor. Although, she manages to poke fun at herself whenever she starts to feel a little self-conscious. I don't care much for that. Her likeness in some instances causes my stomach to twist. Cindel was a pleasure to be around, I like spending time with her, but I needed to crawl into the little cracks that appear around her vulnerable edges. The ones that go deeper than surface pleasantries.

After our meal, I take Cindel for a stroll alongside the harbor. As predicted, she begins to shiver in response to the sea breeze. I offer my jacket; our hands briefly brush against one another as I drape it over her shoulders. Despite the temperature, I felt uncomfortably warm. This is already so much more taxing than I thought it would be. Our hands found one another as we turned and walked back toward the valet. My insides knot by the time we arrive at her apartment building, but I can't circumvent her questions any longer.

"I was an idiot… I didn't want to upset you… and I didn't have cell service." Were all I could come up with in response to why I ignored her texts this past weekend. She seems content, but I could tell she was holding back too.

Her body naturally gravitates toward the car door as she fiddles with her nails. To my surprise, she invites me upstairs. I was both nervous and pleased the night wasn't over yet, especially with the timetable my father laid out for me.

Her apartment is quaint, with a few flares of her artsy personality, expressed by vintage food magnets on the fridge or antique rugs between rooms. Cindel arranges the roses in a vase while I meander around the room. Her roommate is working late, which apparently happens quite often from what she's said.

I see a familiar glow that urges me deeper into the apartment. Upon a bookshelf, adjacent to the living room couch was a garnet lit tank with an active little tarantula, perched atop its faux skull.

She walks over to my side, "Would you like to feed Thelma?"

I nodded, unable to form words at that moment.

She quickly retrieves a couple of waxworms from a lower cupboard and places them in a tiny dish.

I flip the enclosures lock with ease and lower the creature's food onto the bedding of its home. The arachnid taps her front legs. Cindel smiles but also watches me with mild curiosity, as I close and lock the top.

"You're very good at that. Did I tell you I had a tarantula?"

I rub my jaw, instinctively putting some distance between us. Then I continue, touring her place. "Yeah…you mentioned it briefly."

She nods her head, as if to convince herself she must have forgotten the conversation. "Did I mention she was my brother's?"

Biting the inside of my mouth, as to not say anything stupid, I settle on shaking my head no. "Do you have any other family you're close with? Distant relatives? Long lost cousins?"

She giggles, but her eyes don't lie. Her thoughts are carrying her off. She walks past me and puts a kettle on the stove. "Not really. The only family I have left in town is an uncle."

Right. She mentioned that before.

"We have breakfast once a month to catch up. I like those days, because he actually doesn't mind me talking about my brother. My parents have distanced themselves so much, it's like they don't want to remember the past."

I lean against the fridge while she looks in different containers for what I can assume are tea bags.

"What about you, are you close with your family?" She fires back.

That's a loaded question. "Not really. My dad's a bit of a loose cannon and my sister is unbalanced, to put it nicely."

There's that smile again that meets her eyes.

"How about your mom?" Soon she pours the hot kettle into a mug of tea. The scent of orange blossoms fills the space.

"She's not around anymore."

Cindel stops pouring, placing the pot down.

"Oh, I'm so sorry."

I reach toward her, taking her hand in mine before reminding myself to get close. Learn what I need to. I kiss the top of her hand, then take the other and repeat the action. Her eyes became heavy with lust or exhaustion; I'm not sure which was the lesser of two evils. She peers into my eyes as her hands remain in mine, then slowly her gaze lowers to my lips.

I'm no priest. I know what she wants. Will kissing her help? I'll give her what she needs, if it means gaining her trust. I pull her to me and close my eyes, her glossy lips easy to part. My tongue finds hers. Deepening the kiss, I continue exploring just enough that I have her panting in my arms. We part gradually, her once shiny tinted lips, now puffy and smeared. I wondered if I performed okay, it felt different.

"I should go," I admit before pulling on my discarded jacket. I was feeling conflicted. If I stayed here… if I thought too much about it, I might lose that expensive wagyu before I made it out to my car.

"Do you like music?" She calls out.

I halt just in front of the door. "Yeah. Mostly just enjoy it as background noise, but I like it."

She bounces the teabag in the mug of hot liquid, then sits down at the wooden table in her tiny kitchen.

"How about Stone Temple Pilots? Do you like them?"

I consider and nod my head, side to side. "They're not too bad. I don't listen to them very much anymore. I prefer stuff like MUPP or Sadfriendd."

She squints her eyes, seeming to analyze my answer. As if it is some graded points scale. She shakes away whatever was transpiring in her mind and blows on her cup. "Goodnight, Eamon. Thank you for a lovely night."

I show myself out, hoping my time spent wooing Cindel wasn't lost on my inability to get my head into the game.

NINETEEN

CINDEL

My date with Eamon went surprisingly well. Initially, I went along with it simply because I wanted answers, but somewhere along the evening things changed. He listened to me, asked me about myself, and even understood how the pain of losing someone is ever present, despite years passing. Maybe it's just because I've never seemed to find a partner who showed more interest in what was in my mind than between my legs. Eamon was a gentleman and very easy on the eyes. Could I see myself going on a date with him again? Probably. Is dating your boss breaking some kind of ethical work code? Most definitely. Do I think Eamon is my musical stalker? I. Don't. Know. However, one question has repeated itself in my mind multiple times. "So you think there was foul play?" What an odd question.

Emerging from my bedroom, I find Andrea bumping around the kitchen, making herself a sunrise smoothie. She is dressed in a wide legged pants suit vs. her usual athletic wear, which tells me she has meetings today. She is a go-getter. If my roommate wasn't working crazy long hours, she was arranging consultations with potential customers to take on even more projects. At least, that's what she tells me.

If I'm being honest, I've never even been to any of the buildings she works from. Not even during a lunch break. The thought made me wish for our college days, when she only worked twice a week at Scoops. Thinking back on how close we were then makes me feel like we're practically strangers today.

Just behind me, I dangled the basket of goodies from my parents' trip to Martha's Vineyard. I clear my throat loudly, but she continues scooping powder into the blender. Her back still to me, she asks, "Where'd the flowers come from?!"

Luckily, I already had my hearing aids in. "Eamon. He came over last night after our date—"

The blender comes to life, tearing through chucks of frozen fruit and ice. It's an obnoxious way of getting her point across, but message received.

Pouring her orange-colored drink into a to-go tumbler before turning to fully face me. She sees that I have something behind me. "What's that?" Nodding her head in my direction.

I bring the basket to my front. "I haven't had a chance to talk to you since I got back. It's from my parents. Soaps and dressing from Martha's Vineyard."

Andrea smiles and steps forward to take the basket from my outstretched hands. Peeking inside the woven bin, before looking at me with a raised eyebrow. "You didn't want them, did you?" Her ability to sniff shit out is unparalleled. Setting the gift down, she begins to lift soap bars of various sizes and colors to her nose, exploring each scent.

"Can we talk?" I sit on the first piece of furniture we found together, when we started living here. It was a pedestal dining set we discovered on the side of the road, after someone moved out of the building. Three of the chairs were unstable, but after we lugged it back up to our apartment, we set to work. A little wood glue and a few nails, it was gold! It's been extremely reliable, holding our asses up through countless meals.

Andrea finally sits across from me, pushing the vase of roses to the edge of the table. For a fraction of a second, I expected her to send the whole thing shattering to the ground. Lackadaisically, she peeks at her rose-gold watch then seems to study every inch of the room, while she sips from her frozen beverage. I breath out audibly causing her eyes to finally snap back to me.

"I shouldn't have said what I said. That was dick of me. Who you're with is your own business..."

She's right in front of me. I know she hears me, but she remains neutral as she examines her black fingernail, while tracing the outer rim of her drink.

"I'm sorry," I repeat, truly meaning it.

Her eyes wander back to me. How is it that she can manage to be both melancholy and irritated, all wrapped into one? "So, you're dating him now? You and... Eamon?"

I glance briefly over at the two-dozen long stem roses on the edge of our kitchen table. "We went on one date."

Her arms fold on the table in front of her. "Do you plan on going on another?"

I mirror her body language, not meaning to copy her, but I don't care for her tone. "I guess, yeah. If he asks me." It's quiet for long moments, as we look at one another across the dependable surface.

"Don't bring him here again," she declares, then stands with her drink.

"Wait... what? Why?!" I spin in my chair and watch with confusion as she grabs her work bag and slings it over her shoulder. Is she not going to answer me?

She reaches for the front door before turning and speaking. "If you've ever cared about our friendship, you will do this one thing I ask."

The inside of my throat feels thick, making it difficult to swallow or even respond. She just stares at me as my mouth opens and closes, but nothing comes out. I'm dumbfounded! Shocked! My parents telling me what to do is expected, but from Andrea?! I shake my head with confusion. "Why?" My question comes off more as a plea. My roommate. My best friend. My once, ride or die, groans with frustration as she opens the door to our apartment, steps through, and slams it shut.

Jeez Louise! What's crawled up her butt?! Imagine if I told her that someone has been following me, leaving me messages and gifts over the past few weeks! I have no fucking idea why she has such a vendetta against Eamon. I mean, she doesn't even know the guy! Okay… I may not know him much better but still. Could the man in question be the one playing all these mind games with me? He literally came out of nowhere and has been showering me with attention. It sort of adds up. Do I want it to be him? I do seem to be going along with everything, all the same. Does that make me the insane one or him? You know what… it doesn't matter. Either way, being vague with Andrea was a necessity, because I have no doubt, she would lock me in my room and feed me burnt waffles under the crack of my door for the rest of my life.

Thinking back to other guys I've been with during my college days, doesn't exactly validate my choice in men. I was seeing someone who kind of dealt drugs. One time he was so high, he wouldn't take no for an answer. He brought me back to his place. I tried to leave. He forced himself on me. It wasn't our first time together and I was his girlfriend at the time, but I said no. I didn't like it when he wasn't himself. I dumped him once he sobered up. Consent is important. I felt taken advantage of. Like my power was stripped away. I remember that night I went to Andrea's. She lived in a rinky-dink apartment before we lived together. I was extremely upset. Crying and shaking, I told her everything. Well, like some freaky coincidence the next day, he wasn't in class. One of his buyers told me he had moved back to Connecticut. Like overnight! Even his social media was gone. I never saw or heard from him again. That week, Andrea and I got this apartment together. She's been my guardian angel ever since. My heart aches when I think about how loyal and fierce a friend she is. I never want to take that for granted, but I don't want to be controlled either.

This weekend is the Craft Bazaar, so I spend what little time I had left tagging and organizing all the projects I plan to display in my booth. Andrea, like the celestial being she is, had my custom sign ready. Even managing to borrow a folding table from one of her jobs. I sit on my bed surrounded by piles of clothes, tags, and accessories, when I feel a sudden vibration. I move and shift heaps, searching for my phone that has somehow become buried. Finally extracting it from a collection of shirts, I see a message notification from an *Unknown number*. I let out a slow controlled breath as I slide my finger across the screen.

Unknown: Long stem roses? Very cliché.

My fingers hover over the keyboard, ready to respond. Wait… Why would Eamon have a different number than the one I have saved? I consider for a moment before I type back. Maybe it's a burner phone? My thumbs dance along the keyboard, then I hit the send arrow.

Cindel: So is a bed full of candy!

I hold my breath as I await a response. Please be Eamon, I repeated again and again to myself. Dots appear indicating their typing, then the message pops through.

Unknown: Perhaps… but you seemed to have appreciated the walking stick.

I forget how to breathe. This couldn't be the same man. Could it? Eamon never asked me about my injured foot when I returned. Is he clever enough to…

Another message appears breaking my train of thought.

Unknown: Be a good girl and wear your earbud. See you soon, Princess.

I stare at the thread of messages, rereading each word. As if a tiny fire has been ignited inside me, I switch over to the thread of messages with *"It's Eamon Actually."* I can't find any similarities between the two. Different pet names, conversations, mannerisms! It's viable that there are two different people. Instead of turning my phone off or changing my number, I let myself be in charge. I click the button to add the contact and save this number as: *THE STALKER.* Whomever this may be, I'm not going to sit ideally by and let them make my life into some kind of sport. Thanks to growing up with an older brother, I'm competitive. "Game, set, match," I say aloud.

Tonight was a little unusual at The Black Sheep. Connor wasn't on the schedule, and I haven't seen Eamon all night. Not wanting my stalker to have an upper hand, I wore the damn earbud. If more things seem to go wrong when I don't wear it, perhaps having it in would be beneficial. I manned the helm with Brittany, who seemed to be warming up to the idea that this position was thrust upon me, along with the two new girls who were hired recently. They were friendly and attentive to the customers, while not too shy to ask questions if they didn't understand something. I believe they make a great addition to the team.

At some point during the night, Eamon's buddies take up residence at the bar. They keep to themselves after ordering a round from Brittany. I was popping in and out of the back, keeping on top of Connor's barback duties, when I hear an unusual commotion on the floor. I emerge from the back to find one of the new girls, Leslie, arguing with a customer. The large man's face and shirt appear to be dripping wet with an empty mug lying on the table beside him. The man, much larger than the new girl, towers over her. Before I could think better of it, I quickly put myself between the two, since it's my job as manager to settle these matters and protect my staff. I didn't plan on what I would do once I was here. Standing even shorter than Leslie, I had to look straight up, to see the face of the brutish, beer drenched man.

"Bitch needs to learn her place!" the bearded man slurred.

Leslie yells back from behind me. "Slapping my ass does not make me get your drink faster, fuck face!"

Jesus! I liked Leslie, but shush! His face turns a deeper shade of plum from the slander, causing him to push toward Leslie. Placing my hands up and stepping back, I attempted to create distance between the drunkard and us, but instead he grabs my wrist in response and squeezes.

"This deaf little cunt won't listen, either!" The grotesque man holds up my arm to his friends at the table, making them cackle. His hold on me was too tight.

Suddenly, I feel his hand release. I step back with Leslie in tow, attempting to make sense of what is unfolding. Bodies moving, I was taken aback when the pig of a man was on his knees with Dax holding onto his contorted arm. The vial man wailed like an animal caught in a trap, begging to be released. Dax just held him like that, looking at me before he all but dragged the drunkard with him, out the front bar door. Garron's usual playful nature was long gone. He commands the room, beginning by rounding up the horrid man's friends and instantly escorting them out. Luckily, they don't object. Garron is intense when he's like this.

Brittany and Leslie were soon on me, asking me if I was okay. The other new hire, Maya, notices me rubbing my wrist and takes off to retrieve ice. I am a little shaken up, but turn to Leslie to make sure she is okay, seeing how she was the one man handled on my watch. There is still an hour til closing, however Garron marches back into the bar, flipping on and off the bar's lights and hollering for everyone to go home. Can he do that?

Garron jumps right in, helping with closing tasks as if he's done this before. I wasn't going to object, as it allowed the girls and I to close up in record time. Dax didn't return. I hope he's okay. The belligerent drunk was the size of a house! As we are getting ready to lock up, my phone vibrates. I pull it from my bag and read the message.

It's Eamon Actually: Are you okay?

I smile to myself, knowing that his friends are the ones who likely reported the incident to him.

Cindel: Yes, I'm fine. I'm glad your friends were here.

Another response follows immediately.

It's Eamon Actually: Garron will be walking you home. No exceptions.

"Ready?" Garron appears at my side, just as I turn the key on the big red door's lock. He walks me home, actually quiet and reserved for the first time.

When we reach my building, I finally ask, "How long have you known Eamon?"

He moves the signature toothpick side to side in his mouth before answering. "Since we were kids. My mom was a junky back then, so his family kinda took me in. He's more of a brother to me than anything."

I couldn't imagine. That must have been hard. I didn't have anything else to ask, but I appreciated Garron's honesty. "I'm glad that you were there tonight. Where'd Dax go?"

He removes the toothpick and swipes his hand in front of his body. "Aaaah… Dax can handle himself, don't you worry, Princess." He flicks the toothpick to the ground, with a slight nod downward he wishes me farewell, and continues down the street.

Did I just hear him correctly? Did… he call me, Princess? I don't even thank him for walking me home. I'm virtually frozen in place as he disappears just past the next cross-street.

As if on cue, the piece of technology comes to life in my ear as I stand on the darkened street, outside my building. A harmonic guitar riff starts and the familiar lyrics from **The Flys – "Got You Where I Want You,"** play into my right ear. I glance up and down both sides of the street for anyone possibly watching me, but there's no one. I rush into the safety of the building, taking two steps at a time, before pushing through my apartment door. It's vacant, empty… Andrea is most likely still working. I go to the window and glance down at the street one more time. Someone passes beneath the window walking their two dogs, while another hooded figure walks toward them. When the shadowy man passes beneath my window, he stops and looks up.

Their features darkened beneath the hood of the jacket, but I swear I can see an unsettling smile.

My blood runs cold as I force the curtains closed and hurry to my bag to retrieve the phone. The song is over now and I'm left with only the ringing in my ears to keep me company. I open the message thread and quickly write.

> Cindel: Where are you?

Do I chance another peek out the window? Instantaneously, a response buzzes through.

> It's Eamon Actually: Tied up at the Club. Did you make it home okay?

I send a thumbs up then switch over to the newest contact in my phone.

> Cindel: Where are you?

I type out again.

Dots appear. Disappear. I shake the confounded piece of technology. "Come on!" The message comes through after what feels like forever.

> THE STALKER: What's your favorite song?

It was him.

I slide down the door, sitting right where I land on the entry rug. With my back to the door, I let the words from the song dance through my mind. He literally has me right where he wants. Either Eamon has one fucked up sense of humor, or this is most definitely, two completely different people. I had no intention of telling this psycho my favorite song.

I could barely sleep that night, my mind mulling over the messages, all the songs leading up to this one, and everything else that had been happening lately. My psyche was a storm of chaos with more questions than answers.

When the sun rises the next morning, my window coverings have trouble keeping out the piercing light. I want nothing more than to go back to simpler times. When all I desired was for my parents to take my brother and I to the park. We loved to ride the carousel until we were green in the face. Theo always ran faster, claiming the fiercest animal he could find, either a dragon or tiger. While I enjoyed the stationary creatures like a giraffe or even the small little bench, nestled between the more thrilling choices.

Lately, I feel like I've been on a ride that I can't get off. No matter how hard I hunt for something that holds still in the circling madness, I'm given no option. Making up my mind, I decide to clip the little belt along my lap and hold on for dear life.

145

THE STALKER'S PLAYLIST

option. Making up my mind, I decide to clip the little belt along my lap and hold on for dear life.

145

TWENTY

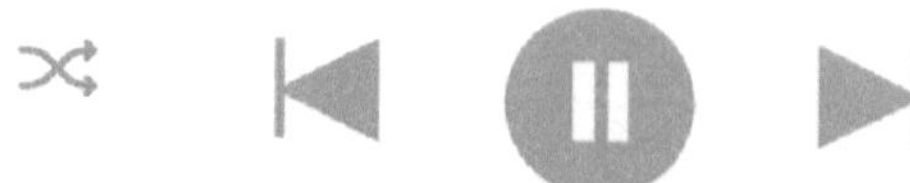

ANDREA

Once I'm out of our apartment building and on the street, I take a sharp right down the first alley and chuck my smoothie against the brick wall. I scream. I kick the dumpster, and I give two quick jabs to a stacked collection of cardboard boxes. I'm sure someone has heard me, even stopped to watch the crazy girl in the alleyway, but I don't fucking care. How?! How the fuck has he managed to get his slimy hands on her?! This is my fault. I should have been more thorough. I've looked into each job she's had up until now. They all checked out. Nothing was tied back to them. I could have sworn Connor was the owner of The Black Sheep, but this! "FUCK!" I kick the stack of boxes causing them to finally collapse in on themselves. Should I inform them? No. If I do tell them, I need to know more information first. She's not just working for a Murray, but now she's dating the prodigal son! He must know who she is. Cindel should have moved to New York, but I understood why she wanted to stay. For the memories ingrained within the very bricks of this city... so, she would never forget Theo. Cindel thinks that's why they left. To forget. If she only knew the truth... she'd hate me.

Picking up my bag from the place it fell in the alley; I shove past the collection of people who gathered to watch the short woman in business attire lose her shit on the building's garbage. I did, in fact, have a meeting this morning, but it wasn't involving graphic design projects or freelance work. That only takes a couple hours of my time and maybe two designs a month tops. No, the rest of my time is reserved for the primary job. The reason why I'm here.

I make it across town in record time before entering an upscale restaurant on Northern Ave. They weren't open to the public yet, but I knew my appointment was already waiting for me at a table in the back. I set my bag down, across from the boy in a red hoodie and pants low enough they rested more on his thighs than his waist. Sitting down, I cross my legs to the side and lean onto the small table with my elbows.

"What have you got?"

The young man from a local barber shop sits before me. He's just one set of eyes and ears I have around the city. "Not much. He came for a trim. Seemed anxious about some kind of date with a girl named Kendall," he informs me.

"Cindel!" I correct, already irritated he's getting shit wrong.

"Right!" He tries to pacify me with a shy smile. "Said something about his father being here… said he's going to fuck things up."

Wait, his father? "Are you telling me Patrick Murray is back in the states?"

The kid's eyes are downcast before looking back up to me, this time with conviction. "Yes! I remember he said; My father is back in town, and this girl means everything."

Fuck. Now I have two Murrays on my radar. From what I understand, the other sibling isn't involved in anything having to do with the family business. "Anything else?!" I press, irritated that I need to make more arrangements when I'm already stretched thin.

"No, ma'am."

Ugh, ma'am. I'm not that old. "Fine. I'd like you to hand out some business cards for your shop on their side of town. Keep your ear to the ground. If anyone gets chatty about anything involving the Murrays, be sure to let me know."

He nods. Right. On to stop number two. Without so much as a thanks, I drop a small roll of hundreds on the table for the kid to continue being my little snoop and head out.

I walk all the way to Park Street, before getting on the Green Line to head out to Boston College. I had a source who wanted to speak in person. I find myself reflecting on everything Cindel has been through. All she's faced, all she's lost. I know she struggles. She's terrible at hiding things, especially her feelings. If I continuously insist, she doesn't see Eamon, I know it's going to make her want to be with him more. She's also incredibly stubborn… and ridiculously naive. No fault of her own. Cindel has been kept in the dark about everything. Why can't she just listen when I try to warn her? I mean, look at that block head Brodi. I tried convincing her time and time again that he was no good, but did she listen?! No… seriously, I question why she stayed with him so long. I'm the one who told her parents about him in the first place.

Terri was in the car before I even hung up the phone. Cindel was very surprised to see her mom show up unannounced for a visit. After a long conversation, her mom returned to New York. I think Cindel was able to placate everyone, insisting she found happiness with the grease monkey. Although, I had a feeling she was trying to regain some kind of control over her life. Her choices. Cindel convinced herself she was content, but really, I believe she was settling. He was a cheating piece of shit, and I should have dealt with him myself, but I don't think I could have lived with that. Little did I know he would just up and vanish one day. Maybe it was the tiny buddha I found on the subway that week. Like a good luck charm, Brodi was, poof... gone!

I was introduced to Cindel in our first semester of college. She had this magnetic personality. Everyone adored her. She dreamt big and wanted nothing more than to create art and enjoy her life with the people she cared about. I believe in karma, but I still don't understand why good people are robbed of a full life, while the scum of the earth are resilient as a cockroach riding a twinkie into the apocalypse. It's been three years since her brother died. I've tried my best to lift her up, but it was actually Brodi who helped her smile again. That's why I couldn't bring myself to do anything about it. Over time, Cindel started changing. Whether she was still working through the loss of Theo or something about her relationship with Brodi, she just wasn't the same. She jumped from job to job, sometimes working multiple positions at the same time, but she never put her fashion degree to good use. Could it be that control thing again? Maybe. Perhaps she figured if she didn't take chances, she wouldn't be disappointed. Brodi disappearing was the best thing that could have happened to her. Familiar with characters like him, he's probably stolen enough money to move off grid and start that new life he always told Cindel about. Thank fuck, because I was days away from putting a small slit on the brake line of his Harley.

I manage to grab a seat on the subway, positioning myself to watch the scrolling text until Boston College is displayed. I have a connection there, someone who has knowledge beyond my reach. I hoped they could shed some light on my current situation. I had to know what Eamon's intentions were with Cindel. If I wanted to stay one step ahead of the Murrays, I needed to go back further.

The name of my stop rolls across the screen. I stand with my shoulder bag and step onto the platform. After about a two-minute walk I'm on the college campus, right on time. I find the bench before the woven patinated fountain and take a seat. Chilly moments pass before a thin framed, older woman stands before me. Her thick red glasses are a stark contrast to her pale blue blazer and pencil skirt. She stretches out her freckled hand, offering one of the hot, to-go cups in her hand.

"Nice to finally meet you in person, Andrea," she greets with a mousy voice.

Taking the warm offering from her, I stand from the bench. "Hello, Mrs. Kent."

She gives a tight-lipped smile, with a downcast glance and a nod. "Miss. Divorced, some years ago... please call me Moyra."

TWENTY-ONE

CINDEL

Yesterday's shift at The Black Sheep was perfectly tedious. No bar fights, no injuries, no unexpected deaths, and no drama. Connor worked the back and Eamon dropped by to have a drink. His buddies weren't with him for once, which was kind of nice. I'd like to think that Eamon was more open with me when they weren't around. Probably just a guy thing, can't lose face with his bros! He asked more about Thelma and if I'd ever been to "Spooky Flicks," at the local theater. When I told him, I loved going when I was younger with my brother; it was settled before he even asked if I'd like to go. We were going to see *The Lost Boys* next week. Obviously, he knew my schedule, being the boss and all, so I figured he'd just pick a day, I didn't work. I mean, what else did I have to do besides watch reruns of *The Sopranos*? I haven't been to the theater in a while. It holds so many special memories for me, I was a little anxious but also excited to revisit.

On my walk home, I had that unsettling feeling again… was I being followed? Everyone on the same side of the street as me probably thought I was crazy; due to the fact I kept spinning around every couple steps. My erratic behavior even caused one couple to cross over to the other side of the street. Even though I never saw anyone lurking from the shadows, I still couldn't forget that sinister smile I witnessed from my apartment window.

Tonight, I organize bins full of inventory, pulling out the dusty headless mannequin, and piling everything into the living room for an easier morning. Andrea volunteered to help load up, but there is still thick tension between us. We work quietly, side by side, piling the cart full of what is needed for tomorrow. When I get hot, I push my sweater up to my elbows, revealing the yellowing bruise on my wrist from that pig of a customer who grabbed me. Like a hawk, she spots the injury and gets immediately in my business.

"Did Eamon do that to you?!" She finally speaks, her tone accusatory, borderline enraged.

"What? No! It was some asshole customer that was harassing one of the new girls. The guys jumped in and—"

She looks from my face to the insignificant injury again.

"Why do you even work there, Cindel?! That place is a hole in the wall. I'm going to find something more suited for you."

I abandon packing away embroidery hoops and stand from the floor. "What?" I ask, confused and mad. Actually, madder than anything! Since when does she get to tell me what to do?!

Her chest rises and falls, while her brows remain furrowed and her jaw clenched tightly. "You heard me," she scolds. "If your parents knew what you've really been up to, they would have taken you back to New York with them three years ago!"

My body is rigid, despite the chilly floors I feel heat flowing through me, starting at my neck. I had heard enough! "What the actual fuck, Andrea?! You're supposed to be my friend, not my parents' spy! Why do you suddenly have a problem with everything I do?!" I wanted to run to the bathroom, close myself in. Splash water on my face. Anything to make this destructive, whole-body feeling go away, but I know I can't run from this.

She folds in on herself, her jaw relaxes slightly, but the tiny lines between her eyes remain. "Things are different, Cindel. I'm just trying to look out for you."

I look away briefly, my gaze bouncing between a photo of us in our caps and gowns after graduation and another of us with my family. When my attention returns, her eyes are glossy. For once she looks... scared. I know she cares deeply for me... for all of us. "I know you are. It was you who held things together, when we lost Theo. It was you who helped me to carry on after Brodi, but now... now it's like you're pushing me away!"

Her arms fall to her sides and the tears she fought so hard to hold back now careen down each cheek.

"I'm tired," I admit. "The morning will be here before we know it. We should try to get a few hours of sleep."

She signs '*goodnight*' ahead of me, turning and closing the door to my bedroom.

Laying out my outfit and getting everything ready the night before was a smart idea because I forgot to set my alarm clock. I fly out of bed when I see the sun is up, realizing the Bazaar was set to open in an hour! No matter how much planning I do, something is bound to shake up my carefully laid plans.

Andrea helps me to load the wheelie cart I borrowed from a neighbor. Like the mother duck she is, she also manages to grab a couple bananas and two nutritional shakes from the fridge. I secretly hope they aren't the ones that taste like chalk.

Despite lugging a mannequin, clothing, accessories, clothing rack, signage and more; we manage to make it to the Craft Bazaar in record time. Probably had a lot to do with us sprinting while taking turns pulling the wagon. Many vendors are already set up in their booths with signs and merchandise, so we still have to hustle. I find my spot on row three, booth C. We work together to extend the legs of the table and, erect the wire display wall. The vendor to the left was kind enough to let us borrow their step ladder. Andrea stays to help hang the custom: *Craft or Crime banner*, on the front of the booth. I and just in front to admire the edgy black lettering with yellow background. I felt really proud of myself at that moment. It was a step in the right direction, no matter how small it actually was. After the big stuff was up, I insist I can handle the rest on my own. Andrea gives me a feeble hug before dashing off to the gym or whatever she does with her days lately.

The upcycled pieces I brought were already on their designated hangers, so once I extend the pole for the hanging rack, that part was ready to go. I lay out a yellow tablecloth on the folding table along with an acrylic sign, displaying the prices and my online handles. Earrings dangle upon a wooden display stand, alongside woven baskets filled with handmade bracelets and woven hats.

I took to knitting last year when I was having my usual struggle, during the holidays. Instead of sinking into a dark place, I dove into another craft. That winter I cranked out twenty hats. I was still sad but had a solid start to my inventory for this very event.

The mannequin was positioned closer to the front of my booth, starring my favorite upcycled pieces on the bust. The one and only bedazzled, Lisa Frank jean jacket, cropped *True Crime Enthusiast* shirt, and a lace trimmed leopard mini-skirt. I place a purple, woven beanie from the collection, on the headless figure to finish off the look.

Just in time too, the Bazaar appears to be open. Before I go through the effort of hanging the embroidery hoops on the back panels, I want to entice shoppers by adding twinkling fairy lights along the top of my tent.

I had a lot of *peopling* to do today, so I turn to music while I waited for shoppers to engage with me. Taking off one of my aids, I throw it in my bag and dig around for MY earbuds. I could have sworn I packed them. Pulling out a singular earbud, I turn it on its side to find the annoying little star that loves to follow me everywhere.

"Fine. Uncle. You win." I put the device into my right ear and instantly there's music! How long has this been playing? I recognize the melody but I'm not sure what the song is, until it replays from the beginning...no!

OMC – "How Bizarre," plays. Then it plays again... and again!

"Are you fucking kidding me?!" I whisper-shout as to not scare away any potential customers meandering by.

Before it could roll over to a fourth time, I take off the earbud and hurl it back into my bag. I groan. It's worse than having a brother. My stalker is literally going to torture me to death! Either he never learned about homophones in school or he thinks he's just fucking hilarious!

People walk by in droves, giving me a nod when we accidentally make eye contact. A couple potential customers come into the booth to explore the table of goodies. Within an hour, the place is packed and my tent is seeing a lot of foot traffic. Once the wall of embroidery hoops is up, a gang of grandmas stroll right in. Some cackle while others clutch their pearls as they read from the slew of sassy, embroidered sayings hung before them. I sold six snarky hoops by ten o'clock!

After ringing up a young couple with a pair of woven tassel earrings, a familiar face appears. A creamy skinned, freckled faced young woman, with a bun full of red wild hair stands on the other side of my table. She smiles widely, throwing open her arms and coming around the table to embrace me in a friendly hug.

Mairead was wrapped in a fur coat, but when she stretches her arms wide, it reveals a scantily fitted, red dress within. It might be a teddy. Isn't she freezing? I myself am double layered this morning.

"Your space looks so pretty! I love the twinkling lights!" She spins around, returning to the front of the table. She latches onto an older, well-dressed gentleman nearby and begins dragging him toward me.

Oh no... does she even know this man or is she pulling random people against their will into my tent? The strange pair stops just in front of the table.

"Daddy, this is Cindel." Oh, thank god, they're related! Wow, you'd never catch me wearing anything like that around my dad.

He extends a massive, calloused hand, and I place my hand in his. The sharply dressed man gently kisses the top of my fingers before releasing me.

"Pleasure to make your acquaintance. I've heard a lot about you."

Mairead is already moving around my tent, oohing and awing over everything she touched.

"I love your accent, where are you originally from?" I inquire.

"Here originally, but I've been in Ireland the past couple years. I guess an accent has set in, during my time away."

I politely nod and smile, "well, it's a pleasure to meet you. Sorry... if you would excuse me."

Someone holds three bracelets and a hat, ready to pay. While I check out the customer, I can hear Mairead chatting with her father about how amazingly talented I was. She's a very sweet girl, odd, but sweet. I try not to stare as her father hands her a stack of bills, before he regards me with a tip of his hat and continues, down the row of tents. Mairead giggles and places down a hundred-dollar bill. I watch as she removes the shimmering jacket with two hand-painted porpoises, off the mannequin and squeezes it to her body with a high-pitch squeak. Removing her black, furry coat, she places it onto the displayed ensemble and pulls on the jean jacket. She spins and squeals with excitement, causing lots of looks from passersby.

"This is the best day of my life!" She exclaims, pulling me into another hug. "I'll text you about going shopping next week!" Mairead rushes out.

"Wait, you paid too much! The jacket is only sixty-five." But she is already skipping off toward the direction her father went. Mairead also left her clothes behind, but I think that part was intentional. The headless bust doesn't look terrible with the long fur draped over the animal print miniskirt and screen printed top. Although, if I had to guess, that coat is worth more than everything in this tent, including me!

During slower times over the course of the event, I desperately want to play music, but my earbuds are missing and all I have is this possessed tech that will not stop playing *How Bizarre!* Poking around in the settings on my cell phone, I manage to pair the purple starred earbud with my own phone.

I feel a pang of loss after completing the pairing, wondering if I would ever hear a song from my stalker again. I couldn't explain it, but it's like having a one-way walkie talkie with your best friend next door. When you are having a bad day or maybe you're a tad bit afraid of the dark… you knew someone was there with you. Sometimes they would talk, or play music in my case, but you weren't completely detached from them. I'm confused. Why do I care if I miss something? I'm sure the lunatic will just mail me another one when he realizes he's not getting his point across any longer. Clearly, it's a "he," right? I mean, I'm not sexist, clearly a woman would be perfectly capable of being a stalker too, but I am team sausage, so I kind of thought the person in question would be male. If I'm being honest, I hoped it was Eamon, but my gut told me this may be a completely different person.

A lot of the other booths are busier than mine, so I am happy with the little foldable stool and my tunes, while I wait for my next sale. A teenage boy appears in my booth, just as I finish the sawdust tasting drink Andrea brought for me. He seems nervous or uncomfortable, based on the way he picks up items, quickly places them down, then looks around for something.

"Can I help you find something?" I round the table to come closer to the nervous boy.

"Yeah, umm… how much for this black furry thing?" His voice cracks as he holds up the sleeve of the coat Mairead left behind.

I smile. "That's actually a display piece, but if you like fur, I can show you this jacket on the rack over there." I point to the rack full of clothes behind the table.

He nods, appearing happy with the offered help.

"Are you shopping for yourself or a friend?" I slide the hangers to the side as the tall lanky boy stands between me and the table.

"Friend!" He nearly shouts.

"Okaaay. Do you happen to know their size?" I lean forward between articles of clothing to check the tags of the inside of each piece, before lifting them off the rack for the customer to see. "I have two pieces here with fur trim. One is large and the other is extra small." I announce as I hold them up.

Oddly… the boy wasn't in front of me anymore, he was running away? The little shit is fleeing from my booth with what looks like my purse!

"STOP!" I shout, fleeing my booth. The isle is so full of people there is no way I could tell which way he went. "Little Shit!" I scream after him, standing in a crowd of potential shoppers that will probably be avoiding my booth for the rest of the day. If I could have kids, I still would never have them! I stomped back to my tent, so thankful that I removed my phone from my purse before the kid showed up. "Goddamnit!" Any cash transactions I made today were in my purse, so the little thief made off with at least two hundred and fifty, plus my debit card, and license!

I put my head in my hands, attempting to slow my heart rate and focus on my breathing. No cops, I told myself; they never help. What would be the use anyways, report it, answer a bunch of invasive questions, as I defend myself over something I didn't do. My belongings would never actually be recovered. Then, I would have to cancel my cards and get a new ID regardless. I'll take the less aggravating route, thank you very much.

It was thirty minutes till the end of the event. I had a few pity buys from onlookers that witnessed me running after the punk kid, but no big sales to speak of. I don't wait. I start folding and placing clothing and hats into the bins I brought, ready to head home, when I hear something drop on the table behind me. I spin around to see no one, but when I stand to full height, I find my purse sitting on the table between the earring display and hat basket.

"Holy shit." I pick it up and shuffle through, first locating my wallet. I count each bill three times and to my astonishment, not a dollar is missing! I walk out of my booth to the aisle, purse in hand and look in each direction. Who I was expecting to see, I don't know… but I was elated no matter who brought it back to me. Without my purse being returned, I would have been in the hole for my tent rental and booth fee, but having the money back means I had enough to be in the green and a little extra to buy some delicious take out this week.

Wheeling my little cart slowly back toward home, I encounter an adorable, older lady in a coral, cashmere sweater. "Excuse me. I wasn't able to make it in time to the craft event, but I understand you have lovely embroidery hoops for sale. Would it be too much trouble to make a purchase, my dear?" I glance back at the boxes and precariously stacked items in the wagon.

"Ummm, sure. I just need to get that box out." The one on the bottom. "Just a second." I let go of the handle, on the wagon. "Oh, not here, dear. Are you able to deliver?" I face her, confused how she's going to know which one she would want without seeing them first. "Not really. I could show you—"

"How much for all of them, dear?"

I don't think I heard her right. "All of them?"

She nods.

I quickly calculate how many I brought with me; versus how many I sold. Then multiply the average price, times how many I have left. Four hundred? No. I pull out my phone and check my math. It seems too high… but the calculator on my phone said it was right. "Four hundred and eighty?" My math is terrible, but I checked twice to be sure. Why did Eamon want me as manager again? It's a miracle I haven't messed up the drawer yet.

"Wonderful. She reaches into her pockabook and hands me a thick envelope. I look inside to find crisp fifty-dollar bills. Significantly more than the price I just gave her. "The extra is for the delivery fee and the slip of paper within has the address. Please deliver at your leisure." She snaps her little latch shut with a click, gives me a warm smile, ahead of continuing down the avenue.

I glance at the money again, then back toward the older woman who all but disappears. This seems too good to be true. I slip the envelope in my bag and walk a little faster toward my apartment.

After getting everything up the stairs and through the door, I was starving and exhausted. I throw a frozen burrito into the microwave and collapse on the couch with the envelope of money. I count it multiple times, only to realize not only did I have enough for takeout, but I have enough in my hand to cover my share of this month and next month's rent! I would be lying if I said I didn't smell the money, but I would deny any implications that I rolled in it. I did, though… roll in it.

The burrito tastes like burnt beans, with spots of ice throughout. I don't care at this point because I am ready for a shower and nap before working at the bar this evening. I start to undress, leaving my aid and earbud for last. When I reach for the earbud, a soft melody begins playing. I recognized the song. It's **Radiohead – "Creep."** Who doesn't know this song? I cover my face for a moment in utter disbelief… then I smile. I don't know how he did it… but I'm relieved. I didn't sever how my musical stalker communicates with me. Sure, he could text, but this felt special. I found myself swaying as the song plays only for me. The room fills with steam as the shower runs while I dance. I wipe my hand across the mirror, staring at my reflection. Could my musical stalker be the one who recovered my bag? Does he really find me that special that he would go through so much trouble? For once, I didn't find the idea of him creepy.

TWENTY-TWO

CINDEL

Keeping up with a perpetually pleasant facade can be draining. On top of it, people consistently expect you to communicate, making the task much more laboring when you're hard of hearing. Whether I'm at work or out and about, I'm going to be surrounded by the 98% of the population who don't need assistance to hear. So, when I have a day off, where I can drift through a city of unfamiliar faces, with no expectations of me, I relish it. Of course, Andrea knows where I am. I wouldn't be shocked if she tracks my phone or has a drone tailing me from high above. She can be brazen at times, but I know it all comes from a good place. I just wish every conversation with her lately didn't turn into an argument.

The Lantern Festival at the Boston Zoo has stunning exhibits of paper covered lights that wow children and adults alike. My family and I would attend each fall, being sure not to skip a single display. Brodi took me once, although we kind of rushed through most of the exhibits because he got bored and wanted to go back to his place so I could give him head. That's always how it went. Pleasure him first, then I sometimes get a turn. Maybe that's just how relationships go. One side makes out better than the other, or it's hot and heavy at the start, then it slowly fizzles out. For once, I was relieved to be unaccompanied. Going at a pace that pleased me. Perhaps that's the era I've entered in my life. Doing what I want.

My face is pretty, but I'm not hot or sexy. I learned a while ago that I flourish when it comes to dressing my body.

This evening, I pair my long dress-like, *Smashing Pumpkins* tee with an oversized, olive-colored army jacket and black tights. I was warm enough despite the cutting temperature. With the forecast of a light drizzle, it was apparently off putting enough to discourage people from visiting the lantern festival. This gave me a wide berth and plenty of time to walk at my leisure. Halloween was less than a week away and many of the trees were nearly bare. My boots crunch atop collections of leaves, as I stop to admire lanterns in the shape of panda bears, nestled between bamboo trees. A girl with pigtails comments on the bears to her parents. "It's broken!" She whines, "It's not brown." As innocent as the comment was, it's a stark comparison to how society views something other than what you perceive as 'normal.'

Continuing down a path of fish, I am engulfed in a sea of color. It was like something from a fairytale, floating between lantern-shaped lily pads in a kaleidoscope of color. Not quite the same presentation as when I would visit with my family, but I explicitly remember racing my brother down similarly lit paths. The ocean setting morphed into a garden, as blooming lotuses cascade from the sky. This creates tiny stars along the pathway as if moving onto an otherworldly place. The farther I go… the fewer people I see. Just past the school of sea creatures and tranquil twinkling ponds was the greatest marvel. It was the only consistent display at the Lantern Festival, the dragon.

The enormity alone is astounding, but it was all the fine details along the back and tail that could keep me awestruck for hours. I don't know how long I've been standing here as soapy rain covers my hair and shoulders, but my clothes are beginning to cling to me. With the dropping temperature, I soon find myself rubbing my arms to keep warm. Perhaps only wearing a giant shirt and a pair of sheer leggings wasn't the best choice, but I looked adorable damnit. Cold, but adorable. I should really organize my closet and find my raincoat.

All at once, opaque clouds of gray begin billowing from the dragon display. I don't recall this feature from past visits. This must be a new addition. Slowly, the ground becomes covered with a rolling fog as the creature releases a continuous stream of smoke. It was rising higher up my legs, causing my boots to disappear. No one is around, as the haze gradually swallows me within the secluded alcove. Pins and needles start at my fingertips, working their way up my arms and into my torso. My heart thunders in my chest and it feels impossible to take a full breath of air. I am frozen in place, instantly brought back to that smoke filled room when I was a child. The ever-present ringing in my ears surges, while my hold on reality shrinks. Lowering myself down to the ground, I hug my legs into myself. Rocking softly, I try to find my way back, repeating that word that changed me forever.

"Explosion. Explosion. Explosion."

I'm back in that playroom. Alone. Strong arms scoop me up from my huddled position, lifting me into the air. I must have forgotten to breathe this entire episode, because I could have sworn, I was floating right before everything went black.

I open my eyes; vision still blurred and try and take in my surroundings. I'm lying on a couch in a small office. A worn chair sits in front of a large office desk, flanked by two metal filing cabinets. The only light comes from a green banker's lamp perched on the corner of the desk, casting a muted glow across the room. Trying to lift my hands to my face, I find my left arm restricted.

Following my arm down to my wrist, I discovered I'm cuffed to the leg of the couch. I tug, causing the metal to clank loudly. Taking in the whole, dimly lit room, I see no sign of another person. Sliding my body off the couch and to the floor, I was ready to lift the sofa and free myself, but the goddamned leg was bolted to the floor! I search around for something to use. Anything to free me from this situation before whomever put me here returns.

Windows are high above me, each containing a wire grid, embedded in frosted glass. Am I in some kind of office or backroom? Was I still at the Zoo or did someone bring me to a different location? With nothing in reach, I attempt to pull my wrist free from the cuff, only to be met with disappointment and raw skin around the top of my hand. I pull and kick at the other latch, hating the metal against metal sound. I'm just happy it makes a sound at all. That means my hearing aids are still secure and working.

Without warning, I hear footsteps. The growing sound means whoever put me here, is coming back! I urgently wedge my body within the tiny opening between the couch and the wall, despite my anchored hand, hanging awkwardly in plain sight. I am trapped, but I still felt safer in this corner than out in the open.

I listen to the sound of the squeaking door gradually opening. It stops, then a different tone screech tells me the door is closing again. A deep metallic "THUNK," indicates the room is locked.

Fuck. Fuck. Fuck.

My body is curled inward on itself; I don't dare look up. My captor approaches with massive squeaking boots before grabbing the chair and wheeling it in front of me to sit down. I assume this is a man based on the heavy way he sat and the sheer size of his footwear.

Unexpectedly, the crinkling of a plastic wrapper is the only sound that fills the room. What is that? What does he have? More rustling and ripping ensue, then chewing? Is this psychopath eating? Lifting my head slightly, I dare a peek. A large menacing form sits before me, suited in head-to-toe, black tactical gear. Literally, from top to bottom. From shiny combat boots, all the way up to his ballistic helmet. I couldn't even identify his face, as the man has on a balaclava, helmet, and goggles. He either planned on going to play paintball later, or he was ready to face a riot. Oh fuck, is he military? Police? I look down at my handcuff. Am I being detained?

Trying to remember what happened before my blackout episode. I recall smoke and how I felt like I was back in my childhood home… brought back to the explosion that took away my ability to hear. My past, once again, has whisked me away from sensibility. I use my uncuffed hand to smooth my hair as I face the masked stranger.

"Is this about the explosion thing? I swear, I'm not dangerous. I have flashbacks sometimes. When I was little, I kind of went through some fucked up shit. All the smoke made me—"

The shadow of a man extends his arm, revealing the source of the noise. He shakes a small box at me, causing its contents to rattle.

It's... it's a box of sour gummies? I look between the box and his concealed face; he's offering me candy?

He reaches his gloved fingers into the box to retrieve a red and yellow sweet, pulls the mask just far enough away from his face to slide underneath and inserts the candy into his mouth. He pushes the box back into my personal space and shakes its contents again.

"Umm, no thank you. I will however take a key, since this all seems to be some kind of big misunderstanding."

This person... this man is a massive statue, filling the entirety of the chair with his silent protest. He's not going to take no for an answer, is he? I stretch my free trembling hand out and reach into the box. Reluctantly, I plucked out a blue and orange, citric acid covered gummy, before popping it into my mouth. I make the 'Mmm' sound and nod. "Can I go now, please?"

The sculpture breaks form, standing to fetch my purse off the desk.

"Hey, that's mine!"

The man clad in black hasn't spoken a word to me, which makes everything that much more nerve wracking. He dumps the contents out onto the desk, causing my compact to roll off the table and shatter upon the floor.

"Hey! You're breaking my stuff!"

He locates what he was searching for. Holding up the white piece of tech I forgot was buried at the bottom of my purse. He approaches my folded form in the corner, as I attempt to scoot deeper into the crevice. No. He squats right in front of me. I hold onto myself as he reaches out. Gently, he removes my right hearing aid and nestles the earbud in its place. Is he...? Still, he remains voiceless. Pulling out a phone from his pocket, he presses the screen a couple times, then moves his thumbs across the bottom. He appears to be typing. Who was he talking to? Without warning, the quiet room ceases and words start filtering from the little earpiece.

"Sour candies help with panic attacks. It distracts the brain from negative thoughts," a deep male voice whispers in my ear.

He picks up and points to the box again, urging me to comply. Never have I ever thought eating candy would be such an unwilling task but here I am... secured to a couch and eating sugar on the floor, with a muted kidnapper who may or may not hurt me. Against my better judgement, I take the box from his outstretch hand. He watches me from the chair, as I eat slowly. One bite at a time. I don't take my eyes off him. Steadily, I started to feel better. My heart rate slows a bit, my breathing levels, while my mind becomes clearer by the minute. Is… is this my stalker? I dropped the box between us.

"Are you… him?" I ask.

No answer. He remains sealed off, unmoving, facing me in the rolling seat like I'm his evening entertainment. I free my legs from their cramped quarters.

"HELP!" I holler. "HELP!" I try again to pull my hand free, kicking aimlessly toward my captor.

Unfazed, the man stands to his full height and pulls something black from the back of his holster. It wasn't shaped like a gun. Was it a weapon? Oh god… it's a taser! I'm fucked if I don't get out of here!

I begin screaming louder and flailing my legs to keep him away, when the earbud starts speaking again.

"Do you have anything dangerous on you, Miss Mari?" A baritone male voice says.

Too busy figuring out how to get the hell out of here, I didn't realize he had his phone in hand again. He must be using one of those 'text to speech' apps, changing the voice option. I'm familiar with the program.

I shook my head feverishly at his question.

His hold tightens on the black instrument.

"Please…" I beg. "Let me go. I don't have any weapons, I promise." He points to the couch.

I shake my head, refusing his request. I try to position myself farther back in the safety of my corner.

"Lie on the couch," the voice demands.

Each time he has to type into his phone for the message to read in my ear. Why won't he just speak? Is it because he knows I would recognize his voice? Maybe it could be…

"Eamon?" My voice comes out shakier than I mean.

He leans toward me, each forearm resting on his wide-open legs. Inches from me, he types another message.

It whispers in my ear, "Follow directions. I won't hurt you."

Awkwardly, I stand and twist my body back into the position I had been in when I first woke. Wishing I could shake myself from this 'Jigsaw-like' fever dream. I lie back down on the couch, close my eyes, and force myself to stay calm.

I can still hear him, the Kevlar of his uniform shifting and tightening as he positions himself, kneeling before me on the couch. A soft click sound comes from the item he holds above me.

I jerk in response. With his gloved hand, he takes my free hand and places the item in my palm. I watch as he guides my hand to one of the carabiner clips on his uniform. The smooth item in my hand vibrates suddenly upon contact and I startle. He does it again, guiding my hand away and closer to the hook. It's not a taser! Is it a metal detector? He's showing me it's not going to hurt. Just like he said he wouldn't.

"So… you want to look for something, like what, a weapon? Are you one of those 'rent-a-cops' who take their job too seriously?"

No response. I thought my stalker was funny… what if he was *actually* law enforcement? I huff out a breath and submit to the search. When I listen, he usually leaves me alone.

Taking the vibrating metal detector back into his own palm, he starts at the crown of my head, scanning my hair… for what I'm not sure. Gradually, he moves down my neck, barely hovering the device above my skin. It pulsates against my clavicle, and he stops. His masked face turns slightly, as if curious.

"It's my necklace." I blurt out.

He studies me then proceeds down my arm, rotating and patting the loose jacket as he goes. Next, he sweeps my other arm before progressing, across my chest and down my middle. I stopped breathing. Willing my chest to cease rising and falling as he skates just above my breasts. Moving down my body painfully slow on the outside of my leg before reaching my shoes. He actually removes each boot, checking the inside for anything that could be seen as dangerous, I suppose.

"Satisfied?"

He shakes his head no.

The first form of communication I've received from him besides text to speech. After retying my laces, he presses the handheld device just above my footwear, on my inner leg. I can't help but lift my head somewhat, to watch as he glides the plastic casing up my thigh, till it's at my center. The device vibrates. I'm instantly mortified!

"It's not a weapon!" I'm… umm, it's…ya know?"

He turns his head like a confused dog, forcing me to say it out loud.

"I have my VCH done."

Like a cartoon, the masked man turns his head the other way.

"Ughh!" This man is infuriating! "My vertical clitoral hood is pierced, okay?!"

I shuffle onto my elbows, hoping that I am done and ready to be released, when he swiftly presses the battery-operated item back between my legs. It vibrates… right there! I try to squirm away. His free hand lands on my shoulder, pressing down just enough to say, "stay" without actually speaking. I'm overwhelmed, likely in shock. Confusion soon mingles with pleasure. Questionable feelings racing through me.

It was as if this was a game for him, chasing my movements, as I fidget and attempt to move away from the vibrating device.

"Fuck." Oh, that felt good. Wait, this is wrong. "Stop." My resolve is weak. My pleas come out shaky and frayed at the edges.

The puzzling man won't let up. In fact, he presses the end of the device firmly into my bundle of nerves. Despite the contraption being above my underwear and tights, it vibrates deliciously. My protests soon transform into moans. It feels insanely good. The balls of my piercing rattle in a frenzy from the metal detector, and I know my clit is becoming engorged Without a doubt, my panties were wet... my hips instinctively begin to buck in a rhythm that drives me closer.

Although this soundless shadow is covered, I know his breathing is coming heavier by the way his chest rises and falls. If this was meant as a form of torture, clearly, I was the masochist that unknowingly agreed to the terms. This man is restrained. Determined. Patient. Brodi never seemed to have the time to wait for me to cum. He often commented that I "took too long," so he always came first. By the time it was my turn, he complained that he was too tired to satisfy me.

This masked stranger is dragging me to the very edge while silently communicating, as long as it takes.' My legs shake and muscles ache, but he never lets up. Concentrating on the task at hand, I try to ignore how my hair must look... how I might be sweating, or how this whole thing is insane.

However, I didn't feel rushed. He wasn't judging me based on my ability to cross the finish line, but some cardinal need we both share. He holds right there, not changing a thing, until I just can't combat what's happening any longer. My hands claw and grab at the couch, desperate for anything to keep me grounded. I broke with a scream.

The enigmatic man watches me, waiting until each wave of pleasure runs through me, before removing the gadget. I swear I could hear him panting as I came down from my high.

I was a mess, and I can confirm by my reflection in his mirrored goggles upon his face. My hair was in fact frizzy, while the eyeliner I applied earlier made me look more like a raccoon at this point.

He stands, keeping his gaze trained on me while he removes his gloves. His pants are thick and look to be military grade, but I can still make out the faint outline of his erection.

Suddenly, I become self-conscious of how heavily I am breathing as I stare..., unsure what was to come of me.

Dropping his gloves, he methodically pushes up his sleeves, just enough to reveal corded forearms. Tiny cuts and bruises on his massive hands. His physique, quite similar to Eamon's, especially his hands. Could this man in front of me be Eamon? I wasn't entirely sure. He drops a pillow to the floor and bows in front of me like before.

I'm still coming down from my orgasmic high, too intrigued to object.

Still lying horizontally on the couch, he opens my thighs. His big hands move to my center, massaging the fabric that covers me, before pulling up and out. The tights run, creating a hole, it rips an entry straight at my crotch.

All rational thoughts sidelined, I am panting… unable to get enough air. Dizzy with need, still wanting more of what this mysterious man had to offer, but sex? I… I don't think I can.

He swings my legs off the side of the couch, wrist still affixed to the leg of the furniture. My feet hit the floor. He taps his combat boot between my shoes, instructing me to open.

I look up at his concealed face. The tinted goggles hold only my reflection. I'm disheveled, needy, unhinged… silently I obey, opening my legs for him. I'm exposed. With torn tights, only a thin layer of fabric covers my throbbing pussy.

His head falls forward. I hold my breath. He inhales deeply.

I wonder if he can pick up on how hard my heart is working, because I've never had a partner do *that* to me before. A gasp escapes me as his thick finger hooks the side of my panties, exposing me to the cool air. Was I going into cardiac arrest, because the pounding in my chest was beginning to hurt. All at once, his solid tongue presses against my wet heat. He must have lifted the lower part of his mask, just enough to perform the task. All without revealing an inch of his face. Only I was on display, regarded, and vulnerable. The second stroke of his tongue travels from my ass to my clit with the perfect amount of pressure before he pulls away.

I strain to watch as the masked stranger grips the handle of the sleek, plastic detector and places it just in front of my entrance. He pauses. I can't see his eyes, but he seems to be looking back at me, poised just above my opening… waiting. Is he asking for consent? I temporarily forget how to breathe, let alone think.

Finally, I take a shaky breath and speak, "Don't stop."

Without hesitation, he pushes the thick device into me, to the hilt.

I can feel the top of his fist on the handle, pressing against my lips. I swallow. When my lips part, a moan tumbles from me in response to the full, intense invasion.

He pulls it from me painfully slow, before shoving it back in. Heavy breaths fill the space. It was solid. The mask stranger, unyielding. But I want… no, I need more! I didn't want to think, only feel in this moment.

"Please," I beg between fervent moans. I flourish in a realm between pain and pleasure.

Brodi only ever chased his own release despite my earnest pleas for a spanking, here or there, he never did more for me. He was the very definition of vanilla.

Women's bodies are a force to be reckoned with, as I quickly become adjusted to the size of the foreign object, I crave more.

Abruptly he withdraws the makeshift dildo, before pushing back in with a slight upward angle, as to kiss my cervix. Apparently, he can read me like a book. He keeps it there, deep within me, pushing gently against that sensational spot. Then I hear the small click. The machine buzzes to life.

My body reacts. Unable to keep still, it's too much and not enough all at once.

Without missing a beat, he picks up the pace. The shaft of the sleek molded object drives into me, causing reluctant whimpers of pleasure to fall from my lips. Just when I thought I hit my limit, he adds the pad of his thumb to my clit, forming small circles that grow in speed.

It was all too much. Too sensitive. Too overwhelming. My mind awash with pleasure but also a healthy dose of fear, since I literally can't identify the man on his knees before me. I was getting in my head again, causing the ecstasy I desperately sought to be entrapped within my own thoughts.

As if he could sense my struggle, he takes the same hand that is teasing my bundle of nerves and positions his palm above my pelvic bone, putting pressure on my bladder. How does he know…before I could think more on the matter, his enormous hand spans my mound, reaching my piercing with his finger. He commences flicking it back and forth, while he continues to fuck me with the metal detector, all while maintaining compression on my lower belly.

With three more totters of my piercing, I explode. My cry was the first thing to rip from me, followed by a rush as my walls clamp down on the foreign device. I am floating, unable to hold back the force that surges through. I unravel right there, unashamed, and without reservation. My throat burns and my vision hazy, nevertheless, I could make out the dark stranger before me. His goggles dripping with my release.

"Oh fuck." I sit up taking in everything that just transpired. "I'm… oh god. I swear that's never happened with anyone before."

I put my forearm across my face, embarrassment radiating through me. I'm apologizing to a masked man that just handcuffed me to a stinky couch and played me like a fiddle, until I squirted all over him! I was weird… this was strange. These types of desires were only shared within the pages of my journal.

To my surprise, when I lift my arm, the man was unmoved. Still positioned before me, wet and traumatized? Wordless, he reaches for his phone and clicks the screen a couple times, making the little earbud play a melody.

A drum beat along with a xylophone plays before the words come through, "Never met a girl like you before." **Edwyn Collins – "A girl like you"** fills the awkward silence. Automatically, I shield my smile beneath my arm, stealing glimpses of the man as I listen.

When the song finishes, he stands going to the metal desk; he opens a drawer fetching a key for the cuff around my wrist. After removing the clasp, he places the key and cuffs in his cargo pocket before passing me a tissue box from the desktop.

"Thanks."

We manage to clean ourselves in the most uncouth manner. I was confident I would perish from awkwardness alone. Finally able to stand, I adjust my tights and begin to collect my belongings.

The chair squeaks softly, as the covert man faintly rocks, watching me pack. He acts as if nothing had transpired between us. I wish he'd say something, anything, but I, myself, didn't know what to say either.

"Ummm… will I see you soon?"

He nods once, crossing his arms over his chest.

Pulling my bag over my shoulder, I go to the door. Turning the metal lock, I pull the door inside, and step through. We are in some kind of back-office area, still at the zoo. No one in sight, I back out... closing the door gradually, transfixed on the stalker who speaks to me through music.

TWENTY-THREE

CINDEL

I fall into a routine over the next few days; pulling long shifts at The Black Sheep, watching garbage cable TV, and finding the time to text both saved contacts: *The Stalker* and *It's Eamon Actually.*

Not to automatically jump to the conclusion that I've entered a polyamorous relationship… it could still be the 'same' person. One man. Eamon hasn't been to the bar in a while, either occupied with the Bay Boxing Club or his family being in town. My contact, saved as *The Stalker*, will only give brief replies. Simply answering two questions a day on average. Texting him is like some outlandish game show, where you spin the wheel and are forced to mindlessly clap no matter where the pointer ends up.

> Cindel: Did I gross you out? Because I'm still mortified! I've never done that with anyone.

> The Stalker: THAT WAS THE HOTTEST THING I'VE EVER EXPERIENCED. Don't you dare feel embarrassed. Now I have a barometer for your body.

That was one of his lengthier texts, to date, and I was glad for it. I felt empowered… even sexy. I also inquire about the day of the Craft Bazaar.

> Cindel: Are you the one that returned my purse?

> The Stalker: Yes.

Another time I ask…

> Cindel: Was there a message behind the song "Loser" or is it just your favorite song?

The Stalker: No message.

Followed by the devil horned emoji.

The Stalker: Although, I like the song… it is not my favorite.

I may have learned the hard way that *The Stalker* won't text back if I ask two or more repetitive questions. For two days I missed opportunities to get answers, by asking the same repetitive question.

Cindel: Did you kill my manager, Craig?

After numerous "no responses," I figured out how he works and moved on from the nagging question.

Although my musical stalker didn't always make sense, I want to know what makes him tick. Why he felt so compelled to not only follow me all over the city, but hours away as well. Why me? When I think of the masked stranger, my body instinctively reacts. My stomach does somersaults and my panties become wet, just by simply thinking back to how he made my body bend for him in that cramped office. I've all but killed the batteries in my vibrator with how often I've been using it lately. I know it sounds insane, but I'm drawn to him. Maybe it's the mystery of the unknown, but I want him. I need to see him. I just hope that once I learn his true identity, these feelings won't change. This morning, I wanted to know one thing. As soon as I woke up, I sent *The Stalker* a text.

Cindel: Can I see you today?

It took him longer than usual to reply.

The Stalker: Not if I see you first.

Leaning over the bathroom sink, I ready myself for my date with Eamon. I applied a bold burgundy lip and a messy *slept-in-look* for my eyes. With a generous amount of mascara and a velvet ribbon fitted snuggly around my neck, I achieved the 90's grunge look I was going for. Once I am presentable, I tiptoe out of the bathroom, hoping that Andrea was still MIA…

"You look cute," my roommate blurts.

As if glued to the spot, I gradually spun in place to face her. "Thanks! Just gonna go to a movie."

Willing my feet to press forward, I make my way to the door. The room remains quiet as I bend over, pulling on one red converse at a time, before reaching for my messenger bag on the entryway table.

"By yourself?" She watches me from the kitchen, slurping up leftover lo mein noodles, while flipping through one of her magazines about women's health.

"Mm-hmm."

She abandons her food and starts to get up. "Lemme grab a coat, I'll come with!"

I put up my hands, taking a step forward. "No! I want to... I just need some time to myself." Fuck, now I was lying. I wonder if my fib sounds justified as I finish tying the laces. She's the one who threatened to involve my parents, all because she's not happy with my choice in men. Andrea has pushed me to this point.

"Oh... okay." She sits back down at the table and proceeds to continue flipping one page at a time.

She is my best friend. What is happening to us?

Not looking up from her magazine, she calls out, "YOU have fun, now." Drawing out the 'YOU,' it's clear she doesn't believe that I'm going by myself.

No matter. I close and lock the door from the hallway, expelling all the air in my lungs at once. Fuck, did I misinterpret her? Is she actually hurt that I didn't want her to tag along? I am the world's worst friend!

Approaching the local cinema, I'm instantly brought back to the days my brother and I would buy a ticket to a "PG" movie, with the intention of hopping from screen to screen, sampling all the vulgarity, violence, and sexual content that "R" ratings had to offer. The best part of this theater was if you simply stated you wanted subtitles for your showing, they obliged. Standing in front of the little run-down theater, with a classic marquee and at least three bulbs burnt out, is Eamon. He wears a long gray, tweed coat with quintessential suede, elbow patches. That is the thing about him... he wears the clothes; they don't wear him. Everything he dresses his body in is like a second skin. It only makes him look that much more.... MORE! I'd ask if it was vintage, but I had a feeling that it was new and probably cost more than my entire month's rent.

When he sees me approaching, he throws down his smoke and stamps it out with his shiny shoe.

Brodi had a similar habit and wouldn't quit, no matter how often I pressed the issue. I didn't mind the smell at the time, I work in a bar after all, but it was the taste of it that bothers me.

Eamon immediately throws an arm around me. "You look like you're ready to help refuel at the next Formula One race."

My hand goes to my chest, mouth agape; I back out of his embrace. "I'll have you know that this is a jumpsuit and it's the epitome of fall fashion!" I can be a bit overzealous at times.

His amused look causes the green of his eyes to sparkle with mischief. Somehow, the sight of him fills in the tiny cracks of my heart, originating from my dishonesty with Andrea.

"Is that so? Well, I hope to see them next season on the runway, during fashion week. Now my interest has piqued! "Have you been?!"

He casually nodded, pushing his fists into his coat pockets. "I'm invited regularly; however, I rarely show."

I was in awe over this man's ability to have it all but not give a rat's ass unless it suited him. Sure, he was a walking billboard of designer labels and drove a teenage boy's wet dream of a sports car, but the more I got to know him the more he surprised me. In spite of his 'all business' persona at work, he can be quite sweet when he's away from it all. I can't fault him for wanting to "keep up appearances." Especially in a city like this, where people only seem to be impressed by how hard you work and how little sleep you get. The grind is a way of life, until life is taken away. With time, I hope Eamon's shell can fall away. I see slivers shining through the cracks, each time we're alone together.

At the box, I politely ask for subtitles during our show. Our tickets for the nine o'clock showing of *Lost Boys*, already had a queue full of other eager movie goers, including some couples hand-in-hand. I find myself suddenly looking for something to occupy my hands. As the line gradually moves forward, I celebrate silently as I remember my stylish jumper has pockets. I slide my hands on each side of me, thankful that they have a place to be.

In the lobby, Eamon notices me eyeing the candy display as we make our way to the theater three. Without a second thought, he diverts us over to the counter, dragging my hand from the safety of my pocket. I look down to find our hands joined together. I like how my hand feels in his.

"A box of chocolate clusters and sour candy for the lady." My lips purse. Odd choices. "Chocolate clusters were my brother's favorite," I inform him as he pays.

He hands me my box then proceeds to rip open his selected treat, rattling a handful into the palm of his hand, ahead of popping them into his mouth. "No kiddin'," he says with a mouth full of chocolate. Extending his bent arm, he escorts me to our assigned auditorium. Any previous smile is long gone; he seems more withdrawn than before.

Did I do something wrong?

We sit down front and center, nibbling on our candy, while waiting for the classic horror flick to start. A few teenagers sit behind us, as the theatre slowly starts to fill up. I could tell they were boys based on the different pitches in their tones, not quite settled with a deeper masculine voice yet. I also couldn't make out what they were saying.

The movie begins after a short preview, and the subtitles appear across the bottom of the screen. It makes it so much easier to follow along with the character's dialogue, especially when the actor is speaking "off screen." I look over at Eamon. He seems on edge, turning occasionally to glance back at the rambunctious adolescents behind us. Eventually, their words become loud enough for me to hear. The teens are booing and yelling for the staff to, "Turn off the stupid words at the bottom of the screen?!" This wouldn't be the first time I've had others complain about simple accommodations that cause no harm to them but make a world of difference for people like me.

I turn around to find three pimple-faced boys, tossing popcorn at one another, while taking turns hollering their distaste for literacy in a movie. They seem to notice me staring, which only makes their heckling worse. Insults get thrown around like: "Deaf people shouldn't come here, and no one goes to the movies to read a book!" I never saw Eamon leave his seat, but in an instant, he had two out of three teens by the scruff of their shirt, raising them off their seats. The other teen looks as though he may cry, immediately apologizing right as the theatre staff show up. Calmly, Eamon explained the situation. I believe he even dropped his last name just as the manager approaches. The uniformed man apologizes profusely. Permanently banning all three of the boys from ever stepping foot in their establishment again. The manager even offers us complimentary tickets for the whole year, but we kindly decline. It wasn't their fault some parents didn't teach their kids not to be blatant assholes.

When we finally sit back down, he turns to me. "I'm sorry. I shouldn't have allowed them to say those things to you. It should have never gotten that far." He seems disappointed in himself. He's so protective. I take his hand and weave our fingers together between the two seats.

"You can't control what happens, Eamon, only how you respond to it."

He nods and gives a tight-lipped smile. His emerald eyes are duller than before. My awareness of the man holding my hand in the dark causes pictures to form in my mind. I imagine him in tactical gear, reaching his gloved hands over to me, he begins unbuttoning my jumper. Exploring my body, much like his masked version did, just days ago. My fantasy has Eamon doing this to me... in a room full of people, no less. Yet... he isn't making any moves to do so. In fact, he wasn't quite as *touchy-feely* without his stalker gear. I mean... sour candies, really? It must be him. His large hand all but swallows mine, as I spend more time recalling the man that was previously between my legs, than I do watching vampires reign over Santa Carla.

It's a cult classic, but I just can't buy how every problem is instantly solved by killing the head vampire. There has to be some kind of residual issues. I mean the character Lucy, likely has trauma!

We watched the rest of the movie without interruptions although at one point, I could have sworn I saw a tear stream down Eamon's face. Maybe it's all in my head, but each time I'm alone with him, it's as if I understand myself better. After the movie concludes, I invite Eamon to my go-to place, Benny's. Sometimes, the easiest way to get to the center of a person is by sharing a slice of pie.

In the brightly lit diner over a large helping of cherry dessert, Eamon and I take turns exchanging nuances from our childhood. He grew up in Boston, just like me, however he wishes he had more say when it came to his career path. Between forkfuls of compote and crust, he tells me about his college years. That was one stark difference between us. Even though my parents weren't thrilled about me pursuing fashion, they never decided for me. I'm sure it wasn't easy, putting my brother and I through school. Eamon briefly touches on his mother and how her death created a rift in his family. That… I can understand. My parents up and left after my brother passed. We weren't a picture-perfect family; they worked a lot and relied heavily on Theo to watch over me. My relationship with them has only grown more obscure over the last three years. I got lost in my own head, wondering if my parents leaving was because there was nothing left to keep them here. I always thought Theo was the *golden* child but abandoning me nearly validated it.

As if he could sense that the conversation had become too heavy, he redirects to 'favorite food stops around the city.' We agreed to disagree about who serves the best lobster roll while it was an unequivocal, *yes*, that we both root for the Red Sox. I like how his eyes had little lines at their edges when he laughed. Honestly, I don't think I've ever heard as much as a chuckle out of him, before now. It's as if he's a different person outside of The Black Sheep. This side of Eamon is nice. It feels like a warm hug in this cold city. Would it be strange to say that being around him reminds me of hanging out with my brother? Just fewer noogies and fart jokes. I shake the unsettling comparison from my brain, as we exit the diner. Out of things to say at this point, I find myself standing before him, yearning for a more physical connection.

"You're incredible, Cindel. I truly enjoy getting away from all of my responsibilities and spending time with you."

My idol hands fiddle with the seam on the pockets of my romper, as I wait on pins and needles for this gorgeous man to make some kind of move. A man who is very much, NOT my brother, I remind myself.

Clearly, he can read my thoughts, because he places his hands on each of my hips and pulls me forward. My cheeks warm over the close proximity to him. Towering over me, I look up into his evergreen eyes. They resemble closer to a solitary rain cloud in a park, vaguely their usual brighter color.

Eamon leans down, while I tilt my head up and to the side. He hovers just a breath above me, as if thinking better of it. I hold my breath for what feels like minutes. Finally, he pushes the last inch, slamming his mouth on mine. It's light and sweet at first, tasting like the tangy fruit we just shared. Then as the kiss deepens, his tongue forges its way into my mouth. Exploring. Curious. Notes of whiskey and smoke invade my taste. The kiss feels new... exotic. He is a force.

I wish for Eamon to be able to move toward what he wants in life, and I think I'd like to be one of those motives. Perhaps it's because things are new or he feels vulnerable without a mask, but something feels... off. As if he's void of the desire, he had for me just days ago.

We just kiss, nothing more. He even tries to walk me the rest of the way to my building, but I tell him I'm good. There's a possibility that Andrea is waiting for me. She could see us walking up the street from our apartment window. I'm 'supposed' to be alone. He kisses the top of my hand. "Goodnight."

Our apartment is dark, aside from the crimson glow of Thelma's light. I soundlessly make my way to the bathroom undetected. Could Andrea be asleep already? It was pretty late, considering she was an early riser. My lipstick is smeared, and Eamon's smell still clings to me, so I opt for a shower before bed.

Putting my hearing aids on the sink, I climb into the shower and briskly wash. The mirror wasn't even fully covered from the steam, so I knew I wasn't long. I slipped on a robe and wrap my hair up in a towel before making my way to the kitchen for a glass of water.

I startle when I notice a shadowed figure sitting at the table. Taking in a sharp, choked breath, I can feel the sound resonant from my throat.

The figure reaches for the switch on the wall, illuminating the table in a vague wicker-like cast from the pendant light above. Andrea's intense stare and clenched jaw keep me fixed in place. All at once, she begins to move her hands erratically, mouth moving a mile a minute, but it's hushed.

I regarded her, pointing to my ear, as to indicate... I'm not wearing my hearing aids. The onslaught of her voiceless words pauses. Then she proceeds to speak in sign language.

You lied to me. She motions forcefully with her hands. *You were out with Eamon!* Each movement is meant to feel sharp; her hands are quick with razor sharp precision. *You're putting yourself in harm's way.*

When she is done, I take a moment to consider my friend. The things she's said to me over the past two weeks... how she claims to care about me, but I know one thing. Actions speak louder than words, but her words have cut me! She's the one who's never around lately. Always running off to work or whatever she actually does. Right now, I'm struggling to understand who's right here. Our once solid friendship has been reduced to a pile of rubble, and I'm the only one left to pick through the pieces.

I recede within myself, feeling cornered, wanting desperately to hold onto any sense of self I have left. I repeat internally; *I deserve better*. Eventually, I faced the scrutiny and signed back with just as much punch as she gave me.

I'm so sorry you're jealous. Worried I have someone new in my life. I'm not apologetic and I know my delivery made its mark.

Her lip curls while her brows narrow. The kind of look that someone would give you if you just spat in their meal.

Despite her scowl, she remains seated. Her body may be disciplined, but I know her mind is stuck. Solely focused on my last message. She's always shown how she feels on her face, without even saying a word. When she signs back, it's filled with trepidation; her muscles flex with each gesture. Like the weight of the letter or word is too great. *I'm not jealous. I'm worried about you.* She pauses briefly, taking deep slow breaths as if this is all laborious. *Please...* she continues. *Stop seeing this man. He's dangerous! You're NOT safe!* When she signs "not," by closing her fist and brushing her thumb under her chin... her head shakes left to right. Eyes red and glistening.

I don't bother signing... I yell, "If he's so dangerous, give me one good reason why I shouldn't see him!"

Her lips tighten and she blinks. Nothing more. Unwilling to explain herself. Once again, I say what her ears are only able to hear, but I can feel them burning through me.

"What aren't you telling me, Andrea?!"

Her face is like stone, only her eyelids flutter.

I'm confused and hurt, but then I realize something is missing. Shadows across the space between us settle just as I catch on. The roses... where are the roses? I narrow my gaze at my 'once best friend.'

Where are the flowers from Eamon? I sign, feeling the slap of contact from hand to hand as I scrutinize her every tell.

Andrea's arms cross, she leans back in her chair, and her eyes narrow. Still silence consumes the space, although my ears begin to ring out in protest over the lack of respect. Understood. Even if she did have a reason, she's unwilling to give it to me. I tightened the strings of the robe, abandoning why I was in the kitchen in the first place. Then sign one final message before closing myself in my room.

How about you butt out of my life? I turn and stomp loudly toward my bedroom and I do just that... slam the door on this conversation. I crawl in bed, the only light peeking beneath my door from the living space.

I see her shadow shift around the room as if she's pacing. Slowly the shadow grows, only light in the far corners, as if she's positioned right outside my door. Is she coming to talk to me? Knock? I couldn't hear her anyways. Just like that, the shadow narrows, moving farther away until the light source is turned off. Once I know she is closed in her room for the night, I connect my phone and hearing aids to their chargers. Finally, I set my alarm. I had an important errand to run before work tomorrow.

Reviewing the address within the envelope again, I discovered that I can make the walk without having to bother with the city's transit system. The location was within business... well a P.O. Box to be exact. A pack and ship store, where people can purchase Bubble Wrap, stamps, and drop off packages. They even have a wall of shiny, keyed mailboxes just like in our cramped apartment building lobby. As I scroll through the photos online, I have a vague recollection of accompanying Andrea there once. I never understood why she wanted to go all the way there, instead of just dropping her letter in the blue mail bin on our street.

To my surprise, I managed to fit the entire collection of snarky, embroidery hoops into one large box. I know the older woman said I could "take my time" delivering them, but she overpaid, and I felt obligated to get them to her asap. I wonder what she plans to do with all of them.

It was a strange exchange; she already had more than enough cash and the address ready for me, as if she knew I'd accept. No "attention to" or name was included on the slip of paper, so I hope an employee could shed some light on who pays for the account.

I have two unread messages on my phone. One from *It's Eamon Actually* and the other from *The Stalker*. Both were slightly different, but they shared the same underlying tone. *Are you okay?* I was exhausted and not in the mood to explain in detail, so I settle for a thumbs up to my bipolar man... or men.

Although I had some initial trouble falling asleep last night, I felt slightly more energized this morning. There hasn't been a single trace of my grumpy roommate so far. Even though I told myself it was a new day, the sour feeling of last night's interaction carried over. Our once effortless friendship teetered near toxic, causing the taste of bile to crawl dangerously close to my mouth.

I attempt to tamp down this sick feeling with something besides acidic coffee. Bread! Some kind of simple carb. With a full mug and slice in hand, I shuffle to a seat by the window, watching with vague curiosity as people bustle about the streets below. In three large bites I finish the square of whole wheat, hopeful it will keep the queasy feeling at bay. My friendship with

Andrea used to be so easy. We've been as thick as thieves since the first time we met.

A knock on the apartment door startles me from my thoughts, causing coffee to spill onto my hand. "Oww, fuck shit!" I carefully place the mug down on a side table and rush to the sink to run cold water over the scalded area.

The persistent visitor on the other side knocks again.

"Be right there!" I grab a tea towel, run it under the faucet before ringing it out and wrapping my hand.

Hand still throbbing, I peer through the peephole to find a middle-aged man in uniform on the other side. He appears to be an officer with the Boston PD. Were Andrea and I too loud last night? But we barely spoke! Did the neighbor just below us really call the cops over my stomping?

I open the door and greet the unexpected officer. "Hello…" He assesses me. Glancing from the plaid towel over my hand, then back up to my face.

"Miss Mari?"

I nod.

"I'm Officer Kent, with the Boston Police."

I nodded again, still unsure why he's here.

"May I come in?"

I look over my shoulder remembering that I'm alone, then turn back to face the man in uniform. Chewing on my lip, I reply, "Umm, I think I'd prefer right here." I didn't mean it to sound so meek.

He gives a curt nod in response.

I stepped out into the hallway, leaving our apartment door ajar.

"I'd like to ask you a couple of questions about your time working at the Star Mart off Washington Street."

My heart begins to pick up pace, like a slow jog transitioning into a sprint.

"I understand you worked there for an extended period of time," he continues.

Shit. Why does he want to talk about that place? Then it hits me. What Mairead told me. The question I've asked my stalker multiple times, but he never gives me a direct answer. *Did you kill my manager, Craig?* I quit slash "got fired" right before he turned up with an earbud down his throat!

Is this… an interrogation? Do I need a lawyer? I all but stopped taking in oxygen. Act normal. Calm down! I shout at myself. You didn't do anything! Although, I may have an inkling as to what happened to that vile human.

I give him a tight-lipped smile and dip my head a few times, to indicate I was listening and not having an existential crisis on the spot. Fuck. I probably resemble a bobble head. Stop nodding!

"Are you aware that your manager," he pulls a notepad from his breast pocket and flips a few pages in, "Mr. Craig Moore... was found dead on the morning of October 20th, at your previous place of employment?"

I'm still as a statue.

"The PD has been investigating the incident, following leads, as all evidence is pointing to homicide. I'd like to go over your time working there and how you left on poor terms."

See! This is why I hate cops! Always thinking the worst of the guiltless! I feel like I am in a glass fishbowl, trapped within a translucent prison. All I can do is watch helplessly as the situation unfolds. The questions start off easily enough.

"How long did you work at Star Mart? Did you work with Mr. Moore often?"

Then the line of questioning turned.

"How was your relationship with your previous manager? What led to your release from the position?"

Of course they would think I was fired! Each question is more invasive than the next, eventually leading him to ask, "How was your last interaction with Craig Moore?"

I attempt to steady my heart. Taking a deep breath in, ahead of letting it out slowly through my lips. My shirt is wet from where the saturated towel still rests against me. I know this officer already came here knowing all the answers to his questions, but I'm forced to obey regardless. Calmly as I can muster, I tell him everything that happened, including the sexual advances Creepy Craig made on me. I also informed him that 'I quit,' not the other way around.

He jots down notes, making noises like, "mhmm," then glancing up from his notepad from time to time. The pen was moving, but I swear it seems more like doodling than forming actual letters or words. Mid-sentence, he cuts me off.

"I think that's all I need, Miss Mari. Thank you for your time." At the point he begins to walk down the hall, while I recede back into the safety of my apartment, when he turns suddenly. "Do you have both of your earbuds?" Like a punch to the gut, that uneasy feeling returns despite the toast. "A coworker of yours said you were listening to music the day you stopped working there. They also said you only wore one. Is this because of..." He gestures to his own ear drawing a swirl to represent what I can only assume is him mimicking a hearing aid. A wave of frustration and worry crashes through me.

Can a fish drown in water, because that's exactly how I feel at that moment! I arm myself with a half breath before responding, "Yes. I was listening to music, and I still have both in *my* set." My voice shook, but I knew the best deceit came from half-truths, because I did in fact have MY full set. I just didn't disclose that I also had a single earbud, delivered by a possible murdering stalker, where its matching pair most likely resided deep in the throat of my predatory ex-manager. The officer studies me for long moments. What he was looking for, I'm not sure, but I wasn't going belly up, despite his tactic of 'shaking the tank.'

"Very well." He surrenders. I try not to sway over the quick shift in his demeanor, suddenly sounding chipper. "Enjoy your day, Miss Mari." Just as abruptly as he came, he was gone again.

I slip back inside and lock the door. Temporary relief washes over me, but deep down... it was tortuous. So much has changed over the past couple weeks, I couldn't make sense of anything. I may have fended off drowning today, but I was a fish out of water. Fighting to survive in an unforgiving world.

TWENTY-FOUR

CINDEL

About a twenty-minute walk in the wrong direction of the bar, is a small postage store with a hanging metal sign that reads: *Mail Haven*. Bronze mailboxes line one side of the establishment, embossed with numbers and individual key slots for each one. Customers could easily come in, grab their mail and leave, all without interacting with a single soul.

An older gentleman with an inky black comb-over and orange embroidered polo greets me upon entering.

"Hello, hello, hello. What you here for?"

Bilingual got it. The man seemed wide-eyed, almost shocked I was there. I hope this is the right place. I gave a polite wave before stepping forward, placing my box on the counter. Hastily, he puts on his readers as I hold up the slip of paper with the address, from the lady's envelope. Holding the note much farther out than necessary, he finally speaks.

"Ah, yes. I know, I know, I know."

He scurries to his computer, types on the keyboard, and a label begins to print from a machine, off to the side.

"I'm sorry, but do you happen to know who this box is for?" I smile very sweetly.

"No," he replies without a hint of warmth.

"It would be wonderful to thank the person who purchased such a substantial amount from me."

He fetches the label, peels the sticker, and slaps it on. Before I have a chance to see what the white rectangle says, he transfers the box to a back counter; farther than any pair of human eyes could possibly make out.

"No," he replies again, before returning to the task of folding and forming cardboard boxes.

I mirror the man's position on the opposite side of the counter. "Please."

He shakes his head and gives a slight eye roll. "No. We mail drop for customer. Forward to new place. Customer no pick up here."

I understand what he meant now. He simply didn't have the information. The new address would be another courier service.

"Oh. Okay. Well, thank you anyhow," I reply.

The steadfast shop owner has no idea who this client is. The underhanded business most likely doesn't cater to the average Joe. Who would need that level of anonymity? I doubt the man would even tell me if he did know.

Before The Black Sheep opens, Brittany and I use step ladders to hang spider webs from the pendulum lights above the bar. We pull them across and down, stretching them to the beer taps below. The new girls, Leslie and Maya, work on covering the wall sconces in off-white gauzy fabric, making the already dimly lit atmosphere increasingly darker. We work together to set up life-sized skeletons at the end of the bar, complete with top hats and copper mugs in hand. The place looks qualified to host the annual Halloween Bar Bash. I have a fondness for the holiday. Looking forward to everyone's creative costumes and eating enough candy to make myself ill the following day. This year, I have my costume ready on time. No need to pull an all-nighter with my sewing machine.

I was so caught up drawing a cauldron on the chalkboard, I didn't realize Eamon and Connor had arrived until they both came out of the backroom. Eamon stumbled just past the threshold. Appearing more like a newborn giraffe than his usual poised self. Was he... drunk? I mean, he did own a bar. It wasn't foreign to see a whiskey in his hands. Even if he went from *Mr. Neat* to *It's Eamon actually,* I've never actually seen him inebriated.

Connor went out the front door, mumbling about the impossible task of finding candy the day before Halloween. I was relieved to see Eamon made it to a chair, plopping down next to the skeletons at the high counter.

"Whiskey!" He slaps the countertop.

The girls and I must all be thinking the same thing. Looking between one another, no one makes a move to serve our already drunk boss.

"Alright then." He does a lazy sweep of the room before he leans forward, extending his body across the bar and grabs the first bottle available. It wasn't his usual top shelf whiskey, but he didn't seem to mind.

I steal glances as I finish writing the specials on the board.

Eamon tips the bottle back, not bothering with a glass. His gaze bounces around the room, looking at nothing and no one in particular. There were no two ways about it; he was blitzed and at the rate he was going, he would need a lift home, a cold shower, and a good night's rest.

I try to mind my own business as my boss drains the cheap spirits, but he wasn't just my boss anymore. Over the past few weeks, I've come to know him on a deeper level.

Brittany appears beside me, "should we text Connor to get back here?"

I shake my head, not wanting to undermine Eamon.

"Cindel!" Eamon beckons me over to him, pulling out the stool to his side when I arrive. "Did you enjoy yourself last night?" Leaning back slightly to face me. He can't seem to focus on any one place for long.

"Yes. I did. Thank you for taking me out." I smooth my skirt down, unsure how to phrase the next words.

The glass container is nearly empty at this point; he totters the bottle from side to side on its base. "Did you know… I knew your brother, Theo."

What? He never mentioned anything before. We've been on two dates; I've brought Theo up a number of times and now is when he tells me this?

"What…?" I finally voice. "How did you know him?"

His eyes are glassy. Truely, it was a wonder Eamon can even sit up straight.

"Remember at the diner, I told you about not even having a choice in my major? Well… I went to Boston College."

I finally take the seat next to him, feeling like my knees may buckle over this news.

"You… met my brother at college?"

He nods. "Didn't like him at first. Thought he was too cocky for his own good. One of those 'do-gooders' who wanted to chase a story until the truth was printed in black and white, for the world to see."

That was Theo. It sounds like he *actually* knew him. My brother graduated from Boston College with a major in Communications. He was working toward a career in investigative journalism. My eyes sting when I contemplate where he'd be today.

"I graduated the same year as him, but in business. It was the course my parents chose for me. Theo and I connected after graduation. Our paths crossed and we found common ground. We—" He takes the last swig from the bottle in his hand. "We became close… right before he died."

Why didn't I know any of this? My heart fractures over the fact that there are parts of Theo's life that I will just never know. Instead of asking something, I just sit there. Staring dumbfounded at Eamon, like he's just handed me an unconventionally shaped jigsaw piece, for which I have no idea what the final image is supposed to be. What am I supposed to do with this?

Eamon sways slightly as if he's been set adrift on a boat. All at once his flush face focuses on me, and he smiles widely. He's absolutely plastered. If I don't ask something soon, he might just blackout right here. My mind was teeming with questions. Shit. What do I ask? Did my brother seem happy? Do

YOU believe my brother died from a drug-overdose? Do you know something I don't know?

Eamon's blinks are becoming longer, so I blurt out.

"Why didn't you tell me you know my brother from the beginning?!"

Slowly he blinks, his eyes soften, and he puts an elbow on the bar to hold his head up in his hand. "You have the same eyes." His voice is barely above a whisper.

Without warning, Connor appears next to us and tosses a five-pound bag of candy on the counter. "Come on, big guy, let's get you home." He wraps an arm around Eamon's middle, whisking him off the stool and toward the exit. I watch as he stumbles out the door with help, turning back at me with a wistful look.

I was on autopilot. Like when you don't remember the walk from your apartment to your job, and now you're questioning if the last three cross walks had a person or a hand displayed, when you stepped off the curb. The entire shift was like that. I couldn't tell you what drinks I made, who I spoke to, or what my biggest tip was that night. All I could focus on was how Eamon knew Theo. How am I just learning this? This charming, handsome, mysterious, yet confusing man has so many surprising layers to him, I'm unsure if I'll ever reach his core. Will I like what I find? Does Eamon knowing Theo connect us somehow? Did my brother's death affect both of us? Eamon was not himself this evening, although only officially meeting him less than a month ago, doesn't exactly build confidence in me knowing him all that well. Does he usually get smashed on a weekday or was something bothering him? The date went well last night. Maybe it's his family or perhaps business troubles at the boxing club? Whatever the case, I am eager to learn more about Eamon and his past.

Theo and I would talk weekly on the phone when he moved out. Although, he's always been vague about his life in general. Aside from the one time he got suspended from school, he never had any serious issues. Rarely did he invite friends over and come to think of it... I don't remember him going on a single date when he was a teenager. One time in high school, my folks dropped me off at the movies to meet a boy. For a month, my brother teased me about my date looking like the character, Steve from Blue's Clues! If I was more private with my life... I could be settled down by now, happily wed to the guy in the green strips with a blue dog. Perhaps my brother was wise to keep some stuff to himself.

Theo made growing up easy when he was around. I felt like we talked a lot, but now I question if his conversations with me were on a superficial level. It sure didn't feel that way at the time. As children, we laughed over Sunday morning cartoons, physically wrestled over who got the last Oreo in the house, and told each other impossible fictional stories, within forts made of sheets and pillows. I cherish the fond memories we had. Sometimes thinking back to them hurts, because I feel robbed. Severed from creating more memories together.

The walk home is bitterly cold tonight. Pulling my coat closed tightly, I lift my hood to shield my face as hot tears rained freely. I cry when I'm mad or sad. However, this isn't a sorrowful cry. I'm livid. Pissed at Eamon for keeping things from me. Irate with Andrea because every interaction with her is instantly sour. Lastly, I'm resentful of my brother. For fucking dying and leaving me to face this life alone. He was more than just family. He was my teacher, my friend, and my hero. I miss him every goddamn day and I'm reckless for it.

The apartment may as well be a dim icebox. I adjust the thermostat once inside, with hopes of warming my fingers and toes soon. Thanks to the extra money from the unexpected sale on the street, I could finally bump the heat to 60°F.

As per usual, no sign of Andrea. Honestly, I didn't even care what she was up to. I change into warm flannel sleepwear then search the fridge for something that won't have me hugging a toilet in four hours flat. Disappointed by the cold options, I move onto the shelf of nonperishables, settling on a mason jar of pistachios for tonight's 'brinner.'

You know… the time between dinner and breakfast? It will catch on one day.

I peer into Thelma's tank, finding her nestled in her little fortress of solitude. She really loves that skull my brother added for her, all those years ago. The little spider was usually more active at night, so it was strange to see her cozy in the hide at this hour.

"Damn. I really need to freshen your substrate, girl." I made a mental note to swing by the pet store within the next week.

Precariously juggling my phone and the jar of seeds, I collapse onto the couch. Then, select the next episode in my marathon of *family drama with weapons*; pull the coffee table to the edge of my seat and begin shelling the green, tear-drop shaped fruits. I try to tell my body; this is good for you. I even said, "Mmmm," to convince myself, but it was no use. My stomach is in knots from thinking about what Eamon said.

After eating no more than a handful, I was done willing myself to 'nourish my body.' It did, however, keep my hands busy. Soon, I found myself with a pile of ivory-colored shells and a mound of uneaten pistachios. My stomach growls, unimpressed that I can play with food but not actually ingest it.

The phone vibrates next to me. I dust off my fingers and lifted the phone to check the notification.

The Stalker: Why did the pistachio get fired?

What? I jump up, immediately searching the dark street outside my window. No one's down there… but I know he can SEE me! Just in case, I pull the drapes closed. My phone vibrates again from the couch. Another message. I know it's him again.

The Stalker: It kept cracking up at work.

Is he? No! I type back.

Cindel: Was that a joke?

The Stalker: Yes.

Brodi thought he was a comedian, too. Most of his jokes were extremely inappropriate. Could he be…? No. Fuck that. Even if my stalker wasn't shielded by layers of Kevlar and cotton, I would still know it wasn't him. Brodi never took care of me the way that this man has. Once the crazy notion passes, I text back.

Cindel: Are you drunk?

The Stalker: Not currently.

At the beginning of my shift, Eamon was wasted. Has it been long enough for him to sober up? If my stalker is Eamon, then he should know the answer.

Cindel: How well did you know my brother?

While I wait for a response, I start counting how many seeds I cracked. *Cracking up at work.* I bit my bottom lip.

"Not funny." I declare to no one. Minutes go by. No response. One hundred and thirty-one shelled pistachios.

I put down my phone and paced the room. Pick up the device, still no response. This is maddening! Fine. I turn off the television, clean up and restore my uneaten 'brinner' on the living room table, then brush my teeth. After checking again for a response from *The Stalker*, I abandon any chance of "piece of mind" for today and crawl into bed.

"Watch me sleep for all I care!" I say within my darkened room. My body is tired, while my mind is restless. I try to readjust, elevate my head, put a pillow between my knees, but all I seem to do is toss and turn. Sleep doesn't welcome me. I even try playing games with myself, pretending the roaring in my ears is a swarm of crickets on a summer evening. The sound morphs into a school bell that rings incessantly. Counting sheep is pointless.

Sometime between three and four in the morning, the sandman finally accepts me. I dream of Theo. Not flashbacks but memories that 'could have been.' It was one of those realistic dreams. The ones that make you question whether or not this actually happened. Twinkling lights illuminate our Christmas tree, while the carnage of wrapping paper and presents lay strewn throughout the room. Laughing echoes in the distance, and I move toward it. Like a movie playing for me, I observe as our family gathers around a table filled with delicious holiday fare. Everyone is so happy. Laughing and talking. Just watching them was enough to warm my heart. Theo left the room briefly, only to return with a silver platter, which he lays in the center of the dining table. Everyone looks at one another smiling, excited for the feast ahead. I wish I could stay within this moment for the rest of my days. Theo lifts the tray's lid to unveil the main dish. It wasn't ham or turkey, but a skull. Everyone gasped at first, but then they started to chuckle. Upon closer inspection I could tell the skull was not real. Its surface decorated with tiny chips of paint and black outlines. Unaware that something was within, I jumped back when a tarantula came out of its eye! Everyone roared louder... Mom... Dad... but not Theo. That's when I notice he's changed. His eyes now black. Hollowed voids where his blue eyes should have been.

I startle awake from the vibration of the alarm on my phone. My body is overheated. Sticking to the sheets from the strange delusion. The whole room feels warm. Shit. The heat was on all night. I pull myself from my sweat covered bed and immediately head for a shower.

Once dressed, I head to the kitchen.

Andrea is sitting at the table staring at a bottle of wine adorned with a ribbon around its neck.

"Little early for a drink," I state dryly, walking toward the sink for a glass of water.

She stands and thrusts the bottle into my arms. "It's for you actually. From your darling Eamon."

I examine the tag on the bottle of expensive French wine.

I'm sorry. Please allow me to make it up to you by making dinner.
- E.

The door closes to Andrea's room before I'm able to utter a word. Well, this sure adds fuel to the already blazing fire.

It's a sweet gesture but I've told him before… I don't drink. I'm inclined to look past Eamon's drunk transgressions and poor selection of apology gift, if only to spend more time with him. Even if the driving factor was to learn more about my brother, I still enjoy my time with Eamon.

Looking from the wine to the big calendar in our apartment, I'm reminded that today is the best day of the year. Halloween! I consider for a brief moment, striding over to Andrea's door and knocking, but I didn't want to start off my favorite holiday with an argument.

In fact, I didn't feel like hanging around here for a moment longer than necessary. I grab my costume for this evening, a coat, something essential from the freezer; shove everything in my bag and head out.

It was the perfect day to feed the ducks in the park. In the middle of the Public Garden is a large pond. Most of the benches are full, but I am fortunate to find a seat in the sun on the east side of the lake. Soon, this body of water will be mostly frozen, causing birds and other feathered friends to fly south for the winter. Oh, how I hated the cold. The holiday season always coincides with brutal, cutting temperatures. I sometimes wish I could leave like the wealthy do. Go down to Florida and soak up the sun, only returning to this place once its frozen conditions have melted away.

Ducks make infinite circles, quaking merrily in the water, while some dunk their heads, kicking their legs to the sky. I cherish this time. It's even more enjoyable if you bring a bag of frozen peas with you. That's their favorite! Many park-goers have the common misconception that you should bring bread for the ducks. When in actuality it lacks nutritional value; unnecessarily filling their belly to the point that they forgo searching for *real* food. A quick internet search is all it takes. Then everyone would have the proper "quack snack!"

I was in stitches when I learned that Andrea is petrified of anything with wings. For being someone who is incredibly resilient, I was shocked when I witnessed her take cover over a pigeon who flew too close to our campus.

Brodi wasn't a fan of feeding the ducks either. He complained it was lame, in turn spending his time scrolling on his phone while I distributed peas alone. So, this has become a solo activity.

I started coming here after I lost my brother. It was cathartic. I needed it. Time away from condolences and people who expected me to "talk through it." Better than therapy. It was here, among the ducks, that I also decided to swear off drugs and alcohol. Even though I couldn't fathom that Theo would ever want to take his own life, I still made the promise. More for him than myself. "Use this as a lesson and keep going." The words ingrained in me since I was little. Now, whenever I'm feeling overwhelmed or depressed, I make my way to the park… frozen veg in tow.

Over the years, I started recognizing some ducks. Even naming a few. The one with the janky wing and black feathered tail is Filber. The two white ducks that sound like they're laughing are Betty and Wilma, and last but not least is the loudest duck. It has extra plumage around its head and is always squawking incessantly for more peas. Never fully satisfied with anything it's given. That one was dubbed, Brodi. Sometimes I ask myself if there was anything I could have done differently. He was the one that came onto me after all… but as time progressed, he just didn't seem to want to be with me as much. Always had something better to do. Like putting in extra hours at Rick's or meeting buddies for a drink after work. When he started another job, I barely ever saw him! Stupid boxing scene turned him into a different person. I wonder if Brodi ever went to The Bay Boxing Club that Eamon runs? It's not like his club is the only boxing place in town. The possible parallel is laughable.

My mind just keeps folding in on itself, like an endless origami that never transforms into a swan or frog. Thinking about a solitary issue is impossible. Every painful thought eventually doubles. Soon, I'm so ensnared in a weave of thoughts; I can't seem to navigate myself back to the beginning.

Once the bag of peas is empty and the rolling trills of ducks become distant, I head into work early. Tonight is the bar's bash. I'm sure there's something I can do to prepare. There was a time not too long ago that the idea of isolation seemed scary. Now flying solo seems like a luxury I will never reach. Between Eamon and my stalker, who may be one in the same, I've had little time to experience detachment. I'm not trying to be bleak; in fact, I feel wanted. Confused, yes, but I know he's watching, and I don't think I'm ready for it to stop.

TWENTY-FIVE

IN THE SHADOWS

Tonight, the bar is having its annual Halloween Bash. At first, I was worried I wouldn't even make it, since everyone was still held up in a meeting about the "Lombardi problem." Though I don't care much for parties, I do appreciate being able to conceal my identity from a certain someone at the bar. At least for a little longer. Cindel is still unsure of exactly who I am, which makes this evening all the more fun.

The Black Sheep is already packed with slutty fairies, pathetic super-heroes, and an egregious number of green faces that could be either turtle fighters or swamp ogres. This wasn't even half the people wanting to spend their night here, as a line snakes from the entrance of the door to the deli around the corner. Everyone is in costume, including the staff. No one pays me any mind as I easily maneuver between dancing bodies to the beat of "Somebody's Watching Me," all while looking for my mark. I wasn't here for the atmosphere nor to drink, although the music was hilariously on point. No, I came for her.

Two of the songs I've sent her so far were more of a warning. Although I didn't directly tell her what the message was, I'm hoping her subconscious uses caution, because both the songs, *Loser* and *Creep* are about me. She's already confused and overwhelmed, but she's figuring out things faster than I ever anticipated. I'll give her everything she could ever possibly need. All in good time.

For now, I was laying out each piece, one by one. It didn't take long until I finally laid eyes on her. My jaw clamped so tight, I thought I might crack a tooth.

She was mostly covered compared to the other more risqué costumes on the floor. Cindel expertly balances a tray of toxic green cocktails, garnished with candy gummy worms. I watch as she struts back to the bar top in pinstripe pants, a brimmed fedora, suspenders, and a white dress shirt open so low, I could see the edges of her breasts and the top of her navel. What the hell was she wearing? Was she some kind of old timey banker?

Her playful smile is a jolt of electricity to my already shortened fuse, finally allowing my jaw to relax, despite my disapproval of wandering eyes on what's mine.

She pushes back her long brown waves behind her ear, and I see it. The little white earbud. Good girl. Each time I interact with her, she's wound up wearing it more.

The way the shadows play in the decorated room makes me nearly invisible from my position. Pulling out my phone, I easily connect to the personal device in her ear; playing her another carefully chosen song. **Radiohead –** **"Karma Police"** begins to play, moving the progress bar along my screen as I watch her expression morph from carefree to attentive.

Her eyes widen as she starts to scan the room.

My face aches with how big my smile is under my cover. She's looking for me. It takes her nearly half of the song, but she spots me. I'm in a far-off corner of the bar, leaning against the wall. Her eyes become slits. Come to *the piper* little one. Dressed the same as the first time I made myself known, tactical gear and all, I'm thankful for the bulky attire. I could already feel myself growing stiff beneath the thick material of my pants, as she nears, recalling how I buried one of my devices inside her. God, she's so fucking beautiful.

As she stalks toward me, the rhythm perfectly coincides with her pace. Like the source music in a movie, she's aware she plays a part in all of this. When Cindel finally reaches me, she stops only a few strides away. Her wordless, assessing stare feels like ropes, wrapping and pulling tighter. I can't help but drink her in.

Stepping forward, her head falls back, allowing me to appreciate the view from above. An ivory valley of skin. Too bare for others to see. The room is alive but there's stillness between us. No words needed at this moment. I surely didn't plan on speaking. This wasn't the place for two people to have a conversation anyhow; it's way too loud in here. How does she tolerate all this noise on a regular basis? I want... no, I need to be alone with her.

Not wasting a moment, I take her by the hand. She doesn't object nor pull away. Cindel comes willingly, just like I knew she would. I lead her down the small hallway and into the women's bathroom. She follows obediently, clenching my gloved hand tightly until we're within the vacant room. I lock the door and take my time to fully appreciate the goddess in front of me.

Her buttoned shirt is just barely doing the job of covering her chest. I'm overcome with desire. Jealous when I realize just how many other men have looked upon her this evening. My muscles have become rigid. I have a cardinal need to not only shield but protect this woman from anyone who may mean her harm. Her eyes search mine, although she can't exactly see them through the rainbow iridium goggles.

As if on cue, she realizes what I'm ogling at. Cindel crosses her arms, blocking the wide valley between her modest breasts. How I'd love to run my tongue between them.

"Why didn't you answer my question last night?"

My eyes travel back up to her face. Her words are clipped, brow furrowed, and stare narrowed. I reached for my phone, bringing up the conversation I had with her, before turning to show her the screen with our thread of messages.

She looks from my masked face to the screen and back again.

I hold up one finger slowly, then another, finally the third.

"Shit." She drops her arms from their barricaded position and begins to pace. "Okay, fine! I asked three questions. It's a new day now! Okay, first question. Were you close with my brother?" Her innocent eyes make it so difficult not to simply give her an answer.

That's not why I've come here tonight. Am I being selfish? Yes, but this girl makes me feel things I never thought possible.

Frustrated by my lack of response, Cindel goes for the lock on the door. I'm trained faster than most. In one swift motion, I pin her arms behind her back before she even realizes what's happened. With one hand, I'm able to hold her tiny wrists, freeing up the other hand to explore my little princess. Her hat topples to the ground, unable to remain on her head as she tries to look up to me.

A throaty growl reverberates from her, as she wiggles and mutters profanities. Like a wild animal caught in a trap. Unable to resist the initial lure. Her fate is sealed. She never tells me no, so I persist. I sense she's conflicted… but so am I.

Despite it all, I've vigilantly been swimming against a current… focusing on getting what I've wanted for far too long. On the outside this may seem *wrong but* damn the consequences. Fuck what I'm told to do. She belongs to me. Always has… always will.

I tap my boot gently between her inner ankles, indicating I need her feet parted. Like the good girl I know she wants to be for me, she widens her stance.

My lower jaw is sore with the perpetual grin I've had since she started searching for me. Once again, I'm thankful for being shielded. Her body doesn't lie, chest rising and falling so quickly, I'm more than aware I've awoken something in her. She grumbles softly yet never protests.

Facing the mirror, she watches with feigned curiosity, as I take a gloved finger into my mouth and pull off the glove in one swift motion. Much harder of a task with a balaclava on, but I need to feel her flushing skin beneath my touch. Like someone seeking water in a desert, eager to quench my hunger.

With my ungloved hand, I skate past the useless shirt and take her warm breast within my palm. My fingers move to caress her nipple when I realize she has pasties on. Now that just won't do.

I release hold of her wrists, then spin her around so that her perfect ass is pressed against the counter instead of my groin. Her hands find the sink counter behind us; our bodies face one another. Finally, I press against her. Cindel is so small compared to me, but watching her as long as I have, I know she has the ability to be fierce despite her stature. Her pupils dilate and I relish the moment when she realizes I'm hard. I want to drown in those sparkling blue pools of hers.

Impatiently, I unfasten the belt clips of the suspenders, before untucking and pulling the dress shirt from her body. Her shape is flawless. Perky, natural, just the right amount for my hand. No fake shit. Huge knocks don't do it for me. I'm already envisioning what they would look like when they bounce. How fast can I make them move?

Her chest continues to surge. As rapid as the tempo of the muffled music that plays beyond the walls. I wonder if she can sense how fast my heartbeat thunders behind my rib cage. Superior to any marbled Grecian statue, I trace a finger from the notch of her neck, slowly trailing down to just above her waistband. Cindel's still, quiet form watches me with such intensity. It is hard to keep myself from spinning her back around, pulling down her pants, and driving into her. I can't rush this.

Reaching around her to the faucet, I turn on the cool water and soak my hand. Dripping palm, I cup each breast one at a time, saturating the pasty that keeps her hidden from me. Rogue droplets trickle down her stomach, before disappearing beneath her covered lower half.

I never expected to envy water like this.

Removing my other glove, Cindel views our reflection as I carefully peel off each adhesive covering, revealing tiny pink nipples. I take her into my hands, rubbing soft circles around them with the pad of my thumbs. Gradually, I change the direction of my teasing fingers, rocking her nipples back and forth with just enough force to make hard peaks. Her mild discontent turns into soft moans, tumbling from her now slack jaw. I want to tell her how beautiful she is like this. How turned on she was making me, but I couldn't. The best I could do was show her.

I reach around her body, retrieving one of her slender hands and position it over my cock. It felt good to have her finally touch me. Even if it was over thick material.

Her eyes bounce between my hidden face and the area her hand now rests. If she starts rubbing, I don't know how long I could last.

"Is it my turn?" She coos.

Fuck, this woman is more than I could have ever dreamt up; I'm not religious but she is my deity.

She drops to her knees in that bar bathroom, bare breasted, looking up at me for what I can only assume as permission.

If Cindel knew what I kept from her, she would probably stab me. However, if she looked like this while doing it, I'd let her.

All it took was one nod from me, and she was unfastening the button to my pants, then lowering the zipper. The way tiny whines spill from her as I massaged her nipples, or even her actions, reveals just how eager she is. Despite the material of my pants pulled back, the belt lies against my lower belly, still fastened, as my cock stands at attention for her. I was thankful for my choice to go commando this evening.

Tentatively she licks her lips, as I collect her silky chestnut hair in my hand and tug gently for her to move closer to me. Her mouth opens, tongue slightly jutting out; she starts working on teasing the tip, popping on and off, causing my lower spine to tingle with pleasure. Perfectly happy with just the head being played with, but then she goes further.

Not progressively, but all at once she dives forward, takin all of me in her mouth. The sensation in my lower back turns into fire! Wanting desperately to touch her, play with her nipples, which I know are still rock hard, but too far.

Instead, I let my hands dive into her velvet strands. I thought I'd lose myself right then. The head of my dick petting the back of her throat. She moves, repeating the motion, but not even letting the tip leave the warmth of her mouth. The delicious sounds she makes as she bobs on me cause my vision to blur.

Cindel leans back for a moment and glances up at me. Little ribbons of spit connect from the head of my cock to her moist, pouty lips. Fucking glorious. God, this woman will have me cumming faster than a pubescent teen with his first nudie magazine.

Her lip tugs upward in one corner. Is she teasing me?

Not allowing her to get off track, I give her hair a little tug, egging her on. It's cute that she thinks we're done here. I'm sure her jaw is tired, but I plan to fuck her mouth until I explode.

She leans in, taking me deep into her throat before pulling back. This time she meticulously sucks and licks the head of my cock, all while her hand works my wet shaft. My legs feel like Jell-O. The pressure building at my core, a heat raging to escape. I'm so fucking close. My hips jerk involuntarily.

A loud knock comes from the other side of the door. "HEY! Let me in! I need to pee," a high-pitched voice complains.

Cindel doesn't falter, in fact she must feel challenged. Popping off ahead of licking me from tip to base with that talented tongue of hers. All at once she takes me back into her mouth. I am so deep, her nose scrunches against my groin. Fuck! Running my fingers through her hair, I draw her back to search those watery arctic eyes, causing a strained breathy noise to escape my chest.

My willpower falters as I initiate fucking her mouth with abandon. She takes me beautifully. Gargled moans break the silence, as I move at a punishing pace. At last, the coil releases; I come apart, unloading down her throat; she stays right there with me. Taking every drop I give her.

Those eyes… they gaze up at me with a hunger I knew only I could satiate. She leans back on her heels, as she takes her bottom lip into her mouth.

I help her to stand, wanting so desperately to rip off this mask and take those soft, pillowy lips into my mouth. Knowing who I am before she even learns who she really is could be disastrous.

I tuck myself away while she fixes the smeared eyeliner from the corners of her once tear-filled eyes. The impatient gal outside continues to bang and holler, as I lazily pull Cindel's shirt back on and button her up, much more conservatively than before. With her suspenders and hat in place, she appears put together and ready to exit our temporary haven. She hasn't said much, mostly because her mouth was busy doing other things, but she studies me before stepping forward.

Her hands explore my torso. Moving from zippers to clasps, even trying out one of the pockets on my gear. She's like a cat discovering that not only can they lounge on the couch, but they can scratch at it too. Eventually her exploration moves upward. She attempts to take hold of the goggles hiding my face, but I pull back, just out of her reach. I shake my head.

"Will I ever get to see you without the mask?" She asks tentatively.

Eventually, just not today. I nod because that's all I'm able to do right now. Unlocking the bathroom door, the nuisance nearly falls inside.

"About time!" The woman dressed as a slutty cowgirl pushes past us, diving into the nearest stall and proceeds to relieve herself, without even shutting the privacy gate.

I wish I could stay. I'd take her home and hold her in my bed till the sun rose, but we can't. Shit. I don't know if she'd ever want that.

We part ways, I head out the back door of the bar, and she goes back to work like nothing ever happened. Was this anything more than lust?

Back at my place, I pulled up the camera feed on my surveillance monitors from The Black Sheep. Watching my girl until I know she is home, was a nightly routine at this point. I spot her instantly on one of the cameras. I swear to fucking god, if someone ogles her nipples through that white shirt, I was going to remove their eyes with a cocktail fork. Lucky for me, more scantily dressed women were on the menu to keep their attention. Cindel still has the little earbud in, and the shirt buttoned up to the top, as I left her. Good girl.

I try to busy myself with anything that wouldn't cause me to go straight back there. Settling on hanging new wall decor in my room; then, moving onto answering a unread emails, and eventually attempting to read. I can't help but be distracted by her as the bar party rages late into the night. My sweet princess sneaks fun-sized candy bars, instead of the offered shots, while the rest of the crowd happily knocks them back. The candy was more for her anyhow. Her commitment to sobriety shakes my foundation, making me question everything I've worked toward.

Discipline knows no bounds when it comes to the ones we care about. I'm transfixed on the way she glides through the bar, making sure customers are happy and watered. I suddenly realized something as I watched her, pulling out my phone; I send her a message. Live footage displays Cindel removing her device from a deep pocket. Her head shakes. Then she puts the phone back. I would willingly cut off pieces of myself each day, if it meant seeing that smile. Even for just a moment.

She finishes off the eventful night with her team's help. Cindel really is a natural within this manager position. Changing into something less obvious, I opt for a black hoodie and jeans, then head out with just enough time to tail my better half as she walks home. I will never let her leave my sight again. I'm thrilled when my phone vibrates; Cindel is just a block ahead of me.

> Princess: You really didn't know I was dressed as a gangster?

She finally responds to my earlier message. When I remembered her favorite show was *The Sopranos*, I realized what she was aiming for.

> Pawn: Not like any gangster I've ever seen.

I add a winky face to the end of the message, because I do love to get her worked up.

She continues walking toward her building, all the while holding her phone out, perhaps thinking about what to write. All at once, she stills, then turns to look behind her. Quickly, I duck between two buildings before she could see me following. Dots appear in the chat as I wait to hear footsteps continue toward her apartment.

> Princess: Please tell me more about my brother.

Before I overthink it, I give my sweet girl what she continues to press. One piece at a time, I tell myself.

> Pawn: Your brother was a good man. Pay attention to who you surround yourself with. In time, you'll learn things others have tried to keep hidden. Don't believe what you haven't seen with your own eyes.

I peek around the corner to find Cindel frozen in place.

Without warning, she takes off like a rocket, running down the street, one hand on top of her hat, while her bag bounces aggressively with each stride. She may be fast, but I'm faster. My girl likes playing and I'm here for it. Her pounding footsteps slow as she reaches her building and slips inside.

Once I see the windows brighten from the third story of her building, I know she's safe. I picked this out earlier, when I was watching her finish out the night. Within range, I connect to her little earbud and hit play. Our covert way of communicating is still nestled in her ear as the upbeat song, **"All Day and All of the Night"** from the English rock band **The Kinks**, streams from the playlist. I'm not good with words. Lyrics have a way of conveying my message better than I ever could. As if on cue, her silhouette appears within the lit window. Turning to her side, I get a glimpse of her perfect body. I step from my hidden position allowing her to see I'm here. Clad in black, I was a mere shadow beneath the streetlamp.

She raises her chin like it was some unannounced game of chicken, as the song continues to play for her. Slowly she begins unbuttoning her shirt. Is she? No, she wouldn't. Slowly, she moves down each button until she's at her navel. I move. Not toward her, but away. Back into the shadows. She pauses the progression, unbuttoned completely but still covered. I'm like a moon in her orbit. Pulling away was damn near impossible. However, I won't let any passersby see what's mine. Far enough away she can't see me; Cindel pulls her curtains closed almost instantly. She may have won this round, but there won't be any room for her to be a brat next time.

If I thought having any part of her would dull this steady craving, I would be lying. Not having my hands running through her hair or cupping her ideal breasts is causing me physical pain.

Micro-sized nanny cams give me a portal to Cindel as I watch her shuffle about her apartment before settling into her bed. As her movements cease, chest slowing to a steady rhythm; I can't help this protective feeling that comes over me.

Anger bubbles to the surface as I consider past events and all the pain she has faced. If she only knew these, *accidents* that have befallen her were intentional. The mental anguish would poison her gentle spirit. I'm no saint either... solely responsible for at least one of the atrocities and because of that... I'll never be the same.

How will she see me once she knows? Can she survive all these truths as she unknowingly unravels them? Will she still want me then?

Her leg kicks out from the sheet as she repositions herself. I toy with the idea of going over there and joining her in bed but think better of it. Sometimes she has trouble sleeping. She's exhausted. I'll wind up giving this poor girl an embolism if I keep up with all these unexpected encounters. The carved walking stick I gifted her in the Catskills, is just under her bed. It makes me wonder if she's grown sentimental or if it's simply within reach to club anyone who invades her home. Which will only be me, from here on out.

Time isn't on anyone's side right now. Others want answers, and I don't think Cindel has uncovered enough to keep herself safe. She's running headfirst toward the danger… she just doesn't know it yet. I need to do something to point her in the right direction. If Cindel doesn't learn about what really happened to her brother, she's going to wind up just like him. I'm not going to let that fucking happen. Things are different now. I couldn't give two fucks about what I was brought up to do. Whether or not I was refined to be a weapon.

My father has been tirelessly planning. His first play was the explosion. What a fortuitous turn of events, to have landed this jewel in my lap.

From the moment I laid eyes on her, she had a hold on me. She's been ingrained into every cell in my body, no longer am I able to follow my directive. Now it's time to shed some light on what her family is capable of.

TWENTY-SIX

CINDEL

Last night, I fell asleep envisioning who the man behind the mask could be. I definitely smelt smoke on him last night, but it was a musty odor, closer to a cigar. Sometimes Brodi smoked them with his friends when they went out. Of course, I know this man is not Brodi. Now, that I've had his dick in my mouth I can confirm, this is NOT him.

Everything with my stalker is new. Better than I've ever experienced. Even with his face completely covered… I can tell when he's looking at me. Whether he's checking in or asking permission, I want to say yes to everything. Yes, because unlike everyone else… he seems to care about me.

When I wake alone, thoughts of the man clad in black still looming, my hand inadvertently travels beneath my sleep shorts. I rub lazy circles with the latest memory of my stalker in those opened cargo pants. What could have happened afterwards? If there wasn't someone banging on the door? If we had all the time in the world…? He's beginning to consume my thoughts and now my dreams. It's been so long since I can remember a pleasant dream. The unknown, once a shadowy corner I steered clear of, now beckons me. I'm drawn to it. Drawn to him. I'm falling for this man and I'm not even sure who "he" is. I'm not scared, though, but intrigued. What does my stalker have in store for me? The feeling of being watched brings me comfort. Like no matter how shitty of a day I may have, I know I'm not facing it on my own.

My calendar reminds me I have plans with a certain someone who has trouble with recognizing boundaries. She wandered into my room without permission once and I may have been an accessory to petty theft after our visit to the tea party ship, but she's genuinely really easy to be around. Today is the first Friday I've had off in a while, however I was unequivocally "busy" according to Mairead's text.

After nearly being dragged to Salem, I was almost too afraid to object to her plans to go shopping. I'm also going to try and return Mairead's coat she left in my booth, at the Bazaar. Surprisingly it smells of cigars too. I shouldn't fester here with my thoughts, which is pretty much all I would do if I wasn't forced outside. Some *girl time* might do me good.

I sure wasn't hanging out with my roommate much anymore. With Andrea's panties in a twist about me seeing Eamon, I just figured I'd give her the space she needs. Maybe it will work itself out? I was given a time more than a destination from Mairead, so I'm dressed and ready in front of my apartment, per her instructions. I knew I was in for an interesting day when a shiny BMW pulled up to the curb.

The driver steps out of the vehicle, rounds the car, and opens the door for me. Instantly, I text Mairead. Wondering if she meant to send a fancy car with a chauffeur and not a cab. A thumbs up emoji was all I got.

When I climb into the back, I was surprised to find leather seats and sparkling water with glasses. Why in the hell did Mairead ever choose to work at Star Mart? Shaken from my thoughts on my friend's finances, the driver informs me that we were heading to Copley Place.

It's an enclosed shopping mall. Multi-story, glass ceilings, luxury stores, and incredible views overlooking the city. After paying rent, getting my bank account to a positive balance, and going grocery shopping this week, I might be able to afford a salted pretzel. Not used to 'being in the green,' I want to keep a buffer, in case I ever find myself without a job.

During the ride over, a puzzling text comes in from my uncle.

> Uncle: Hello, Cindel, I know this is unexpected, but would you be available for an earlier breakfast date? I know you're a busy girl. I've just been a little lonely lately.

I smile at myself, knowing my uncle has never asked for anything. Him wanting companionship from me is touching. I will always find the time for him in a city that nearly swallowed me whole, three years ago. I respond immediately.

> Cindel: Absolutely! I would love to have breakfast with you! I'm so happy you asked.

He sends me a peach and a winky emoji. Making me laugh so loud, it causes the chauffeur to peer at me in the rearview mirror, the rest of the drive. I'm confident my uncle has no idea what some of those little symbols truly mean.

The driver parks the sleek black car beside the upscale shopping plaza, then proceeds round the vehicle to open my door. I suddenly feel out of place as I look down at my thrifted, grungy attire. I wasn't expecting to face an outing so… opulent.

As soon as the door opens and the driver helps me out, a tornado of red hair comes hurtling toward me. Mairead wraps me in a hug, before lifting me off the ground with surprising strength for such a little thing.

"Aaaaah, girls' day!! I'm so glad we finally can hang out again!" I reach back into the car to retrieve her fur coat but waves it off as nothing. She insists I leave it in the car for the driver to handle. This is her personal driver! It blows my mind how some people have enough money to hire drivers.

Meanwhile, I'm hoping for a few extra singles in my wallet, to afford the two-ply toilet paper. Stop it! I tell myself. You don't know her life or her situation. Don't be so judgy.

Mairead takes me by the hand and hauls me toward the shiny glass entryway of the mall. Man, she's excited!

As soon as we enter the mall, it's like a punch to the gut with festivity. Decorated fir and pine trees line the lobby; twinkling icicles pass between railings overhead, and the wafting aroma of winter spice and fresh tree invade my senses. It's only November first for fuck's sake! I hate the holidays. This is going to be a trying day.

By the time we finish half the shops on the first floor, my feet are killing me. I should have chosen more practical footwear, as she insists, I accompany her to every single store. I did learn something new today. Apparently, you can buy stuff and have the store hold it while you shop. I guess it's common practice for someone who likes to go shopping.

Mairead bought something literally, every place we went. I honestly don't even know if she likes what she's buying; it seems more like crossing items off a checklist than an earnest transaction. When Mairead finally decides to take a break from spending a small fortune, I am thrilled to stop walking and get something to eat.

Near the food court, I hop in line for that pretzel I've been craving all day. She scoffs and all but pulls me away from my coveted treat.

"Eww no way. We're going to an Italian place around the corner."

Taking me by the arm, she escorts me toward the white linen restaurant with employees in a black and white uniform.

"Mairead, I can't afford this. You enjoy, I'll grab a pretzel and peruse the bookstore."

Despite my protests, she continues pushing me toward her desired place.

"Oh, don't be silly. My treat!"

She's more generous than any previous friend or boyfriend... also seemingly wealthier than anyone I've ever been around. She attempts to wine and dine me, I order the least expensive thing on the menu and insist on water to drink.

After she downs two glasses of wine prior to bread arriving, she attempts to 'wine me' some more. I politely decline, even though I've told her at least three times; I don't drink. Mairead is confident, witty, and carefree; especially with her spending. I should consider her a good friend, even if it may be just for a season. People don't seem to stick around long with me. So, only time can tell.

"So Cindel, any special someone or someones in your life?"

She sips from her large wine glass while indulging in a cheesecake topped with a decorative honeycomb. Mairead ordered two desserts. I could never say no to dessert.

"That's a complicated question." I slowly chewed the last bite of my cannoli, savoring every delicious morsel. It's incredible, but Mike's Pastry in the North End still gets my vote for best cannoli.

I can pull truths from the situation.

"He thinks he's funny. Sometimes a little reserved and puzzling too. It's like two sides of the same coin; I just never know which version of him I'm going to get."

She drains another glass, raising her hand to motion the waiter to refill her drink.

"Have you fucked him yet?" She asks pointedly as the poor server tries to keep their composure. Her expression morphs in a fraction of a second from light-hearted to interrogative.

The water I drink goes down the wrong tube, allowing me long enough to think while I cough.

"I… I haven't yet."

She swirls the rose liquid, by holding the delicate stem of the glass.

"Soooo… you've done other stuff? Do tell!" She tucks her hand just under her chin, leaning forward as the intensity she once displayed just melts away to giddy interest.

"Well…" I begin pushing the cuticles deeper into their beds, just beneath the table's linen. There's no harm in telling her about what I did with the mystery stranger, while weaving in Eamon. It's not like I have anyone else to talk to about it anyways.

So, I kind of unload it on her. Telling her about the office-like detention center at the zoo and how he first explored my body. She's shocked but insistent that I keep going. I move onto the steakhouse date and the movie followed by shared cherry pie. Then I recall the steamy rendezvous at last night's Halloween Bash. I left out the part about his face being covered because, rationalizing that there may or may not be two people in this story. Sorting through that just isn't in my wheelhouse right now.

Her mouth hangs open and for a moment I was a little worried about being too graphic, considering our new friendship and current setting.

"Huh. No shit?"

Her reaction was similar to how I responded in college when I learned; dresses and skirts were considered *gender-neutral* up until the 18th-century.

I shake my head, "No shit," repeating her words right back.

"Well... Sláinte! I guess it's good that we get along so well." She winks as she raises her glass in a celebratory gesture before draining the Rosé.

I smile politely and nod, unsure how to counter the odd choice of words.

When lunch is through, Mairead moves at a slower pace. She is also in the mood to try on clothes. The spending crazed-girl gawks over mannequins draped in sparkly, sequin dresses and literally squeals, whenever we come across a collection of furs. My friend has a very particular taste in fashion, but to each their own.

Peeling a hot pink, cocktail number off the display, Mairead skips off to the dressing room.

"Wait right here. Tell me what you think when I come out."

I make myself comfortable on the circular ottoman, within the horseshoe of changing rooms. Checking my phone to see if I have missed any messages, I confirm there's nothing.

She pops her head out of the small room. "Can you zip me?"

I stand despite my aching feet protesting for me to sit back down and go to assist the sprightly girl in the extremely loud dress, covered in strawberries. As I glide the zipper up and fasten the clasp to the dress, I can't help but notice a thin lined tattoo on her shoulder blade. It's a skull with shamrocks for eyes. I, myself, don't have any tattoos, so I wonder what encouraged her to pick this particular design. I didn't want to be rude and question her choice in body art, especially when she's already treated me to such a lavish day. I keep the question to myself and tell her she looks nice in the outfit.

She, of course, bought the dress. Using the same black shiny card to pay as all the other times. Could it be her father's card? I wasn't jealous. Just curious... what it's like to have parents that help you out. Her dad seemed nice when I met him at the Craft Bazaar. Dressed in head-to-toe designer labels, it kind of explains his daughter's ideology.

My parents worked very hard. We always had a roof over our heads, food in our bellies, and truly everything we needed. After I got out of the hospital, we moved out of my favorite childhood home and into something much more conservative. Maybe the house was too badly damaged after the explosion, but it never really made sense why we constantly moved.

The house I still see in my dreams was my grandparents originally. They decided to move back overseas, where their ancestors originated, to spend their remaining years living on a houseboat along the Mediterranean Sea.

Back when my hearing was intact, I remember my mom playing a grand piano in the great room. If my memory serves me right, my dad used to cook in a massive, shining kitchen with a chandelier above the island. I was little so some things were a little fuzzy, but after I the accident and the relentless bells began… we led much different lives. No more music in the halls, no more grandiose cooking spaces. Things were simpler. Nothing flashy. As soon as I became acclimated with a new house or school, we moved again… always within Boston.

I know my parents were trying to do right by us. Instilling the importance of family over lavish things. Anytime I was sick, dad made his homemade Italian penicillin to make me feel better. He learned the recipe from his father. My mom tried to be present, never missing a school function. As I got older, our parents worked longer hours.

I still had Theo, and I wouldn't ever exchange my time with him for any designer bag or sports car. I just wish I understood why they cut me off. I've always had the sense that Theo was the favorite.

Yes, they offered us both college but sometime between him graduating and his death, it changed. Like I did something wrong and now my parents won't help me. Do they blame me for their favorite child's death?

Okay. Spiraling. Get a grip Cindel. You're loved. You're here. That should be enough… but why do I feel like it's not?

By the time we get to the third floor, I didn't feel so good. Maybe because I was having an existential crisis over why my parents didn't love me as much as I wanted them too. Yet, my body ached and I found myself feeling both overheated and freezing. Regardless of the number of times I took on and off my sweater, I just couldn't regulate my temperature. A mild headache was starting to set in that quickly began to wrap itself behind my eyes, causing my vision to become slightly distorted. I took up residency in a small chair in the corner of a high-end jewelry store.

Mairead has her eye on a set of pink, diamond earrings to go with the eccentric fruity dress she just purchased. I can't continue on like this. I've hit my limit.

"Mairead!" I called over to her from my seated position. "Hey… I'm not feeling so well. Could you please call that driver to come?"

She makes a pouty face but seems to realize my poor state. Fortunately, she pulls out her phone to make the call. Without stopping at any more stores or retrieving her previous purchases, she wraps her arm around my waist and walks me toward the closest exit; where we find the chauffeur waiting for me.

"Feel better, sis'! Tell that lover boy of yours, Mairead says 'hurry up!'"

I must have been running a fever, because nothing she said made any sense. She gently helps me into the car and kisses my forehead before waving us off.

The driver is very kind, insisting he walks me all the way up to my apartment door. Maybe he started growing concerned when I asked to pull over so I could empty my guts onto the side of the interstate or perhaps the fact I stripped off three layers of clothing and was down to only a tank top on a frigid, autumn day. Either way, I was thankful for him and Mairead's generosity.

Once inside, I drop my bag, shoes, and everything else I carry as I make my way to the bathroom. I shakily draw myself a cool bath and check the medicine cabinet for anything to help bring down the fever. Expired Tylenol will have to do, until I run to the store or have some kind of delivery service bring something stronger. I felt as though my head was being crushed within an invisible vise.

My teeth chatter as I lower myself into the tub, my body throbbing as if I fell down a flight of stairs. I just need to stay here long enough for the medicine to do its job. When my fingers start to prune, I reluctantly lift my trembling body from the tub, just managing to wrap a towel around me. Instantly, another wave of nausea consumes me. Lucky me, the bathroom has anything and everything I could need.

After multiple episodes of heaving in the toilet, nothing is left in my stomach. Regardless of how close I was to my bedroom, I gathered clean towels from the shelf, along with an extra bathrobe; dropping them right onto the floor. I didn't want to be far if another bout of nausea courses through me. The only thing I brought into the room with me was my cell phone. It lies somewhere in this room. I barely have the energy to claw at the piles of random linens to form a soft nest for my body to collapse into. I also didn't bother putting my hearing aids back in. Not only was I too weak to care, but I honestly couldn't remember where I set them.

Was Andrea home? Would she stumble into the bathroom and find me like this? Did I have work tomorrow? What day is it tomorrow? The room was bright, light still on, but it didn't matter. Sleep consumed me.

When I finally managed to pry my eyes open, it only felt like seconds had gone by, but I wasn't in a pile of rogue fabric any longer. I was in my bed, and it was light out. The sun still hung in the sky. Was it the same day?

Instinctively, I reached for my phone to find it on the nightstand, plugged in. Today was Saturday, November 2nd. A whole day has gone by.

I sit up trying to get my bearings and notice three separate medicines next to me. They're all new and unopened, with a full glass of water within reach.

I scan the room to find most of my room in order, but more in order than usual. Clothes that normally litter the floor now sit neatly folded on my vanity chair. The trash bin beside it has been emptied, and even the closet doors are closed. One of the accordion door tracks is usually janky, never lining up properly, so why does the closet actually shut tight?

I look down to find my normal swirl of blankets is laid out, smooth and tucked into the edges of the mattress. Is my bed made? Am I made into bed?! I search for my hearing aids, thankfully finding them nestled on their charger beside me. There's no way I did all of this! Maybe Andrea took care of me? She must be home.

Carefully, I put on my aids, tear open one of the packages of cold and flu. Then drain the water from its glass. Pulling my shaking body from bed, I'm surprised to find that I'm no longer naked, fresh out of the bath, but I'm dressed. In duck pajamas? What kind of time travel paradox took place between the bathroom floor and now?

My stomach grumbles and I smell something delicious, wafting through the house. Gingerly I pull myself from bed, making my way through my room, when I find something on the floor next to the foot of my bed. Holding onto the mattress, I bend down to pick up a tiny splinter of wood from the floor. Where did this come from? It's a toothpick. I flick it into the fresh garbage bag and follow my nose to the kitchen.

A large pot sits on the back burner of the cooktop. I take a quick look inside the simmering pot, I wonder if I'm hallucinating from the fever. Inside is an orange broth with tiny little stars. Italian Penicillin! Honestly, I don't even care how it came to be. I grab the ladle from the spoon rest and give the pot a stir. Perfect creamy consistency, pastina pasta, and even a rind of parmesan bobs within. Just like when I was little.

I serve myself a heaping bowl, then shuffle over to the table. "I really want to keep this down," I whisper to my stomach. I try to start off slowly but it's difficult. Switching between blowing and inhaling the soup, I'm instantly brought back to a cozy kitchen where my dad stood over a stock pot and hummed a merry tune. Soon, I find myself serving another helping. Filling my belly to its capacity before turning off the stove and letting the meal cool. I'm pleased that everything seems to be staying within my gut, where it belongs.

Andrea walks through the front door as I begin to rinse my bowl. Her face contorts as she takes me in.

"Oh my god! What happened to you?!" She drops her bags where she stands and rushes to my side.

Man, I must really look like shit. I turn off the faucet and turn to face her. "Sick. Maybe food poisoning? Not sure. I took the medicine on my nightstand."

She cradles my arm, escorting me to the couch. She has a quizzical gaze as she searches my face, like she's seeing me for the first time.

"You didn't know I was unwell?"

Her lips point downward, and she shakes her head from side to side.

"Where were you?"

She helps me lower onto the couch. Then proceeds to turn away but speaks loudly for me to hear.

"My team has been working tirelessly to meet a deadline for a client. Most of us crashed at Todd's place last night." Her back was to me, as she busied herself putting away items, she previously carried in. She continues talking quickly about what the project entailed, really not looking at me as she spoke.

"Todd?" I press.

She stops what she's doing, turns and glances at me over her shoulder, giving a tight-lipped smile. "Ya, Todd. He's new to the firm."

I suck in my cheeks and nod, realizing she either didn't care enough to tell me the truth or she doesn't care enough to lie better. Either way, I felt the valley between us grow increasingly wider, each time we communicated.

She goes over to the stove, lifting the lid of the pot and inhales deeply. "Mmmm, that smells incredible. You made this?"

My turn to evade the truth. "Yeah. Just like Dad used to make." I remain on the couch, while attempting to listen to Andrea cite all the work she's done recently and the long hours she's putting in, around mouthfuls of her own bowl of pastina. I dip my head from time to time, but really my mind is trying to figure out who dressed, fed, and cared for me last night.

Did Mairead stop by to check on me? No, I don't think it was her. Where did that toothpick come from? Or it could be…was it him? My stalker?

Back in my room, I message Eamon. I knew I was too sick to work this evening. Did he already know that? I keep it simple.

> Cindel: Hey. I'm pretty sick today. Unfortunately, I don't think I can make it into work.

His response was jarring. No, he wasn't a dick nor did he threaten to fire me like previous bosses would when I was calling out on short notice. Not that at all. In fact, his response was kind, even worried for me.

> It's Eamon Actually: Oh shit. I'm sorry to hear. Can I help in any way? Do you need me to deliver anything? Food or medicine perhaps?

He also included, *not to worry about my shift*. With the two new hires, him, and Connor, he was confident they could handle a Saturday night rush.

No, Eamon's response was unsettling because he didn't know I was unwell. There's no logical explanation for why Eamon would secretly visit, care for me, make me soup, and then act surprised when I say, *I'm sick and can't come into work.*

How does he benefit from all of this? Why pretend to be two separate people? Eventually I responded to his text.

> Cindel: No, thank you. I have everything I need.

Which means… my face feels numb.

Eamon didn't take care of me either. It wasn't Andrea; she was just as surprised to find me unwell. So, unless Mairead made a copy of my apartment key, became unnaturally strong and determined to care for me, the only explanation is... there's two of them.

The paralyzing feeling courses through me when I realize I truly and unequivocally have no idea who the masked man is.

Initially, I thought it was Eamon playing some kind of game. Plus, the coincidence with the sour candy... after I blacked out at the lantern festival my masked stalker offered me the candy to calm me, then Eamon picked the same movie treat on our date. Does he have a clone? A twin?

All at once, images flash like a flipbook.

The things he's done to me. Fuck, the things I've done to him! I let a stranger drive his cock down my throat. How am I not dead? I must be the biggest idiot in all of Boston. I bury my face in my pillow and scream. Then cry and then scream some more. I am exhausted, trying to recover from whatever ails my body while my mind is a tangled mess of embroidery floss. All the colors, mixing and weaving together into impossibly complicated knots. Instead of being patient and sorting through them like a sane person would... I just shove my hand into the metaphorical sewing box and swirl them all around until it is impossible to make sense of where one thread starts and the other ends.

Mairead also reached out, in between bouts of me screaming into my pillow. She sent photos of herself in the intense strawberry print dress, with a disgruntled looking fluffy, white bunny. The creature had this *save me* look about it, while Mairead squeezed the poof of fur to her chest. I hope that's her pet and not some poor wild rabbit she found in a park on the way home. Each time we hang out, I speculate if her free-spirited personality is something to be coveted or medicated. After the slideshow of candid photos, she texts.

Mairead: Hurry up and get better. We're doing an Escape Room next time! Bring along your grumpy roommate too.

I've visited more attractions with Mairead over the past few weeks than I have in years! I send a thumbs up emoji, silence my phone, and attempt to sleep.

One eye pries open, instantly spotting movement. I blink a few times before my vision clears, finding people coming and going within the brightly lit room.

Layered crisp, white sheets cover my body against the cold temperature of the room.

A woman with buttery hair holds her head within her hands, as a tall man in a dress shirt, tries to make her feel better. The woman is my mommy. She cries at my bedside, while Daddy rubs circles on her back. They look tired, like they haven't slept in a while. Mommy's hair is sticking in different directions, while Daddy's top is wrinkled. I've never seen him wear an unpressed shirt before. I don't know why I'm here or what's wrong with my parents, but I don't like it.

Where's Theo? I glance around for my brother, finally spotting him across the room, asleep in a chair. My uncle stands by the room's door frame causing my daddy to leave us and to go to him. I don't see my uncle very much, so I'm surprised he's here.

Uncle Nicholas would sometimes stop by during the holidays. I remember when he brought me a present once. It was a stencil kit, where I could change the plates for the top, middle, and bottom of a dress, then lay down my paper and color on top. It was one of my favorite things because there were endless varieties of dresses I could make.

Another time, my uncle visited late at night. Theo was already asleep in his room, but I was still up. When I went down the stairs to get a glass of water, I heard Daddy and my uncle arguing in the study. When I asked about it the next day, my daddy said they were just discussing work. He told me, "Being a grown-up is complicated and to try and be sweet for as long as I can."

I didn't understand what he meant at the time, but I was happy to learn anything from him. I wish I was at home right now, making new dress combinations. If it was Christmas, my family would be all together, including my uncle. There would be songs, games, and laughter. All while enjoying hot cocoa with marshmallows.

Right now, is not a time for merriment. I watch as my uncle and daddy speak with big hand movements. They're too far to hear, but my mommy is close and she's talking to a nurse now, but I can't hear them either.

The lady in a blue uniform has kind eyes. She comes to my side and takes hold of my wrist, while looking at her watch. She smiles at me. The corners of her eyes look wrinkly. I realize that her mouth is moving but still no words come out. My daddy suddenly noticed me. He walks over and plants a kiss on my forehead as I sit up. Mommy squeezes my hand from her seated position. Their mouths move, but still, I hear nothing.

Something is wrong. I try to listen harder. Maybe I'm not paying enough attention. I can hear something! Like a ringing bell off in the distance. The noise gets louder the longer I try to listen. Like a fire alarm sounding, but no one is trying to evacuate the building.

I try to tell them it's too loud as I cover my ears at the same time. Pleading with anyone in the room to make the noise stop. No one is doing anything to help me! All they do is shake their heads and frown. The lady with the gentle eyes motioned for me to lie down. My brother is awake now and has joined my parents at my bedside. A tear streams down Theo's face. I've never seen my brother cry before. I look away toward the wall of windows that looks into the hall.

My uncle never entered the room and now he's leaving. I wish he'd take me with him. Away from this room full of sadness with the itchy sheets. I watch as my uncle meets a strange looking man at the end of the hall and a boy. The boy is older than both me and Theo. He stands next to my uncle as the two men speak.

Another nurse and doctor come into my room, checking wires and screens, making it hard to see my uncle... to see the boy. At one point, the boy looked at me. He seems sad. Sad like me. Maybe my uncle could bring the boy next time he visits.

They all leave together. I wanted so badly to leave with them. I didn't like it here. There was an awful noise that wouldn't stop, but no one else could hear it! It was too bright and cold. I don't want to be in this hospital bed; I want to go home! Everyone cried. The doors at the end of the hallway swung shut. Closing me out. Keeping me in.

TWENTY-SEVEN

CINDEL

I sweated buckets last night. My sheets are drenched, but I feel as though my fever has finally broken. At least there was one sliver of light at the end of this twisted tunnel.

Dreams like these were reoccurring. There's no escaping them, just as much as there's no avoiding sleep.

I drain the water beside my bedside, not giving much thought as to how it miraculously became full again. Then, I ventured into the kitchen, a blanket draped over my shoulders, finding half of the living space bathed in sun. It's late afternoon.

A folded note lies on the counter. In crude handwriting,

I hope you're feeling a little better. Leftovers are in the fridge. I picked up some elderberry tea and honey for you. See you tonight. -A.

That was really kind of her. My stomach twists a little thinking about how we've been acting toward one another, but I know deep down, we both would do anything to help one another. I put the kettle on and grabbed a mug from our vast collection. Still weak on my feet, I know I'd need at least one more day of rest before returning to work.

Honestly, I couldn't afford to not work.

I dunk the tea bag into the hot water, while scrolling mindlessly on my phone. I read through posts from old college friends, who were now growing their families or flourishing in the fashion world. When I have enough of comparing my insignificant accomplishments to others, I switch gears to something more productive. I investigate when the next Craft Bazaar will be. I did really well all things considered and next time, I'm wearing a fanny pack! Looks like the next one will take place, early spring.

Is that enough time to embroider a whole new collection? I had hoped the upcycled pieces would sell better. They were much less time-consuming and sincerely more enjoyable to make.

Fashion has always been my passion! Cheesy…? Very! Our professor in art school would say it before each class and it just kind of stuck. Andrea and I caught ourselves saying it way too often. Eventually turning into a superstition that if we didn't say it while dressing up for a night on the town, we would have a fashion crisis.

When's the last time we actually did something fun like that? I feel like it stopped after we graduated. When all we seemed to do was work, work, work.

Seriously, if I knew what a scam being an adult was, I would have held onto my sticker collection. No one says "good job" for paying your taxes or vacuuming your room. Those nauseatingly cheerful Lisa Frank stickers would have been a great incentive right about now! "Look how well you did, not punching that customer in the face. Here's a sticker!"

Even though I was making more money as a manager than holding two different jobs, I knew this wouldn't last. As of right now, I can cover my bills, but I have other things to consider. Big adult things. Like… should I go on another date with Eamon if he asks me?

If what I believe is true, Eamon and my stalker are in fact two separate people, then I should stop seeing one of them… shouldn't I? I mean… I like Eamon. I feel at ease with him. It feels familiar. He's protective, generous, and really kind. However, he did keep things from me. Like Cassie's passing and that he knew my brother. I still haven't received a sober answer about any of that yet.

Wait… I texted the stalker about my brother. Holy shit! Does he know Theo too?!

I realize I've been bouncing the tea bag in my mug for far too long. Resting the little string over the edge of the drink. Then leaning forward over the hot beverage, I bring my arms up and press my palms into my eyes, willing my mind to settle.

Okay, deep breath, Cindel. Filling my lungs to capacity, I hold everything in for long moments before letting out a smooth and steady stream. "Count back from ten," my therapist would say.

Focusing on what I know to be true, as opposed to the "what ifs." I bring up my recent job searches for vacant positions in the area. Staying long term at The Black Sheep will be difficult. Whether I'm "with" Eamon or not. It's funny… I had no idea he even owned the place, up until recently. What changed? As I see it, there's no harm in continuing to spend time with Eamon. Both of these men know more than they're letting on about my brother. In addition, I've made no such commitment to be exclusive to anyone. It's a wise decision to start hunting for a job. I can't stay there forever. I need something to cushion my fall, because like so many times before, I will fall.

A twinge in my chest suddenly has me blinking away unwanted tears. When do I stop picking myself up? From what I've had drilled into me, Theo stopped trying.

I've had so many odd jobs over the years that nothing was off the table if it paid well. Well, besides that! I may be technically involved with two men, but I wasn't about to sell my body to the highest bidder.

Scrolling past server positions and sales associate offerings, I filter by pay and begin clicking through various listings. I have no experience in the human resources department, but the idea of having a tidy little rule book to refer to was intriguing. Perhaps this is one way to get back into the driver's seat of my life, instead of holding on for dear life in the trunk. As I continue searching, I don't bother entertaining jobs with descriptions containing Designer I or Fashion Internship.

Isn't that what you went to college for? Why yes… Yes, it is! So, why am I not applying for any positions? Easy, because everything I love gets ripped away from me and I just don't think I could face the disappointment of losing one more thing I care about. If I fail in that… I don't know what I'd do.

Breezing past those postings, content with only dabbling in fashion as a hobby, for the foreseeable future. Perhaps using my degree as a means for making a living causes it to be less enjoyable? I hate feeling vulnerable. So… I'll continue to keep the idea at arm's reach. No one's let down. No risk.

Brodi never understood my appeal to fashion. He said it was a "waste of time," especially since all he wanted to do was take the garments off me, when we were together. Still, the fiery passion we had in the beginning fizzled out. Intimacy was one-sided, and I was always the one left wanting.

It's hard to admit that maybe Andrea was right. She has the ability to see things I can't. When she made up her mind about something, everyone else had better watch out! Early on in my relationship with Brodi, she made it quite clear where she stood. Only tolerating him for short stints, I could tell when she had hit her limit. I've witnessed his puerile sense of humor cause her knuckles to turn white. Somehow, I convinced her to go on a double date with me and Brodi. She brought along a delightful coworker from one of her recent design gigs. We all got along great until Brodi had a little too much to drink. At the pool hall, he made juvenile comments about Andrea's date. Even thinking back to it makes me uncomfortable, I could only imagine what my best friend and her date must have felt. Andrea looked murderous, cracking a pool stick over her knee before storming out of the place with her date in hand. She didn't come back to the apartment that night either.

Brodi and I fought. I was ready to end things, but he pleaded with me and said it was the alcohol talking. Stupidly, I forgave him. I did that a lot actually, excusing his behavior. Accepting his obvious lies. Who am I trying to kid?

Andrea was right. Maybe it is better off that Brodi just vanished off the face of this planet.

I applied for a grand total of *zero* jobs. Too bad there isn't a job in the department of *poor decision making*, because I could be the CEO of that fucking establishment.

After my mug is drained, I head to the bathroom to peel off the duck pajamas. I am looking forward to washing off last night's sweat that still clings to my skin. After removing my hearing aids, I climb under the hot pin pricks of water, bringing the bar of soap to my skin for a lather. I did feel stronger today but was sure to hold onto the railing while climbing in and out. Steam covers the mirror despite my express shower. I'll brush my hair at my vanity table. I don't think I can hold myself up much longer.

Wrapping the towel around me, I carry what I need back to my room. Pushing open the door with my foot, I shuffle to the vanity and dump everything onto the counter, before the mirror. I all but collapse onto the stool and begin to brush my wet tangles from the tips of my hair, working up to my scalp. As I move the brush to the opposite side of my sopping-wet head, my vision shifts from my reflection to what lies behind me.

Springing up from my seated position, the small stool falls over and I back into the nearest wall. My heart hammers in my chest, but I dare not draw breath. Positioned on my bed, looking like he was posing for the centerfold of a magazine, was the man clad in black. My stalker. Is he? Wearing that eighteenth century hat?

Of course he was covered. In his usual balaclava, goggles, gloves, pants, and shoes that kept me from seeing any part of him. The only difference was his hat. The usual helmet sits at the end of my bed since he's wearing the colonial hat, from Mairead's crazy Boston bender.

Like an engine finally turning over, I sucked in air and rushed out, "Get your boots off my bed!"

Really, Cindel? That's the first thing you say to the deranged stalker that's broken into your home again!

He looks from me to his feet and slowly sits up, bringing his large boots to the floor instead of my comforter. His movements are exaggerated, like a cartoon character unsure if the next frame is going to lead him to something unpleasant. I can't see his mouth; my hearing aids aren't on. What if he's speaking to me? I can't hear anything, but I know he can hear me.

I clutched my towel, feeling oddly exposed, caught off guard. Even though this man has seen a lot more of me than in this moment, I'm not a fan of surprises. Also, I did those things with him, back when I convinced myself he was Eamon. Now, I know better.

He remains fixed in place on my bed. Studying me, probably waiting to see how this scenario plays out. He's once again letting me decide. The bedroom door ajar; I briefly wonder if I am fast enough to make it out. Should I find something to defend myself? He's never hurt me before... I survey the room, realizing subtle changes around me.

A full glass of water on my nightstand and... did he change my sheets? I can't help but shake my head at the gall of this man. He has to be a psychopath. Why else would someone they don't even know go through such great lengths to care for a stranger? Peeking out to the living room, I find long shadows stretching along the space. Could Andrea be walking through the front door at any moment?

The shadowy figure watches my every move. Finally, I pipe up, "Who are you?!" If he said anything, I wouldn't know. I can't see his mouth.

He raises off the bed, crossing the room so swiftly, I don't have time to think let alone respond before he reaches me. Without my shoes, he's even bigger. He has to crane his neck down just to see my face, when he's this close. His gloved hand extends, revealing the little purple starred tech within his palm. Peering up to his covered face, I arm my lungs with air before letting out a choppy breath. If I do what he wants, maybe he'll leave before Andrea comes home.

Reluctantly, I took the offered gadget and nestled it into my right ear. I startle and step back just as he reaches for something. He must take notice of my reaction, because he moves more slowly, as if to tell me not to worry.

The masked stranger pulls a phone from his pocket, then begins pressing its screen. I wish my winter gloves worked on my touch screen devices. I try to peek at the screen, but he quickly hides his phone away into his pocket once again.

Drums kick-off, followed by a catchy guitar solo that could only be one song. **"Two Princes"** by **Spin Doctors**.

Motionless, he regards me as I listen to the newest message within. It seems like all his song choices hold some kind of meaning. We're both still, standing mere feet apart in my room, just taking in the other. When the song concludes, the lyrics are still playing on repeat in my head. I know this song like the back of my hand, so I didn't need to hear it a second time.

Memories of my brother and I, jumping around our playroom with the boombox blasting, dancing our hearts out to artists like Spin Doctors, Beastie Boys, and Reel Big Fish. He's always had impeccable taste in music. After the explosion, we didn't really dance anymore.

I wish I could see the man's eyes who stood before me. Even his gaze could tell me so much. His intentions. His truth. I'm at a loss of words.

Nervously I fidget, switching hands to hold my towel closer to my body, when I accidentally drop the whole thing! The towel falls to the floor around my feet. I soundlessly gasp as he steps forward, bending down before my naked body.

Why didn't I mind him touching me in the women's bathroom at The Black Sheep? Maybe it's because I'm feeling unwell or is it due to the fact that I have no idea who he is? I feel exposed and unsure of myself. Uncertain of my ability to make good decisions as of late. Especially when it comes to this strange man.

He stands to his full height with my white towel in hand, wrapping his arms around me to secure my towel in place, all without actually touching me.

"Thank you," I say on a shaky breath. I can feel the reverberation through my chest.

He nods before moving toward the doorway, freeing up space for me to move about in my room. I opt to sit on the bed. My thoughts waning enough for me to feel the illness still present in my body.

"You're not Eamon?" It comes out more as a question than a statement.

He shakes his head from side to side.

I knew it! If I weren't already sitting, I'm confident my knees would buckle. I study the floor while asking the next question; my throat vibrates as I enunciate each word. "Are you here to hurt me?" Slowly, I drag my attention up his massive body, to his covered eyes.

He crosses his arms, as if offended by my inquiry, shaking his head deliberately *no*.

"Are you royalty or something? Is that why you don't talk? Do I know you?"

He's not answering anything else. Did I ask too many questions? Did I say the wrong thing? I push myself to stand. Closing the space between us, so tired of constantly being in the dark.

"Please... I need answers."

Just one more step closer and I would be pressed against his chest.

His head tilts downward, so close to him that he can only view me by putting his chin on his chest. As I study this immovable mysterious man, the grip on my towel instinctively tightens, causing my hand to tingle and ache. After long moments of us silently facing off in a weird ying yang of dark versus light, he tilts his head to the side. Nothing more.

This is beyond frustration. "I don't understand." I nearly cried.

He steps around me, going to my vanity, and returns with something in his hand. Standing just behind me now, he pushes my hair back behind my ear and gently removes the earbud. Clearly, no more songs will be played. Tenderly, he begins brushing the ends of my hair, gradually working his way up, to remove tangles from my still damp strands.

I hadn't had a chance to finish, being caught off guard when I saw him in my bed. He's so close. My fight or flight slowly ebbs away, and in its place, contentment is causing my eyes to become heavy. The brush running over my scalp and the fact that this man has only brought me pleasure, every time we're together.

Heat radiates off him like a furnace on a winter's day. He smells masculine. Also, a little like black licorice, which really has a bad rap, in my opinion. It's such a sweet and intoxicating odor.

My eyes fly back open when the brushing stops. With gloved hands, he places one of the hearing aid cases behind my ear; then carefully wraps the tube around, positioning the inner receiver just inside my ear.

Aside from my parents or doctors showing me when I was little, no one has ever done this for me. Never so intimately. Not like this.

Delicately, he does the same thing to my other ear.

It's odd how much I crave this stranger's touch, more than he probably even realizes, but knowing now he's not Eamon, feels like I've somehow wronged everyone involved. Does my stalker know Eamon? Has he watched me go on dates with him? Is this enigmatic man some bar patron who has slowly become obsessed with me?

The absence of his touch causes me to groan. I continue standing in the center of my bedroom, now hearing his footsteps leave only to return just as quickly, with a robe from the bathroom. He drapes it over my shoulders, guiding my arms through. Swiftly, he tugs the towel away and pulls the garment closed with the tie in the middle.

My face feels hot. Am I running another fever? How is he able to withdraw such intense feelings from me? Despite all the things I've let this man do to me, I'm still reluctant... fascinated... eager. Am I bothered he hasn't touched me or impressed he's trying to care for me?

He takes me by the hand and escorts me to the couch, as if I'm a visitor in my own home. I may be able to hear now that my hearing aids are on, but he has yet to speak to me.

Placing a blanket over my shoulders, he leaves the room.

What would Andrea say if she walked in right now? She already seemed to have a distaste for Eamon; how would she react when she found me shacked up with a random masked stranger?

He returns promptly with a glass of water and a box of flu and cold tablets. Placing down the glass in front of me, he shakes the box and proceeds to the kitchen. It's unsettling how effortlessly he moves through the space, finding everything he needs with ease.

Well... he's been here before, but how long has he been watching me? Does he have cameras in here?

He stops what he's doing, pulling me from my thoughts, and points to the box of medicine and then to me.

Bossy. I hold up the blister pack of pills, exaggerating each motion, as I unpackage, wave the pill at him, and swallow the set. Not because he told me to, but because it has been multiple hours since I last took a dose.

He fetches the leftover pastina soup from the fridge and proceeds to ladle a portion in a bowl before microwaving. Cementing the fact, he is the one who made the soup. He's clearly taking care of me. It seems like the more interactions I have with this man, the gentler he becomes.

That or it's a textbook case of Stockholm Syndrome and I need to resume seeing my therapist at once. Is it wrong that I don't have regrets about the things we've done together?

The microwave stops humming, and he carries the piping hot bowl over to my seated position, placing it on the coffee table before me. He extends a spoon, indicating he wants me to eat. Apparently, this man has superpowers to command his will.

I can eat, suck, and take orders like a good girl; just with a few subtle prompts. Really, I'm just being facetious, because he's always given me a choice. He's never MADE me do anything. It's my play. I decided how the pieces move on the board.

I start eating as he grabs the remote, powers on the TV, and queues up my comfort show, *The Sopranos*. I actually haven't watched it since he last griped at me for *rewatching* the wedding episode. As I predicted, he already knew I haven't watched any further; beginning the next episode in season 6: *Live Free or Die*.

I wonder if he's overheated in all those layers, as he lowers himself to the couch next to me. His heavy body causes me to tip slightly toward him. He then drapes his arm over the back of our seat and proceeds to cross his ankle onto the other knee. Are we really snuggling up on the couch together to watch a show? This all seems strangely normal. Aside from him being decked out in full militant gear and me looking like a disheveled cat lady who hardly ever leaves the house… you'd almost think we were a couple.

We silently watch the episode about a family disgraced by the actions of two consenting adults. Lies, built on lies, creating conflict for everyone involved. Pride and an *obligation to family* make people do stupid things, blood or not. I can't help but glance at the door frequently, expecting my roommate to appear at any moment.

My nonchalant stalker watches on, the epitome of composure and self-control that near strangers shouldn't have with one another. Was there some sort of message here I was supposed to be decoding? All his curated songs seem to have held some kind of meaning or temporary comic relief. Was I overthinking all of it? Maybe this wasn't anything more than two people spending time together.

Reaching for the remote when the episode ends, he shuts off the television, and I find that our legs are touching. I stare up into his goggles, that just reveal my own tired reflection.

"Did that episode represent something? Like in real life? To me?"

He shakes his head up and down.

Yes? I think back to all the questions I've asked him prior to this moment. "You never answered me. How do you know my brother?" My mind reels, as one question leads into another, before he has a chance to respond. "Does all this have something to do with him?"

He bows his head again.

I'm so fucking tired. I attempt to temper my thoughts, while carefully forming my next question. The reason why I hated the impending holiday season, why I haven't been quite the same for multiple years.

"Did my brother kill himself?"

He considers me, marginally angling his head. I couldn't see his eyes, but I knew behind the covering they focused on me.

Time froze and I felt as though I couldn't take a full breath, while waiting for this stranger on my couch to respond. I silently plead with the universe, promising anything it wants. Please give me answers.

His posture stiffens while his leg spontaneously starts to bounce.

I knew it. I've sort of always known. I shatter; hot tears stream down my face. Theo did not take his own life.

Without being asked, he wraps his large arms around my body, pulling me closer to his firm Kevlar covered chest.

I unravel teetering between loss and solace, unsure which one holds more merit.

He just holds me. My only pillar in a world that falls around me.

Once I'm able to collect myself, I pull back abruptly. "How?" I sob, proceeding to bite down on my tongue, only to keep from crying again. "HOW?!" I don't know why, but I smack his immovable chest, like I was capable of harming this man. As if he's ever tried to hurt me. He is a wall and I, a feather caught in a breeze colliding against his strength. "Tell me!" I idly push on him, expecting too much from the still shadow.

He locates his phone, wakes the screen, then seemingly types out a message. Using a text to speech feature, the phone reads his words out loud. Just like it did in the office at the Lantern Festival. A deep male voice reads: *Your brother started poking around, where he didn't belong. He discovered secrets. I strongly believe he left something behind for you.*

"What?"

Just then, I heard the jingle of keys just outside the apartment door.

Swiftly, he stands, sliding open the window, and ascends the building's fire escape. Despite my stunned state, I managed to close the window, just before my roommate crosses the threshold.

"Hey." She rushes.

"Hey," I reply, while trying not to look directly at her.

"Feeling any better?" She asks, setting her bag on the table.

"Mhmm." I peek over my shoulder to see if there's any trace of the shadow, I'm beginning to feel more attached to by the day.

"Need anything?" She asks, now walking over to me.

I curl the blanket around my face and shake my head. "No thanks, just need more sleep. I'll be right as rain tomorrow."

She gives a tight lip smile, folds in on herself, and halts her advance. As if she could tell, I was pushing her away.

Quickly, I say goodnight and find my way back to my room. Sleep is a welcoming diversion, releasing me from my spiraling thoughts.

"What secrets?" I whisper into the darkness.

TWENTY-EIGHT

ANDREA

Stakeouts are so boring! I've spent the last two days watching Patrick Murray attend meetings around the city with enough muscle to instill fear in anyone who may see him as a target. I doubt anyone would be dumb enough to try anything.

My guy at the barber shop came through. He had two bits of information that could be helpful in figuring out Eamon's intentions with Cindel and why the fuck Paddy Muscles is back. Apparently, Daddy Murray is unhappy with his son's business model. There's talk of moving their gambling virtual to evade the law. Although, I'm pretty sure that's all been done before. It sounds like Patrick is off his rocker.

Now, the second piece of knowledge was much more concerning. In a little over two weeks, the red wolf is being released. Now, what does that mean... I don't fucking know yet, but what I do know is I've spent all my energy and resources on the Murrays, so I haven't had time for much else.

My friendship with Cindel is in shambles. Every time we interact, it's some kind of argument. I get it. My protective nature may come off more, *domineering thunder-cunt*, but I mean well. God, I'm a shit friend, but she's playing with fire, being involved with a Murray. Ultimately, she won't just get burned; she'll be incinerated. I know what they're capable of.

It's been a long weekend and although I want nothing more than to head back to the apartment and check on how Cindel is doing... I must head back out to the college. Moyra will only talk in person, never corresponding via email or phone, unless it's to arrange a time and location. I guess being married to a cop as long as she has been, can make anyone a bit paranoid. Nevertheless, she has the backstory I need. So, I must stomach the transit system and her conditions. I am grateful though that she wants to meet indoors this time. Not only could the wind chill cut right through you, but a storm was rolling in. That's all I needed right now, was to wind up with pneumonia when I had some kind of obscure timeline to have answers by.

At precisely 4 p.m., I sit in the coffee shop on the southwest corner of campus. This time I bought, and for once, she was late. This is the third time we've met in recent weeks. I desperately need to know more about her time working here. The things she's heard. The things she's seen. When we last met, we got a little off topic. She apologized but I led the conversation there. See, I like to know who my sources are in addition to what they know. Knowing their characters and a little history makes all the difference in the world, because after all, what they're telling you is already hearsay. If their background could skew the information they gave me, I needed to catch that upfront.

Moyra Kent was married to Karl Kent for a whopping twenty-five years. I'd say being together with someone that long is impressive in itself, but they weren't happy years. Karl's real personality started rearing its ugly head, shortly after they eloped. At first it started off as gaslighting. Then, isolating her from her friends, as well as her sister who she said was her best friend at the time, but she couldn't leave. She stayed for the baby.

He developed a drinking problem while on the force. The job took a toll on him. Shitty excuse if you ask me. He chewed through their savings, but there was a silver lining for Moyra, because it meant she was able to go back to work. She's been teaching journalism at Boston College for twenty years now. "I've always dreamed of being a journalist. Karl wasn't too keen on the idea. So, the compromise was teaching."

Eventually, the conversation circled back around to the whole reason I came to see her… Theo. "We're not supposed to have a favorite but… he was a natural," she recalls the memory, looking melancholy. "His papers were so intriguing, I commonly used them in other lectures as examples…" she told me while we strolled around the campus grounds during one of our meetings. "His brilliance didn't just catch my attention but others who weren't even enrolled in my class."

This is it! Something leading in the right direction. Toward answers about Theo. Cindel never believed he took his own life. She's not the only one who felt that way. "I recognized the young man who sat in the back of the class. You see… he's, my nephew."

Moyra enters the coffee shop looking not quite as put together as usual. Her merlot-colored hair roughly pulled back while her outfit is mostly wrinkled. I stand when she approaches, already having finished my latte.

"Moyra, are you okay?" I try to ask casually rather than alarmed at her state.

"Sorry, I'm tardy. Please, sit."

We sit at a modest table off to the side. It's a busy time of day. She seems to scan the room. Did she want the place to be full of people? What was she concerned about?

"I'm afraid your drink is cold."

She swats her hand. "No bother, I'll still sip at it. Thank you, dear." She pulls out her red framed glasses and fidgets in her chair, generally looking unsettled.

I lean closer to ask, "Is something the matter?"

She looks down to the purse she clutches in her lap before looking up at me with an apologetic smile. "That's not why you came all this way. I don't want to bother you with my personal woes."

I rest my hand on the table. "You, are why I came all this way."

The same somber smile comes back, before it's gone again. "Karl called me." Her ex-husband. The bastard that secluded her from everyone abused her mentally and physically. I nod. "He... he said he wants to get back together. He says it was the biggest mistake of his life, letting me go..." She looks up to the ceiling, breathing deeply before continuing. "He says he's making enough money now with his side gig, that if I came back to him, I wouldn't have to work anymore. He's such a fool to think I'd want to have anything to do with his dirty money." Tears gathered in the corner of her eyes as her face scrunches up.

This isn't exactly the direction I expected this meeting to go. I was in fact here to learn more about Theo but...

"Karl never caught me listening to his calls, but I understood... my sister lived a similar lifestyle, so I was familiar with how business works. Somehow, Karl found himself as an insider for a mobster."

I may faint. I think I just hit the informant lottery.

TWENTY-NINE

CINDEL

Muddy puddles gather along the streets, overflowing from drains clogged with leaves, while the sun stays hidden behind a heavy blanket of gray clouds. It seems as though the comforting warmth I sought shall remain hidden for another day. Although I felt physically stronger, the combination of weather and disturbing information from my dark visitor left me feeling weak-willed. *Your brother started poking around, where he didn't belong. He discovered secrets.* He even said Theo may have left something behind for me. A deep chill lingers in the very marrow of my bones, no matter how hard I try, I can't shake it. I couldn't stay in bed any longer.

Getting ready for work, I polish off the rest of the eerily, nostalgic soup, pack some extra cold medicine, and slowly make my way to The Black Sheep. The onslaught of frigid rain wasn't going to let up anytime soon, so I dress accordingly. I finally found the missing yellow rain jacket in my closet. Paired with some galoshes and I am shielded from the elements.

When I arrive, I hang my coat, noticing they've already taken down the decorations from the Halloween Bash. Now, Fall is in full swing. Muted leafy garland weaves between velvet pumpkins, on the glass liquor shelves behind the counter. I'm overjoyed that they didn't skip right to the Christmas decor.

Connor emerges from the back, holding a stacked tray of clean glasses; Brittany replenishes napkins, while Garron and Dax take up residence at a table in the back.

Garron was carrying on about how the hook and ring game is rigged, and the real test of skill lies within darts. I think he was just being a poor sport about losing to his accomplice. It's not the first time I've seen Garron throw a fit due to Dax besting him in a tabletop game.

As I approach the table, I realize another body occupies a third chair. My rubber boots squeak with each step, causing the hidden form to peek around the pillar.

Her assessing eyes travel down to my footwear then back up to my face.

With a curling lip, she turns back to the table before leaning back into her chair.

"Jada... Back already?"

Her booted foot is elevated within one of the adjacent chairs. The look of distaste morphs into a tight, high-cheeked smile, as if the brief review was all in my head.

"No, not yet," she responds, closer to a bad-mannered child. "I just wanted some quality company," she announces, looking between the two bruisers at the table.

Garron smirks then winks at Jada before landing the little metal ring on the hook in one perfect swing. He spits his usual toothpick he carries in his mouth to the floor and hoots. Then proceeds to stick out his tongue at Dax. The man on the receiving end appears unfazed, easily giving his friend the middle finger.

I look down to the toothpick on the ground. Suddenly brought back to the sliver of wood I found near my bed. I tossed it, thinking nothing of it, but now I gawk between it and the nonsensical man before me. Could he...

"You look like that little girl from the salt container!" Garron shakes me from my train of thought. I regard him as he lifts his chin slightly toward the rack that holds my yellow, dripping garment. Dax leans forward, whacking Garron upside his head. "Ow! It's a joke, *Ax*!"

A forced giggle tumbles from Jada; one I've heard too many times over the months working here. Men often take notice of her, it's easy when you have ample cleavage, pouty lips, and long eyelashes.

"Just a few more weeks till I'm out of this damned boot," Jada shares. "Till then, you'll find me hobbling around this place. If I'm not at home watching Real Housewives."

Eamon unexpectedly appears at my side, causing me to startle. "Hello, Cindel, glad to have you back. Are you well?"

I nod. "Yes, much better."

I can't help but notice the way Jada sits up straighter and adjusts her shirt when Eamon is nearby. Is no one off limits for her? I mean, not that he's off limits, but we have been on two dates now. I know we aren't a couple. Getting to know Eamon more intimately, he's different than I expected. Kind, familiar, and even special. She's not good enough for him. Jada doesn't care who looks, as long as someone is looking. That once icy center in me melts with fiery possessiveness. Eamon doesn't seem to notice, plucking a speck of dust I can't even see from the sleeve of his jacket. He turns to me, looking more like himself than last time I saw him, completely sloshed.

"Did you get the gift I sent over?" He asks me.

Jada's once dreamy gaze toward Eamon, suddenly shifts to me with a look that could kill. "Yes, thank you," I answered softly. I'm uncomfortable having everyone listen in on how my boss was courting me with gifts.

"And...?" He insists.

"Umm, I consider all the eyes on me around the table, some with jealousy, others with boredom.

"About the dinner invitation?" Right. The bottle of wine he delivered to my apartment with the note.

Is it hot in here? I feel hot. I push the stray hair behind my ear.

"Ummm..." I look between the four pairs of eyes on me. Jada seems beyond pissed. I don't know what comes over me, but I stare into her eyes and answer, "Yes. That sounds really nice."

He brings his hands together, causing a loud clap. "Wonderful! It's all set. I'll send a car next Monday, at six."

I swear I see a vein bulging from the side of Jada's neck and I'm fulfilled by the sight. Dax stands abruptly, causing the chair to nearly tip over, and then walks straight into the torrential rain, entirely composed.

Garron comments first, "Guy is moodier than a woman."

Jada snickers at Garron's comment, placing her hand on his, before slowly rubbing upward toward his shoulder. Her movements are intentional, methodical, as she continues laughing over nothing, fluttering her eyelashes while assessing the two men who are left. Jada is starving for attention. Garron doesn't seem to mind the obvious play, letting her body remain on him for long moments before announcing he's going to make a cash run for the till, since Dax is on the rag.

"Is he okay?" I ask Eamon softly, in regard to the man that just stormed out.

"Yeah, he'll be fine. Needs time to work through his shit. He always returns sooner or later."

I follow Eamon behind the bar as he talks, happy to get far away from Jada's unsettling aura.

"Dax isn't too keen on communicating. He hasn't been the same since the incident." Eamon begins setting up the clean glasses, still covered in condensation, onto the bar mats along the back wall.

"What happened to him?" I keep myself busy next to Eamon, slicing apples for the new cider-bourbon drink that's been added to the fall menu.

"I've known Dax for multiple years now. He's furiously loyal and ungodly stubborn. Last spring, Dax and Garron were sent to collect on a debt..." He pauses briefly as if deciding on his next words. "The situation took a wrong turn..." he finally reveals.

I've stopped chopping, only focusing on Eamon's mouth as he forms each suspenseful word.

"The guy they were sent to collect from pulled a knife. Dax was just following orders, like so many times before." Eamon has also stopped his monotonous task. Now facing me fully. "Every time I look at him, I wish it would have been me instead."

I picture the man in question. His perpetually reserved state... the intriguing scar... it all suddenly made sense now. The first time I interacted with him, I shouted at him. Told him to stop washing dishes behind the bar. That was before I knew who Garron and Dax were. This narrative makes me question if I really know who any of these men are, or what they're capable of.

I can't keep the question from falling out. "Did Dax lose his ability to speak?" I watch Eamon's head and shoulders droop, then he nods.

"What about the other guy?" I had to know, why...? I'm not sure. "Did he go to jail? The guy that pulled the knife..."

His mouth tilts upward on one side, causing a crooked smile. "He's where he belongs," Eamon declares.

Connor appears from the back. Coming between us, he places down another plastic pallet of glasses. "Hey. Could use some help in the back with the ice machine. It seems to be on the fritz again." Eamon raises an eyebrow and tilts his head toward me.

"I'm good." I lie through a smile no less convincing than Jada's inability to use tact.

He follows Connor to the back, leaving me with my thoughts and a lot of fruit to pack into condiment containers before opening.

Jada eventually hobbles out of the bar, being sure to only hug Brittany goodbye as her eyes pin me with an assessing glare. I secretly wish she fractures something else on her way home.

This is one of the slowest nights I've worked to date. Not many people are willing to brave the weather just to try out a few seasonal, apple themed drinks. Dax eventually shows back up. Soaking wet and looking more ornery than usual. I can't help but watch the way residual rainwater clings to his face, before finally dripping down his jaw, and past the purple scar. Everything about him is intense, even without him uttering a word.

I couldn't imagine not being able to speak. Although, I'm sure a lot of people wonder what it's like to be someone who can't hear without assistance. Is one really any worse than the other? I doubt there's any surgery that restores your voice. Is there? All at once, I realize I've been staring at him way too long. Now, he's watching me.

Shit. I scrambled to keep myself busy, wiping down the bar top that wasn't even dirty. Dax leaves shortly after my awkward bout of gawking, with an ever-foolish Garron at his side.

Eamon spends most of the night in the back, probably repairing the unreliable icemaker. After what seems like forever, they finally emerge and announce that he put in an order for a replacement. It should arrive sometime next week. In the meantime, he encourages us to wear slip resistant footwear. Ha! Look at who's wishing they had rubber boots now!

The Morton salt girl on the navy-blue packaging wasn't actually dressed for the rain, aside from the umbrella she held. A lot of people think it's the Mandela Effect. They're convinced the company simply took away the nostalgic imagery of a little girl in a yellow raincoat and boots. In all actuality, she was always in a simple yellow dress and Mary Jane shoes. The mind sometimes has a funny way of recalling something. Having such convictions you saw it one way, only to be told it's completely different than what you swear it actually was.

My boots slosh through ankle high water, as I trudge past flooded, dark streets. The rain hasn't let up all day. As I approached my home, I notice a police cruiser parallel parked on the other side of my apartment. It looks as if someone was in the dark car, just sitting there. It's hard to see who was inside the cruiser. Was it a dummy, just to deter people from breaking the law? Not wanting to be on the street a minute longer, I hurry past the vehicle and slip inside my building. From my window, I watch as the cruiser's headlights turn on and pull out onto the street. Clearly, someone was inside. What's the point of waiting around in dark vehicles? Why leave now? Nothing law enforcement did made any sense.

"You're dripping all over the floor." I turn from the window to find Andrea in the middle of the room; arms interlocked over her lime-green top, paired with ghost patterned sweatpants. I look down to see the small puddle I made, thanks to my soggy coat and shoes.

"Shit."

She tosses a tea towel for me to dry the floor. Removing my outerwear, I hang it near the door, then collapse onto the couch. My head feels heavy with the chill returning; I reach for another blister pack of cold medicine. Throwing them back with a half drank water on the table.

"That was mine," she quips, jutting out her hip, still standing some distance from me. "You should have stayed home. You don't look so good."

I drained the hijacked glass before facing her fully. Perhaps it's all the things that have come to light, my perpetually concerned best friend, or a bout of delirium from the bug I picked up, but I knew these pseudo truths needed to end. No matter what the status of our friendship may be, things were getting more complicated as time went on. I need my friend back.

Nothing made sense anymore. Could Garron be my stalker? It's clearly not Eamon... But how do they both know my brother? Worse, they both seem to know things I don't. Things about Theo. I want to tell Andrea everything.

"Andrea, don't freak out..."

Her eyes narrow, but she remains quiet, now leaning against the frame of her door for stability. Good, she might need it. I steel my nerves by taking in a large breath and holding for ten seconds, just like previous therapists have conditioned me to do. I remind myself to speak slowly. Be concise and don't get overly emotional, right off the bat.

"I think someone killed Theo."

Her once slim gaze widens to the size of dinner plates. I continue before I think better about it.

"All these weird things have been happening. First my ex-manager from Star Mart turned up dead the same weekend I quit. Then, some cop came by the apartment and started asking me questions about my time working there. Now, I'm involved with not one but TWO men!" I take a moment to catch my breath, wishing the glass in front of me had more liquid. Andrea's mouth hangs open, but she remains silent. I begin to speak faster this time, hoping to get it all out before I think better of it. "Actually... I'm not too sure if either could be considered a relationship. I also learned very recently that Eamon knew my brother! Well, here's the kicker... I found this earbud at the bar; it started playing music! Even though I tried to get rid of it multiple times, it kept coming back! Then, I realized I was being followed. It's actually my stalker that sort of told me my brother didn't kill himself and I needed to find something Theo left for me. I can only assume that this thing I need to find will shed light on what actually happened to him." I may have left out some parts, and I'm glad I did.

The color from Andrea's face has drained. She stares blankly in my direction. My roommate is here, but not really all there. I think I broke my friend. I was so used to her jumping in and trying to solve everything; her shock was almost cathartic. Right now, I don't need to be told what to do. What I lack is the occasional freedom to unload the mental baggage I'm lugging around. Her simply listening... hearing my words is more than enough, even if I did sound certifiable. The air felt thicker somehow as all my truths wafted out in the open. Taking air in felt taxing. As I waited for her to say anything, I panicked internally. Would she retreat further away? More than she already has been?

"I need a drink," she finally declares after long moments pass.

"Please... allow me." I rise from the couch, zip past her to the kitchen, and locate the bottle opener from the drawer next to the stove. Clutching the bottle of wine from Eamon, I pop the cork before pulling down two glasses from the cabinet. I then proceed to pour the deep red liquid to the brim of BOTH glasses.

Shock and concern are plastered across her face. "Did I miss that you're drinking now too?" she guesses, sitting upon the dining chair with a heavy thud.

I set both glasses onto the table and sat before the very vice I swore off three years ago. I've never been into drugs, and I barely ever drank besides the occasional long island iced tea, but when my brother unexpectedly died... I felt compelled to make a commitment. More to him than anyone else. Even in death, I didn't want to disappoint him. I watched what Theo's passing did to my parents... Mom and Dad sold everything, moved away, and withdrew. They mourned, but they did it behind closed doors. It's like my parents didn't want to talk about it. I may have been an adult in my first year of college, but I've never been more unsure of myself. That year was a whirlwind, but the decisions I made were to keep me safe. To survive another day. It seems almost silly that I did things back then to appease others. No drugs or alcohol for my parents and brother. Even staying with Brodi as long as I did was probably, so I didn't disappoint him.

I'm so tired! So fed up with worrying how my fuck ups will be perceived. I've known it all along, somewhere deep down. He didn't kill himself. It wasn't an overdose and after these past few weeks, I would like a goddamn drink.

"Today seems like a good day to start," I decisively retort. Causing the corner of her mouth to curve slightly upward. Rotating the steam of the glass between my thumb and pointer finger, I watch as the maroon liquid sloshes along the edges of the glass.

Andrea extends her arm over the table, ceasing the spin of my glass as she places her hand on mine. "Are you certain this is what you want?" Her tense body leans forward as if toying with the idea of snatching it from me.

"My brother didn't overdose. I made that commitment, uninformed. Someone took my brother from me. Now, I have a new promise. Find out what happened to my brother." I watch as her body visibly relaxes, and her hand withdraws to her side once more. "I deserve a drink." I say with steely nerves, ready for any disagreement she may be ready to throw my way.

She shakes her head and actually snickers. "No, it's not about that. You just took cold medicine, you're not supposed to drink, nitwit." There she is. There's my overbearing best friend. I've missed her.

"Just one glass, then," I agree.

We say nothing as we sit across from one another, periodically sipping from our oversized glasses. The last time I was truly intoxicated was the summer after high school graduation. Never a party girl by any means, however, it felt freeing to be out from the watchful eye of my family. Mom and Dad became super paranoid about my safety as I became older. If I wasn't meeting with a therapist, I was to report my whereabouts, checking in often if I wasn't with my brother or at school. I sometimes wish I had other parents. Ones who weren't so uptight. If they just spent more time with us, they'd see that we were fine, but they worked so much. It seemed stupid they always had to know where we were, but never tell us their agendas. They were different when we were younger, more carefree, and happier. My brother and I rarely saw them by the time my senior year in high school rolled around. One shrink told me, stop holding back my emotions. Let them pour out of you and free yourself of that weight. Well, if I actually emanated what was going on in my head, they probably would have sent me to a facility with padded walls. Little girls aren't meant to have wild, depraved thoughts.

I tried journaling when I was younger. Just my luck that I would forget to put the notebook back under my mattress before my mom came into my room. Naturally curious, she read it. For the next year, I was forced to endure an extra day of counseling each week. Apparently, documenting fantasies about being restrained, kidnapped, and fucked till you lose control of all bodily functions, isn't considered "normal" hormonal urges. Good grief, when I think about it, I pity my poor mother, but that troubled teenager was the most honest version of myself to date. The rebellious phase is a balancing act of coming into your true self and learning what's socially acceptable, while trying not to be too harshly judged by others. I wonder what my parents think of me now. Are they proud of me yet or will my mother always see me as some damaged thing?

When Theo left us, I felt my conflicted, 'adolescent self' trying to claw its way out. Already feeling so broken and lost, I desired safety and consistency in a world that seemed to be perpetually unpredictable. Starting by taking away anything that inhibited my ability to remain intact, like booze or narcotics. It was the one last component; I felt as though I had a hold on. Also, I didn't want to dishearten my mother. Not again. I'll never be Theo, but maybe... Who am I kidding, they're the ones who left. I'd love to know why I still seek approval in every facet of my life.

When Brodi crossed my path, he made me feel appreciated. I hoped he could be that special someone to me. The one who accepted me as is. No returns. No refunds. He was the one to approach me. In a strip club, of all the places. I was a part of the bachelorette crew, rampaging through Boston's finest establishments, like Cha-Cha's. That friend is now divorced. Maybe having the starting line of your marriage with tits and ass, should have been some kind of red flag... but I was giddy over Brodi's pursuit. He wasn't like the other guys I've been with... Tattooed, muscular, oozing confidence, and rode motorcycles. It was like edging myself with danger. I was helpless against him. Andrea wasn't a fan right off the bat, and I'm pretty sure Theo would have hated him, if he had been around to meet my boyfriend. As if I was a defective faucet, I allowed who I was to slowly trickle out. Drip by drip. It was fun at first. He took me out. Fucked me in exciting places and even introduced me to his friends once. Over time, I opened the valve more, needing connection on a deeper level. I wanted him to know my desires. Learn the real me. In spite of me pouring myself out, while grappling with who I was and who I should be, he withdrew. Sure, he stayed with me, but I felt more like a commodity. We saw less and less of each other as time went on. I think the turning point was when I got my vertical clitoral hood pierced. I always wanted it, but I could tell he didn't like it. He said he liked his woman *natural*, which was a crock of shit. I've seen his search history. Nothing was natural about anything he was viewing. I was crushed, but for some reason I stayed. I also kept the piercing. Looking back, I think it was my way of saying, "fuck you," don't tell me what to do with my body or how to be.

As each month passes, since Brodi up and disappeared, I have clarity. Like I was caught in a haze, unable to see what was right in front of me. I deserve better, I gave it my all and he rarely showed up. I like me. Bedazzled pussy and all! I shouldn't be ashamed of who I am, especially with someone who is supposed to be my partner. What I wouldn't give to be able to go back and spend just an hour with that chaotic, teenage version of myself. Give her a glimpse of what is to come and ensure her that she will survive this.

With both glasses empty between us, Andrea is the first to fracture the still moments. "Who do you think did it?" Andrea's finger runs along the mouth of the drained glass, smearing the glossy, mauve lip stain across its edge.

"I'm not sure," I divulge. Honestly, I don't even have a heading. My brother didn't have any enemies. He wanted to work in journalism. From what I understood, everyone adored him. He was the golden child so to speak.

Andrea stands and disappears to her room temporarily. I was briefly worried she wouldn't come back. Next thing I know, she's rolling a whiteboard from her room.

"Where did that come from?"

She clicks the lock on the wheels and uncaps a dry eraser marker. "Closet," she says, before scribbling words on the white, shiny surface. *Theo, Eamon,* and *Stalker.* "Okay, we know Theo died almost three years ago." She writes *three years* under his name. Andrea points the uncapped marker toward me. "When did you start working at The Black Sheep?"

I think for a moment, "Around six months ago." I had just lost my job as the hotel receptionist. Star Mart didn't pay enough; I needed that second job. Within a week I was offered the position at the bar. Connor was actually the one who handed me a flyer, when I was just happening by. It was Cassie who offered me a job on the spot. That's why I thought she owned the bar, not Eamon.

"How about this stalker guy, when did that start?" Andrea inquires.

I look back through my phone's calendar and messages. "I found the earbud less than a month ago."

She steps back to admire the chicken scratch of notes across the board. It's barely legible; she should have pursued a career as a doctor. "Wait!" She yelps.

I startle, because she's not one to display sudden bursts of energy. I'm drained, too tired for jump scares.

Andrea looks at me. "Didn't Brodi disappear right before you started working at the bar?"

I guess... Yeah. It is a really odd coincidence. It was a rough time for me. Having two jobs and keeping busy helped me get through the onset of his departure. "That's right... I did start at The Black Sheep shortly after."

She's at the board feverishly annotating, like a professor that's finally made some headway on that career halting equation. "You said Eamon and your stalker seem to have known Theo?"

I nod.

She draws lines, connecting *Theo's* name to *Eamon* and the *Stalker*. I chew on my lip as the story unfolds, right before my eyes. It's just all loosely based associations. None of it makes any sense. Nothing related. Who are we missing?

"Can you add two more names?" I suggest. "Garron and Dax... they're like Eamon's right-hand men or friends, not sure what to call them."

She adds the two names with two shorter lines, connecting them to *Eamon*. The toothpick I found... could the man behind the mask be Garron?

Andrea finally sits down in the chair beside me, as we both study the board with what can only be described as a disorganized collection of acquaintances. What are we doing here? Figuring out what happened to my brother, surmising who my stalker is, or cataloging my questionable choices. Perhaps all three?

My roommate turns to me after a long stretch of us staring at the board, trying to make sense of this perfectly illustrated chaos I call my life. "Has your stalker ever made contact with you, beyond using technology?"

Shit. I knew this would come up. I think it would have been easier to tell her I was fooling around with Eamon, who she clearly has a distaste for, rather than disclosing I've been intimate with a masked man, whose identity is still a mystery even to me! Getting ready to say it out loud made me feel stupid, for engaging in such a potentially dangerous activity. When I was with my stalker, it just felt right.

I speak my truth. As it turns out... She listens, no judgment. No snide remarks. Just hops up from her seat, pulling the easel closer, and changes to a different colored marker. She has to be part machine.

"We should list the songs he's played for you. There may be some kind of message there, that helps us." She writes the words *The Stalker's Playlist* on the top, right side of the board.

It takes me every bit of an hour, looking through my phone, checking calendars, and messages to recall everything. Racking my already, very tired brain, was a chore to list all of the songs he has played for me, up until this point. The list barely fits on the board.

"Cindel. All of this…" She motions toward the insane amount of information. "Goes deeper than you could possibly know."

Here comes the power of reasoning. I hold my breath before she continues, worried she's already made up her mind.

"But we're gonna figure this out. Together."

Okay. I didn't expect that.

"Cindel, I've only ever been concerned about your safety. I'm begging you… please stay away from these men."

I can't promise her that. Like a moth to a flame, I'm drawn to him. Drawn to both of them. Maybe for two separate reasons, but I can't really explain it. My eyes sting, as exhaustion from this day consumes me. "I'm tired. Let's continue this tomorrow."

She caps the marker, then pulls me from my seat. My first real friend wraps her arms around me. I needed that. To know, we're okay. Before closing the door to her bedroom, she signs *I love you.* With that, I know that if everything else goes to shit, at least I have her.

THIRTY

CINDEL

Over the next week, Andrea is curiously home more than usual. Each night she and I go over our conspiracy board, accumulating notes, names, and songs. Puzzles were never considered 'fun' to me, but this one might as well have no image on display, identical shapes, and pieces lost to the vacuum. We even had to add paper taped on the sides of the board, because we've run out of room. *Officer Fucking Kent* was one of the additions, with *Creepy Craig* below. We're confident my boss's untimely demise doesn't have anything to do with Theo, but we want to list every possible variable.

Ironically, with my roommate back in my corner, Eamon has been scarce. Even the text messages aren't more than a goodnight or emoji here and there. The subtle change only causes me to become even more anxious about our approaching dinner date. I can't discern if the nerves are apprehension or something else entirely.

Andrea has gone all "Nancy Drew" on my ass and insists I should be *wired,* when I go on the date. Honestly, where does she get this stuff from? I agree to her plan, if only to put her mind at ease.

Jada came by the bar again, conveniently during the only time Eamon was there this week. Watching her forced laugh and idle hands explore Eamon's shoulders and arms, while he attempts to work on his laptop, was a true test of everyone's patience. It's not like Eamon is mine or anything. I technically didn't belong to anyone, so how can he? We haven't even been physical with one another, aside from the one kiss and even that felt forced.

I've never kissed the masked man. Not on the mouth, at least. I wonder what his lips would feel like on mine. Once the mask came off and the games were over, would there be anything left? Anything real? Did I unknowingly accept terms when I took that earbud home? Was I... his? I can't.

Committing to anything from here on out, will be kept at arm's reach. Too many unknowns.

Presently. I am fed up with Jada. She continues barking orders at me to bring her random things since she can't move around easily. When she demanded a Cosmo and a tonic for Eamon, I was done. I may have accidentally put down the drink too quickly, splashing the pink liquid onto her phone and down her white miniskirt.

"Oops."

As she shuffles off to the bathroom, muttering profanities the whole way, Eamon gives me a knowing wink paired with a devilish smile.

My lower belly somersaults. Fuck, this man confuses me. Cold for nearly a week, then undeniably smooth when he finally comes around me. I shouldn't feel guilty, no one's getting hurt. I'm simply having some fun, while also getting answers to questions I've had for years.

Eamon's comrades seem to hang around The Black Sheep habitually. If Garron isn't drinking or challenging a group of frat boys to a game of darts, he is distracting the new hires. It seems like each time the new girls, Leslie or Maya, deliver drinks; they go out of their way to pass by the boy's table. More often than not, I find one of them sitting at their table passing the time. At first, I was easily able to redirect the girls by having them grab something from the backroom. However, after the fifth time, I realized the catalyst was Garron. Redirecting my focus, I warned him, if he didn't stop monopolizing my waitresses' time… I would dress him in a low-cut top and have him serving tables.

Garron wags his eyebrows at me and tells me not to threaten him with a good time. Fuck... it better not be Garron behind the mask.

Still, his friend never engages me. I feel uncomfortable sometimes, when Dax is around. His features are always severe, right before he takes off somewhere. Those nights without the drama of Jada or the fluctuation of Eamon's moods, between flirting or ignoring me, go by easier. Nonetheless, I felt more like a babysitter than a bar manager.

The only song I can add to our list this week is, **Elastica – "Connection."** The stalker played it for me one night, after Andrea and I went round and round, trying to make sense of how all these names are connected. It was actually Andrea who pointed out that Theo and Eamon went to the same school, Boston College. How did she know that?

I surmised since we pretty much grew up in the same city; our families had to have some sort of loose connection. Andrea intermittently became quiet when I would go on a tangent about Theo or Eamon. I can't deny the feeling that she may be withholding something. It's probably just in my head, trying to automatically make connections when there probably aren't any.

When I told my roommate about the newest song, she ripped apart the apartment, looking for cameras or microphones. Cursing ensued and now we need to buy new throw pillows because she disemboweled each one with a kitchen knife and sheer determination. Nothing was found to indicate we were being watched, but I knew my stalker was always watching. Andrea was pissed. Personally? I was relieved he could still watch me.

I open the texts with my stalker. Rereading and trying to carefully form questions that could help in my search for answers. He wouldn't answer any questions this week. In fact, he didn't respond to anything I've sent. Since when did these roles reverse, the pursued became the pursuer. Had I done something wrong?

Wow, Cindel, are you concerned about your actions against him? Maybe I do need to start journaling again. Clearly, I'm more disturbed than before.

With the masked stalker MIA, I try to shift my focus to getting ready for dinner at Eamon's. It's tomorrow. So, many questions run through my mind.

How should I act in the privacy of his home? What do we talk about? Will he want to…? You know… how far am I willing to go with Eamon? Was agreeing to this date smart if I wasn't willing to go all in? Was I simply using him… trying to shed light on my brother's life, before he passed?

Good grief, I think I am! Didn't Eamon deserve a sincere connection, with no strings attached? I attempt to sort through my feelings as I ready for bed.

What are my feelings about Eamon? Genuinely, it feels more like hanging out with a sibling than anything sexual. Maybe I'm overthinking it. He is successful, charming, good-looking, and a skilled kisser. Ughh! My inner unrest reminds me of a game of tug-of-war, rationalizing between my brain and my heart.

On the sidelines is the cloaked stranger. Every time I feel as though my mind is made up, the stalker trickles into my thoughts. MY stalker.

The wave of memories hit me. How he made my body sing like no one has ever done. The whole situation should be considered unhealthy, ultimately dangerous. Yet, his furtive engagement has me longing for him in every dark alleyway I enter. Lately, I find myself thinking about him whenever I have time to myself. In the bath, in bed… last time he was near, he took care of me while I was ill. I appreciate the tenderness, but I also feel like I'm overdue. Now I only conjure up emotions about his touch against my skin. Somehow, this nameless man has me in a chokehold.

After I quiet my cravings, I emerge from the bathroom a few minutes before six...

Andrea nurses a bottle of Moscato in the kitchen, as she watches me do a last-minute fit check in the hallway mirror. The tight-fitting, black cocktail dress hugs me in all the right places, since I took in the bust to accommodate my small chest.

"You look hot. I'd fuck you," she announces unabashedly. Setting the bottle down, she comes behind me and proceeds to zip up the garment. "Are you wearing it?" I turn, facing her fully, then point to the small rose brooch, affixed on the top of the dress. "Good. Make sure you're close enough so I can hear what's being said. I want to know if you get into any trouble." I look up to the ceiling and nod. This feels wrong, but I agreed to put her mind at ease.

"Yes, I know, but will you be listening if things get... ya know, serious?"

Her eyebrows furrow, then shoot up. "Oh. Right... umm, no. Eww. Love you, but no. I promise not to listen if you cross that bridge with him." Andrea tells me when she hears the beep of a horn, just outside.

Simultaneously, my phone vibrates, indicating that my ride is here.

"I'm going to stay up and wait for you to get home," she adds.

I sign to her *thank you* as I made my way out the door.

Eamon sent a car, since he needed to pick up a few last-minute things before our date. The driver shares that Eamon's place is on the posher side of the city, overlooking picturesque sunsets on the Boston Harbor.

I smile but remain quiet, recheck my small clutch once in the vehicle. Phone, check. Earbud, check. Pepper Spray, check. Pepper spray? Damnit, Andrea! I don't need that. Just because Eamon was sometimes complex, didn't mean I was fearful for my life. My time with Eamon was enjoyable. Being around him feels effortless. No matter how tonight turns out, I know he won't hurt me. I also recognize that Andrea is listening... I tap roughly on the rose brooch in lieu of her sneaky, 'self-defense' addition. I hope it makes an uncomfortably loud sound for her.

Considering the purple starred tech in my purse, I replaced my hearing aid. Not sure why, but I don't want to be without it lately.

The car pulls up to an enormous, glass building that sits overlooking the bay. The modern structure has a marbled wall, with black lettering displaying Twenty-Two Liberty. The whole thing oozes class and money. A doorman instantly welcomes me inside the breathtaking premises. From the colossal decorative planters to intricate chandeliers, the lobby entrance is swankier than any hotel I have ever stayed in, but this is a place people live! My heels click along the smooth floors as I make my way through the vast room and over to the concierge.

"Welcome, Miss Mari. Mr. Murray is expecting you."

The suited man with note-worthy posture escorts me to the elevator, holds the doors open as I enter before he swipes a card onto a reader. The light inside indicates we're heading up to the top floor. As we ascend, I wonder if Eamon's monthly rent is more than a year's worth of the place Andrea and I split. How can the owner of a rundown bar and boxing club do this well? The elevator dings upon reaching the twentieth floor. The poised man once again, politely holds the automatic doors for me. I'm pretty sure the censors don't allow the mechanism to squish people. Having an escort for guests is a tad excessive.

Exiting the lift, I find myself inside a well-lit, contemporary apartment with trendy art and windows as far as the eye can see. The water below looks like paintbrush strokes from an impressionistic painting. Boats bob on the water, as the last traces of warmth disappear below the horizon. Lights from residing buildings emit gold and traces of yellows against the contrasting black and blues, of the choppy waters beyond. I would never leave this place if it were my home. This view is everything Boston has to offer.

Banging pans in the kitchen bring me farther into the apartment, toward its source. "Hello?" To my surprise, Connor pops around the corner, holding a wood crate.

"Hey, Cindel. Just dropping off some bottles of whiskey for the boss."

It makes sense that Eamon would not only want his bar well stocked, but also his own. I wonder if he entertains often. Am I just one of many? Not sure how I feel about this realization.

"Enjoy your little soirée."

Holy hell, now everyone knows Eamon is hosting me. He rushes to the elevator, sliding a card much like the attendant, and disappears behind the closing doors.

"In here!"

I round the corner to find Eamon in the kitchen, with what I can only assume is his entire collection of pots and pans, littering the pristine, marble island.

"Wow!" He proclaims. "You look magnificent." Stepping toward me, he opens his arms in greeting.

This is new. The hug is almost awkward, we are trying to decide between facing each other fully or a quick side squeeze. In the end it was a mishmosh of both, but he quickly remediates by leaning in and kissing my cheek.

He's dressed smartly. Crisp white shirt, slightly rolled up sleeves, showing off just his wrists, and black slacks that are tailored so dangerously perfectly; it should be a sin.

Eamon returns to rummaging around the kitchen, pulling out various ingredients from the fridge.

I find myself appreciating his backside for probably longer than I should have.

"I wasn't sure if you wanted steak or pasta, so I picked up all the ingredients. I can make both, if you'd prefer."

I fight back a laugh, trying to be polite with my response. "Both?"

He nods. "So, what will it be?"

I tap my finger on my chin as I consider. "Well… I never say no to pasta."

He smiles, revealing an adorable cheek dimple; I never noticed prior. "Of course. Pasta it is!"

I take that as my cue to take a seat at the island to watch the man work his magic.

A faucet above the stove pours into a large stainless-steel pot, as Eamon washes ripened tomatoes at the sink. When the pot is nearly full, he turns the lever, then proceeds to dice the red fruit atop a wooden board. It's like watching a cooking show, but with a painfully handsome chef.

"You must be quite the chef in a kitchen like this," I remark, as I scan the massive room that's probably the size of our entire apartment. The place is brimming with state-of-the-art appliances, including gadgets I'm not even sure I know how to use.

"Actually, I'm not much of a cook. I usually eat on the go."

His response astonishes me, seeing how incredible the kitchen is. "You're kidding, with a space like this… I could be the next Martha Stewart!"

The newly discovered cheek dimple deepens. "Yes, I know… shocking!" He jeers, looking up at me briefly ahead of returning to his chopping. The next words come out with an unusual level voice. "The last person I was with liked to cook. We were always in the kitchen together. Frankly, this room has sat untouched for quite some time."

I watch on as he absently scrapes the tomatoes into a shiny sauce pot and pushes them around. He hasn't wanted to be in his own kitchen since his last relationship? How long ago was that? Eamon seems as though he's drifting away with past memories.

I try to pivot the conversation. "Well, I bet you could run circles around Martha," I remark matter-of-factly.

His smile doesn't quite meet his eyes, but I'm hoping it's moving things in the right direction. Eamon punctures a package of premade Italian meatballs, instantly making me eat my words. Premade? Oh man, he really wasn't kidding about the whole *not cooking thing*. It's like a crime against Italians!

In a skillet, he works to brown the abominable meatballs while forming a thick sauce with olive oil, tomatoes, and a little water. While he cooks, I inquire about his other business, the Bay Boxing Club.

Eamon explains how his grandparents acquired the failing gym and how they planned to expand their successes to other parts of the New England area. Unfortunately, they never grew past Boston. When he took over the family business, it was his efforts alone which made the gym more profitable than ever. I knew his family was visiting, but what I didn't know was that it was more for business than pleasure. Eamon would like to expand someday, but any conversations of growth have been frozen, until an outstanding issue has been resolved. Whatever that means. He seems to have a good head for business, although as I learn more, it's apparent he'd rather spend his resources and energy at the boxing club than the bar.

Will he ultimately close the bar once the issue is resolved? I might need that backup job sooner than later. What I still can't wrap my head around is how either of these businesses would merit someone "owing a debt." Who would have such a deficit that Eamon would have to send his goons to collect? Obviously, I don't pry on the subject. At some point during the conversation, he invites me to come by the club sometime for a *beginner's boxing class*. My mind wanders to Brodi, recalling how he too enjoyed recreational boxing. Would it be rude to ask Eamon about past Bay Boxing members?

Sure, Cindel... let's see if your last boyfriend went to my club. Okay, okay. I drag myself back from the impulsive thought, as this seems like the wrong time and place, to be thinking about my absent ex.

Abandoning the food, he pours himself a finger of whiskey, adding a perfectly clear sphere of ice in the center. "I remember you saying that you don't drink... otherwise, I'd offer you one," he explains.

Now he finally remembers? "Actually, I've had a bit of a reawakening. I'm going to try to make some changes, starting by not making promises to myself that hold little merit."

He instantly takes out another glass, pouring the same amount of amber liquid, and adding an ice ball. All the while his eyes are assessing. I take hold of the drink from his extended arm across the island. He raises his glass to mine, "Sláinte."

Just then, I notice gray smoke billowing from behind Eamon.

"Is something burning?"

Setting down the glass, he urgently reaches for the cooktop to remove the lid from the skillet, finding the meatballs no more than blackened briquettes at this point. A procession of unintelligible curses pours from his mouth while he turns every knob to its off position. Next, he investigates the sauce which had apparently overheated to a rolling boil. As if this was one of those blundering rom-com moments, the bubbling concoction erupts outward, splattering onto everything in its path... including Eamon.

"Fuck, I've ruined suppah!" He faces me with a look of defeat. "Sorry, little fish. Lemme order some Thai." His entire front, including the once-pristine shirt are covered in a fine spray of scarlet.

I cover my mouth, trying to squelch the laugh, over this usually refined man looking so... normal.

To my surprise he smiles, causing another dimple to appear in his left cheek. There's two of them?!

Although dinner may not have gone according to plan, he looks at ease. Happy. Like he finally allowed his carefully placed mask to slip away. "I hope

I haven't ruined this night for you." He stands beside me, towering, even with me upon this extra-tall bar stool.

I have to crane my neck back just to gaze into his eyes. They're an alluring sage green. Hours could pass, and I would never tire of staring into them. "Of course not. I'm not here to rate your cooking skills, sir." Holy smokes; this man's face is all sharp lines and bedroom eyes.

"Oh? Then why are you here, Cindel?" His words are no more than a whisper.

Maybe because we're alone or the smell of burnt meat is going to my head, but I feel bold.

"Well… I'd like to get to know you better," I propose.

He tilts in and reaches a hand out, only to play with pieces of my bangs that have grown into my vision. We're only a breath apart.

"I could never tire of those eyes," he admits as his hand presses gently against my cheek. This close, I can't miss how his expression drops slightly. How is it possible that someone can switch so quickly between passion and pensive?

My body moves instinctively, attempting to close the narrow gap between us. He smells of whiskey, with a hint of smoke. I should be relishing his scent, but I'm unable to. Thinking back to the way my masked stranger makes me feel. How I want to be wrapped in his black candied flavor.

"I'm going to get changed," he blurts, immediately withdrawing when we were just a hair's breadth away from one another.

He strides down the hall, most likely to his bedroom, and I'm finally able to shake myself from this spell-bound state.

What am I doing? I don't know what's come over me. I'm conflicted. Lost to the pull of another without a name. I should go, this was a mistake. Standing, I slipped off my heels, and padded down the hall in the direction his figure disappeared. Let me tell Eamon I'd like to go home.

Only one door was ajar in the long hallway. I push past to find a dimly lit room. Dark walls surround a shallow bed; all cast in a familiar crimson glow. Curiosity has me slipping into the room, where I find Eamon shirtless before his closet. Just as I am ready to speak, I find the source of the red light. Inadvertently, I edge toward the glass box, holding what air I already had within my chest. Within the enclosure of plants, I locate a fuzzy creature, almost identical to my Thelma. In the corner of the tarantula's home is a skull hide, just like I have back in my apartment.

My stomach twists, causing the air to rush from my lungs all at once. An audible noise falls from my lips, just as a hand lands on my shoulder. I spin around to find Eamon, eyebrow raised, and still shirtless. My mouth opens and closes but no words form. That's when I notice something even more odd than a twin spider in my boss's home.

On his upper forearm, a stark, black skull with shamrock eyes looks back at me. I've seen that before. "There's something you need to know," he confesses.

When my brain finally fires up, I spit out. "Why do you have an identical set-up and pet to my brother's?" The world tips on its axis. Without realizing, I have progressively been backing up... I'm taken off guard when the back of my calves hit soft material and I fall back. I've guided myself to his bed.

Eamon now stands positioned between me and the door to his bedroom.

What is happening? What could he possibly need to tell me besides; *I've been hiding things from you.* Oh my god! Does he plan to...?! My heart painfully thunders in my chest. Think! Think! My phone is in the kitchen, but I know Andrea must be listening. If I were in danger, she could help me. Right?

Eamon must have noticed me looking from him to the door. "I'm not going to hurt you. I just need you to... understand some things." With arms folded, I'm now angry with myself for agreeing to come here in the first place.

"What do you want from me?!"

Then it hits me, how he knows so much about me, why he keeps me close. "Did... did you kill my brother?!"

His features change from soft to jagged in the blink of an eye. His knit eyebrows and curled lips tell me all I need to know. "What?!" He takes a step back.

On shaking legs, I stand and point my finger toward him, "You heard me!"

His jaw begins to tick, as if chewing on something invisible. "I would never hurt Theo," he says through gritted teeth. "I fucking loved him."

Wait... what? I sit back down onto the bed. Memories of my brother swirl in my mind. How? Could this be true? Too many imperative questions to pick out just one. Long quiet moments pass without either of us speaking. He's keeping his distance. I focus on the present, what's in front of me, and how I should begin. "What's its name? The tarantula."

His shoulders noticeably lower. "Louise," he says a breath above a whisper.

"Thelma and Louise?" Eyes downcast; he confirms my hasty revelation with a head tilt. "You were... like, together, together?"

His body moves to the closet, pulling a shirt off the hanger ahead of advancing toward the floor to ceiling windows, toward the endless dark horizon. He's telling me without his voice.

"Oh. Oh!" I look for something to busy my hands, finding a loose thread on the hem of my dress to fiddle with. This man makes me question how well I actually knew my brother. Through childhood we were thick as thieves, but as we grew up, he made room in his heart for others, I never considered. Was he scared to tell me? Theo meant the world to me; I would never judge him over who he chose to love. Is Eamon the secret I'm supposed to find?

"Are you a prince?" I wondered out loud, thinking back to the song my stalker played for me. I probably sound unhinged, but I suppose it's better than telling him why I'm asking. Well… a song by Spin Doctors informed me you are in fact, not my stalker, and I was wondering if you were of noble blood? Yes… let's avoid that.

A shy smirk works its way across his face, and I can't help but chew on the inside of my cheek. Slowly, he makes his way to my side; his attentive glare trained on me. "I'm sure my father would consider himself a king, but no, little fish, I'm no Prince Charming." His words were hushed but spoken with conviction. I feel like even his answer has a riddle woven throughout.

The bed dips with his weight as he sits, naturally leaning me toward him. The shirt he now wears has the top few buttons undone with the sleeves rolled up to his elbows; past the ink on his skin. His large hand takes hold of mine, ceasing my ability to wind the rogue string on my outfit, around my finger.

As if he knew my plan to wrap it around, until it turns the tip of my finger white. Even now, he is tender with me. I seem to understand the dynamic better. Unable to meet his eyes, I settle on assessing the hollowed, shamrock sockets of his tattooed skull.

"You have so much to learn, little Princess. This much I can say, I wouldn't touch a hair on your brother's head. Unless he asked me—"

My hands shoot up to cover my face. "Oh god! Please don't finish that sentence!" I absently feel for the flower shaped brooch, while trying to do anything but picture my brother with the man before me.

Removing his hand from mine, he stands abruptly. "Other things are at play. Everything goes far deeper than you could possibly fathom. There are people who want to hurt you, Cindel." Each new revelation is more disturbing than the last. "Your family aren't who you think they are."

An unpleasant shiver works its way up my spine. "I've been trying to get close to you. Working up to telling you all of this… because Theo shouldn't have left us. Now, it's my job to protect his kid sister."

I watch as his arms move, trying to convey his message as the word "sister" gets stuck on a loop in my brain. Hold on. That tattoo… Mairead! She has the same one on her shoulder. Mairead is Eamon's sister! Like connecting toy bricks, everything snaps into place. Is he aware of my friendship with Mairead? Alarm bells began to sound in my ears. Everything is connected! Nothing is by chance… I need to get out of here. I try to control the tremor that quakes through my body. If not Eamon, then who wants to hurt me?

Fidgeting with the rose pin on my chest, I remind myself that I'm not alone in all this. I roll my shoulders back, mustering all the confidence I can, then stand to walk toward the bedroom door. "Fake it till you make it," my mom would tell me. Especially whenever I was too nervous about what others would say.

The windows and low-lit room play with shadows. Eamon's silhouetted frame watches me inch toward the door, as he remains fixed in place against the dark navy sky.

Within the door frame to the hallway, I demand one more thing before I leave. "Who is my family, Mr. Murray?" I wait on bated breath with posture so rigid, it makes my neck ache.

His hands ideally find their way into his pant pockets. His gaze distant, not just physically but detached from the present conversation.

I ran my hands down the length of my dress, smoothing the wrinkles from sitting most of my time here.

He nods to himself before glancing down at the floor then back up to me. Even from across the room, his eyes appear lethal, like an invisible switch flips from my inquiry. "Look up... 'Lombardi' when you get home." He pivots away from me, facing the water, as if that is my cue to leave.

I don't waste a moment longer, I make my way to the kitchen, grab my belongings, and head for the elevator. Fortunate to find an already parked cab, I am on my way home shortly after exiting the ritzy apartment complex.

I clutch my chest, willing my heart to settle when I feel something is missing. Shit. My pin! The microphone rose brooch must have fallen off in Eamon's room! My fingers find their way up to my mouth, as I begin to chew on the sides of my nails. A habit I commonly resorted to in my younger years; when I feel trapped or when others didn't seem to want to accept me "as is." Was Andrea able to hear clearly? Will she know everything that was said between Eamon and I?

Oh no... what if he finds it and knows it has a microphone? I'm not even sure what he would think. That I'm untrustworthy, a spy? At that point I realize something even more horrifying. Worse than Eamon, finding out I had a mic hidden within my flower pin. I've kissed my brother's lover. I feel automatically queasy, either from not eating or partner sharing with my sibling, I can't tell. Right before I'm about to christen the backseat of this taxi over my very own episode from the Jerry Springer show, I find a rogue mint in my bag to settle my stomach. Seriously, I couldn't have made this shit up in my wildest dreams.

As soon as I pay the taxi driver, Andrea is bursting through the front of our building with half of her coat on, a sneaker on one foot, and a rain boot on the other.

We notice each other at the same time causing her to run the rest of the way to me. "Oh my god, I thought the worst! When I couldn't hear you any longer, I realized it must have fallen off you... I got ready as fast as I could!"

I place my hands onto her shoulders trying to soothe her, when I'm not sure I look any less frazzled myself. "You didn't even know where I was," I say with a laugh.

"Of course I know," she proclaims through labored breaths. "There's a tracker on your phone."

I point my finger toward her. "I knew it!"

Shortly after our interesting reunion on the street, we find ourselves back at the white board, as a frozen pizza cooks in the oven. I add a heart with a lame-looking spider between Theo and Eamon's name.

"I didn't hear anything after he spoke about *not harming a hair on your brother's head*. Was there anything else we should add to the board?"

There's so much I still don't understand, so I take a moment to reflect.

I first met Mairead at Star Mart. My ex-coworker is Eamon's unbalanced sister. How is each new thing I learn connected to something I thought I understood? What does Mairead know about all this? I decided that I need to see Mairead. We have tentative plans to visit an escape room. I wouldn't be "lying" to Andrea, only withholding a couple pieces of information until a later date. Hanging out with Mairead, without Andrea thinking we're in imminent danger, could shed some light on this situation.

This board sure is a poor excuse for mystery solving, although likely still better investigative work than any 'officer of the law' in this city.

I catch myself before sharing the last thing Eamon said to me. The first lead I need to follow in regard to my family. This feels too personal and until I look up what "Lombardi" means, I didn't want to involve my roommate any more than she already was.

She's been like a sister to me since college. She loves me and my family. "Nothing else to add," I insist.

Her face speaks volumes, never hiding how she really feels. I can tell she doesn't believe this is all I know, but she must understand. That's all I'm going to give her for now.

Peering into Thelma's tank, I find her nestled within the faux skull. It's so strange how she's been sleeping during the night and out during the day. She's nocturnal after all. I whisper against the glass, "Are you feeling, okay?" She remains immobile within her hide. "I met Louise today, your partner in crime."

The oven beeps reminding me that the pizza is ready. We eat at the table, only the sounds of chewing fill the space. My eyes are going to cross if I stare at that board a moment longer. After we each polish off our half of the pie, I reveal, "I'm going to go through some boxes of stuff my mom gave me a while back. Maybe I can find something that gives us an idea of who would want to…" I stop myself before I think out loud.

Andrea tilts her head while taking the dishes from my hands. "I got this. Go get some sleep. You're making less sense than the whiteboard."

I do appreciate the way she can be mothering at times. Once the door to my room closes, I peel myself from what I realize is an extremely inappropriate dress, considering who I learned Eamon was to my brother. I think I may need to burn it.

The chilled floors are only going to become more frigid as autumn morphs into winter. At the top of my closet, I pull down extra blankets for my bed and even use some leftover washi tape, to seal the cracks around my windows that allow our expensive heat to escape.

Tomorrow, I'll continue my hunt for answers. The day will be busy from the start… including breakfast with my uncle, earlier than normally scheduled, work at The Black Sheep, and then finding time to look up "Lombardi."

THIRTY-ONE

THE LOMBARDIS

Over Thirty years ago...

"Come on numbnuts, keep up!" I bellowed to my little bastardo of a brother.

We shot down one of the alleys trying to flee the sirens, wailing from all directions. I just got done paying a visit to the Irish territory. I hated the way their shit family crests were displayed outside their bars and clubs. Lucky for them I have impeccable taste, helping them to redecorate their fronts with a brick through each window.

I stop just short of emerging from between two buildings, when brilliant lights and wailing alarms streak past us. I put out my arm, stopping my incompetent brother from running headfirst into the side of the passing police cruiser.

Once the coast was clear, we barreled across the street, raced along the river, and continued fleeing that defiled part of town till our lungs burned.

Tears streamed down my fica brother's face.

I thought about leaving him there after I threw my last brick but knew my father would murder me on the spot if I returned home without him. What's poetic about all this is, he looks up to me, therefore the little turd will always keep his mouth shut. It'd be touching if I actually liked him, but I'd rather see him fileted from navel to sternum, tied to a cinder block, and thrown into the Boston Bay. Not by my hand, of course.

When we arrived home, our parents were waiting.

We both got walloped pretty good.

Pops already knew what happened, of course. He has eyes and ears everywhere in this city. He carried on about how our families are allies, and he'll be damned if he lets me trifle with their crucial network.

My face healed in a couple days, but the marks across my body took *almost a month. The baby of the family didn't undergo nearly as many lashes as I did.*

That night, we both got sent to bed without suppah.

I heard Ma sneak into my little brother's room with soup and bread, after Pops went to sleep. I however got an extra whack upside my head from a wooden spoon. She's a wise woman. She knew it was all my idea, even though Charles didn't say a word about anything. Ma cried for a long time, both from frustration and sorrow.

I'll never forget the day they brought Charles home. Mama thought I was too young to remember, but how could a boy forget when his ma had a swollen belly one day, then found in a pool of her own blood the next. They took her to the hospital to heal.

When she came back home, everything was different. She didn't want to play hide and seek anymore or push me on the tire swing. She wept whenever she thought no one was paying attention, but I saw.

I knew what happened even at that innocent age.

About a year later, my Nonna came over to watch me while my parents took a trip. I liked it when she visited. She let me help make lasagna from scratch and even taught me to be somewhat fluent in Italian.

I remember Mama walking through the door with Papa at her side. Her smile was bigger than I'd seen in a while.

I thought they brought me home a puppy because Pa had a large basket in his hands. I'll never forget peering into the large, wicker basket and not finding a pet, but a person. I was so mad, I ran to my room and screamed into my bed until my throat burned.

Then, I grabbed the paintbrushes and new paint colors my Nonna brought me from Sicily. I snapped each wooden handle in half and threw all the wreckage into the bin. I felt like I cried forever. At one point I sobbed so hard, my pa came in and hollered at me to quiet down before I woke the baby, or he'd really give me something to cry about. Everything hurts and I hate him. Not my father who clearly didn't give two fucks about my feelings, but the new child my parents brought home. I have nothing but resentment for the imposter who took my life from me.

As I grew older, it became more and more apparent who my parents preferred. Although when I was small, I told myself if I was good, said my prayers, and made good grades; I could become their new favorite, but it never happened.

My teenage years were a bit more colorful. I was quite rebellious and turned to drugs. It's easy to be a delinquent when your family has the drug market cornered. If I was never going to be the best, I might as well be the worst I could possibly be. I'm a committed guy when I put my mind to something. Isn't that what Pa always wanted? For me to excel at something? I will admit, I was kind of a loose cannon at times. Anyone who pissed me off or even remotely looked at me wrong, found themselves beaten to a bloody pulp.

Generally, my father knew what I was up to, he just didn't fucking care anymore, as long as I left his precious boy out of it.

There was another time I crossed the line, when I tried to pursue a red-haired girl, at a family function. My father said, I had no business going near a girl like her. Even though she was underaged, the puttana was already promised to another. I think Mr. Lombardi was more upset that I could have put a rift between his precious connections. I was upset that I didn't get my dick wet.

On my ceremony day, when the knife and pistol sat on the table, I took a blood oath to honor this family. My father, the captain, and other inducted members in attendance watched on as I became a man. Everyone must have somehow forgiven me for all my fuck ups or their Don threatened them if they spoke against his decision.

Charles was younger, so I was elated to finally have something he didn't; but I knew it wouldn't be like this forever.

For a while, I was on the straight and narrow. I listened when my elders gave advice, thought carefully about my actions, and strived to be the son my parents saw fit to take the reins, all in the name of the Lombardi family. I also learned about how our family had their web stretching far across the city and how we had a symbiotic relationship with other groups like the Murrays. They pointed customers our way and vice versa. I was a dumb kid when I chucked stones at their business fronts.

I kept my nose clean and my head on straight, but that fiery haired girl never left my mind. What was her name? No matter how much time passed, she wouldn't get out of my head. I needed to find out if that was her natural hair color.

Omerta is the most important code in the mob. If you're not in the family, you're not going to know much about us. Civilians remain blissfully unaware of who controls every major construction project in the Boston area. We get kickbacks from new projects, since our family had ranks within the union leadership. Having the association in our back pocket meant we monopolized the entire industry. If contractors or the big developers didn't pay on time, we had the ability to bring all development to a screeching halt. That's not the only way the Lombardi family gained power, we also had middlemen circulating narcotics within our terrain. Connections from Southeast Asia allowed an ample supply of heroin and opioids to the states. Mr. Lombardi drew the line at cocaine. Too many hands in the dope business, not a safe bet. It was easy money, the drug business; it doesn't dry up either. Our granddad always said Americans are avid consumers... there's always a market here.

Eventually, Charles came of age and completed his ceremony as well. He instantly became the star pupil. I was naive to think I had a shot at rising to the top of the mob.

My Ma and Pa were so proud to have their baby, finally learning the family business. The kid could have lit our home on fire, and they still wouldn't be deterred from giving him the world.

Everything that was rightfully mine. I am the first-born son after all. An actual full-blooded Lombardi, unlike my bastardo brother, Charles. I'm not meant to be a fucking solider, I'm supposed to be the Don! Not him! Someone who never belonged in this family in the first place.

As I stood watching my legacy handed over to someone who never deserved it, I made an oath to myself. I'll play my part for now, but when the time arrives, I will squeeze every ounce of happiness from Charles. It's like playing chess at a snail's pace. Slowly, I will take back what I'm owed, piece by piece.

In the meantime, I'm not going to sit around, letting life's pleasures slip through my fingers.

One summer evening, I found the red-haired princess just happening by. Like the stars had aligned, I'm going to take something for myself.

Far enough away so as not to raise suspicion, I followed the little fox all the way to the South End of the warehouse district. Then right into Club 114. I remained camouflage behind crowds of people, as she made her way through the club, looking for something. Maybe a group or a friend? If this was going to happen, I needed to make my move before she found someone she knew. Before I entered the club, I spotted one of our dealers, who I purchased a cap from. He was happy to oblige, especially when I threw an extra hundred on top, for discretion. As my target moved through the dancing bodies, I slipped close enough to administer the small syringe into her arm. She never saw me coming. No one batted an eye as I took what looked like an inebriated girl, out by the arm and into the fruitful night. She was everything I hoped she would be. I'm also happy to report the carpet does indeed match the drapes.

I learned much later that my midnight romp was a little more complicated than I anticipated. Although I already knew the girl's virtue I took was promised to another, I didn't know who she was destined to marry. A rather esteemed alliance of ours, actually. The heir to the Murray Empire. I thought she was a nobody, a loose acquaintance my father forbade, but she would someday be someone my family worked with regularly.

Fuck. I already didn't care about the relationship our families had. The way they conducted business was shoddy and most of their clientele were destitute has-beens or drunks. The whole Murray family was a shameful bunch of bogtrotters. If it were my choice, I would get rid of them all together.

While I was sent to do the shitty grunt work, my brother was tasked with expanding the family. It seemed as though everyone had a prized daughter to offer up to the great Lombardi legacy. It didn't take long until he was smitten with one of the capo's girls.

I had zero interest in settling down. In fact, the relationships I sought were more of the business variety. I'm no rat, but finding a foothold within the Boston PD was imperative to regaining control of this city. I understood this venture could take a considerable amount of time. People in Southie have big mouths and small imaginations.

A little birdie told me the "Virgin" Mary wanted to devote her time to a church in Ireland, in turn, delaying her marriage to Patrick Murray. A few months short of a year, she returned to marry her betrothed.

Doesn't take a fucking genius to realize what happened. She went there for a reason and was forced to leave something behind.

Despite my better judgement, I attended the wedding being sure to sit in a far-off pew. I guess that's one of the benefits of being a do-boy, rather than the face of the family. No one really knows what I look like. The wedding was so grand that all the flower shops were sold out of yellow roses for weeks. I schooled my features as I listened to the bride in white, made promises of chastity and commitment to her new husband. The church may be bursting with roses, but this young lady had already been deflowered by yours truly. A surge of intense heat consumed me, while the newlyweds kissed.

All these false pretenses surrounding me makes me sick. I need more players in the game if I'm ever going to become king.

THIRTY-TWO

CINDEL

I have time this morning to sort through old boxes stuffed full of letters, drawings, and photos. Most are from our childhood, while I know at least one of the boxes belonged to my brother. Our mother couldn't bear to hold onto any memories after Theo passed. So, they're mine now.

My face aches from a perpetual smile, as I reminisce over goofy photos of my brother and me. One candid image shows us wearing feather boas and costume heels.

There is also a collection of burnt CDs he made during his teenage years. Labeled compilations such as *Friday Night Jams* or *Viva La 90's.*

Tears trickle down without my consent, recalling a time my brother and I would study the lyric booklets that came within the CD cases, then we'd battle against one another to see who sung the words correctly. He was always victorious. Theo was amazing at whatever he did.

After exploring multiple boxes and emptying a container of tissues, I found nothing out of the ordinary. Honestly, I didn't even know what I was looking for. It could be staring at me right in the face, and I wouldn't even know it.

"What did you leave for me, Theo?" I whisper toward the withholding capsules.

I check the time, "Shit." I was going to be late if I didn't get moving. I pull my unwashed hair into a high pony, splash some cool water on my face, and tug on something 'semi-clean' from the corner of my room. Throwing the messenger bag over my shoulder, I head out. I don't bother checking my bag anymore for the earbud, because no matter how hard I try to get rid of it, it always comes back to me. Sure enough, as I retrieve my keys to lock the door, I spot the white piece of tech in the bottom of my bag.

Benny's looks busier than unusual, this morning. As I draw closer, I spot my uncle through the glass-walled diner. He is already at our regular table, but someone was sitting across from him. I slow my pace as I approach.

Did I get the time wrong, was I too early? He texted me again early this morning to confirm. It was, in fact, the right time.

To my surprise, I recognized the person sitting in the booth across from my uncle. It is the same officer who came to my apartment. Officer Kent. He wanted to know about my time at Star Mart and what happened the day I quit.

Do they know each other?

I didn't want to enter the restaurant, at least not yet. Instead, I chose to remain concealed, positioned so I can see them, but they can't see me.

Uncle Nicholas looks flustered; he keeps pointing toward the door as if insisting the other man leave.

The uniformed deputy stands abruptly, turning to walk out, causing me to step even farther back between two buildings. The officer throws open the diner door, causing pedestrians on the street to startle. Standing in the middle of the walkway, people are forced to part around him as he lights a cigarette. He looks back toward my uncle with a sneer before making his way toward his patrol car. As soon as he gets in the vehicle, he flicks the butt to the ground and takes off down the avenue at dangerous speeds.

Once the squad car is gone, I count to ten before coming out from my hiding spot. I cross the street and enter Benny's diner. My uncle's tight knit brows and wrinkled forehead ease when he spots me. Slate eyes soften, and he immediately puts on a smile, waving me over to our booth in the back corner.

"Cindel, you look well. Did you just arrive?"

I slid into the vinyl covered booth, nodding promptly like a child who tried to deny eating a cookie before dinner. "Yup!" I accidentally pop the p. "Just arrived, sorry I'm a little late."

His body visibly relaxes as he slings an arm across the bench's back. "Good. Thanks for meeting me early."

A twinge of guilt ricochets through me, for spying on my uncle. He has been understanding and a great listener as I talk incessantly about the same topics. I trust my uncle. "Anytime. I look forward to breakfast with you," I affirm.

The corner of his eyes creases, as he reviews his phone before setting it back onto the table. "How's that boyfriend of yours, Eamon, right?" He has an incredible memory.

I play with the corner of the plastic menu at its edges.

"He must have been the one playing you songs, right?"

I inadvertently bend the corners of the menu, making an irreversible crease. "Well…" Why did I share this in the first place? It feels too personal now. "It's not him. It's… it's actually someone else."

He licks his lips and reaches across the table to pluck the menu from my hands. Kinda rude, but I was surely ruining it. "Have you called the police?" He presses.

"No. You know how I feel about them."

He nods, folds his hands atop the menus, and leans over the table. "Do you know who this someone else is?" He implores. His jaw ticks slightly as he waits for me to answer.

"No," I admit. I wish I knew.

The grooves in his forehead deepen. He's slightly older than my father, probably overworked since he's yet to retire like my parents. My uncle can be reserved at times. His eyes searched my face, for what I'm not sure. At the drop of a hat, his eyebrows invert and his mouth tips downward. "Cindel, this is serious. You could be in danger. I have a friend in the precinct, maybe you could talk with him."

I wonder if this was the same man I just saw leaving in a rush, moments before I entered the diner. Even so, I have no plans of ever confiding in an officer of the law.

"Can I do anything to help? It hurts when you keep things from me... I just want to keep you safe. Let me help you!" My uncle looks more desperate than concerned. I remain silent, as he continues. "I read in the paper about that manager at Star Mart. Maybe it's time you leave the city. Go stay with your parents in New York."

What? No way! My uncle has never endorsed that. All the stories I've told him over the years. He's never encouraged me to leave. I take a deep breath in and let it out gently before I respond. "I'm not in danger. Maybe it's just some kind of admirer, like you suggested... but I have no plans of leaving Southie. In fact, I feel like I'm onto something big."

I didn't mean to let the last part out, but there it is. Hoping he doesn't press, I nervously find one of the zippers on my jumper, opening and closing it, to give my hands something to do. The sound brings me instant relief.

"Big?" He asks, raising an eyebrow which adds to the already present valleys along his forehead.

"Yeah. Something big," I admit. Here I go... "Since our last breakfast, I learned Theo's death wasn't an overdose—"

A chipper waitress appears next to our table, placing down two waters, while smacking her gum. "What can I get you two?"

My uncle practically barks at the young girl, who's just trying to do her job. "We need more time!" He returns to his posed position; fists now clenched on the table.

The waitress rolls her eyes before shuffling away, muttering under her breath.

"What do you mean... not an overdose?!" He sounds aggravated over this revelation, compared to my initial shock.

"Eamon, my boss. He told me he knew Theo. Was even close with him."

My uncle's smoky eyes become more midnight sky than cool gray. "You can't possibly believe Eamon. From what I hear, he has a poor reputation. Furthermore, you barely know the boy!"

He wasn't wrong, but how would he know his character better than me? I only met him a little over a month ago. I mean… I've been on three dates with him, until I learned he was actually my brother's lover. That part I plan to keep to myself.

I can't help but notice the way my uncle's knuckles have now turned white. He's acting rather strangely. Maybe his blood sugar is off?

I chew on my lower lip, readying to speak my truth, despite his unwilling-ness to believe me. "Well… I still don't believe that my brother would have taken his own life."

He reaches across the table, grasping my hands in his pale frigid fingers. "Cindel. We've gone over this. Your brother was in a dark place before he passed. Have you been seeing your therapist lately? Would you like me to call your mother?"

I pull my hand back, speaking concisely but respectfully. "I'm not a child. Please don't disregard my feelings."

Like flipping a switch, he sits back, unbothered by my words. "Suit your-self." He beckons the waitress over and orders a black coffee.

I've lost my appetite, so I stick with the drink in front of me.

She takes the menus and leaves, probably frustrated. We're taking up a table for only a cup of coffee.

An awkward silence settles between us, which is a first. The coffee arrives, and he sips only briefly from the piping hot drink, before removing a five-dollar bill and placing it on the table. Is he leaving already?

I can't help but speak up. "Why did you want to meet earlier?"

He wraps a black and gray plaid scarf around his neck and stands to pull on his long overcoat. My uncle's once miffed demeanor is now indifferent. His flat expression, tense shoulders, and downcast mouth are unsettling. I've never seen him appear anything other than warm, attentive, and caring. His body language speaks volumes, making my stomach feel as though it's twisting into knots.

"Silly girl... you should have left with your parents when you had the chance."

Like a slap across the face, his comment stuns me. I am at a loss for words. He's only ever supported my decision to stay here in Boston, when my parents left, after my brother passed. Why? Why would he ever say that to me? I try to play back everything that's transpired, since I first walked into the diner. Did I do something wrong?

"Do tell your folks I say 'Hello.'" Then he just walks out. Leaving me just like that. I watch as he heads down the street without a second glance back.

I down the water in two big gulps before leaving Benny's. As I walk toward The Black Sheep, a lot earlier than necessary, I have this eerie feeling that everything was going to be different moving forward.

My shoes crunch on the sidewalk over little granules of salt. The impending freeze sends the city into preparation mode.

Theo dared me to try the salt one time. My throat burned and I think I even threw up. I swear the taste buds on my tongue are still permanently damaged from the incident. Zero stars… do not recommend! My cracked lips pull into a pitiful smile, thinking about something as stupid as a dare from my brother, but that's what this city does to me. Every building, fallen leaf, and grain of salt holds Theo's memories. I could never abandon this place. It's my home. I refuse to forget. Fuck my uncle for thinking I should have left. If there's some kind of clue or message that could shed light on Theo's untimely death, I will find it. I'm nothing if not manically stubborn.

A shaky hunger courses through me, due to my inability to back down, I skipped breakfast all together. I know I'll need my strength for the long shift ahead. Making a pit stop at a hot dog stand, I managed to find just enough money in my wallet to cover the cost of the delicious smelling meat log. I handed the cart owner the exact change, then found a remote bench to eat. Knowing I'm going to be indoors for hours on end, makes me willing enough to brave the temperature just a little longer.

A man in a bright cobalt coat passes by me twice.

I grew up in the city, I may be sheltered, but I'm not stupid. It's important to be aware of your surroundings. It's definitely the same man, not two separate people in a similar colored coat.

I am just finishing my hot dog when the figure goes to pass a third time but, instead, stops in front of me, sitting down on my left. The looming man in blue, reeks of booze.

"Heeeey!" A haggard voice blurts.

I stand as if on autopilot, familiar with panhandlers' tactics. Giving a half-hearted apology for not having cash on me, I toss my trash, then continue toward work.

"Your overalls are cute."

They're not overalls, but I wasn't going to argue a moot point. I hit my quota for the day. I give a small smile. "Thank you. Have a nice day." I started to walk toward The Black Sheep.

"What's your name?!" He shouts, apparently jogging after me.

"Sorry, I'm not interested. My boyfriend is waiting for me," I stammer through the lie, while trying to increase my strides.

He's trailing me despite my pace.

Stay on the busy streets, you're only a few blocks away, I tell myself. Weaving in and out of people, I glance back to find the drunken Smurf keeping up with me. I can see his mouth moving, but he's too far to hear the incessant banter. His deep-set eyes remain fixed on me, looking almost predatory for a midday drunk.

I need to lose him without risking going down less crowded streets. The Black sheep is only a few hundred feet away, so I take off like a shot. With an instant muscle spasm under one side of my ribs, I practically fell into the bar. Pushing the door closed, I stand against the exit, attempting to catch my breath. I peek out the small porthole of the red door. "Please go past, please go past," I whisper to myself. Luckily, the man ambles by. I knew I would be safe here. I didn't exactly want a deranged man following me to work. I have one of those already, thank you very much.

Turning, I find everyone together at a table, staring toward me with a look of pure confusion. Apparently, I was so early... I must have stumbled into some kind of meeting between Eamon, Garron, and Dax.

Eamon was the first to speak. "What's wrong?" Between breaths I just manage to get out.

"Someone... following... me."

Eamon snaps, causing Dax and Garron to stand to attention. They both wordlessly make their way out of the bar to find the man in question.

"Blue!" They freeze upon my word. "He has a blue coat," I add.

Garron nods and they both march out into the streets.

Eamon pats the seat next to him, and I oblige, mostly because I really need to sit. How he treats me makes so much more sense now. Eamon never considered me a lover but closer to a sibling. It's because of who Theo was to him and how he believes he must carry the burden of looking after me. I still wonder, though... why try to pursue me in the first place? There are still so many pieces missing here. Too many unanswered questions.

"Did you look up what I suggested?" He immediately inquires.

"No, but I looked through a few boxes of family keepsakes. I haven't found anything noteworthy yet, but I plan to look up Lombardi after work."

He nods, closing the laptop that was previously open and facing the group of men, before I arrived. "I'm needed at the boxing club this evening. Because of Connor being off today, I'm going to leave you in the capable hands of Dax. Garron will accompany me to the club. Brittany will be in before opening."

Not him. Garron at least engages me. "Okaaay. Should be a slow night." I try to say it without sounding entirely disappointed.

Beginning with my opening tasks, Eamon takes down chairs as we wait for Garron and Dax return. With a shrug from Dax, followed by an apology by Garron, it seems they couldn't locate the man who tracked me. Just as well, I hope to never see the unhinged person again. When Brittany arrives, Eamon and Garron head out.

Dax finds a table far off in the corner to inhabit, as opposed to his usual spot at the bar. Am I really that off putting? It's fine because I don't really care about him either. We didn't exactly get off on the right foot. Me yelling at him to get out from behind the counter, when he was only trying to get us caught up on clean glassware.

This just seems to be the ongoing trend with men and I. Destined to be pursued by troubled men yet alone… starved of meaningful connection.

Which reminds me, I need to pick up double AA batteries for my vibrator. With my stalker practically ignoring me as of late, I've been left to my own devices. Literally!

The brooding introvert nurses a Guinness far from anyone, while Brittany and I have a pretty good handle on things behind the bar. It's so dead tonight that all the customers just come up to the counter when they want to order.

Brittany asks me for some pain relievers at one point; she appears unwell.

"Are you sure you're alright?"

She tries to play it off at first, saying she drank too much the night prior, or she just needs to hydrate better, but after three waters and two Tylenol, she is looking worse by the minute. "Brittany, I think you should go home and rest, you look sick. It must be going around; remember I was out just over a week ago?"

At this point, she doesn't have much fight left in her and agrees to leave early.

I just have to make it through two more hours, until closing. I can practically do this with my eyes closed. Also… I am not entirely alone; the bar's silent lackey lingers nearby.

Tonight, wasn't yielding many tips with so few visitors, but it made an effortless shift. A pair of women who ordered two dry martinis left a few minutes ago. With no one currently in the bar, I take the opportunity to carry some dirty glasses to the dishwasher in the back.

There's a light in the backroom that indicates when any of the outer doors are open in the bar. When I see the red-light flash, I emerge seconds later to greet the customer and let them know it was ten minutes till the last call.

My hold tightens on the edge of the swinging door, now faced with the unbalanced man in the cobalt coat.

"There you are!" He stammers. "I've been looking for you." I look to the table where Dax once occupied, but he's not there! Where is he?

"Stay away from me!" I bellow, slowly inching toward the bar where I know there is an alert button for these types of situations. In all the time I've worked here, we fortunately have never used it. I had to believe it would work if pressed.

The vagrant drunk must have sensed what I was up to, because he was in front of me faster than I was able to get fully behind the bar.

Where the fuck was Dax?! Is he in the bathroom? Just outside? My head pounds in time with my heartbeat… so hurried it's painful. No one else is here, but me and this deranged guy.

I grab a handled corkscrew within reach and wave it toward him. "Get back!"

All I smell is booze weeping from this man's pores, as he steps closer to me without an ounce of fear. Within a split second, he is near enough to have the tool pressing against his blue covered torso. He knew I wouldn't do it… predators like him can sniff out women, who don't have the nerve to drive a weapon into their assailant. I wish I was stronger. To protect myself.

Putting up both hands, I begin to push. Trying anything to get away from this maniac. "Help!" I wail, just as two blue arms wrap around me.

The bottle opener falls to the floor. Of course, he's bigger than me, managing to swipe my feet out from under me and I go down hard. White hot pain pulses within my vision as my head hits the floor first. My vision blurs at its edges, and he's on top of me within an instant.

He smells me, breathing heavily over my face. His hot and putrid mouth opens as he initiates licking down the side of my face. I fight, shove with all my strength, I even scream despite my head feeling like it's split open… but he has me pinned. He's too strong!

The pig of a man smiles above me with yellowed teeth, as he straddles my body. He begins to fumble with the zipper on my jumpsuit, grasping at me with his dirty hands. Squeezing roughly at my chest. Then the zipper slowly starts to move downward.

A choked, desperate cry works its way up my throat. "Please! Please don't do this!"

His nose wrinkles, while his crazed grin nauseates me. I brace for this man's vile hands to touch my skin… to knead my exposed breasts, but he does something even worse. Painfully my hearing aids are yanked off my ears and thrown out of reach. I watch in silent horror as the man's mouth begins to move. I can read lips. Understanding fully when he says, "I'm going to fuck your deaf cunt."

My sobs are soundless, but the ringing in my ears grows increasingly louder, as if leading up to an ear-splitting crescendo. I am powerless, struggling for breath from the weight of this man's body. If I pass out, it's all over. Breathe, Cindel! Keep fighting!

The tears make it impossible to see straight, but… we're not the only ones here anymore. A dark figure stands behind him. One second the disgusting man is looking down at me, and the next his face is turned in an unnatural direction. The weight of his body is pulled from me.

Blinking back tears, frozen to the floor, until… I'm lifted into the air. I cling to whoever my savior is, gradually I'm lowered. I'm in a chair a moment later, with a stack of napkins set before me on the table. Patting my eyes, I try desperately to slow my racing heart. Deep breath in… steadily letting it out, just like I've learned in therapy.

Before me, on his knees, is him. Dax is my savior. Unmoving from the shock, he gingerly takes the zipper from below my belly button and carefully pulls it up to cover me. I regard him voicelessly.

Although he's wide-eyed, his features are soft. The pinkish raised scar etched across his neck is such a striking contrast to his pale features. He signs effortlessly, *Are you hurt?* Dilated pupils, tense jaw, and chest moving with heavy breaths, he waits for my response.

I shake my head from side to side, but I'm still unable to use my words.

Remaining on his knees, unmoving, and patient he signs again… *I'm sorry. I should have never left your side.*

I chew on my bottom lip and nod in understanding, because that's all I seem to be able to do right now. Move my head. I glance over to my attacker in blue, whose body lies contorted, unmoving… lifeless. I stare back at Dax and now he's the one nodding. Confirming what I already suspect. The man's dead. Dax did that. Staring at my rescuer, he stands and proceeds to the front door of the bar, locking it from the inside then flipping off the neon, *open* sign.

The reality of the situation is sinking in. I feel like I'm going to be sick. Finally, my body remembers how to function, I run to the bathroom and make it just in time to empty my street hotdog from hours prior, into the toilet. I'll never be able to stomach one again. After splashing some water on my face, I emerge from the bathroom to find Dax leaning against the bar counter, spinning keys on his finger, with no *body* in sight. I find my hearing aids placed together on the counter for me. It takes me a few moments longer than usual to place both devices back on my ears, because my hands are still trembling.

"Where is he?" I whisper. I can now hear the jingle of the keys as he continues spinning them, not answering the question. Suddenly, he pushes from the counter and tilts his head as if telling me to follow him. "No way! Not until you tell me where he went!" I cross my arms, feeling fed up with men telling me how it's going to be. I want answers.

He makes a pouty face. His features almost appear boyish, when he isn't moody. Medium length, honey brown hair that he's constantly pushing out of his face. Sharp jawline, prominent brow, and wide full lips, that rarely split to speak. Unexpectedly, he reveals a devilishly handsome smile.

If I was in high school and I found his face in one of my teen magazines, perhaps advertising some ridiculously expensive cologne, you better believe I would be tacking him up on my wall. Ghastly scar or not, this man gave Casper's real boy form, a run for his money. Man-age though, no ghost boys. Get your mind out of the gutter!

Pull it together, Cindel! Dead body. Nearly assaulted by a lunatic.

He steps toward me and takes my hand, and I yield to this gorgeous man without so much as an explanation. Dax leads me out of the back door, locks it from the outside, then pulls me toward a black 69' Camaro parked in the alley. Going to the back of the car, he stops at the trunk. Using a key from the ring, he unlocks and lifts the hood to reveal a mound of blue limbs, nappy hair, and the unpleasant aroma of cheap liquor.

I can't help the gasp that escapes me.

My reaction triggers a crack in his usual steely facade. His hand combs through his unruly hair. Pulling the trunk shut, he rounds the car with me in hand, opens the passenger door, and signs *home*. I lower myself into the seat, ready for this fucktastic day to end.

THIRTY-THREE

CINDEL

Eamon texted me this morning to ask how I am doing. I was a nervous wreck when I first arrived home. With my overactive imagination playing out scenarios where Dax didn't rescue me, I wind up making myself sick. I brushed my teeth multiple times to get the taste of my stomach acid off my tongue.

I barely slept, tossing and turning most of the night. Fortunately, Andrea never left her room. If she saw me… if she knew what happened, she would have packed my bags and had me on my way to my parents that very night.

Eamon told me to take the next day off. I didn't object. I'm certain Dax told Eamon every uncomfortable detail of what transpired. I've seen some pretty crazy shit as a bartender, but I've never been attacked before. Obviously, I was upset… I mean, who wouldn't be?!

Yet, I couldn't discern if I was angrier with the guy who was supposed to keep watch, the abhorrent man in blue, or myself. Reflecting on what happened, I feel like it's my fault I didn't fight harder. Even if Connor was there, I still would feel the same. I made a promise to myself that very day… when I'm facing the impossible, I will fight. No matter how bleak the situation may seem. I can't allow my fears to paralyze me because next time, there might not be someone to come to my rescue.

It's ironic how I can make this badass vow while I still couldn't get the image of contorted limbs tucked inside a trunk out of my head. The way Dax handled the circumstance was unnerving. Previously, Eamon informed me how Garron and Dax were sent to handle collecting a debt. Was this just a regular thing for these guys? Killing people?! Who the fuck are these men? Andrea did try to warn me.

Opening up the tab on my phone with the recently conducted job search. I made a point to apply to at least five vacant positions this morning. Although, nothing I choose is in line with what I went to school for. Keeping my options 'open' seems like a wise choice. I need *safe* options right now. I mean… what if the FBI came in one day and shut the whole bar down over these men's crimes?

Jiminy Cricket, I witnessed a murder. It was merited, though…wasn't it?

Holy shit balls… am I justifying that some people deserve to be killed? It was self-defense. Although it wasn't me doing the defending. An unsettling chill skates through my body as I consider all of these moral dilemmas. If I actually reach out to my therapist to work through all this, I'm confident they would book me an extended stay at the *white-walled, no sharp things inn…* or jail.

Aside from the breathing techniques, they couldn't help me right now. Despite last night, I have been sleeping better lately. Which is wild considering all the fuckery that's been going on over the last month. Having the day off, I am ready to tackle the *Lombardi* topic as well as finish going through the remaining boxes from my family. I wonder if my parents had anything else squirreled away at their place? They quite literally liquidated everything and moved to the Catskills shortly after my brother's funeral. They're not known for their nostalgic nature.

Dusting off my dinosaur of a laptop from college, I found the charger and went through a series of overdue updates. Being in the service industry didn't exactly entail computer work, so this relic was struggling, after I summoned it awake for the first time in ages. It takes well over an hour of me shouting vulgarities at the screen, that I did not in fact want to purchase any kind of anti-virus and I could care less that my PDF reader was out of date. Once the computer boots up and the background screen is displayed, it is like a punch to the gut.

A picture of me in a maroon cap and gown, on the front steps of my high school, with my brother beside me. He's yucking it up for the photo, by pinching my cheeks and making an exasperated *awww* face. He took every opportunity to point out that I was the younger one, but he never made me feel incomplete or unwanted. I remember my parents being too busy with work on this day. As soon as I walked across the stage, they took this photo and were back to their *oh so important* obligations.

My brother's the one that took me out to celebrate that evening. I had my first martini. I said, "it tasted like pickled dog water," in turn earning me the name "Sparky," the rest of the night.

Clicking on the internet icon, I type in the word *Lombardi* and hit search.

The first hit was for a news article, well over fifty years old.

"The Mafia wars made for difficult times in the 1960s. While smuggling was a lucrative business, crime families spread to the states where they could control distributing networks. Historical records are not kept on such secretive organizations; however, it's believed that such crime families are present today."

The next website I scroll through covers Mafia origins, dating back to the mid-19th in Sicily. I need to narrow down the information to just the Lombardi family.

Unreliable resources had news from twenty years ago about the Lombardi family, referring to them as *mobsters still at large* in the Boston area. The journalist goes on to say, *they were likely not the only crime family in the area.* Right...? So, some guy like Tony Soprano, was running around Boston knocking off people when I was little?

I love *The Sopranos*, but this shit is far-fetched! I fall headfirst into the rabbit hole, clicking on site after site, skimming through dubious reports about real-estate inflation thanks to illicit activity from the Mafia. Current articles highlight how the average Joe is unable to afford property in the Boston area, due to fraudulent schemes still taking place. I guess it's possible the Mafia is still present today.

It feels as though I blinked and it's lunchtime. Now I know way too much about the Mafia, however, the last name 'Lombardi' just seemed to vanish about twenty years ago. Eamon has been extremely kind and helpful, but I still hadn't the foggiest idea what all this had to do with my brother.

When I finally stand from my bed, my legs have pins and needles from sitting in one position for too long. I manage to shuffle into the living room as the blood flow slowly returns to my feet.

Spinning the whiteboard toward me, I consider all the evidence that Andrea and I have on display so far. I uncap a dry-erase marker and write the name *Lombardi*, along the top. Not sure how it ties in, but there it was in loopy cursive.

I stand back looking over everything we've theorized, feeling like today's hyper fixation was a huge waste of time. Still, we're no closer to figuring out what happened to my brother. We don't even have a person of interest.

The front door swings open to reveal my silver-haired roommate carrying in so much stuff; she can barely see in front of her. I rush to help, relieving her of multiple bags.

"What is all this?" I inquire, lugging the heavy packages to the counter.

"This and that," she replies.

I peek into the bags to find not just groceries but brand-new home security items, including glass break detectors, doorbell cam, and motion sensors. "What is all this for?"

She quirks an eyebrow as if I should know, while proceeding to unload her monstrous number of purchases.

"How'd you pay for all this stuff?" She proceeds to quietly put the few groceries away.

On the counter remains; spaghetti, two Roma tomatoes, a bulb of garlic, and olive oil.

"Are you making pasta? Who are you and what have you done with my culinary challenged roommate?!" I defend myself by holding up one of the security monitors to my chest and playfully point my finger in her direction.

She cracks and a smile breaks through. I miss our games, jokes, and just laughing with her.

Andrea grabs the box from me and sets it back down with the others. "I should have you know that I am an excellent cook. Just not the best with frozen waffles." Her grin fades as her tone switches. "All of this is to make you feel safe. No more cops showing up without you knowing. Also, no more surprise visits from you know who."

I wasn't sure how I felt about that. He really wouldn't ever surprise me again?

"I should have done this years ago," she adds.

Pulling out a large sauce pot, she stops suddenly as her gaze catches on the board in the sitting room. "Did you write that?" She walks over to the board and points to the word *Lombardi.*

"Yeah. Eamon told me to look it up." I joined her, staring at the way the lines connect to names.

"And?" She looks at me with rapid blinks.

"Nothing much online. Just that it's some kind of Mafia family that had a heavy presence in Southie, from the sixties to early nineties. Apparently, the real estate market is still suffering despite the family name all but disappearing when I was small."

Andrea sucks her teeth, then saunters back to the kitchen to continue preparing to cook. She seems off... lost in thought or bothered, so I spin the whiteboard toward the wall and tuck it away for later.

Just as Andrea put the water on the stove, a knock comes at the door. Automatically, she pushes me aside and checks the peephole. She pulls back and motions me toward the door, before signing, is *that who I think it is?* I look through the opening to find a head of vibrant auburn hair and a familiar nineties jean-jacket, bouncing just in front of our apartment door. We both let out a long breath before opening. I can tell from Andrea's body language that she wasn't exactly delighted to have her visit. Knee bent, foot and back against the entry wall, her eyes travel up and down the spunky girl with such scrutiny, I am happy not to be on the receiving end. She clearly remembers Mairead's last visit here, when she took the liberty to explore the apartment herself. Or maybe it's how she nonchalantly told me our manager was murdered, on her way out. Lucky for Mairead, she doesn't seem to even notice the way Andrea assesses her.

"Hi friend! Are you ready?"

I look at Andrea, then back to the oblivious girl atop our welcome mat. "Umm... Ready for what?" I ask.

She steps between us and lets herself migrate deeper into our apartment. My roommate already appears flushed, her complexion matching that of the produce on the counter. Following the unannounced visitor inside, we find her helping herself to the fridge, popping open a can of flavored seltzer water, and taking a seat at the kitchen table.

"Mairead! Ready for what?!" I press. My thoughts are pulled in various directions; I honestly can't figure out why she's here.

She takes a sip of the poached drink before answering. "For the escape room, silly. You promised me we'd go after you got better… Remember?"

Andrea stands just behind Mairead's seated position mouthing, "*what the fuck?*"

"I know you don't work today."

Ok? Weird. I was supposed to work. How would she know? My best friend's face might get stuck like this, because her perpetually puzzled expression hasn't fallen since Mairead entered our home.

"Come on, sis! You can bring your cranky roommate too."

Holy shit, Andrea might take a swing at this girl. Then I'll have to deal with two murders in a one-week stint. Since when did my life become a *B grade* episode of Law and Order?

"Okay. We'd love to go." I look at my roommate who all but throws her arms up in the air, allowing them to quickly fall down to her sides with a thud. All subtle cues must go over Mairead's head because she squeals and instantly hugs each of us.

"Today is going to be perfect! I have it all planned. Hurry up and get ready, we hit the town in five minutes."

I am not keen on going, but since I learned Mairead is Eamon's sister, I need to learn more about the Murray family and how they may play a part. I will learn what happened to my brother. Even if it means keeping a bit more information from Andrea. Let's hope that bringing her along won't turn around and bite me in the butt.

Mairead skips just ahead of us, like someone who just pounded several energy drinks. Her purple Doc Martens and pink zebra print leggings, really compliment the bedazzled Lisa Frank piece. She definitely has an eclectic taste in fashion, to say the least, but she makes it work. We look as though we are following a magical unicorn into battle, as we all make our way to the first stop on Mairead's perfect itinerary. I just hope this time doesn't involve petty theft or counting gravestones.

Andrea turns to me. "The code word is porpoise. All you have to do is say the word and we'll leave."

Mairead disappears into a restaurant with a wooden sign that reads: *Tequila & Oyster Bar.*

"Chill G.I. Jane… everything will be fine. We haven't gone out to do anything fun together in forever!"

She considers me, lets out a long sigh, and nods; before we follow her into the restaurant.

The hostess leads us to a large table.

Once seated, Mairead insists lunch is on her. She demands that we each get a flight of tequila to make the experience at the escape room more enjoyable. "I've been to Jalisco before, where they make tequila. I actually went down there to ID someone. Pretty hard when they've lost their head." She casually remarks as she nibbles on complimentary chips.

Andrea mouths to me, *"say… the… word."*

I shake my head with a reassuring smile, knowing a lot of what Mairead says doesn't make sense… but now I've learned what kind of man her brother is, I'm hoping her words aren't literal.

I can't help but notice how Andrea has spent most of her lunch, studying Mairead, while I attempt to keep the conversation light.

We touch on just about every subject; from animals to fashion and even movies.

I would never have taken Mairead for a Sandra Bullock fan. She was all over the board and there wasn't a subject she didn't want to cover, especially once she pounded through each brightly colored shot glass.

Somewhere along the line, a laugh bubbled from Andrea's serious state.

Since I inadvertently made a promise to stop all depressant substances years ago, I have become quite a lightweight.

By the third shot, I am definitely feeling the effects, and I still had three more to go.

Words pour from Mairead at an unnatural rate with no inkling of being intoxicated, other than being chattier.

Nothing damning or significant is shared during the flight of top shelf tequila and birria tacos.

Although it's become even more apparent, Andrea does not care for Mairead. Each of her sharp-tongued quips is laced with either sarcasm or intolerance.

Next stop is Escape Goats. Mairead is giddy, I am concentrating on appearing not as drunk as I actually am, and Andrea is… well, her usual ornery self. Unlike me, she is fine and prevents me from running face first into a light pole on the way over.

When we arrive at the escape room, I become a little worried the teen boy working at the counter will deny us entry. There must be some kind of rule about being intoxicated while playing, especially when I'm unsure if I could find my way home at this moment. Shockingly, he could care less about my condition, instead informing us that they are booked for the rest of the day.

Mairead isn't too pleased with this development. Deciding to remedy the situation by leaning through the sliding window and whispering something into the honest kid's ear. Maybe it was her feminine wiles or something she said, but his story changed. Now, the most popular experience is suddenly available for us. Candy colored lip gloss is smeared on the teen's cheek, as he leads us to our assignment door.

We each grab a laminated instruction sheet from the wall pocket, before stepping inside the fully immersive escape room.

It is a quaint office setting with a large desk, bookshelves, floor lamp, and two chairs. A grandfather's clock ticks softly in the corner of the room, while we get to work exploring the maps and books lining the walls. This place emanates Sherlock Holmes' vibes.

Mairead spins in a chair and Andrea tugs at each of the desk drawers, while I read from the handout.

"Callaway is notorious for getting away with his crimes. You have one hour to visit his office before he returns. Find out who his accomplice is and locate the explosive devices around the city before it's too late. Don't forget to escape the room before Callaway finds you here."

My throat suddenly feels tight, and it isn't because of the shots.

Andrea is already standing in front of me, tilting her head back slightly to look up to my face.

She knows my triggers, my weaknesses. How a single notion could bring me back to that room when I was a little girl. The explosion. Just saying the word makes my chest constrict. Last time, the smoke from the lantern dragon made me panic and blackout.

I want to leave this room, even if I don't get anything from this outing. Maybe I was just kidding myself, about gaining insight from the Murray family tree. What does it matter that Mairead is Eamon's sister? It's probably just a weird coincidence. Our meeting, her working at the same grocery store as me, it could mean nothing.

"Mairead, I'm not feeling so great. I think I should go."

She's still spinning in an armchair before the bookshelf, her head lulling back; she faces ceiling. I would have barfed by now if I were in her place. She lifts her head and stops the chair. "No way, we're locked in here for an hour. We have to solve the murder mystery!"

Andrea crosses her arms. "I'm sure they can unlock the door in an emergency... plus, it's not a murder mystery, we're finding where the ummm..."

"EXPLOSIVES are!" Mairead pipes up.

"Yeah," Andrea says hushed.

I need to sit. I perch on the edge of the desk and start fanning myself with the laminate sheet.

Mairead swivels her head toward me. "What's wrong?"

I'm dizzy and I can hear the whooshing sound as my heartrate starts to pick up. Everything in the room moves at a snail's pace. Why did I drink so much?

Andrea's sagging mouth and downcast eyes tell me, I look pitiful.

I point to my bag I dropped near the door; she immediately goes over and brings it up to me. I shuffle through items looking for the one thing that I've learned can help with these episodes, *sour candy*. I rip open a bag of sour Skittles and start popping two at a time into my mouth.

Andrea quietly watches me, likely unsure how this could possibly be the remedy.

"Damn, I wish I had thought to bring snacks." Mairead pouts.

Once I feel like the walls aren't closing in and the rushing sound subsides, I speak. "Sour candies can help with panic attacks. Someone taught me that recently."

They exchange glances then look back at me.

Mairead still seems just as confused as before.

"There was an accident when I was young."

Andrea rubs her temples, knowing how hard it is to share this story; however, Mairead is unaware of my struggles.

"A gas line exploded next to my house when I was around five. I was in the hospital for a while; fortunate to be alive, but not everything healed. They said I have noise-induced hearing loss from the blast. I've been wearing hearing aids since."

Mairead taps her chin, still sitting in the paisley print chair. Leaning forward, she grabs the armrests of her seat, her face a mask of concentration. "Explosives are the worst!" She declares, enunciating each syllable. "I'm more of a knife girl myself."

Andrea and I make eye contact with the same perplexing expression. Did she really just say that, and are we actually stuck in a room with her for the next hour?

While the candy works its magic, I tell myself this little outing is for a reason. Pushing down my past, I focus on the present. What I need to gain and how Mairead might have insight.

"Your aid thingies are so cute! Do they come in different colors?" Mairead stands and begins flipping through pages of a book she pulled from the shelf.

"Umm, thank you? I suppose they come in different styles, depending on your needs."

She pushes the book back onto the shelf and begins checking underneath tables and chairs, for what I'm not sure.

Andrea sticks out her tongue, tilts her head to the side, then swirls her finger next to her ear, as to indicate *she's crazy*; while Mairead is poised under an end table.

She pops up suddenly. "Okay, we have less than an hour! Let's figure out who killed Mr. Callaway!"

Andrea's palm hits her forehead so loudly; it echoes through the room.

"Let's find clues," I announce, trying to run interference before Andrea voices what her face already says.

We spend the next thirty minutes checking every possible nook and cranny of the mock office set. We've found a skeleton key, a letter from Mr. Callaway to a "Mr. Simmons," and a cipher to decode some kind of message. Checking the handout again, I notice that we're locked in one of the most challenging rooms in the establishment. Five lightbulbs across the top, indicating it's the hardest.

Great... I can't even figure out where to write the one and zeros on my W-2 form, but I'm supposed to figure out some theoretical plot before the city is blown up? Andrea and I study the letter we found, paired with the cipher, but came up short.

Mairead on the other hand hasn't given up looking for secrets and finds a hidden compartment within the office desk, which we previously missed. She holds up a black and white photo, displaying a bunch of gentlemen in business suits. "I am having such a good time!" She proclaims, but in the blink of an eye, her lighthearted tone turns cold. "I never expected that finding my mother's *actual* murderer would be such fun," she says plainly.

Did she just say murderer? Andrea and I share a mutual gaze. Okay, I heard it correctly. Arming my lungs with air, I ask Mairead the most obvious thing. "Did someone kill your mom?"

"Yup," she says with a pop of the p. She grabs a magnifying glass off the desk as she studies the monochrome photo. Suddenly, standing ramrod straight with the lens in front of her eye, she declares, "Let's solve that mystery instead!" Mairead gingerly sits down at the desk and shuffles some papers around, tapping the stack on its end, to collect them into one neat pile.

"Where were you on the night of December the 31st, three years ago?"

Wait! What? "Mairead—" I don't know how to answer this. Although, I knew exactly what I was doing around that time. Unintentionally, I become defensive. "Are you for real right now?" It comes out more derisive.

"Answer the question!" She holds the glass to the other eye with all the severity of an alley cat, who spots an unsuspecting bird within reach.

Okay, fine. I don't have anything to hide from the obviously delusional girl. "Probably mourning my brother. He died only days before."

She sets the prop down loudly. "I know!"

My eyes try to find my roommate, but she's no longer in the same place. Instead, Andrea is edging around the perimeter of the room, ever so slowly. Maybe she's trying to find a way out. Do we need to get out?

I focus on Mairead, trying to rationalize what to say next. "What do you mean, *you know*?"

Her bottom lip juts out, and she blows one of the red curls from her eyes. "I mean, I know, that your brother died. I understand. No one wants their family to die… but someone killed my mother and I'm 100% sure your family is to blame!" Now Mairead stands from the desk, looking as if she's ready to pounce.

Andrea's now by the only exit, pulling something from her pocket before positioning her front toward us. She appears to be fiddling with the door lock behind her back. Keeping my eyes trained on Mairead, I try to defuse this unfathomable situation.

"My family? My family are nobodies…they didn't kill anybody. My parents are glorified real estate agents, while my uncle is an investor." This whole conversation is unhinged, but I keep my tone calm and my words concise.

She throws back her head, laughing maniacally. At first, it's a high pitch chuckle, eventually morphing into a low sorrowful groan. "Nobodies? You naive storybook princess, they've left you in the dark, haven't they?"

Wow… maybe Mairead is one of those people who get angry when they drink. I can't help wondering if the liquid courage that everyone flocks to consume each night is more of a filter remover. How easy things could be if everyone was simply more forthcoming. Is it really so hard for others to come clean without a catalyst?

Where has the light-hearted girl gone, who easily befriended me when she started working at Star Mart? What changed? This person before me is cold, calculated, and seeking vengeance for a murder I had no part in.

Why didn't I let Andrea know that Mairead was Eamon's sister? Well, probably because I knew how she would react. She already didn't like Eamon, why would she have less concern for his sister. Fuck. I was more worried about my friend than myself.

Just the same, I empathize with Mairead… so consumed by grief, she's become disconnected, even paranoid.

Something twirls in her fingers that catches the light. It's iridescent and long. A letter opener perhaps?

Mairead is focused solely on me, paying Andrea no mind. My roommate remains steadfast; her shoulders rise and fall as she works. Can she pick locks?

"Daddy and I agree… you're the reason mother is dead! You're only still breathing because my brother thought he could get information. He had this stupid notion that we could get answers without anyone getting hurt… but I'm done waiting! His time is up."

I hear a faint metal on metal click, just as a slice of fluorescent light pours into the dimly lit room.

Without delay Andrea moves, grabbing me by the shirt and dragging me into the hall. She slams the door behind us.

The distant sound of Mairead's wild laughter is unsettling.

All at once, the door starts vibrating, likely banging from the other side.

Andrea and I take off down the hall, away from the worst escape room of all time.

The street is now illuminated by yellow streetlights.

Straight away, I find the nearest trash reciprocal and regurgitate all the skittles, tacos, and tequila that was left inside me.

Andrea holds my hair while rubbing quick circles on my back. I need a moment, but she knows better. "We have to go," she rushes out… "now!"

We practically sprinted the whole way home from downtown. Despite the wintry temperatures, we both have a fine sheen of sweat on our brows.

Andrea fixes us both a cup full of water with baking soda, then procures charcoal tablets from bathroom medicine cabinet.

After we've both hydrated and regained a normal heart rate, she pulls out the whiteboard and uncaps a pink marker. "Who is Mairead?!" It's not a polite question; it's an accusatory one, filled with hurt and mistrust.

Shit. I rub my fingers along the cord edging of the last couch pillow in the apartment. Taking a large breath prior to letting it all out in one go. "She's Eamon's sister."

The marker in her hand falls to the ground. "You've got to be fucking kidding me! I told you Eamon was dangerous… why would his sister be any different?! For fuck's sake, Cindel!"

She paces the room, while running both hands through her shiny silver strands. She looks spent.

This is all my fault. I put my roommate, my best friend, in harm's way, all because I wanted information that could *potentially* help me figure out what happened to my brother. I'm such an idiot. I can't operate on hunches. What if Eamon was lying about knowing my brother, and it was all a facade, just to get close to me?

Eventually, Andrea scribbles Mairead's name on the white board, just beneath Eamon's, with the words *"Crazy Red-headed sister,"* below.

I can't help but pick at the edges of my nails while Andrea stands back, surveying the board. I almost rather her yell than be unnervingly quiet.

"Could that stalker of yours be the one responsible for Mary's death?"

Abandoning my tender nail bed, I stare up into my roommate's frustrated face. "No." This I was sure of, with every bone in my body. "He's trying to help. He's the one that told me to search for something Theo left behind." I sigh as I glance down to the floor. Wait. I look back to my roommate. "How did you know Eamon and Mairead's mother was named Mary?"

She tilts her head then shakes her hair out of her face, "You told me. Remember?"

Did I? You know… so much has happened as of late, I probably did tell her and just forgot. I squeeze my eyes shut and exhale. "I'm sorry, Andrea. This is my fault. You'll be happy to hear; I've applied to other places. You're right, I shouldn't work there." Saying it out loud feels more matter of fact, than just applying to a couple job postings.

"We should leave town for a bit. Mairead is clearly unhinged. I need you safe." She has a good point. A lot of what Mairead said earlier is certifiably, but can I really go back to living with my parents? They have themselves to worry about. They don't even technically have a home to welcome me to. They're house sitters.

I also don't want to leave the city. My thoughts spiral, soon I find myself thinking about my stalker. Would I be leaving him too? He's followed me wherever I've gone thus far, but why haven't I heard from him in days? My head throbs. It feels as though icy spoons are pressing against the backs of my eyeballs.

"I'm tired," I declare.

"Well, I'm too worked up to fall asleep. So… I'm going to stare at this board until something makes sense," she asserts, tapping the marker into her other hand. "Are you sure that's all the songs your stalker played for you?" Of course she would be focusing on the mystery man. Why do I continue to trust him? Trust everyone?

I am already disappointed in myself, the least I can do is ease her mind. "Let me write down everything thus far and we'll cross reference what we have."

She agrees, but I can tell she's not pleased with me. I grab a few slices from a loaf on the counter in advance of heading to my bedroom.

As I chew on the final slice of bread, I commence jotting down each artist and song that I recall being played through the found earbud. I'm up to fifteen songs but I'm not sure if one of the songs count. One I'd never heard prior to my drive to the Catskills. The words are memorably haunting. After a quick search, I find the *Lil' red riding hood* song. It's from a group called *Sam the Sham & the Pharaohs*, released in 1966. The strange song plays… which I most definitely DID NOT add to my driving mix. Despite my exhausted state, I relisten to each and every song my stalker has played for me up until now. From the first song by the *Pixies*, to the most recent tune by *Elastica*. I lose track of time.

Even with bready carbs absorbing the residual tequila, my stomach still suffers. Brain and body at war with one another. My mind screams, "go to sleep," but my entire being burns for the masked man. He makes me question myself, rethink everything; but I know one thing for sure… he doesn't plan to hurt me.

As my eyes begin to grow heavy, I lay on my pillow; however, a piercing light keeps me from sleeping. The earbud glows like a beacon, beside me on the nightstand.

My hearing aids are already out for bed, so I easily nestle the little bud into my ear. There and then, music streams into the once peaceful space.

"Possum Kingdom" by the **Toadies** plays, sending me right back to those confusing, teenage years.

Not so long ago, I had trouble making decisions, even for the simplest things. My taste in boys relied heavily on how wide the hem of their pant leg spanned. They were selfish. Telling me just about anything I wanted to hear to get what they wanted. Funnily enough, I didn't even know what *I* wanted, mostly because I was young… scared.

Today, although not quite as 'inexperienced,' I'm still apprehensive but I recognize what I need. I'm a woman willingly being lured into a dark space. This time, it's more about what I crave rather than what he has to offer.

I covet what this lyrical message has to offer. What if he's watching me right now?

My hand finds its way beneath the sheets and under my panties, as the song repeats for the second time.

The phone vibrates next to me, just as I dip a finger inside myself. Using my free hand to read the notification. It's from *The Stalker.* I click message.

> The Stalker: Stop touching yourself, Cindel, and go to bed.

My eyes widened as I reread the message. I knew he had cameras in my room!

Dots appear, then another message comes through.

> The Stalker: Tomorrow, Paddle Boathouse, 6 p.m.

Per the song that just had me all hot and heavy, he's supposed to reveal a *dark secret* to me. I type out a message before vowing to turn off my phone for the night.

> Cindel: It might be kinda hard if the Boathouse is closed for winter.

Without missing a beat, another message pops through before I can power down my phone.

> The Stalker: Don't you worry about it being hard. Go to sleep, Princess.

I hold the two buttons, causing the screen to go black. I've made up my mind... I want my stalker to 'treat me well.'

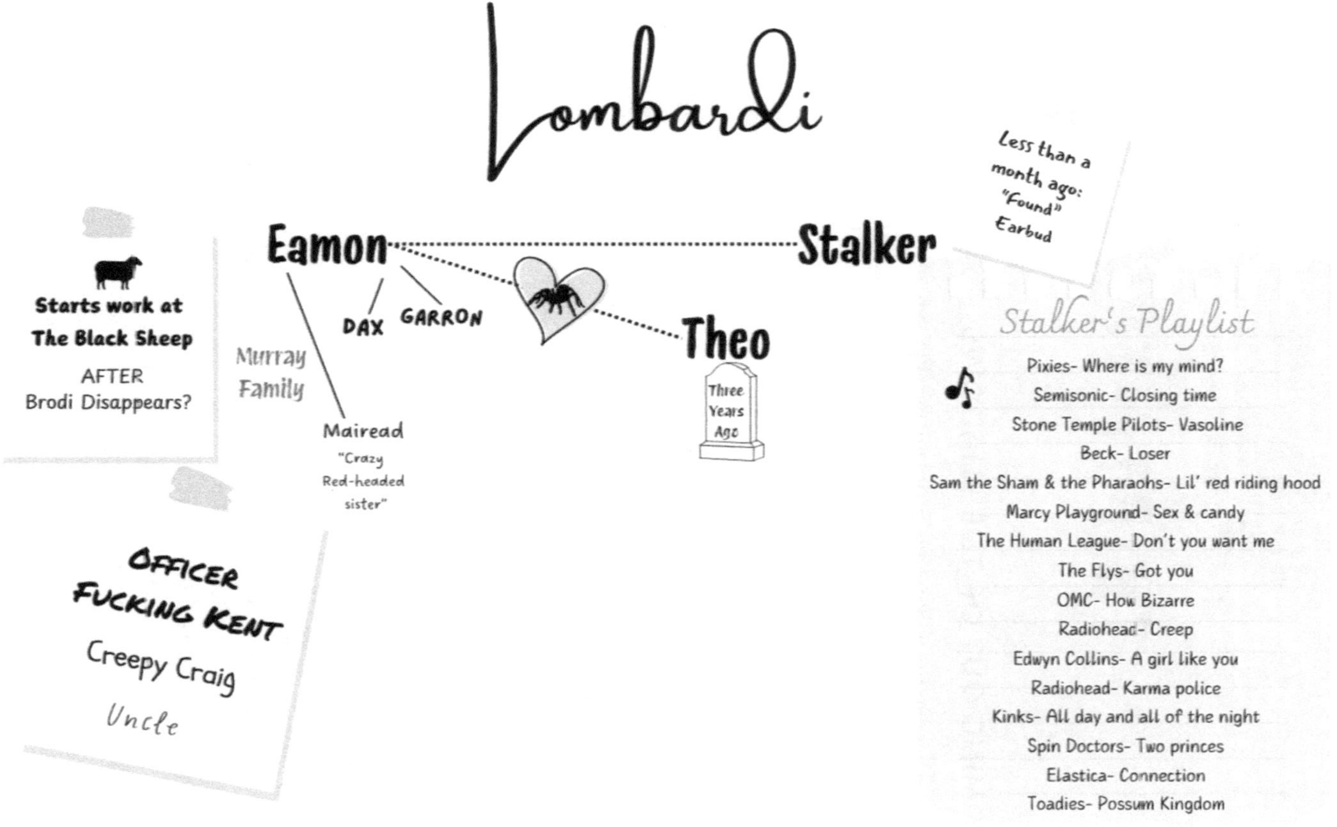

Lombardi

Less than a
month ago:
"Found"
Earbud

Eamon .... Stalker

DAX   GARRON

Theo

Three
Years
Ago

Murray
Family

Mairead
"Crazy
Red-headed
sister"

Starts work at
The Black Sheep
AFTER
Brodi Disappears?

OFFICER
FUCKING KENT
Creepy Craig
Uncle

Stalker's Playlist

Pixies- Where is my mind?
Semisonic- Closing time
Stone Temple Pilots- Vasoline
Beck- Loser
Sam the Sham & the Pharaohs- Lil' red riding hood
Marcy Playground- Sex & candy
The Human League- Don't you want me
The Flys- Got you
OMC- How Bizarre
Radiohead- Creep
Edwyn Collins- A girl like you
Radiohead- Karma police
Kinks- All day and all of the night
Spin Doctors- Two princes
Elastica- Connection
Toadies- Possum Kingdom

THIRTY-FOUR

COMING OUT OF THE SHADOWS

Normally, I have no problem passing out despite living next to the highway. The blaring sirens and honking of horns have become almost a lullaby during my years living here. Despite staring at the ceiling, listening to brown noise for hours on end, I barely sleep. Thoughts of Cindel's angelic face and crystal blue eyes looking up at me flood my mind.

When I saw her touching herself on the camera, it took a great deal of self-control to not simply go over there and take her. Instead, I eased the tension by picturing all the things I wanted to do to her, none of them are what I was employed to do.

"Watch her, don't let her learn the truth." I've been instructed, that was before I decided she's mine.

Everything I do is monitored, well, he tries to, but I have ways of circumventing the system.

For such a long time, living the life of an 'agent of espionage,' never knowing acceptance… constantly grappling with any form of a moral compass. I spent the beginning of my childhood in an orphanage, learning real fast that you can either eat or be eaten. Never growing attached to anyone or anything, I became accustomed to change and insurmountable strife. To avoid emotions that deemed me weak or vulnerable; I became detached, violent, and unruly. My time consumed in that place was either with my nose in the corner or with difficulty sitting from being walloped. They managed to break multiple wooden paddles on me before the ripe age of eight.

I heard the nuns talking one evening in the courtyard about a crimson-haired lady who revisited, years after dropping off her baby boy. Gossiping about how she was too young, too pretty, and made the right choice. I saw the woman in question earlier that day, when I was playing ball with the other kids. They said the child was the product of rape and shouldn't have come to be. Later on, I learned what that meant. The baby was a mistake. A sin from the beginning. The child was me. How could someone who looks so pure, deliver something so undesirable. Being insignificant was familiar territory;

learning that I was conceived in such a fashion, just validates my brilliant reputation.

A few days after the nice woman visited, I found one of the nuns with an affinity for whooping me, packing a modest suitcase with all of my belongings. She explained how some generous guappo wanted to adopt me and take me back to the States. Her jeering tone told me she was glad to be rid of me. I was immediately skeptical, always thinking the worst of everyone without giving them a chance to fuck me over first. I was so young... a small part of me still had hope for a family. Naturally, I was thrilled to flee the deplorable living conditions of chilled porridge, uncomfortable bedding, and stale biscuits which could literally shatter a window.

The man who took me in had me call him sir. He lived by himself in America, in a state known as Boston. No siblings or mother waited for me, but he did have a whole extra room for me to sleep in. To my relief, he wasn't a pedo, but that doesn't mean a guaranteed magical childhood.

When I started maturing, I realized something. Uncooperative hair, familiar gait and stature, identical iron eyes; I was looking more like him each day. I wasn't blind. The man kept me mostly hidden from the world; home-schooling and private combat lessons were the only time someone else was welcome in our home. I was meant to be his *secret shadow* and nothing more. That time spent on my own made me long for a friend. Even a weak conniving one, like I could find in the orphanage.

For the longest time, I was under the impression my guardian was a sales-man, because of all the places we went and new people he'd meet, but I never understood what he was selling. One day he took me for a long stroll in the park. Which was unusual because he never normally took me anywhere. When we finally got in the car, he didn't drive us home, but to the hospital. I wasn't sick or anything, but he said he had to "make an appearance." He told me to wait in the hall with one of his weird friends. I didn't like the people he knew very much. In a room at the other end of the hall, I could see a small, young girl in a hospital bed. She must have been sick, but she looked more scared than anything. The people in the room wouldn't stop crying, and the girl screamed as if no one could hear her. I couldn't look away.

Those sapphire eyes have been ingrained into the very fiber of my being from that moment on. I'm confident she doesn't even remember that day. All the same, I will finally get to make myself known to her tonight. Her undivided attention on me alone. I already knew Eamon offered Cindel another day off work. I, myself, didn't sleep for two days straight, after seeing my first dead body, but to my surprise it was well past ten in the morning and she was still sleeping like a rock. My little princess was made for this life; she just didn't know it yet.

My phone vibrates with a notification.

I agree with him there, she is asking a lot of questions, mostly because I'm leaving her the trail of breadcrumbs. My monitor displays multiple images of Cindel in her apartment from various angles. I love that she still hasn't found a single camera. Be that as it may, she is aware I'm watching. Sleeping beauty is so close to revealing the truth, she simply needs to open her eyes. Until then, Princess... rest, you'll need your energy for this evening.

I reply to *Warden* with a thumbs up emoji. In turn putting MY plan into motion.

I watch the surveillance feed as Andrea pours another cup of coffee, not yet making it to her own bed. She has a notepad full of theories including the song names, durations, and researched lyrics. She's been a good friend to my woman, yet I recognize that's not why she's stuck around. Even though Andrea doesn't care much for me, I'm going to throw her a bone. She's spent so much time and energy looking into the Murrays, she's completely missed what's right under her nose. As strange as it may seem, my playlist wasn't meant to be anything beyond a creative way of communicating with Cindel. Somewhere down the road... the collection shifted, carrying messages of relevance.

Sure... it may have scared her at first, causing her to become slightly paranoid but that's my way of showing I care. I appreciate her roommate's dedication to the cause, so I toy with the list. Using artist names and songs, until I construed some kind of meaning. Just another breadcrumb for Cindel. I transferred her entire contacts list, into my phone, during one of my previous visits. Texting her roommate a series of numbers, holding cryptic information.

Rubbing at my stubbled jaw, I watch the camera in their living room. Andrea grabs her phone, reads the message, and finally sits down for the first time in hours. Yahtzee.

I'm glued to the feed as she scoots the kitchen chair over to the whiteboard and begins by writing the numbers, then circling letters under the list labeled: *Stalker's Playlist.* I like the name. It would make a great title for a novel.

Before long, her overworked friend has strung together the letters: *eilsalohcinelcnu.* Her head tilts to the side, she erases, then rewrites the nonsensical characters, but inverted. *Unclenicholaslie.* Almost there. She feverishly removes and modifies the letters with spaces in the right places. *Uncle*

Nicholas Lie. I send her exhausted friend one more message before I go back to focusing on the screen, where Cindel lies in bed.

> The Stalker: You need to tell her. Before it's too late.

Andrea's wild eyes bounce around the room, like I'm hiding in a corner.

Sorry… you'll never find the cameras. Her overworked form can barely stand, as she initiates searching the room. She's going to crash hard at some point. Rest easy comrade, I'll take over the next watch.

I never got presents for Christmas, or any holiday for that matter. If I ever did, I'm sure I would have been sneaking peeks every chance I got. That's how I feel right now, as I watch Cindel dress and ready to meet me at the boathouse.

After showering, she pulls on a cropped shirt, form fitting skirt, her usual boots, and a bomber jacket. I rewind the footage just to confirm, the naughty little minx didn't bother putting any underwear on. Fuck, I am already hard. No self-control when it comes to surprises…. so eager to sink into her after waiting for what feels like a lifetime.

Before Cindel is scheduled to arrive, I let myself into the festively lit boathouse to arrange everything the way I want. A sign hangs on the front entrance: *closed for the season.* Wintery conditions make it difficult for anyone to navigate the water, so they aren't open to the public during these colder months. An ideal playground for this very occasion.

Paddle Boston is decorated accordingly, lit up with colored lights and holiday wreaths, as are many homes and businesses in the area. I easily pick the lock of the side door and get busy rearranging the space. The wind over the lake makes the outside air to feel closer to thirty degrees, so our tentative walk around the property will have to be more of a brief meander, on the dock within the boathouse.

First on the agenda, create a space warm enough for Cindel and I. The boathouse is designed for storing all kinds of water vessels. Although it's enclosed, it is still considered an 'outside structure,' hovering just above the lake. Kayaks are secured in rows along the wall, while two covered boats are winterized and suspended high above the water. The dimly lit room has so much potential, especially with all the entertaining pulleys and wooden rafters at my disposal. I locate an electric patio heater and switch on the tower to begin warming an area, away from the open water.

Tonight needs to be perfect, just like her.

I collect two strands of white lights from shaped topiaries just outside the building and string them between trusses. It's not my best work, but time is passing too quickly, otherwise I would have wrapped the beams for a cleaner look.

Unpacking the small basket which I brought along, I lay out a blanket, wine glasses, a charcuterie board of cut meats and cheeses, and a bottle of Moscato; since she always likes things on the sweeter side. I checked the space before I committed to bringing my girl here, so I already know most of what I need is on hand. I'm curious if she is familiar with Shibari; a Japanese art form of rope bondage. If not, she will be after tonight.

Keeping my identify hidden up until this point was necessary, tonight however, I relinquish the helmet and tactical vest. I'm still covered, but not for long. I still can't believe she thought I was Eamon. It makes me wonder though, if he has ever considered being with her; would they have made a better match? I shake the radical idea from my mind. Nope. Fuck that. I don't have any qualms with Eamon, but I would have killed him if he took what he was doing any further. It's bad enough he kissed her. I know he didn't do it willingly, but I still plan to punish him for it later.

His father Patrick is playing him like a marionette. Mairead, on the other hand, is more of a danger to Cindel. She's unpredictable and quick to react when her feelings come in to question. Once, I witnessed her floss a guy's teeth with one of her many petite blades, just because he ate one too many slices of her pizza. I felt queasy trying to floss my teeth the rest of that whole week.

A soft knock on the side door shakes me from the disturbing flashback. Crossing the hollow space, I open the door to find Cindel dressed exactly as expected, only without her usual smile. She moves into the boathouse one step at a time, eyes roaming the unfamiliar space. She's unusually quiet. She locates a source of warmth and immediately starts toward the heater. I watch warily as she studies the room, her face scowling at the doctored lights that hang among the rafters.

I look from the lights to her. Fuck, did I really do that shitty of a job?

She folds her arms over her chest. "Did you put those up?"

I bow my head, cautious that any wrong movements could frighten her away. "I hate Christmas," she declares, finally facing my direction.

I tilt my head slightly, hoping she'll elaborate as to why.

"Theo died just after Christmas. I despise the lights and festive trees, basically anything that reminds me of that time." She turns away and commences rubbing her hands together, near the warming tower.

Fuck. How did I not realize this? Without a second thought, I take a running jump to grasp the string of lights and tug them down in one swift motion. Just as hastily, I wrap them in a ball and store them beneath a nearby tarp.

Her face slowly brightens and I can already tell she appreciates the gesture. "You said you'd show me a dark secret, is it about the message you sent Andrea?"

I stride toward her, my weight causing the floating wooden floor to creak with each step. I'm having trouble keeping my distance from this angel in front of me. I motion for her to sit on the floor where the blanket lay. She stands before me unmoving and quirks an eyebrow. Soon I realize my poor planning, not accounting for her pencil skirt.

Holding up my index finger, I jog up a set of wooden stairs before grabbing two folding chairs from the narrow loft above. Returning to the mock picnic, I unfold the chairs, ahead of spotting a giant wooden spool that could act as a makeshift table. Flipping the spool on its side, I roll it next to the blanketed area and arrange the items I brought onto the circular surface. Now, we have a proper table setting.

Shaking out the sheet, I relay it down beside us, basket within reach. I have so much in store for her this evening, but all in good time.

I pull out one of the chairs for Cindel, because I am, in fact, a gentleman. I hold it in place as she comes down to sit. Her mahogany waves cascade down her back. I can't help but stare as I make my way around the makeshift table and sit in the adjacent seat.

She pushes her hair behind her right ear revealing what a good girl she is. Wearing the earbud with the Sharpie star shows how she's become familiar with me, aware I'll use it to communicate with her. It's so much more intimate when I can whisper in her ear.

Despite the heat source, Cindel is still shivering. My attention lingers longer than I had anticipated on her thin shirt, David Bowie's face nestled between raised nipples. Regardless of the goggles, she knows exactly what I am staring at.

Looking up through long lashes, she reaches across the table for a grape. Gradually she presses the fruit into her mouth, pausing just as the round green food creates an "O" with her lips. Tease. She knows exactly what she is doing.

We watch each other wordlessly from across the impromptu dining table, her savoring each morsel of cheese and prosciutto, while I long to be the object that makes her mouth water.

"If you take off the ski mask thingy, you can eat." She extends a cracker, waiting to see if I'll take the bait.

I kindly refused the offer. Patience, woman.

Once she's had her fill, I remain seated as she explores the boathouse. She lifts the coverings of boats, opens boxes, and investigates inside of every nook and cranny available. Such a curious one.

When I sense she's comfortable within her surroundings, I type out a message on my phone before hitting play. The message siphons directly in her ear; the only sound is the lapping water against the sides of the structure.

"What scares you?" The husky curated voice whispers to her.

She lets out a small gasp, dropping the rope she was previously fiddling with and turns to face me. An elevated boat and span of open water separates us, but I notice how the question makes her chest rapidly rise and fall. Her breath is visible before her, temperature dropping by the minute.

"Being lied to," she rushes. The answer, just as intriguing as she. "I hate when I'm treated like I'm some fragile thing that can't handle the truth. It's not reality that scares me, it's being deceived that makes me want to run." Her words carry so much weight; I can't stand it.

Rising from my chair, I stalk toward her. She watches me with both interest and caution. I stop mere inches from her and type out another message, opting to show her the phone screen this time.

Do you trust me?

Cindel's eyes bounce from the phone to my shielded face, she reaches for me, laying a hand on my cheek.

I can feel her icy touch through the thin fabric concealing my identity. Can she feel how hot my skin is? How I'm burning up from the inside out? I need her more than the very air I breathe. Fuck everything I'm supposed to be. Nothing else matters but her. Before I continue, I must make sure… she wants this too.

Little droplets collect on her bottom eyelashes and I'm unsure if she's forgotten to blink or if I've somehow upset her. I dare not move, as I await a response.

Eventually, her other chilled hand joins my face as she cradles me within her hold. "Please," she begs.

This woman could bring me to my knees with one word; but I remain still allowing her to finish.

"Please… never lie to me."

Fuck! I am a goner. She could ask me to cleave off my hand and I'd oblige. I nod unhurried; more to myself than in reply. I vow to never be dishonest with her again.

Straight away, I wrap my arm around her middle before lifting her into the air. She lets out a small squeak of surprise as I carry her back toward the warm sanctuary. Not wanting to wait a single moment longer than I already have. The make-shift table rests too closely to the soft fabric. Needing more space, I toss the wooden spool on its side causing the food and drinks to topple to the ground, breaking on impact.

Laying Cindel's shivering frame down on the blanket, I can't help but quiver as well, not from the temperature but from how hard I'm fighting to maintain control in her presence. Like some kind of brainteaser, I assess which article of clothing to remove first. It would be so much easier to just rip it all off. Although, I don't want her to be indecent for anyone but me, and she still has to find her way home. I took a cab here, not wanting my car to give me away or raise suspicion about anyone being on the closed premises. I opt for removing her articles of clothing, meticulously.

I start at the bottom, unlacing her shoes, I slip them off one at a time. She watches without a sound. Her chest rises and falls faster, with each scrap of fabric I discard. Without reservation, I work my gloved hands up to her skirt.

She's either become impatient or has little faith in my abilities, because she arches her back to help unzip the deceptive covering. Apparently, the zipper is along the back and down the curve of her ass.

Sliding the black spandex skirt down her long creamy legs, I'm welcomed home with her scent. Just as I anticipated, no underwear.

Without batting an eye, she removes her jacket, balling it up and placing it beneath her head. Cindel lies back against the sheet... she's a fucking vision, the only thing covering her is the meager white shirt.

I should level the playing field. This will be the first time she sees me, all of me. I suddenly realize, I'm nervous. As casually as I can, I remove my black jacket and long-sleeved shirt, taking care to not expose my face while pulling the top over my head.

I add my shoes next to Cindel's and it just looks so... right. Having something as simple as our boots organized next to one another. I want to do ordinary things with her, like placing my footwear beside hers in our home, each and every day.

Control yourself. She's right here... you haven't driven her off. This realization helps to diminish any residual nerves.

Unfastening my belt, she shifts to her knees prior to putting a hand on my thigh.

"Let me." She all but purrs.

Fuuuck, she's magnificent. I can hardly wait to feel her skin again.

While she tugs the belt from it's loops, I begin working off my gloves, which are much more difficult to get off when your hands are as sweaty as mine. Staring down at her, I desperately pull at each finger to wiggle out of the article of clothing, while she unbuttons my pants.

A seductive smile plays on her lips just ahead of the pants falling past my ankles.

I too, have forgone underwear. My cock already at attention. If she was just a breath closer, I swear I would have poked her in the eye.

Her sweet smile causes my chest to tighten.

Finally, I manage to pull off both gloves and drop them to the ground beside the belt.

Licking her colored lips, she leans forward, just as I step back with a "tsk, tsk" sound.

I point to my chest then spin my finger above her, indicating it's my turn and I need her to swing around.

Her burgundy bottom lip juts out in a pout, but she complies.

Stepping out of my pants, I kick them to the side then go to the basket. Inside, I locate the trinket I had specially made for my girl. With Cindel's back to me, I can't help but appreciate how the backside of her is even sexier than the front. She's still sitting on her heels, not quite the desired position, but we're moving in the right direction.

Next, I retrieve a small bottle from the collection of items and open the cap. Squeezing a generous helping of the viscous liquid onto the handmade gift; I tuck the bottle away and move toward my obedient subject. With the item in hand, I kneel just behind her. I run my free hand from the base of her spine, up between her shoulder blades, where I give a small nudge downward.

Cindel obeys. Bringing her hands to the floor before her and adjusting onto all fours. I notice when she tries to peek over her shoulder, but I don't want her to ruin the surprise.

I deliver a swift warning smack to her exposed ass.

Sucking on her teeth, she inhales sharply before facing forward again.

Very responsive. I had a feeling she'd be like this. Wanting direction. Craving a little bit of pain with her pleasure.

Gel drips down the head and base of the custom-made, glass butt plug. Shadows play on the curve of her hips in the dimly lit boathouse. Holding the plug before her backside, I leisurely make small circles to start.

A gasp escapes her; however, she lowers her belly causing her spine to dip and her ass to raise slightly. She stays in place... asking for it.

Inside the glass toy I ordered, uniquely for her, are rainbow sprinkles. It has a flared base just wide enough to encase a tracking disk. If something happens... I need to be able to find her. I will never allow anyone to hurt what's mine. When she gets home tonight and has a chance to remove the plug, I hope she appreciates it.

A bead of cum drips from the head of my cock, as soft whimpers fill the space as I orbit her tight hole with the cool, wet glass. I never expected her to be inexperienced, but I am captivated with how eager she was to play with me. I make a mental note to find and kill anyone else that has touched her before me.

The plug is modestly sized, not too big... nor too small. I push it in little by little until I've reached the girthiest part.

A deep seductive moan has Cindel throwing back her head, causing me to involuntarily grab her hip. I coax the toy out gently and repeat the process. Her soft skin no longer cool to the touch, but hot with a blooming red mark on her cheek.

The next time I tease inward with the plug, I'm taken aback as Cindel rocks backward into my hand. Her ass swallows the plug whole in one swift motion. Greedy girl. I may have had it specially made for her, yet she holds the power. She decides how to use the tools I provide her. She's a daydream in this nightmare.

My cock throbs and it would be so easy to just drive into her, but there is something I have to do first. I help her to stand, guiding her toward my next desired location.

Between two trusses of the hammerbeam roof is a tie rod, lift system.

Cindel holds onto me like a fawn on new legs, trusting as she follows without question. In the near future, we'll have to have a more serious discussion about stranger danger.

My face is still covered, but I take a moment to hold her by the chin, becoming lost in the varying hues of cool blues. Leaving her side briefly, I roll the electric heater over, grab my phone, and the nautical rope which already holds a few preliminary knots.

Out of the corner of my eye, I see her reach around trying to touch the base of the plug, nestled inside her.

Snapping my fingers, she straightens with an irritated growl. Despite it all, she remains where I leave her… waiting for me.

Once I have everything in position, I stand before her and play the new message. "You can see your present when you get home."

Her jaw opens and closes a few times, obviously at a loss for words.

She can't see it, but I'm grinning beneath my mask. Setting my phone on the ground, I commence wrapping the thin marine rope, into different loops and patterns around Cindel's torso to create a chest harness. So cooperative, she even holds out her arms for me. This is just one of the many skill sets I learned growing up. Making and undoing knots is cathartic. Eventually, I stumbled into Shibari. Bondage made it easier for me to get close to a woman. I suppose a life void of hugs and affection could make any person uncomfortable with intimacy. I wasn't ready for her hands on me. It's been some time since I've been with someone. Years actually. I'm a little out of practice but I am determined to see how distorted I could make the image on her shirt. Accentuating Cindel's petite breasts within the confines of the ropes.

She watches in silence, her breath steady but heart rate hurried. That sultry mouth of hers hangs slack with an inviting O-shape that has the capability of making me cum, even before I finish tying her up. Intricately placed knots weaved together, running all over her top half, arms tightly bound to her back.

Each breast resembles a white-chocolate candy kiss, all packaged and ready to bite into.

"Please," she whimpers.

Reality is finally catching up to her. She's exposed, tied up, vulnerable, and alone with someone who she can't even identify. Unless law enforcement conducts a line-up of perps without pants, there is honestly no telling *who* I am. Nevertheless, you can't rush art, so she'll have to tolerate my preparation a little longer.

With her top half restricted, I walk her back until her heels touch the end of the wooden platform.

Cindel's eyes are like saucers, legs trembling, all the while I keep her there… right at the edge of the ice water.

My finger brushes against her lips before continuing downward past her sternum, between her breasts, sliding over her stomach, where my touch ends just above her pubic bone.

She monitors me as I fetch more of the silky rope.

Creating a series of new knots and shapes; I wrap and secure an equal measure of rope around each thigh, finishing just below her knees. A single-column tie with a loop behind each bend will allow the bight to act as a pulley system.

I check her hands, legs, and other extremities to make sure they are their *usual* color. When I'm confident nothing is too tight nor too loose, I connect her to previously suspended ropes and pulleys, on either side of the wooden pillars. Before suspending her above the dock, I check in.

She looks at each connected rope before peering over her shoulder at the dark water. Her hooded eyes consider me; the tangle of ropes in my hand, my hidden face, and a stiffy that's beginning to throb painfully. Again, she bites that puffy bottom lip of hers, then tilts her head back.

God damn, if that's not a yes, I don't know what is.

I pull hard on the ropes, tying the loose ends to a cleat hitch, located on the wooden berth. Levitating at just the right height, her body is splayed wide for me. She's willing, but is she able to face all hard truths to come?

Cindel resembles a rotisserie in a butcher's knot… but sexy, and I am hungry. Eager to devour her.

I chuckle silently to myself, over the irony of it all. Hear no evil. Speak no evil. If I actually obeyed orders, I'd simply run my blade across her throat and leave her here to bleed out. Too bad I've never been good at playing by the rules.

Cindel allowing me to string her up like this just validates that she trusts me. She's ready to play and absolutely fucking perfect like this.

I pick up my phone from the ground, typing out what I can't voice before hitting play. The words murmur in her ear, "I told you I'd make you my *angel* tonight, but not before you know whose name to scream."

A shiver wracks through her suspended body as she focuses on me.

Removing the goggles first, I chuck them off to my side.

Cindel squints in the dim light, first taking in my eyes.

I step closer to her hanging form. Ever so slowly, I drag the balaclava up and over my face... holding the material by my side with a clenched fist. What if she rejects me? Screams even? I've concealed who I was up until now. Frankly, I've kept who I truly am a secret, not just from her, but everyone.

Her eyes are unblinking. I don't even think she's taken a breath.

Time is frozen as I clutch the mask tighter in my hand. There's nothing to say, no readable expression, just parted lips that I so desperately want to taste. Maybe this is a mistake? I drag my fingers through my hair, knowing what an unacceptable mess I must look.

"It's you," she states plainly. "Has it been you the whole time? But... what about the toothpick I found in my room? I thought you could have been Garron!" Her voice becomes high-pitched on the last word.

Crap, are my knots too tight? How could she possibly think I was that buffoon? I must have tracked a toothpick into her room on my shoes. I attempt to wet my chapped lips, still grasping the small piece of fabric like it's a life-line. I bend my head downward instinctively... attempting to hide my scar. Did she want it to be him? Was showing her my dark secret a poor decision? I can't tell.

When I finally find the courage to look back up at her, we just stare at each other. This goes on for so long, I start to believe she's ready to tell me to take her down.

"Can you speak?"

I look to the floor and sign "*no*" with my three fingers.

I picked up some sign language after my accident. Now she knows I'm Eamon's mangled friend, I can finally use my hands to speak again.

I peer up at her, just as her eyes retreat from me, seeming to remember that we're fully naked and I'm perpetually erect.

"Dax." Her eyes are heavy. "Please," she begs, facing me again with fervency.

My name sounds more like a prayer than a curse, coming from her mouth. She... she still wants me?

The tension in my chest eases. Knots I never knew were present begin to unfurl in my belly. Cindel accepts me, defects and all. More than passion at this juncture, I feel an animalistic desire to protect... to possess. No one will ever hurt her again. Her simple plea is all the consent I need.

Rapidly, I bridge the gap between us, taking a hip in each hand, I press my body forward.

She's soaked, the head of my cock gliding over her opening with ease. It's fortunate her ass is occupied, because I have no doubt that I would have accidentally slid in on this angle.

Her breathing is uneven as I tease her entrance. Small moans tumble from her parted lips, as I push inside her, advancing forward, inch by inch, until I'm fully seated in her fucking heavenly pussy.

She whines between breathy pants as she attempts to wiggle regardless of being midair, unable to touch me or control her movements. It makes all of this, that much more enjoyable. It's an act of trust. Despite her helpless and vulnerable state, she's still in control. Buried inside her, I take one of her ass cheeks in my hand and push lightly on the base of the plug with my finger, reminding her how full I've made her. With my other hand still on her hip I shift her back and forth, effectively bouncing her on my cock.

Her moans and pants fill the space, each time my tip enters, making contact with that one spot inside her. I'm not hung like a horse, but her shallow canal doesn't have any more room for me. Any deeper and I would be hurting her. She's so fucking tight. I try desperately to think about ducks in a pond or taxes, literally anything that won't have me filling her prematurely.

Cindel's head lolls back, mouth agape, but still, she watches me. Her intense eye contact makes me feel coveted. Wanted for once in my life.

I reposition the hand once pressing on the plug's base, to between our bodies. I know my girl needs more. Rolling her clit with my middle finger, her piercing moves with it. I'm enamored by her every sound... her every movement.

All the while her gaze becomes languid. She's drenched, aroused, but not to the point of exploding. I want her walls tightening around my cock, in tune with my name being torn from her throat. I will continue pushing all the buttons and twisting each knob, until my girl loses control.

Focusing on random shit, like how waterfowls aren't able to claim dependents on their taxes, I can't help notice the drool escaping the corner of Cindel's pretty mouth.

Now we're fucking getting somewhere!

One hand remaining on her hip, keeping her from swinging away from me; the other shoves between us, applying pressure on the area above her pubic bone, with the heel of my palm. My finger switches directions, continuing to circle her engorged lady boner.

"I... I can't."

Goddamnit, I wish I were an octopus! I desperately need an extra set of hands at this moment to relay to her, "it's a boathouse, everything is meant to get wet."

My heart is beating too fast, but I maintain the perfect rpm as I stimulate her, not changing a thing, until she comes undone. My dick remains deep inside her, despite it no longer driving in and out. Bringing my face close to hers, I nose her cheek just ahead of sucking on her bottom lip. Feeling my mouth on hers is everything I hoped it would be. Sweet, soft, and utterly divine. I long for those desperate noises she makes right before she tips over the edge. She's only shared them with me at the Lantern Festival, but I've listened to her draw them out countless times prior, when she pleasures herself.

"Oh my god!" Legs quaking, she cries out, "DAX!" Her scream echoes through the space.

She breaks beautifully for me. Her warm release drips down my legs, as wave after wave of pleasure, tugs at my cock.

Thank fuck it's late and this place is secluded enough that no one is around, because my girl is a screamer.

The ripples of her orgasm subside causing her body to become torpid within my arms.

Stay with me, Princess, it's my turn. I grip her ass roughly, convinced she'll have ten tiny bruises by tomorrow. Thrusting forward I fuck her at a punishing speed.

No longer do I need to concentrate on business savvy birds, as I'm finally able to chase my own release.

Wet slapping sounds echo in time with her short, heavy gasps.

My vision begins to tunnel. Her scent, all consuming. Like metallic rain. Every muscle in my body tightens as I bounce her on my dick. My throat aches, attempting to create sound, as my resolve snaps and I spill inside her.

To my surprise, Cindel has yet another wave of pleasure storm through her. Bared teeth hold in pleasure filled groans. Her weary body is decorated with red splotches, while her muscles give one last punishing squeeze to my well-spent cock.

I could die happily like this, buried inside her. It's all I could ever want from this life. Being accepted... needed. I will worship this woman till the end of time. My conquest. The queen I hold above all else.

Unhurried, I deliberately untie the knots, easing her down to the wooden floorboards.

I know her hips ache from being suspended in that position for so long, so I lower her restrained form carefully.

Reaching for my phone, I play the song I have chosen for tonight. This feels like the right moment. I select the song within my newly renamed collection: *Stalker's Playlist*. I couldn't help myself.

Her once listless gaze expands with wonder as the music plays straight into her ear.

The song is from **Highly Suspect – "My Name is Human."**

She's reserved... listening tentatively as her breathe steadies; staring blankly toward nothing in particular.

During the time the song plays, I remove the artfully placed ropes from her upper body.

I should have brought extra blankets, silently scolding myself for not bringing enough to make her comfortable.

Scooping up her tired body, I carry her over to the solo blanket, positioning the heater to give her a warm space to clean and dress.

Her sedated assessment has braids beginning to form in my lower belly, again.

Now the lustful thoughts have subsided, is she second guessing herself? Is it me she actually sees? Why would anyone want damaged goods? Does she only see the jagged scar across my neck?

Without my mask, I feel exposed... shameful. She may know my name, but she still doesn't know who I truly am to her.

Despite my internal struggle to understand, her hands reach for me. Her light touch rests on either side of my face. Such a contrast to my flawed character; she's too pure.

"Can I keep you?" she whisper-shouts.

I... what? The question catches me off guard and I can't help but turn my head, still baffled.

Her eyes look more, blue-gray at this moment, and I'm unsure how someone so flawless would agree to have me. I'm overwhelmed. Awestruck by how she has thrown me a metaphorical ring buoy; unknowingly rescuing me from a sea of doubt I've been drowning in my whole life. She's my salvation, in a world that has never seemed to have space for me. Of course she can keep me.

I fervently incline forward, taking her mouth in mine. The kiss is all consuming. A mix of tongues and teeth, battling to find purchase in each other. I could kick myself for waiting so long to kiss her like this, but maybe it was necessary. To make sure we belonged to one another.

My cock engages too, unabated regardless of the emotional turmoil I just battled.

Her teeth rake my bottom lip as she pulls back, looking over me with such tender resolve.

Wait... all at once I remember why the question sounds so familiar. Where I originally heard it from... a movie I watched on cable TV, one Halloween.

Did she just pull a quote from Casper? The part where Christina Ricci sees her ghost friend as a real boy for the first time?

As if she can read the realization across my face, a devious smile blooms on hers. Her once flushed skin seems to be diminishing... although the marks will soon leave her body, I'm confident what we shared tonight in the boathouse will stick with us.

I would willingly be stuck in purgatory… giving Cindel my only soul if she requested.

I pull back just enough to sign, *Time to go home.*

MARY

Over Twenty Years Ago

The driver has me back home by three in the afternoon, on a beautiful Sunday. I'm jet-lagged, exhausted from traveling, but my mood immediately boosts when I open the door and see my boy running toward me with open arms.

I drop my bag right there in the entrance and embrace my little Eamon with a spin. Twirling around he gives me an award-winning laugh, while his little fingers stretch out to enjoy the ride.

My husband strolls in, carrying my gorgeous baby girl, who just turned one this past summer.

"How was your flight, Mo Shearc?"

I gather the gummy-smiled girl in my arms while the boys muscle my luggage into the house.

I've only been gone for a week and my precious girl has her first reddened curl coming in, just like her mama.

"Long," I replied. "Didn't get much rest."

Patrick tells Eamon to take his sister and go play in the den.

Taking me by the hand, he leads me into the house and pours me a glass of champagne with a splash of OJ as I take a seat at the long counter in the kitchen.

My husband can be thoughtful and gentle... but only with me.

It was a smart match our parents made. My sister should have been the one to wed first. She was older, but argued she wanted a career more than a husband. Moyra was never going to go along with any arranged marriage.

Then, right after she graduated, she secretly eloped. To a police officer of all people. I must have asked her a hundred times after I had heard the news. Why? Why him?!

Immediately, my parents cut her off. "No daughter of theirs should be *involved with a copper," they declared. Whether it was her husband or simply because our family values didn't align with that of an 'officer of the law,' my older sister became estranged.*

It crushed me. Especially once I started a family. Someday, I hope my children will get to know their aunt. She's not only an amazing friend, but a mother herself... I wish she had confided in me the way I had her, all those years ago.

My husband never isolated me, in fact, he mostly sought my advice when it came to delicate business matters. He also consciously tries to put me and the kids first. There is no question if he loves me, but I worry he would see me differently if he knew the real reason I flew back to Ireland.

I left under the notion I was "visiting family" and to help care for my ill nanny, which was true. Equally important, I visited a place I previously buried in the darkest corners of my mind. My folks were privy to the real reason I went; they of course were the ones who arranged everything.

This secret I carried, held the power to ruin family names and destroy partnerships. Even prevent stipulated marriages.

I was promised to Patrick Murray and my parents sought to keep that arrangement intact, until I came of age. My family wasn't wealthy by any means, but my father was a smart businessman and worked his way up the ladder, rubbing elbows with all the right people.

Before my sixteenth birthday, my Pa' informed me that I was promised to his boss's son. This wasn't too foreign of a concept back then, especially if the deal meant your family would be taken care of for as long as business was good.

Patrick came to my birthday that year. He was handsome with a charismatic smile and a confidence that made all the girls at my party swoon. I was happy and could see a promising future as his wife.

Sundays, we saw each other at church, the occasional family function, and whenever business partners, like Pa, were invited. Everyone over-embellished at these parties, so they rarely noticed when Patrick and I snuck away to share a kiss, beneath the large, twisted oak outback. My sister caught us once. She was actually the one to lecture me on the birds and the bees, so to speak.

I felt like the luckiest girl in the whole city.

A little before my eighteenth birthday, I went to meet a friend from school, in the club district, at a place called Club 114. My parents thought I had a study group and planned to spend the night at Sheila's. Sheila was a straight

'A' student who would never be caught dead in a sketchy club such as this. So, she was my alibi.

I never intended to be naive, prey in a city of wolves.

As I navigated my way through the first club I'd ever been to, I felt a sharp pinch in my side. My arms and legs felt instantly fuzzy, while everything around me started going in and out of focus. I was sleepy but also content.

Without realizing it, I was moving. A large body escorted me back onto the dark streets, all without ever finding my friend. It was like watching a movie. There... but not really present. No pain, just pure, disconnected euphoria.

Snippets of the person stayed with me. Those steely gray eyes that looked like they belonged to a beast. His gaze was hollow, empty, and after he had his fill of me, he disappeared. I was a husk of a woman. Broken... I've never been quite the same since that day.

I guess that's part of growing up.

When I finally clawed my way out of the hellish nightmare, I awoke to an enraged man shouting at me. He was convinced I was some homeless drifter who'd made camp in the back seat of his car. My skin itched from head to toe, and the stench of vomit clung to my hair. Still, despite my wretched state, I managed to snatch up my pockabook and sprint all the way home.

I told my sister first. When I finally confessed to Ma' and Pa' they were beside themselves. Moyra held my hand the whole time, never leaving my side. After the verbal lashing of a lifetime and a few encyclopedias thrown my way, they went into rescue mode.

I don't deserve them.

My parents made excuses in the beginning, explanations for my absence due to "sickness," but as the problem grew... it became harder to conceal, especially from my future betrothed. Ma' formulated a plan to send me to my Nanny and Pop-Pop's in Ireland. They told my future in-laws and close friends that I wanted to take some time to help the church, back in our home country.

It was a half-truth, because I did go to Nanny and Pop-Pop's, however, the church helped me, not the other way around.

On the coldest day in January, on the sacred 3rd day of the month, I delivered a healthy baby boy in the local, catholic hospital. Such a joyous time for most new mothers... on the contrary, this day had rapidly become one of the most difficult moments of my life.

They set the red skinned babe in my arms for just a moment. I counted ten fingers and ten toes, before a nurse whisked him away to be cared for, until the nuns from the orphanage came to retrieve the baby.

I cried and screamed into my pillow every night for the next two weeks, until my voice became hoarse. Then it was time to fly back home to the states, back to my new future with my husband-to-be.

A piece of me remained in Ireland when I left, a secret that should never cross the Atlantic.

My doting husband rubs a tense area in my shoulders, bringing me out of the memory. Rubbing outward with his strong hands, hands that I know for a fact have killed multiple men, although he never discusses such matters under our families' roof.

His squeezes and strokes quickly morph into playful nibbles on my earlobes and neck. He's missed me and I, him. Hot against my ear, he details how he plans to welcome me home properly, once the kids are in bed, tonight.

Patrick had some paperwork to catch up on and I was desperate for a nap above all else.

I kissed my babies on the top of their heads, before informing our au pair I planned to lie down for a little while.

Removing my heels, I crawl into the tightly made bed to settle my exhausted mind, at the very least. When I closed my eyes, I was flooded with images of the young boy, multiple years older than Eamon. The boy probably didn't even take notice of me, as I watched him play ball in the field with other children. Just outside the orphanage, I stood with the nuns as they shared what little they could with me.

They named him Daxton, Dax for short. "He'll be nine next January," they shared. Of course, I already knew that. The day etched into my memory. I never lost count. Even though the visit was short, I could see he was quite the leader, out of all the children. Heading the charge toward the leather ball in the grassy field, eventually catching it midair and scoring on the opposing team. At one point, the ball rolled just in front of the nuns and I. Of course, Dax was the one to retrieve it. He was right before me. All I had to do was reach out and... what could I possibly say?

His eyes were gray; not cold or empty, but full of curiosity. It wasn't his fault. He had no say in the man who meddled in our lives. The dirty-faced child regarded me, although only a brief moment, I could tell his soul did not match his father's. Only managing to deliver a tight smile before he fetched what he came for and ran back to the others.

In my dreams, I imagine Dax happily running around and playing. A day hasn't gone by without thinking about the baby I gave up. I prayed that it was the right choice for me... and for him.

Later that evening, we went to the Lombardis for Sunday gravy. They were a lovely young family like us, with kids of similar age and gender. Mrs. Lombardi and I had weekly playdates with the kids and our whole family had regular get-togethers. Our husbands even attended baseball games together, when they weren't working.

Terri and I sat at the table, talking about the best schools in the area, while Patrick and Terri's husband, Charles, smoked Cigars on the back patio. I could hear their heated discussion becoming progressively louder through the sliding glass door. Arguing about who will be coming out on top, in next week's boxing match. I swear, men are too passionate about their sports. To each their own I guess, but we weren't too far off with our chatter. Daydreaming about who our kids might be when they grow up. I believed our families' friendship would last a lifetime.

Little Cindel dashed through the room, holding colorful ribbons in her hand, while Mairead eagerly tried to crawl after the action. Eamon and Theo were two of the sweetest boys in town. They loved to spend their time together, coloring or watching cartoons. As long as they were together, they were content. It just seemed like we were living the American dream, with the perfect friends, home, and work-life balance.

This was the life I desired. I smile, blinking back tears. Fighting off the pang of guilt; keeping secrets so consuming from my loved ones.

I suppose it was only a matter of time before my past caught up with me. Secrets never stay secrets forever. Especially when the unfathomable strolls right through the front door of your best friend's home.

A well-dressed, olive skinned man with slicked back hair and reflective dress shoes, stood in the kitchen where Terri and I sat.

"Nicholas! How are you?!" Terri stands to greet the surprise newcomer, by kissing him on each cheek. "Mary, I'd like you to meet my brother-in-law, Nicholas. Nicholas, this is Mary Murray."

He looks down at me with stormy, calculated eyes. Eyes that I see often in my nightmares.

"Mary Murray?" he says slowly, like he's tasting the words as he speaks. "Such a pleasure."

I feign a smile and politely extend my hand, to not cause Terri to suspect anything other than two people meeting for the first time.

The suave man leisurely kissed the back of my hand, as I willed myself not to rip it away from his poisonous touch. It felt like an eternity, until he released his hold of me and announced his intent.

"So sorry to intrude on your little affair, but I wanted to tell my brother something in person. It's quite pressing."

Brother? This man looks nothing like the fair featured Charles, just outside.

"Ladies..." he bows his head slightly, as a leering grin contorts his mouth. He moved like a serpent through the space, making his way out to the

men who still readily exchanged insults about who deserved to win the coming match.

My stomach soured after the interaction, and I excused myself to check on my kids. I said a little prayer, that the horrendous man leaves without damaging my life any further.

Once dinner was plated and we wrangled the kids into each highchair, the three men made their way to the table to join us.

"Hope you don't mind, dear, Nicholas will be joining us for dinner."

Terri wrinkles her nose and smiles, waving a hand in front of her. "Of course not! The more the merrier."

Perfect. Now I had to sit front and center with my family and friends watching me pretend that everything was fine, when in fact I'm battling a tornado of feelings and memories. Will this Nicholas character say anything about how we know each other? Divulging secrets so dark, they could fracture our family apart. I simply did not know how I was going to make it through this meal.

We took a group photo, which our friends regularly do. It was a tradition we started when the boys were small, to witness how we grew each time.

I positioned myself as far away from the depraved man as possible, both in the picture and at the table.

The men laughed and joked, while Terri and I spent the better part of the meal, fussing over the kids who thought eating with their hands was pro-quo for the best spaghetti experience around.

No one seemed to notice that I just pushed my food around the plate but never actually ate. I couldn't stomach it. To my relief, nothing nefarious was said during dinner. I was cautiously optimistic that this whole uncomfortable night could be behind us shortly. Now, I simply had to ensure our paths wouldn't cross again.

If only I were so lucky.

After dessert, we put the kids in the den where a playpen was set up for the girls to share and a small sofa for the boys to lay down on.

It was too early for Patrick. I knew he wasn't ready to head home just yet. I tried to make myself scarce by excusing myself to the powder room. After spending a brief time alone, I opened the sliding pocket door, only to be pushed back into the small room.

Nicholas stood before me in the half bath. His narrowed gaze and predatory smile made me want to flee. I could hear laughing and music through the door. "Hey, little fox." Without a doubt, he recognizes me. His words felt like hot tar as they slid through the cramped space. "Remember me?"

How could I forget? I bite my bottom lip, trying not to make my situation worse than it already was, by saying something stupid. Just like my parents taught me, keep your mouth shut, if you know what's good for you.

"I heard you just got back from a little trip. Any particular reason you chose to visit Ireland?"

Sinking my teeth harder into my flesh, I now tasted blood. I shook my head no, hoping that's all he wants to know and he'll leave me alone.

He tsks. "That's no place for a modern girl of your stature. You belong here, with your beautiful children and loving husband."

I pull in my bottom lip to conceal the mark I inflicted. Nicholas was unmoving. I had to say something, then maybe this would be over. "My Nanny was ill; I went to take care—"

He pressed into me, I could smell stale smoke on his breath, he was so close. "Was she?"

I nod like an obstinate child, wanting to be done with this conversation.

"See, I know you're lying, little fox. I know the real reason you were there."

No... he can't possibly know!

"I've had eyes on you since you ran home crying, after I painted your thighs in blood." His words were toxic, making my heart hammer violently in my chest. "Tell the truth, Mary."

I tried to arm my lungs with air but I could hardly breathe, in this cramped space. He's too close. Lie. "I... I went to a church while I was there. I volunteered—"

My head suddenly jerks back and I felt as if my hair had been ripped from my skull! I let the anguished scream get stuck in my throat. I don't want the others to hear. They can't know! I face up toward the ceiling in the small bath, as he rests his stubbled face against my cheek.

"Sweet, sweet mother Mary... what's our child's name?" He fists my curls so tightly, tears start to collect in the corner of my eyes. I Can't. I can't tell this horrible man a thing!

"Mary..." he sing-songs my name. "You wouldn't want to keep Patrick waiting. I just need a name." His words weren't the only vile thing sliding over me, his free hand began pawing at my breasts, then eventually inching up the hem of my dress.

"Please. Please don't." Not again! Do I call out? Hollar for Patrick?! Of course, he would come to my rescue but what if Nicholas spins the story, says I was coming onto him, or worse, spills my dark secret. Our secret. This man was the epitome of pure evil, but I had to protect this life; my two children sleeping in the other room. I needed to continue keeping my adoring husband, blissfully ignorant to my sins.

I had this eerie feeling that I would die at the hands of this man, not today but sometime in the future. I asked the lord for forgiveness, as I spoke the three-letter word that I promised to leave on the other side of the ocean, "Dax."

THIRTY-SIX

CINDEL

Tiptoeing into our apartment with the stench of sex and curated meat isn't exactly how I envisioned the night ending. I'm not sure what I expected… but I went to the boathouse knowing I trusted him.

The house was silent. Andrea must have passed out after being awake for hours on end, combing through the information on the board. I couldn't do any of this without her help, however I am glad to not come home to a barrage of questions.

I scurry to the bathroom after closing and locking the front door. These kinds of insidious activities are going to be much more difficult once Andrea installs the security system. During the taxi ride home, I couldn't help but shift in my seat… keen to remove the keepsake *he* pressed into me.

He is Dax. I let his name sit with me for some time. Dax is my stalker. How had I not considered him before? Always so close by. I was naive to think the man in the shadows was Eamon, but it all made perfect sense now. Why he never spoke. Garron never closed his mouth long enough for anyone else to get a word in edgewise. The only reason I considered him was because of the stupid toothpick. Which Dax must have tracked in on his boot. I mean they are almost always together… everything clicks into place. How he knew so much about me and why he was able to funnel me songs nearby without me noticing.

I drew a bath, easing sluggishly into the balmy water. My body aches in new places from the ropes which bound my body and suspended me midair, merely an hour ago. I liked it. More than liking, I can't stop thinking about it. The way I was restrained yet, all he wanted to do was lay himself bare. His form was very nice in itself, but I saw the vulnerability in the way he looked at me. The way he recoiled when he unmasked. He was apprehensive… probably expecting I would reject him. How could I ever… when everything that's ensued over the past month has made me feel more myself, more empowered than I've ever been? Dax doesn't make me feel damaged, he stokes the fire in me that had gone out, once upon a time. I've never been more sure of myself and my decisions. Finally confident in who I am. I may have lost my ability to hear long ago; except I suspect I've been going through life blindly. I can see now. Thanks to Dax and I have no plans of closing my eyes to reality, ever again.

After soaking for a little bit, I find the edges of the flared base, covering my clenched hole. Taking in a large inhale, I draw out the toy, tensing on the widest part, I try and remind myself to relax… exhaling slowly, I'm finally able to remove the plug. Truthfully, pulling it out felt so much better than the initial invasion. It's funny how I didn't even mind it being inside me. This is the first time I've actually enjoyed having something there. Previous times just fucking hurt. I roll the toy in soapy bubbles, eventually examining it above the water. It is heavier than expected, speckles of colors that could only be sprinkles, encased within the glass object. This was obviously custom-made. I've shopped online, been to sex shops, and I've never encountered anything quite so unique. Rotating to the base of the object, I notice something unusual embedded. I've definitely seen this thing before. Not in person but like in pictures or videos online. The theme is generally to caution you about 'possible dangers.' People who could follow you, even track you down. Well, this menacing device was encased within the base of the see-through sex toy.

"What the fuck?!"

Emerging from the tub, I briskly towel off and stalk toward my bedroom to locate my phone. There's a new message from him.

> The Stalker: How are you feeling, beautiful?

Ignoring his question, I type out the reason I vacated the bath so quickly. Hitting send, before rereading. "Damnit!" Spellcheck corrected my words.

> Cindel: You ducker! You put a tracker inside me?

No one means to say ducker! They really need to update phone software to include profanity!

Dots appear, then his response follows.

> The Stalker: Technically it wasn't "in" you.

I retort,

> Cindel: Semantics.

Another text appears almost instantly.

> The Stalker: Do you like it?

Well, I did before I knew I was the equivalent to a sea turtle, being tagged and tracked off the Atlantic. I was livid and turned on? Just fucking conflicted… unsure how to reply.

My sheets are currently rolled into a messy ball. I kind of liked when they were made up, tucked neatly into the corners. It's more inviting… warmer. A smile now plays on my lips, but I remember how scared I was when I first found him stretched out in my bed. Dressed in a towel, no less. When I close my eyes, the smokey stare finds me… no trepidation under his assessment, but something closer to tenderness… he almost reminds me of Kingston. Just a big dopey dog who means well, but can't help tugging roughly on the rope when you play or drooling onto the floor when you present his meal. I replay the moments his gaze transitioned from measured to unbridled as he plunged inside me… fucking me until I saw stars. Was this tracker just another screwy way of showing me he cared? I did enjoy the sensation of fullness. Intensity paired with his ability to play my body like a fucking instrument. I'm never going to forget the things we did together in that boathouse.

My phone vibrates with another message.

> The Stalker: Seems like you need more time to think in it.

What? I think he meant, "on." Before I can respond, another message vibrates the phone in my hand.

> The Stalker: Next time you're at work… wear the plug.

He can't be serious?! I generally don't like being told what to do. Stubbornly, I retort.

> Cindel: What if I just carry it in my bag? You'll never know the difference.

Lowering the bright screen I squint, trying to see further into the dark corners of my bedroom. Wondering if he's watching me as we speak.

> The Stalker: I plan to check, Princess.

The first thing I sense in the morning is coffee wafting into my bedroom. Sleep came effortlessly last night and I don't recall a single nightmare, either.

Installing my aids, I drag my body from the comfort of my bed, with the promise of go-go juice on the horizon. Andrea faces the table askew with various papers, alongside the whiteboard on wheels.

She peers up from her task, "You look... different." She raises an eyebrow. "Did you enjoy your night?" She tries to hide a knowing grin, while sipping from a mug.

Of course, she knows I went out. Even when I think I'm being sly, nothing gets past her. I chew on the inside of my cheek, recalling all the delicious ways Dax explored my body, making me feel like I was something to be cherished.

I lick my lips, make a fist and bob my wrist up and down, signing *yes*. Over the counter, I reach for a mug as I decide when and if I should tell Andrea my stalker's true identity. She's literally hated every man I've been with since I met her. Sometimes, she manages to be more overbearing than my own mother. Two of the past guys I've been dated, have dropped off the map completely. What if she doesn't like Dax too? A man who lured me in with mind games, broke into our apartment, and has kept his identity hidden up until yesterday. Yeah... I don't exactly expect Andrea to roll out the welcome mat for him either.

When I pull down the last clean mug off the shelf the lettering reads, *Serenity Now!* Damn it all to hell... fine. The universe has spoken. I spin around, ready to tell her when I notice the board has something new added. Various letters are now circled within the *Stalker's Playlist*.

"What's that?" I walk over and point at one of the circled letters.

"A code," she declares.

I give her an incredulous look. "A code? Did you figure this out?" I inquire.

She stands to join me next to the whiteboard. "Not really. Your stalker boy texted me a string of numbers. Then this message. She points to the words *"The End is the Beginning."*

I examine each circled letter, following how she counted over from left to right, through the artist and song title. The chosen letter matches the number of spaces, based on the random string of numbers she wrote down. Dax sent this...?

"Your boy likes games."

I take notice of where she erased the transposed message, then reordered the letters backward.

"The end is the beginning," I whisper to myself. "What do you think *Uncle Nicholas Lie* means?"

Her shoulders raise and drop. "Beats me. I just wish that stalker of yours sent that to me instead of having me decode dumb riddles all night."

I sit down at the table, this time with brain fuel, overlooking everything we've jammed within a small area. What does my uncle have to do with any of this? My uncle has been there for me over the past few years, more than anyone else. What would he lie about? New pieces with vague connections, now some far-fetched message about my uncle?

Feeling particularly brazen, I casually note, "Dax seems to have a rhyme and a reason for everything he does. Maybe he has to be careful. I've learned recently it's very easy to be watched without your knowledge."

Her painted finger taps on her chin. "I don't think that's a good excuse to make me jump through hoops when he could have simply…wait!"

I nonchalantly sip from the mug as her almond eyes widen.

"Did… did you just say Dax?!"

I lower the drink to the table, all the while pressing my lips firmly together, in an attempt to fight the grin that pulls at my mouth.

Her beautiful features contort… caught in a whirlwind of confusion, then realization, followed up with surprise.

"Holy Shit," she proclaims. "I did not have Cindel getting more action than me on my bingo card." Her head shakes, in advance of using a hair tie to pull back her short silvery bob. "Eamon's Henchman… how did I miss that?!" Andrea appears absolutely drained, clearly fed up with not being any further ahead than where we were previously.

"Don't beat yourself up, Nancy Drew, it's not like you're my security detail or anything."

Her face screws up for a brief second, before it slips away just as quickly. "Well even if I were, clearly you don't need me when you have someone watching you twenty-four seven!" She waves into the empty room. "Hi, Dax, glad I finally have a face to the man fucking my best friend!"

My mouth drops over her blatant truth bomb.

"What?! Like I didn't realize what you were doing after you were returning home looking well satisfied and actually happy?!"

Seriously, I bet she figured out where Carmen Sandiego was as a child!

Andrea now sits across from me at the modest table in our kitchen. She reaches across the surface and takes my hand in hers. "We'll figure out all the rest of the stuff… I promise. Until then, you still need to be careful."

She's not wrong. Mairead is manic, while Eamon mentioned something about people wanting to hurt me! Clearly, I need to be more selective about who I surround myself with. Why is it that every time I see red flags, I think to myself, *oooo… it looks like fun over there*! I can't just go along with everything. Dragging my only friend into this was a poor decision. What if she gets hurt?

I rub at my temples.

First, my ex-manager tries to blackmail me into some kind of sexual favor. Barf. Then, my free-spirited co-worker confronts me in an escape room, convinced my family and I are a bunch of murders?! Nothing connects. Initially, I thought it could have been Mairead who killed Creepy Craig, but now... I know better. It was Dax, without a doubt. I've witnessed firsthand what he's capable of. Plus, the earbud down his throat? I mean... who else could it be? The memory of a blue contorted body in a trunk, flashes through my mind. There has been countless hazards lately, but I don't fear him. He's protective and has been watching over me for a while, although I wonder if it's been longer than I realize... in some cases, I think he knows me better than I know myself.

It's hard to believe that a little over a month ago, I was still working through Brodi's disappearance. I actually convinced myself he'd come back to me. Now I find the notion hilarious. What a fool I was to think he loved me. I can see clearly now, that I was no more than a commodity, my thoughts never considered.

Dax communicates with me better than Brodi ever did and he can't even fucking talk. If Brodi showed up today, I have choice words for him. Andrea never liked him. Always said, "he didn't deserve me." With my stalker, Dax I mean... he gives me his undivided attention, it makes me realize my roommate was right.

I straighten in my seat, gently squeezing my friend's hand back. "You're right." I meant this on so many levels, but I keep it simple. "We will figure this all out," I reaffirm.

Over the next few hours, we go over everything that has happened as of late, making sure we don't miss any details that should be added to the board.

My brother died three years ago... soooooo much time has passed. How were we supposed to find clues for a case that law enforcement declared as suicide?

Out of nowhere, I remember the cop who I have encountered twice in the past month. His name is something with a K. Kyle... no. Kevin, that's not it... Kent! What's so odd is, it's not the first time I've heard that name. Like I should know the name from somewhere, but I'm not sure from where. Maybe I've seen it written down before? I wasn't sure, but mentioning the strange exchange I saw between him and my uncle seems noteworthy.

"Remember the police officer who showed up to question me?"

She dips her head, causing the silver bun on her head wobble.

"Well.. two days ago, I saw him again. His name is, *Kent*. He was in the booth with my uncle at Benny's, right before we were supposed to meet for breakfast. I saw them but they didn't see me. Then, Kent left in a hurry, looking very displeased."

Andrea's nose scrunches up and for once… I've rendered her speechless.

"That wasn't even the weirdest part… my uncle seemed irritated when I told him I was positive that Theo DID NOT kill himself. He all but growled at the waitress when she tried to take our order. We didn't even eat! He just told me I was silly and should have left with my parents when I had the chance. Then he left, just like that."

Andrea's cheeks puff out, leading up to a long-drawn-out exhale. Leaving no stone unturned and accounting for Dax's cryptic message, we add the word *Uncle.* Right underneath the other names which don't appear to relate to anything.

My stomach twists, seeing his name up there, next to *Officer Fucking Kent* and *Creepy Craig.* It might as well be a puzzle piece that's been soaking in water and is now expected to fit within this monochromatic puzzle. Somehow, this is all a part of a bigger picture… I just can't seem to figure out where anything goes.

Reviewing the board for the hundred-millionth time, I notice something I hadn't realized before. Something within the word *"Lombardi"* written in loopy, cursive lettering along the top. Standing before the whiteboard, I uncap a marker. As if I'm before one of those 'depth perception pictures,' the longer I stare at it, the letters become almost 3D. Popping out to me. Showing me the hidden message.

I begin to circle letters within the name, *"Lombardi."* M-A-R-I are now circled in purple. My hand shakes, causing the marker to fall from my grasp as I take a staggering step back. "Holy shiitake!" My last name is right there! Burrowed within the confines of the name Lombardi!

I don't even realize Andrea is next to me. One minute she's at the table and the next, she's in front of me. She bends down and picks up the marker I dropped on the floor. She has a rueful look about her, the corner of her eyes wrinkle, while a vague frown flattens her lips.

"Come… sit down, Cindel." Her words are soft but firm.

This isn't the moment to object but to brace for something unexpectant. The ringing in my ears is already at a solid five; as I'm guided to the couch, the volume escalates to an ear-splitting pitch.

My roommate doesn't sit, instead she remains before me, pacing the length of the room. It's like watching a tennis match with one player and no ball. "There's something you should know."

Here's where she would normally pause and allow me to respond, but she doesn't, instead she rolls right into the topic as if it's too heavy to hold back any longer. She rambles, her gait has me agitated already.

For starters, she affirms how my family is all she has. Her sloppy hands move about expressively, all without making actual words but expressing overwhelming emotion. This makes following along increasingly difficult.

Next, her babblings become profound lectures… touching on 'tough decisions' and 'hard truths' in life, all of her statements are vague and unclear. Honestly, it's come to the point that I'm unable to figure out what the Sam hell she's going on about.

"Andrea," I try to interrupt, but she persists with her info dumping. I strain to listen and even still I can only process every other word she says.

Wait… did she say… Mafia?

"Andrea," I say again, but it's like I'm not even here, as she tries to race through all the things she has to relay. Even though I'm actively trying to listen, watching her mouth, while using context clues… fragmented words tumble out like… hiding, safe, and… bomb.

My temples are throbbing and I'm beyond overwhelmed. I've had enough! Stepping up onto the coffee table, I scream, "Andrea!"

Her mouth remains open, but the words have finally ceased. Horizontal lines appear across her forehead and it's almost as if she just realized that I am present too. Tears well on the bottom of her lids.

I lower myself from the table. "I don't understand. Please slow down and look at me when you speak, for crying out loud!"

She blinks as twin tears roll down each of her cheeks. Shit. I can likely count on one hand how many times I've seen Andrea cry. I want nothing more than to console her and tell her it will be okay, but that's not what's happening here. This egregious display is because she has something big to share. I just don't know what that is…

Using the corner of her shirt sleeve, Andrea dabs the wetness from her face. Her head tips back as she looks up to the ceiling, before proceeding to shake out her arms as if warming up for something that could prove exerting. Schooling her features, her next words were utterly impassive.

"Cindel… you are a Lombardi. You're effectively a Mafia princess."

Icy pin pricks blanket my face, and the room suddenly begins to sway back and forth. Not wanting to hit the floor, I lower myself back onto the sofa until the world stops spinning.

She continues, "everything changed after the hit against your family."

I feel like I am aboard a boat, bobbing and swaying in an unforgivable sea of uncertainties. After extensive moments of practiced inhales matched with slow exhales, I ask the most obvious question. "What hit?"

She crouches before me, meeting me at eye level before speaking to ensure I hear her response. "Remember the…" Her lips draw to the side, and I know precisely what triggering words she's trying to avoid. "Remember the day you lost your hearing?"

My eyes blink rapidly. There's no need to answer the rhetorical question.

How could I ever forget? The infernal ringing in my ears, hearing aids, and recurring nightmares act as a constant reminder of the event. Ironic how the deafening sound, in the aftermath, is the only thing I can hear without my aids.

"It wasn't an accident," I state matter-of-factly.

"There was never a gas leak," she adds to my realization, while placing a soothing hand on my knee. "Someone… maybe a rivaling gang… tried to cut off the Lombardi bloodline."

The swaying feeling fades, only for the air to be ripped from my lungs.

"Your brother wasn't in the room with you like the assailant had hoped."

I glance down at my hands. The raw sensation has reached my pale fingertips. I'm sure my face appears just as ghostly, all the blood in my body rushing to my heart to keep it beating, in response to the shock.

What I need right now, more than anything, is sugar. Perhaps a candy cane… the fruity kind, not the festive peppermint shit. I crave sugar when I am stressed. Hell… maybe I could craft the treat into a shiv! Ready and willing to stab whomever harmed me, went after my family, and possibly killed my brother!

Looking up to Andrea's assessing stare, I figure out how one crooked piece fits into this confounded puzzle. "How?" A small curious flame ignites within my icy form. Before she's able to speak, I cut her off. "Not how did it happen, but how do YOU know all of this?!"

Her tender touch on my leg becomes stiff, as if she's taken aback by the question. Removing her hand from me, she sits back onto the table and begins to rub at her opposite arm.

"Your parents are like family to me." This I already know. Andrea's upbringing was unstable. She was moved around in the system, spending most of her teen years on the streets. She may have a tough exterior, but she's forged a precious relationship with my mom and dad. Sometimes I think she's closer to them than I am. "They never wanted this for you."

As if the *Distress Express* wasn't clear enough when it mowed me over with the news that I am a Lombardi, the thing backs up. At which point, I realize that makes my parents Lombardis too. The notorious Mafia family I read about, with a questionable presence in these parts. Oh. My. God… my parents! Dad? No? No… no! My cinnamon roll making father with his terrible dad jokes and notable gardening habits is… a Mafia boss? One time, my dad rushed his dog Kingston to the vet after he stepped on a pile of thorn bush clippings. He sounded like he was ready to cry when he told me the story over the phone that very night. That's who the Don of Boston is? Well… was the Don, apparently. I've watched enough Sopranos to understand how the hierarchy works. Maybe that's why I've always found it to be more of a comfort show…? I'm spiraling again. Right now, wasn't the time to analyze myself. I need to move forward with this information.

Fuuuck! What about my mother?! The woman who prioritized work or fluffing throw pillows over attending her own daughter's art show. Appearance was everything and I never seemed to do anything right in her eyes. Theo was the favorite. Even when my GPA was higher and I never got in trouble at school, my mother still only recognized his accomplishments. Maybe it was a form of reverse psychology because he really did turn his grades around near the end of high school. Mom was especially proud when he graduated from Boston College with a degree in journalism. When I admitted I wanted to go to school for fashion design, I felt like an utter disappointment. It's funny… I can actually see her rigid routines, mannerisms, and drive being excellent characteristics for a mob wife. She's just overbearing enough to pull it off… but my dad? I just can't picture it.

Andrea extracts me from my wandering thoughts. "After the incident, business was conducted, "differently." Your family went into hiding, without actually leaving the city. Shortening your last name and continuously moving your home every couple years to stay safe."

I just thought my parents hated being stagnant and the nonstop moving was such a pain. My life might as well compare to a daytime Spanish soap opera. No less intelligible and cleverly dramatized. Comic relief aside… my folks up and left , relinquishing everything right after my brother's death. Apparently, they've always been running from their past, while doing a shit job of including us. Without my permission, hot tears descend onto my chilled face. What stings the most are the lies. Humorously, I can hear my mother's voice in my head, telling me how *omitting* something isn't a lie but deception.

When I was around twelve years old, she caught me in the bathroom applying one of her deep ruby lipsticks. *"I found it!"* I embellished. Which was true, but I left out the part about me purposely going through her vanity to procure it. *"If you become good enough at deception, you'll start fooling yourself,"* my mother told me. I never understood what she meant until I grew older. Whether you label it a deception or a lie, the results are always the same. Trust issues and a lifetime of "what ifs" because you're too scared to take chances.

Using the front of my nightshirt as a makeshift handkerchief, I wipe at my streaked face. "That means my uncle is a Lombardi as well."

Andrea tentatively nods, because I think she knew I needed the confirmation. Why would my uncle lie? Does Dax know what I'm supposed to find? Why won't he just tell me! Everyone seems to know more about my family and past than I do. So why am I tasked with collecting the data and writing a thesis? I'm no investigator… I went to college for fashion design for crying out loud!

Thinking back to a time when things were straightforward, my brother was alive, and the house was filled with laughter… I don't recall my uncle coming around much when I was a kid. I've seen more of him in the past couple of years than I ever did back then. He was the only family I had left. My parents pleaded with me to move out of the city, but I refused. My life was here. My apartment, my best friend, and… Theo. Theo's memories are still here. I wasn't going anywhere. I perceived my uncle as a very busy man, but I still had hope that when the holidays came around, he'd show up. Occasionally, I even put out an extra place setting just for him at the table. All the same, he never showed, at least not when I wanted him to. Only coming around during odd times actually. Like bird watching with the goal of witnessing a bald eagle land in front of you. It's never going to happen, but if you did see one, it wouldn't be on your terms. Notably, he was there after I woke up in the hospital.

My father never spoke ill of his brother, in fact, he would retell tame versions of the no good they would get into, back in their day. One time, I remember them arguing… it was late at night. They were downstairs and I was supposed to be in bed. It wasn't too long after my accident, but I was able to put my own hearing aids in after a lot of practice. I crept down the stairs and stood quietly just outside the parlor door. I even held my breath so I could listen better.

Uncle Nicholas was yelling about something not being fair. I just chalked it up to being something about grown-up stuff; real estate, money, or work. Now I know it probably had something to do with the family business, the Mafia to be exact. Moses on a motorboat, my daddy is a full-fledged Tony Soprano!

Andrea carries over my cold mug of inspiration and sets it down before me. She must have noticed me staring blankly at the wall for quite some time, while drowning in my own thoughts. I sip from its disappointing contents, ahead of setting down the drink and rubbing at my temples.

"Okay!" I finally proclaim.

Andrea puts a hand to her chest in response to my sudden outburst.

"Sorry…" I force a smile, understanding that she too must be on edge. "But why would my uncle be lying?"

She sits next to me, with her third cup of jet fuel since I emerged this morning. How is she not jittery as hell? "That's what I've been trying to figure out," she reveals. Continuing with the theme of deception, I see.

Apparently, we're both veering around the question… about *how she knows so much*. I lean back playing along, while remaining transfixed on the whiteboard. Andrea replicating my motions. I so wish Theo was here. He loved this shit. Figuring out things way before it should be humanly possible. Playing the game Clue with him was the worst!

I stand to study the board closer. The names we have displayed and how all the lines in the middle connect. The papers off to the side with *"My start date at the Black Sheep"* correlating to *"Brodi's disappearance"* on one and *"Officer Kent," "Creepy Craig,"* and my *"uncle"* on the other.

My father was adopted. I have fond memories of my Nonno and Nonna before they moved back to Italy. They were so giving… always trying to feed us. From what I understand, they wanted a big family. My father joined the family as a baby; however, no more siblings ever came along. It was just he and his brother.

This still doesn't explain the message on the board, *Uncle Nicholas Lie.* Is he lying to himself? The family?

"I looked into the *Lombardi* name recently. The articles speculate that the Mafia must have worked with another crime family, seeing how similar criminal activity was happening, simultaneously throughout the city. Maybe there was a falling out or the rivaling gang wanted more power?!"

Andrea sips from her mug for an exceptionally long period of time, as I follow her eyes hopping from either side of the room.

My gaze narrows… I know that look. "Just say it!" I implore.

She tilts her head back, draining every drop of liquid from her cup, before attempting to speak. "I know who the 'other' gang is."

I can't help but spin away from her, my hands naturally tossing themselves skyward. "Damnit, Andrea… we're trying to figure out what this all means in regards to Theo. Can you stop withholding every other thing from me?!"

She shows me her bottom teeth with a stupid grin. Then continues, "remember how I told you to stay away from Eamon?"

I raise an eyebrow. "And…?"

Andrea gestures with a suggestive tilt of her chin toward the board.

My eyes scan the writing on the wall. "The Murray family?!" I exclaim.

Her face winces all the while her waving hands raise to the air, twisting at the wrists, as she signs *applause.*

I groan, hand dragging down my face, as if it could wipe away my exhaustion. A padded room is looking more like a vacation by the day. In my wildest dreams, I never could have made this shit up. Not only do I reign from a Mafia family, but I'm also employed by a group of criminals, who just so happened to have worked with the Lombardis in the past. Uncapping a cobalt-blue marker, I write *"Murray Family"* between Eamon and Mairead's name.

I recap the marker, turning to face my roommate but she's disappeared into her room, probably trying to avoid the impending question. *How do you know so much*? Not long after she shut herself in, she emerges once again. Andrea holds a strappy briefcase in one hand; while dressed in an all-black pantsuit, obviously heading off to work.

"I have to go," she informs me plainly.

As if it was a regular day, as if she didn't just turn my world upside down moments prior. I'm beyond repair. Shattered to pieces by the sheer weight of the reality that has been thrust upon me. Now she just wants to mosey off to work?! I can't just grin and bear, I need answers.

"We're going to revisit this whole subject on how you know so much about all of this." Unable to face my supposed best friend, I survey the white board. For what? I have no idea.

Andrea ignores my declaration. "I plan to install the security system tonight. Please, don't let anyone in and I strongly suggest you don't bother going to work."

That's rich! She gets to run off but I don't? I chew on my lip... still focused on the board, "Whatever you say." Without even looking in her direction, I'm able to hear the exaggerated exhale, followed by the sound of the door slamming and the dead bolt turning.

She can't possibly believe I will stay put. If she gets to come and go as she pleases, while keeping secrets from me, then I will find my own answers. Which means... I will be going to work today, instead of sitting on my hands and doing nothing. I've gotten this far haven't I?

Even as I shower without my hearing aids, it's still never fully silent. My ears ring with bells I don't wish to hear. Over the years, I've tried to drown out the sound by listening to music, practicing therapeutic techniques, or even praying for that thing my ears do when they go offline... only then am I rewarded with a few blissful moments of quiet.

It's funny how others perceive being hard of hearing means your world is tranquil. Nothing could be further from the truth... at least for me. There's no optional mute button. Facing the shower head, I fill my mouth with water and spit it out. I used to do this as a kid. Back when I had little to worry about other than what I should draw next... holding the water briefly, until it trickles from the corners of my mouth as a smile forms. A pained chuckle rattles through me under the warm rain. How the hell did I get here? Never in my life had I expected to come across the real-life Mafia, let alone be the child of a mob boss. If Eamon and his family are or were accomplices to the Lombardis, clearly Dax must know about everything. Without fault, he's always come to my rescue. He... the nickname rushes back to me. He calls me Princess. Of course, he knew who I was, but... who is he? Other than a part of the Murray gang. How does Dax fit into all of this? Good vs. bad... there's no black and white here, but a spectrum of gray where these men lie.

Eamon has been helpful, but the Murray family has been painted almost enemies to the Lombardis. Are Dax's intentions with me pure? I can't help but question motives, when there are still so many unknowns. Pushing ahead I need to be careful, not only with my life, but my heart as well. My once delirious laugh has morphed into practiced breaths through tiny streams of water. Attempting to work past the deep wounds, all the lies have cut into me. I haven't been able to rely on my ability to hear for a long time, instead I need to put my trust in what I see.

I watch as the sudsy water swirls counterclockwise down the drain between my feet. Like an omen that everything I once held onto, will likely be swept away and lost forever. I have to believe Andrea is on my side, but it's also very convenient how she only reveals what I first stumble upon myself. Deception is lying and it hurts even more when someone you thought you knew is the creator of your mistrust.

With the edge of my towel, I make a portal within the condensation of the bathroom mirror. My reflection is a canvas of both my parents. High cheek bones from my father, clear eyes courtesy of my mother, and a stubborn cowlick which seems to have only graced my brother and I. While I'm stuck with school-age bangs for the foreseeable future, Theo had an effortless shaggy hairstyle which looked great even when he just woke up.

My chest pulls like taffy, thinking about him in any context. He's still here with me, just not physically... This city is an echo of him, and I won't leave nor rest until I find answers. There's no length I wouldn't go, because I know he would have done the same for me.

Against Andrea's wishes, I'm going to work... not only do I need the money, but I also need to talk to Eamon. I'm confident he knows more about my brother than he's already revealed. I just hope he's actually there, so I can speak to him. He may have been closer to Theo in his last years but, that's my fault... I should have called more... arranged more lunches. Outside of my guilty conscience, Eamon and I both recognize the fact that Theo would never take his own life. Especially with drugs... he never touched the stuff! At least, I think he hadn't.

I shake the heavy notion from my mind, focusing on the present while I dry and style my hair. Back in my room, my attention falls upon the sprinkle filled plug, taunting me from the dresser. Heat floods my cheeks when I think about where it was, who put it there, and all that happened just last night at the boathouse. Dax expects me to wear the plug while I work. I'm torn. While the idea excites me, making me feel insanely aroused... I also worry I'll be uncomfortable serving strangers with a sex toy buried just inside. I check the messages on my phone while securing my aids on each ear. I missed quite a few while I was away.

The Stalker: You've made progress. I've been watching… you need to find some kind of proof. I believe your brother left something for you to find. Now, be a good girl and put your present in that pretty ass of yours.

Jesus! My lips feel dry and chapped, tongue jutting out to rehydrate them following Dax's dirty text. I feel compelled to change his current contact. I suck my bottom lip into my mouth, recalling how he's prompted me into a rollercoaster of emotions. Causing everything from fear, to pain, and then pleasure. Given the option, I still want to stay on.

Somehow without my knowledge, he managed to give me my power back. I asked to keep him, because as much as he's pursued me… I get the impression that I've longed for him, just as long. Although, now I have a name for who I yearned for. Editing the Contact, I change the text from *The Stalker* to *Dax the Friendly Stalker.* Eat your heart out, Kat Harvey, the ghost boy's mine! I smile inward, rereading through his words one more time before moving onto the other missed texts. I was surprised to find one from Eamon.

Eamon: Don't worry about coming in today, I found coverage. We'll talk later.

Umm, how about no! Nothing will stop me from going into work today. I have bills to pay and he has some explaining to do. Last we spoke, I left with too much unsaid. The date at his posh apartment was the last time we were alone together. The more I learn about him, the more clarity I gain. Of course, my boss is a crime lord… how else could he stay afloat with a hole in the wall bar, a boxing club, and still manage to afford a life like that?! He must think I'm pretty helpless if one text could keep me away. Well, I'm nothing if not persistent. I plan to live my life as I see fit. Not bothering to offer either man a response, I plan to unapologetically show up for my shift and learn what I can.

I have one more missed text. It's from… Mairead? Sitting on the edge of my bed, I think back to the escape room. How worked up she was. Arming my lungs with air, I open the message.

Mairead: I figured it out… who set the explosions off around the city! It was Mr. Callaway's sister!!! I'm super bummed that you and your pretty friend left before we found the answer. No worries, though! We'll get to play together again soon.

There is so much to unpack within this message. Even more of a reason to see Eamon. Especially since his sister seems to think I killed their mother. I mean, what the fuck?! I click the contact and select "block." She's certifiable! I've never killed anyone! How is the reserved, level-headed Eamon related to 'Strawberry Nutcase?!' A sense of dread sinks like a weight to the bottom of my stomach, when I call back her words at the Escape Goat. *"Daddy and I agree… you're the reason mother is dead!"* I had never seen her like that before. Pupils blown out, like an animal that had just cornered its prey. I've met their father before too. He accompanied Mairead when she visited my booth at the Craft Bazaar. There was a faint Irish accent when he introduced himself. Patrick I think? Why would they think I'm responsible for Mary's death? Each new pebble of awareness builds upon an avalanche of curiosity. One thing I can interpret… without a shadow of a doubt, I need to stay the hell away from the father-daughter duo.

Lombardi

**Starts work at
The Black Sheep**

AFTER
Brodi Disappears?

Eamon

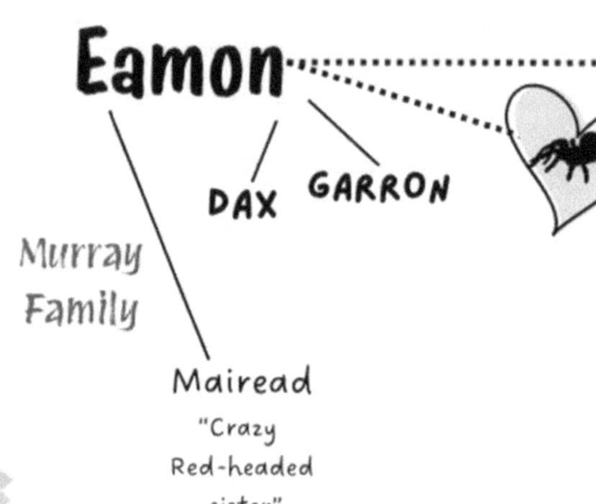

DAX **GARRON**

Murray
Family

Mairead
"Crazy
Red-headed
sister"

The End is the
12-11-7-7-7-5-4-3-2

OFFICER
FUCKING KENT

Creepy Craig

Uncle

Less than a
month ago:
"Found"
Earbud

Stalker

Theo

Three
Years
Ago

inning

7-2-7-10-4-5

Uncle Nicholas Lie?

Stalker's Playlist

Pixies- Where is my mind?
Semisonic- Closing time
Stone Temple Pilots- Vasoline
Beck- Loser
Sam the Sham & the Pharaohs- Lil' red riding hood
Marcy Playground- Sex & candy
The Human League- Don't you want me
The Flys- Got you
OMC- How Bizarre
Radiohead- Creep
Edwyn Collins- A girl like you
Radiohead- Karma police
Kinks- All day and all of the night
Spin Doctors- Two princes
Elastica- Connection
Toadies- Possum Kingdom

THIRTY-SEVEN

CINDEL

Maybe I should respond to the messages…? No. That would be unwise. Fuck, I don't know! I need… I need time to think! For now, I'll compartmentalize and do what I do best… style my figure to conceal the ruinous feelings within me! It's my ultimate superpower.

Today, I feel cheeky. I select a cabled knit sweater, pull atop a white-collared button-up shirt, tweed breeches, high socks, and a pair of brown saddle oxfords. It is a smart outfit and thrifted too! I resemble a woman who went against the norms in the forties. Answering to no one while never taking no for an answer. A gray beret crowns my head, forcing my fringed bangs to lay flat. Fashion is sometimes intentional, and I was tickled pink; due to the fact I had multiple defensive layers.

In spite of Dax's instructions to "plug up" before leaving, I was more determined to rebel. If he did decide to check, he'll have a hell of a time getting through all of this. I hope he doesn't have a brat kink.

Three hours till my shift starts and I am going to make good use of the time I have. After avoiding the inevitable, I carry a collection of disorganized boxes from our childhood, out and into the living room. Making piles to remain organized, I section our lives into personal, family, school, and miscellaneous.

My childhood mementos were significantly lacking compared to Theo's, but somewhat less chaotic. I reminisce over old report cards, doodles of the 90's universal "s" on notebooks, and become teary eyed from tiny inked, baby feet on Theo's birth certificate. That one gets put to the side because I realized my mother should have it.

Time flies by and I feel an unsettling sense of dread as I work through the last box. Despite the giant piles of papers and photos around me, nothing thus far has stood out. How was any of this stuff significant in my search for answers?

"What did you leave for me?!" I say, into the empty room. Leaning against the couch, I rub at the back of my neck before shifting forward, peering back into the almost empty box. Pulling out a drawing of a wolf, I put it in Theo's pile before noticing a tinge-yellow photo just beneath. The edges of the photograph are worn. It's a group of people.

At first glance I don't recognize anyone. Four small children shoved between what looks to be family or friends, before a table of food. One of the toddlers looks familiar. I reach for the "family" pile, searching for a much younger picture of myself. Got it! Comparing the two photos together, that's definitely me. I haven't really seen any photos of my parents when they were younger, so I can only assume the woman holding me is my mother and the man next to her, my father. That means that one of these boys has to be Theo. He's five years older than me. Who are these other people?

Beside our parents, is another man. Gradually, I recognize the younger version of my uncle. Thinner, same sharp features, and steely gaze. It's hard to believe this is the same man that I sit across from each month at Benny's. It's only a picture, but he looks irritated? I suspect this because I witnessed the same look on his face when I last saw him. When I wouldn't simply accept the past for what it was.

The other woman in the photograph has red wavy hair. She's holding a baby and there's another little boy by her side… but I don't recognize them. Actually, I don't recall my parents even having friends. Especially ones that came over to the house. The man beside the mystery woman looks so familiar. Holding out the photo, as far as my arm can reach, I gradually bring the image closer to me. Between Andrea's sparse insight and what I've learned about the Lombardis… "they worked with others in the past," I remember.

Holding the photograph mere inches from my nose, I rapidly realize who the family is… "Oh my god, that's the Murray family!" Mr. Patrick Murray, a younger and significantly fitter man. With his wife… Mary.

From what I understand, Mrs. Murray was murdered. That must mean that the baby is Mairead. I can see the resemblance between her and her mother. Soft features, button nose, and wily hair that's just starting to grow. So, that must mean the other boy, beside my brother, is Eamon. They've known each other since they were kids!

Well, technically we've all known each other for a lifetime, but why do I have no memory of them at all? What happened to cause such a fall out between our two families? Everyone looks so happy. Well, most of them do. My uncle has a sort of scowl, while Mary appears almost distant. Like the smile is hard to keep on. Perhaps I'm overthinking it, however I've always been particularly good at reading people.

This photo is important. I fold the curious picture and slide it into the front pocket of my breeches. I don't believe this is what Theo left for me to find, but I planned to show Eamon when I saw him. Reaching back into the box, I find a story Theo wrote in high school with a B+ across the top and then... that's it. The bottom of the container. It's empty.

I turn to find no new bins left to sort through. I'm out of boxes, there's nothing left. I've gone through everything I had and I didn't find a single thing.

"Argh!" I slam my fists into the couch. Glancing at the piles around me, a sense of shame crawls through me. How easily a life could be divided by categories... that my brother can be equated to nothing more than a few bins and insufficient mementos. Anger is easy. Of course, I'm teed off that my parents didn't save more of Theo's stuff, but moreover I'm disheartened. It's as if I'm losing him all over again. Worse than that, I haven't found anything he may have left for me. What if I'm letting him down?

Flopping back onto the couch, I notice how the shadows have grown longer. The sun is lower in the sky, and I need to leave soon for The Black Sheep. My weary eyes survey the room, skating past the board, then over to the bookshelf where my gaze catches.

Something's different... the glow of red light is absent. "Shit." I pop up and race over to the other side of the room. "Dammit. Did we lose power?" I've been so busy searching for answers, in addition to handling multiple personalities that I've forgotten all about Thelma! My sense of time is all out of whack, I don't think I've checked on her in a few days... or has it been a week?

"Shit. Shit. Shit." The surge protector appears to be working. Perhaps the terrarium light burnt out? How have I not noticed?! Opening the lid to the darkened tank, I begin searching each corner, even within the plants for any sign of the little arachnid. I'm a terrible pet owner, why did I ever agree to take her? I can't even keep a cactus alive! Thank fuck I can't have kids.

At last, I lift the skull-shaped hide, which I know has been her favorite spot as of late and there she is. On the substrate, just beneath her choice spot, her pint-sized, furry body. Unmoving. The tarantula's little legs curled inward.

"No... fuck! Noooooo... why?!" Slamming down the faux skull onto the coffee table, it shatters to pieces on impact. My chest aches as the last connecting thread to my brother has severed. I killed Thelma. This is all my fault. I consider the splintered pieces of resin around the living room, convinced that my heart is no better off. All at once, my mind jumps to Eamon. He might be more devastated than me. No longer is there a Thelma to his Louise.

My brother bought his Chilean rose tarantula, as soon as he moved out of our parent's home. Any pets that could hide within a shoe, were not allowed to reside within my mother's home. I remember him being so excited to finally have his dream pet, that he sent me photos and videos of Thelma for a week straight!

Eamon seemed to be much better at caring for his tarantula. Why didn't I just offer for him to take Thelma too. Then maybe she would still be alive. I dreaded the thought of having to tell Eamon that his partner spider has passed. Might as well grab the salt to rub in my already opened wound. I'm a horrible sister.

Descending to the floor, I can't help but lower my head into my hands. The space seems even darker without the ambient glow…

Journals from my teen years would read, *I deserve this. My world is a dark room and I'm bound to reside within.* The younger me felt shameful for how I thought and what I liked. Retreating within myself, journaling helped little. It shoved me into a tiny digestible box. Lately, I've shifted my way of thinking, realizing that I seek out approval, apologize too often, and hold onto guilt like it owes me money. I have no control over these things. Being confident in my choices is hard… but I like me. Yes, it absolutely blows chode that the little tarantula is gone, but I didn't do it intentionally or with malice.

Emerging from my hands, I push up from the floor and make for the kitchen to retrieve the hand broom and pan. I need to stop moping, clean this mess up, and get to work. Gathering most of the pieces in the tray, I walk back to the kitchen to dump the contents into the trash bin, when I notice something unusual within the fragments. This object, unlike the others, has letters and numbers. It's flat, black, and rectangular, whereas the rest of the pieces are jagged and mostly off-white. Picking out the unique item, I flip on the light above to examine the piece that doesn't quite fit the rest of the wreckage. The corner is angled, while on the opposite side of the lettering has gold lines. Rotating the item in my hand the tiny font reads, *SanDisk.* It's a microSD card. What's this doing in Thelma's enclosure?

The microwave clock reads, ten to six. I need to hurry or I was going to be late for my shift. If I was going to insist on staying to work, I better at least arrive on time. Pushing the tiny SD card into my other front pocket, I dump the debris, grab my purse and phone, then head out the door for the bar. Just as I'm about to lock the door, I remember the message or should I call it, the advanced warning. "Shit." Sprinting back to my room, I quickly locate the sprinkle filled glass-plug and toss it into my purse prior to locking up.

By the time I finally arrive at The Black Sheep, I am out of breath but on time. I really should start doing cardio; my side aches with a stitch, and not the calming kind you fix with a needle and thread. I definitely need the largest glass of water we have.

Already the regulars at The Black Sheep line the bar, enjoying their habitual after work drinks. Brittany is behind the counter and Jada is working the floor. Jada?! When did she come back? I thought her boot wasn't coming off for at least another two weeks?!

Just as I had hoped, Eamon was here. He sits off to the side of the bar with his laptop, probably answering work emails or whatever gang bosses do. When he spots me, one of his eyebrow's arch, causing creases to form along his forehead. As I cross the room, his troubled gaze trails me the whole way. Right as I pour myself a drink Jada saunters up, as if to intercept me before I'm even able to speak with Eamon. Casually as a feline stretching when it first wakes, she leans on the opposite side of the counter.

"Cute outfit." Jada is not usually one to give compliments and I'm absolutely not in the mood for her games. Everything would be so much more straightforward if she could just be civil with me, however, I think those days are in the rearview. What changed? When did I become public enemy #1? My eyes stay trained on her, as I drain the giant glass of water, waiting for some kind of follow up insult.

"Are you like, a paperboy or something?"

There it is… Good old Jada. If anything has been consistent lately, it's her ability to be a bitch whenever she engages with me. It makes me wonder if I've tolerated her acting this way toward me all along or has my threshold for bullshit been maxed out?

Once my water is gone, I ease the glass down to the bar. I allow her time to become bored over my lack of response, anticipating she'll walk away. Nope… she's still poised across the bar, playing defense.

"You're back," I finally admit with a heavy sigh. "Isn't it too soon? I wouldn't want to see you injure yourself… again."

Her eyes narrow in response to my terse comment. Jada's lips jut out in a pout. In the next moment, her eyes become slivers, just before she runs her tongue along the top of her teeth. "Made a miraculous recovery! Doc said he's never seen anything like it." The subtle smirk and patronizing tone is already grating my nerves. "Came back just as soon as I heard MY Eamon needed help. It's a shame how the help around here isn't as reliable as we all hoped for."

I regard Eamon who is now suddenly on his phone. Briefly his eyes catch mine, as if he knows what this is and he isn't about to get dragged into it. Between the ambient music and Eamon being farther down toward the end of the bar, I'm confident he can't hear what's being said between Jada and I.

"Anyways," she continues, while tracing the grooves in the top of the counter, "I'm here. So, you can go back to delivering papers or whatever," she quips. All the while positioning herself so her breasts rest upon the wooden surface, allowing her ample chest to be even more on display thanks to her low-cut yellow top. Her eyes drift to Eamon then back to me. She's trying to make me jealous. Funny.

"Yeah… how about, no. I will be staying tonight." Without much forethought, I'm now leaning unwittingly against the high top, bringing my face no less than a foot from hers.

We stare at each other for long moments before she speaks again. "Suit yourself," she announces, pulling back from the counter and stretching up to the ceiling. Her mere presence irks me, but when she continuously looks to Eamon in an attempt to get his attention, it causes me to envision her shoved into a trunk.

"Do watch YOUR step today," I blurt. Wow… I actually just said that. Not only am I impressed by even opening my mouth, but I delivered it without my voice shaking. Honestly, I've had this strange feeling since I started here. That Jada has never meant well toward me. Whether I took the manager position or not, this hostility was bound to happen.

Jada seethes, "don't you worry your breeches boss… I will take great care of everything when your absence arrives." She looks over her shoulder toward Eamon, who seems adamant about taking his call in the furthest corner from the bar.

Bitch. Plus, he's sooooo far out of your league, Jada. Turning on her heel, she stomps off toward a table of rowdy guys who just came in. Clearly her injury wasn't as severe as everyone was led to believe.

Brittany catches me up on things such as what needs to be ordered, since I had the last couple days off. After the debriefing, I go to work replenishing napkins, cutting lemons, and stocking clean glasses, before the night gets super busy.

Jada is glued to Eamon's side, every chance she gets, while Brittany and I handle things just fine without her pulling her weight. I swear Brittany even seems less tolerant of her. She even paid me a compliment, telling me she likes how I delegate tasks. When it's convenient, Jada limps. For instance, when I ask her to grab ice or serve the table on the far end of the bar. She doesn't give two shits about my appointed position and seems to have made up her mind that despite my title, she is going to bitch, moan, and complain every chance she gets.

Dax hasn't come by this evening, and neither has his chatterbox buddy, Garron. At least that's one less thing to worry about. I am not really sure how to act, let alone what to say to him. How I feel about him hasn't changed, although now I know who he is. Dax. The man who's always been around… watching… protecting.

With Jada being present as her unfiltered self and Eamon all but avoiding everyone, I have yet to speak with him. I have questions and I need to show him what I found. I let Brittany know I'm stepping off the floor for a moment and head to the bathroom. After all that water, I am going to burst! Once I finish and wash, I go to step out of the women's room, only to be thrust backward.

"Hey!"

The metal lock clicks into place. In front of me stands Dax, a solid dark force. My eyes climb up before settling on his face. The corners of his lips curl upward as he peers down with an unsettling intensity. That wide mouth makes my belly summersault. Cool-toned eyes travel the length of my body, ahead of his brow lifting suggestively.

"What?!" I insist.

His shoulders begin to shake slightly as if he finds me humorous, without me saying anything. Is he laughing? It's like watching a silent film from the 1900s.

Pushing up onto the balls of my feet, I press my lips to his cheek. Tonight, I'm not myself. Bolder than I usually am, allowing my anxious overworked brain to take the back seat for once. I attempt to maneuver around his large body, remembering that Brittany was pretty much by herself on the floor, but Dax shifts into my path.

He holds up his hand and wags a finger at me, making a clicking "tsk" sound with his tongue. At that point, he proceeds to point downward, while swirling his finger. Oh. shit. He can't be serious! I thought he was joking. Dax wants to check if I have it in. The plug.

"I… I can't right now," I stammer. "I need to get back to work." I try to argue with the silent, immovable man.

His response…? Leaning back and crossing his arms against the door. He might as well be a cartoon character, checking a nonexistent watch all the while tapping their foot.

"Really?!" I fold my arms and growl through gritted teeth. "Right now?"

His head nods forward once.

Unbelievable.

My muscles clench around nothing, as if my body is anticipating his touch. I turn around, unbutton my slacks, and drop trou. Warm hands grasp at my hips. I pull my lips within my mouth and press down, in an attempt to match the stillness in the room. No words. No breath.

Next thing I know, his hands are traveling up the back of my shirt, stopping just as he reaches the base of my neck. Gently, he urges me to bend down farther.

Obediently, I pull my head toward my knees. I want. No… I need him to touch me.

In an attempt to break the tension, I declare, "no drugs. I promise." I'm met with silence. I know full well that I didn't listen to his earlier request.

The same "tsk tsk" sound echoes within the close quarters. I'm a mere ragdoll, exposed and positioned just how he wants me. I'm unsure what he's doing, but I think the faucet is running? A second later, something smooth presses on my clenched hole. I didn't have to see it to know exactly what it is.

Between my legs, I look on as he crouches just behind me. He moves to feather a kiss on one ass cheek, right as he gradually slides the moist, cool plug inside me.

No longer can I keep the sound in. An unexpected moan tumbles out of me. If this is an attempt to punish me, I will only be disobedient from here on out.

Warm lips press against my other cheek once the plug is fully seated just inside me.

Slowly, he pulls up my panties and then the bottoms. Like I'm the puppet and he the master, he spins me around only to button the front of my tweed trousers. This man has bent me to his will time and time again; however, each new encounter has been overlapped with extreme devotion.

My body aches for him, but all I do is stare as he stands to his full height and rolls his shoulders back. Strands of streaked, ash blond hair fall partially into his eyes, as he tilts his head and leans toward me. Dax lines my neck with soft kisses, then pulls back and considers me. Those slate eyes cause my knees to feel weak and I wonder if I behold them long enough, if I can glimpse into his very soul. His lips part slightly and the air feels charged. Lust fills the modest room, in spite of everything that has transpired. My mind and heart battle yet, I have to remind myself that everything is so new. Too many uncertainties. I'm positive more secrets are waiting just around the corner.

"I found something," I let out, cutting through the thick sexual aura that engulfs us. My fingers dive into my miniscule pocket, retrieving the SD card, putting it into his now outstretched hand.

He observes the foreign item in his hand, then looks back to me, as if urging me to continue.

"Thelma died."

His brows scrunch together and dammit his beautifully pitiful expression, better not make me start crying.

Taking a deep breath, I press on. "Everything that I love seems to die. I should have checked on her sooner, especially when I noticed she wasn't coming out of her hide anymore."

Deep lines mar his forehead, ahead of a staunch frown.

Don't cry. I point to the card in his hand. "It was within the pieces of her hide. I... I smashed the skull hide. I don't know how to see what's on it."

He nods thoughtfully.

"Do you think it's from Theo?"

He hands it back to me.

Immediately, I push it back within my front pocket for safe keeping.

With his hands free, he signs: *Be careful around Eamon. I've seen what he can do.*

Of course, he would know Eamon better than me, but I believe that he'd never hurt me either. Him and my brother seemed to have something real.

They were special to one another. I don't think I've ever left a toothbrush at a partner's place, but my brother had a serious enough relationship to keep twin tarantulas with someone. Theo was always better at everything, even dating apparently.

"Okay. I will," I conceded.

Dax exits the women's bathroom first and I follow a few moments later. With so many unknowns, it felt kind of liberating to have my own secrets for once. My only wish is that one of them doesn't cause me to become aroused, as I labor through this night.

Dax takes up residence in a far corner of the bar, positioned so he can watch me. Has he always monitored me so openly or have I never realized it until now? What if someone notices? Like Eamon... would he be upset? Happy for us? Fuck me. Everything was so vague, but also so real... intense. His relentless observation causes me to feel unease, teetering between both desire and modesty. Whatever this thing is between us, I don't want it to stop.

As I pour the shaken liquid into its glass, I can't help but wonder how long we're supposed to keep up this charade. Pretending that we aren't anything more. Like many parents, my mom explained that there's a difference between good and bad secrets. Good secrets are the kind you keep to yourself for a little while, then eventually share, like a surprise party or a present. Bad secrets are when you keep the information to yourself forever. Funny how they were the ones who kept the biggest secret from me. Did they ever plan to tell me? Did Theo know? What category did this situation fall into? Was being with Dax a good secret or a bad one...?

My internal unrest comes to a screeching halt as my gaze snags on Jada's suggestive position, all but leaning over Eamon at the end of the bar. I don't know why I feel more slighted by her pursuit of him than anything thus far, but I have an overwhelming urge to smother her. Truthfully, I don't even feel remorseful for thinking this way... I do reign from a Mafia family after all.

Heedlessly, I march over to separate the delusional girl from the counter. The poor thing wouldn't accept rejection, even if it was court ordered and delivered in a manila envelope. "Jada, we need more vodka and rum behind the bar. I need you to pull them from the backroom." I flutter my lashes because our boss is present after all.

She smacks her gum, ample cleavage on full display as she remains unmoved against the countertop.

Eamon visibly relaxes, almost as if he was waiting for someone to intervene.

"I'll get to it later, boss lady." She stretches and pops the gum while continuing to make bedroom eyes at Eamon.

He's still on his computer, however his brief side glance and lifted brow goads me.

"Now, Jada!"

I could have done without the eye roll, but she heeds my request.

"Fine." She groans. At a snail's pace, she makes her way to the backroom. Limping of course.

Finally, a moment to speak with Eamon. I pull the picture from my pocket, carefully unfolding it to show him. Without looking up from the screen, he lectures, "You're not very good at following directions, are you?"

Likely referring to the fact I came into work tonight, despite him telling me to stay home. My mouth pulls to one side, but I remain fixed in place, photo extended out to him.

Inevitably, he peers at the photograph. "Wow. Where'd you find that relic?" He takes the image within his hand. First looking delighted then gradually morphing into a sort of pained expression.

"I found it in some of my family's memory boxes. Not sure where it came from. It was a mess of childhood items from Theo and I… but I couldn't recall ever seeing that photo before today."

He makes an *mhm* sound, clearly transfixed on the worn memento. "I don't remember this day, but I have a subtle recollection of our families getting along."

That makes sense. He's older than me, maybe five or six in this picture, so he must have memories as far back as when the Lombardis and Murrays got along. "I was young, but I'm certain I overheard something that wasn't meant for my ears."

I know I shouldn't get overexcited, especially over long-lost memories, but I was hanging onto each word like it was a lifeline.

"Off and on… things jog my memory, like a scent or even a photograph. I swear I retained more from childhood than I ever did as an adult. Some things are better left forgotten. My mother was a saint. Always putting us first, ensuring we had everything we needed including friends to play with. I remember you. Just a little older than my own sister. I also remember Theo. Just snippets, but they were definitely real. One night, when I was supposed to be sleeping, I woke up to the sound of my father yelling. Even from the top of the stairs, his voice carried up to me. He was mad about the police raids. He even suspected another group was trying to sabotage his livelihood." Eamon stops briefly; eyes scanning the room. He continues, "shortly after that, things changed drastically. No more playdates. We didn't leave our side of town much.

Ingrained in my memory was the day of your accident. When I first heard about it, I thought I lost you both. It doesn't make it any less significant, because you were still hurt. You were too young to get caught up in our parents' world. Too innocent to understand everything that was evolving around you. Your family all but vanished overnight."

I feel my lungs burn for air just as I realize I've been holding in a breath the entire time he's been speaking.

"My mother cried for weeks. She mourned the loss of our family's friendship and the future we were meant to have. My father threw himself into work. While, the Lombardis just faded away, after they nearly lost their daughter." Eamon leans in closer to me, speaking just above a whisper.

Jada emerges from the back, with an exaggerated hitch and two bottles of liquor. She sets the bottles on the counter, all the while she pins me with a look of pure discontent. Oh, for fuck's sake, I will *Old Yeller* this hoe if she interrupts! Lucky for her, she proceeds to hobble her way back through the swinging door to recoup more bottles.

Eamon resumes his story. "When the cops started busting in our doors, we suspected some other kind of gang or sudo mafia was trying to take us out. Law enforcement seemed to know too much. We tried weeding out the bad apples in town, questioning involved parties, and tracking down anyone who may have a grudge against us. Nothing ever surfaced. Until... I was led to you, little fish. My father—" He shakes his head as if struggling within himself. "My father... so blinded by his rage, thinks the Lombardis duped him into a false sense of security. Somehow convinced you killed my mother as penance for Theo."

A gasp slips from me, before I can cover my mouth. "You know that's not true. I'd never do that... my family could never do that!" The words pour from me as if my urgency could validate the claim. "I didn't even know I was a Lombardi until recently!"

He searches my face then nods with finality. "I know that."

Thank fuck! I fill my lungs which I seem to be depriving as of late.

"But my father and sister are convinced you're at fault. They won't listen to reason. I was given a timeline. To learn what I can. Get close to you... but I'm out of time. My hands are tied without any proof that you're innocent. For some confounding reason, he believes your family is still running this town. Even from afar."

I feel ill. What am I supposed to do with all of this? How am I going to find answers about Theo's death and prove that my family aren't murderers? Why does everyone only tells me things on a *need-to-know basis*? So much confusion could have been avoided if everyone was simply more forthcoming!

Eamon pursuing me, taking me out, kissing me, only to validate I was or was not some sort of assassin? Rude. Feelings aside, I should be more concerned about the potential impending war between two powerful crime families, and me being somehow caught in the middle. Why can't my life be more like a Sandra Bullock film as opposed to a Soprano finale?

Eamon closes his laptop just as Jada appears and sets down two more containers of vodka. "Have you found anything?" he mouths each word, so only I understand in this busy room.

I dry my sweaty palms down the front of my pants, feeling the tiny rectangle in my front pocket for safe keeping. This is not leaving my side until I identify what's on it. Before I can think better of it, I tell him no. I glance over my shoulder to the man that has monitored me. Even though Eamon seems to "believe," that my family is innocent in all this, I still heed Dax's warning. Eamon was a prince, for all intents and purposes, to a powerful family empire. I need to proceed with caution.

Eamon rubs at his eyes, clearly exhausted. He begins gathering his items within a leather case. "Don't give up… you're bound to find something," he delivers with a forced smile.

Jada reaches Eamon, just as he pulls the case onto his shoulder. Maneuvering around her, he heads out the red door of the bar. I have trouble holding in the chuckle at Jada's pitiful attempt to get our boss to notice her. If looks could kill, she'd have me mounted on the wall.

Brittany pops up and asks me to bring over five Smithwick's to table six, so she can use the restroom. Just as I'm rounding the counter, Jada materializes before me. I try to balance the tray while avoiding her, but she moves into my path, intentionally bumping my arm that carries the drinks.

"Oh fuck!" Half of the beers tip over, drowning me in amber colored ale. My clothes are saturated, all thanks to her. Regardless of the icy liquid, my face swells with red-hot frustration.

Jada knowingly puts a hand to her mouth and gasps for dramatic flair. "Oops! How clumsy of me. I didn't see you there." She continues to the back, not sparing me a second thought.

Brittany tosses a bar towel to me and I begin dabbing at my clothes the best I'm able. Screw her, if she thinks that will make me leave. I'm finishing MY shift. Dax, like some sort of mind reader, has kept a healthy distance from me. He doesn't have to speak for me to know. I see it in his eyes. It's not a sympathetic stare… no. It's a look that tells me, *you got this. I'm right here.* Dax reminds me of a watchdog. The capacity to delete the nuisance animal that brazenly walks the fence line of what he's meant to guard, however he hushes the internal beast, the one I know lies within him. Each new interaction with this man has been unexpected, but I've never felt safer. Somehow, he coaxes me to step out of my daily comfort zone. I'm becoming more assertive, even if it means my choices don't come with guarantees. He has me distracted… unable to help stealing glances at his beautifully-shadowed face. When our gaze meets across the room, it causes every muscle in my body to tighten. I'm reminded of what he did to me in the bathroom. The secrets we share and all the ways he's made me succumb. I have no apologies for any of it.

That night, after a well-deserved shower and finally being able to remove the custom toy Dax reinserted, I'm able to focus on what I found earlier. My imagination runs wild with the possibilities. What will I find on the SD card? Pulling a massive hoodie over my cleaned body, I climb into bed with my outmoded laptop and enough adrenaline to pull an all-nighter. My phone lights up next to me.

Dax the Friendly Stalker: You should leave it off.

I bite my top lip to keep from smiling. Of course he's spying on me. Setting down the phone on the bed, I begin looking at all the different cavities on either side of the laptop. I need to figure out what's on this thing! Turning over the tiny card in my hand, I begin sizing up the item to each port.

"Damnit! Which hole does it go in?!" Instantly, my phone vibrates.

Another text from *Dax the Friendly Stalker.* A series of emojis... a taco, a peach, and lips, followed by a shrugging man.

"Har, har!" I sneer to the obviously empty room.

Wait... he can hear me? I'm curious how many times he's heard me moan from my vibrator, before I even knew of his presence. Shaking the thought from my mind, I bury the phone beneath my pillows, now, stubbornly determined to get the device to read without intervention. No cavity appears compatible. Nothing is the right size or it's already occupied. God, I'm glad I didn't just say that out loud. I have no doubt Dax would climb through my window looking to put all those innuendos to the test.

With my nail, I push on one of the ports that has something thin and plastic within. The part pops out, a bigger version of the microSD card I found in the tarantula tank. The words read: *San Disk Adapter.* Of course... there wasn't a place for the tiny card, it needed this converter thingy! I remove the smaller card within and slide in the found microSD card into the adapter. Like a glove, it clicks into the side of the computer. Nothing happens. Shit. Did I break something? Should I remove it and blow on it? It worked for the Sega cartridges.

I take a deep breath in and tell myself to be patient. Waiting for something to happen makes me want to get up and pace the length of my room or throw up. Probably both with an undertone of all consuming dread. I begin clicking around the desktop frantically, looking for any sign of a file or anything that I could have missed. Is it blank? Ruined from sitting in Thelma's hide for years?! No. I can't think like that. Something has to be on it. I inadvertently began nibbling at the skin on the side of my nailbed, all the while staring unwavering at the home screen. Was I about to learn something awful... like how my brother died or was this as unimportant as a compilation of Theo's poetry? I can't deal with more dead ends, especially when half the Murray family is ready to blame the Lombardis for Mary's death! My stomach pitches and drops like a raging rapid, when I recall everything that's come to light this week. I'm a Lombardi. The notorious Mafia family.

"Ssssss... Ouch!" I peer downward to find the side of my thumb now raw and bleeding from my incessant chewing. Frustrated, I grab the computer and give it a shake. "Argghh... give me something!"

Without warning, a notification pops up just above the taskbar. My hands begin to quake as I lower the laptop back onto the bed. I dare not breathe for fear that the small window could vanish. Carefully, I use the track pad and right-click the bar on the bottom of the screen, selecting *Read Removable Disk*. A new window instantly appears, containing only one folder. Choosing the first document, I notice it's named: *"I'm Sorry."* I suck in air, desperate to fight the overwhelming clash of emotions. Hot tears of relief begin streaming down my cheeks. Holy shit. It's from Theo. There's actually something on it!

As much as I crave answers, a minor part of me is panicked. What if I don't see my brother the same way anymore? I have a sinking feeling that everything is going to change after viewing this file. I suck in a deep breath and click *Open*.

THIRTY-EIGHT

THEO

"Two Princes"
Three Years Ago

I'm mesmerized by the way flecks of light glide across the horizon. Waking the past week during the witching hour, has me reflecting on the way stock finds its way into Boston, under the cover of the night.

Cargo vessels drift along the harbor waters, burdened by their heavy load. While most of the city sleeps, some work thankless jobs. Laboring for the greater good and never being able to share their plight of traffic jams and unnecessarily long lines, all for a regular to get them through their day.

I'm Disconnected. No more than a ghost above the city in a haze of my own subconscious. Obviously, I wasn't a specter, but I'm sure I'd give someone a fright if they happened to look upon the twentieth floor, finding me stark naked before the massive window. The cloud of smoke around me was meant to be more of a stress relief than a health risk, but nothing I seem to do lately falls into my better judgment. The more I draw from this vape pen, the more it takes on the taste of burnt toast, so at odds with its cinnamon bun claim. Nothing could compare to the swirled pastries my dad would make with my little sister.

I grew up in this city, although that seems to be the only consistent thing about my childhood. My family moved around a lot. Changing addresses meant changing schools. Hell, my folks even revamped our last name at one point. Their behavior was as erratic as the weather in Boston, yet because of them, I am who I am. Strong-willed and inquisitive to a fault. Always questioning everything. Simply put, I can't accept the direction of my sail until I understand where the breeze is coming from. Even before a storm rolls in, I can feel it. It makes my bones sore.

Currently, I can't sleep. Tormented by my mind and body. No dark looming clouds, yet I can sense a force on the horizon.

"Hey," calls a deep-groggy voice behind me. "Come back to bed."

I let out the inhale of charred bread before tossing the vape pen back onto the dresser. My hand bats away the lingering mist, prior to making my way back to the bed. The chilled-satin sheets urge me toward the other warm body inside. It's remarkable how a simple touch can ground me. Causing all my cares to instantly melt away. Arms wrap around me, as I press myself flush against my partner. Turning my gaze upward, I playfully lick across his stubbled cheek. Causing a devious grin to grow on his face. Swiftly, he moves putting me into a chokehold. Despite the lighthearted position, I still struggle to be released. Ultimately waving my free arm as a way of saying, "uncle."

He kisses the top of my head and frees me. Instantly making me miss his tight embrace. Eamon leans back, basking in the red ambient light of the room, with a smug look of victory painted across his face.

I was all in when it came to him. He's actually the one that pursued me at first, but it was fate that ultimately reunited us. We've been together just under a year, but I was determined to get him something that reflects how much he means to me. Eamon now has an identical set-up to mine. Louise the tarantula, extends her tarsal claws atop the skull hide in her tank. It took a few weeks of planning, but I think I killed it on his birthday present. He's not a fan of celebrating since the holidays seem to shroud his special day. Didn't stop me from spoiling the hell out of him by cooking dinner each night. Everything from broccoli and cheese soup, to penne alla vodka, and even a short rib ragu. Honestly, he's a terrible cook, although I also don't mind watching him swallow what I serve him.

"What's wrong?" Eamon has learned my tells. One of his hands supports his neck, while the other skates over his scalp, as if attempting to rouse himself from his previously tired state.

"Well... besides Brenda nagging me as usual. I'm great!" I lied. My stomach plummets in response to the sympathetic smile that pulls at the corners of his handsome face.

"I get it. Intern jobs are shite work," he agrees. Sitting up, he reaches for me. Pushing back long strands from my forehead, while managing to look straight into my very core. "You're going to get that journalism gig. I just know it," Eamon speaks so matter-of-factly.

Lately, it's been hard to view the glass as anything but half empty. Quickly reeling in my pessimistic thoughts, I position myself back against the headboard and gaze upward at the mirror, all in an attempt to escape Eamon's assessing stare. Eventually, I pulled a truth from the illusion. "Investigative journalism can be extremely competitive. I wouldn't doubt there will be at least a hundred applicants."

Eamon throws the covers off his naked form. Moving onto me by straddling my legs and resting upon my thighs. When he gets like this... there's no escaping him. He doesn't like when I'm hard on myself. When I believe I'm no better than the next guy. He takes it to heart, seeing it as an attack on what's his. I wish I understood what he saw in me. His hands trace my navel, working up to my chest before tracing the length of my neck, where he eventually rests just upon my jaw.

"Listen to me."

I can't fight the pull of his hypnotic focus.

"Any place would be lucky to have you. Now… why don't you cut the shit, little prince, and tell me the real reason I caught you watching boats at three a.m., instead of in my bed."

My other half knows me too well. Regrettably, he can't know what's truly going on. At least not until I know more. Eamon's world, although dangerous all on its own, is pretty black and white. I learned early on the kind of life he led. If it meant being together, I was ready to dive in headfirst.

In college, he thought he was slick at first. Attending a journalism class as a business major. I knew he didn't belong there, but as much as he watched me, I was considering him. Maybe it was our youthful pride? Attempting to fight the pull we had toward one another. It was actually after graduation that we started seeing each other. We tried to keep our relationship private. Not just because he was a gay man who was the son of a crime lord, but because our families have a complicated history. Our memories resemble two slices of Swiss cheese. Overlapping at some points, even if gaping holes leave us questioning whether or not we remember things correctly.

While my folks have attempted to present themselves as hardworking, loving parents. I've always known something wasn't normal. The Murrays are a known name on the streets. I know what they're capable of. They may deal in racketeering, gambling, and tax evasion, but that's small potatoes compared to what my family has accomplished. They played their part well, trying to hide who they truly are from my sister and me. Real estate and investment? Come on… Really? No one works that much. I'm a nosy motherfucker, so once I had access to a computer, I looked up the name I was supposed to forget.

"Lombardi."

Our grandparents came over from Sicily, immigrating to the States where they quickly made a name for themselves. Between research and collecting old articles, I've learned that I'm the descendant of people who got rich from extortion, intimidation, and manipulation. I've always known something was uniquely different about our family. Why else would we have to move every couple years and change our name without explanation? Cindel was little, she probably didn't even realize it was altered.

Come to think of it, it's kinda crazy my parents even supported the idea of me pursuing a career in communications. They knew full well I planned to minor in investigative journalism. If Mom and Dad wanted their true nature to stay buried, why encourage such an education? Either they're blatantly naive or they knew precisely what they were doing; forging the path for me to uncover truths... all on my own.

Regardless, my kid sister Cindel is in the dark about everything. I can only hope that, after what my parents' choices had brought to our family's doorstep, she never learns about any of this. She deserves to stay blissfully ignorant, chasing her love of fashion and staying the hell away from anything or anyone who could bring her harm. Not living at home makes it difficult to find the time to talk to her, more than once a week. We've grown distant... her starting college and me chasing the high of 'why the wind blows.' It's better this way. Keeping her at arm's reach and away from me. It's for her own good. I would be lying if I didn't say it kills me when I think back to how close we used to be. Cindel has a good head on her shoulders. If she just stopped getting in her own way, she'd be alright. She has to be alright. Someday I might not be around to protect her.

When I started college, more specifically, interning with news outlets, my uncle Nicholas started coming around more. He said he wants to "help me." Repeatedly telling me he has connections that could be beneficial in my future career in journalism. I couldn't fathom how he could help me with a job in financing or whatever he did. Each time he tried to convince me that he could advance my career, I politely declined. At one point, he offered me a hefty salary if I took some time off from my schooling and came and worked for him. If I've learned anything over the years, it's that nothing is what it seems. "If you take everything at face value, you'll never have a story." My first journalism professor drilled that saying into her students. She even wrote it on top of one of my papers. Signed, "Moyra." I ripped the message off the top half of my paper and taped it onto my bedroom mirror. Reminding me each and every day, to keep asking questions until the truth reveals itself.

So, there I was, tailing my uncle around Boston for weeks on end. He commonly met with one particular character in uniform. Clearly, he was an officer of the law. I managed to learn his name only by asking the barista at the coffee shop he frequented. Kent. Odd. The professor who made a lasting impact on me in college had the same last name. Was Kent really that common or could they be related?

When I find myself over analyzing the minute detail, I push the thought aside and focus on the clear evidence before me. My uncle has befriended a cop. That's clear as day, but to what end? How does working in finance involve secret rendezvous with a copper in an abandoned warehouse? Things weren't adding up.

When I started looking into my uncle's place of employment, like who he worked for, or any colleagues... you know what I found? Nothing. Bupkis! There was never any job in investing, banking, or however he spun it. Was he trying to shelter me like my parents did? I already knew I was Lombardi but my folks were done with that kind of life. Weren't they? I might be out of the loop when it comes to Mafia's codes of conduct, but I'm pretty fucking certain that being chummy with a cop, gets you a one-way ticket to the bottom of the bay.

However involved my parents may currently be, surely, they can't be okay with what my uncle is doing. I never wanted to look further into what my family used to do, especially because it resulted in Cindel getting hurt. I may have been young at the time of the explosion, but I understood without anyone spelling it out for me. Someone wanted to hurt us because of who my family was and you know what? My parents did a shit job of keeping us safe, after the incident. What does redacting letters from our last name and moving around all helter-skelter within the city do for protection? Maybe Mom and Dad never stopped the family business... that would explain why they consistently expected me to watch my kid sister.

For a while, I hated my parents. Refused to answer their calls. It was even more confusing when my uncle would invite me out to breakfast the day after I ignored them. I never went. Unwilling to be spoon-fed whatever shit he conjured up. Eamon would one day inherit his father's empire; I didn't want to concern him with theoretical scenarios and my own family drama. Keeping all this from him felt like a rock in the pit of my stomach. A steady-painful burden. I admired how easy it was for Eamon to share with me. Despite my chosen career path, while adhering to an ethical code involving truth, accuracy, fairness, and transparency, he knew I would never report a thing. We have history. He was my beginning. My forever person.

I was frustrated with myself for taking so long to notice it, but I finally saw a pattern. The day after my dear old uncle would meet with Officer Kent, Eamon's family business would face some kind of raid or arrest. Almost like clockwork, Nicholas would have an audience with the man in uniform from the Boston PD, again one of Murray's soldiers would be taken in for questioning. Sometimes one of the Murray guys would just up and disappear! None of the charges ever stuck, but the coincidence was too convenient to overlook. I had a new theory... Uncle Nicholas has taken the omertà, the code of the Mafia and pissed on it. I should give my parents the benefit of the doubt.... maybe they did try to step away from the family business, but clearly Nicholas assumed control.

My father was adopted into the Lombardi family, although unlike their first son Nicholas, Charles had been deemed the dependable son. The one fit to take the reins one day. I wonder how Nicholas felt about all that? Clearly, it seems that he carved out a little space for himself in this city. Convenient for him, that my family went into hiding after a supposed "gas leak." The explanation never sat right with me. What happened to my sister was the start of many doubts I had. After that day, I never stopped demanding answers and I never will. It's one of my driving factors. The reason why I wanted to become an investigative journalist.

After multiple sleepless nights, I've come to the conclusion that Nicholas is the reason behind the Murray's troubles. He slighted his own family, starting by generating chaos. Classic totalitarian mindset. Nicholas Lombardi plans to obliterate any and all competition. Pulling the strings from behind the curtain, this man will wind up killing off the Murrays and ruling Boston with an iron fist. Still a working theory but a viable, fucked up one.

What I was doing was time consuming. Fully invested in my research and reconnaissance, I made the decision to quit my temp job. Just last week, while looking through a box of old photos, I was taken aback when I stumbled across a photograph of our families together. What could have caused the notorious Murray and Lombardi alliance to stop? Everything should point back to the day my sister could have died, but I have this sick feeling it goes even further back. Possibly when our parents were young, around our age. It looks to be the start in a long series of events. The first domino to fall. It may seem like a slew of loose connections but there is always one consistent variable. My uncle.

Kissing, biting, and teasing away Eamon's concern, he eventually forgets how I never answered his question. I managed to close my eyes for an hour or so, thanks to Eamon's arm draped over my torso, pinning me to the bed. He was up with the alarm, then straight to the shower, whereas I headed into the kitchen. Bright light now floods the spacious room, as I set to work all in an attempt to cook away my concerns.

Eamon eventually emerges into the kitchen just as I pull out the baked Eggs en Cocotte with Smoked Salmon. "Mmmmm, tell me I get to eat that!" Eamon commands respect in any room he enters. Not just because of the expensive tailored suits, but the confidence, charisma, and eye contact he maintains without fault. Setting down his briefcase in the chair beside him, he adjusts his cufflinks as he sits down at the island.

"I think I know the way to your heart by now..." I wink in his direction.

Taking one of the piping hot ramekins off the baking sheet, I balanced a baguette on the rim and placed the delicate dish in front of him.

"Don't tell anyone." He scolds.

I sit beside him as we take turns sharing what the day holds, in between hot spoonfuls of the eggy entree. I push down the buzzing thoughts involving my family as I struggle to focus on Eamon's words. He mentions having to handle an 'ongoing issue' with their bookie at the boxing club. Speaking freely about his world, never hiding the ugly parts from me.

Waiting patiently for a lull in the conversation, I comment, "Hey... tonight, I'd like to show you something I've been working on."

He attempts to reply around a bite of food, "For work?"

I shake my head, "No, this is more of a personal vendetta."

He nods with understanding, just as he swallows the last bite.

I smile seeing the white dish empty.

Pushing out from the counter, Eamon stands and presses a kiss atop my forehead. "I'm gonna head out. A new guy joined the crew, so I need to show him the ropes. Get him acclimated." He grabs the keys from the bowl on the table and considers me. "Are you good?"

Occupying my mouth with a large spoonful, I give him a thumbs up. Lines crease along his forehead. He may not be buying it, but he doesn't stick around to argue. I hear the elevator door chime as it opens a moment later. Before I'm able to reconsider my mission for the day, I swiftly clean up, throw on yesterday's clothes, and head out.

I should feel regretful about misleading Eamon in regards to my whereabouts, but I am "working." Perhaps the apple doesn't fall too far from the tree... my folks were capable of shaping deception into an art form.

I gave Brenda the middle finger more than three weeks ago. Putting my energy to better use, I've had ample time to log all the shady shit my uncle does. I would have liked to tell Eamon sooner, but it just didn't feel right, since his birthday had just passed. Plus, I still had a few more things to figure out.

I'm back at my place, grabbing a few items to aid in today's research. Retrieving the microSD card from my tarantula's enclosure, I slide the additional memory card into the larger space in the back of my phone, before snapping the case together again. I'm not paranoid, just proactively cautious. I catch a glimpse of myself in the mirror, realizing I look dressed for a job I no longer had. Turning back to change, I opt for a black hoodie and matching running pants. Now I could easily disappear into the shadows.

Today, I planned on following my uncle to one of his frequent stops. A neglected warehouse located in a less desirable part of town, not too far from the interstate. Until recently, I never dared to get closer, but I needed to determine who these other people were. The simple meet ups with Officer Kent have grown into small congregations of unfamiliar faces. Before, I'd have to follow him to know the location; now it's almost as if he isn't even trying to hide anymore. Meeting at the same creepy building for the past two weeks. I dare say, it's impressive how he's able to move like a phantom through this city, no one the wiser to what he's up to. There's no way the rest of the family knows about this.

The cab dropped me off about a block away from the deserted warehouse district, on Tudor Street. I didn't want to chance being seen by unloading too close to their meeting location. By the time I arrived, my uncle was already outside of the building with two other men. The older one I could have sworn I recognized. While the other dude appeared younger, likely around my age. Close enough to actually see faces, I still couldn't place who either man was. The younger guy didn't seem to want to be there. Earbuds nestled in both ears; he looked like he wanted to tune out everything around him. They moved inside of the building where I couldn't monitor. I needed to find a way to see inside.

Checking the adjacent building, it appears to be abandoned as well. It was easy enough to pull the handle from the weathered door, allowing the padlock and chain to slip free. No need to pick any locks. The vast space sheltered an old printing press, maintenance parts, and crates upon crates of yellowed newspapers. From the looks of it, it seems this place hasn't been touched in more than twenty years.

Once I scaled the small ladder to the top of the scaffold, I moved from window to window, in an attempt to find the best vantage point. Precariously stacking buckets of ink, I use my phone to view from the transom window. By the time I hit record, the inexperienced fellow had left. I zoomed in as much as possible, on my uncle and the mystery man poised within frame. My calves ached from balancing and this very well could be an utter waste of time, because not only could I not hear a thing, but I couldn't read lips either. Regardless I was compelled to stay, not wanting to miss a thing. I remained there; grateful I inserted an additional SD card. This gave me enough storage space to record until the two men emerged from the desolate warehouse.

When each man pulled away from the area in their designated cars, I felt it was safe enough to leave my spot and get the hell out of this place. Back on the main road, as I waited to hail a cab, I noticed another vehicle parallel parked across the street. It definitely wasn't there when I first arrived. The vehicle looks vaguely like my uncle's, but since he already left, I was probably worrying for nothing.

At home, I removed the microSD card from my phone and connected it to my computer using an adapter. Adding to my running log, I entered today's findings. It contained my uncle's whereabouts over multiple weeks, detailed descriptions of what I witnessed, along with dates and times. I think my professor would be pleased to see how I've put my degree to use already. It's a well-organized report, which could prove useful as I move to uncover the truth. This wasn't school though and I wasn't writing a mock column with construed opinions sprinkled throughout, this was real life, and it was fiercely personal. He was inadvertently ruining the Lombardi name while simultaneously tearing down the Murray's empire.

I watched today's recording, no less than ten times, but I couldn't make heads or tails of what either man said. Fuck! I can't lip-read, but I know who can. No. I can't drag her into this. I'll figure this out. I plan to tell Eamon, but... what if my hunch is wrong? What if he's just some freaky swinger or just dealing drugs?

"Argh..." I argued with myself, trying to justify my actions for spying on my uncle or being dishonest with the one person who understands me better than anyone. I opened up a new document and began typing. It read more like a script, apologizing Eamon for not telling him what I've been up to. Even if he didn't read this, it was cathartic, nonetheless. Compiling the recording, poignant letter, and logs; I thought it was a wise decision to make a backup microSD card. What if this one got lost, damaged, or even stolen?

I wedged the original memory card back inside Thelma's hide, where I usually store it. Except... where was I going to conceal the other one? It needed to be somewhere outside of my apartment, yet a location I knew I could get to. I ran my fingers through my hair, leaning back in my chair, as I watched Thelma move about her tank before finally settling back inside her favorite spot. At which point, I knew exactly where to put the duplicate SD card.

Later that night, after picking up some Chinese takeout, I texted Eamon on my walk home.

Without awaiting a response, I tuck the phone back into my pocket and retrieve the keys, only to realize the front door to my apartment is already unlocked. "Shit." Did I forget, again? I push the door open and set down the paper takeout bag, prior to moving farther into the dark living space.

"Hello Theo."

Startled, I grab the first thing within my reach which just so happens to be... a curly willow branch from a floor vase. The shadowed figure pulls the chain of the floor lamp beside them, revealing a tall frame cramped into an armchair.

What was my uncle doing sitting in my dark apartment?! All at once, I realize I have a decorative stick ready for battle before humbly setting it back down in its designated spot.

"Uncle... hello. What are you doing here?" I'm not scared, just surprised.

Without meaning to, I raise my chin to the air, rolling my shoulders back, I stand a little straighter than usual. In the usual cozy setting of my apartment, my uncle looked more like an awkward giant in a doll house. He's taller than me and wider, but I'd like to think my trips to the gym made me denser.

"Can't I pop in on my nephew from time to time?" The room seems to shrink in size.

I haven't moved from my position; however, my estranged family member takes up an unsettling amount of my space. I clear my throat, "Well... yeah, but you could call or maybe knock before letting yourself in."

Inspecting his suit, he picks something off that causes his lip to curl upward, as he sprinkles the invisible speck onto the floor. His eyes shift slowly through the room, climbing up my frame, where a cold-hollow stare settles on my face. "Seeing how you come around without such formalities, I only thought this was the new norm."

Shit. It was his car I saw. He knows I followed him today. I try not to panic, although I can't help but scan the apartment still glued to the floor. Suddenly, I'm thankful for my compulsive habit to always put my research away. He'll never find a thing.

My mind goes a mile a minute, I don't know what to say... how to proceed? Taking in a seemingly level, yet shaky breath, I tell myself to chill. Yes, he knew I followed him this one time, but he can't possibly know how long I've been tailing him... can he? I force my body to move toward the kitchen counter, where I begin unpacking the to-go containers of chicken lo mein and crab rangoons. They taste terrible when they're cold.

Nicholas remains seated, silently watching me as I unpack my dinner. Pulling out the chair, I lowered myself down to eat at the modest table. Seriously, if I didn't sit down, I believed my knees would buckle, from the sheer strain. Peeling the paper off the chopsticks, I begin shoveling food into my mouth. If I ignore the elephant in the room, maybe it will just leave. Each swallow is labored. Never had I thought, eating in front of a family member could feel so uncomfortable.

Halfway through the container, Nicholas finally stands. He paced the room, as if unaffected by the unease or the prolonged silence. "Ya know... when your dad told me you wanted to pursue a career in journalism, I thought to myself, great! A wonderful way to bond with my nephew. I suspected we could make a great team one day." His stride stops now that he's pointing at me. "You could uncover essential information with your skill set. Finding all the dirty little secrets from our illustrious town officials. We'd have the blue-

prints for the inner workings of the city, thanks to you! While I continue doing what I do best."

The most recent bite of crab rangoon became lodged in my throat. I choke it down, causing an unintentional coughing fit. When I'm finally able to speak, I ask the most obvious question, "What exactly do you do best?"

He levels me with a stare that resembles a bottomless pit of ash. "I think you have a pretty good idea about what I do, dear boy. You've been watching me for quite some time. Let's not play these games."

I extend the takeout container to the disconnected family member before me, hoping to ease the tension in the room. "Noodles?"

His thick eyebrow quirks up just ahead of a sickening grin, which gradually spreads across his face. "I'll pass. Too sweet."

I shrug and proceed to shovel more of the brown long noodles into my mouth.

"Have you been keeping a record of my whereabouts?"

I shrug again, keeping my eyes downcast. Although, I can just make out his arms crossing over his chest in conjunction with a long audible sigh. I don't think he's going to let this go, as I originally hoped.

He moves closer to me. "Does your little boyfriend know what you've been up to?"

Something switches in me when he brings Eamon into this. Clearly, he knows what buttons to push. I try to stand, only to be met with a firm hand that pushes me down into my chair. Immediately, the chair moves back with force. He's in front of me with his foot on the seat between my legs. Casually he leans toward me, an arm atop his bent knee. "Let me make myself... crystal clear. I haven't worked as hard and as long as I have, for all of this to go belly up because of my bastard brother's, faggot son has grown a conscious!"

Not the first time I've heard those names. It doesn't faze me, but what's more unsettling is how his words are dripping with malice. When I face something challenging, I try to put myself in a happy place. I imagine Eamon. Our first kiss. How his handsome face looks so at peace, in the morning light. How perfectly our hands fit together.

*I reach for the phone in my pocket. My uncle simply hovers above me, watching, waiting, most likely thinking I'm about to give him what he wants. I have no intention of handing over a single thing. Instead, I connect to the speakers in my apartment, because I'm a passive aggressive little shit. I opened up my current playlist, choosing the most fitting song for the occasion, and selected 'repeat.' These were songs I picked to pass the time, when I was keeping an eye on my dear old uncle. **Nine Inch Nails – "Terrible Lie,"** fills the apartment with industrial sounds as my uncle's once deadpan stare shifts to something darker.*

A long irritable sound escapes him ahead of speaking, "Suit yourself." He leans farther into my space. His head came parallel with mine, whispering into my ear as though we weren't the only two in the room. "This would have been a lot simpler if you died like you were supposed to. If I just handled things myself, the bomb would have taken you both. Consider this time you've had my gift to you." His words are like molasses, heavy... thick... dark.

Everything moves even more slowly. The words, "terrible lie!" echo off the walls, and I wonder whether this is the song's first go round or if it's already repeated. I'm unable to react, accordingly; his cold, boney fingers grip my jaw. Anchored in place, I suck in and spit, landing a loogie on its mark.

Unruffled, he uses his cuff to wipe his face. "Tut Tut," he lectures. Pressing firmly into my cheeks, he causes my mouth to painfully come ajar. With subtle movements, he retrieves a small item from his coat pocket, using his free hand.

Not waiting to see what's in his hand, I attempt to move away only to be pinned back in place by his shoe, savagely pressing against my groin. I'm completely at his mercy.

"Does Cindel know?"

Now the object comes into focus. A syringe hovers just above me, while his fingers relentlessly dig into my cheeks. My words are garbled but they fall on deaf ears, switching to an urgent throaty, "No!"

His iron eyes narrow. In the blink of an eye, the needle travels toward me, piercing my tongue. The stabbing pain is nothing compared to the burn of whatever he just injected me with. Lifting my foot, I kick back from the table, causing the chair to tip over. My world tilts on its axis. What... what'd he do to me?!

"Why are you doing this to me?" At this point, I didn't know if I was saying the words or if it was a part of the song. My head pulsed to the rhythm and my mouth felt dry. I pushed up from the floor, attempting to stand. My legs refuse to cooperate, feeling as though my bones have turned to smelted wax. My eyes ricochet around the room until I find him, wiping the syringe off on a handkerchief and gingerly placing the vial next to me on the floor. Paralyzed, I watch from the ground as he removes the memory card from my phone, pushing it into his pocket, before tossing the phone next to me. I know the microSD card he's taking has nothing significant on it, but he doesn't.

"Terrible lie!" Reverberates off the walls of my home. My heinous uncle crouches down beside me, I can't move a muscle. "I will strip my bastardo brother of every shred of happiness he's ever known... then I will take back what's rightfully mine."

I sense the vibrations as he moves farther away from me, following the culminating "click" of the apartment door closing. My face tingles and my vision swims. These tears aren't for me.

I'm back in our childhood home. I feel the room shake followed by the deafening sound of an explosion. I ran to the playroom just as fast as my little legs would carry me. No longer am I the one laid out on the floor. I can just make out her small, fragile body lying lifeless in the lingering haze. I thought I lost her. My sister. I can't do this again. I never want her to experience what I saw. She... she'll find me. Just like this. Our parents raced past me. "Please be alive." I begged. Clouds surrounded me. No longer could I see straight. I squeeze my eyes shut, hoping to escape this fever dream. Incapacitated, I focus on my breathing.

Despite my shut lids, lights shoot across my vision. Moving in sync with the far-off rhythm... as if dancing. It's proving difficult to take in a full breath.

I think of Cindel, moving across the starry emptiness, merrily spinning just like she did when we were young. "I need someone to hold onto..." she stops and all the lights wink out.

THIRTY-NINE

CINDEL

The drive held three files inside a folder named, *"un."* UN? What did that stand for? United Nations…?

Inside the folder are two text documents as well as a video. I start by selecting the one named, *"I'm Sorry."* It looks like it's a letter…. to Eamon. Theo's always been an eloquent writer, earning a few of his papers to be published in the local paper, even before graduation. This letter, however, feels rushed, containing words out of context and minor spelling errors. It's still a heartfelt apology, nonetheless. Theo goes on to admit he hasn't been working as an intern but following someone of interest for many weeks. Could this person be the one responsible for my brother's untimely death?! I read through the entirety of the letter but not once is the name mentioned. Minimizing the letter, I opened the next file. This one has dates, followed by brief descriptions. It's a log.

November 11th: Person of interest meets with Boston PD.

I skipped a few entries that have similar descriptions.

November 18th: Person of interest meets with the now named Officer Kent.

Hold on. That's the name of the officer who came to my apartment. Alarm bells commenced blaring in my head. I press on.

November 29th: Person of interest has frequent meetings in abandoned warehouses in the bay area. Associates unknown. Keeping distant for now. Eventually I need to record interactions.

December 7th: Person of interest has breakfast at Benny's.

Oh great, now the person he was following frequents at my breakfast spot too? Super.

December 10th: Person of interest meets with new man.
December 13th: I have learned that the new man is affiliated with the Irish gang family, known as the Murray's.
December 16th: Person of interest meets with Officer Kent. The meeting seemed informal and hurried.
December 20th: After inquiring, with my source. The Murray's are unaware of any infiltration at the present.

Fuck me sideways. The person of interest is in cahoots with a rat! Are they still around? I should tell Eamon.

December 22nd: Person of interest meets Officer Kent at new location. The Murray family faces another raid at their Boxing Club.

December 29th.
What?
That's... the day my brother died.

Person of interest meets with accomplices at a warehouse. I believe the older man, has wormed his way into the Murray family. The younger man is someone I've never seen before. The newcomer leaves prior to recording.

The words: ***See Recording*** are bolded next to the date's entry.

That's it. The last date he wrote in this log was the same date he was pronounced dead.

I do as the note says, switching over to the little reel icon in the file. It's the only video on the microSD card.

"Please," I whisper toward the glowing screen on my lap. A silent plea to find something, anything that can shed light on this entanglement of information.

Double clicking on the icon, I take a deep breath, as if to brace myself for whatever I may see. The video begins with a jostling picture. It appears the video is being taken with a phone; someone attempts to steady the camera. As if a loose thread has been tugged from the stitches holding my heart together, I catch a brief glimpse of my brother. Theo accidentally flipped the camera. Just as swiftly as he appeared, he was gone again. Finally managing to reverse shot, he presses the phone to the glass. It appears he was trying to see into another building. Through the smudged window, he zooms past bricks, beyond panes of glass, and into the residing empty warehouse. It's too blurry.

The camera struggles to focus on the dirt upon the window versus the far-off subjects. Coming in and out of focus until eventually the image becomes clearer, as the lens is ultimately able to pick up movement in the distance. I check the sound to make sure my computer has its volume turned up, but I hear nothing.

The movie is silent, everyone is so tiny, I'm forced to zoom in closer. Two men take center stage. One of them has their back to the camera, while the other mystery man is speaking. There may be no sound, but I can already tell by the man's face and body language he is frustrated, even nervous. I've spent most of my life reading people. Observing them while picking up subtle details that others may miss. The man's fists clench often while he talks; his posture rigid as he shifts his weight from foot to foot. When you're unable to rely on hearing, it's important to hone in with your other senses. I study the squirrely man, watching his thin lips form mumbles of speech. I have no idea who he is, but I feel like I've seen him before. He speaks quickly, but I can make out a few words like, *she knows* and *it's time to do something*. My brother's vantage point can't change, so I anxiously wait for the conversing party to pivot, so I can read the other person's lips.

At long last, the other figure turns. Ice floods my veins. That confusing grin. Those somber eyes. It's… our uncle. I pause the video. Considering the name of the file, *"un."* Uncle Nicholas. He's the person of interest? But… he's family.

I tap the cursor to continue the video. Transfixed on each man's mouth, I dare not blink. My chest aches, as though the ice is expanding inside my lungs. Unwavering, I decode my uncle's steady words. *"I'm relying on you to feed me information about the Murray's. Keep close to Mary… I don't want her talking."* The other man waves his arms, firing back insults at my uncle. Both men appear to be at a standstill, frustrated and unwilling to budge. The unknown man speaks again, quickly. Either he says, *she's known the new kind of sin,* or *she knows the new kid's your son. Neither* make sense.

I replay the video multiple times for clarity, but the last part has me stumped. My uncle had no children. He never married either. I go back to the beginning. Skimming the letter then rereading the log. In an attempt to de-ice my core, I check the side table drawer. Rogue Twizzlers from Andrea's incredible skeleton candy board sit in bags. This is exactly what I need at this juncture.

Staring at the screen, I gnaw on the waxy treat, rewatching the video. I hope the sugar can kickstart my tired brain, aiding in rationalizing everything I just saw, in conjunction with what I already know. My brother was watching… no, not watching; following my uncle.

Nicholas is a Lombardi. That means… Nonno and Nonna brought these questionable traditions over from their home country. My father became a part of this family as a baby, back when my grandparents adopted him. So... was my initial analysis wrong? Was Nicholas the one who ran the Mafia all along? Are my parents aware of this? For the past three years, he's been the only family I've relied on. Leaning heavily on him when I felt as though my parents wouldn't listen to me. I used to look forward to our monthly breakfast. He let me vent, never interrupted me when I talked about my brother. I can't say the same about my parents. Always switching subjects as soon as I uttered his name. How could he just sit there and say nothing? Month after month, year after year, impassively listening to me pour my heart out. What was the point? Why bother?

Unless... I think the copious amount of candy just hit me. He was monitoring me.

Theo went to school to be an investigative journalist. All of this can't just be by coincidence. One time, he told me that journalists follow a code, sticking to the truth, reporting accuracy, offering fairness, and being completely transparent. I can't accept that anything my brother logged is fabrication. In fact, now I'm suspecting he went into this field on purpose. Did he have a hunch about Nicholas, even before the log was started? There's no real way of telling. He's not here. I've laid over his grave crying enough times to know, the dead don't talk. I knew my brother well. Clearly not everything, but he was never unhappy. He loved music, was within reach of his dream job, and had a committed partner... Theo did not take his own life. This I know to be true, with every bone in my body.

At the end of my rope here... licorice that is, I switch to picking at the edges of my nails. When my thumb slips off the nail bed and skims my ring finger, I feel the tiny scar from childhood. One of the few parts of me I adore, because it reminds me how we only grow through pain. Theo taught me that. Glancing through the log again. I review each entry with more consideration.

November 15th: Person of interest visits business just past Flaherty Way.

"Flaherty Way?" I feel like I've been down that street recently. Opening the web browser, I type in the road name. Dropping down to street-view, I stroll down virtually. Townhomes, a few restaurants, and a mail store. *Mail Haven.* I went there to drop off the embroidery hoops, after some lady bought all of them. I never expected to sell anything on the way home from the Craft Bazaar, but then she handed me an envelope full of money and the address, which led me there.

Holy crap... it's like the waterlogged, symbolic puzzle has inevitably dried up and the pieces are fitting together!

This time when I rewatching the video, I have a notepad, ready to record every word I can make out from my uncle and his accomplice.

Next thing I know, daylight is pouring into my bedroom and the alarm is vibrating next to my bedside. I must have fallen asleep at some point. My face feels sticky and damp. Fingers glide across the sides of my head, finding hearing aids still in place, "OWWW."

Rising from the puddle of drool on my pillow, I noticed my laptop screen is dark. A notepad lies next to it… everything rushes back. Dragging my sore, languid body from bed, I stumbled into the kitchen to find Andrea. I had so much to share; I didn't know where to begin. Without coffee or even visiting the bathroom, I unloaded it on her. This burden was too heavy to carry alone. I needed my friend, even though she hadn't explained herself. After I brought her up to speed on the microSD card, the evidence, and even the old photo I found, she seemed… off.

No rebuttals. No lectures about 'going to work' when she insisted I stayed in. Nothing. Did I break it? The only indicator she was still with me was the periodic chewing on her bottom lip.

Like a wind-up toy had finally been released, she stood from the table we both sat at. "I need to go."

My mouth hangs open, unable to form words.

"Stay home," she insists.

What? No… "We need to talk about how you know so—"

The door closes to our apartment, with my complicated roommate on the other side.

"Rude!" I call out, hoping she can hear me through the walls. Sure, I'll just put a pin in the fact that my 'con artist' of an uncle may have been the driving force behind my brother's death.

In line with me pulling my phone from the oversized hoodie pocket, a call comes in. *"Take a Deep Breath,"* fills the screen and for once I don't ignore the call. I press the green button.

"Cindel dear, are you alright?!" my mother cries.

"Yeah…? I'm fine. What would make you—"

She interrupts, "your uncle called. We're worried about you. He said you're showing the same signs as Theo. Are you home? Is Andrea there with you? She didn't answer…"

What? She called Andrea first, even though she's worried about me?

"Oh god, this is all our fault! We should have never let you stay in that awful city. Your father and I are coming to you. Pack a bag, you'll be returning to New York with us."

I didn't know if I wanted to scream or throw the phone across the room. Now? Of all the times I've expressed to my uncle how much I miss Theo.

How I wish it was me and not him that died... this very week is when he contacts my parents with concerns about my safety, right as I'm making progress? Right as I'm sure—

"Mom," I rush out.

She continues ranting, all the while barking orders at my father in the background. "Mom!"

She finally recognizes that I'm, in fact, still on the phone.

"I'm fine," I insist. "What did Uncle Nicholas say, exactly?" I can just make out heavy breaths on the other side of the phone. I'm apparently not the only one who needs to practice soothing techniques.

After long moments, she continues. "Well... he said you were acting odd. He's very concerned. He... ummm." The phone goes quiet.

"MOM," I bark.

I hear a popping sound through the receiver, as if she's letting out a long aggravated breath. "He said you've been drinking and sleeping around with strange men."

I throw my head back and laugh. At least he's finally telling the truth. Once I'm able to collect myself, I pivot the questioning toward my mother. "Do you believe everything he says?" Because I surely don't. At least not anymore.

"Of course, sweetheart. He's always had our family's best interest at heart. Yes, he can seem somewhat blunt at times, but your uncle wants to protect what's most important."

"What's most important—" I start, then stop.

Instantly, I see everything clearly. The facade he carefully put in place. How he moves around like a snake in the grass; ensuring no one notices the deceit, before he gets what he feels he's owed. Jealousy is an ugly emotion. One that has the ability to eat away a person from the inside out. My uncle.... Nicholas has likely been resentful throughout his entire life, regarding my father being welcomed into the family. Although Charles wasn't a full-blooded Lombardi, Nonna and Nonno chose my dad as the heir to their empire. It's always been about family! Just not in the way my parents think.

"Put dad on the phone!" I demand.

"Dear, your father is currently getting the luggage down from the attic, please just—" I don't allow her to continue.

"Now mother!" The phone goes silent. I check to make sure the minutes are still counting, before my father finally speaks.

"Cinnabun?"

I blow out a slow breath. Fighting against the urge to retreat, because it's the easier thing to do. If I'm wrong, what I'm about to say would be like opening Pandora's box. Things could never go back to the way they once were.

Good. I couldn't let Nicholas go on, getting away with… murder.

"Dad." I consider my next words before I start. "Your brother has never seen you as a Lombardi." The phone is silent, but he's still with me so I continue. "Nicholas has been running the family business. He's monopolizing the whole industry. Taking out competition, in an attempt to have some kind of strong hold over the city. Theo found out—"

My father's voice drops an octave, "Cindel."

I've had enough of treading carefully. "You lied to me!"

Silence. Time painfully lingers, as unnerving quiet filters in.

"Is Andrea there?" he ultimately asks.

My steely resolve splinters ahead of tears filling my vision. "Really?" my voice cracks. They want to know where she is? I understand I'll never be like Theo. The cultivated golden child, but have they replaced me? Is Andrea the daughter I never was? I always suspected they liked her better. My family is beyond twisted. No better than a storybook where the princess has been banished to a tower or cursed.

My father clears his throat, speaking more gently this time. "Cinnabun…"

No. I'm no damsel in distress. I will save myself this time. Pushing the red button, I end the call.

♪ ♫ ♩ ♫ ♪ ♫

Splashing water on my face and pulling on some pants, I tuck the microSD card into the front pocket of my jeans. I made the executive decision to head to Mail Haven today. After bashing a couple of keys on the alarm panel, I eventually figured out how to arm the damned thing and slipped out the door. Danger was still looming, and I thought it wise to at least utilize the confounded security system. It's odd really… how I've been brought to Mail Haven, twice in less than a month. Does Nicholas have a mailbox there? Would I be able to convince the shopkeeper there to tell me anything? I am *family*, after all.

When I entered the store, I found the same gentleman as before. Meticulously combed back hair embroidered polo shirt, all the while working diligently to take care of each customer as if he's being graded on his efficiency. Today is busier than last time.

I join the line, patiently scanning the room as he helps customers label and package items. I'm happy to see at least one of the customers in front of me has their box all taped up and ready to go. After a while, I've taken inventory of every poster and packing option around me, I begin absently tracing the outline of the tiny drive in my pocket. Even though there's a lot of people in the store, it's still fairly quiet. As if a librarian is ready to hush anyone that speaks above a whisper.

I hear something… distant. Are those drums or maybe bass?

I pivot, glancing out the windowed front, half expecting a car to slowly be driving by, with their windows open and music blasting, but I see no such scene. There are no speakers in the mail store either. There's definitely music... is it coming from me?

I dive into my bag to find the culprit buried at the bottom. Bingo!

Removing my hearing aid, I drop it into a pouch and pop the bustling device into my right ear.

The line moves up as I actively listen to the musical message. A harmonious male voice joins the beat of drums, producing a rock and funk sound in conjunction with the electric guitar. **311 – "Don't Stay Home"** plays through and it takes everything in me not to bob my head along. I can't help that it's a catchy song. I haven't communicated with Dax since I read the microSD card. Each song thus far has been cryptic yet laced with meaning. The current message is pretty straight forward.

I peer over my shoulder, again scanning the street. Why does there always seem to be some form of danger awaiting me around every turn?

The line moves forward, bringing an elderly man to the counter who wants to mail socks to his grandkids, but has nothing but an address.

I rock onto the balls of my feet, as the music unsettles me. Why can't I go home? Diving back into my bag, I search for my phone to text Dax.

"Next!" The small man behind the desk motions for me to move forward. Abandoning the task at hand I step closer to the counter.

"Yes. Hi, remember me?" I put on a sweet smile but he just looks back at me with a flat expression. Shit. I forgot what to ask.

As it is, my parents already think I'm spiraling out of control, meanwhile Dax is suggesting I avoid going home, and I'm fairly confident Nicholas would not appreciate anyone else seeing this. This is my only option.

"I'd like to mail something please." His face remains neutral, aside from one eyebrow rising. "Oh right." I shove my hand in my pocket, realizing I have to actually produce what I'd like to be sent off. "It's quite small, but extremely important. I need it to be discreet." I lowered my voice on the last part.

With all the composure of a qualified, seedy mail clerk, he nods once and shuffles over to another area behind the counter. Using a key adhered to his wrist coil, he opens a locked cabinet to reveal a collection of black boxes, each with a small padlock. He removes one of the containers before walking back to the counter, opening the lid for me.

"Place item inside." He closes his eyes and turns away in succession.

Okay…? We're the only two people in the shop, but I appreciate the notion.

I place the microSD card into the black box.

"Done?"

I nod before remembering his eyes are closed like a child playing hide and seek.

"Yes," I announce.

He snaps the metallic box lid shut. From his back pocket he places a worn spiral notepad on the counter between us. "Write name and address here." He taps his finger on the lined paper next to a pen on the counter.

Not much for small talk I see. I bet Dax would get along great with him. "I can do that. Thank you." I wrote down the address of the house I stayed at, when I visited the Catskills. My parents need to see this. I know they're still residing there. This card should be kept safe, especially if my uncle, half the Murrays, and maybe even Officer Kent may pose a threat.

The man hastily puts on the readers which hang from his neck. Reviewing the addressee, then glancing back at me, "Lombardi?" His once neutral expression softens, eyes widen, as the corner of his mouth raises gradually. A "hmm" sound escapes him despite his tight-lipped expression.

In the blink of an eye, he slips the paper with the address into the box, shuts, and locks the box with an even smaller key in his collection.

That's it?

He migrates over to some kind of label maker and begins changing over to a fresh roll.

Do I not pay because my family is a known Mafia name around these parts? Okay… this is awkward. I feel like I'm taking advantage. I should buy something. Clearing my throat, I pull out my wallet. "While I'm here. Could I purchase a book of stamps, please?"

He nods a few times and proceeds to the adjacent counter to retrieve the item. Giving him my card, he hands me a strip of forever stamps with festive Christmas trees. His face naturally creases when he smiles, nodding once again.

"Thank you." I leave with the stamps, feeling as though the universe is giving me the middle finger. I really fucking hate Christmas. Now all my outgoing mail will be christened with holiday cheer.

Outside Mail Haven, I finally have a moment to text Dax, but I find he's already sent me a message instead.

> Dax the Friendly Stalker: Don't go home.

I type back.

Cindel: I figured as much.

A few dots dance at the bottom of the thread, just ahead of another message.

Dax the Friendly Stalker: Where are you? You're not wearing your present.

Is he for real? I'm not wearing a plug whenever I'm not in his presence. My phone buzzes,

Dax the Friendly Stalker: Do you like being punished?

Christ… between him, my family, and the Murrays, I'm going to have a head full of gray before thirty! I look down at the taunting stickered trees in my hand. Punishment does seem to come naturally to me, as of late.

Dax the Friendly Stalker: Don't worry, Princess… I'll always find you. I have to run a quick errand, then I'll pick you up.

I began wandering, not sure where exactly, since I can't go home and I wasn't on the schedule. About three blocks from the mail store, I stop walking. Right in the middle of a crosswalk, people part trying to avoid running into me; I realized I forgot to get my credit card back.

"Fuck. Me." I turn on my heel to high tail it back to the store, before I'm forced to report the card as lost or stolen. Ugh! Can the cosmos please cut me some slack?!

I arrive back at Mail Haven, rather quickly. Out of breath, I push the shop door open, causing the little bell to ring overhead. The once well-lit store now has its front blinds drawn and half the lights out. Do they close for lunch?

"Hello?" I move toward the counter, finding no sign of the shop owner who helped me earlier. "I left my card here, by accident!" I call out, just in case he is in the back.

In a flash, the back door swings open, and the man comes out. He looks different... Wide eyes that bounce everywhere, damp under arms, and paler skin than earlier. "We closed!" he proclaims.

"Oh, I'm sorry. I just left my card here by mistake."

He shakes his head feverishly, "No. No card here! You leave." The once adept shop owner seemed dismissive, even aggravated that I am in the store again.

"Please, I was just here. Could you take a look?" I insist, with a service smile that has been perfected after many jobs in the industry.

The same door swings open from behind the counter, the man recoils just as a gum popping Jada walks into the room with us. "Is this what you're looking for?!" she asks, holding up the microSD card I just dropped into the pitch-black box, not ten minutes ago.

I couldn't form words nor coherent thoughts. What is she doing here and why the hell does she have that in her possession?! Too shocked by her sheer presence, I don't even notice the gun in her hand, pointing haphazardly at the shop owner. Now that he's turned, I spot his bound hands.

"Jada…?"

Her gum crackles between her teeth. "The one and only."

I'm confident that's not true, but her ego never could handle reality.

Removing the gum from her mouth, she saunters over to the shorter man, pressing the pink wad into his neatly styled hair. She then proceeds to drape an arm around his neck, positioning the weapon just under his chin. She looks too casual, as if she does this all the time.

"What are you doing here?!" I rush out. Too lost as to why this crazy bitch has a weapon; when I know for a fact, she mixes up whiskey versus rum, stating, "Well, they're both brown."

Jada tilts her head, in sync with pouting lips. "I was sent here. For this." She waves the tiny drive in her hand.

How… who? I final speak, "who sent you?"

She begins to laugh maniacally. Like, way too long.

The poor store owner looks terrified. I'm unsure if it's the gun or the gum, lodged within his thinning hair, that has him more upset.

Stepping back from her hostage, she gives me a wink right before she places the microSD card into her wide-open mouth. Positioned just between her molars, she crunches down like it's another stick of gum.

"NOOOO!!!"

The gun pivots from the man to directly at me.

I freeze.

The sound of cracking plastic between her teeth fills the space. Puffing out her cheeks, she spits the pieces to the ground.

More than wanting to cry out, I want to bash her face into the countertop.

A smirk blooms on Jada's face, in parallel with her eyes fluttering in triumph. It's more obvious than ever, the disdain she has for me. The way her misplaced feelings have grown into something equal to loathing.

"I think you know who sent me," she says, each word clipped.

Do I? At this point I believe anyone could have some kind of hand in this.

The once subdued man moves swiftly, like someone half his age, he moves toward Jada, drawing back his leg and kicking her hard enough to make her fall back onto a display of assorted boxes.

I dive for the counter, hopping over and down on the other side. It can't be lost! Maybe the microSD card can be fixed? The drive… it's not only crushed, but broken into pieces. I look to Jada who is already managing to right herself, then I realize the gun is on the floor.

Straightaway, I attempt to reach for the weapon, but she gets to it first. She raises her arm, barely aiming.

I cover my ears ahead of the thunderclap of the bullet being released from its chamber.

I don't feel hurt. I check myself; no blood. I turn. The target wasn't me, but the shop owner just behind me.

His once orange shirt now has an expanding crimson blot across his shoulder. Ultimately the red cascades down to his chest; red complimenting the orange. I watch in horror as he falls to his knees, unable to catch himself due to his tied hands. The wounded man lays face first on the floor. Unmoving.

"Is he…?"

Jada snickers.

Red fills my vision and I lunge for Jada. I don't know what's come over me. Maybe I am through feeling defenseless in every situation, or perhaps it's the way I just witnessed an innocent bystander get shot… but I am done being perceived as a broken girl, too fragile to handle anything. Driven by my pursuit for answers, regardless of how ugly this world can be. Theo taught me that life is precious, and I'll be damned if I let this crooked bitch fuck with mine!

We wrestle for the gun. Jada may me strong but I had an older brother who tussled with me, just for shits and giggles.

She pushes me and I push back, causing the gun to spin away from view as we both battle for it. On our feet, she turns to pick up the weapon, right before I grab a handful of her braids and pull.

She smiles, barely able to perceive me from the awkward angle I have her; somehow the gun is in her hand!

I let go of her hair and step back, hands raised.

The part between her eyes wrinkles as we stand facing one another. I used to think of her as confident and sexy. Now, I see the real Jada. Cold-hearted with nothing but heinous intent.

I turn and gasp at absolutely nothing.

Using the moment from the diversion I created, I step forward, thrusting my leg between her stance. I curl my calf behind her knee and push on her chest.

Jada loses her balance, tumbling backward and dropping the gun on impact.

Instinctively, I kick it away. I've never held a gun in my life, let alone used one before.

I lower myself onto her legs, pinning her in place. One arm secured beneath my weight while the other is caught behind her own body.

"You destroyed the only proof I had!" My teeth hurt with how hard I was clenching them.

She laughs, although marginally weaker this time. The smug girl licks the top of her teeth and I'm nearly compelled to position a box over her head, just so I didn't have to look at her.

"When Nicholas recruited me… I was more than on board to ruin your pathetic excuse of a life. Getting paid was just a bonus."

Nicholas? My Uncle Nicholas hired her to do this?

Lost in thought, she catches me off guard. Managing to free her once pinned arm, she sinks her nails into my forearm, like the savage little bitch she is.

The gun is too far, while there's not much else in reach without chancing Jada getting loose from my hold. On the counter above us, sits an industrial sized roll of green, stretch-plastic for shipping. I suck in through my teeth as she manages to dig her nails into me even more. "Ah, fuck!" Little swells of blood appear, preceding trickles of crimson, dancing down my arm. Goddamnit! What would Tony Soprano do?

"You don't deserve it! I should be the manager! The guys were mine, way before you ever showed up! Who would want a defective, flat-chested girl like you?!" she spits attempting to squirm out from under me. Her words are like venom. Jada's hold on me is relentless, showing no sign of being released. Clearly, she has no intent of letting me walk away from this.

With my free arm, I reach toward the heavy-duty packing material, wiggling my fingers till the wrap gives way. I yank toward me, allowing the roll to unravel its stretchy contents. In my peripheral, the idle shop owner is now lying in a pool of his own blood. I won't let that be my fate. With the opaque plastic, I make quick use of it by swinging my free arm around Jada's head.

Finally, her nails rip free from my arm, as she attempts to remove the wrapping from around her face.

My arm burns but I know she can hurt me with only one free hand. Lifting my knee, I shift my weight to her chest, then settle once again on top of her. With one arm still pinned behind her back, she switches between pulling the plastic from her face to clawing at my jeans.

Jada battles to free from her airways.

I want… no, I need to be the one to survive this. For Theo. For myself! Extracting more of the stretch-cling from the roll, I tirelessly make wide circles, encompassing her entire head.

Her trashy stiletto nails claw at the suffocating layers, but it's puncture proof to ensure packages are nice and secure.

Good luck breathing. I don't know how long I've been wrapping her, but I hear the hollow tube spin as I reach the end of the roll. I can't help but glance back at the shop owner. There's blood everywhere. I grasp the clingy wrap on either side of her head and push downward, so it's flush with her skin. Tiny rivers of blood flow down my arm as I press with all my might. Her body bucks and arms flail, but it's no use. I have her pinned to the ground. A fragment of the microSD card sits next to us. It was the last thing I had of my brother! The only way to prove he didn't take his own life! I inch upward, onto her chest with my full weight.

"AHHHHHH!" I scream, and it becomes my battle cry.

I scream at her, at my family, I scream for Theo. They're supposed to be my family. Why? Why all the lies?! I strain, fantasizing how I'm able to extract all the answers from those who have wronged me. Finally reaching retribution. Drops of my blood eventually make it onto the green plastic, just as the fight leaves her body and her arms fall to the sides. Everything is still. Mouth fully open, her eyes seemed to bore into me, despite the egregious layers of translucent emerald film.

I reach for the counter and pull myself up. Another dispenser catches my eye. Peeling off a sticker from the reel, I slap a *"Fragile"* sticker over her creepy stare. I chuckle to myself, "Who's breakable now?" My hands shake, clearly adrenaline still surges through me, and the room wobbles. I lower myself to the floor and crawl over to the shop owner. Remarkably, his chest is still moving.

The bell above the door jingles.

Oh fuck! Someone's here! What if it's Nicholas? Or worse… Mairead and her father!

I curl up in a ball. I'm going to jail. Shit. I can't just sit here. I crawl closer, peeking through a small crack in the partisan, where I find a wild-eyed Dax, taking in the scene, just past the counter. He takes out his phone, appearing to be typing something, then puts it back in his pocket. By the time I realize I can't see him through the seam any longer, he is next to me.

Extending a hand, he helps me to stand, taking in my bloodied arm. His eyes darken, looking murderous over my minor injuries, heedless of the carnage around us. Leading me through a back door, we exit into an alley where I find his car. He doesn't stop, as if not allowing me to overthink what just happened. Ripping from Dax's hold, I try to make it to one of the trash cans, only to come up short, emptying my stomach onto the cracked concrete beside. A hand gently presses to my back. Small circles soothe me as the other holds back my hair, just ahead of another wave of sickness pouring from me.

This time, bile speckles my shoes. I must be a sight. Gross and disheveled, however Dax handles me like I'm something precious.

Carefully, he escorts me to his vehicle, helps me in, and buckles my belt. Next, he rounds the Camaro and turns on the car. We drive smoothly away from the scene, although my body still quakes. His hand rests on my thigh, as if saying, "it's going to be okay," all without a word. Multiple blocks from Mail Haven, an ambulance rushes by as we head toward the interstate. Did he call for an ambulance?

I'm glad the store owner was still alive, but can he survive such an injury? Too rattled to actually speak... I close my eyes, only to visualize a body surrounded by a growing ruby puddle. My eyelids pop open.

"Where are we going?" I ask, voice hoarse.

He removes his hand from my thigh to bring his fingers and thumb together, to form a flat "O" shape. Pressing his hand beside his mouth, then moving slightly upward toward his ear, touching again at the top of his jawbone, with the same closed hand. *Home,* he signs.

NICHOLAS

"Sir, there's a lot of activity over here on the Murray's side of town. I think your little problem is going to take care of itself." I rub my thumb across my chin feeling a spot of stubble, I neglected to shave this morning. "Ouch! Be careful, woman!"

The manicurist fumbles with the nail trimmers, apologizing profusely while tending to my feet. This is just one of the many ways I have to care for my health, at this stage in life. Another burden I must bear.

"Next time you call me, make sure you have actual confirmation and Kent, keep watch! It seems my son's loyalty has switched sides as of recently." I hit the red button on my phone, watching as the nervous girl tries to shape my nails exactly as I instructed. My usual nail tech is unavailable. Kids these days, no work ethic.

I alternate between watching people rush past the salon window on the busy streets and playing Candy Crush on my phone. This shitty little game is extremely addicting. Ironic how just a handful of sweets like these could put me in an early grave, but it passes the time, nonetheless. Maybe I indulged in too many delicious things at a young age and this is my retribution... a cunning spawn of a child and bouts of neuropathy from the knee down.

I only made the new girl cry on three occasions, by the time I left. Amy said it was on the house this week. Why is it that people only try to do better, after you threaten them?

Even though I have eyes on the streets and informants where I need them, I need to confirm that my secrets are buried, along with the ones who carry them. I've worked too hard to watch all my plans go to shit over my illegitimate niece, happening upon information she has no business learning. You know how many breakfasts I've had to sit through, just to ensure she was every bit in the dark as I've orchestrated for her to be?

As oblivious as she may have been, it was only a matter of time before she found anything her brother left behind. The problem is, I don't know how much was recorded. I knew he was tailing me for a few weeks before I finally confronted Theo in his apartment. Such a shame. He had so much potential with his skill set. It was all too easy, making his murder look like a drug overdose. There wasn't a dry eye at the funeral. I may have implied to dear old mom and dad that the Murrays were behind the death of their beloved son. They never said yes… but they didn't say no, either. I made the hard decision because I'm a good big brother like that.

That was a very happy New Year indeed, because I got rid of not one, but two problems within a few days' time. Mary's slender neck fit so beautifully between my hands. She was just as fiery as she was thirty years ago. I couldn't take all the credit though. I had to keep the reputation squeaky clean and all. Who else would be around to finish off the entire Murray family? Years ago, I planted one of my top guys in the Irish gang. He quickly worked his way up to 'protection detail' of the immediate family. It's a shame he had to take the fall, but he was in the right place at the right time. When he told me about Mary recognizing her son, I had to quiet her. Patrick, the hot head, popped my guy in the back of the head before he could even ask him a single question. Everything wrapped up so nicely. This city was as good as mine…

Chess is rather simple. Now… you would think it's ideal to have all your best pieces closest to you, protecting the king…. but the trick is to disperse your force across the board. It's harder for your adversary to anticipate what's coming next.

My brother was always a shit chess player and a sore sport. Even as a child my end game was never winning, but seeing him lose. Seeing the look of defeat on his face, was like igniting a flame in the depths of my darkened soul. There was a brief time that I tried to be good. Play by the rules. Yet, no matter how hard I tried… attempting to prove to my father that I was born for this role, Charles still came out on top. The son they always wanted.

When my father decided to leave the family legacy to him, I promised myself that one day… I would squeeze every last ounce of joy, from my bastardo brother. I'm a patient man, so I started small. Growing the list of names in my own book and beginning a side business, so to speak. While my brother was busy playing devoted husband, I extended my reach to office officials in the city, including the Boston PD. He may have thought he ran the family business from his position but I was the one operating the levers.

There came a point when I had to drive a wedge between the Lombardis and Murrays. The two families were growing close. Enjoying weekly dinners. It made me sick. An alliance so strong could ruin my carefully laid plans. Be my undoing. I needed some kind of leverage. My people advised me that

Mary Murray, the girl I had a quick romp with as a young man, wound up running off to Ireland. Allegedly, she delivered a secret child while away. Our child. That was many years ago, but when she went back to visit, news found its way to me.

Thereafter, I paid a quick visit to one of my brother's weekly 'Sunday gravy's' with their dear friends the Murrays. I kindly explained to Mary what I could do, how I was very capable of still ruining her life. She eventually came to her senses and I had a name for our bouncing boy. That week, I hopped a plane to Ireland so I could bring home the kid. To this day, Daxton still believes his mother was some whore I picked up in a bar. Told him I didn't even know about him, but once I did I came straight to Ireland to get him. Which is still a half-truth. I didn't know for sure.

He had my eyes. There was no doubt the spawn was mine and I was going to use him to my full advantage. Keeping the boy mostly out of sight, until he was ready. Homeschooling and private lessons helped him grow, while I had the freedom to continue coming and going as I pleased. When my idiot brother started confiding in Patrick Murray more than me, I decided it was time to take away the most precious thing in the world to him. His children. Business should stay 'in the family.'

Outsourcing the job was the best option to keep everything neat and tidy, but they did a shit job. What was made to look like a gas explosion, left only one kid injured but both very much alive. The result wasn't too bad though; it caused my brother and his wife Terri to go into hiding. It's funny how mistakes can sometimes work in your favor... my brother became paranoid enough to change their name! Good. He doesn't fucking deserve to hold the Lombardi status.

He wouldn't leave the city though, still holding onto the reins tightly. They moved a lot, in an attempt to stay hidden from whoever tried to harm their little ones. Ironically, the one who actually called the hit, knows exactly where they are at all times. Charles may have looked up to me at some point in our childhood but I had a feeling he never trusted me.

With my brother, somewhat out of the way, the Murrays became the biggest threat. Their gambling operations were sloppy at best. After learning as much as I could from the inside, I arranged for the Boston PD to come knocking at their establishments, no less than twice a month. Officer Kent was a vital asset, ensuring the Murray family stayed just beneath my thumb.

Currently, I'm questioning if I ever should have taken Dax in the first place. He's disobeying orders and has been damn near unreachable, far too often. When I placed him within the Murrays' inner circle, it was only a means to an end. It would be nice to eradicate the Murray family as a whole. Haven't I waited long enough?

The queen was knocked off the board and Dax was perfectly positioned to finish off the man who considers himself a "king." That was until he ran off to Ireland, heartbroken and put that boy Eamon in charge. I knew he'd be a thorn in my side as soon as he and Theo found each other again at college. Theo was a smart boy, but he should have kept his nose out of my business.

With Patrick gone over the past couple years, his boy did a fairly decent job of vetting the people he surrounded himself with. Surprisingly, Dax permanently earned the Murray's trust after a nearly fatal injury while on a job. While he was recovering, Eamon learned about a hidden Lombardi. His family still believes they were to blame for their business woes and now, for the death of Mary. A little birdie may have spread the rumor to move things along.

The Murray's sole focus has been on the Lombardis… on Cindel. Dax was tasked with watching her. He's been instructed to report back to me on anything she may have learned, especially any evidence she stumbled upon. If she caught on to what really happened to her brother, my protégé was instructed to neutralize the threat. I'm still unsure what incriminating evidence Theo had on me, but if it ever got out, Charles would hunt me to the ends of the earth. Fuck my brother! He doesn't get to have it all! He couldn't even put his pathetic family aside for a second, to embrace the power he was so freely gifted.

That Jada girl was a last-minute addition. She practically begged me to let her kill Cindel, but she had to deliver first. Find whatever evidence Cindel has and destroy it, then she is free to do whatever she wants with her. Jada had better succeed, because Dax hasn't exactly been forthcoming in matters that pertain to his cousin. As Kent put it over the phone, "My problems are about taking care of themselves."

Apparently, Patrick and his daughter are on their way to Cindel now. They actually believe being a Lombardi makes her at fault. I'm not going to argue with their logic. My brother has defaced our family name and he doesn't even use it anymore. Even though I am a full-blooded Lombardi; I opted not to use my real name with my accomplices. Patrick in his prime, went by "Paddy Muscles," I however am unknown. I don't ever give my subordinates a name. I'm a ghost. Better than my ancestry. Fuck my father and fuck Charles for dirtying the bloodline.

On the walk back to my place, I text the saved contact, *Spawn*. Quickly, typing out the message.

> Ghost: I'm disappointed in you, son. I thought you would be the one to handle this.

I hit send, then place the phone back in my coat pocket, before rubbing my hands together in an attempt to keep warm. Every year, I swear it is colder than the last. I should be somewhere tropical at this age, but my stubborn nature and desire to take back what's rightfully mine keeps me going. I've had men tell me; I survive purely out of spite.

Just ahead, I see one of my sales reps on the street. He's a chatty guy who seems to know everyone's business, no matter what part of town they're from. I tolerate the incessant rambling in small doses because, not only does he have good intel, but he can push drugs faster than anyone else in Southie. If he plays his cards right, he could be climbing the ranks by next season, when the books are open.

"Hello sir! Brisk day we're having."

I nod continuing to rub my hands together without relief. Damn neuropathy.

"The crew says, you may be celebrating the holidays early this year."

I check my wristwatch then cross my arms, hoping he'll get to the point faster.

"What I'm getting at sir is… I hope you keep me in mind when you get what's yours." He extends an elbow to bump me in the arm.

I sidestep the gesture.

"I'm very familiar when it comes to the gambling department," he adds with an over exaggerated wink.

Fuck it, he's more obnoxious than useful. His body will be nestled within a slab of new townhouses going up on Fifth Street, by next week. My irritated breath condensates between us just before I turn and walk away. I don't even bother with pleasantries as I continue toward my warmer destination.

The corner gossip shouts after me, "Have a nice day, sir!"

With a hot, black coffee and the feeling returning to my extremities, I reexamine various upcoming contracts and loans. I have two developers and three construction firms working with me on a two-billion-dollar condo building going up on Harrison Avenue. Acting as the middleman, I should be able to skim hundreds of thousands of dollars off the top, once development has concluded. Still, all this effortless money hasn't brought me a shred of joy. That is until I dismantle the brick and mortar that surrounds the Murrays. With the shell company in Delaware and a fictitious name holding a trust fund, it's been quite simple to buy up land around the city for a fraction of the price. All you need is a couple unfortunate incidents to occur, making the area less desirable. Thanks to my friend in the Boston PD, raids should drive down the land value. In comes a developer to buy up the insolvent land, level those red-headed mick's bread and butter, and bada bing bada boom, I'm the last man standing with an incredible bay view. Now that my brother is living out of state, it's even easier to run things my way. Just as I drain the mug, the bottom of the cup reveals grinds.

My phone chirps.

> Kent: Sir, the Murrays are heading to Cindel's apartment.

As we expected.

I lean back in my chair, pleased as pie my once obstacles are now collapsing in on themselves. Like a blackhole, the girl seems to suck everything in with her. Even people who have nothing to do with her turn up dead, just from being in her orbit.

I sent Kent to question Cindel on the matter of Craig Moore. I suspect that wackadoo, sister of Eamon's, had something to do with it. Little minx is the spitting image of her mother, yet wild as a hungry polar bear. She may be just crazy enough to get rid of Cindel for me. What I can't figure out is, why was that slob Craig significant enough to assassinate? Did he know something or did he just piss off the wrong person?

With both Lombardi kids gone, I may not even have much of a use for Dax, any longer. He hasn't been following orders. If Jada accomplishes her task, maybe she'll replace the useless boy.

One last play will put me in check with my dear brother Charles. I plan to take my sweet time, ensuring he reflects on his transgressions against "his family." If I'm feeling generous, I might let him watch as I make his wife scream my name. Perhaps I'll record the session. Then I can rewatch as the light leaves his eyes, again and again. My game, checkmate.

FORTY-ONE

DAX

I'm not sure if it's the smell of the jerk chicken or the adrenaline coursing through Cindel, but she manages to throw up two more times between my car and the front door to my apartment.

My arm steadies her quaking body, wrapped firmly around her waist, as we steadily climb the small staircase beside 'Caribbean Cuisine.' I can't say I've ever felt more self-conscious than right now, but having her here in my home makes me feel… exposed. This life has conditioned me to keep my true-self concealed at all times. I'm not sure if I know how to let my guard down.

Her eyes bounce around the room nervously as she lowers herself onto the couch. She's quietly assessing, rigid despite the soft seat. I leave the room for only a moment, to grab the first aid kit in the bathroom, coming back to find her legs pulled into herself, still surveying the space. I give a low-intensity whistle just as I enter the room, so as not to spook the already uneasy girl. She's had a rough go in recent days. I wouldn't trust anyone at this point, especially not me.

Unhurried, I clean and bandage the wound on her arm. Then head to the kitchen to fetch a glass full of water and a half-eaten box of sour, gummy worms from the counter. It's a new habit I picked up from the blue-eyed goddess in my living room. I never allowed myself to enjoy something as trivial as candy until I was entrusted to watch her.

When I turn the corner, I find Cindel is no longer where I left her. After checking the hallway, the bathroom, and the office, I find her in my bedroom of all places with her back to me, frozen before my bed. She's still, simply taking in the space including the wall surrounding my bed. Shit. I was hoping to disclose this at a later time. I place the drink and most likely stale candy on the dresser beside me.

She doesn't even turn to acknowledge my presence, instead, she steps closer to the wall, reaching out to trace the circular, wooden frame. I remain motionless, patient. Unsure if her current state will yield a negative reaction to this new finding. Long moments pass as she takes it all in.

Suddenly, she turns to face me. "How…?" she marvels. Her vast ocean orbs, teeming with red swollen exhaustion. She looks down to the floor, then back up to me. "It was you! You're the one who bought them." More of a realization than a question.

Her skin appears a touch paler, and I worry she may start to cry, pass out, or even puke again. It could be any of the three, and I gauge how far away I am from catching her versus the closest bin.

Cindel returns to scanning the wall that was bare up until recently. Her gaze eventually travels back to me. Color returns to her cheeks, reassuring me she's not about to fall over. I roll back my shoulders, bracing for however she may react. I'm not ashamed of what I've done, but how she feels, what she thinks… matters more than anything at this point. This is all so new to me.

The next question out of her mouth makes things more complicated, "Why?"

I didn't even know why. How was I supposed to answer that? As I reflect, I try to look anywhere but at her tired, desperate face. I'm drawn to an intriguing dark knot that resembles a sheep, on one of the wooden floorboards. My throat feels tighter than usual. Instinctively, I rub at the irregular, raised scar across my neck. Ultimately, my eyes climb back up to hers and I shrug. Yeah… I'm a full-fledged asshat.

With eyes blown out, mascara slightly smudged, her face is unreadable… a sleeping volcano, of possible cataclysmic destruction. I watch as her face morphs. The corners of her eyes wrinkle, pink lips turn upward, and her cheeks puff out. She folds in on herself, grabbing her stomach and laughs. A full-on belly laugh, complete with an animated head toss.

Damnit. I think I broke her. Decisively, I remain unmoved, just watching as she ultimately collects herself, and wipes a rogue tear from under her eye.

"What a crap-tastic week. Seriously, I don't think anything else could possibly surprise me at this point."

If she only knew.

She moves past me, as if nothing had transpired, nabbing the box of sour worms on her way out.

I follow her out of the room, a few steps behind. Cindel drops a yellow and red gummy into her mouth, after plopping back down onto the worn sofa. Following suit, I position myself on the arm of an adjacent chair, watching this incredible creature go from zero to sixty, with only one citric-acid chew. Phone in hand, I type out a message for her to read, as she continues to polish off her snack.

I extended the screen toward her. *Do you want to talk about it?* My phone vibrates at the same time as she views my message. Tipping the screen back toward me, I catch the banner across the top.

Warden: I'm disappointed in you, son. I thought you would be the one to handle this.

I can't help but notice how Cindel lowers her gaze even farther. She definitely saw that. Crap. Nothing too damning was said, right? I mean… aren't all fathers disappointed in their sons to some degree? I wish I knew what she was thinking. Subtitles that just materialized right above her when she wasn't speaking. There's no stopping this trajectory. It's inevitable. Cindel will find out the truth. If given the option, I would remove the only one who knows how I truly relate to all of this. That answer was clear… but could I really kill my warden?

Everything is different. No longer will I be forced to do his bidding. She's mine. Fuck the game plan. She unwraps one of her arms from her body and drops another colored worm into her mouth. All at once I realize, I need her more than she needs me. Yes… I pursued her. Watched her. Manipulated her… but she's come this far because of her own determination. She never changed. I did. Cindel simply recognized who she's been all along. When I swore to protect her, she was the one to save herself. I may have destroyed plenty of lives over the years, but she has the power to destroy me. I wish we could hide from all of this. I want nothing more than to throw her over my shoulder and worship her for days in a remote cabin in the woods. Regardless of how I want time to stand still, I know she needs closure. She is within arm's reach of answers and I am not about to pull her away. I couldn't live with myself if I robbed her of this. My only question now is, will she still want to keep me, once she knows who I am?

"Jada destroyed it," Cindel finally asserts. She sounds so broken. "The only proof I had." It's hard to tell if she's about to cry or is completely disconnected from reality. I fight the urge to reach for her, I know she has more to disclose. "There was a recording on the drive. It was a video at some old warehouse, by the bay. My brother witnessed my uncle and two other men meeting."

I can't breathe. Warehouse? The warehouse? Was I there?! Could she have seen me in the video? I dare not draw breath. I wait, listen, and try to remain still as she shares at her own pace.

"I didn't see one of the men in the video. Theo logged that the younger man left, before he was able to start recording." She chews her bottom lip while collecting her thoughts. Cindel licks her lips and continues. "The man my uncle was talking to looked familiar. I don't know how, but I could have sworn I've seen him somewhere before. Maybe an old friend of his?"

I know exactly who she is referring to and yes, he was indeed a long-time accomplice of my father's, but he's not around anymore. He's the one who took the blame for Mary's death. Nicholas placed him into the Murray's circle, years prior. When my father found himself needing an out, he pushed his *"friend"* to the front of the line. He took the blame for a senseless act of violence. Shot on the spot. Years later, I still can't fathom why he took the life of Mary Murray. Maybe to start a war? There's no questioning what drives the great Nicholas Lombardi.

Cindel was supposed to remain hidden from her condemned past. I suppose there is no keeping her from this, once the Murrays learned Cindel was a Lombardi. Craig Moore had a very loose tongue when I paid him a visit. Exposing his cousin was in fact Alex, the conniving snake who was loyal to no one but himself. He's the one who told Brodi that Cindel was a Lombardi. Information is currency. They worked out a deal so neither party would get caught stealing from the house. It was supposed to be their ticket to freedom. Too bad, shit always has a way of catching up with you. Before I could ensure Cindel's identity stayed hidden, Brodi pulled that fucking knife. Garron didn't follow the plan. He was supposed to wait in the car so he wouldn't learn about a Lombardi in the midst of all of this. Good thing he never listens... I wouldn't be here right now if it weren't for him. Eamon learned about Cindel, pulling her into his world immediately. Things began to quickly unravel as the Murrays suspected corruption in their midst. Alex was brought in for questioning. I was tasked with protecting Nicholas' interests, but instead, I kicked a hole in his face for her. He was the reason she couldn't continue to live out a seemingly normal life. A small part of me believes in fate. If these events hadn't happened, she wouldn't be here with me.

"Theo's logs..." she continues. "The video he took... everything was centered around my uncle. My brother wasn't depressed, nor was he paranoid. He chased the truth and apparently died trying!" Her shoulders shake as she grips the edge of her seat. A tear falls free, then another slides down her cheek, just as she attempts to wipe them away with her wrapped forearm. "Will you help me?" She insists. "With my uncle that is... I know who you work for and I've seen what you're capable of." She believes I'm only employed by the Murray family. "Please!" she begs. "I can't go on not knowing if my uncle played a part in all of this... in my brother's death. What if he's some kind of serial killer? This might not be his only kill." She lowers her voice, practically whispering her next words. "What if he killed Mary?"

My woman is so fucking smart, she's gonna have it all figured out in no time. How unfortunate for me.

Cindel rests her head atop her knees, merely staring blankly out the hazy apartment window. Using the text to speech app, I write out what I'm unable to say.

"If you follow this path, there's no going back. He will answer for what he's done. With that said, I can't shield you from hard truths. I can only promise I will be right there, by your side."

Her small body unfurls from its position and she reaches for me. Without hesitation, I pull her onto my lap, sliding my hand up her back and cradling the base of her neck. I draw her closer, taking her bottom lip into my mouth. Her salty flesh reminds me just how selfish I can be. How those tears are just the beginning of what I will bring. My cock grows beneath her, as I take in the sweet notes of honey from her hair, combined with a lingering scent of industrial-grade plastic. The unique aroma echoes both life and death. Cindel was made for me.

Her delicate hand raises to face, "We can't." She pulls back, head turning from me as she speaks. "I need to make sure Andrea's safe. I dragged her into this mess and now she's at risk."

It's hard. Physically and metaphorically speaking, as she drags herself off of me. I'm set adrift, without her touch. She heads toward the door, freezing before she touches the handle.

"Will you come with me?"

Did Casper ever abandon Kat? Never. The question was adorably unnecessary. I would follow her until the end of time. Even when she hates me. It's just a matter of time until she learns the whole story.

The drive back to her place is quiet, but I can tell by the way she wiggles in her seat she's anxious to get to her friend. She attempted calling, even texting Andrea with no response, but that's not too unusual for her.

We walk up to her apartment floor; she gets out the keys and proceeds to unlock the door.

"That's strange. It's not locked."

An uneasy feeling creeps up my spine, causing me to instinctively pull Cindel behind me. I push open the door, revealing the dark apartment. She follows behind, fisting the bottom of my shirt as we enter. Nothing seems out of the ordinary… yet.

She gently knocks on her roommate's door, muttering, "Andrea?" I motion to her; finger raised to my lips. Turning the knob, I enter the room first. Right away, I notice a lamp has toppled on its side, glass litters the area rug.

Cindel gasps as she peeks past me. Did I just lead her into a trap? My phone vibrates and I ignore it. At this point, I don't care who's trying to reach me. The once ajar door creaks, gradually closing on its own. The heat kicks on in the apartment right before the door slams, relatching itself with a metallic thunk.

Pivoting toward her, I quickly cover her mouth and pull her close to my body, just as her muffled scream escapes. Someone could still be here. On the back of the door is a note affixed by a switchblade. The knife is dug deep into the wood. I release Cindel. Clearly, whoever was here is gone.

She steps forward and pulls down the note.

"IF YOU DO NOT PROVIDE PROOF OF INNOCENCE BY SUN UP TOMOR-
ROW, YOUR FRIEND WILL BECOME MY NEW PLAYTHING —M."

Tears begin to stream down Cindel's face again. I've never seen someone cry so much and it guts me. I don't know how this girl has any tears left at this point.

"This is all my fault. I have to do something!" She pulls out her phone, mashing a number from her favorites, before holding the phone to her head. "Eamon!" Cindel's voice cracks, as she tries to clear her throat before speaking again.

He's saved as a favorite? I make a mental note to delete that from her phone later.

"They took her," she blurts. "They took Andrea! The evidence I found is gone too."

I can hear a deep muffled voice from the other side of the phone.

"Okay. Yeah… I'm heading over now." Once she ends the call, Cindel faces me. "Eamon thinks he knows where they took Andrea. He said something about a tracker."

Well, this is an interesting turn of events. Eamon helping Cindel, against his family's wishes? Won't he be in for a surprise when he goes from unable to reach me to me showing up in tow. I'm sure he won't mind that I now hold Cindel's romantic attention. It's not like Eamon was ever competition to me on that front. I know he only pursued her on his father's order. The daddy-daughter duo had grown impatient.

Now, I'm not sure how we're going to convince them that neither Cindel nor her family had anything to do with Mrs. Murray's death. The only concrete proof was destroyed.

I called Garron in to clean up the mess at Mail Haven. Fucking Jada. Leave it to Nicholas to always have an extra insurance policy. I never saw her coming. My attention has been solely on Cindel as of late and I've clearly grown too comfortable.

On the ride over I can make out Cindel's stomach so clearly, I make a detour to the best deli shop in town. After I encourage her to pick something off the menu that isn't doused in sugar, she finally selected a ham, egg, and cheese bagel. She demolishes it right before we arrive, the pink hue to her cheeks fades back to normal.

I used to care about this car, now with faint traces of blood and bagel crumbs scattered throughout the passenger seat, I notice my priorities have changed. I throw the keys to an attendant at Eamon's swanky apartment off the harbor. Eamon never bothered me much. I even grew to like him over the years, but as soon as we entered that elevator, something instinctual comes over me. I move, pinning Cindel against the metallic wall to make a point to everyone and destiny itself… mine. Even once she discovers who I am to her. She'll hate me, but I'll always belong to her.

As expected, she instantly succumbs to my will. Melting from my touch as I take her earlobe into my mouth, soon moving across her jaw, where I finally land a consuming kiss onto her lips. I'll never grow tired of her. She's so sweet. I can't understand what she possibly sees in me. I might as well enjoy it while it lasts. The elevator chimes as it reaches Eamon's floor. We turn to find Connor standing before us.

"Hmmph…" a throaty sound comes from him. "Never thought you'd bag this one," he muses.

What's he doing here? Cindel looks up to me with pure confusion, just as Eamon rounds the corner joining Connor's side, as we continue this peculiar standoff.

"Hey, you got here fast," Eamon stammers as he tucks in the tail of the dress shirt into his pants. "Come in."

A coy smile plays on Connor's face as we trade places, him entering the elevator as we invade Eamon's home. For a moment, a similar expression paints Eamon's features. A look two people share, when they know each other intimately. Connor nods to us as the shiny doors to the elevator close, leaving the three of us alone.

Cindel and I regard each other. How the fuck did we both miss this? Of course, Eamon has moved on from Theo. It's been three years. Good for him. Connor's a stand-up guy.

"So… how long has this been going on?" Eamon ask, now leaning against the kitchen counter, his arms crossed in an assessing stance.

Cindel fiddles with the bottom of her hoodie, while I settle onto a seat at the fancy marble island. "Oh. Well, it's umm… it's relatively new?"

She's fucking adorable when she gets like this.

Eamon looks at me, gauging if I could be more than what I appear. If only he knew. He turns his attention back to Cindel.

"I suppose with you learning more about the past, it was only a matter of time before you discovered my motives with you were purely transactional. Forgive me for courting you under false pretenses. I was trying to keep you safe." He looks sincere yet full of regret. "You're too good for any of us, Cindel."

The comment instantly sends heat crawling up my neck. Okay, enough of the kumbaya bullshit. We don't need to state the obvious right now.

"Eamon." Cindel all but reads the room, steering the conversation elsewhere. "The evidence I told you about. It was a microSD card… it's broken. Jada—"

Eamon holds up a hand, cutting her off mid-sentence. "I know. Garron told me. He's the one your boy-toy called in, to clean up."

Cindel bites her bottom lip at the pet name. I've always known Eamon was a smart guy. I should have figured he'd know about us, before we ever got here. Cindel moves to my side before she continues.

"Andrea's been taken. I think it was Mairead."

Eamon leans forward, placing his hands upon the massive polished counter between us. "I have no doubt that she's behind this. My father's gone off the deep end... ever since my mother died. As soon as he was back in town, I put a tracker in a box of cigars I gave him. He doesn't go long without one, so wherever he goes, I know he has his trusty box of smokes. I can show you where he's taken your roommate." He opens an app on his phone, displaying a map of the area. A green dot is positioned on the other side of town, looks to be in the old club district.

"Eamon, I don't know how to prove my family didn't kill your mother. The only proof I had is ruined. It was the only thing I found in Thelma's hide." Cindel begins to pace the length of the room. We watch in silence as she darts back and forth across the kitchen.

Eamon rubs at his five o'clock shadow, before he asks, "You found the drive in Thelma's tank?"

She nods.

His face is difficult to read. "Come on." His words are rushed as he grabs a jacket off the back of a chair. "My sister can be a wicked thing when she has someone beneath her knife."

Any progress I've made at helping Cindel return to her usual coloring has reverted, thanks to Eamon's dark premonition. She resembles an animatronic as we make our way back out to my car, simply functioning but without resolve. I could care less that Eamon is on board, because I've been waiting for the right time to play this song for Cindel. When I was on my way to Mail Haven, I planned for the worst. However, when I found her upright, alive, and capable of shrink wrapping someone till suffocation; I knew I'd found my soulmate, then and there.

Connecting the Bluetooth through an updated sound system, I queue up the ideal song, **Deftones - "Change."** I can see one of Eamon's eyebrows lift from the rear-view mirror, but he knowingly keeps his mouth shut. Cindel is uncommunicative, gazing through the window as we make our way to the location on Eamon's map.

I park far enough away, so we aren't seen upon approach. Following Eamon through an alley between two brick buildings, he enters the building first through a back door. Cindel enters next, followed by me. Noiselessly, we navigate the dark halls filled with stacked stools, tables, and wooden crates of dust covered bottles.

As we venture deeper into the building, we start to hear voices. When we reach a turn, Eamon stops. He motions for me to look around the corner as well. Cindel remains a few steps behind as I move forward to see just beyond. Eamon and I must share a similar look of dismay, because I never would have anticipated this.

Andrea's silver hair shakes from side to side as she sits cross-legged upon a desk, with Mairead opposite her. An open box of pizza sits between them, while they share a laugh about god knows what. Patrick, their revered father, is asleep on a tattered couch on the other side of the room.

Cindel pushed past us, blurting out the question we all have on our minds, "What the fuck?!"

FORTY-TWO

ANDREA

"Where is she?!" My fingers are so tightly clenched into my palms the tips start to lose feeling. I peer through the apartment window again, down the street, and STILL no sign of Cindel. The security system is armed, but it seems she left hours ago.

I specifically told her to stay put. I went back out to see Moyra; this time we met at the bus stop. In her hand is a suitcase. She's leaving town for a bit, but she wanted to meet in-person one more time.

"I know who you work for, Andrea," she announces as I walk up and sit beside her on the bench. "The way you carried yourself, even before you spoke, I knew who you were employed by."

I lower myself to the bench, allowing her to continue without interjection.

"He was such a good student. Always wanted to find all the possible information, before delivering the story. I still use some of his papers today, as examples." Moyra scans the people around us. She has on gloves and a hat, almost in an attempt to stay anonymous. Hidden. She smooths out her knee length skirt with her hands. "Your time is valuable and since this will be the last time we meet, I will cut right to the chase."

I cross my legs and lean forward toward the uneasy woman.

"My ex-husband was assigned to Theo's case. I overheard what he said on the phone." Her voice cracks, barely above a whisper. "He was paid off to report it as a suicide."

I sit for a while. Long after the Greyhound pulled away with Moyra inside. My phone buzzing nonstop; however, I just can't bring myself to answer any of them.

I make a pit stop at the barber shop and ask my contact if he can get the squad car number for Officer Kent and send it over as soon as he could.

Eventually, I get home to find Cindel MIA. Of course, nothing is ever that simple. A police cruiser pulls up and parks by the curb, adjacent to our building, as I check out the window again for my principal. My phone vibrates and I check right away, hoping for signs of life from Cindel. It's not her.

Barber Contact: E3.

Glancing down at the squad car, a giant E3 is stickered atop the roof. "Hello Kent." I want... No, I need to ask him a thing or two.

I go to the apartment door and yank it open to find someone on my doorstep. Rookie move! I chastise myself for not being armed, but also for not checking the peephole before stepping foot outside.

"Cindel isn't home," I blurt, slamming the door on the unwelcome guest.

A leather cowboy boot, trimmed in turquoise, prevents the door from latching shut. Pressing my back against the threshold, I push with all my might to shut the door, only for it to be catapulted open by a very unexpected force. I hit the wall, falling to the floor.

"I think we'll check. Just to be sure." The unbalanced redhead above me coos with an unnerving smile.

An entourage of suited men, pour into my home. The shortest of the men, kisses Mairead on the cheek as he enters. Patrick Murray... or should I say, Paddy Muscles. The years haven't been kind to him.

One of the brutish men lifts me up by the arm, then proceeds to guide me by the clavicle to my own living room. The thud of the lock resonates through the room as Mairead shuts the five of us inside. In this moment, I'm grateful for Cindel's absence. Mairead immediately makes herself at home, grabbing an apple from the fridge before plopping down on the couch. Her outlandish outfit of clashing western with blue sequins is such a contrast to the muted colors of our living space. Fruit in hand, she produces a rainbow butterfly knife and begins to flick the blade open and closed, with her free hand.

Clearly, I'm outnumbered, but optimistic I'm not outwitted. Making a quick assessment of where everyone was situated, I determine the best course of action and act swiftly. Slamming my heel into the top of the large man's foot who still holds me, he instinctively releases his grip. I make a beeline for my bedroom and lock the door. My room is the best option, as I have more weapons than any ordinary kitchen. Before I can reach the Glock beneath my bedframe, a foot comes flying through the flimsy-hollow door.

"Shitty construction," I groan. With the useless door now opened, I commence throwing whatever is within reach at the intruders who are now piling into my bedroom. The tips of my fingers graze the polymer-frame just ahead of hands seizing my ankles and pulling me out from under my mattress. Learning their lesson the first time, now TWO brutish men bring me to my knees before Mairead and her father.

"Daddy, I like this one... she's feisty." The other man beside them, has a folded white cloth in his hand and I know exactly what is coming next. Tapping into those core muscles, I push and thrash in an attempt to break free from their hold and get the hell out of here.

All I manage to do is kick over my lamp, causing the globe to shatter around us. All at once, the colorless material comes into view, draping over my nose and mouth. I try to hold my breath but it is no use. Dark swallows my vision.

When I finally manage to open my eyes, my limbs feel like they've just completed their twentieth rep and need to rest. My head throbs and I attempt to focus on my surroundings.

Beige walls, vintage office desk, dingy couch, and every ceiling corner is laden with cobwebs. Where the fuck am I? I'm alone, in some remote location. There's a good likelihood this is the last room I see before I die. Like a flipbook animation, flashes of the events leading up to this moment come back to me in succession.

"Fuck," I blurt. I'm bound to a wooden chair, and for all I know, my roommate could be facing the same fate, in an adjacent room. What if they've had Cindel for hours? Regardless of my languid extremities, I twist and pull, in an attempt to free myself, but the knots are just too tight. "Arrrghhh!"

Facing a wall lined with awning windows, I scan the room for anything that can help me escape or tell me where the hell I am. A layer of dust coats every surface. It is clear this building has been abandoned for some time, verified by the fifteen-year-old, yellowing newspaper that suppresses the only natural light.

To my relief, the neglected place smells of fish like the Boston Harbor. At least I wasn't taken far. I hear footsteps. I'm out of time… the door screeches open and in saunters a petite psychopath in leather boots.

Mairead's smile never falters. Just pleased as punch to be here. What I wouldn't give to have an ounce of that dopamine trip she's perpetually on. This time, no beefed-up penguins escort her, which means I might still be able to get out of this. She's yet to say a word… unhurried Mairead circles me. Without warning, she stops before me, straddling my legs, and lowers down to sit on my thighs. She runs her fingers through my short bob with a surprisingly tender touch. I recoil.

"Your hair is pretty."

Considering the situation, how I was just chloroformed and brought to a random location, her behavior is unsettling. I can't help but notice the way her iridescent nails catch the fluorescent light. They appear to match her butterfly-knife from earlier.

Her bottom lip juts out before she takes a giant breath in through her nose. "I wish we would have met under different circumstances, but here we are."

Her hand shoots up to hold my jaw. Nails slightly digging into my skin, she gives my head a little shake moving even closer to my face. "We need to talk about that Lombardi roommate of yours."

Normally, when someone kidnaps and restrains you, your concern should be for your own well-being… I however don't have that luxury. My energy is always focused on Cindel. Every second wasted in this room could be her last. I have to get out of here… I have to find her! Tipping my head back as far as possible, I thrust my face forward making perfect contact with Mairead's nose. She topples backward, clutching her nose. Gradually her eyes travel up from the floor to my face. I wait for screaming or a slew of curse words… but neither come. Lately, nothing seems to 'present' as it should. Mairead begins to laugh maniacally, turning away only to pull a compact out of nowhere and examine the damage. She smiles at her reflection. Snapping the mirror shut, she rises before me with such resolve, I actually find it hard to swallow. She's fucking certifiable. Blood stains her teeth as she beams down at me, like I'm the challenge she's always wanted. I can't help but wonder… how many victims have suffered at her hand? Does she always play with her food?

"Get it over with!" I spit.

She clicks her tongue. "And here I was putting all this time into your roommate… only to realize that you are much better. I do love how everything always seems to work out in the end."

I've officially kicked the hornets' nest. As the feeling of impending doom sinks in, adrenaline floods my body, and I wrench at my restraints with everything I have. "Stay the fuck away from Cindel!" I snap.

Hands on her hips, she inclines forward, mere inches from my face. Her tongue glides over her top teeth, cleaning the red from her smile. "Or what?" she taunts.

To my surprise, the door to the reckoning room bursts open, sending dust swirling around us. Patrick Murray enters, setting a wooden box on the desk while casually puffing on his cigar. His gaze shifts from me to his daughter, and he nearly rolls his eyes. "Leanbh… what have I told you about getting too close to the captives?"

She lets out a small huff, crossing her arms and turning to her father. "I'm not a child," she argues. "Plus… you said she was mine to do with as I wished!" She practically twirls, causing her shiny skirt to momentarily hover around her.

Apparently, she's like this with everyone. His endeavor to lecture her is quickly lost. The once revered kingpin lets out a long breath ahead of taking another toke from his smoke.

"Pumpkin." Clearly mustering up as much patience as possible. "Can we move this along please? I have other things to tend to."

Her shoulders raise to her ears, in succession with her wrinkled nose. This girl clearly has no limits when it came to her daddy. Is no one capable of putting this brat in check? "Fine." She agrees, seeming to calm once again. "—but no more interfering!" Her manicured nail wags in his direction, and I can't help but gawk over the way she has unbridled control.

Patrick kisses his daughter on top of her head, just ahead of pinning me with a narrow stare. The corners of his mouth turn downward and he leaves just as swiftly as he came, through the only door in the space. A cloud of smoke trails behind him, leaving his daughter to her own devices.

As if I could see the collection of sand dwindling within the hourglass, I understood my time is running short. I have to try something 'irregular,' since I won't be able to fight my way out of this one. She's unstable... but if I can shift the balance. Maybe she'll believe what I am about to tell her. Tread lightly Andrea. I clear my throat. "You know... you're pretty lucky to have your family."

Wordlessly, she revolves around the chair I'm tied to. Lips pursed. Nose finished bleeding. She doesn't deter from her course.

I press on, "I didn't know my parents..." She doesn't falter. "I'm also fairly confident I have no siblings either." In fact, each pass she moves nearer. My throat is dry, but my voice is all I have left. "My childhood was shit. My own mother didn't want me."

Her gait falters.

Before I can overthink it, I continue. "The system that was meant to protect me... It failed. I couldn't trust anyone. I..." A knot was forming in the pit of my stomach. "I left. Constantly on the run.... it was only me for a long time."

Mairead stands before me, no longer circling me with a predatory gaze, but something similar to consideration.

"When they found me... they didn't see a lost cause, but a fighter."

Her reddish eyebrows rise slightly, but I don't need her to simply listen... if I am going to walk out of here with all my fingers and toes intact, I need to be concise. "They accepted me for who I was. Showing me compassion, I didn't even have for myself..."

Her head tilts to the side.

"Cindel only learned she was a Lombardi, this week. Her family isn't to blame for Mary's death."

In a blink, she lunges toward me. I never saw the blade coming. Its unforgiving pressure threatens to split my cheek, as the rest of her hovers over my restrained body.

"Keep my mother's name out of your mouth!" Each word drips with venom.

Fuck. I went there too soon. I need to see things from her perspective. Proof. She needs validation. My words are softer, careful, so as to not gash open my own face. "Losing someone you love hurts. Cindel knows this better than anyone, but she's innocent in all this." The knife remains pressed against me with each passing word. "I don't know where I would be if it weren't for them. That's why I was happy to do the job. To protect their daughter after unfathomable loss. Although, I would honorably accept any punishment in her place… can I at least show you what I learned?"

Her jade eyes bounce around my face, her expression unreadable.

"Allow me to bring in the person responsible for all of this. It will explain everything." My words hasten. "If you still aren't happy, you're welcome to do whatever you want!"

Her eyes become big as saucers, the strain on her knife increases, causing the blade to progressively slice into my flesh. The warmth of blood, so at odds with the stinging chill of the metal. She withdraws. The slice burns. Just behind it, blood dribbles and collects around the collar of my shirt.

Situating the balisong spectrum between us, she proceeds to open her mouth, extends her pink tongue, and cleans the side of the blade. She licks her lips and I involuntarily repeat the action. "Hungry?" she asks.

♪ ♪ ♫ ♩ ♫ ♪ ♪ ♫

I'm so stupid. All this time. Fuck… thinking back on my years living with Cindel, I've been a shitty friend. Too engrossed with my own mission, proving my self-worth that I never considered how I affected my client. No… my friend… MY FUCKING BEST FRIEND. I just came and went as I pleased. Never taking the time to reflect on how my behavior hurt her. Not only did she lose her brother, but she's struggled with depression, and even has recurring PTSD episodes! I didn't soothe her fears; I made them worse. Why did I disregard her concerns... our friendship?! Cindel deserves better. A relationship can't sustain itself on just protection. Especially, when I have frayed the connection at its source. I mean… her biggest pet peeve is liars and I've been the worst offender. The wolf in sheep's clothing. Just because others offenses are worse than mine, doesn't make it okay. It makes me a hypocrite. I should have told her a long time ago.

♪ ♪ ♫ ♩ ♫ ♪ ♪ ♫

An hour and a half later, two slices of cold pizza lay in a grease laden box, between me and Mairead. We face one another atop the steel top desk in the neglected room. I told her everything. From the time Charles and Terri found me living on the streets as a runaway, to them taking me in, training me, and eventually hiring me as a full-time companion and protector for their daughter. No one was the wiser. I was simply Cindel's best friend from college. Seeing to her safety wasn't my only mission. I was also tasked with investigating their son's untimely death.

At first, I believed the Lombardi's judgment was clouded by their history with the Murrays. I was dead set on finding evidence that the Murrays were behind Theo's death… However, the more I learned… the more I understood why Charles and Terri wanted their daughter protected. I've been at this for years and still never found proof that Theo was murdered, but thanks to new sources, I know who has been pulling the strings. I've worn multiple hats to get to where I am now. Then some mystery man shows up, having more answers than any outside party should. Nothing is by chance.

In truth, if it weren't for the song-slinging hacker, I'd be just as lost as Cindel was. Except, he revealed something I don't think he meant to. I spent a lot of time going over the information on the board. Decoding the songs he sent to Cindel. Reading between the lines. He intended for the songs to be eerie, sure, but behind the catchy chorus of The Spin Doctors- "Two Princes," were buried truths. It took me being knocked out, strapped to a chair, and a daft redhead wielding a pointy thing to realize it, but… he wasn't referring to Theo.

Mairead relished in my stories about interrogation tactics and stake outs. I schooled her on how I've handled numerous situations, all without a weapon, simply by knowing how to use my body to its advantage. She insisted using a blade has brought her faster and better results. It's not often my trade gets messy, but she has some pretty intriguing tales herself. She resented her brother for trying to push her out of the family business when their mother died. Eamon probably thought he was saving her, then again, even the best intentions can't prevent the butterfly from emerging from their chrysalis.

It felt nice to finally be able to say some of this shit out loud. Someone to understand. For some confounded reason, I even told her that I interrogated and disposed of two of the guys from the Murray crew. What is wrong with me? It's like I have no filter when she's present. More importantly, she was on board with proving Cindel and her parents' innocence. Mairead also managed to tame her father into submission. Patrick Murray is currently passed out on the couch alongside us, thanks to a sleeping pill she served him, under a slice of pepperoni. I made a mental note to never accept food from her again, in the future.

Just as I was about to ask her how well she knew Dax, I hear something. It's coming from the hall. Footsteps cease before the doorway and a bewildered Cindel stands at the entrance of the room. Eamon and Dax, peer in from either side.

"What the Fuck?!"

It took well over two hours to explain to Cindel everything that transpired, including who I was to her. My stony heart crumbled within my chest by the way she regarded me. I know our friendship will never be seen in the same light, especially because I was placed into her life with intent. Her head nodded as she listened, but she wasn't really there. She was withdrawn. Spending a majority of the time, staring at a broom and dustpan in the corner.

Cindel looks hollow and I am the cause. Eamon paces as I speak my truth. I've never cared for him but I know he's calculating. Figuring out how to do all of this on his own. Dax, the enigma that he is... remains distant. Arms crossed over his chest, leaning against an adjacent wall, focus trained on Cindel.

It's obvious he doesn't want any harm to come to her, but what are his other motives? If my suspicions are right and he's had a part all along... this whole plan could go to shit. Mairead sits on the arm of the couch where her father snores, despite the lengthy discussion taking place around him. How strong were those pills?

Cindel chimes in occasionally with, "how" or "why?" When she finally glances up from the unclean corner. She too has something to disclose. Unfortunately, it isn't good news. The microSD card that she found, with evidence of her Uncle Nicholas meeting with accomplices, has been destroyed. I can't believe it was right under our noses, all this time. Just when I think I've hit my limit, Cindel nonchalantly shares that she killed somebody!

Mairead jumps from her spot and shakes Cindel's hand while congratulating her on, '*popping her cherry*.' Eamon, chimes in, assuring me the situation has been handled by one of his best men. I still don't trust him or any of his goons.

Cindel can't even look at me, but at least the interaction with Mairead brought her out a little. Despite all the different personalities in one room, we formulate a plan. To bring in the only person who can provide a full account for the events. It wasn't a great plan, but it was the best one we had. Cindel is going to invite her uncle for breakfast at Benny's. Then, we have to dangle an enticing carrot to get him to come to this very location. I know Cindel was planning on just questioning him, maybe even scaring him. However, the other people in the room understand what needs to be done. We just don't say it out loud. For Cindel's sake. The logistics are messy and a lot of this is built on hopes and dreams, but without that microSD card, Nicholas will have to face the music.

With everyone in agreement and a temporary truce in place, we go our separate ways. I immediately go to Cindel's side, only for her to lean into Dax. He may not be a danger to her, but I'll be damned if I let her leave this place with him. The little prince seems to understand, encouraging her to accompany me home in a taxi. Her body migrates away from me on the ride home. The fare was fucking ludicrous too! The Murrays will be reimbursing me for kidnapping after hours!

When we arrive home, I see no sign of the asshat cop, so we go up to the apartment and I set the alarm. Cindel goes straight to her bedroom and shuts the door. She hasn't spoken to me since we left the warehouse. She has every right to shut me out, I've been dishonest for years. I don't think it matters that it was for her own protection, she has every right to hate me. Sometimes, I hate myself too.

I stand just before her closed door, hand raised in a fist, just short of knocking when I hear her voice. I'd bet anything she's on the phone with Dax. That would be a very one-sided conversation since he can't speak. I can't believe I let him rope me into his juvenile games. Was the series of numbers even intentional or was it like going through the discount bin at the thrift store, hoping to find two matching shoes? If I know one thing… that jagged scar across his neck holds a story and I'm sure it's not a pretty one. Even without the mask, I'm positive he's hiding more.

Cindel is so much more than what she's endured, she's a survivor. In spite of that, hairline fractures are apparent. I fear they are slowly going to continue expanding until she crumbles to dust. I don't know if I can mend her. It's ironic how her well-being is now out of my hands. From the other side of the door, there's music. It takes me a moment to realize the song. It's **Silverchair - "Tomorrow."** Dax has a knack for picking them. I stay and listen, the song playing out loud on her phone. A damn near perfect premonition.

Tomorrow will be hard to swallow, for everyone. With Officer Kent missing in action, it's possible Nicholas still doesn't know the evidence has been destroyed and Jada's dead, so we plan to use that to our advantage. Earlier, Cindel composed a clever text to her uncle.

> Cindel: "I can't get ahold of my roommate, and I think someone is watching me! I'm scared. Can we meet at our usual place, tomorrow at noon? I found something."

She's so fucking smart. I can't help but feel proud of the woman she's grown into. Once the music stops, I jot down a note and leave it on the counter for Cindel to find in the morning. I grab a pair of boots by the front door, pull on a black hoodie, and leave the apartment for a midnight romp.

FORTY-THREE

CINDEL

It rained most of the night. I'd blame the change in barometric pressure for my fretful sleep and raging headache, but I know that isn't why. My skin crawled as if I couldn't find comfort within my own body. I was questioning everything. What I've done. Who I am. How I am about to bring down the hammer on someone who I once considered family.

When we arrived home late last night, I closed myself in my room. I was so drained, I couldn't fathom hearing Andrea try and explain herself further. Apparently, my uncle isn't the only one who has been lying to me for years. My brain simply couldn't process anymore. The entire time… our friendship has been a sham. Like one of those artificial, cardboard cakes in the window of the bakery. It looks nice, but the inside is void of what you actually desire. Sustenance. Something real. The icing on this metaphorically fucked up cake is, she was hired by my fucking parents! No wonder they always want to talk to her. Fuck me! Is anything as it seems?

I used the found earbud as a security blanket, keeping it in as I watched the rain beat against the window. Each waking hour, Dax played me a new song. At 1 a.m. it was: **Ozzy Osbourne - "No More Tears,"** 2 a.m.: **Depeche Mode - "Policy of Truth,"** and the final song I recall was: **Incubus - "Pardon Me,"** right around 3 a.m. That song ripped me to shreds. I cried until I passed out. When I checked the time again, it was eight in the morning.

Music has always been a form of therapy for me. Whether these songs were meant as a distraction or a nudge of encouragement… I have this strange feeling that there are layers I have yet to discover.

The weather is dreary and the rain relentless. It make the notion of leaving my bed that much bigger of a challenge. The white tech rests beside me, upon a rumpled pillow. To think… just a little over a month ago, this rogue earbud presented itself to me. Everything before was so much less complicated.

As turbulent as things may currently seem, I'd rather be here, than continue navigating this life in the dark. Being *blissfully ignorant* is an illusion, coveted by those who are wary of compassion. Surely, I'm not lacking there. I feel sorry for my uncle. Hell, I'm apologetic to ducks when I run out of peas. It's hard to swallow that Nicholas would rather kill off the people in his life than be benevolent. Humanity would cease to exist without understanding… without change. Sure, it can be troublesome and also really fucking unclear at times… but without a little discomfort, we don't grow. I believed I was stuck, up until recently. Forced to struggle based on someone else' s design. After everything… all the deception and lies… I'm just as guilty. You can't know your true self if you constantly seek others' approval. Well… no more lying to myself! Pain is no stranger to me. I wouldn't be who I am without it. Uneasiness is mandatory. Our time here is supposed to be messy. Filled with self-doubt and risks with no guarantees. I'll never be able to go back to the person I once was… and you know what? I wouldn't want to.

In a matter of hours, I'm expected to meet my uncle at the diner. Dropping the earbud into its charger, I force myself from the warmth of my bed, in search of headache relief. The pressure in my cranium, causing a head-splitting swell. Our apartment is still… no sign of Andrea. That's when I find the note on the kitchen counter.

Cindel,

Had to run out & pick something up… I'll see you at the meeting point.

P.S. I'm sorry.

Your forever friend,
Andrea

I crumble the note into a tight ball, before tossing it into the trash beneath the sink. I simply don't have the mental capacity. I check my phone again, confirming my uncle still has not responded to my text from earlier. Today, truly is built on hopes and dreams.

♩ ♪ ♫ ♩ ♫ ♪ ♪ ♫

Right at noon, I'm sitting in our usual booth in the back corner of the diner. My feet are wet because I was unable to find my rain boots. The yellow raincoat I wore, hangs with other dripping coats and umbrellas beside the entrance. The downpour is likely keeping people from venturing out because the diner is nearly empty.

I opted for all black attire today. Unsure if I am dressed to be taken seriously or if I am just prematurely mourning. He doesn't deserve the extra effort, but how I dress directly affects my mood.

Twenty after, just as I am about to go home and give up, he walks into Benny's. Like so many times before, he strides in without reservation. Casually he removes his coat, places it on the back booth, then lowers himself to sit across from me.

My uncle has a spot of toilet tissue on his face, likely from nicking himself shaving. Pointing to the spot on my own face, I hope it serves as some informal ice breaker. He takes the cue, batting away the white dab of paper. I can't help but watch it as it flutters gently to the floor. Deep breath, Cindel. I remind myself; *you're supposed to seem scared.*

"Uncle, I'm so glad you came." I try to make myself seem panic stricken. Looking out the windows. Scanning the room every few moments. "I didn't know who else to tell." I fidget with the cuffs of my long-sleeve shirt. "The guy I told you about…" This next part I conjured up, while in the shower this morning. When I considered that my *deceptive uncle* could have been monitoring me. I decide to work every possible angle. It may be the only way to get him to accompany me to the warehouse district. My hair cascades over my right ear, to cover the purple starred earbud. I somehow felt more confident when my *friendly stalker* was with me. Yet, I realize this was my web to spin alone.

Knowing what my uncle is capable of, I feel protective over the ones I care about. Including Dax. Which is why I need Nicholas to believe that he's not a part of this. "Well... my musical stalker has disappeared. I—" Leaning slightly forward onto the table, I lower my voice. "I think someone in the Murray family is to blame. One of my coworkers is trying to kill me." My teeth clench and grind together.

Normally, the diner was busier around lunch. With minimal distractions, it is difficult to sell my fear, without calling attention to our booth. My uncle's mouth pulls up in the corners and his eyes glisten, he looks pleased for a fraction of a second, before schooling his features.

I continue, "I found some kind of disk thingy. I... I got scared. Between Jada and the Eamon, I decided to hide it elsewhere. I found an abandoned building and stashed it there last night. Will you come get it, with me?" Take the bait. Take the bait. My eyes feel dry. Not daring to blink, in case I miss any subtle tells. Beneath the table my hands busy themselves by pushing the cuticles, even farther than necessary. I worry the beds will bleed if he doesn't answer soon.

The man who I once considered my closest family, remains hardened. His eyes narrow to slits. A surge of panic runs through me. Shit. Knowledge doesn't mean you're credible. He doesn't believe me... I've always been a shit liar. Was I not convincing enough? Is it possible he knows about Jada? I know he's the one who sent her. She told me so herself.

"Be right with you," the waitress says as she passes by to another table.

In sync with the interruption, the man before me softens. His features smooth out, while his next words are honeyed. "Sweet girl. Why ever did you wait so long to tell me? You found something, you say? A disk... did you see what was on it?"

Play dumb, Cindel. "I don't know what it is." I fib while simultaneously lowering and pulling together my eyebrows. "I thought it was a computer part. Like a broken piece off a motherboard. Could you help me see what's on it?"

He scratches away the dried blood on his cheek then clears his throat. "Why not just bring what you found to our meeting today?"

Shit-fuck, he has a point. Think, think, think. "I saw a cop. The one who came to my apartment asking questions about my last job. I got spooked. You know I don't trust the police. I couldn't risk anyone taking it. Maybe it has the answers I've been searching for... insight on Theo's death." I can barely hear the words leaving my mouth, I speak them so softly. The ringing in my ears trumps any present sound. "I hid it in the old club district. No one knows but me... and now you." I wait with bated breath.

My uncle's jaw ticks. Urgently I review what I've already said. Did I say the wrong thing? Was my face giving me away? Without a sound, he slides from the booth and stands. Reaching for his coat, he pulls it onto each arm, and adjusts his tie. "Well then... take me to it."

Per Dax's request, I share a cab with my uncle to the warehouse, instead of letting him drive me. He only agreed because of my "insufferable paranoia". Neither of us is particularly communicative on the ride over, but Dax did play a song for me. **The Verve - "Bittersweet Symphony."** It was the ideal song.

Funny... I was here less than twenty-four hours ago, yet instead of a rescue, I'm leading someone to their reckoning. I played my part to the best of my ability... he's here. Now the rest was in the capable hands of people who apparently interrogate and murder. Okay... technically, I could be lumped into that category, but I did what I had to do for survival! I can't deny... I am thrilled I don't have to deal with Jada's bullshit anymore.

As my 'so-called' *uncle* follows me deeper into the warehouse, my mind wanders. How will this all end? Will he admit to everything or will it take some coaxing to draw out the truth? Could I handle what's about to happen? Turning left at the end of the hall, my belly feels like a wave pool; churning and crashing against the walls of my insides. What if I get to the room and no one is here? Then what?! Was coming here with my *'liar'* of an uncle a dumb decision?

I take a deep breath and slowly let it out, hoping he can't hear me attempting to calm myself. I glance back at him with a reassuring smile, just as he checks his watch.

"It's just through here. I put it in the drawer of an old desk." I enter the familiar room first, with the office desk right where it was the night before. Along with the aging couch, which no longer has a slumbering Patrick Murray upon it. At first, the room appears empty, but once we were both in, I quickly realize we weren't alone.

In a shadowed nook, nestled behind a stack of boxes, is a tied and gagged man. Once the man sees us, he begins mumbling uncontrollably while trying to scoot his restrained body from its darkened corner. His eyebrow is split, hair in all directions and both sides of his face are a purplish-black hue. Regardless of his state, I know exactly who he is.

My uncle's wide eyes jump from me to his haggard accomplice, before he pivots and proceeded to flee the room. Faster than I can process what is happening, he is blocked by my sterling-haired roommate, framed within the only exit of the room. My uncle steps back, more confused than frightened. He balks at the barely five-foot hellion with both knuckles wrapped in black boxing tape.

Hey… are those *my* rain boots?! Something glints as she waves, resembling a possessed doll at a haunted house. A pair of brass knuckles affixed to one of her hands. Clearly, Andrea has been busy, since we last saw each other, using Officer Kent as a punching bag, before our arrival. I may be upset with her, but I can't deny she is sort of a badass… also, a little scary.

The man I once considered my uncle turns to me, his upper lip twisted just as he lifts his too large nose toward the ceiling. "Is this the dumb leading the blind? Do you honestly believe that you and your feral friend can keep me here?"

Andrea turns to look down the corridor. A smile gradually grows on her face, as she turns back toward us. Relief washes over me as Eamon appears just behind her. My petite yet menacing roommate steps aside to let him pass. His expression is serious, unbending posture, confident stride, while dark pink skin runs along his neck and cheeks.

I've seen Eamon upset before. Like, when he handled those rude teenagers at the movies, but this is different. He appears murderous. One look into his eyes, and I even stepped back a foot. Grabbing the man of the hour by his shirt collar, Eamon backs Nicholas into an open chair. My uncle begins to laugh… an unsettling, tear-filled chuckle, at a joke only he knows the punchline to.

Eamon doesn't waste a moment securing him to the seat with rope, I didn't even notice till just now.

I can't contain myself any longer, his blithe attitude makes me want to slap him. "Why?!" I all but scream. "Why did you kill him?!"

His humor melts away all at once, morphing the unstable individual. Long gone was the man I shared gossip with, in the diner booth. In his place was a cruel, calculated man. "You'll have to be more specific." Each word pointed, he knew who I was referring to. Nicholas looks at the other people in the room. "Is that why we're all here today? Fences mended over the loss of your pansy brother?"

Oh… no! Did he really just say that? I want to hit him. Beside myself with rage…before I have a chance to react, Andrea steps forward her fist winds back and drives into his face with a satisfying crunch to the side of his jaw.

Nicholas' face flies to the right and he spits blood onto the floor. "Bitch."

Do we have duct tape or something? Why hasn't Eamon gagged him yet?

Rhythmic footfalls echo down the hallway, getting louder upon approach until the next guest makes themself known. Mairead stands in the doorframe, somehow looking both adorable and menacing at the same time. She seamlessly twirls into the space, first visiting the prisoners with a pat on the head, before settling right next to Andrea. "This guy? He looks like an accountant," the redhead teases, hopping up onto the desk surface. Promptly, she pulls out a colorful blade and proceeds to flip it open and close with ease.

Andrea wipes away residual blood from her knuckles with a small towel, before throwing it in a corner. I can't help but glance back over to the splatter of blood on the floor. My arms fold over my stomach, eager to keep the sickening feeling at bay. Why did I think I could handle this?

"Looks can be deceiving." My roommate informs the newcomer.

With his mouth ajar, my uncle moves his tongue around as if searching for any missing teeth. We all watch as he sucks at his teeth and regurgitates even more blood onto the linoleum. "Well… Isn't this a lovely site?" The words slither through the room. Despite his current disadvantage, he's unable to censor himself.

Kent mumbles something off to the side; I nearly forgot he was here.

Andrea lets out an audible groan. Looking straight up to the ceiling. "Shuuuut upppp! You'll get your turn soon enough."

Without notice, the light from the hall is dimmed. We all turn to find Dax, poised just within the room. What took him so long? He was supposed to be here when I arrived. It doesn't matter, he's here now. The restrained man's eyes narrow. I hate the way he's glaring at Dax, following his every move as he strides into the space, coming straight to my side. My body instantly relaxes from his mere proximity. Maybe I can stomach one more punch to the *'worst uncle ever.'* His finger brushes against the back of my hand, stealing my focus. As if we were alone, my eyes crawl up his broad chest, over his unique scar, where I find solace in his flawless gaze. He has the ability to tell me exactly what I need to hear, all without a word. My lighthouse in this storm.

Just past Dax, I watch as Eamon approaches us, stopping when he lifts his arm and puts a gun to Dax's head.

"Uh-oh… Trouble in paradise?" Nicholas taunts.

This time, Mairead hops off the table and kicks him in the shin. "Shhhh-hh…. not your turn linguine!" she scolds, before springing back onto the desktop. Then she proceeds to eat a handful of popcorn. Where in the Sam Hill did she get that from?!

"Eamon…" I speak evenly. "What are you doing? This isn't a part of the plan." Gradually, I stalk around Dax's position, to face a fuming Eamon. His skin is redder than when he first came into the room. Eyes boring into the side of Dax's face. "Dax didn't do anything. Nicholas is responsible… remember?"

I wasn't meant for this. The most mediating I've ever done was, when I took a summer job in high school as a camp counselor. I never realized how highly regarded Pokémon trading cards were, before using them as a bargaining chip between a group of wild six-year-old boys, who wouldn't stop hitting each other with sticks. This couldn't be much different, right? I raise both hands slowly, showing Eamon I'm not a threat.

"For so long, I couldn't imagine you having a hand in this." Eamon starts. "Not the seemingly innocent, little sister… but then, I found the brooch on my bedroom floor, after the night you came over. I didn't think much of it at first, but once I thought about what you said…. I gave the pin another look. Quite to my surprise, I found a microphone inside the metallic flower."

My eyes jump to Andrea for a moment, then back to Dax.

"Who was listening on the other side of the microphone, Cindel?"

Dax bares his teeth, but it was actually Andrea who rose and spoke. "It was me. I told her to wear the mic."

Eamon regards my friend standing her ground, just beside his very entertained sister, as she shoves another mouthful of popcorn in. "I didn't trust you." She continues. "I thought for certain you were behind the Lombardi's adversities."

Stepping forward, he towers over her, still; she levels Eamon with equal intensity. His gun never lowers from Dax. Neither party breaks from their unofficial, stare-down for long moments.

To my surprise, Eamon folds. Stretching his neck to each side, he returns his attention to the person his weapon was pointed at. "You're capable of a lot more than I initially gave you credit for Cindel, but Dax has pulled the wool over both of our eyes!" He's speaking to me, but not bothering to actually look in my direction.

My eyes jump between Eamon's gun and Dax. Fuck. Should I do something? Say something? Dax is just standing there… like, he's not even surprised that a gun is being held to his head. Instead... he watches me with a pained expression... as though his concern is for me and not himself.

"Everything. All our misfortunes... they lead back to HIM!" Eamon's shouts. His sleepless, bloodshot eyes water in their corners. This is crazy! He's not thinking straight.

"Eamon, you're wrong!" I finally interjected. "Dax wants to help. He's only ever tried to help." My vision adjusts past the men before me, to the man tied within the chair. His disquieting smirk gives me chills.

Eamon doesn't seem to hear me, nor will he even consider my objection. "Would you like to take a guess at what I found last night?" Eamon inquires. "I'll give you a hint... it was in Lousie's hide."

A nauseous realization courses through me. My hands shoot up to my mouth, trying to hold in anything that may accompany my sickening astonishment. Eamon nods to himself more than me. Clearly, my physical response was enough of an answer.

"Yes, Cindel... I saw everything!" He leers at Dax. If looks could kill... I wouldn't be as concerned about the weapon, as I would the man holding it. "In fact, I watched the video thirteen times. Just to make sure I had every detail memorized."

Dax's jaw ticks, pulling his shoulders back as he audits the people in the room. Why is he just standing idly by? This conversation is completely one sided. He's not even trying to communicate!

Eamon's arm shakes faintly, but he never lowers the barrel from Dax's face. I need to be his voice! The rationale to all this madness. My influential words could be the *Jigglypuff card*, ultimately making the boys stop. When in the hell did I become a Pokédex? I rest a hand on his arm.

"Eamon..."

He wrenches his gaze from his target to look at me.

"I've watched the recording too. I read over the log and the letter my brother wrote..."

His lips part followed by a strenuous swallow. As if whatever he was about to say is lodged within. "I'm sure you did, little fish... but you didn't know what to look for." His words are filled with heartbreak. "Did you recognize the other man in the video?"

I consider Dax, whose eyes remain forward, glossy and distant. Has he even blinked?

"No..." I answered, but then thought better of it... "Maybe? He looked familiar, but I don't know who *he* is, per se."

Eamon steps closer to Dax, pressing the pistol's end flush against his temple. Oh my god.

"Well, let's go back a few years then... back to when Dax magically showed up." Eamon doesn't falter, as though he got a second wind, his arm steadies.

Mairead pulls her legs in, sitting cross-legged, carrying on with her random snacks. Andrea isn't concerned in the slightest. She migrates over to Kent, ensuring he stays put in the corner of the room. All the while, my uncle's smug face makes me feel queasy. I was completely ineffective. No weapons and not a single person to back me up. My only option is to listen, to believe he'll calm down and eventually lower his gun.

"As if he fell off a delivery truck, Dax shows up at my boxing club, one day. No one had ever seen, nor heard of the guy before. Of course I was ready to send him packing, but then one of our families' best guys vouched for him. We believed him. Fiercely loyal, he was with my family for years! I gave Dax a chance. To my surprise, he fit right in. Took each job I threw his way. Hell… even my old man liked him and he hates everyone." Eamon pauses, sucking in air until his cheeks puff out, then blows it out hastily. "I stayed by your side the entire time you were healing. Always felt like it was my fault. My call did this to you… I made you a part of my family... My. Fucking. Family!" he bellows; as he shoves the piece against the side of Dax's head, causing it to tilt to one side.

I gasp and squeeze my eyes shut. Holding the threatening tears in place. Dax remains silent. His chest rising and falling is all that moves.

Eamon continues, "shortly after Dax showed up, my mother was murdered. No… it wasn't him! His hands were clean, because the guy who assumed blame was shot on the spot. This video was recorded just a few days before my mother died. The older gentleman, with whom your uncle met, is the man who shouldered accountability. The same man who supported hiring Dax." With his free hand, Eamon pulls his phone out and holds the screen up to my uncle. "Never would I have suspected that a Lombardi had planted a mole in my house for years. Until I saw this guy's haunting mug come across my screen. Now, all those raids made perfect sense."

My uncle watches the video play, likely the first time he's ever seen it, then looks to Eamon with an impish smirk. "Did you know the boy was there too?" With his chin, he motions toward Dax. "Even then, he was a disappointment."

That's an odd choice of words. Nicholas looks between the two men, looking positively delighted with how the tables have turned. Disappointed. Wait. The text! The one I saw on Dax's phone, when he was showing me something on the screen, at his place. It said, *"I'm disappointed in you, son."* No… no. My attention jumps from the allegedly blameless Dax to my subdued uncle. Nicholas' stare pins me in place, as he watches the discovery wash over me. What I never noticed until this moment. I force myself to look up. Dax's brilliant silvery vision floods in the corners. Those eyes. They were almost identical to my uncle's.

"He's…" I couldn't breathe. "He's your father?"

Dax's once blank stare falls. His downward cast eyes tell me everything I need to know. The room turns on its axis, but I manage to stay upright by leaning against the closest wall. My stalker. This whole time? He followed me. Spied on me. Manipulated me. We… I thought this was different! Fuck. I'm so stupid. Why? Do I have, *Lie to Me,* tattooed across my forehead?

Mairead pops up from her discarded snack pile, brushing off her hands with a loud succession of claps, and then proceeds to drag an empty chair behind my uncle. I can't move, as I watch Eamon escorting Dax to a vacant seat. The two men sit, back-to-back. Pistol permanently positioned at his temple. He doesn't even put up a fight… not even attempting to deny the allegations. Dax simply does what was expected of him. Sitting down in the chair behind his father, he waits for the Murrays to finish tying him up. The wall was the only thing I have left to support me.

"Soooo, does that mean you've fucked your cousin?" Mairead probes, when she's done helping her brother subdue Dax.

Preceding my reaction, Andrea gets involved and whacks the callow girl upside her head.

"Oww!" she grumbles.

"You had that coming," her brother quips. "Be happy it wasn't with the brass knuckles. Now keep quiet and let the grown-ups talk."

Mairead regards Andrea with admiration, as she saunters over to the tied father-son duo. She stops in front of Dax and leans in close, whispering something in his ear. I can't see her mouth; she speaks too softly for anyone to hear. Dax's eyes go wide just before he returns to staring off at nothing in particular.

Andrea reaches to the ceiling, folding her fingers together before tilting to either side. Stretching for what, I wasn't sure. "I have reliable intel in the city." My roommate declares. "Your weasel of a friend over there was very informative, once we became acquainted… isn't that right?!"

Officer Kent screams in short bursts behind his gagged mouth, clearly displeased with her commentary.

She bends at the waist, leaning forward into Nicholas' face and clutching each arm of the chair he sits upon. "Do you know what I learned, daddy Lombardi?"

My uncle's lips pout into a sneer, directed at the authoritative woman above him.

"I know why you killed Mary… did you really think a mother wouldn't recognize her own son?"

The reddened hue that Eamon's face once held is now void of color.

Mairead is still putting two and two together, while I'm on the verge of vomiting into the closet garbage pail. She raises her hand to ask a question, like we're in some kind of impromptu lecture. Mairead speaks out regardless, "did mom have an affair with the lasagna accountant?"

Andrea smacks her forehead, "No you beautiful idiot. Nicholas raped your mother before she wed your father. I've spoken with your aunt, Moyra."

Everything seems to move in slow-motion. Mairead's forehead scrunches. Her eyebrows furrow. Then next thing I know, she's hurtling toward my disgraceful *family member*. Knife in hand, she drives the rainbowed blade into Nicholas' thigh. It happens faster than anyone could have seen coming.

A blood curdling scream fills the space, followed by a string of profanities in Italian. Eamon intervenes just as she removes the blade and aimed toward my uncle's crotch. Taking her by the elbow, he walks his sister over to the couch to sit.

Dax brings his head as far forward as possible before throwing it back into his father with such force that I would have thought at least one of them would black out.

"Figlio di puttana! Fuck all of you!" Finally… something I agree with. Nicholas Lombardi looks deranged. Bruised and bloodied, with his hair pointing in every which direction, his wild eyes find me. "None of this is yours! My father, the stronzo, gave it all to Charles. That bastardo of a brother! Not even a true-blooded Lombardi! It was supposed to be mine! This city belongs to me!" His face is a canvas of indigo and burgundy, while a bulging vein snakes up his neck as he continues to scream, about what he believes he's owed. He's no uncle of mine.

"He gave everything to me for a reason, brother." Like a scene from a movie, my father enters the room.

No matter how old I get he's my safe space. I push from the wall and run to him. His arms welcome me in his warm embrace, just like he did when I was a little girl. "Hey Cinnabun. I'm so sorry you had to learn everything this way, kiddo." I glance up at the man who raised me, just as tears began to fall without my permission.

"We kept you in the dark to keep you safe." My mother appears. Joining his side, in a room too full of ugly truths for one day.

Against my better judgement, I turn from my parents and approach the rotten man I once confided in. I had one more burning question. No one dares to stop me. "Are you responsible for what happened to me as a child? The *gas leak* that stole my ability to hear?!"

Dax's head hangs low; he doesn't even try to regard me. My heartbeat thunders louder than any ringing in my ears, and I wonder if anyone but me can hear it. The man who was supposed to have our *best interests in mind*…

protect us… love us. The only family I had left in the city. Now I see him for what he is… a callous, bitter man, driven by greed.

The thinning skin on his jaw moves from side to side, as if grinding his teeth. Seconds, minutes drag on as I wait for an answer. His Adam's apple bobs, before delivering a clear-cut, "Yes."

My hellish nightmare. The day I'm brought back to every time I close my eyes, was it intentional? Liars. Con artists! Every single one of them! It sounds like blaring sirens in my brain. Tears cascade down my cheeks. I glance at Dax, one last time. He can't even look at me. In spite of the fact that everyone in this room has disregarded me at one point or another, they stare. As if I decide the next course of action. I need to get away from them. Desperate to free myself of any responsibility to this. Fuck them. They can do whatever they want... with BOTH of them. I need to be anywhere but here.

I move toward the door, causing Andrea to step aside with a rubber squeak. My eyes shoot down to her feet. "Keep the stupid rain boots."

Yanking the earbud from my ear, I let it roll from my hand and onto the floor. Leaving the room without looking back. My ears roar as I move down the hall, past a distraught Patrick Murray. I don't bother stopping. Pushing past the heavy steel door, I'm met with drops of icy water against my skin. The air around me seems to freeze as I look up toward the gray sky. Without warning, the ringing in my head dies off. Stillness. Dampen in solitude, I knew where I was heading next.

FORTY-FOUR

CINDEL

Two months later…

For weeks, the ground has been blanketed in snow. What was once a colorful valley of trees is now barren. The only signs of life are the birds and squirrels, with the occasional deer passing through. Floorboards flex with each step I take. I'm almost confident I'm alone.

Last time I stayed here, I questioned my own sanity. Locking each door, drawing the drapes, and checking the tree line for movement. Now I allow the reflective glow to pour from the cottage and onto the still grounds. No longer do I hold misgivings for the shadows. There's no room for that. I've accepted the hole in my heart as my own. This is what I need... time.

My parents were overjoyed when I agreed to accompany them back to New York. Straight away, they volunteered to move out from *their* place and into one of the more spacious homes, nearby. Turns out that they weren't glorified house-sitters after all, but own multiple properties in the Catskills. If that wasn't enough of a shock, they gifted me the entire storybook house I stayed in last time I was here, watching Kingston.

"Cinna… it's Thanksgiving," my father says.

I push the plate away from me at the giant table surrounded by family and *friends* I barely even knew. Why the fuck would they invite the Colbys over, if they knew I wasn't even up for this?

"They're our guests, Cindel. Don't be rude," Mother chastises.

I lean back in my seat at the table filled with glass flutes, polished cutlery, and more food than necessary, wondering why I am the one being told to practice modesty. How incredulous of them.

"I don't see the point. Why bother with appearances? Everything else has gone to shit. Let's take off our shoes… hell, let's eat with our hands!" I scoop up a fist full of cranberry sauce, lick it from my hand, and then rubbed the residue across my chest with David Bowie's face. Well… it used to be my favorite shirt. Now it just reminds me of the boathouse… of him.

I think I'll burn it in the fireplace tonight. For once in my life, my mother's rendered speechless, while my father can't even look at me. Everyone has stopped eating.

"Don't let me keep you from enjoying your holiday." Without so much as a goodbye, I leave the table and make my way through the second kitchen, toward the door which exited to the attached parking area. Just as I reach for the door, a metallic thud sounds behind me; I spin around to find Mrs. Colby.

"I figured you needed these." She glances down at the ring of keys she just dropped onto the butcher block.

I completely forgot the keys after storming from the dining room. She pulls out two wooden chairs and positions them next to the hearth. Sitting in one, she reaches over to pat the other, while smiling sweetly.

"Come on. I won't bite."

Overcoming my urge to lock myself back in the cottage until the valley is green once more, I sit with the woman by the modest fire. "You know they love you… don't you?"

I nod, though tight-lipped and ever stubborn.

"They never abandoned you. They had certain measures put in place, to ensure you were always taken care of."

My face feels icy even though the fire dances not even a foot from the masonry. "I am already well aware of the bodyguard posing as my friend."

The woman next to me chuckles and shakes her head, causing her brown curls to sway. "No child. Not her." She regards me with a warm chestnut gaze and smiles. "Do you know who my boy is?"

I search her face, trying to recall who I may have forgotten, but I come up short.

"No, I'm sorry." Her eyes squint causing the brown to become more golden. "Losing a child is something I wouldn't even wish on my worst enemy… but your parents didn't just lose one child… they lost you too."

My face scrunches. Clearly, this woman sees me before her… right? She smooths out the material covering her legs.

"Not like that. They let you go. To protect you."

No, they didn't. They wanted to run away… forget Theo and the memories that Boston held here.

"I've known your parents a long time and I can tell you this much… every choice they made was for you both. Theo learned who he was long before your parents expected him to."

Of course he found out. He's always been keen at solving things.

"This life is dangerous, as you're well aware. They didn't want that for either of you. In the beginning, they tried to evade danger while continuing their businesses, but their obligation to Cosa Nostra wasn't going to damn their children."

What is this lady going on about…? The woman around my mother's age turns more toward me in her seat, the silver strands in her hair shimmer from the flames.

"Mr. Colby and I have worked by your parents' side for a long time. What seemed like a gift to your father was closer to a curse. Following the line of succession from grandparents to parents, it is the next generation that is expected to take charge. Charles and Terri wanted this to stop with them. They wanted you and Theo to pursue your own dreams, while they handle the rest."

I stand from my chair causing it to rock. "Then why not just give it all to Nicholas? Then everyone would have been happy!"

She tilts her head upward to face me and reaches for my hand, still stained magenta from the cranberry sauce. Her warm hand gently squeezes mine. "Your nonna and nonno knew the kind of man their son was. It's why they gave their legacy to Charles. It took your parents a little longer to come to terms with that. Although, they always suspected he was up to something behind their backs. Don't blame your parents for just trying to do their best; it took a lot of people working together to bring justice. Even now, they would rather shoulder the burden than expect you to give up your dreams."

My chin quakes, but somehow, I hold back. "Then why didn't they help me? Why did they let me struggle, if they were trying to give me a better life?!"

A reserved smile creates deep curves in the older woman's cheeks. "Oh, sweet girl, they weren't withholding to watch you fail; they were allowing space to help you flourish." Mrs. Colby squeezes my hand one last time and stands from her seat beside the fire.

I watch as she passes through the room, before she turns and speaks.

"When you return home, do tell Connor that his mother says to call more often." She gives a forced smile before leaving the room.

I haven't set eyes on another person since Thanksgiving. I refused to come out, especially when Christmas came around. My parents mailed me a letter, continuing to give me my much-needed space. It explained how they tried to *secure my future* without looming over me. Letting me *figure things out*, yet still keeping an eye on me, from a distance. Connor was another player in the game. He was not only reporting on me to my parents, but also keeping an eye on the Murrays.

Despite ties being severed years ago, my mother still cared for Mary and her family. The letter describes how they felt it was their duty to protect the Murray children. However, they never knew about Dax. Even Andrea was unaware of the precaution. She was busy enough with her own assignments: protecting me and investigating Theo's death. Honestly, all of these moving pieces were no less complicated than solving a dodecahedron-shaped puzzle, with twelve faces. How did mom and dad keep track of anything?!

It took me weeks to digest everything. I screamed. I cried. I slept... after the soul-stirring smoothie I was force fed, I felt nothing. Void of emotion. I was convinced my whole life was a simulation and I never was presented the choice of a red or blue pill. I tried to unplug from everything... I rewatched *The Sopranos* and even explored new crafting endeavors that I've never had time for in the past. First, I tried turning plastic bottles into wire stem flowers, with only a lighter and sheer determination. It proved to be a lot more challenging than I initially expected. After burning myself an unspeakable number of times; then, piercing my hands with eighteen-gauge wire, I was done.

With my extensive collection of embroidery thread, I decided to adorn every piece of clothing I had packed. Some displayed simple colorful edging or tiny emblems. Others had words or phrases. My favorite to date were the high-top Converse, which were embroidered with *"Fuck You"* in pink thread. Very therapeutic.

Reaching "Made in America," the final episode of *The Sopranos*, I reflect on how Tony had declined as a whole despite all of his efforts. All the mobsters went round and round, pointing fingers, arguing about who is to blame for letting the war get out of hand... but the truth is, even the best-laid plans don't go smoothly. When the screen goes black, it's not the end... at least not for those who are still here. It's a new beginning. Just not the one you hoped for.

I managed to burn a frozen apple pie. The house smelled like burnt sugar for days. More importantly, I didn't get triggered when smoke bellowed from the oven. My growth may look different from others, but this charred dessert is proof that I'm trying.

Aside from Eamon's message, reassuring me that I should take all the time I need... all else was left *unread*. I don't think I can go back to working there. Pretending like nothing happened... as if everything hasn't changed. Dax sent me a text. I didn't open that one either. In fact, after I compiled a playlist of my own... I shared the compilation and blocked his number. The music was potent enough to ensure he wouldn't try to contact me again. I named the playlist, *The Queen's Collection*. I included: **Chevelle - "The Red", Blink 182 - "Dammit," White Town - "Your Woman," Primitive Radio Gods -**

"Standing Outside a Broken Phone Booth with Money in My Hand," Our Lady Peace - "Superman's Dead," and **No Doubt - "Don't Speak."** I know, I know! The last one was unnecessary and a week later, I felt like an asshole, but I was in a really bad place when I made it.

During my time here, I fell into a routine of feeding birds and squirrels in the morning. Reading in the afternoon from one of the books Mairead bought me along the Freedom Trail. While the evening proved difficult to occupy my mind, so I resorted to journaling. When I got bored of that, I pleasured myself. The damn vibrator stopped working on Christmas!

I was running out of things to do, ways to ensure I didn't think about him. Oddly enough, my duration here in the snowy mountains was coming to a close. I received a call about a job offer. An interview for a fashion intern position. The thing is… I don't even remember applying for it. The old me wouldn't have applied. That version of myself is long gone, so I agreed to an in-person meeting in a few days. I've spent enough time alone with nothing but my thoughts. No longer could I avoid the inevitable. It's time to go home.

The day before I planned on heading back to Boston, I decide it was time to catch up with emails. The starred one on top was from Andrea.

"Like a Band-Aid," I say as I open the long overdue message. A small box pops up in the center of the screen. The email is encrypted. Of course, it is.

First, I try our apartment number as the key. When that didn't work, I enter each of our birthdates. Then… the year we graduated college. "Fuck." I groan, rubbing my eyes. Then it hits me. What she always insisted we watch, every movie night. I type in the word, *Sandra.* The words magically appear. Of course, the password is her favorite actress.

I pull the woven cream-colored blanket over myself, as I drain the last of the liquid in my mug. "Ready as I'll ever be…" I curl into myself as I read the lengthy email.

```
Cindel,

    I'm glad you had time to visit Theo's grave
before you left town. Calm down, I didn't follow
you… I pinged your phone. I know you need your
space and that's why I tried to cram everything
into one email, instead of blowing up your phone.
This way, you could read it when you were ready.

    The apartment is still standing! I haven't
burnt a single waffle in your absence. As you
know, a position will always be waiting for you at
The Black Sheep, however Eamon needed
```

some help in your absence. Connor was promoted and Eamon brought on his sister to assist at the bar. From what I understand, she's enjoying it… only had one infraction so far. She learned it's frowned upon, to threaten to "shave someone's balls and feed them a pube-cupcake if they don't stop reaching over the bar and helping themself."

Garron now keeps a healthy distance from Mairead, while Eamon is questioning an early retirement.

Now that I'm not tasked with espionage work, I've had time to apply myself in commercial illustration. Yes, it was always a real thing, but now I'm actually doing it full-time.

Please don't rush home on my account. All our bills are covered. Your parents weren't ready to tell you, but I believe it's important you know… our apartment building is owned by your family. All the money you've put toward rent has been put in a savings account for you.

I may not have had a 'real-family' most of my life, but I do know what it's like to feel lonely. For me, you're like a sister. The most consistent relationship I've ever known. I'm not asking you to forgive or forget, but I hope with time, you can at least understand how much you mean to me. I miss you. Especially our movie nights together, where you binge on candy and I fangirled over Sandra Bullock. By the way…good job figuring out the password!

Your folks have held multiple sit-downs with the Murrays. It seems they have worked through past indiscretions to create a new working relationship. I somehow doubt they plan on retiring anytime soon.

Dax is still around, although initially, I really wanted to kill him. In the warehouse, he was given a choice. Leave the city and agree to never return or prove himself. Fall in line,

right the wrongs of his father, and work together
to set the city straight. However you look at it…
he chose you. Dax has been doing whatever is asked
of him, all for the chance of exoneration. He
didn't make this decision lightly.

First, he was tasked with torturing his own
father. Each victim's cause of death was delivered
by his son's hand. We all laid witness to Nicholas'
fate. Multiple doses of insulin were administered
to your diabetic uncle, as punishment for Theo. As
the plethora of drugs coursed through him, Mini
Cannon, firecrackers were packed into his ear
canal, before being ignited. It was quite the show.
That one was Dax's idea… on your behalf. Finally, a
rope was suspended with just enough slack to
provide a slow strangulation in Mary Murray's
honor. Mairead may have turned his body into a
piñata, despite others' objections.

Nicholas got exactly what he wanted. His blood
money will be used to repave the South Boston
Waterfront, with his ashes mixed in. It's his city,
although we are the ones to walk upon it. Over in
the old club district, you'll find a small area of
sidewalk that's been demoed and fenced off. In the
spring, Mairead and I will plant American
chaffseed. A federally endangered plant in
Massachusetts. Below the future garden will lie,
Karl Kent and Craig Moore. A sign will be displayed
as a designated "spit area," since general law
usually prohibits such behavior on sidewalks. I'll
wait until your return so we can spit on their
graves, together.

I know it's not my place, but I needed to say
it. Dax was conditioned to be a weapon. A pawn
awaiting his next command to move. Even though he's
found family… the feeling of abandonment doesn't
give way. I understand that more than most. I can't
help but notice how each passing day seems to

chip away at the usually resilient man. He seems
lost without you. I thought you should know.

> P.S. Be sure to let me know when you're coming
> home. I also have a gift for you.

> All my love...
> Your best
> friend, Andrea

I was packed and heading back to Boston that very day. If traffic was in my favor, I could make it back to the city before it was dark. This way I have enough time to unpack and eat before bed. Who knows... maybe she'll be up for a movie.

While I drive, I settle on the 2013 movie, *The Heat*, for a little comic relief before dealing with the reality of being back home. I return the rental and make it in record time to Southie, considering people may still be traveling close to New Year's.

Dropping the luggage in the entryway, I find the apartment just as it was before I crammed two duffle bags to the brim and left town. The whiteboard, once bursting with life-changing information, is now wiped clean. Pushed into a corner of the living room as if nothing came from it.

Drawing closer to the panel, I find traces of residual lines and letters. Symbols that once engulfed my mind... I was blind. So determined to learn the truth, I didn't consider the cost. How it could alter everything. If I stayed, where would I be today? Blissfully alive, or bloodlessly well-informed? Somehow, I've landed between the two.

Just barely, am I able to make out *"The Stalker's Playlist,"* among the brownish swirls of negative space. Some of these lyrics were deeply felt. A pang of guilt rattles through me over the harsh list of songs I sent him. The way I disregarded him and his messages. How I left...

From out of nowhere, a drawn-out sigh comes from inside Andrea's room. Eager to surprise her, I spin toward her room and push open the door to find Andrea awake in bed. Emotions battle for purchase, joy that she is here, yet guilt for waiting so long to come home. She has a way about her. Just three minutes hanging out with her could make me feel like everything will be okay. Andrea's eyes meet mine, she appears more startled than delighted by my intrusion. That's when I notice the sheet covering her lower half is moving, unnaturally, just between her legs.

"Oh… oh?!" I try to back out. "Shit. Sorry!" I try to excuse myself from the very awkward situation.

"Cindel?" I hear my name in a voice that doesn't match my roommate. The other person beneath the sheets, pops their head out. Tousled red waves are pushed back from the face of the girl, who has a knack for making shit get weird, real fast. She climbs atop the covers, before settling on the bed beside my friend. Holy. Shit.

Andrea pulls the covers high over her chest, looking between Mairead and I, as if one of us should be the first to speak. Is… is Mairead wearing the Prince tee, I bought Andrea for her birthday?!

Dimples appear in her cheeks, paired with a devious smile. Like the cat who just caught the canary, she beams while pulling up her flaming locks into a top bun.

"Sorry… I should have knocked. Ummm, I'm going to go…" I retreat quickly, closing the door to the far-fetched scene I just stumbled into. From the other room, I can still hear clipped words, along with the slamming of drawers. A few moments later, Andrea and her *current* partner vacate the room. This time, I am pleased to find them, more clothed than before.

My roommate pulls Mairead in close to her. Despite my presence, Mairead takes the opportunity to lick up the side of Andrea's face. She groans, wipes away the spot with her shoulder, and faintly smiles.

Mairead grabs her bag from the table, which I didn't even notice when I first arrived. She gives a princess parade wave. "Got to run! I have to meet up my stupid brothers. Text me later, Silver Bullet. Bye Cin Cin!!! I'm glad you're done being grumpy!"

As soon as the door to our apartment closes, I pierce Andrea with a look of dismay and a touch of, *what the actual fuck*? "Silver Bullet? Cin Cin?!" I mimic.

"I know, I know! It just kind of… happened." She paces the length of the living room, all while giving me the rundown. Rattling on about how the daft girl saved her, using phrases like, 'it's different' and 'she gets me.'

"Soooo. This is the first time?"

She halts in place and begins to chew on her lip.

"Oh. Wow… okay. I thought you didn't like her? You called her crazy… remember?"

She comes to join me on the couch, facing me fully. "She's like… the *ying* to my *yang*."

I've never heard anything so… so sentimental, come out of her mouth. Let alone, something pertaining to a partner. It's always just been a fling.

"I really like being with her. She's just wild enough that I don't need to constantly worry about her. No need for protection."

I can't stop the words from spilling out of my mouth. "Like me?"

Andrea's eyes widen, her hand extends toward me, and lands on my knee. "You know I didn't mean it like that."

I can't help but feel as though I've been more of a burden to her, than a friend of her choosing. Taking her hand in mine, I remind myself to work through these emotions, as opposed to bottling them up. No more running. I've chosen to return. To repair whatever is salvageable. I refuse to be filled with, *What ifs?* Constantly questioning if I should have put forth more effort. I'm putting all my chips on black. I'm all in.

"I'm happy for you." I say with my whole being. We're all reshaping our lives. One choice at a time. "But if she hurts you, she's going to be the one who needs protection," I proclaim.

Her eyebrow lifts, followed by a playful grin, then she squeezes my hand. "Take it easy killer! Let's keep it to one cling-wrapped body a year, kapeesh?"

Ugh, is nothing unknown to this woman!

On my bed sat a pair of purple rain boots with a bow. "Surprise," Andrea sing-songs.

I pull her into a hug. We stay just like that, for long moments. It wasn't about shoes but what they represent. How our friendship is more than just an accessory, but the foundation of the outfit. I now understand, she wasn't here because she was expected to be... Andrea stayed because she's, my friend.

Together we strip the sheets from my bed and unpack my bags. After everything is put away, we move onto the kitchen, to scrounge up ingredients for dinner. I was so sick of soup, but was grateful to stay in. Somehow, vague ingredients of pasta, broth, and expired spices from the shelf became a delicious meal. Seems like no one has grocery shopped in weeks!

Andrea tells me about all I've missed, during my time away. It almost slipped my mind... I reveal the other reason, why I came home. The interview.

"It's strange... I remember doing a job search, but I don't recall applying for this. All the same, I'm actually excited."

An indent on Andrea's previously licked cheek forms as her lips migrate to one side. Her downward cast stare makes me immediately on edge.

"What?" I narrow my gaze, trying to figure out what that *look* means. "What'd you do, Andrea...?" I cross my arms in response to her obvious, *I know something you don't know*, expression.

"Meeeee?" She disputes with a slightly raised voice. "I didn't do anything. For once. Although, I may happen to know someone who applied to a couple jobs in the area, with the belief you would come back to Southie."

No. Dax? He did this?

"You know... I see Dax kind of regularly at the boxing club. I started taking lessons there. He's given me some great pointers."

I nod, unsure of what to say at the mention of his name. Taking a deep breath in, I ask. "Is he... well?"

Andrea's mouth forms a straight line, while her eyebrows draw up at the bridge of her nose. She sets her spoon gently in the bowl, gazing into the empty dish, as if it holds answers. "He'd be a lot better if you gave him a chance to explain himself." Her words are spoken so softly, they weren't meant to cut but to ignite curiosity.

I run the tip of my thumbnail over my lip, as I think. Focusing on the numbing feeling the perpetual movement caused. "I'll sleep on it."

When climbing into my bed, my phone accidentally tumbles to the floor. My hand reaches down to the floor, feeling for my phone, instead finding something unusual. My stomach flips. It's the earbud... with its purple teasing star. I thought it was gone. Left in the abandoned warehouse where I dropped it. Placing the white tech into its charging port on the nightstand, my thoughts drift to the songs I've heard with this. The man clad in black. My friendly stalker. I wasn't even sure how to approach a conversation with Dax, let alone be in the same room as him. Where do I start?

"I told you I only wanted the truth" or "did you ever plan on telling me that my uncle was your fucking father?!" Both seem a little rocky as a starting point. Andrea already gave me an idea of when I could see him again. The Murrays, now including Dax, seeing how Eamon and Mairead are his half siblings, commonly grab a meal together, once a week. She says I should come to their next one. It just so happens; there's one on the same day as my interview. I told her that I'd try my best to swing by afterwards.

The idea of seeing him is already overwhelming. Perhaps, having extra buffers in the room was wise, especially with how things were left. Two days till the interview and the hours seem to drag on and on. Aside from the essential grocery trip, I stay home. I am just not ready to bump into anyone, unexpectedly.

Mairead comes over again. Both her and Andrea help me decide on the outfit for my big day. It is kind of nice. We make a night of it, ordering lukewarm takeout and trying on outfits, nobody in their right mind would leave their home wearing. When I say, Andrea was mortified in a pink boa and heels... I mean, she gave us the impression that she may burst into flames if we didn't insist, she change.

Mairead's infectious giggle didn't remedy the vulnerable moment. I doubt Andrea will ever try pastels again. The selected outfit for the interview is a long sleeve, cream colored top, and a pair of dress slacks. Toward the end of the night, Mairead surprises me by producing the bedazzled, Dolphin Jacket, she bought off the mannequin at the Craft Bazaar. She insists I show them what I'm capable of. The outfit comes together perfectly.

Glimpses of what Andrea likes about the sometimes-unhinged redhead, shows through today. Although, I'm pretty dead set on never participating in another escape room with her, even if the opportunity presents itself.

Twenty minutes ahead of my scheduled interview, I find myself on the curb with a hand on my forehead, attempting to see the top of the enormous office building. Like a child's first time going to school, I feel swallowed by the sheer size of the place and its ability to make me feel insignificant.

With traffic, it is a solid thirty-minute drive to the sustainable starter company in Chestnut Hill. I'd either need to buy a car or take the train, nearly doubling my commute time. Arming my lungs, I let out a smooth calming breath. *One foot in front of the other*, I tell myself. Hiking the strap of my bag higher up onto my shoulder, I enter the building armed with my portfolio from college, various notebooks full of custom designs, and a pathetic excuse for a resume.

Without my permission, my hand reaches up to my right ear, as it has so many times before. Whenever I find myself anxious or mildly lonely in a crowded room... the knowledge that I held a tether to someone who had my back, injected me with confidence. The thing is, I wasn't wearing it. My fingers skate across the hearing aid in its place, gracing me with the sense I lost long ago. It's twisted, really... how I can't hear while he can't speak.

Technology makes everything so seamless these days. Despite endless connectivity, people are more disconnected than ever. Armed with nothing more than outdated papers and the reminder that I can only thrive by throwing caution to the wind, I straighten my shoulders and press the button in the elevator.

No more than twenty minutes later, I'm back in front of the shining building that beckons me, just as a sea of commuters' part around my inconvenient position on the sidewalk. I gaze down at the parting gift from the lady with the jet-black hair in the plum blazer. A minimalistic business card reading only her name, *Margaret Steely*.

Regardless of any compulsory compliments, this interview was a fruitless attempt. It was quite clear from the beginning, that my lack of experience wasn't what they were looking for. After plastering on my service smile and retrieving the "better luck next time" token, I leave. Might as well throw all my stuff in this trash can.

No… NO. We aren't using the monster voice anymore, Cindel. Positive thinking. I take a deep breath in. The polar air makes my nose instantly start running. Right now, I just want to go home and lick my wounds. Be that as it may, I told Andrea I would meet everyone for lunch, after the interview. She made me 'promise' this morning. "No matter how things go… You're coming," she demanded.

As usual, I didn't want to disappoint anyone. Arranging for another car to pick me up, I head across town, to the address Andrea gave me this morning. It was a new place, best known for their Baja-inspired small plates and fruity cocktails, according to reviews. The silver lining to this bleak outing was, I may beat everyone there, allowing me time to drown my sorrows in a lavender-colored guava drink. It better come with a paper umbrella, like the menu indicated online. No one is ever glum with a miniature parasol! Now I just have to figure out how to circumvent any questions about the worthless interview.

Well just my luck… traffic is terrible. I arrived no earlier than the set time and the restaurant appears incredibly busy. Groups of people wait to be seated, while the hostess seems to disappear for long stints, causing the line to snake out the door. I take it upon myself to take a look around, just in case anyone else arrived before me. Every table I passed is occupied beneath an endless strand of zigzagging lights. Wooden shelves adorn a massive brick wall, holding no less than fifty miniature cacti. All the while, vibrant murals pull your focus in every which direction. It was a visually pleasing orgy of color and light. On top of it, the food smelled incredible! My mouth salivates as I make my way through the establishment, feeling better with each new discovery. Why have I never checked this place out before?

On my second loop around laughing patrons and plated tacos, I am ready to give up on the search when I notice a pink neon sign that read: *The Patron Room*. Maybe they rented a space in the back, since we were a larger party? I slide the massive wooden door along the metal track, revealing a room with an oval table, covered in every possible small plate you could order off the menu. The feast had velvet, fuchsia chairs surrounding the perimeter, but not a single person within the room. Enticing smells invite me inside the secluded space.

All at once, the door slides shut with a thud and I spin around to find, I'm no longer alone.

Dax stands before me, in a form fitting, button-down shirt and perfectly tailored slacks. His finger hooks a matching dark jacket, slung just over his shoulder and my breath catches. Damn it all to hell, if he doesn't look more god than man in that form fitted attire. Silent as always, he approaches, stopping beside me to pull out a chair.

"Where is everyone?" I inquire, ignoring the offered seat. I sidestep him, setting my heavy bag into another vacant seat, and refuse to sit.

As if it's all a game, he rounds the table, pulling out the seat directly in front of me and lowers himself into it. He fills the pinkish furniture, leaning forward onto his elbows, while bringing his hands together to create points among his fingertips, then simply shrugs. The miniscule smirk in the corner of his mouth and slightly raised eyebrow, however, tells me this was always the plan and I fell for it. That conniving... I know exactly who will be taking out the apartment's trash for the next six months. He gestures for me to sit.

"You know... I just don't think I can do this. Great catching up." I spin on my heel, ready to flee the room, but he's out of his seat and before me, in an instant.

"Cindel," a graveled voice whispers. My heart stops. "Please." The words are soft and deep; however they sound as if laced with pain.

"Can you speak?"

He rubs at his throat and nods. His intense gaze shifts toward the floor. I clench my teeth.

"Please..." I beg, with what little air I can muster. "Tell me that you haven't been able to talk this entire time..." Despite his towering presence, I steel my spine. Arms locking over my chest, I back just far enough away...

He reaches into his pants pocket, pulls out his phone, and opens a prewritten message. Eyes meeting mine, he presses play. "I shouldn't have lied to you. I've spent so long pretending I'm someone I'm not, I lost sight of myself. It's not an excuse, I know that... but I'm trying to right the wrongs. Repair what's been broken. Even if it takes the rest of my life. I'm sorry." I can feel myself unraveling as his automated words continue. "I've sought help. To speak again. Some days hurt more than others, but I'm able to vocalize a few words a day. The specialist believes I'll get better with time, although never quite the same as before."

It's hard to believe anything he says! Whether it's from his text to speech app or from his mouth. This is beyond mending, no matter the apology.

His eyes bounce back and forth, assessing me. Likely looking for any indication of how I feel. No longer am I brittle. Closer to stone. Yet still empty. Hardening myself in spite of life's cruelty. For survival. For me. His pupils grow wide, seeming to realize my stance, his thumbs dance over the screen of the phone.

"Did you get the job?" The message asks.

I bite my tongue fighting the urge to curse or even scream. My mouth hurts. My shoulders ache. My resolve is weakening. "I'm so fucking tired," I say more to myself than the man in front of me. I look past Dax. Down to the chair where my messenger bag resides. Papers peek from the corners of the flap, so full of ideas. I was such an optimistic soul. Full of hope laced with a sad desire to prove myself. Even these past sketches no longer reflect the person I've become. Still focused on the sac of my former self, I shake my head *no*. Long moments pass before I glance back up to his face. My stomach twists. How is it that he seems more destroyed than me? I'm the one who was handed the *better luck next time*, business card. I take my pretty painted nails, which I did just for the interview, and press them into the palms of my hand. I tighten my fists, staying this way until they feel numb. Savoring the sting which grounds me.

"Thank you," I proclaim. "Andrea hinted it was you, who applied. You can stop trying to help me. I need to do this alone."

His eyes narrow. In a heartbeat, Dax steps forward, closing the space between us. The first few buttons on his shirt are undone and he smells even more appealing than the wafting scent of cumin and chili powder in the private space. Mere inches apart, I lift my chin, meeting his intense steely gaze.

"You've. Never. Been. Alone." Each word is sharp. His deep voice resonates with torment. In one fell swoop, he drops himself to the bright chair, taking me with him. My legs straddle his lap and he scoots us toward the table. He positioned his phone to rest against one of the plates of food before us.

I'm caged between the table and his body. If I'm going to be forced to be here, I might as well fill one of my needs. I reach for a mini empanada, paying no mind to manners or anything other than the impending flavors reaching my mouth. I hum as I chew, happy to finally taste something from the spread of delicious foods. Beneath me, I can feel his chest rumble, unsure if he's flustered by my unwillingness to cooperate or something else entirely.

With the phone resting horizontally before us, he reaches past, opening up the pictures app. Making his selection, he presses the center play button… The song **"Otherside,"** from the **Red Hot Chili Peppers**, plays along with a slideshow. Each photo has me in it. Whether I'm walking past the hot dog cart on my way to work or feeding ducks by the lake at the park. I'm the subject. Some shots were way before I ever found the earbud. Like the one of me and my brother, arm in arm on the steps of my high school after graduation. The empanada was hard to swallow as I discovered just how wrong I was about everything. He didn't start watching me recently... he's been stalking me even before I was an adult! I need to get out of here, my flight winning over my fight.

"Thanks for validating you're a creep! I'm leaving."

As I go to rise off him, his arms lock around me like a vise.

"Let. Me. Go." I try to push free, but escaping his hold is useless. My teeth clamp together paired with heavy breath. Was this some kind of litmus test? Ultimately deciding when it was 'the right time' to pursue me? This wasn't fate. He made it so it was inevitable that I would fall for him. He manipulated me! Dax is a liar. How could I forgive this?

Stuck in place, I lean forward toward the feast, he releases me just enough to pluck a jalapeno tortilla chip from its basket. Then, reaching for the molcajete bowl, I scoop a substantial amount of guacamole onto my chip. Bringing the overflowing bite toward me, I pause, hovering just long enough for the lumpy green mixture to fall from my chip and land on his fancy pants.

"Oops," I taunt.

A grumble resonated from his chest again.

I smile, knowing I can provoke him so easily.

The song is about struggle. Battling invisible demons that are present for some, day in and day out. If I plan to survive this life, I must embrace change. Doing the same things time and time again, expecting different results... that's the definition of *insanity*. This time when I reached for the dip, Dax eases his grip just enough for me to grab only chips. Denied guac... I make it my personal vendetta, to be as messy as possible.

I don't want to be here, but I also can't look away from the unusual slideshow. There's a candid shot of me at the Bazaar, right after my purse mysteriously found its way back to me. Followed by photos of me of my recent stay at the cottage in the Catskills. No matter how distant I make myself; my stalker is allegedly there. Even before I knew of his presence. He's always been watching. I should find this terrifying... but for some confounded reason, I find comfort in knowing that he was always there. Never truly alone. I've tried cutting this invisible thread which steadily cinches us together, but there's no point. Our lives are meticulously woven together. I can't change what's already happened, but I'm stronger from it. If I stay, I need to take risks. I don't want to look back and regret how I lived my life.

The song concludes, halting on one final image and I drop my chip. On the screen is a photo of me as a young girl, gazing into the bakery window at Mike's. Obviously, I'm unaware my photo is being taken, but the angle reveals someone else's reflection. The photographer. A young boy. Same unruly mop of hair. Identical steely-stare. I incline closer to the phone. It can't be. Glancing back at Dax, he releases his hold, freeing me to twist toward him.

"You're the boy from the hospital. The one that was with my uncle, after the explosion." I'm malfunctioning. Unable to breath.... to move.

His arms come between us, not to hold me down, but to keep me up. Large hands cradle my face so tenderly as he searches for something I'm not sure of. I can't help but notice how different his eyes are from his father's. Dax's center has never held anything but regard, commitment, and desire. His pupils now dilated, are rimmed in thick bands of bluish silver.

In an instant, he closes the rift, consuming me with a punishing kiss. I need him more than air. Biting and licking, tongues battle for purchase. I relinquish the fight against the predestined, becoming subdued within his hold.

I've wanted to know him since I was a child. Always hoping one day, my uncle would bring him around. Nothing is by chance. He is my past, my present, and my future.

Before I even realize what is happening, he guides me to stand and turn. He brings me down onto his lap again, but this time I'm straddling him. His erection rubs against my center. That *droppie* feeling hits the bottom of my belly, in anticipation. Like when you careen down the crest of the roller-coaster. I haven't felt his touch in so long, I can hardly stand it. Unabashed, I rock my hips, appreciating all he is. All he's done. His hands find my hips. This day definitely didn't turn out the way I thought it would. In fact, nothing seems to go to plan anymore... nonetheless, I couldn't be more content.

Some could say, I'm throwing caution to the wind but, it's better than having decision paralysis. In fact, I'm more sure of myself than ever; these past few months, I've felt more alive than I have in years. Yes, a lot of fucked up stuff has happened, but living a half-life is so much worse than not living life to its fullest. I was barely holding on and it's because of Dax, that I was able to sort through the broken pieces and rebuild.

Goosebumps emerge down the length of my arm, as he pushes loose strands of hair behind my right ear. He smiles with his eyes, tilts his head and kisses the freckle on my neck. With him, there are no flaws, only beauty marks. A chill wracks through me, just as he brings his lips to my ear.

No louder than a whisper. His bruised voice struggles to ask, "Can I keep you?"

My chest constricts. Before I can even answer, Dax stands to his full height, bringing me with him. His massive hand holds me up by my ass, while the other clears an area on the table before us. I'm laid down in the middle of the spread. His body cages me in, while his lower half presses between my legs. Breathlessly, I wrap my legs around him. Locking my ankles together, he leans into me and hums his approval.

I can't help myself... dipping my finger into the bowl of queso beside my head, I dab it onto his nose. "I've always been yours. Now... are we finished with all this cheesy stuff?" I jeer, in unison with unbuttoning his dress shirt. This time when the reverberating sound moves through his chest, I knew exactly what was to come.

Epilogue

DAX

Preparations for today start early this morning. It was almost our first anniversary, and I am determined to make it an unforgettable one. The idea came to me a while back, however her best friend insisted I wait. She can be quite persuasive, especially when she threatens to put my kidneys on ice if I don't listen. It wouldn't be the first time she's made one of Cindel's boyfriends disappear, I guess we have a lot more in common than I thought. I wasn't the only one who had a hand in today's arrangements.

Mairead kept Cindel occupied most of the day with lunch, nails, and thrift shopping. Meanwhile, I wrapped up a few loose ends at work before taking off to prepare for the surprise. The next Mur-Lo's was opening in a mere two weeks and there was still so much to do. These wine bars were a hybrid business, run by both the Murray and Lombardi families. The choice in name also pays homage to Mary Murray, whose hair resembled the color of merlot, in her later years. I wonder what she would have thought of the place... or me for that matter. I never suspected she was my mother, when I agreed to spy on the Murrays. I hurt people. People I care about. All because of my blind devotion to a man who only used me as a piece in his fucked-up game... a pawn. Even his death doesn't erase the deep seeded feeling of regret. I don't deserve forgiveness.

The wine bars have occupied a lot of my time lately. They were the ideal front; a members-only establishment which served top-shelf wine to an upscale clientele. A sort of 'middle-ground' where sit-downs could be held, including the occasional family meal. It was a fresh start to a relationship that was formerly irreparable. The second floor of Mur-Lo's was a compromise between father and son. Patrick relinquished command, giving his blessing for Eamon to keep operations in-person. Like newer movies be digitally rendered, the art of the process is lost. Eamon offers gambling of every kind from roulette, crabs, and even classic poker. Each week brought in a bigger crowd. Not three months after the first Mur-Lo's opened, we started construction on the next. Eamon practically had me overseeing all the recruitment and equipment installation. He was too busy between the first wine bar, the Bay Boxing club, and The Black Sheep. It was important I didn't fuck this up.

I also swore to Cindel that I would keep my nose out of anything having to do with her future in fashion, but I can't say the same for my siblings. Not only did they insist she accept payment for designing their staff's uniform, but they may have had a role in securing Cindel a position with a company known as Gemini. She's now the lead textile designer, as well as, a renowned fashion blogger. From what I coaxed out of Mairead, the person who held the position prior is now living a modest life, somewhere in Anchorage, Alaska. I kept my promise. My sister... not so much. Cindel is incredibly talented, excelling despite everything life has thrown her way. She truly earned all this on her own. No need to focus on the fact that anyone who wrongs her would disappear without a trace, in less than 48 hours. She's confident in herself along with her choices. Cindel's folks may have wanted to keep her far from this life, but they've learned not to make choices for her.

After interviewing multiple applicants and rejecting two dented wine coolers, I manage to slip out of Mur-Lo's with enough time to get across town. Cindel will be meeting me soon.

Right at six p.m., the bell above the door jingles as my girl enters the darkened shop. I'm pressed within a darkened corner, where I'm able to see her form, moving around obstacles with greater ease than I expected. This place has recently been remodeled. I'm curious how she's so familiar with the layout. I opted to change from my everyday business attire to the balaclava and dark tactical gear from the first time I made myself known to her. My heart picks up, thundering against my ribs as I watch her body slowly advance toward me. I rented out the whole place for this occasion. Leaning slightly from the shadows, I realize that not only has she not called out to me, but she's stopped progressing all together. Two reflective orbs scan the area. What the...?

Through the maze of tables and bins of sweets I see her rooted in place, simply waiting for me to reveal myself. Is she wearing night vision goggles? I can just make out the smile as it blooms across her face.

"My, my... Has the wolf become fair game?" she taunts ahead of spotting me. Red glowing eyes lock onto me and she takes off in my direction; similar to a predator who's locked onto their target. Too focused on me, she doesn't pay attention to where she's going. The environment betrays her; body lunging forward, she screams. "Oh, fuck!" Arms flail attempting to steady herself as I witness her tiny frame go down. A series of cracks and crunches along with the pitter patter of spilt candy, gradually dissipate. Straight away, I race over to Cindel, finding her in a heap of contorted limbs among smashed baskets. Skin-tight clothing hugs her body with some kind of fishing vest on her torso, topped with military grade headgear. What in the hell is she wearing? Kneeling at her side, I notice her boot caught within one of the baskets, most likely the culprit for my little lioness being brought down in the first place. Colorful candy litters the surrounding floor; I aid with untangling, before pulling her upward.

"What's all this?" I mutter, studying her as she pulls off the pair of night vision goggles.

"I can be mysterious too..." she grumbles, surveying the damage around us.

I chuckle to myself. "Yeah... in the, how did that Skittle get in my bra? Kind of way." She grimaces and I try my hardest to fight back a smile. She turns away from me, hastily removing the ridiculous vest. A cute frustrated noise fills the space. I can't help but feel revered; how sweet of my Cindel, attempting to swap roles with me.

Using my voice isn't easy. It took a great deal of hours and painful practice with a speech pathologist to speak this well. Although I'll never be the same as before the accident, I'm grateful to have come this far. I did it for her. Sometimes, I open my big mouth before thinking. In moments like those, I wish I could return to having no voice at all. Cindel's a spit fire. I know whatever dumbass thing I manage to say, she can give it back tenfold. I just can't get enough of it. She's brazen and stubborn, even at the best of times. On the contrary, she's also a good listener. Staying present and attentive when I recall my shit childhood. Even though I can now vocalize thoughts, it will never be above a roaring whisper.

Our favorite times are the still ones; spent intertwined during the early morning hours. Just her and I. Helping Cindel to her feet, I can't help but appreciate the way her choice in outfit clings to her subtle curves.

"When I saw the address for Sugar Drop, I figured you wanted to play... I dressed accordingly."

Fuuuuck... the ideas that ran through her mind. I plan to worship this woman for the rest of my life. I'm always in the mood to play with her.

There was no question that this would be the venue for today's special occasion. From the first time we went to Sugar Drop 'Candy Shop,' I bore witness to her transformation; from an overworked woman to the state of a carefree child, among the blanket of multicolored sweets. Despite everything that's happened, Cindel still manages to shine brightly... no matter how bleak things may appear. She keeps me grounded. I'm thankful she came back to Boston of her own accord, because I had no plans of ever letting her go.

I pull her into my arms, my concealed face resting atop her head. "As you wish, Princess." Just the idea of pursuing her makes my cock grow. "You have until the count of twenty," I share. "You hide. If I find you in under a minute, you do as I say. No objections. No argument."

She raises a little higher off the floor. Still substantially shorter than me, her challenging glare makes me that much more worked up to find her. "What about if I win?" She insists. Not a fucking chance I'll let that happen, but I entertain the notion.

"I'll buy you this entire diabetic retreat," I whisper into her ear.

Her eyes double in size. "Promise?"

No more stalling. Holding up my fist, I display one finger at a time, indicating that her timer has begun. She beelines for the other side of the massive candy store, trying desperately to find a spot she can squeeze into. I like to play fair, so I turn around and even close my eyes. I didn't need an advantage. I will always find her.

When I get to twenty, I give a high-pitched whistle, so she knows I'm coming for her. The building is dark, but I'm confident she's chosen an area away from the front window. I have less than sixty seconds before I'm the proud new owner of a sweet shop. I stand still, listening for any sign of movement before I progress toward the center of the room. Deliberately, I pass the giant gummy bear statue where I check beneath the display table. Not here. Shit. What if I go around the perimeter of the room? Just as I was passing a vat of jaw breakers, I caught a glimpse of a platform heel, disappearing within a collection of stuffed animals. Before my minute is up... I swiftly lower myself, reaching into the plushy filled shelf, feeling for any part of her. Bingo! Grasping onto her leg, she lets out a squeak as I pull her from her hiding spot. Of course she tries to argue, saying I was cheating and this round didn't count.

"No matter where you go. I will always find you, Princess." Retrieving a pair of handcuffs from the holster of my belt, I press each bow of the cuff to a wrist in front of her body. A tiny growl works its way up her throat. I know all too well what she desires. Cindel is sweet, but she can also be a brat if I don't restrain her. She'll need to hold herself up, but also not have access to anything. Her face may display a pout, whereas her body begs for more. I guide her onto her knees, hands positioned beneath her.

On all fours, she slightly wiggles her perfect ass. I move behind her, extracting the 'special gift' from one of the cargo pockets on my thigh. Fortunately for her, this skintight number has a top and bottom. I have no problem tearing her clothes at the seams until I gain access to all of her.

Gradually, I edge down her leggings, along with her panties until they reach the top of her boots. Those can stay on. I know how much she loves her Docs.

"Dax..." she groans knowing this particular position can only mean one thing.

"Shhh... you promised to be a good girl if I found you. This is just the first step." I pat her cheek to reassure her, taking the personalized present into my mouth, ahead of lining it up with her tight little hole.

She rocks forward with a hiss. Soothing her with my hand on her lower back, her body visibly relaxes. I tease the entrance with the shiny stainless-steel plug. Spitting on her ass, the saliva slides downward, ensuring it will glide in smoothly.

"This one is bigger than any I've put in before." Her breaths are already quickening. "Once it's seated inside you, it will make everything else feel that much better."

A quiver runs up her body. Pushing on the keyhole base, I release a steady stream of drool onto the Lotus plug, causing the precious item to gradually disappear. "AH! Fuck, Dax…" she cries. I twirl the toy at its foundation, until it rests fully inside her.

I smack her round ass. "Beautiful."

"I plan to watch you pleasure yourself."

Her neck cranes to consider me. I can't help but appreciate the way her eyes glisten, complementing her reddened face.

"I… I can't. Not in this position with my hands cuffed together."

There's no use hiding how much I enjoy pushing her past her comfort zones… toying with her. The corners of my mouth pull upward.

"No… I have something sweeter in mind." I stand, returning to the front of the store, I leave Cindel curiously waiting. Securing what I need from a tall, cylindrical display; I deliberately take my time. Her skin is dotted with goose-bumps, as she attempts to identify what I've brought back with me. "Eyes forward." I demand. I can't have her ruining all the surprises. She lets out a 'humph' but obeys. Keeping her body in place, facing forward. I can only imagine how her arms are growing weary from holding herself up, but we've just got started. She'll have to stay strong.

Dragging over a wooden drum full of candy, I set to work with my pocketknife. Whittling a small hole into the keg, at precisely the appropriate height. The metallic snap of my blade closing, causes Cindel's body to jerk. A throaty chuckle escapes me. My voice, already partially hoarse. "So jumpy." I taunt.

Unwrapping the rainbow swirled lollipop, I run my tongue up the length of every ridge. The flavor makes my cheeks cinch. It's too sugary and not the flavor I crave. Once it's slick, I jam the treat's stick into the narrow cut I created. The once seemingly innocent lolly will soon bring pleasure in a different form. Little by little, I push the barrel of Tootsie Rolls between Cindel's legs. "Scoot back, Princess. I'm going to watch you enjoy your candy, in a whole new way." No longer can she fight the urge to look behind herself. She looks to me then down at the barrel holding the long, spiral lollipop. She gapes, realizing what I've orchestrated. "Remember… no argument." Her glistening pussy is inches from the makeshift dildo.

Kneeling down by her side, I run my fingers through her chestnut hair. Helping it to fall on one side of her face. Placing one hand on her waist, I help guide her backward. Tiny gasps paired with incomplete breaths leave her parted lips, as the sucker slowly enters her. Once Cindel's lined up, I lean back. Allowing her to set her own pace. The way she moves, is fucking enchanting. She lowers her torso on shaky limbs. Leaning onto her forearms, the shining plug puckers as her form inclines artfully, toward the barrel. Her body comes to life, happily accepting the multiple invasions. I can't help but touch her. My hand settles on her lower back, right in the spot where dimples form when she's turned on. She shifts back and forth… lengthy moans tumble from her pretty mouth as she progresses, taking the lollipop a little deeper each pass. Red, green, orange, blue, yellow, then indigo appear. Only to then witness as, indigo, yellow, blue, orange, green, and red disappear inside her. The twisted treat is coated with her ecstasy, all the while I hunger to take their place. To taste the rainbow.

"Dax…" My name sounds more like a plea. "Dax! Please…. I can't… I… I need more!"

My cock is painfully erect from all the pants and moans. It revolts against the zipper separating me from her… but today isn't for me. It's about her. It's always been about her. Hastily I remove my face mask, positioning myself on my back, just under her trembling body. She raises up onto her hands again. Beneath her, we are nearly in a 69 position, although I don't expect her to touch me this time. Taking hold of her hips, I soon realize I'm not able to reach my mouth to her pussy, as she is skewered on a candy pyre. I look to my side, finding the avalanche of stuffed toys just within reach. With my foot, I kick one up to my hand, then place the makeshift pillow beneath my head. When I extend my tongue, her clit just glides across. This perfect woman moves rhythmically, as she works the dick shaped candy, all the while using my tongue as a scratching post. She's so fucking wet. Her juices literal euphoria, combined with sweet secretions of sugar.

"Dax! Dax! Oh fuck…it feels too good."

I flick my tongue to the cadence of a song I've studied for some time. Her body sings just for me, as she rocks backward and forward. I close my mouth around her piercing and suck. I'm well-educated in how to make Cindel lose herself. Sometimes she just can't get out of her own way. Steadily her walls crumble, but I dare not rush her. Waiting a lifetime to feel wanted… accepted as I am. Cindel submits to me. I'm nothing if not a patient man and those orgasms are worth their weight in gold. I discern the change in her cries, from opened mouthed moans to teeth clenching growls. I take the cue, reaching around, and pressing lightly on the base of the plug with two fingers, giving her that pressure that consistently breaks through her dam. All at once her rocking ceases. Legs convulse violently around me. I transition without delay to a pattern of licking and sucking, in line with pressing firmly on her lower pubic region with my free hand. I am a means to an end. As unusual as our beginning may have been, she's always been the one in control. She just didn't realize it at first. Cindel's hold on me is boundless. I'm just the man behind the curtain; pushing and moving dials in unison with her signals. Her taut body slams back one final time, consuming every inch of the twisted knob and her barrier fractures. Screams fill the room in time with tremors of pleasure, reverberating through her body.

I dare not stray, ensuring I ring out every last drop of Cindel's release. I'm a starving man, surviving solely on her. My face is warm and I fucking love the way she extinguishes my thirst. Without even being touched, the screams falling from her lips, cause me to lose myself. I'd be lying if I said, it was the first time she's caused me to cum in my own pants.

In an improvised bed of stuffed animals, we lay side-by-side. Between the bodily fluids and the sweat, I'm going to have to buy the whole lot. It's a small price to pay for Cindel's happiness.

I didn't have much time left. Raising off the ruined fuzzy ducks and christened teddy bears, I pull a remote from my pants pocket and hit play. Cindel's eyebrow raises as she too sits up. Music pours through the candy store's sound system.

Her face beams when she realizes, **"Maps"** by the **Yeah Yeah Yeahs**, was resonating through the entire shop. She moves to kneel before me, taking my sodden face into her still bound hands. She whispers, "You figured out my favorite song."

I produce a key for the cuffs from a metal ring on my belt, freeing Cindel to pull up her bottoms. Standing before our temporary haven, her body sways, moving liberally as I watch her dance about the room. I don't correct her. I've always known her favorite song. She listened to it on repeat when she was younger. Belting out lyrics while leaping on the bed. I've always been watching… she just didn't know it at the time. This song was saved for today. As the music carries her away, she turns from me, positioned right between the sugar fill station and the wall of jelly beans. So distracted, she doesn't notice when I move to a clearing and take a knee. When she twirls around, her eyes lock onto mine. Long moments pass as I fight the urge to move from this vulnerable state, unsure what she's thinking. Have I progressed things too quickly? Is this not what she wanted?

From this distance, I notice a slight tremor in her hands. She steps closer… closing the gap between us, agonizingly slow. Reaching for her, I can only hope that she doesn't discard me like everyone else in my life had. Taking her hand in mine, I attempt to steel my nerves, unsure who's more fragile at this moment. The soft musical outro matches the juncture in which I push myself to speak.

"Cindel..." I say, before closing my eyes. "You've been my beacon of light, when I've faced nothing but dark waters." My throat feels tight, making it even harder to form words. "I've barely been treading water, most of my life. So lost, I couldn't make sense of up from down. When you walked through that bar door, I knew you were capable of guiding my ship to shore or sinking the vessel upon unforgiving waves. I will undoubtedly accept any fate you bestow upon me. Even if I drown, I would still love you from the bottom of the ocean."

Tears begin to spill over her eyelids, peppering her cheeks with emotions I can only assume are in my favor.

Decisively, I continue with what I've been waiting a lifetime to ask. "Will you stay... swim by my side for the rest of our days?"

Cindel looks up and blinks rapidly, appearing to fight back the fresh surge of tears forming. Her mouth becomes tight however her bottom lip quivers. At some point her gaze shifts from the ceiling, back down to me. She shakes her head, *no*.

My eyes lower to the floor, unable to show her how much this kills me. I feel as though my heart is emulsifying; veiled beneath rejection, just like so many times before. It's likely something I said... I'm terrible with words. That's why I let my playlist do the talking for me. Cindel's boots shuffle closer to me. I almost wish this checkered ground would swallow me whole.

She lowers herself onto her knees, lifting my chin, insisting I consider her. What a sight I must be... the bird comforting the beast for exercising its freedom. Her small hands rest on either side of my cheeks, leveling me with a look of discontent.

"You beautiful, ridiculous man... give me a moment to speak." Her lip no longer trembles, instead her resolute glare keeps me pinned in place. "From the first song you played for me, I was ensnared within your game. What I didn't anticipate was how much I wanted to be pursued. As time went on and I learned more about my past, somewhere along the way... things changed. I changed."

My head feels like it's trapped in a vise, slowly increasing pressure. Not wanting her to see me like this, I attempt to look past her. Cindel must notice my diverted stare as she pulls me closer, trying to refocus my attention. "Despite everything, the one constant that kept me waking up each morning was you. You've helped me in ways you couldn't possibly imagine."

My neck throbs from the sheer force in my skull. I'm having trouble taking a full breath.

"You should know..." she lets go of my chin and eases back on her heels. "I can't swim." What...? Wait. Is that why she said no?

In a flash, I wrap my arms around her. Pulling her into me and squeezing tightly. I didn't want to let her go, for fear that all of this could possibly be a dream. I push up from my knee, taking her with me. Her legs wrap around my waist. My mouth devours hers. Cindel is the very air I breathe. I wouldn't be able to go on without her. Before long the fervent kissing transitions to a soft embrace. I dry any traces of salted tears upon her cheeks. Her adorable giggle rings out as I skim down to the nape of her neck, landing on her freckle. I pull back to take in her raw features. Blotches of rosy hues glitter her skin, smeared makeup, and puffy-bruised lips. Fucking perfection.

"You know what this means?" I hint.

Her head vaguely tilts.

"We get to practice water sports more, now."

Her eyes narrow before she removes a hand from the back of my neck, taking a finger into her mouth and slowly drawing it out. Next thing I know, she is jamming that same finger into the canal of my ear.

"Ah! Why?! Violation…"

Cindel throws her head back and laughs. "Oh okay… so, I can squirt all over your face, but a wet willy draws the line?"

The lights abruptly blink on and we find ourselves no longer alone in Sugar Drop. Time's up.

Just as I set Cindel down, my brother, sister, Connor, and even Andrea invade our once intimate space. Shouts of "Congratulations!" and "I'm so happy for you two!" fill the space.

However, as soon as they reach the area we occupy, the comments quickly morph into, "What the fuck?!" followed by, "Dear god!" Cindel's sparse patches of pink became a more uniformed shade of red, much like the gummy bear statue near the front of the store. I honestly couldn't discern if her new wave tears are from happiness or horror.

"Man… if Theo were here, he'd kick your ass!" Eamon announces, before turning right the fuck around and exiting the building with a clearly amused Connor at his side. Andrea simply stares at the lollipop still protruding out of the wooden barrel, then looks to Cindel, finally landing on my luster face. Promptly, she excuses herself to the little girl's room. Mairead however sticks around, grabbing a tootsie roll from the drum of candy, unwrapping the chocolate treat meticulously, and popping it into her mouth.

She holds out a hand to Cindel. "Well… let's see it!" Mairead demands. Cindel looks from me to Mairead. The spirited redhead proceeds to pick up a fist full of tiny rolls and starts throwing them at me. "You didn't get her a ring?!"

I hold up my hands, trying to block the onslaught of chocolate chews, pelting me in the face with incredible accuracy.

"Woah! Ow! Woah! There's a ring! There's a ring!" I try to speak as loudly as possible.

Dropping the remaining ammo, she proceeds to put her hands on her hips, in a *WELL* kind of stance. "It's just… indisposed at the moment." I admit.

Cindel's hands pop up, covering an audible gasp. Mairead hops in place while clapping her hands loudly together. "You. Two. Are. So. Fun. Together! I need to tell Andrea about this!" Mairead all but runs toward the restroom, leaving Cindel and I alone once again.

"Are you seriously implying… that there is an engagement ring in my…" I reach out, squeezing her butt cheek, causing her to squeal and swat my hand away.

"Not implying. Your engagement ring is unequivocally in your ass."

Her mouth falls open and I can't help but imagine what else I plan to put in there, once we get home. "Ah, one more thing…you can only remove your trinket, after I feed you and show you the 2009 film, *The Proposal,* starring Ryan Renyolds and Sandra Bullock. Andrea's rule."

Before she has the chance to object to anything, I sweep her off her feet, scoop her in my arms, and carry her out the back door. I am anxious to get back and show her the ring. I set her on her feet; her smell is intoxicating. Before I can open the car door, I pin her against the side of my Camaro, delivering a punishing kiss. It was unshakable, a promise passed from lips to lips. Mine.

Just then, the alley door screeches, stealing our attention. Andrea and Mairead pop out into the night, hand in hand, stopping just before us. Cindel is the first to speak.

"Really?... a Sandra Bullock movie?"

Andrea's eyes narrow. The corner of her mouth turns slightly upward. "Sandra should always be included in important milestones! Even if we aren't living under the same roof anymore."

Cindel's lengthy breath forms a cloud from the plummeting temperature. At that she holds out her arms to wish the two farewell. Mairead falls into her open arms, with giggles and squeaks, but Andrea however stays in place.

"Raincheck on the hug. I'll get you next time you're… washed." Cindel sticks out her tongue at her stubborn friend, just ahead of climbing inside the car. I round the vehicle, as Mairead and Andrea walk in the opposite direction toward the street.

"You're no Keanu—" Andrea calls out to me. "But you're not so bad either." I turn to find her walking backward down the alley, my sister skipping beside her in the dirty, week-old snow. "If you hurt her though… there'll be nowhere you can hide."

I don't doubt that. Giving her a curt nod, I lower myself into the driver's seat. I can still make out Mairead's voice. "Why don't you ever threaten me like that?!" she whines to her partner.

Slamming the door before I'm subjected to more of their squabbling. They're like oil and water, but somehow, they're meant for one another. Looking at my future wife in the passenger seat, I remember something. Removing two uniquely shaped keys from my ring, I set them in her lap.

"What do these go to?" I throw the car into reverse, ignoring the initial request. Heading toward our apartment, I take corners with enough liberty that Cindel has to grab the 'oh shit' handle on a drifted turn.

"How else am I going to open the Lotus?" I confess. Her mouth falls open making it extremely difficult to keep my eyes on the road. I am greedy. Needing the prerequisites out of the way and my sweet Cindel beneath me. The ring was just a symbol. We've belonged to each other for a lifetime.

An extra thousand gets added on top of renting out the candy store, for 'damages' to inventory, along with cleaning expenses. I may have also added a thousand on top of that for discretion.

Cindel's parents are still very powerful within this city, and they don't exactly need to know what was entailed with their daughter's proposal. The Lombardi's took back their full last name, since there was no longer a threat against their family. They keep to themselves in the Catskills, although they come around a lot more than in recent years. Most weekends they'll make it a point to drive out to us, fabricating excuses about how they had a meeting, or the Murrays needed them. I know why they really visit. With Eamon, Connor, Garron, Mairead, and I handling most business affairs these days, it allows the Lombardis to make up for lost time together.

When I initially told Eamon I planned to ask Cindel to marry me, he pulled me aside. "Does she know...? About her ex-boyfriend?" I knew exactly what he was suggesting, but I shut it down before he could continue. "She's never asked and if you keep your mouth shut about it, I won't have to tell her either." He's been a little hot and cold with me over the past week, but we've worked it out in the ring. He blames it on dehydration, but I knocked him out so hard that Garron had to crack open the smelling salts. Consider it payback for kissing my future wife. Having siblings is fun.

With the Christmas holiday on the horizon, I have made it my seasonal duty to help Cindel enjoy the holiday again. Even the idea of a tree in our home makes her on edge. It's not her fault what happened to her brother, was just after the holly-jolly date passed. If I had known sooner, I probably would have killed my father that very day. Maybe my mother would still be alive.

I pack a string of lights in my duffle bag, in preparation for our stay in the Catskills. Cindel loves staying at the cottage, so we've cleared our schedule to be there for a whole two months. Scrolling through my phone calendar, I realize we'll be away for my birthday. I never really celebrated in the conventional way. Thanks to my asshat father, I don't think I've ever blown candles out on a cake before. It was just another average day that passed each year, where I got older, and no one was the wiser. Contrary to my desire to have another cycle around the sun go unnoticed, Cindel felt very different on the matter.

When she happened upon my license, learning that she missed the date, she swore the following year that we would celebrate properly. With us being shut away, in the snowy mountains this time, I just might escape the party wrath; she's conjured up.

Continuing to pack, I layer sweatpants with wool socks on top of the compelling decoration, and zip the bag closed. I can hardly wait to string Cindel's pretty little body up, in the colored lights. I plan to make her moan to the tune of; "*Baby it's Cold Outside.*"

While we were away, Mairead volunteered to watch our place. It's a fairly simple task for most people. Collect the mail… water the houseplants… but this is Mairead we're talking about.

So, I wrote down explicit directions, along with friendly reminders. Such as, *the koi fish do not need to be rescued.* Last time we were away, she put two koi fish in our bathtub. She said *they looked cold.* Thankfully, the botanical garden did not press charges.

Patrick Murray surprised us all by announcing his retirement this past summer. Once his affairs were in order, he returned to Ireland, leaving his legacy in the capable hands of his children. Eamon has already been at this for years. He was more than capable, where our sister needed to be 'reeled in' every now and then. Somehow, she's become more renowned than *The Barber*, inheriting her own name on the street, *Red Smile.*

Patrick hasn't quite closed this chapter of his life. Recently, we discovered Moyra flew out to spend some time with him in the countryside. What started off as commiseration, Patrick's once vengeful heart softened for her sister. Not too long ago, the ornery man called me. Mostly he reminisced about his younger years between sips of scotch, eventually confessing that he always knew Mary had a child out of wedlock. Moyra told him. He loved Mary and respected her privacy but he never knew who I was, nor who my father was. I listened quietly as he let go of shame; understanding that he can't change what has passed but is willing to work toward building relationships with the ones still in his life. Cindel and I agreed… we want to hyphenate our names once married, acknowledging both sides of our lineage. Never wanting for more, I'm pleasantly surprised each day with the amount of understanding and compassion Cindel has for everyone around her. It makes me want to do better and be better. No one knows what the future holds, but as long as she's with me, little else matters.

Realizing I haven't packed my toothbrush, I cross the bedroom to our connecting bathroom. It's not by the sink or on the small shelf beneath the mirror. As I scan the room, spotting it teetering on the edge of the tub. Stepping closer, I reach for the toothbrush, when suddenly the curtain is jerked open. A figure in all black stands before me, face hidden by tinted goggles and a mask!

"What the—?" Before I'm able to react, the mystery person lunges forward with a taser. The intense burning sensation shot through my body, as the current seized my muscles, causing my knees to buckle. I fall to the tiled floor, as I watch the shadowy form withdraw from the shower. The inky silhouette crouches low before me.

"Did you think I wouldn't find out?" A breathy, sultry voice coos. I know that voice. My eyes once again focusing, I turn my head slightly to see the figure is much smaller than I first thought. "No secrets! Remember?!" Shit. Where'd she get the…? "Mairead was more than happy to lend me her taser." As if she could hear my thoughts. She's always been a whizz at reading me. "And don't you dare blame your siblings! One of the girls over at Cha -Cha's found me. They got worried when Brodi stopped coming around. Garron also confirmed he was with you that night."

Fuck me. Garron can't keep his mouth shut for anything.

"What happened that night is obviously something you'll never forget, but I'm pissed I had to find out what really happened from a hooker instead of you." She raises to her full height, looking like a sexy villain in her dark form-fitted outfit.

I may feel tingly at this moment, but I know blood is rushing to my dick.

"You should have told me. I would have liked to teach him a lesson myself. Maybe stitch a hundred anchovies to his cheating ass and drop him off in the middle of the Montana woods. Just like he always wanted."

The sensation of pin pricks travels through my hands and feet. Cindel pulls off the goggles and balaclava; right hand glinting with the giant stone that looks closer to a watermelon candy. Her hands disappear into her long hair, then she gazes down at me. "I'm looking forward to our time in the mountains, my love. Be sure to pack the plug with the tracker inside and an extra string of lights."

Wait… how does she know—

"It's my turn to pursue you. Then once I find you, I will make it a birthday you will always remember."

Fuuuuck… definitely hard, although there's a hint of sarcasm laced in there. My little vixen drops the taser onto my crouch, hitting her mark. I curl inward, grimacing in pain. Left with only the image of her backside sashaying away.

Once the dizzying nausea subsides and my limbs regain their strength, I pull myself up beside the toilet. There in the bowl… floats my toothbrush. I can't help but grin ear to ear.

Despite everything…. the hardships, pain, and loss… Cindel emerged not with a darkened heart, but with the strength of a polished stone. She's a diamond. If one day she decides to participate in the game her ancestors started, she would make a ruthless queen.

** BONUS PLAYLIST**

ABOUT THE AUTHOR

This is D.C. Powers' debut novel within the dark romance genre. Her desire is to not only create stories that are inclusive and diverse, but also humorous… sometimes questionably inappropriate. I mean, are you really expressing yourself if people don't question your sanity? When D.C. Powers isn't writing, she's spending time with family or hyper-focusing on some random new interest. She will always be obsessed with shiny things, candy, and her very own MMC.

Follow D.C. Powers on her socials…

AFTERWORD

A special thank you to my Beta Readers…
I couldn't have made this story into reality without your words of
encouragement and invaluable insight.

Andrea… You believed in me from the start. "Love your face!"
Corinne… Your feedback left me both laughing and crying.
Jackie… I'm so happy you were confused and even shocked!
Danielle… Your knowledge was essential to making this FMC relatable.
Mairead… You've got the musical touch! Thanks for letting me borrow your
name too.
Jordan… I'm so pleased you not only read it, but helped create the perfect
cover!
Amber… For not only being an ARC but helping to polish this story 'til it
shined!

THANK YOU ALL…
From the bottom of my sugar-filled, black heart! 

Last but certainly not least... Thank you to my readers.
I appreciate you taking a chance on an indie author. Hope you enjoyed reading
this as much as I did, writing it!

D.C. Powers